Bridge to To.....ow
Cold Peace

A Novel of the Berlin Airlift
Part I

Helena P. Schrader

Cold Peace: A Novel of the Berlin Airlift, Part I

Cross Seas Press
91 Pleasant Street
Blue Hill, Maine 04614
www.crossseaspress.com

ISBN: 979-8-9871770-0-6 (paperback)
        979-8-9871770-1-3 (eBook)
Library of Congress Control Number: 2023 9078 53

Bridge to Tomorrow

Cold Peace

A Novel of the Berlin Airlift
Part I

Table of Contents

Foreword

On 24 June 1948, the Soviet Union imposed a blockade on the Western Sectors of Berlin. This cut off roughly 2.2 million civilians from food, fuel, electricity, and all other necessities of life. The Western Powers faced the choice between withdrawing from Berlin or using force to bring the vitally needed goods across the Soviet Zone to the people of Berlin. Withdrawal would have rewarded Stalin's callous use of two million civilians as hostages and enabled the Soviet Union to absorb all of Berlin into the communist East. Yet the use of force risked provoking an armed response in the heart of Europe. The world stood poised on the brink of the Third World War.

Rather than risk war or concede defeat, the leadership in London and Washington decided to attempt to supply the city entirely by air. At the time, this was seen as a stop-gap measure. It was intended to buy time for diplomacy. No one in Washington, London, or Berlin seriously believed it would be possible to supply more than two million inhabitants by air alone. Yet against the odds, the Airlift proved successful, and the Soviet Union gave up the Blockade after eleven months. The Berlin Airlift represented the first Western victory in the Cold War and remains to this day a dramatic example of a successful, non-violent response to aggression.

Yet while people may have heard of the Berlin Airlift, few realize how close it came to failing or fully grasp its significance. The Berlin Airlift brought about a fundamental transformation in the character and ideological orientation of post-war Germany. It transformed enemies into allies. It contributed materially to the establishment of the Federal Republic of Germany, NATO and ultimately the European Union.

As a long-time resident of Berlin, the Berlin Airlift always inspired me, yet I did not study the topic in earnest until The History Press in the UK commissioned me to write a book for the 60th Anniversary. At the time, many German, American and British participants were still alive.

4

So, in addition to the usual scholarly research, I contacted eyewitnesses, starting with those still living in Berlin. I had the great privilege of corresponding with Gail Halvorsen, the famous "Candy Bomber" himself, and I also travelled to the UK to interview many British participants. These encounters planted the seeds for this novel.

Yet while the topic attracted me, it daunted me as well. The situation in Berlin in 1948-1949 was extremely complicated. The cast of characters was great and diverse. The relationship between the various actors was fluid and nuanced. Focus on a single character or plotline promised only to distort and oversimplify the historical situation. I chose, therefore, to create an expansive, inclusive and intricate novel intended to do justice to the complexity of the situation.

The richness of the material demanded breaking the story into phases. The Airlift cannot be appreciated without first comprehending the situation in Berlin *before* the Soviet blockade. Berlin in 1948 was unlike any other place on earth. The scale of destruction and the depth of the psychological trauma exceeded that of Tokyo, Frankfurt, or Rome. In addition, the simultaneous presence of all four wartime allies in the city created unique political pressures and fissures. The result was a poisonous cocktail composed of crime, terror, mutual suspicion and widespread hopelessness.

Instead of a single volume, a trilogy subsumed under the overarching title *Bridge to Tomorrow* evolved. The title springs from the German term for the Airlift, "Luftbruecke," which translates literally as "Air Bridge," and the fact the Airlift was a pivotal turning point between the post-war era and the Cold War. *Cold Peace* is the first volume in the trilogy and covers the period from late 1947 to the end of June 1948. It introduces most — but not all — of the major characters in the complete work *Bridge to Tomorrow*. Because the series is meant to show not only how the Airlift changed the course of history, but how it changed the lives of those who lived through it, one character who does not arrive in Berlin until the second book in the series is included in this volume. This enables the reader to develop an understanding of his character and situation in the pre-Airlift period. On the other hand, the biographies of the two main American characters were too divergent from the European focus of this volume to justify inclusion. Their introduction was reluctantly deferred until Volume Two, *Cold War*.

I wish to take this opportunity to thank my editor, David Imrie, my graphic designer Anna Dahlberg, my layouter Matthias Wille, and all my test readers for their patient and helpful contributions. Without any of them, the final product would not have been possible.

Helena P. Schrader
Blue Hill, Maine 2023

Maps

7

Detailed Table of Contents

Chapter Null
Zero Hour

Per Ardua Ad Astra
Adastra House, Air Ministry, London
Tuesday, 18 November 1947

Berlin. The very belly of the beast. The seat of evil for six long years of war and half a decade before that.

In the pit of his stomach, Squadron Leader Robert 'Robin' Priestman felt revulsion bordering on rebellion. He'd had disappointing postings before. His current job at the Ministry had hardly been his first choice. Yet a posting to Berlin filled him not just with disappointment but also with anger.

His first thought was defiant: he would *not* go to Berlin. His second thought was realistic: what was the alternative?

The RAF didn't need insubordinate, uncooperative officers. Great Britain was bankrupt and the Empire crumbling. The ruling Labour Party wanted to retrench and spend money at home rather than abroad. Britain, the government said, should not attempt to play policeman in a complex post-war world; it was time for America to assume that role. Nor should Britain try to hold on to an Empire it could no longer afford, much less do so by force of arms. In place of imperial grandeur, the British people wanted prosperity for the common man. It was time to grant the colonies independence and reduce the 'bloated' military establishment so revenues could be redirected toward social services.

As the ranks thinned, the competition for each job increased. No one was going to retain officers who said 'no' to assignments.

"Very good, sir." The words came out automatically, the façade intact.

"Should be very interesting for you," the Air Vice-Marshal continued. "The Ivans can't be trusted, but although the Americans can be rough at the edges they're generally on the same page as we are. Gatow itself is a bit sleepy. It has one grass and one of these new PSP runways."

"PSP?" Priestman asked, unfamiliar with the term.

"Perforated steel planking — rather like steel mats that are rolled out over the grass. The Americans developed them during the war. They're quick and easy to lay down, cost a damn sight less than concrete, but are quite adequate for light traffic. We've only got a single Spitfire squadron at Gatow and a BEA flight from Northolt every day but Sunday. Otherwise, all you'll see is the odd VIP swooping in for a meeting of the Allied Control Council. I think you'll find it a refreshing change from the stuffy halls here at Adastra House." He winked and laughed shortly.

Priestman's dissatisfaction with staff work had obviously not gone unnoticed, but after admitting, "Indeed," he concentrated on the new job. "May I ask, sir; is this an unaccompanied assignment?"

"No, not at all. I believe most of the staff have their families with them, and apparently, there's a British school there as well. As Station Commander, you will be expected to do quite a bit of representational entertaining, so you'll certainly want to have your wife with you."

Priestman nodded. Since Germany had no government and the Allied presence was still a military occupation, it was hardly surprising that senior military officers had to perform some tasks normally undertaken by diplomats. He simply did not particularly relish "diplomatic duties" and doubted whether he'd be any good at them.

The AVM caught his look and made a vague, calming gesture. "Don't worry. The British City Commandant, Lieutenant General Herbert, and the most senior RAF officer in Berlin, the Air Attaché at the Allied Control Council, Air Commodore Waite, will bear the brunt of the representational burden. Nevertheless, because of the extra diplomatic duties, the job comes with a number of perks. The housing is quite good. Requisitioned, of course, and the Station Commander's house comes with a staff of four or five. Also, your wife will be entitled to a car and driver of her own. There are other extras such as allowances for food and clothing as we don't want to look like the impoverished cousins. I can't remember all the details, but you can look them up." He made a vague gesture to indicate the information was in a file somewhere.

"Sounds excellent," Priestman agreed in what he hoped was a

convincing tone while wondering if after nearly two years of working together the Air Vice-Marshal seriously thought that "perks" were what motivated him.

His superior was continuing, "Officially, of course, you'll report to Air Marshal Sanders, the British Air Forces of Occupation commander, but with BAFO HQ in Bad Eilsen, you'll have a free hand most of the time. As it happens, Sanders has been summoned to London for the upcoming Foreign Ministers' Conference, so you can introduce yourself to him while he's here and get his instructions before you go out to Berlin. It will save you a trip to Bad Eilsen."

"That sounds excellent, sir," Priestman agreed, before asking, "When am I supposed to report?"

The AVM drew a deep breath. "I'm sorry to say that Group Captain Sommerville, the current station commander, has taken ill. Apparently, unbeknown to us he's been unwell for some time, which probably explains why he's kept a low profile and did not engage with his counterparts as much as we expect you to do. He is being flown back to the UK for surgery later this month and any transition will have to take place here in the UK after he's out of the hospital. His deputy can manage Gatow in the meantime. You should plan to wrap things up here in the next four weeks and take Christmas leave in the UK before meeting with Sommerville early in the New Year. We want you reporting at Gatow no later than 10 January."

"Very good. Was there anything else?"

"Not at the moment."

"In that case, if you have no objections, I'll take off a little early today. I want to tell my wife the good news."

"No problem at all. Give my regards to Mrs Priestman."

"Thank you, I shall."

S/L Priestman put his cap back on his head and returned to his narrow office where he wrapped a long, white shawl around his neck and grabbed his attaché case. He left Adastra House just after five pm. Because he needed time to sort things out in his mind, he chose to walk to his flat in Chelsea.

Fortunately, it wasn't raining, although a chilly breeze chased clouds across the sky. Priestman paused long enough to look up and wish he were flying. Then he briskly passed St. Clement Danes, crossed the Strand and carried on down to Victoria Embankment. Here he turned right and with his head down against the wind he started walking vigorously.

Of all the RAF airfields in the British Empire, why did he have to land in Berlin? The word conjured up Hitler's voice and the unique way he harangued and threatened. It brought back the sound of unsynchronised engines groaning across the sky, the jangling of the telephone, the squawking of the tannoy, the sirens and the crump of bombs. He had only to look around to see the scars left by those bombers. London had "taken it," but at a high price. Gaps like broken teeth marred every row of buildings as far as he could see.

More insidious, however, was the association of "Berlin" with the Gestapo — the ominous threat over seventeen months in captivity during which the Luftwaffe guards hinted that they would have been more comradely, more compassionate, more generous, if only "Berlin" weren't looking over their shoulders, if only "Berlin" didn't threaten to kill all the prisoners, if only "Berlin" with its torture chambers did not await the rebellious and the runaway....

Yet such feelings were irrational, Priestman reminded himself. *That* Berlin had been obliterated, crushed, eradicated. Hitler was dead, his minions were arrested, tried, and hanged. The Gestapo did not exist anymore. The victorious Allies controlled Berlin, and their joint occupation forces patrolled the streets and the skies, a constant reminder of Germany's utter defeat and unconditional surrender. Why on earth should he dread an assignment to Berlin so viscerally?

Was it just the fact that he was being grounded again? He'd been counting on a posting where he could fly. He was a good pilot and he liked leading in the air. The best assignments of his career had been commanding a Hurricane squadron during the Battle of Britain and then the Kenley Wing later in the war. There were no positions like that in peacetime, of course, but there were still flying jobs to be had.

Maybe, if the RAF was unwilling to let him fly, he should throw in the towel and try to get employment in civil aviation. Except that he was a fighter pilot, an erstwhile aerobatics pilot, and he didn't have the qualifications on heavy, multi-engine aircraft that the airlines wanted. Not to mention that there were tens of thousands of ex-RAF pilots from Bomber, Transport and Coastal Commands, who *did* have those qualifications. There was no point in chasing fantasies. He was not going to get a flying job anywhere in the UK.

Some of his former colleagues had found work with the air forces in the colonies — South Africa, Kenya, India, Burma, Malaya. Sometimes memories of Singapore haunted him with alluring images of the tropics and sailing on the South China Sea. But he had no friends or relatives in influential positions in those distant places. What was he supposed to do? Spend his last shilling to go to the ends of the earth and then — find nothing? Even if he hadn't been married, he would not have risked it.

And he *was* married. Emily had been his mainstay practically from the day they met. Without her, he would not have held up so long in the early years of senseless and costly fighter sweeps across France, much less been able to withstand the strain of commanding a Wing through most of 1943. He'd clung to memories of her while a POW. He'd made two escape attempts as much to get back to her as out of a sense of duty, pig-headedness and boredom. When they were finally reunited, he had felt whole again, and she had given him hope for the future.

Yet he had never been able to talk to her about being a prisoner, about how it made him feel naked, worthless and helpless. He'd certainly never told her about the brutality he'd experienced on recapture. That silence had been compounded by the fact that his current job entailed working with many official secrets. As a result, they talked and shared less, until, over time, they seemed to coexist on parallel courses without being connected — or not the way they had been before.

Emily had a degree from Cambridge and had been working when they met. Then, during the last half of the war, she'd flown for the Air Transport Auxiliary. He'd been excited when she developed the same passion for flying that he had. He'd been inordinately proud of a wife who was contributing to the war effort by delivering service aircraft to the RAF, including not only his beloved Spitfires but medium bombers, too. He knew that this important and demanding job had enabled her to get through the difficult period when he was MIA and then a prisoner of war. What he hadn't fully anticipated was the extent to which, when the war ended and her services were no longer needed, the loss of purpose would leave her restless and depressed.

As a woman, her chances of a flying job were even fewer than his, so she had looked for other work. He understood her desire for gainful employment. She had a sharp mind, and she wasn't suited to doing nothing. He'd encouraged her to look for a job. Yet, deep down, he'd been relieved each time she was turned down because he was secretly afraid the work would thrust her into the company of other men and a world without him. She read the relief in his eyes, and he saw resentment and disappointment building in hers. Neither of them was where they wanted to be in their lives or their relationship. A change would do them both good.

So why did this posting fill him with a sense of dread bordering on panic rather than enthusiasm?

He stopped dead in his tracks as it hit him: because he was afraid. Being a prisoner had shattered his sense of invulnerability and destiny. His unsuccessful escape attempts had underlined the fact that he could fail -- and fail again. The staff work he'd been doing since had done nothing to restore his self-confidence because it was too easy and too safe. It was easy because he had a first-class education and he'd gone to Staff College. He could write lucidly in support of any argument — or the opposite — with equal aplomb. The job was safe because the work was collective. Everyone contributed to it, yet no one was responsible for it. So much of it was political and theoretical anyway, which made success or failure entirely subjective. Robin had been lucky to have a direct superior who liked his work so much he took credit for it. That left Robin unexposed to criticism and completely detached from his duties. He'd hated every minute of it.

Going to Berlin meant leaving the cocoon of a safe, boring staff job. It meant putting himself to the test again. It meant exposing himself to the opinion of men who mattered to him — other airmen. It was an assignment in which he could *fail*.

Furthermore, it came with those extra "diplomatic duties." He would be expected to flatter the Americans, to not let the French know what he really thought of them, and even to be nice to the Germans. Christ, he'd never been good at coating his opinions in politeness. His candid remarks had got him in the cart more often than he cared to remember. If he was supposed to suddenly transform himself into a diplomat, he would put up a black so fast that he'd wreck his whole career and be handed a bowler hat.

What priceless irony! He didn't know whether he should laugh or cry. He'd been binding about being stuck on the staff practically since he'd landed there. He ought to be doing loops for joy, not standing by the Thames on a chilly evening feeling like he was in a flat spin. It was time to snap out of it. Take the joystick in his hands and pull out of this self-destructive waffling. He resumed his walk, pounding the pavement angrily.

Before he'd been taken prisoner, the only thing he enjoyed more than flying was commanding men. Humans were more complex and difficult to control than machines. The challenge of making a collection of highly motivated and eccentric men work together for a common cause was the greatest challenge he knew — and the reward of success could be intoxicating. The job of Station Commander offered him a field on which to lead. Furthermore, he would be able to authorise his own flights — and Emily's as well; as a member of the RAF Volunteer Reserve, she was entitled to flying practice. As a crowning benefit, the assignment came with the promotion to wing commander, his last wartime rank restored at last. This amounted to a release from purgatory and the promise of a brighter future.

Not only had he been handed a good job, surely if he did well, he could turn this assignment into a stepping-stone to something better. Everything would be fine, as long as Emily was happy. And why shouldn't she be? She was bored and fractious. She'd always said that she wanted to see more of the world. He would also stress to her that she wouldn't be just a 'camp follower.' She'd have an important role supporting him on the representational front. Success, he reminded himself, was largely a function of determination. It was time to shake-off his post-war malaise and approach this assignment with vigour and confidence rather than these insidious self-doubts.

He looked over at the off-licence on the corner. If he was going to sell this as a great adventure and the door to a better future, a bottle of champagne wouldn't come amiss. He changed direction and entered the shop.

Nothing Left to Lose
Berlin, Neukoeln-Kreuzberg
(American Sector)
Wednesday, 19 November 1947

The interview lasted much longer than planned, and it was already getting dark when Charlotte emerged. She glanced at the narrow band of yellow sky between the banks of clouds and the horizon to estimate how many minutes of daylight she had left. The overcast was worrying. On a clear evening, the light lingered, but clouds would bring the gloom faster. With darkness, the danger increased exponentially.

Charlotte looked at the shattered buildings around her. The shops crouching beside the broken, pitted pavements were closing up. The owners pulled their stands inside, closed and latched the improvised shutters made from shards of furniture, and locked the doors, barricading themselves in for the night.

The nearest underground station was a ten-minute walk away in the wrong direction. At the station, there would be guards of sorts, but they were mostly old men. They often looked the other way when Soviet soldiers swaggered up and chose a victim with the stern command of "Frau komm!"

No, she couldn't face the underground. She would walk. At least on the surface, she stood a chance of running away, and there were places to hide — as long as she kept a good look-out. She started moving briskly in the direction of her apartment, trying to decide whether she was safer on the wide thoroughfares or the back streets. There was more traffic on the main roads, which meant that there might be Germans or even Americans to whom she could appeal for help. Then again, the Russians were more likely to be patrolling there. Yet the back streets were like a rabbit warren. It was easy to become confused by the abrupt jinks and turns or run into a dead-end. She couldn't afford to get lost with night closing in. She would have to risk the main roads.

She turned up the collar of her coat to hide as much of her face and hair as possible. The coat had belonged to her younger brother Connie, who had been killed defending the Atlantic Wall in June 1944. His greatcoat had been sent home with the rest of his possessions. It was too big for her.

It hung almost to her ankles and the sleeves covered all but her fingertips, but it was officer-grade wool and she'd sewn a second lining inside.

The best thing about it, however, was that there were so many men wandering the streets of Berlin in old Wehrmacht coats with the rank insignia torn off that it was almost a cloak of anonymity. Better still, with the collar turned up, it wasn't obvious that Charlotte was a woman — unless someone noticed her little feet. She was tall. Her hair was cut short, and she had strong, angular features that had never been called pretty; by her face alone, she could be mistaken for a thin young man. But her shoes, although flat and practical, exposed an ankle that betrayed her sex. She'd tried wearing her brother's boots, but her feet were simply too small, and the boots made her clumsy. In these shoes, she could at least run if she had to.

As darkness gathered, she reached the point where she had to abandon the dimly lit main road and cut through the back streets. Gritting her teeth together unconsciously, she left the wide thoroughfare. There were no streetlights, and no light came from the houses either. Almost all the buildings here, if not completely destroyed, had lost their roof to fire. The upper floors of many were gutted. Yet, most were still inhabited on the ground floor and some on the first and second floors as well. Behind façades shorn of plaster, people existed more than lived. They cooked a little food over a wood-burning stove, crowded around a radio, perhaps, or read by the light of a bulb dangling from the ceiling. No light escaped onto the street because there was no glass to replace the shattered windows. Instead, the windows were boarded up with plywood and cardboard or simply closed with heavy curtains. Only trickles of smoke and the smell of cooked onions, carrots and potatoes oozing out into the cold, motionless air betrayed the presence of humans hidden in the ruins.

When she reached the Landwehr Canal, Charlotte had only a little over a block left to walk and she started to relax a little. The canal was lined by chestnut trees too massive to be felled for firewood. Only the lowest branches had been sawn off. The dying leaves clinging to the upper branches rustled on the gusts of wind like old gossips whispering.

At last, Charlotte could see her apartment house, number 27. It was one of the few buildings intact all the way to the roof as if some guardian angel had protected it. As she reached for her bag to extract her key, she heard footsteps behind her. Strong, male steps. She stopped fishing for her keys and stretched her stride. The footsteps behind her increased their pace as well. She'd turned onto the narrow path leading between piles of debris and ran. There was no time to find her key because the footsteps had followed her. She pounded furiously on the door as the man behind came nearer and nearer. "Herr Pfalz! Herr Pfalz! It's me! Charlotte Walmsdorf! Let me in!" Pfalz was the house master who lived in the front, ground floor flat.

"No need to rouse Herr Pfalz," a male voice said from directly behind her. "I have a key."

Charlotte felt a rush of relief combined with embarrassment. She tried to compose her exterior as she thanked her fellow tenant, "Thank you, Herr Dr Hofmeier."

Herr Dr Hofmeier was a man in his mid-thirties dressed in a rather shabby and baggy, brown suit. He stepped forward and shone a torch on the keyhole so he could insert his key. Charlotte knew little about him beyond the fact that he worked for the large, electrical appliances firm AEG; he was an engineer of some sort. He had no family and kept to himself.

He stood back for her to enter first, and Charlotte hit the light switch as she stepped through the doorway. The naked bulb hanging in the hallway lit up. As Herr Dr Hofmeier turned to lock the front door behind them, the door under the stairs burst open and a stocky man with an ugly facial scar emerged. He was fussing with his belt as if he'd been caught on the toilet. "Frau Graefin?" He called out anxiously, "Are you all right?"

"Yes, yes. I just misplaced my key. Herr Dr Hofmeier let me in."

"It's already dark," Pfalz added in protective reproach. "You should not stay out after dark."

"No, I know, Herr Pfalz. I did not intend to. I'm safe now." She managed to lift her lips in a kind of smile and nod at him as she added, "Good night."

"Good night," he answered, nodding his head and fingering his brow respectfully, before closing his door.

Charlotte started up the shallow stairs. By the dim light of the single light bulb hanging over each landing, it was hard to imagine how elegant this stairwell had once been. The paint was peeling and covered with smoke. Only broken remnants of the plaster mouldings on the underside of the stairs remained. The beautifully carved banister was badly scratched and broken in places.

On the first floor, Charlotte passed the grand, double-doored entrance to her late uncle's apartment. His grand flat stretched around the courtyard, occupying the entire floor. Four families of refugees from East Prussia, Pomerania and Silesia, a total of 19 people, lived there now. On the second floor, two doors opened off the landing, each leading to an apartment housing families bombed out of their homes. Three elderly couples lived in one and three women and five children in the other. The two third-floor apartments were occupied respectively by Herr Dr Hofmeier and a trio of young men of dubious character. The latter went by names like "Braun," "Schulz" and "Meyer." Charlotte was certain these were false identities and that the young men engaged in questionable activities having to do with the black market. She supposed she ought to befriend them and learn more about their activities for a newspaper article, but her natural aversion to parasites made her shy away from them instead.

Finally, she reached the fourth floor. To the left was the apartment of the Liebherrs and to the right her own. She let herself into her flat, closed, locked and bolted the door. Only then did she feel safe. She turned immediately into the little kitchen, switched on the light and with a match lit the gas stove. She filled a pot with water from the sink and put it on the flame to boil. She did not remove her coat, as it was nearly as cold inside as outside, but she set to work getting the oven lighted so the room would start to warm up a little. When she finished, she returned to close the kitchen door to keep the heat inside. She could not afford to heat any other room, so she lived here except for creeping under her thick, goose-feather comforters to sleep at night.

As she sank down into a chair beside the little wooden table, she heaved a sigh of relief to have made it back without incident, and exhaustion overwhelmed her. It had nothing to do with the long interview, nor the long walk home. The exhaustion was deeper than that. She was tired of living.

With a start, she realised it was 19 November — the day she'd learned that her fiancé Fritz had gone missing on the Eastern Front. It was four years since that day and not another word about his fate had ever reached her. Nothing. After the war was over, she'd made enquiries. She was able to determine that he *hadn't* been a member of the Soviet-controlled prisoner organization called the *National Kommittee Freies Deutschland*, but he was not among the known dead or prisoners either. He was just missing — still.

Yet the more she learned about the Gulags and the Soviet equivalent of the Gestapo, the NKVD, the more she believed that Fritz might still be alive somewhere — enslaved, imprisoned, exiled to the wastes of Siberia. Alone, hopeless, cold, maybe even disabled. When feeling cynical, she supposed he was probably embittered, hardened, even brutalised. So many men came back that way, almost vicious in their cynicism.

But she couldn't think of Fritz like that. He had been too gentle, a man who loved nature and life too much, a man naturally at ease with dogs and horses and every living thing. She had lived for her time with Fritz, and he for his few precious days with her in Walmsdorf, but he was gone along with her brothers, her parents and Walmsdorf itself. All consumed by the war. She alone had survived to see 'peace.' And what had it brought her? Terror, humiliation, and self-hatred. What was the point of living like this? Perpetually on the brink of starvation with nothing to look forward to. Why struggle day after day in this wasteland of ruin and hatred?

Mixed Blessings
Foster Clough, Yorkshire
30 November 1947, First Advent Sunday

While his father-in-law, the Reverend Edwin Reddings made hot toddies, Kit Moran tried to get the fire going in the drawing room. He was having trouble because he was distracted, and his missing foot started to hurt. Always a sign of stress.

"Is something bothering you, Kit?" Edwin asked softly as he handed Kit a cut crystal glass with the steaming toddy in it. "You seem rather preoccupied, lost in thought."

Kit drew a breath and stood up, abandoning the fire as he took the warmed tumbler and shook his leg with the artificial foot attached it to ease the pain. His wife Georgina had made him promise he would say

and so enabling the Soviet Union to become a great industrial nation."

"That might have been true *if* the factories they dismantled here were being rebuilt and operated in the Soviet Union — which they are not. Furthermore, even if they *did* re-assemble the factories, the price would be the impoverishment of Germany, making it perpetually dependent on hand-outs from the West." Jakob dropped his voice. "That, Karl, might be in the interests of the *Soviet Union*, but it is not in the interests of Germany or the German people."

"Defending the Socialist Motherland is in the interests of all working people," Karl countered, more flustered by his father's calm than his earlier anger.

"That's what they taught you in the Lubjanka, Karl. It is not your own brain or heart speaking." Liebherr pinned his son to his chair with his eyes.

After several long seconds, Karl broke free. He jumped to his feet. "How do you know what is in my heart and brain?"

His father gazed at him unwaveringly.

Karl spun about, grabbed his coat and without bothering to put it on plunged out the door, slamming it behind him. From the kitchen, his parents listened in silence to his feet pounding down the stairs at a run. At the bottom, there was a short pause and then the front door also slammed shut.

"I'm not sure it was fair to remind him of the Lubjanka, Jakob," Trude remarked softly.

"Not fair?" Her husband asked astonished. "He has to face up to the fact that *he's* the one being manipulated. That *he* has become a puppet. What do you think he would have said to me if I'd returned from Oranienburg concentration camp spouting Nazi slogans and propaganda?"

"He was 13 when you were arrested," Frau Liebherr reminded her husband, "and barely 16 when you were released. He's only 27 now. When you were his age —"

"I know. I know," her husband admitted with a deep sigh. "I was an Independent Socialist. But there is a difference." Jakob looked sharply at his wife. "When I was a leftist radical, the Bolshevik Revolution was only a year old. Lenin and Trotsky were still alive. Our illusions had not yet been shattered. No one could foresee the horrors that would follow — Stalin's merciless machine, the ruthless eradication of independent thinking within

29

the Party, not to mention the kangaroo trials, the assassination of Trotsky, the forced collectivization, the gulags, the NKVD, the Pact with Hitler......" After a moment of reflection, he spoke again, "I don't understand how Karl, with all the evidence he has in front of his nose, can close his eyes to the true nature of the Soviet regime. He's not stupid and we raised him to think for himself."

"As best we could, but he was conscripted at 18 and became a Soviet prisoner at the age of 20. He spent almost five years in the Soviet Union."

Her husband sighed and then admitted in a small voice, "I'm frightened, Trude."

Trude sank into the chair her son had vacated. She reached across the table and took her husband's hands in hers. Through two world wars, a revolution, and incarceration in a concentration camp, she had never heard her husband admit he was afraid. Gently she probed, "What frightens you, Jakob?"

"The whole situation. I always thought that if we could just get rid of the Nazis, we could rebuild, start anew. I thought we could draft a new social democratic constitution and write new laws.... But look at us! Two and a half years after the end of the war, the country is not only still occupied, it is sinking deeper and deeper into poverty. The currency is worthless. The black-market flourishes, enriching only the dishonest. Honest people have nothing left to sell — except their bodies. And while the Soviets rob us of everything — our food, our industrial capacity, our children, our hope — the Western allies send diplomatic notes of protest! They still view us — rather than the Soviets — as their enemies. I had such hopes when they first arrived. I thought they would protect us from the Red Army and the NKVD. I thought they would support our aspirations for democracy. Instead, they let the Russians lead them around by the nose."

Trude nodded sadly. She had no words of comfort. She felt as discouraged as her husband.

"Ernst Reuter was elected mayor last June." Her husband reminded her, "The Soviet Military Administration vetoed his right to take office in July and it is now December, yet nothing — absolutely nothing — has been undertaken to enable him to govern. Instead, the Soviet-appointed police commissioners grow bolder and Soviet-appointed officials usurp the power of the elected government with impunity."

"The Allied Foreign Ministers are meeting in London," Trude reminded him, grasping at straws. "The American Secretary of State, General George Marshall, is not as naïve as his predecessors. Maybe things will start to change."

Jakob didn't believe that but he knew Trude was trying to cheer him up. Besides, there wasn't any other straw to cling to, so he forced a smile and muttered, "Let's hope so."

Unwelcome Inheritance
London
Tuesday, 30 December 1947

David Goldman and Sarah Goldman Pickering sat in silence in the waiting room until the solicitor invited them into his office and indicated the comfortable armchairs before his massive desk. Although brother and sister, they no long longer resembled one another because David's original face had been lost to the flames of his burning Hurricane. His present face had been reconstructed from bits and pieces taken from other parts of his body and still lacked the suppleness and wrinkles that would have been natural for a thirty-year-old. Not that his new face was in any way grotesque or hideous. Casual observers often failed to notice that there was anything abnormal about it. Still, it was not the fine, elegant face that he had been born with either. His younger, married sister Sarah, on the other hand, was a stunningly beautiful blond in smart, designer clothes perfectly tailored to her slender figure. The wife of a British diplomat serving in Prague, she had flown to London extra for the reading of her father's testament.

"First, allow me to offer my condolences on the death of your father," the solicitor intoned solemnly. "I'm sure it was a terrible shock." David and Sarah's father had been only 57 at the time of his sudden death from heart failure three weeks earlier.

The solicitor next explained that his instructions were to read the testament to them from start to finish, and he asked them not to interrupt him. He assured him there would be plenty of time for questions after he finished. The Goldman siblings willingly murmured their assent, and the solicitor opened the leather folder on his desk.

David felt no particular emotion. His relationship with his father had always been tense, and after his father called him a "failure" for being shot down in the Battle of Britain, David had disowned his father. They'd had no direct communication since, and David had been perfectly happy that way.

The solicitor came to the part of the testament that stated that all Mr Goldman's voting shares in the Canadian bank he had established with two partners went to his eldest son. One thousand preferred shares with a nominal value of one Canadian Dollar apiece were settled on each of his daughters. Sarah nodded her agreement unconsciously. No shares were designated for David. The sum of one hundred thousand Canadian dollars was left to Sarah in addition to her shares.

The Solicitor cleared his throat and continued reading. "To my son David, all claims to property in Germany formerly in the possession of myself or my late sister Anna and her husband Otto, both of whom, along with their children, were murdered in Dachau Concentration Camp and the lump sum of five hundred thousand Canadian dollars which —"

Despite the solicitor's warning not to interrupt, David could not keep still. "Excuse me. Did you say five *hundred* or five *thousand* dollars?"

"I said five hundred thousand dollars, sir."

"That's not possible," David protested.

"The money has already been deposited in an escrow account controlled by this firm, sir. I assure you the amount is correct. It converts to close to 350,000 pounds sterling at today's exchange rate."

David could not grasp it. It didn't make sense. His father had called him a disgrace since childhood. He had steadfastly disapproved of his compulsion to learn to fly. He viewed his wartime service as a failure and had not attempted to contact him after David severed all ties. Why would his father leave him such an enormous sum?

The solicitor finished reading, cleared his throat and asked if they had any questions. Sarah asked about some paintings and furnishings in the family home, and when Sarah was satisfied, the solicitor requested that they provide him with the details of bank accounts into which he could transfer the sums held in escrow for them. Both Sarah and David provided the necessary information. They thanked the solicitor, went out into the street, and flagged down a taxi.

"I told you Father wasn't as bad as you made him out to be," Sarah declared as the cab set off for the Savoy.

"You don't understand, Sarah. I would have preferred him to value me for what I was then to give me five hundred thousand — or even one million — dollars after he was dead. I don't *want* his five hundred thousand dollars — much less any claims to property taken from Uncle Otto and Aunt Anna by the Nazis. I don't even want to think about it — Uncle Otto's beautiful home on Schwanenwerder, his optician's office on the Kurfuerstendam. I can't deal with it — or what they did to him and Aunt Anna and our cousins. I don't *want* to."

Sarah looked down chastened and David turned pointedly to look out of the window although he saw nothing. He was desperately trying to work out what his father had been thinking — and what on earth he was going to do with this unwanted legacy. They did not speak again until they reached the Savoy.

On arrival, Sarah excused herself to freshen up before dinner, and David went straight to the American Bar, where he'd arranged to meet his friend Kiwi at six-thirty. The pianist was playing lively if muted jazz on the piano and a group of well-dressed Americans were at the bar talking earnestly in agitated but subdued tones. Without looking at them, David cocked his ear to listen to what they were saying. They were discussing the latest meeting of the Allied Council of Foreign Ministers, which had just ended. These men, whoever they were, were predicting that tensions with the Soviet Union were going to escalate.

"The problem is that there *has* to be currency reform in Germany, and the longer we delay it, the more damage is done to the economy of Europe as a whole." One of them declared emphatically. "As it is, the Soviets print money without any kind of restraint or accounting. Their bank notes are worthless so people can only live by barter. The real currency of Germany is cigarettes — and since the Germans don't produce cigarettes, we are turning an entire nation into criminals against their will. It's nuts!"

"What I find most appalling is that the *real* thieves — the Nazis who enriched themselves through conquest and theft all across Europe — have the valuables with which to profit from this barter economy." The speaker spoke in a soft, educated American voice, but his words struck David like a kick in the gut. He held his breath to listen as the speaker continued, "The very people who ought to be behind bars are making new fortunes, while honest people have nothing left to sell and turn increasingly to crime — or prostitution — just to stay alive."

David couldn't move as the words played again in his head, "the Nazis who enriched themselves."

One of the other Americans pointed out, "Don't forget the average GI can sell his ration of cigarettes on the black market for hundreds of worthless marks and then get those marks turned into dollars at the post exchange at the official rate. They make a 400 or 500% profit in a couple of hours. We're fuelling this mess!"

"You can't blame some kid from Iowa for taking advantage of the situation. We shouldn't be putting ordinary soldiers in the way of such temptation."

"Banks! There you are!" Kiwi came up behind David, addressing him by his RAF nickname, and clapping him on the back.

Startled from his thoughts, David looked up at the big New Zealander and saw the strain of his recent divorce written all over his face. His eyes were puffy, his face deeply lined, and there was something vaguely rumpled about him. No wife to iron his shirts anymore, David supposed. He also noted that Kiwi had put on a lot of unsightly weight, making the New Zealander look older than 31. On top of that, Kiwi's suit appeared to be second-hand and at least ten years old.

Out loud David welcomed him with, "Good to see you, Kiwi! I hope you don't mind the change of venue." The two men had originally planned to meet at Kiwi's flat, but Sarah had suggested asking Kiwi to join them for dinner at the Savoy.

"Mind? I was tickled pink!" Kiwi's eyes scanned the room around them with an expression of wistful envy. "Can't remember the last time I was in a place like this. And it's warm in here too! I can't afford to heat the flat when I'm not there and it chills out. Feels like an icebox when I get home at night or get up in the morning."

"Let me get you something to warm you up," David offered. "It's on me. I'm celebrating. My father died at the beginning of the month and left me a *ridiculous* amount of money."

"You don't sound as happy about it as I would, mate," Kiwi shot back, not entirely able to disguise a touch of jealousy. David understood; Kiwi needed money and an inheritance sounded like a boon.

"Let's just say I'm a bit stunned. Now, what are you drinking? I've ordered a French 75. Wouldn't you like one?"

"All right. In your honour, but I'm trying to cut down on the hard stuff."

David ordered, telling the bartender to put it on his tab, while Kiwi asked, "Did your dad leave you enough to buy a house so you can move out of that Nissen hut you've been living in these last two years?"

"Kiwi, I don't know how to say this," David started but stopped himself. He had been raised not to talk about money, certainly not how *much* the family assets were worth. He changed tack. "He left me all our property in Germany."

"Now that's *wizard*!" Kiwi remarked sarcastically. "All the property that was taken away by the Nazis and has since probably been pulverised by our bombers. Very generous of him."

David laughed shortly. "I rather hope it *has* been pulverised. That way it won't bring back any memories or cause me any trouble, but I owe it to my aunt and uncle to make inquiries at least. Fortunately, my father also left me some cash."

"So much the better. What are you going to do with it, if not buy a house?"

David knocked down the powerful cocktail and ordered a second. He was feeling very shaky, and admitted, "I don't know yet, Kiwi, but I have this horrible feeling that 'he who laughs last, laughs best.'"

"Meaning?"

"You remember, my father hated the fact that I made flying my career. Then, no sooner had I been shot down than he accused me of failing to contribute to the war effort—"

"Right! Like teaching hundreds of fledgling RAF pilots to fly wasn't contributing to the war effort!" Kiwi shot back sarcastically. "I wish your dad had asked *my* opinion! I'd have put him straight, mate!" There was genuine outrage in Kiwi's voice.

It had been that steadfast support and unwavering loyalty that had made David lean so heavily on Kiwi during eighteen months of plastic surgery. With surprise, David realised that he *still* needed Kiwi. He needed to talk about this inheritance with another flier, someone who could understand. "My father never gave up insulting me and demeaning flying as a profession, all in the hope that I would 'come to my senses' and finally find a 'proper' job. Fifteen years, I stood up to him, and now — from beyond the grave — he has won."

"What do you mean? How? You're still flying."

David nodded but then he drew a deep breath and added: "But not for long. I'm going to have to resign my commission."

"Why? I know the government keeps cutting the budget and the RAF has curtailed recruitment, but..."

David was shaking his head. "It's not the RAF. It's my father's revenge."

"I'm not following you."

David took another deep breath. "He left me *too much* money to ignore. I can't just leave it sitting in a bank somewhere. I *have* to do something with it. And to make things worse, he handed me the responsibility of honouring my slaughtered relatives. If I do nothing, then any assets that haven't been destroyed will be left in the hands of those who benefited from their murder. Even if there is only one little boathouse or a toilet somewhere that was once ours and now enriches some ex-SS or former Gestapo officer, it would be like spitting on my aunt and uncle's grave. I can't let the bastards get away with profiting from their death. I *can't.*"

"I see what you mean," Kiwi agreed softly. After a moment he added, "So you're going to spend the money he left you to go to Germany and try to track down the property?"

David sighed deeply and then nodded. "Yes. I'm going to resign from the RAF and go to Germany to find out what's left. If everything has been destroyed, then the slate is wiped clean, but if some Nazi is planning to get rich with my uncle's property, I will *shatter* that dream!" He was surprised by his vehemence. He hadn't realised just how much he hated them.

Kiwi reached out a hand and squeezed his shoulder. "Damn right!" After a moment of silence, however, Kiwi added, "Just remember, Banks, once they give you that bowler hat, there's no way back into the RAF these days."

David looked over at his friend and saw the raw pain seared on Kiwi's face. After all the things Kiwi had done for him in the past, he wanted to end that pain. Yet the next thought hit him so unexpectedly that he gasped.

He grabbed Kiwi's arm. "Kiwi! Listen! I've got an idea! It's not going to take me a lifetime to find out what happened to half a dozen pieces of property. You might even be right about there being nothing left. In two to three months', I'll have that behind me, and I can take the money, buy an aircraft and set up some kind of flying business. Between the two of us, we can fly anything."

Kiwi laughed.

"I'm serious, Kiwi."

"It's that much money?" Kiwi focused on him, his open face reflecting his disbelief.

"Well," David was embarrassed. He tried to think of some way to say it discreetly, but then simply admitted "Yes." Then a rare smile spread across his reconstructed face. "Remember what I said about 'he who laughs last?' I think — just maybe — the last laugh's mine, after all. My father knew I wouldn't be able to leave this much money just lying around. He thought by giving me a small fortune, he would turn me into a 'proper businessman.' What he failed to foresee was that I could use it to build a *flying* business."

"I'll drink to that, mate!" They clicked and drained their glasses.

David ordered a second round, and then grew serious again as he decided, "But not an airline. That's way too complicated and risky. It would be madness to go head-to-head with BOAC and BEA. Maybe a small charter company of some kind? You did some odd flying jobs before the war. What exactly did you do?"

"Everything," Kiwi answered flippantly, but then his expression changed. Suddenly deadly serious, he looked at his friend and asked. "Are you serious about including me in this?"

"I can't manage on my own," David answered as if he hadn't noticed how much his offer meant to Kiwi. "But we need to find a niche, something that not every ex-bomber pilot with a little extra cash is trying to do. Something unique. What could we do other than passengers or freight?"

"Did a lot of firefighting and crop-dusting in Australia, but there's not much need for that on this rain-drenched island...." Kiwi reflected with a bitter shrug. It hurt David to see him so beaten down. It was as if he was afraid to dream any more. David's imagination on the other hand was on fire. He was sure he was on to something, something exciting and potentially transformational. He shared his thoughts out loud, "Preferably we'd find something we could do with a converted bomber. They'll be cheaper to acquire."

"Air ambulance," Kiwi suggested at once. "Did that in Australia, too. Bombers can be converted easily for loading and off-loading stretchers. The problem with the air ambulance business is you also need some medical equipment on board — you know, stuff to monitor pulse, heartbeat and the like — and oxygen and heating, of course. I think it may be mandatory for a nurse to fly with the patient too. At least the outfits I flew for all had them."

David stared at Kiwi while he digested the suggestion, and then having decided this was the perfect fit he declared enthusiastically, "That's it! It's brilliant!" His thoughts tumbled out in a rush of words. "The very fact that it's complicated will keep down the competition, but it's the kind of business we could operate out of an obscure airfield in the middle of nowhere where the fees aren't so high. Wait. Stop." David held up his hand as if to someone else, but only to stop his flood of thoughts.

Kiwi waited mesmerised yet uncertain.

"We need to set up a company as soon as possible, so I can put you on the payroll," David announced. "That way you can do a lot of the leg work, while I'm in Germany making sure no Nazi is getting rich with my uncle's assets. When could you leave your job?"

Kiwi looked down at his watch. "Hm. It's 7:35. It will take me about two minutes to put a phone call through. Is that soon enough?"

They grinned at each other, and then David answered, "Monday's soon enough. Now, is twenty pounds a month enough for a base salary? Just for the start-up phase." David hastened to assure his friend. "Once you start flying, you'll get flight pay, of course, and once we make profits, we'll split them 25% each and plough the rest back into the company. Sound fair?"

"You bet," Kiwi agreed readily, but then he reached out and put a restraining hand on David's arm, interrupting his monologue about the best legal structure for the company. "Banks!" When he had his friend's undivided attention, he told him earnestly. "I'm not some wizard businessman. Surely you know that by now, don't you?"

David met his eyes. "You don't have to be, Kiwi. That's what my father is forcing me to become. The things I need you to do, you can practically do in your sleep."

"Like what?"

"Well, we're going to have to find out the government regulations for air ambulances and—"

"Mate, you're talking dense paperwork…"

"You didn't let me finish. Find them and post me a copy for some light reading while I'm in Germany." Kiwi laughed with relief and David grinned at him. "Then I want you to find us a couple of options for suitable aircraft and do a little comparative analysis. You'll need to pay careful attention to operating expenses not just acquisition costs—"

"Would you translate that into language a sky jockey can understand?"

"Look into the fuel consumption and the maintenance specs for each aircraft type to see how often essential parts need to be replaced and the like. We'll need erks too, and you need to keep your ears open for an airstrip we could fly from and companies that can make modifications to airframes and find out what they charge."

"Stop! Slow down! I've got to start writing some of this stuff down."

"Yeah, good idea. Can you really resign on Monday?"

"I work on commission, remember? They'll be glad to see me go, seeing how little success I've had as a salesman."

"Perfect, now—"

"Wait a minute, Banks. We've got another problem," Kiwi admitted tensely. David waited for him to spit it out. "If we're going to be flying twins, I'm going to need a commercial license." Fear was written all over his face, again.

David laughed with relief. If there was one thing he was not worried about it was that Kiwi, a born pilot, could master twin-engine aircraft. Out loud he simply told Kiwi with a grin, "I'm not worried."

"It costs money, mate—"

"Kiwi, I've *got* that. As soon as we set up the company, we can start billing expenses to it."

By the time Sarah joined them, they were scribbling down notes and setting themselves deadlines with such intensity that they hadn't ordered drinks for an hour.

Chapter One
Arrivals

Volunteer
Netley Abbey, Hampshire — Gatow, Berlin
2 January — 5 January 1948

"How can you possibly take an innocent six-year-old child to Berlin of all places?" Mrs Harriman asked her daughter indignantly.

"Mother!" Kathleen pleaded, "Gatow is just another RAF station!"

"In the middle of Germany! You'll be surrounded by Nazis!"

"The war has been over almost three years, Mother. Besides, I have housing on the station and Hope will go to school and have daycare there. We won't need to go into Berlin for anything."

"Then why go there in the first place? Why don't you just quit the WAAF and take a nice, sensible job? You trained and worked as a sales clerk before you married, and I see signs in windows saying, 'help wanted' all over the place. There's even a vacancy at Marks and Spencers on High Street! That would be perfect for you, and you would meet lots of nice, respectable people. You and Hope could move back in with us."

The last thing Kathleen wanted was to live with her parents. It was nine years since she'd married and almost five since her husband Ken had been killed. She treasured her independence.

As if reading her thoughts, her mother hastened to add, "Think of how much better it would be for little Hope if you didn't have shift work, Kathleen. As a shopgirl, you'd have regular working hours and could live a normal life again. It was one thing during the war when it was a national emergency and Hope was so little. I understand that working at an airfield helped you get over your grief, but it's time to move on. You're still an attractive young woman. No one would think you were 28 just by looking at you. Your hair is still so dark and thick. It is time to find a new daddy for poor little Hope."

Kathleen reined in her temper and tried to answer in a civil tone of voice, but she was not open to further discussion. "Mother, I volunteered for this posting. It was an urgent request, and I already have my orders. I'll be leaving first thing on Sunday."

"That's only three days from now!"

"Exactly, and I was very much hoping you'd be willing to look after Hope until I'm settled into my new position. There is a daily BEA flight into Gatow, and I've already looked into arrangements for an unaccompanied child to fly on it. All you'll have to do is get her to Northolt when I send you a cable with the date and details."

"You expect Hope to fly alone to Berlin! That's dangerous and must be outrageously expensive!" Her mother protested.

"I can afford it and the flight will be much safer than for her to travel with me via Dover, Brussels and Hanover. I'll be en route for roughly 48 hours. But, if you don't want to have Hope with you for the next ten days, then I shall take her with me." Kathleen left no room for doubt that she meant what she said.

"I would never impose such a horrible journey on a child!" Her mother countered indignantly. "If you insist on throwing your money away on airfare for a child, of course, we'd be happy to have Hope with us until you send word. But I don't understand you, Kathleen. Honestly, I don't. What on earth do you hope to gain by going to Berlin?"

Kathleen drew a deep breath. There was so much she hoped to gain but her mother would understand none of it — not the chance to do radar controlling, or to be the senior WAAF on the station, or to be near Ken, who was buried in the Commonwealth War Cemetery there. Kathleen secretly hoped that going there and seeing the grave would at last free her to love again, but the last person she would ever confess that to was her mother. So, all she said was, "Mother, it's my life."

Four days later, WAAF Flight Sergeant Kathleen Hart reached Brussels in the damp and cold of a dreary northern European January dawn. Travelling outside the UK for the first time in her life, she found herself somewhat intimidated by the large number of passengers speaking French. So, she stuck close to the cluster of men in British Army uniform standing on the platform with her. Being overseas was more daunting than she'd expected, making her a little afraid of her own courage.

When the train arrived, she followed the crowd of soldiers and found a seat in a compartment with four other sergeants, one of whom helped her heave her two kitbags onto the overhead rack. Then she sank down beside the window with a sigh. Now that she was safely aboard her train, her curiosity reasserted itself. As the sun slowly lifted itself over the rim of the overcast horizon, she hoped she might finally see something of the Continent. Yet all the light of day revealed were railway yards, factories, storage sheds and petrol tanks. With a sigh of disappointment, she leaned back against the dusty headrest and closed her eyes. Despite sleeping a bit on the ferry, she was feeling very tired. Soon she dozed.

The squeal of brakes as the train slowed, woke her. She turned at once to the window and noticed that the sun was trying to break through the gloom. Unfortunately, it made little difference to her view because the windows were caked with grime. Beyond the dirty glass, the countryside was dreary in winter dress: naked trees, fallow fields, and puddles of muddy rainwater. There was little traffic on the country roads either.

Yet within minutes, the bleak rural landscape began to give way to a grey-black vista of broken masonry, piles of scrap metal, and burnt-out vehicles. The deeper the train rolled into the urban area, the closer and more ominous the destruction became. The buildings reached higher, but they lacked roofs and windows, and their sides were blackened by smoke. As the train slowed to a crawl, Kathleen realized that messages had been scrawled in white chalk on some of the charred walls. People had done that after being bombed out in Southampton, too, she remembered with a shudder.

The train brakes screeched shrilly, and Kathleen's view was suddenly cut off by twisted rolling stock with shattered windows lined up behind a locomotive lying on its side with its guts spilling out. Kathleen shivered and closed her eyes, but the image could not be erased. The brakes were applied again and at last, they came to a stop beside a concrete platform. She opened her eyes to find out where she was, but she couldn't read the sign at an oblique angle through the dirty glass. She stood and shoved the window down, letting in a blast of cold air smelling of coal smoke. An eruption of angry complaints from her fellow passengers convinced her to close the window rapidly, but not before she had deciphered the name of the stop. They had arrived in a place called Krefeld. It sounded vaguely familiar although she couldn't imagine why. And then it hit her: more than once it had been "the target for tonight."

A handful of passengers boarded the train, the doors clanged shut, and the train lurched forward again. As they continued out of the city, she saw nothing except heaps of grey debris covered with dirty snow. She asked herself, Did we really do all this?

The question repeated itself as the journey continued. The images were unremittingly chilling and with each mile deeper into Germany, Kathleen felt more uncomfortable. What the hell had she gotten herself into? There was so little left standing that it seemed pointless to try to rebuild anything, and there was little sign of life anyway. The few people she glimpsed lurking in the semi-deserted streets hunched against the wind and blowing dust, their heads down, their eyes averted. They undoubtedly looked defeated, but were they resentful too? Angry, maybe? Or bitter? Were they awaiting the chance to strike back? Kathleen turned away from the window. Everything beyond her overheated train compartment full of British travellers had become vaguely threatening.

And each stop was yet another "target for tonight" — Essen, Bochum, Dortmund, Hamm, Gutersloh, Minden. With dismay at her naiveté, she realized she was crossing the Ruhr, the hated "Happy Valley" of the bomber boys.

Her train pulled into Hanover station fifteen minutes late. Fortunately, one of the sergeants in her compartment was returning to Berlin from leave and offered to give her a hand. He took one of her kitbags and together they ran down one set of steps and up another to catch the Berlin train just in time. The train was overcrowded, and Kathleen found a middle seat in a different compartment from her brief companion and squeezed herself in. She was thankful that the last leg of her journey would be after nightfall. She'd seen enough destruction for a lifetime.

Kathleen's instructions were to disembark at Spandau, just short of Berlin, and await RAF transport there. She arrived in the grey of dawn feeling stiff, crumpled, gritty and decidedly nervous. None of the other British passengers disembarked with her, and she realized she was alone among Germans. Not only was everyone around her speaking German, but several of them cast her hate-filled stares.

She turned up the collar of her greatcoat and tried to ignore them as she slung her leather handbag over her shoulder and lifted a kitbag in each hand to descend into a dank underpass smelling of urine that led from the platform to the station. She resurfaced in a building that was little more than a shell with no glass in any of the large windows. A bitter wind blew across the cracked concrete, stirring up cyclones of coal dust and ticket stubs.

"Fight Sergeant Hart?" A pleasant female voice surprised her from behind, and she spun about. With a surge of relief, she found a plump young woman with bright blond hair stuffed under a WAAF cap. She wore the stripes of a sergeant and held out her hand with a smile. "I'm Lynne Andrews, Chiefy. Welcome to Berlin."

"I can't say how glad I am to see you!" Kathleen admitted, shaking the other woman's hand vigorously.

"We're not allowed on the platform, I'm afraid. Here. I'll take your luggage—"

"Oh, I can manage one of them," Kathleen assured her, and with them each lugging a kitbag, Lynne led the way out of the station to the RAF lorry waiting in front.

As the LAC driver set off, Kathleen turned to the other WAAF. "What's your position at the station?"

"Clerk, general duties," she answered snappily, adding with a smile in a pseudo-posh accent, "I'm what they call an executive secretary on civvy street — to the Station Commander."

"Oh, what's he like?" Kathleen hastened to ask.

"Haven't a clue," Lynne answered, laughing at Kathleen's look of bewilderment before explaining, "Group Captain Sommerville, who I served since my arrival, was always very withdrawn and private as long as I knew him. What we didn't realize was that he was suffering from stomach cancer. Anyway, it finally got so bad that his assignment was terminated for medical reasons, and he returned to the UK for surgery in early December. The Station Engineering Officer is acting CO until the new CO arrives on Thursday."

"Have you heard any scuttlebutt about the new CO?"

"Good and bad. Apparently, he's a Cranwell grad and also went to Staff College. He's coming here out of a job at the Air Ministry."

That didn't sound good to Kathleen. He sounded like he'd be all about King's Regulations and "square-bashing" — that is, drill and appearances. "What about his war record?" she asked Lynne.

"That's the good news. He's a Battle of Britain ace, who also flew in Malta, and he commanded a Wing from Kenley until he was shot down and landed in a German POW camp."

As they talked, they were travelling along a good, straight road through a forest. Sometimes, off to their left, they caught glimpses of silvery grey water shimmering under the partially overcast sky. Everything seemed strangely peaceful, pleasant and rural. Because the landscape was too flat to feel like England, Kathleen was conscious of being somewhere "foreign," but she no longer sensed the same ominous threat she had felt during her journey through Germany. Yet there was no sign of a major city either. "Where's Berlin?" she finally asked.

Lynne laughed and gestured with one hand. "Miles away beyond the forest and that lake."

Finally, they came to a barricade manned by men of the RAF regiment, and then the airfield opened up before them. It came as a pleasant surprise to Kathleen. There was not a Nissen hut as far as the eye could see. Instead, the buildings were made of solid brick covered with clean, white plaster.

Lynne informed her, "The accommodations are excellent here. We WAAF are housed in NCO married housing, so we all have kitchenettes as well as baths. There are lots of children on the station. I think it's RAF policy to send families. They prefer us to remain among ourselves rather than get swept up in all the dubious activities that go on in Berlin. It's a veritable vortex of crime and immorality. You'll get the full briefing, but nothing on earth would induce me to walk around the city without a male escort — preferably a drill sergeant from the RAF regiment! Besides, there's not much need to go into Berlin. We've got a tennis club, rugby and cricket teams, a music society and a theatre company on the base, and even stables. They have an odd collection of mounts from ponies to draught horses, and the MO's wife gives riding lessons."

The lorry stopped before a building with a brick walkway flanked by low bushes leading to a glass entrance. Lynne led up one flight of stairs and extracted a key from her pocket to open the door. Inside, a large sunny room greeted them. By RAF standards it was palatial, including the promised kitchenette in a niche near the door. Despite the standard, functional furnishings, the sun flooding in made it look cheerful. More than that: it was warm. What a luxury!

"Since the Station Commander doesn't arrive until Thursday, your only courtesy call is with the Flying Control Officer this afternoon at two-thirty. I'll swing by to take you over to the Sergeant's mess for a meal at half past one and then show you around a bit before ending up at the tower for your meeting with the FCO. For this evening, I thought we WAAF could all meet at the NAAFI for a drink. How does that sound?"

"It sounds perfect," Kathleen assured her sincerely. "I've never been made to feel so welcome before," Kathleen exclaimed enthusiastically.

"Well, Gatow's so isolated, we have to look after one another."

When her alarm clock went off just over three hours later, Kathleen woke feeling comparatively rested and quickly dressed in her best uniform. She brushed and put up her long dark hair, then checked her watch. With time to spare, she unpacked. She'd never pictured accommodation so grand. Most of her service life had been spent in Nissen huts starting as a raw recruit with twelve girls to a room. Her daughter had never had a room all to herself before, either, and as he hung Hope's dresses in the cupboard and put her undies in a drawer she hoped she would not object. To welcome her, Kathleen put Hope's stuffed bunny rabbit on the pillow of the bed under the window. Hope couldn't be parted from her teddy bear and would be travelling with him, but the bunny was her second favourite toy and she'd be happy to be reunited.

In the sitting room, she looked around at the unaccustomed space a little helplessly. Comfortable though it was, everything felt rather empty, not to mention too tidy and impersonal without Hope. She'd start by putting her photos on the side table and shelf, she decided. Her wedding photo took pride of place. It was a large photo in a silver frame showing her in a long, white, satin gown and Ken dressed in the smart, double-breasted, navy-blue uniform of a Chief Mate in the Merchant Navy. Next came a formal studio shot of Ken in RAF blues, sergeant's stripes, and his air navigator brevet. Kathleen let her eyes linger on Ken's calm, square face as she silently promised to visit him "as soon as possible." Next, she set up Hope's Christening photo with Ken again in RAF blue but now a pilot officer. Beside this image, she placed a snapshot of Hope blowing out the candles on her sixth birthday cake. Although small and a bit blurry, she loved this picture because it had been taken after Hope recovered from appendicitis, and she looked exceptionally happy.

The last photo in the folder was one she didn't usually display. It showed a Lancaster and its grinning crew, but it wasn't Ken's crew. This photo showed the only surviving member of Ken's first crew, Kit Moran, along with his second crew. Kit's wife Georgina had sent it to her. She hesitated about displaying it. It might raise unnecessary questions. But the flat looked so empty. It would at least fill a space until she found something more appropriate.

A knock announced Lynne's return. Lynne had brought two bicycles and led the way to the large, comfortable Sergeant's mess. After a sumptuous meal unlike anything in Britain where the rationing was still in force, the two WAAF continued to the main admin building. They left the bicycles in the rack out front and climbed to the third floor as Lynne explained, "The setup here is not standard RAF. The Luftwaffe built the station to their specifications and since everything seemed quite functional, no one made any major changes."

Just off the stairway, they entered a door marked "Operations," and were confronted by a spacious, high-ceilinged room with three, large windows looking out toward the hangars and hardstandings. To the right hung a large map showing the UK and northwestern Europe with Berlin at the eastern edge. On the opposite wall, a much more detailed map of Berlin and its environs was displayed. Both showed navigational beacons and air corridors. In between, along the back wall through which they'd entered, a large blackboard displayed flight information. At present, it contained only a single entry for the daily BEA flight.

A distinguished-looking Warrant Officer with a large red moustache came over to introduce himself. "You must be the new WAAF air traffic controller! Welcome aboard. My name's Tyler." He introduced himself.

Kathleen asked if she could take a closer look at the maps. Tyler happily took her over to the European map first. "So here you see the air corridors," he pointed to three thick lines branching out from Berlin to the northwest, west and southwest. With a glance over his shoulder at Kathleen, he asked, "They warned you about them didn't they?"

"Not really," she admitted.

"Well then, this is important: Our aircraft are not allowed to fly over the Soviet Zone except inside one of these three corridors." Again, he traced them with his finger. "The corridors are 20 miles wide and 10,000 feet high."

"That sounds restrictive," Kathleen exclaimed. "What if there are thundershowers or hail in the corridors?"

"We fly through it."

"And over Berlin? What happens then?"

"Everything in a 20-mile radius of Berlin is open to our aircraft — except within a two-mile radius of a Soviet airfield. Come and look at the Berlin map." Tyler led Kathleen to the map on the opposite wall. Here, thick red lines delineated the four sectors of Berlin, each ruled by a different occupation power. The easternmost sector was the Soviet Sector. Moving clockwise from that came the American, British and French sectors. All fit together like irregular jigsaw puzzle pieces connecting in the centre of the city. Tyler also pointed out Gatow in the lower left, the US airfield at Tempelhof, and the Soviet airfields at Staaken and Schoenefeld. He traced the Havel River stretching from north to south but widening into the lakes of Wansee and Tegel and pointed to the Allied Control Council building in the northern end of the American Sector. "That's where area traffic control is located," he explained, "in what they call the Berlin Air Safety Centre. It is manned by air traffic controllers from all four occupation powers."

After studying the map carefully for another minute, Kathleen ventured to ask, "Where's the Commonwealth War Cemetery?"

"Here," Tyler pointed to a large blank quadrangle east of the Havel but directly beside the main thoroughfare between Spandau and Berlin "Mitte," as the city centre was called. He looked over his shoulder at her with a concerned look. "Do you know someone there?"

"My husband."

Lynne next led Kathleen up the stairs to the control tower. Uninterrupted glass surrounded the controllers on three sides and the view to the runways was excellent. At a long table along the front of the tower sat a sole controller and one assistant, a warrant officer and corporal respectively. Both got to their feet to shake hands with Kathleen. "Delighted to see you," the warrant officer opened with a welcoming smile, introducing himself as 'Willie' Wilkins and his assistant as Rufus Groom.

They happily pointed out the various points of interest on the airfield as seen from this sovereign vantage point.

"Isn't there radar control here?" Kathleen asked.

"Oh, we have it back there," Willie stood and went to the back of the room where he opened a door disclosing a large but windowless space with a single radar set currently switched off. "We only use radar when the weather's exceptionally bad," he explained to Kathleen's disappointment.

They had just started to exchange information about former assignments when a Flight Lieutenant burst in on them.

"What the blazes — Oh. Are you the new WAAF ATC?"

Kathleen noticed the officer was not wearing wings but rather the observer brevet. Fair enough, she thought. The observers on Mosquitos were experts at reading radar and many made first-rate controllers, but this man seemed oddly dishevelled. The Flight Lieutenant approached and leaned toward her as if he was short-sighted and needed to see her better. His smile became almost leering in the process. She caught the scent of alcohol on his breath and knew that he was pickled — and it was barely three pm.

"Yes, sir." She saluted as smartly as she could, forcing him to step back a little and respond in kind, if sloppily.

"Well, I hope you'll be better than your predecessor," he replied, dropping himself down on the long desk at which Wilkins and Groom had been sitting. "We had to throw her out for lack of morals. Slept with everyone on the station except the dogs. Or, who knows, maybe she slept with them as well."

He then staggered toward the window to scan the sky with a pair of binoculars before departing without another glance or word to Kathleen. She stood stunned in his wake. Wilkins and Groom looked suitably embarrassed, but neither seemed to know what to say.

"Is he like that often?" Kathleen finally asked.

The men looked at one another. Wilkins shrugged and admitted, "More and more. He doesn't like it here much."

How ironic, Kathleen thought. She'd been so sure this would be a professional opportunity and all her worries had focused on whether it would be good for Hope. Instead, it looked like Hope would be as well-off here as in England, while she wouldn't be getting the experience on radar she'd hoped for and on top of that would be facing hostility and incompetence from her immediate superior.

Brother of a Hero
Berlin-Kreuzberg
Tuesday, 6 January 1948

"Herr Baron? Is it really you?" Theo Pfalz stood in the doorway of the apartment house on the Maybach Ufer 27 and stared incredulously. The young man opposite exuded health and fitness to an intimidating degree. Pfalz hadn't seen a German looking this good — or this self-assured — since the end of the war. Christian Freiherr von Feldburg was in his mid-thirties, with rough blond hair and a well-proportioned face. He wore a tailored suit and a cashmere coat that was neither patched, ragged nor worn-thin, although by its cut it dated from the thirties.

"Yes, Pfalz, it's me. May I come in?"

"Of course, Herr Baron!" Pfalz backed up into the entrance hall still gazing in wonder at the apparition opposite him. Christian stepped inside carrying two large, bulging, leather suitcases. "Do you plan to stay here, Herr Baron?" the concierge asked stunned.

"Where else should I stay in Berlin?" Christian countered with a raised eyebrow. "I own this apartment house."

"Ah, yes, of course, Herr Baron, but there are refugees in your apartment. Nineteen of them."

"So I heard. I'll stay with my cousin, Graefin Walmsdorf. Is she home?"

"Oh, yes. She never goes out after dark." Pfalz informed him.

"I'm glad to hear that. She's on the top floor?"

"Yes, Herr Baron. On the right."

"Good." Christian took his heavy suitcases and started up the stairs. Halfway to the landing, however, he stopped abruptly and looked back. "Pflaz?"

"Yes, Herr Baron?"

"Were you here the night my brother...?"

"Yes, Herr Baron. The Frau Baronin left very late with Frl. Modenhauer, which surprised me. Shortly afterwards I heard the Fuehrer's speech, and I guessed the truth. Your brother had never disguised his dislike of the Nazis, and only a week or so earlier Graf Stauffenberg had been here. When I heard the pistol shot, I knew what it was. I rushed upstairs, and since no one answered my knocking and shouting, I got the extra key and let myself in."

"Then you were the one to find him?"

"Yes, Herr Baron."

They gazed at one another, but neither seemed to want to go into greater detail. Then Theo added, "I removed his Ritterkreuz and his wedding ring because I thought the Frau Baronin might want them, but she never came back."

"No, she couldn't face this house." Christian let his eyes sweep around the shabby entry hall with its tattered reminders of a better past.

"But she survived the war?" Theo asked hopefully.

"She did, yes. Frl. Moldenauer was able to bring her to a safe house — one of the places where people hid Jews, Communists and others in need of shelter from Nazi persecution."

"Frl. Moldenauer? How did such an innocent young girl know about places like that?" Theo asked in astonishment.

Christian smiled cynically. "You forget, Pfalz. The young are more likely to have ideals — and be willing to die for them. It's as we get older that we become jaded. Frl. Moldenauer, I was told, belonged to a clandestine network that provided Jews with forged documents."

Although his puzzled frown did not fade, Theo nodded and asked, "Would you like your brother's things? The ones I managed to save? I didn't dare take many things. I knew the police were on the way and that the Gestapo would want to turn the apartment upside down in a search for evidence and to find the names of accomplices. Many things went missing in the process. Later an SD officer moved his mistress into the apartment, and as the Soviets came ever nearer, he packed all the valuable things up and sent them somewhere. It was theft, but there was nothing I could do to stop it." Theo's tone mixed indignation with a plea for understanding.

"Thank you for saving whatever you could, Pfalz — and for lying to the

Gestapo about my sister-in-law's whereabouts."

"How did you know about that, Herr Baron?"

"My brother's widow is now a prosecutor for the Americans at Nuremberg. She was able to obtain access to my brother's Gestapo file and it was noted there that you, a staunch and loyal Nazi Party Member and SA man since before the Seizure of Power, had cooperated fully and willingly with the investigation. You were explicitly commended," Christian emphasised, making Theo squirm, before adding, "except, as Alix noted, you lied about where she was and managed to forget many of my brother's visitors. You had, she claims, a remarkable memory for the names of those already implicated, arrested or dead. She asked me to thank you for that, and, yes, I would like my brother's wedding ring and *Ritterkreuz* — and whatever else you managed to rescue from the claws of the Gestapo. But not now. I'm tired and want to settle in. I'll stop by sometime tomorrow or the next day."

"Very good, Herr Baron." Theo was visibly relieved, and he smiled tentatively. "It's good to have you here, Herr Baron. It feels right."

Christian thanked him but could not bring himself to pretend he was glad to be here. He wasn't. To him, everything felt wrong. This was not the elegant, fashionable house he remembered. It was not warm and bustling with life. He could not imagine running into members of the Reichstag, professors, artists and opera singers on these steps. He could not picture the ladies in evening gowns and tiaras on the arms of men wearing white ties and top hats whom he had watched with childish wonder. Instead, the house felt like a rotting corpse, blood-stained, and soulless.

Christian started heavily up the stairs again, but this time it was Theo who stopped him. "Herr Baron?" The baron had reached the landing where the stairs doubled back on themselves. He paused and looked over the railing expectantly.

"Be careful of the three young men living in the left-hand apartment on the third floor," Theo warned. "They're mixed up in the black market. Also, Herr Liebherr's son, Karl, although he doesn't live here, comes around a lot. Don't trust him. He's KPD — SED now."

"Thank you. Who's Herr Liebherr?"

"Oh, that's right, he moved in the left-hand flat on the fourth floor after the war. Herr Liebherr was an SPD member of the Reichstag before the war. He voted against the Enabling Law and spent two years in Oranienburg concentration camp. He was elected to the City Council for Kreuzberg in the municipal election last year. His wife is a senior ward nurse at the Hospital am Urban. Good, honest people, Herr Baron, but their son is a Soviet stooge."

"Thank you, Pfalz."

Christian continued up the stairs to the fourth floor, set down his heavy suitcases, and knocked on the righthand door.

After a few moments, a tense, female voice called. "Who's there?"

"It's me. Christian. Didn't you get my letter?"

"Christian?" A pause. "Christian von Feldburg?" The mixture of disbelief and excitement in Charlotte's voice pierced her cousin's heart. He'd heard terror, loneliness, desperation and sudden hope all mingled together in her gasped questions.

From the other side of the door came the sound of chains and bolts being removed. The key turned in the lock and the door yanked open. Charlotte stood in the doorway. Her apartment was so dark, she was lit only by the lightbulb in the stairwell, and it was not flattering. Christian had not seen her in six years, and he was not sure he would have recognised her on the street. She looked emaciated and haggard. Her hair had been chopped more than cut and it was very short at the back, although in front it fell onto her forehead like a man's. Her skin was rough and raw with patches of dryness. She wore no hint of makeup. Big, dark eyes sunken in their sockets like pools of misery dominated her face.

Christian's shock was so great that he could not find the usual pleasantries. Instead, with a single cry of "Charlotte!" he pulled her into his arms in a gesture of spontaneous sympathy.

She responded by clinging to him like a child. "Christian! Christian! Where have you come from? How did you get here? Why are you here? Can you stay a little while?" She looked up at him hopefully as she pulled away.

"I'm moving in with you, actually. At least for a few weeks," Christian announced and then thought to ask with a smile, "I hope that's all right?"

"Of course! I'm so glad you've come." Charlotte took a step back to let Christian in but hastened to lock, bolt, and chain the door behind him.

Christian meanwhile looked around in the dark corridor and noted that he could see his breath. Without thinking he exclaimed, "It's colder in here than outside!"

"I can't afford to heat anything except the kitchen," Charlotte apologised embarrassed. "Come!" She opened the closed kitchen door and shooed him inside. The kitchen was lit by a naked light bulb hanging over a battered, wooden table.

"I'll buy wood or coal for the other ovens tomorrow," Christian answered setting his suitcases down, while Charlotte closed the door behind him. "What else do you need?" He added surveying the nearly empty kitchen.

"I don't need much, Christian, but what about you? I had no idea you were coming and I have nothing--"

"Don't worry about me. I can organize anything we need tomorrow. Tonight, let's celebrate our long-overdue reunion. Where are the wine glasses?"

She shook her head. "I don't have any, but it doesn't matter because I can't afford wine. I can make some tea. Grandma Walmsdorf sends me packets from England." She started towards the stove.

Christian stopped her. "Don't bother. I brought samples of our Schloss Feldburg premium wine — so all we need are some glasses, any kind of glasses."

Charlotte went to the cupboard, while Christian laid one of his suitcases on its side and removed one of several bottles with screw-on tops labelled "Listerine."

Charlotte gaped as he placed it on the table with a grin. "It's impossible to bring wine across the Zone without the Ivans seizing it for themselves, so I disguised it as mouthwash. Allegedly, some Soviet soldier tried drinking this American mouthwash and nearly died. The word spread among the Ivans that it was poison, and they won't touch the stuff. Come. Sit down and try it!" he urged confidently.

Still looking sceptical, Charlotte sat down and held out her glass for Christian to pour while he explained cheerfully, "We've always produced some wine for our own consumption, but we never tried to make a business of it before. Last year, Mother decided that since it is a high-margin business, we ought to see if wine could put us back on our feet faster."

"Aunt Sophia is amazing," Charlotte acknowledged, referring to

Christian's mother, her father's sister. She lifted her glass to sniff at the pale-yellow liquid tentatively.

"My mother is focusing on the future because, she says, if she thinks about the past, she'd kill herself."

"There are a lot of us like that," Charlotte noted, adding in a barely audible whisper "— or there would be if we could see any future."

Christian wasn't sure if she was talking to him or herself. Her gaze was averted. "Charlotte?" She turned back to him with a weak smile. He could sense her fragility but was unsure how to respond to it. "A toast?" When she remained silent, he proposed one himself, "To a bright future."

Charlotte dutifully lifted her glass, but when she put it to her lips she sipped only timidly, as though she were afraid it might be Listerine after all. As she raised her glass to Christian to close the toast after drinking she admitted, "I'm trying to think when I last drank wine. I think it was Christmas 1944. That was such a sad Christmas. Fritz had been missing for over a year without a word, and we were all so afraid of the future with the Soviets coming closer each day. Father announced his decision to abandon Walmsdorf and try to make it to Berlin. Mother was torn apart by having to leave so much behind. I never dreamed that any Christmas could be worse than that — until the next three found me here."

"Why didn't you come to Altdorf?" Christian asked gently, reaching out to take her cold hand in his. "Surely you knew my mother would have welcomed you with her whole heart?"

Charlotte nodded. "Of course, I knew. It's just…"

When she didn't finish her thought after several seconds, Christian asked, "Is it your work here? I know Altdorf is a boring little provincial town, and Mother says you're a successful journalist."

Charlotte shook her head. "That's a lie I tell in my letters. I'm not successful at all. I sometimes sell stories, but not often. Usually not more than once or twice a week. RIAS pays best. They pay a *dollar* for a good story — and that's hard currency. The others only pay in occupation marks — which are really only useful for toilet paper, but of course, I need that too. If it weren't for Horst and the rations, I would have starved to death."

"Who's Horst?" Christian asked. Given Charlotte's circumstances, he could hardly blame her if she had a boyfriend or benefactor of some sort, but he felt an instinctive alarm, nevertheless.

"You must remember Horst!" She protested. "He was our coachman in Gross Walmsdorf."

"Oh, of course!" Now Christian remembered the coachman with the magnificent Kaiser Wilhelm moustache that he had admired as a boy. He had been a driver in the field artillery during the Great War but had grown up on Charlotte's father's estate and returned there after the last war. He was devoted to the Walmsdorf family.

Charlotte was speaking again, "Horst was driving my wagon when the Soviet fighter found us. He flung me down and protected me with his body. They missed us anyway. He took care of everything afterwards too — laying out my parents and Joseph and Martha with as much dignity as possible, putting down the wounded horse, and even making four crosses. The earth was stone-hard, so he couldn't dig graves, but Jasha helped him cover them with snow. I — I was useless. I wasn't at all brave."

"Charlotte, you'd just seen your parents and two dear friends shot to pieces by an enemy fighter. You were in shock."

"Horst and Jasha managed to keep functioning," she countered, her eyes turned inward, and Christian silently poured her more wine.

Charlotte took another sip and explained in a firmer voice. "I gave Horst the three horses that survived the trip. And the wagon. He set up a business delivering milk. He collects it from nearby farms in the Soviet Zone and sells it here in Kreuzberg, Neukoeln and Treptow. He brings me milk, cheese, eggs, and in the summer apples, onions and vegetables too. He's doing well. At least well enough to keep the horses fed. They're stabled in the second courtyard, where Philipp used to have his horses. You may have smelled them coming in."

Christian shook his head and asked instead, "And Jasha? What happened to her?"

"Jasha got a job cooking for an American officer and his family down in Dahlem. She lives in, so I don't see much of her. Unfortunately, her employer is due to transfer out soon, and his successor is under no obligation to retain her. She's worried she will lose her job."

Christian nodded understanding, but Jasha was a hard-working and resourceful Polish woman. Technically a forced labourer, she had seen what the Soviets did when they invaded her country. Her husband and son had both been killed by the Reds, not the Germans, so she had opted to stay with the Walmsdorfs rather than face the Red Army. He trusted Jasha to land on her feet. Charlotte, on the other hand, was not only his cousin she was clearly in a sorry state. He could not understand why she wouldn't leave Berlin to come to his mother's estate in Altdorf, which was doing comparatively well. Then it struck him. "You're staying here because of Fritz, aren't you? You think this is where he will show up if, by some miracle, he is still alive."

To his surprise, Charlotte shook her head, gazing into the distance. "No, he'd go to Walmsdorf."

"But the villagers will say you're in Berlin."

"Yes, but they didn't know about this house. It's Feldburg property. He'd never be able to find it."

"But you're registered with the police. If he made inquiries, he'd find the address."

"Since we never married, the police would not release the information to him."

Convinced she was telling the truth, Christian tried again to convince her to leave. "Charlotte, things are much better in Altdorf. Agriculture is the one sector that is thriving despite the currency situation. We had seed and livestock, all we needed was labour, and I'm not the only able-bodied male who's returned from internment over the last two years. The Amis pay well for fresh farm produce, and our wine is already turning a good profit on a small scale. As soon as we develop a steady market for it and expand production more, we'll have a good business. Mother could use your help, and you'd get good food, fresh air, and exercise — it's the life you grew up with." He reminded her. His memories of Charlotte centred around visits to her father's estate during summer holidays from school. They were memories of riding, hunting, swimming in the shallow lakes, and helping with the hay harvest. But she was shaking her head firmly. "Why not? What's keeping you here?" Christian wanted to know.

"Nothing's keeping me here," Charlotte told him in a strained voice, not meeting his eyes. "It's just that I can't *leave*." She paused and then gasped out: "I can't travel through the Zone."

"Why not? I just did it." Christian reminded her. "The Soviets can be bastards, but if your papers are in order and we travel together --"

Charlotte was shaking her head, and gasped out, "*I can't!*"

To his horror, Christian realised she was trembling. He jumped up and went around the table to put his arms around her. Her whole body was quivering as if she had a violent chill. "Charlotte, it's all right. Calm down. I won't force you to do anything."

"I'm sorry," she whispered, her eyes closed and her cheeks wet. "Please stay with me, Christian. At least a little while. Please."

"I'm not going anywhere," he assured her, holding her firmly. Never in his wildest dreams had he thought things would be this bad.

The WingCo's Better Half
London-Northolt
Thursday, 8 January 1948

They called the flight shortly after ten o'clock, and sixteen passengers filed past the airline clerk checking the tickets before following another employee across the tarmac to the waiting aircraft. The Dakota sat with her nose in the air, brightly painted in the red, white and black livery of British European Airlines. At the top of the mobile stairs, a smiling stewardess in a smart uniform greeted the passengers as they entered.

Emily Priestman passed through the low door in the fuselage near the tail of the aircraft and climbed up the steeply tilted aisle toward the front with her husband at her heels. Ahead, the cockpit door was closed, and a second stewardess stood in front of it smiling. Their seats were in the second row on the right and she slipped in first and settled herself in the window seat.

As her husband sank down beside her and fastened his seatbelt, he put her feelings into words. "I think this is the first time in my life I've ever been nervous about flying."

They shared a laugh and exchanged a look. They might both be qualified pilots with hundreds of flying hours, but neither of them had ever flown in a passenger liner before. The new experience seemed right for the start of a new chapter in their lives.

While one stewardess closed the fuselage door and reported "boarding completed" over the microphone to the captain, the other went down the aisle checking seat belts and handing out bonbons for people to suck. "It helps against popping ears as we gain altitude," she explained.

"Hm," Robin muttered, "The RAF never issued us with sweets," but he untwisted the paper and popped it into his mouth anyway. So did Emily.

Soon, the other stewardess asked for everyone's attention as she explained safety procedures. She demonstrated how to use the seatbelt and lifejacket. "No parachute," Robin grumbled to his wife. "How are we supposed to feel safe without a 'chute?"

Emily laughed again; parachutes had saved his life five times during the war.

The number one engine started up, distracting their attention. No sooner had the propeller been transformed into a shimmering disk than they swung their heads in unison to look out the window opposite as the number two engine started to turn slowly, fired, and dissolved into a whirr of light. The aircraft vibrated from stem to stern, and the noise seemed louder in the cabin than in the cockpit, Emily thought.

The stewardesses sat down in the two rearward-facing seats just behind the cockpit. As the aircraft taxied away from the gate, Emily peered out of her window, frustrated at not being able to see where they were going. Only by the way the aircraft swung and stopped did she know they had reached the head of the runway. While the Dakota sat motionless, Emily wondered what was delaying take-off. A glance at Robin confirmed that he too was frowning and annoyed by the apparent delay.

Abruptly, the engines started to roar at a higher and more frantic pitch. The aircraft danced nervously like a highly-strung racehorse at the starting gate. Finally, the pilot eased back on the throttles and released the brakes. The Dakota started purposefully down the runway gradually gaining speed. Finally, the tail wheel came up, but the aircraft remained glued to the tarmac.

"What's taking him so long? We're going to run out of runway," Robin growled.

"He's just making the take-off as smooth as possible for the passengers. None of your kind of nonsense." Emily teased. As an ATA pilot, she had been taught to fly 'by the book.' It was a running joke between them that she had a perfect safety record, while Robin had pranged more aircraft than he cared to count.

Slowly, they left the earth behind. Immediately, Emily pressed her nose to the window to see as much as she could. Robin half left his seat so he could look over her shoulder. The view was restricted compared to what they were used to from the cockpit, yet as they gradually gained altitude, more and more of London spread out below them. Excitedly, they pointed out one familiar landmark after another until a layer of cloud blocked their view.

Robin sank back into his seat and reached over to take his wife's hand. Emily turned to him, and their eyes met. There was so much to say, but the engines were too loud for conversation. Emily certainly didn't want to shout her feelings at him, yet sensed this was an important moment for both of them -- and then the mood was shattered by the stewardess offering them newspapers and magazines.

Robin glanced at Emily, and she took a copy of *Vogue* while he accepted a copy of the *Times*. She wasn't very interested in fashion, but the magazine enabled her to look relaxed despite feeling tense with apprehension. They'd been planning this move for six weeks, yet she still found it unfathomable that she was on her way to Germany.

Not that she was afraid of Germany or the Germans per se. She'd been raised on Karl Marx. German had been her foreign language at school. She loved German music and literature and had devoured John Maynard Keynes' "The Economic Consequences of the Peace." Keynes condemned the Treaty of Versailles as draconian and correctly predicted German revanchism. She had been a devoted and active member of the Peace Society; she'd marched arm-in-arm with young men shouting "Hell, no! We won't go!" She most certainly did not believe the Germans were inherently brutal, authoritarian or inhumane. Yet she had despised Hitler and all he stood for long before he became Germany's chancellor. She had abandoned her pacifism in the face of Nazi aggression. She had supported the war effort to the best of her abilities. Yet nothing had prepared her for the images from the Concentration Camps. The evidence they delivered had shattered all illusions about 'civilization' and left her feeling uncomfortably ambivalent and confused about Germans.

Yet, her uneasiness now had little to do with politics. Her apprehension arose from personal concerns. From the moment Robin had walked through the door with a bottle of champagne to celebrate his posting, she'd known that she had no choice but to pretend she was delighted, too. Robin had been miserable in staff work, and he saw this new posting as his escape to a better, more interesting future. He'd explained to her it was a stepping-stone to other overseas assignments. He'd sketched out a future in Singapore and Hong Kong, Rangoon and Bombay, Cape Town and Nairobi. He'd talked of servants and sailing and the wonders of the wide world.

That was so like him! From their first date, Robin had opened doors for her. He had not only rescued her from a dead-end job, he had also rescued her from her loveless and dreary parental home. He had replaced drudgery and duty with excitement and glamour. She laughed inwardly at the memory of a squadron party that Vivien Leigh, Lawrence Olivier and Rex Harrison had crashed. She'd found herself at the bar chatting with Rex Harrison as if they were old friends. For a girl from the slums of Portsmouth that was heady indeed! Robin had literally shown her the sky, and their shared love of flying had always been a bond between them.

She glanced up from her magazine to steal a sidelong glance at her husband. She loved the way he looked in his best blues with the three full stripes restored to his sleeve. He had always stolen the show when they were together, she thought with an indulgent smile. Never having been particularly vain, it did not bother her that most people had eyes only for Robin.

She'd been delighted to see his enthusiasm for this new posting. Shows of exuberance had been sorely missing since the end of the war. In place of keenness, apathy and mute resentment had festered. She had sensed his simmering bitterness in a job that brought him neither satisfaction nor apparent rewards. And while she knew his discontent was not directed *at* her, it had left her in the cold, all the same. She had felt as if they were standing on different ice floes, drifting farther and farther apart on divergent, underwater currents. Her disappointments and frustrations about not finding meaningful work and not getting pregnant had only compounded things. Rather than riding out the tide of their dejection and despondency together, they had fallen into the habit of hiding their feelings from one another through fear of making things worse. This new posting had blown away their mutual and separate dissatisfaction like a fresh gale.

It was a reprieve not just for Robin's career but for their marriage, as well. Emily was determined to make the most of it.

Yet this new assignment was fundamentally political and diplomatic, and that was what frightened Emily. Robin had talked blithely about the representational duties they would have, stressing that the burden would be upon her to host dinners and entertain their counterparts. He'd made it sound like it was important and fun and she should look forward to it all. All she saw were chances to make a fool of herself and wreck his career.

"Excuse me," the stewardess leaned over her with a smile and placed a little tray in front of her with a neat sandwich sliced diagonally and garnished with a tiny sprig of parsley. "Would you like water, wine, beer, coffee or tea with your meal?" the stewardess asked.

Emily took tea as did Robin. As the stewardess continued down the aisle, Robin remarked, "I could get used to having meals served on my flights." They laughed together again, which felt so good. If only it would last!

They had barely finished the sandwich before their trays were collected and they were warned to fasten their seatbelts again. The Dakota started to bank and lose altitude as they descended toward the Elbe estuary. Emily again pressed her nose to the window glass, with Robin breathing down her neck. They spotted several ships loading and off-loading and a passenger liner steaming out. It wasn't exactly the world's busiest port, but it was functioning despite the widespread damage all around it. In contrast, Hamburg itself lay mostly in ruins. She exclaimed, "My God! It looks much worse than London!"

"Yes. We had to close down the docks, the U-Boat pens and the oil refineries," her husband explained without remorse.

"But those are just housing blocks!" Emily protested. "Or *were*. No one could live there now — except birds and rats, I suppose."

"That's from the fire-bombing in July 1943," Robin explained with a shrug.

Emily looked out the window again and struggled with her emotions. For much of the war, the RAF had been the only means of hitting back at Nazi Germany. Robin had been frustrated that his role was indirect and questionably effective. Emily's work with the ATA, on the other hand, had brought her in contact with aircrew from Bomber Command, all of whom seemed proud to pay Germany back for the misery it had caused England. In the papers, however, the air offensive had always been described as "strategic" bombing. The targets had been aircraft and munitions factories, U-boat pens and battleships, marshalling yards and Gestapo HQs. No one had bragged about destroying houses, schools and hospitals.

At Fuhlsbuettel, Hamburg's civil airport, most of the passengers disembarked and five new passengers joined the flight. The Dakota was refuelled, and with just eleven passengers on board, it continued the journey to Berlin. Immediately after the seatbelt sign had been turned off, the cockpit door opened, and the second pilot entered the cabin. He stopped beside Robin. "Wing Commander Priestman?"

"Yes?"

"We understand you're the new Station Commander at Gatow. Would you like to join us in the cockpit for the flight down?"

"Very much!" Robin replied enthusiastically, before remembering to ask Emily, "Do you mind?"

"Of course not!" She waved him forward.

Emily turned back to the window. They were flying below light clouds at no more than 8,000 feet. At this height, she could clearly see the countryside below. Flat farmland interspersed with forest stretched in all directions. Here and there a village clustered around a church, but unlike English villages with thatched roofs, hedgerows and gardens, these consisted of brick or plaster houses with slate roofs crouching low to the ground and surrounded by muddy barnyards. Unlike the graceful Gothic churches typical of English villages, the German churches seemed austere and puritanical with square towers that looked more like military structures than tributes to God. Except for the autobahn, the roads were unpaved and the sparse traffic was horse-drawn rather than mechanised. Emily presumed that was a good indication of the poverty that gripped Germany. She supposed the Germans deserved to be poor for trying to conquer all of Europe, but she could not help thinking how bleak it would make the next couple of years.

Her thoughts drifted back to what lay ahead. Robin either forgot or underestimated the differences in their upbringing. Yes, his mother had been a widow living on a meagre pension, but she'd inherited a large, fully furnished house facing Southsea Common. His grandfather Admiral

Priestman had paid for him to go to an excellent public school, and he'd spent his school holidays at the admiral's stately home on the Isle of Wight, sailing dinghies and small yachts. He'd gone to Cranwell. He'd served in the Far East. He'd been an aerobatics pilot taking part in international air shows. His mother had a picture of him shaking hands with the Prince of Wales. She had considerately removed the many other photos of Robin with various heiresses, actresses and socialites. Robin was at ease in high society, and while he might not always *choose* to be diplomatic, he was not going to make embarrassing blunders of dress or protocol by mistake.

Emily, in contrast, had been raised in Portsmouth's dockland slums, the daughter of Communist activists determined to mobilize the masses for world revolution. Yes, they'd sent her to a fee-paying girls' school, but her weekends had been spent in Portsmouth until she earned a scholarship to Cambridge. Her university had shown her glimpses of the lifestyle her parents so bitterly condemned. She'd been invited to weekends at country estates and attended the odd formal dance, but she had never in her life hosted anything "representational" or "diplomatic." Robin seemed to think a staff of five was a wonderful benefit, but Emily's upbringing rebelled. She might have traded communism for pacifism and then given up ideology altogether to be with Robin, but she was distinctly uncomfortable with the thought of having live-in servants. She much preferred her house to be her own, a place where she and Robin could be alone together and interact without constantly fearing someone might walk in on them or overhear what they said.

Emily felt the Dakota bank gently onto a new course, but she still couldn't see anything that looked like a major city from her little window. Was it on the other side of the aircraft? Or was that something over there in the haze? There was certainly a concentration of roads and railway lines. Yet the aircraft continued over farmland and forest until she caught sight of an airfield ahead of them. Curiously, the airliner did not go into a noticeable descent.

Shortly afterwards, the door to the cockpit opened, and Robin emerged, thanking the pilots over his shoulder. As he came abreast of Emily, rather than taking his seat, he gestured for her to look out the window again. From behind her, he pointed to the airfield now almost directly below them. "That's a Soviet airfield. Easy to confuse with Gatow, the Captain said. We'll be over the Soviet Zone practically to the last minute on this approach."

The "Fasten Seat Belt" sign lit up, and one of the stewardesses told the passengers over the intercom to take their seats. Robin dutifully sat down and buckled up, but he craned to see out of Emily's window. Another airfield came in sight with a large curving building embracing the runways. All the buildings were constructed in the functional yet 'monumental' style favoured by the Nazis. This was no haphazard, wartime aerodrome.

"In the thirties, Gatow was the Luftwaffe equivalent of Cranwell and Halton combined," Robin told her as if reading her thoughts, "both a cadet college and a technical school."

"With no concrete runways?" Emily asked surprised.

"That's right. It was still just a grass field when we took it over. The RAF put down the Pierced-Steel-Plate runway."

"Look!" Emily exclaimed delightedly. "There are the Spitfires!" She looked over her shoulder to share a grin with Robin. She knew he was as pleased about having a squadron of these fighters here as she was. They could both hardly wait to fly a Spitfire again.

The airliner put down nicely and rolled out to the end of the runway, braking gently and evenly. Eventually, it came to a halt and turned to taxi decorously to an apron beside the building with the tower. The engines were switched off and the vibrations died away as they fell silent. "Well, here we are," Emily announced into the comparative quiet. "In Berlin."

"It doesn't feel like it, does it?" Robin replied, peering past her toward the fragment of airfield famed in their little window. All they could see were a perimeter fence and a grey, leafless forest beyond. It felt like somewhere in the middle of nowhere rather than the capital of Hitler's "Thousand Year" Reich.

The other passengers stood to remove their overhead luggage, and Robin unbuckled his seatbelt and started to stand. Emily caught his arm and made him look at her. "Robin, it's hard to imagine what lies ahead. I'm a little afraid I may find myself out of my depth. Will you be patient with me?"

He answered by leaning over and giving her a quick kiss. "Of course."

"Will you also promise to talk to me more?" Emily added. "Like we did in the beginning when you told me everything — even your fears and doubts."

He squeezed her hand. "I promise," then he got to his feet.

Emily was glad she had broached the topic of better communication and she trusted Robin to try. Yet as he set his cap on his head with the visor low, half-shielding his eyes and stepped back for her to precede him down the aisle, she knew that despite his best intentions it was going to be difficult to convince him to abandon the bunker he had built for himself.

Chapter Two
Berlin, Berlin

Eagle's View
RAF Gatow, Berlin
Friday, 9 January 1948

Priestman's first impression of his new command was positive. He and Emily had been met at the foot of the aircraft stairs by a small brass band and a little girl with a bouquet of fresh flowers. They had gone through a reception line composed of key personnel and then been given a full tour of the station. He'd been astonished by Gatow's size, solidity and comparative luxury. Near the runways were four large, modern hangars, along with workshops and a large administrative building topped by the control tower. The hangars were in excellent condition, the workshops tidy and well-swept, and the control tower had a commanding view from pristine clean windows. Priestman was shown his own office, which occupied the tip of the west wing of the admin building with windows on three sides offering oversight of the messes in addition to views almost as good as the control tower's. The operations room and other offices in the building were well-lit by tall windows and functionally furnished with maps, flight boards, telephones, teleprinters and R/T. Behind the admin building, the messes, NAAFI and communal buildings lined a curving road that led to excellent accommodation set amidst landscaping and separated by lawns. Priestman was told by the housing officer that half the units were vacant because current staffing was far below the numbers the Luftwaffe had once stationed here. Beyond the housing blocks came other remnants of the Luftwaffe's tenure, including an auditorium and classrooms that were completely unused at present. There were sports fields, a swimming pool (now a duck pond), tennis courts and stables located near the outer fence. As for the personnel, naturally, everyone had made an effort to get off on the right foot with the new CO, and Priestman had found no cause for complaint.

Yet he had also been in uniform long enough to know that spit-and-polish wasn't what made a unit good. To be sure, a lack of smartness usually flagged underlying problems, but even something picture-perfect could be rotting from within. The problem was that it was impossible to know what to look for without knowing what the station's mission was.

At a fighter station, for example, the most prized qualities were flexibility and adaptability; it worked best with men who were spontaneous, creative, and keen. A bomber station, on the other hand, placed priority on planning, co-operation, and endurance; there you wanted men who were steady, reliable and worked well in a team. A coastal command station, in contrast, fought the elements more than the enemy and your crews had to be exceptionally patient and self-reliant, more introverts than extroverts, and strongly self-motivated. But Gatow was none of the above, despite its lone Spitfire squadron.

During the war, Priestman had served as Station Commander at St. Athans, then the School of Air Navigation and part of Training Command. While that didn't fit into easy categories either, the task of improving aircrew navigational capabilities had been so patently crucial to the war effort, that he'd understood his role immediately. Yet so far no one had been able to adequately explain to him what the RAF's mission in Germany was, let alone how RAF Gatow fitted into the picture.

In his briefing with the BAFO commander Air Marshal Sanders, the latter had emphasized that England was still an 'occupying power,' but practically in the same breath, he had noted there had not been a single incident of civil disobedience, much less rebellion, since German surrender. "All that talk about fantasized Hitler Youths forming guerrilla units to carry on partisan warfare was nonsense. I haven't seen any indication of even passive resistance. The Germans will follow orders no matter who gives them."

"So, what justifies our military presence?" Priestman asked.

"The fact that the Soviets won't agree to any sensible plan for the re-establishment of a German state!" came the exasperated answer. "They veto everything and anything! Nyet, nyet, nyet! We can't end the occupation until we have an alternative for Germany. If we just pull out, that creates a vacuum that the Soviets will immediately fill. In my opinion, that's precisely why the Soviets use these obstructionist tactics. They hope to wear us down to the point where we just throw up our hands and walk away."

Priestman could see that having the Red Army on the Rhine was not a desirable outcome, yet Sanders had rapidly disabused him of any notions that the RAF might be in Germany to deter the Soviets. Sanders complained that he had only four bomber and six fighter squadrons, including the one here at Gatow. It amounted to 134 aircraft against which, he told Priestman, the Soviets had roughly 3,000. To Priestman's question about American strength, Sanders had surprised him by saying. "About the same as ours in the air. Only marginally more on the ground. The US Congress has been demobilizing and defunding the military even faster than we have. Ergo, the Red Army has 18,000 of their veteran soldiers in Berlin alone, and an additional 300,000 battle-hardened troops in the area immediately surrounding it. Along with the French and Americans, we have a total of 8,500, most of whom are post-war conscripts with little or no combat experience. In other words, the Western Allies don't stand a chance of stopping Soviet expansion by force."

"I must be missing something," Robin responded cautiously, "but you make it sound as if our presence serves no military purpose either with respect to Germany or the Soviet Union."

"Quite right! Our presence is purely symbolic. All we do is 'show the flag' — rather like a battleship on a round-the-world cruise."

That didn't sound terribly exciting to the former fighter pilot, but Priestman supposed it was still a necessary job, and one he was prepared to do. He had started to focus on this mission until, just three days ago, he'd met with his predecessor, Group Captain Sommerville. The meeting disconcerted him further.

Group Captain Sommerville was still recovering from recent surgery. He'd congratulated Priestman, while in the same breath drawing attention to his lower rank by remarking, "Quite right of them to appoint a wing commander. No need to waste a group captain on Gatow. It's no bloody use to anyone. If they'd asked me about it, I'd have told them to close it down altogether."

Rattled, Priestman asked, "Why's that, sir?"

"Because it's a hundred miles inside the Soviet Zone, and they don't want us there. When the 284th Field Squadron of the RAF Regiment arrived to take over Gatow from the Red Air Force, they were herded into a hangar and kept there under guard for a whole day! The Soviets maintain checkpoints just outside the fence and every so often they send their soldiers into our Sector looking for trouble. It's a ridiculous situation, the result of bad planning and poor political decisions during the war. Yes, I know all the arguments about having to have a foothold in the German capital, but Berlin isn't the capital of anything!"

"Well, not now," Priestman cautiously suggested, "but surely it will be when the occupation ends?"

"Maybe, maybe not. There are those who would rather see Germany cut up into little pieces with no central government and no capital at all. Certainly, that's what the French want. In my opinion, Berlin isn't worth all the trouble and expense we go to trying to hold on to it. You do realize, don't you, that we provide all the rations for the German population in our Sector and have to transport everything in? The Germans, you can be sure, are not the least bit grateful for what we're doing for them. But, as I've learnt, nobody wants my opinion — or yours. Ours is but to do and die."

Sommerville had been in the Pathfinders, Priestman reminded himself, and they had had less than a ten per cent chance of surviving two operational tours, so Sommerville's sense of being a sacrificial lamb was perhaps not completely incomprehensible. The Group Captain also appeared to still be in pain from his operation, so rather than prolong the meeting, Priestman had resigned himself to finding out more about his function after he arrived.

Now that he was on the ground, it was time to nail down exactly what it was he was supposed to be doing here. With his courtesy calls on the British Commandant and Air Commodore Waite scheduled for the afternoon, Priestman had a few hours to prepare. Given that he'd seen nothing whatsoever of Berlin, he asked Squadron Leader "Danny" Daniels, commander of the lone Spitfire squadron stationed at Gatow, to give him an aerial tour of Berlin.

Priestman had a secondary motive for this request: he wanted to fly a Spitfire again. The last time he'd been at the controls of a Spit, he'd been bested in a dogfight and ended up a prisoner of war for seventeen months. On his return from internment, he'd requalified as a pilot at an RAF Operational Training Unit, but it had been outfitted with Typhoons and Mustangs. Since then, his only flying had been weekend flips on an Anson at Northolt to retain his flying status. He knew he had to erase that last flight into humiliation and captivity with a successful flight on a Spitfire. It wasn't that he expected major problems, but he wanted to get this encounter over with as soon as possible so he'd be free to move on.

Priestman pulled his Irving flying jacket over his uniform and swapped his shoes for flying boots in his office, then with his gloves stuffed in the pockets, he crossed over to the squadron dispersal hut, where Danny awaited him. The Squadron Leader indicated two Spitfires that had already been checked and fuelled by the ground crew.

As they walked side-by-side toward the aircraft, Danny remarked. "I can't tell you what a pleasure it is to have you here, sir. I know the chaps would like a chance to talk to you in more depth, and I was wondering if you could find the time to talk to the squadron one of these days."

"About what?" Priestman asked warily. He had spent years trying to shake off the reputation of an irresponsible aerobatics pilot and playboy. That image had been replaced by "Battle of Britain ace." Proud as he was to have taken an active part in the defence of the realm in 1940, that had been almost eight years ago. He was now thirty-two and he didn't want his greatest glory to be what he'd done at twenty-four. He wanted to have a meaningful future, not just a glorious past.

"Oh, just your wartime experiences, sir," Danny confirmed his fears and Priestman was on the brink of declining when he added, "You won't remember me, but I briefly served in your wing before you were shot down over France."

Irritation was instantly replaced with mortification. Priestman had not recognized the Squadron Leader and apologised at once. "I'm sorry, Danny. I didn't recognise you."

"No reason why you should, sir. I was straight out of flight school and a pilot officer in 148 Squadron, sir. The sweep on which you were lost would have been my third operational sortie, but my oxygen went u/s and I had to abort."

"Just as well. We ran into what felt like the whole bloody Luftwaffe — or anyway, all the FW190s they had." Priestman had seen at least two other Spitfires flame out in the dogfight that had taken him out of the war.

"Yes, I was a bit shaken when four of you didn't return, and the others were badly shocked that you were one of the missing. Although I missed the op, I took part in the efforts to find you."

Priestman looked at him blankly.

"We flew three different sweeps to find your Spitfire and try to determine if there was any chance you'd survived the crash. No one remembered seeing any parachute, you see."

"I'm honoured. I didn't know that. I hope no one was lost trying to find me."

There was just a hint of hesitation before Danny answered, "Not that I can remember, sir." Priestman concluded that either Danny really couldn't remember, or else someone had been killed and the Squadron Leader kindly chose not to tell him.

They had reached one of the two Spitfires being readied for flight. "Your predecessor preferred to fly the Anson whenever he needed to go somewhere, but given your background, I thought you might want one of the Spits assigned for your personal use."

That felt good. Priestman grinned at him. "Thank you. I *would* like that — if it doesn't inhibit your operations?"

"Not at all, sir. Not all that much going on. We do nothing but reconnaissance, really, keeping an eye on Soviet troop movements. We've got fourteen aircraft, all 100% serviceable almost all of the time." Nodding toward the Spitfire in front of them he added, "This is 'P' for Priestman if you like her. She's a Mark XII. Have you flown them?"

"No," Priestman admitted.

"IXs?"

"Yes."

"She feels much the same. Slightly slower rate of climb, and a marginally lower service ceiling at 39,000 feet but almost double the range on internal tanks. She can stay in the air for nearly 500 miles without refuelling."

"That sounds as though it might be useful in this environment."

Danny grinned. "Roger. Shall we mount up?" Priestman nodded.

While Danny continued to his aircraft, Priestman handed his parachute pack to the waiting rigger, pulled on his helmet and gloves, and then reached for the handle to pull himself onto the wing root. To his relief, settling into the familiar cockpit triggered positive rather than negative memories. The sound of the powerful Griffon engine as he pressed the starter button was invigorating and reassuring at the same time. As he gave a thumbs up to the ground crew and started forward towards the grass runway, five years melted away. He could have been 27 again, leading his wing.

At the head of the runway, however, he dutifully slotted himself in behind Danny's starboard wing and followed him into the air. The responsiveness of the controls made him want to lark about and try every aerobatic manoeuvre he had ever mastered. Another day, he promised himself, and he decorously followed Danny.

The Squadron Leader's voice came over his earphones. "Spread out in front of us is the Havel River. It leads south towards Potsdam and the Soviet Zone on our right, and north to Spandau in our Sector on our left. Beyond the river, all that greenery is the district of Wannsee in the American Sector. I'm going to swing north and lead you up to Spandau." As he spoke, Danny banked hard to the left. When they levelled off, the river lay to their right and a forest to their left as they pelted north following a long straight road. They passed Staaken Airfield on their left and then turned right just short of an urban centre that Danny identified as Spandau. They followed a wide avenue running East-West that crossed the Havel via a series of bridges. Dipping their wings to port, Danny pointed out the Olympic Stadium where the 1936 Games had been held; to starboard was a large forest that Danny identified as the "Gruenewald," in the American Sector.

The farther they flew, the more densely built-up the city became and the greater the damage appeared. After they flew over the central park, the "Tiergarten," Danny pointed out the infamous Reichstag, where the Soviet flag still flew, and indicated some ruins that he said were the Reichskanzlei where Hitler had killed himself. Just beyond lay the government district which the Soviets controlled. Danny identified the wide, straight avenue as "Unter den Linden," and Priestman had a glimpse of a series of once elegant and palatial buildings surrounded by large swaths of rubble. The elaborate facades were shattered, and their glass windows were gone, leaving only gloomy grey surfaces pockmarked by artillery and gunfire. They crossed two narrow bands of water forming an island and beyond the city spread out like a vast field of ruins. Almost nothing seemed intact. As far as the eye could see were piles of broken masonry standing between the shattered shells of broken buildings with vacant windows.

The RAF pilots were flying at only a couple of thousand feet, and Priestman could look straight down into entire blocks of buildings that consisted of roofless walls enclosing rubble. At this altitude, the effect was more dramatic than flying over Hamburg in the BEA airliner, and he felt the first niggle of guilt. Of course, the Germans had sowed the wind, but had anyone seriously imagined the whirlwind would look like this?

After a few moments, Priestman noted that lines of people snaked across the ruins. "What are those people doing?" he asked Danny over the R/T.

"Oh, those are the '*Trümmerfrauen*.' They're paid pennies to clear the debris away by hand. Most work in the hope of finding something buried in these heaps of masonry that they can trade on the black market. They're more likely to find a corpse if you ask me."

People also stood in long queues in front of shops, at bus stops, and before government buildings. It seemed as if all the Berliners did was stand in line somewhere.

The only vehicles on the streets belonged to the Soviets; Red Army trucks, staff cars, and even tanks lumbered around the city. Uniformed Soviet soldiers loitered in the streets or walked about in groups. Posters of Stalin hung on the walls, and bright red flags flew from many buildings.

Danny led Priestman on a wide sweep around the eastern suburbs of the city before turning south and finally West. As they flew back toward Gatow over the southern suburbs, Priestman noted that more buildings were intact in the southwestern districts. Yet he was left with the impression that roughly two-thirds of Berlin's buildings had been destroyed. Finally, they slipped back across the Havel and touched down at Gatow just forty minutes after take-off.

Danny met him as he jumped down from the wing root. "I hope that was what you were looking for, sir."

"It was exactly what I was looking for. Thank you. Would you mind giving me another orientation flight tomorrow, extending our range to the corridors?"

"Whenever you want, sir."

Priestman started to turn away, then stopped and turned back. "There's something else I'd like to mention." He paused.

Danny nodded and prompted. "Yes, sir?"

"It may have escaped your notice, but the Voluntary Reserve has opened the flying branch to qualified women pilots."

"Interesting. Is it relevant to us for some reason?"

"My wife is a member of the RAFVR with the rank of flying officer. She flew with the ATA during the war and has close to a thousand flying hours, including more than four hundred on Spits, but she doesn't yet have her RAF wings because she doesn't have enough night flying, formation flying or aerobatics. I'm happy to help her with some of that, but, frankly, it would be better for her to have other instructors as well. I would appreciate it if you or one of your flight commanders could find time to help her out. She's required to fly at least thirty hours per annum to retain her status and is entitled to as many as 60 hours. Usually, that's done at a station with a RAFVR presence, of course, but since I've dragged her over here, I feel it is only fair to bend the rules a little to give her a fair chance at earning her wings."

"We'll do our best, sir," Danny answered obediently, but Priestman sensed he was wary. No doubt he feared Emily might be a difficult pupil, quick to take advantage of her status as the station commander's wife. Robin knew better and wasn't worried.

"I'll take her on her first flight this Sunday, and then maybe you could plan to fly with her next Saturday?"

"No problem about next Saturday, sir, but the tower is closed on Sundays. Because BEA doesn't fly in, the controllers have the day off. There is a duty pilot in the ops room, of course, and a controller is always on 30-minute standby in case of an emergency. Of course, if you want—"

Robin waved him silent. "Of course not. Tomorrow you and I can do the orientation flight, and..." He hesitated and conceded that it was probably simpler to talk to the other pilots about his past than to leave them to speculate and gossip. He only hoped no one would ask about being a prisoner. Out loud he continued, "I'll hang around the dispersal for an hour or so after the flight to chat with any of the rest of the squadron that wants to drop by. Nothing formal, you understand, and certainly not compulsory."

"Understood, sir," Danny saluted with a smile. As Priestman started back toward the main administrative building, he registered that the flight had done him good, but the difficult pieces of the day were still ahead of him.

Disconcerting Duty

Immediately after lunch, the station adjutant, Flying Officer Stanley, accompanied Priestman to the so-called "Kommandatura." This was situated in the American Sector and housed in a low, brick building of unimaginative style dating from the 1920s. The flagpoles in front flew the flags of the four occupying powers, the flag on the far left designating the monthly chairman of the joint body. This month that honour fell to the French.

Priestman and Stanley took the stairs to the second floor, passing and exchanging salutes with several Soviet, French and American officers along the way. They entered a spacious and sunny outer office with two secretaries and Stanley explained that they had an appointment. After waiting no more than a couple of minutes, they were invited into the comfortable corner office.

Priestman noted Lt. General Herbert's KBE, CBE and DSO as well as his many campaign ribbons, while the army officer's eyes scanned the DSO, DFC and bar below the airman's wings. Beyond the medals and other military insignia, Priestman saw an upright and stiff officer who looked like a stereotypical "brown job," as the RAF derisively called their colleagues from the army. Priestman went instinctively into a defensive shell of perfect Cranwell smartness as he delivered his best salute. Herbert returned it and then offered his hand without a smile. He gestured for his visitors to sit on one of two sofas flanking a low table. "Coffee or tea?"

"Tea, thank you, sir," Priestman answered, and Stanley followed suit.

The Commandant opened the door to ask one of his secretaries to bring tea for three, then sat down opposite them. "So how many trips have you made to Berlin?" he asked in a vaguely condescending manner as he seated himself.

"None, sir," Priestman replied, confused by the question; he'd never claimed to be familiar with Berlin.

Herbert raised his eyebrows. "Oh? Most of your colleagues are eager to tell me how many times they visited to deliver high explosives. Your predecessor had over twenty Berlin ops under his belt."

"Group Captain Sommerville was in the Pathfinders. I flew fighters," Priestman answered by way of explanation.

Herbert raised an eyebrow and then dismissed the topic with, "Well, that might be for the best. So, just how much *do* you know about occupied Berlin?"

"I've been briefed by Air Marshal Sanders and Group Captain Sommerville. I've also been reading up a bit."

Herbert nodded but gave the impression he was not impressed. "Did either of those briefings or your subsequent reading include the information that when we arrived in Berlin, the city had no functioning electricity, water, sewage or public transport?"

"No, I don't think I'd realized things were that bad," Priestman admitted.

"Well, you and your colleagues did a very thorough job of destroying just about everything — except the German will to keep fighting, it seems."

Priestman's temper flared and before he thought to curb his tongue he replied. "I was led to believe that much damage was done to the city during the Soviet assault. Furthermore, I was explicitly told that during the period of Soviet sole occupation, the Russians systematically dismantled almost anything left standing in the Western Sectors. I believe I was told they stole an entire power plant in that fashion, along with miles of telephone cables, public transport vehicles, water and gas pipelines, and more."

Herbert snorted. "That's true enough. Because of the way the Germans behaved in the Soviet Union, the Soviets understandably claim the right to massive reparations. The dimensions and modalities of such reparation payments are the business of the Council of Foreign Ministers and not our concern. Unfortunately, every Soviet soldier likewise feels entitled to take whatever he wants from the Germans, and this attitude undermines our efforts to re-establish law and order in the city. Russian soldiers have been known to steal a man's boots off his feet, take a bicycle from a schoolboy, rob refugees of their combs and toothbrushes, and in one particularly shocking recent incident, they shot dead a 14-year-old girl to steal her watch."

"They killed her for a watch?" Priestman gasped.

"Yes, for some reason the Russians are particularly fond of watches. Some Soviet soldiers walk around with six or seven on their arms, but that is not the point."

Priestman bit his tongue and waited expectantly.

"The point is that this behaviour sets a terrible example both for the German civilians and our troops. It has undermined the moral substructure of society at large. With so many weapons still in circulation, violent crime is rampant, while economic crimes and prostitution are endemic. So much so that they take place at all hours of the day and night in plain sight. To be honest with you, Wing Commander, I'd rather have a company of London constables than your squadron of Spitfires. I don't need aircraft of any sort; I need policemen."

Priestman could only nod in agreement. He didn't see any use for Spitfires in this environment either, which was why he was struggling to understand what he was supposed to be doing here.

Herbert continued in a clipped voice. "Aside from trying to keep a lid on all these nefarious activities, my job entails feeding more than two million people, most of whom don't have gainful employment or adequate housing, while simultaneously keeping public services functioning. My predecessor Brigadier Hind performed wonders getting our Sector functioning again, but progress has slowed dramatically in recent months due to insufficient co-operation among the four occupying powers. Decisions—" He was interrupted by the arrival of his secretary carrying a tea tray. She set things out on the table and Herbert indicated to his guests that they should help themselves.

While they poured tea, Herbert continued, "Now, where was I? Yes, decisions about running Berlin must be unanimous, which means that we must find common ground with the Americans, French and Soviets to do anything at all. What that means more explicitly, Wing Commander, is that we have no choice but to cooperate with the Soviets. We fought together in the war successfully, and we should never forget the terrible casualties they suffered. No matter what you and your colleagues like to think, it was *not* the RAF that bore the brunt of the war with Hitler; it was the Soviets. They suffered years of brutal Nazi occupation, losing as many as twenty million civilians. In addition, nearly nine million Russian soldiers died fighting the war. They have legitimate grievances against the Germans that we must respect."

"Indeed, sir."

General Herbert was continuing, "Equally important, it would be suicidal to lose sight of the fact that they have a greater military presence here. You know the numbers?"

"Yes, sir. I believe I was told they had something in the range of fifty soldiers to every one of ours."

"That's about right. It should be obvious, then, that we have nothing to gain from riling the Russian bear. Any 'diplomatic incident' runs the risk of flaring up into a military confrontation, which the Soviets would undoubtedly win. In our own interests, we must be on our guard to calm tensions and show consideration toward the Soviet viewpoint."

"Yes, sir."

"Unfortunately, my American counterpart doesn't seem to grasp fully these elementary principles. He either underestimates the utility of handling the Soviets with kid gloves, or he is simply incapable of behaving with restraint." Herbert's tone had become so acerbic that it betrayed deep animosity toward his American counterpart. Priestman hadn't a clue how to respond.

Herbert, fortunately, did not appear to expect a response. He continued, "You will have an opportunity to judge Colonel Howley for yourself very shortly. As it happens, he is hosting a party at his home tomorrow evening and when he learnt you would be stopping by today, he explicitly asked me to extend an invitation to you and your wife. I would be grateful if you would accept since Mrs Herbert and I do not wish to attend."

"Of course, sir," Priestman rightly interpreted the request as an order. He hoped Emily wouldn't mind being thrown into a full-scale diplomatic event on the third day after their arrival.

"That covers everything for the moment," Herbert announced, getting to his feet.

The RAF officers stood at once. Herbert escorted them towards the door and here addressed himself to the nearest secretary. "Please give Wing Commander Priestman the invitation from Colonel Howley and RSVP positively for him and Mrs Priestman." Turning to Priestman he added, "You'll find all the information you need about address, time and dress code on the invitation." He then shook hands with the two RAF officers and retreated into his office, closing the door behind him.

Priestman refrained from comment until he was in his car. Then he glanced sidelong at his adjutant and remarked. "Well, that was educational. Did Group Captain Sommerville have many dealings with General Herbert?"

"No, sir. He tried to avoid contact with everyone."

Priestman drew a deep breath. He could sympathize with that instinct, but it was equally obvious that he would only succeed in this job and turn it into a stepping-stone for something better if he did not follow his predecessor's example. The Ministry didn't want him to be a recluse. They wanted him to be more "active." Presumably in supporting Herbert's policy of co-operation with the Soviets, countering American irresponsibility, and calming the growing tensions that were reported daily in the newspapers.

After a twenty-minute drive on streets devoid of traffic except for the vehicles of the occupation forces, they reached the grand, former courthouse that now housed the Allied Control Council. Again, the four Allied flags flapped from flagpoles out in front and officers of the four armies of occupation moved about the building like ants around an ant hill. Stanley led the way through a maze of corridors to an office with a tall door and a tall window looking out onto a courtyard.

Air Commodore Waite was a balding man in his mid-fifties with a fine and friendly face. More relaxed than Herbert, he welcomed Priestman with a smile and opened the conversation with questions about Priestman's wartime service, volunteering that he had flown flying boats for Coastal Command, served in the Caribbean and then been part of the planning for D-Day. "I'm not exactly a penguin, but I'm not uncomfortable flying a desk, either," he admitted with a self-deprecating smile. "You can call me 'Rex,' by the way."

"Thank you. It's Robin," Priestman reciprocated and then, taking his cue from the other's tone, risked candour. "I must admit, I'm struggling to understand my function here. As far as I can tell, there is nothing much going on at Gatow except leisurely reconnaissance flights to check on

Soviet troop movements, something that could be done at a lower cost from airfields in our Zone. Given that the Red Air Force outnumbers the Spitfires at Gatow by about one hundred to one, we have no military value. Air Marshal Sanders suggested we are here to 'show the flag,' but my predecessor felt that Berlin is not worth the trouble we go to for that purpose. Indeed, he questioned whether Berlin is important at all, given its location, the level of destruction, and the uncertainty about Germany's future. How do you see the situation?"

"Well, I'm not going to pretend that it isn't expensive to maintain a presence here, but the cost of withdrawing before Germany has been reconstituted as an independent state would be infinitely greater."

"Could you elaborate on that? The papers make it sound as if Germany's future remains controversial."

"True. The Soviets want a Communist Germany that takes its directions from Moscow, and the French want a broken Germany that can never pose a threat to them again, militarily or economically. His Majesty's government and the United States, on the other hand, agree that our interests are best served by a strong, industrial Germany capable of feeding, clothing and employing its population."

"Industrialized? I thought the heart of American post-war policy was 'de-Nazification,' 'demilitarization,' and 'deindustrialization'?"

Waite smiled and nodded. "It was. Fortunately, our American cousins are capable of learning."

"Meaning?"

"The United States — or at least the US Secretary of State George Marshall —recognizes that European economy recovery benefits the US. Furthermore, if Europe is ever to have a booming economy again, it needs German coal and steel, German technology and German markets. In short, European economic recovery would be crippled by a weak, agricultural Germany. That's why Marshall evolved this proposal of his to kick-start European economic recovery with an infusion of cash tied to co-operation mechanisms. The plan is nothing short of brilliant." Waite declared enthusiastically. "It would force the European countries to stop competing with one another and start co-operating instead."

Priestman nodded. It made sense, he was just still struggling to understand the relevance to Berlin and Gatow.

Waite was continuing. "The plan would also enable Germany to be reintegrated into Europe, while we'd gain access to German natural and technological resources. If President Truman and Secretary Marshall can get the proposal through the US Congress, things will start to improve almost at once. Unfortunately, before that can happen, however, Germany needs a sound and convertible currency. You can't run modern, industrial societies on barter."

Priestman nodded but noted, "I thought the currency here was the Reichsmark issued by the occupation authorities?"

Waite smiled wanly, "Only superficially. The Soviets were supplied with the plates for printing the occupation marks and they have done so without inhibition — and without serial numbers. They print money constantly, but it has no value. The real currency in Berlin is cigarettes, American cigarettes. Fortunately, wiser heads than ours are working on a solution."

"So, we plan to introduce a new currency and unleash the German economy?"

"Yes, that's the general idea."

"And how do we prevent an industrialized Germany from engaging in aggression? They've started two wars this century already, and it isn't even half over."

"The key is getting them to draft and accept a new democratic constitution with strong checks and balances."

"The Germans haven't exactly demonstrated a capacity for making democracy work," Priestman noted cynically, all his negative feelings towards the Germans bubbling up.

"I think you're being a bit harsh. Twice in the last year, the people of Berlin have defied the wishes of a powerful and brutal occupation power. First, they stopped the German Communist Party from swallowing the outspoken and independent Social Democrat Party. Second, the Berliners elected city representatives who are not puppets of Moscow by a four-to-one margin. We want to encourage both the democratic process that is behind these recent elections, and we want to support the outcomes that are so decidedly anti-Soviet."

Priestman considered the Air Commodore with a degree of frustration and then noted, "General Herbert just spent the better part of his briefing telling me we did *not* want to 'rile the Russian bear.' He was quite emphatic in stressing the need to be sympathetic to the Soviet point of view. He placed a higher priority on co-operation with the Soviets than on fostering German self-government."

Waite nodded sympathetically. "General Herbert is by nature a cautious man, and he is, perhaps, mesmerized by the imbalance of forces. But there is much more at stake here than Berlin itself. The future of Europe and the UK depends on halting the proliferation of Communist dictatorships controlled by Stalin. Herbert's priorities are backward. Rather than being nice to the Russians for the sake of making things run more smoothly in Berlin, we should be prepared to sacrifice Berlin to stop Soviet aggression. Ultimately, Berlin is expendable, but if the Soviets expel us from Berlin by force, they will have crossed the Rubicon and committed an act of war."

At last, Priestman grasped what he was doing here. "If I understand correctly, you're saying that Gatow — along with the rest of Berlin — is a tripwire. If Gatow or the aircraft using it are attacked by the Soviets, it would trigger a military response. Is that right?" he sought confirmation.

"Yes, but meanwhile, you can use your apparently innocuous position to good advantage by cultivating good relations both with your counterparts from the US and France and with the local population. Especially with the local population," Waite stressed. "After all, we do not *want* another war. It would be far better if the struggle for Germany played out on the political rather than the military plain. Winning politically, however, entails winning sympathy, not just arguments."

Priestman looked back at Waite with a sense of helplessness. He had not encountered any Germans he liked during his seventeen months as a prisoner and that made it very hard to imagine how he should go about "winning their sympathy." He didn't see any common ground, much less any basis for a friendly relationship. He had hoped that his assignment to Berlin would not require any social contact with Germans at all.

Waite seemed to read his mind. "It is hard to put aside our prejudices. I know."

"Prejudices? I'm not pre-judging anyone!" Priestman responded defensively. "The Germans bombed us first, not the other way around. They would have invaded if they could. They certainly tried to starve us to death!"

"That was Hitler's government, which no longer exists."

"Fair enough, but the whole time I was in a prison camp I had to listen to German soldiers — not SS or SA or anyone particularly Nazi — bullying and bragging and threatening. Up until days before the surrender, they were still belittling and demeaning us. These typical German soldiers were sadists and cowards both."

"I suspect the cream of the British Army does not make up the guards at our prisoner-of-war camps either," Waite reflected in a soft voice.

They gazed at one another and for the first time, there was a degree of tension between them. Priestman had come here trying to find out what was expected of him. Now he knew: show the flag, act as a tripwire, and in the meantime be nice to the Germans. Maybe the bowler hat would have been better, after all.

"Let me tell you something about Berlin that may make it easier for you to understand the Berliners and adopt a more tolerant attitude towards them," Waite suggested softly.

Priestman nodded stiffly, trying to get a grip on himself. A bowler hat was not an option. He was here, and he had to not only make the best of it but also turn it into something positive.

"First, Berlin was traditionally a 'red' city, a bastion of the socialist and communist parties. Hitler never won a majority of the vote in Berlin, and Hitler never trusted the Berliners as a result. He preferred Nuremberg for his rallies and withdrew to Berchtesgaden to relax. Berliners were notorious, even during the war, for making fun of their overlords — often at the price of their lives. Second, an estimated 125,000 Germans died in the final assault on Berlin, only 20,000 of whom were in uniform. Many of those in uniform were over sixty or under sixteen. Thousands of civilians were drowned when the Nazi leadership flooded the underground where they had taken refuge. When the city finally fell, I'm told there was widespread relief. There was little mourning for Hitler or his regime. The Berliners preferred, as they put it, a terrible end over terror without end." Waite paused and then added soberly. "And then, in a city where women outnumbered men by as much as two to one, the rapes started. You've heard about this, I presume?"

"Yes, I understand the Russians were quite undisciplined."

"That is an understatement. Even after we arrived in the city, hospitals in our sector were confronted with hundreds of rape cases every single night. Note, that this was in our Sector *alone* and we saw only those women who sought medical attention. The senior British medical officer believes the number of rapes per night easily exceeded 1,000 —"

"But—" Priestman cut himself off.

"Yes?"

"Thousands of rapes per night over a six-to-eight-month period...." Priestman could not calculate the full magnitude much less fathom the impact.

"It comes to about one million rape victims, Robin, and many more instances since so many women were raped multiple times." Waite met his eyes and forced him to confront what he was saying, "We saw women as old as eighty, girls as young as eight, mothers raped in front of their children, girls ravaged in front of their parents. Rapes often took place at gunpoint or in gangs — up to twenty times in a single incident. Women reported being raped repeatedly over days and weeks on end."

Priestman was stunned. He found himself asking, "You said 'we saw.' Are you saying the Soviets crossed into our Sector to commit these crimes?"

"The first explosion of rape took place in the immediate aftermath of the Soviet capture of the city before we had arrived. It naturally spanned the entire city. After we arrived, we gradually asserted control, and the incidents tapered off. But, yes, in the first six to eight months of our occupation, the Russians still crossed over into our Sector, particularly into Charlottenburg, and sought victims after dark. Nowadays, that is rare, but not unheard of."

Priestman was beginning to understand some of the "perks" he had been granted, most especially why the Station Commander's wife was entitled to a car and driver.

"I think you will agree with me, Robin, that nothing the German Army did in the Soviet Union justifies the abuse of children, girls, mothers and grandmothers. Furthermore, and this is the most important point, sexual assaults on this scale over such a long period are not spontaneous acts on the part of undisciplined troops. The Soviet leadership does not hesitate to execute a man for telling a joke about Stalin. They could have stopped this behaviour with a single word. If Stalin or Zhukov or anyone in authority had wanted to stop it, they could have issued an order, shot some violators to set an example, and the orgy of abuse would have stopped. There would still have been the occasional case thereafter, but nothing on this scale. In short, the rape of Berlin was Soviet policy. It was condoned by Stalin himself. That tells you the character of our enemy."

Waite paused and then added before Priestman could speak, "And before you mention the Concentration Camps, many are still operating — under Soviet direction and guards. As for Secret Police, the Soviet NKVD, as it is called, is more pervasive than the Gestapo ever was. Institutionalized murder? It is on a grander scale than anything Hitler imagined. Our intelligence reports suggest that under Stalin between ten and twenty million Soviet citizens have been killed."

Priestman stared at him, his mind refusing to grasp or accept what Waite was saying. He didn't want to believe this. The picture was too dark, threatening and frightening.

"Hitler has been defeated, Robin, but Stalin is a victor, more powerful than ever — and he is expanding his reach as far as he can. He wants control of Germany, the heart of Europe. It is not in the interests of anyone who believes in humanity or Christian values to let him have it. Stopping him means not giving in to his demands. It means not pulling back from Berlin. It means sitting here with 14 Spitfires to 1,400 Yaks, and it means trying to convince the Germans — one at a time — that one reign of terror was enough, that their future lies in working together with us against the Soviets."

"I would have thought after what you just described, the Germans would have welcomed us with open arms. You mean they haven't?"

"Yes and no. When we first got here, they were ready to see us as their saviours and protectors -- until we did nothing to protect them. The rapes continued, the thefts continued, the kidnappings continued, and the concentration camps re-opened. While Soviet propaganda enveloped them in lies about the worker's paradise that their Soviet 'friends' would deliver, we insisted on 'no fraternization' and 'collective guilt.' In short, we have singularly failed to capitalize on their hatred for the Soviets."

"Why?"

"I suppose our natural aloofness or inborn reticence played a role. Or maybe our all-too-obvious dislike of the Germans got in the way of better relations. Another factor, I'm sorry to say, was the bombing."

Robin replied tartly, "As Air Marshal Harris so rightly said, they started the war with the childish notion that they were going to bomb everyone else and no one was going to bomb them. Are you saying they still haven't grown up?"

"Let me answer with the following anecdote. Shortly after I arrived, the crew of a Dakota came to the rescue of a woman calling for help, chased off the Russians, and got her to a hospital, but when they stepped into the nearest tavern for a drink, all conversation stopped. Then one by one the other customers walked out."

"I don't understand."

"They were dressed like you and me. An RAF uniform is to the people of Berlin much what an SS uniform is to us — a symbol of terror."

"And you think there is something I can do to overcome those attitudes?" Priestman asked in disbelief. It sounded completely pointless to him.

It was Waite's turn to draw a deep breath. "I admit, it is no easy task, but I'm saying you should try."

Priestman thought about this for several seconds, stretching his imagination for something, anything, that he might do to alter people's perceptions of the RAF. "Do you think we might do things like — I don't know — soup kitchens for the hungry, or used-clothing drives for children, or air shows for entertainment?"

Waite perked up immediately. "I like your thinking!" he announced enthusiastically. "Given how short we are on food ourselves, I'd probably leave the food kitchens to the Americans; they have more than we do. An air show, on the other hand, is an outstanding idea — if we leave out the usual example of precision bombing, of course. Maybe I could talk someone from Coastal Command into sending us a Sunderland for a day or two. We could land on the Havel — even give free rides, maybe. Now, that would be good entertainment, don't you think? Of course, it will have to wait until the days are longer and the weather more predictable. May or June, I think. For now, let's just give it some thought. We can talk about specific ideas whenever you're ready." He glanced at his watch. "Now, I'm sorry to say, it's later than I thought. I'm going to have to go to another meeting shortly."

"I understand. I'm very grateful you took so much time for me as it is. You've given me a great deal to think about." Priestman admitted as he got to his feet.

"I can imagine!" Waite laughed shortly, also standing. "Before you go, however, I would like to beg a favour of you."

"Whatever you like."

"My daughter is getting married in the UK at the end of this month and my wife and I plan to attend. It means I'll miss the third of this month's Allied Control Council meetings. It's scheduled for January 30th. If you could sit in on that for me, General Robertson and I would both be grateful to you."

That was not a question, so Priestman immediately agreed. "I'm happy to go if you think I can handle it. Just remember, I only arrived yesterday."

Waite made a calming gesture. "Not to worry. There's nothing to it. Robertson will do all the talking. You're just there in case the governor needs some information on aviation issues. I'll be sure you have our file with the transcripts of past meetings and an overview of useful statistics. The meetings take place in this building, and my adjutant will show you where to sit and provide you with the agenda and any briefing papers well in advance. I suggest, however, that you bring a translator with you. The principals all bring their interpreters, of course, but the Russians have a habit of springing new documents on us that *they* have translated. We can't trust those, so you'll want to have a fluent Russian speaker who can check things over if there's something related to air traffic control, the corridors or the like."

"No problem."

"Excellent. I appreciate it very much, and I think you'll find sitting in on a meeting of the ACC an educational experience." They shook hands warmly and Waite closed with, "Berlin probably looks rather bleak at the moment, and you may be having second thoughts about this assignment, but I think you'll find it has its good points as well."

Hope
RAF Gatow
Saturday, 10 January 1948

Kathleen was surprised at how much she was looking forward to her daughter's arrival. She had expected to enjoy being on her own for a bit, and in a way she had. The trip would have been a nightmare with Hope, and her first week had been made easier by not catering to a six-year-old while she found her way around. She'd particularly enjoyed meeting up in the NAAFI with the other WAAF and having drinks in the sergeants' mess with Lynne. Yet when she returned to her flat, it echoed with emptiness. She'd been amused to discover that she even missed Hope's inevitable untidiness; having everything neatly where it belonged seemed rather boring. Mostly, however, she was looking forward to showing Hope her new home. She knew Hope would love the duck pond and the stables and the various toys at the daycare centre run by the wife of Warrant Officer Pierce. She thought Hope was going to like it here, but she wouldn't know for sure until after Hope arrived.

She'd arranged with Warrant Officer Wilkins to come on duty bright and early Saturday morning so he could sleep in late for a change. In exchange, he promised to let her off as soon as the BEA airliner took off from Hamburg. That would give her time to catch a bite to eat before meeting the flight on arrival. She hoped Fl/Lt Simpson wouldn't interfere with this arrangement. Although he had not appeared in the control tower in a drunken state since their first encounter, when he was sober he was either taciturn or caustic. They were all happier when he was absent, which fortunately was more often than he should have been. Kathleen considered him completely irresponsible and a hazard to operations, yet as the newcomer, it was not her place to say something, or not yet anyway. She simply tried to avoid him.

The morning hours crawled slowly by with little activity beyond the WingCo taking off with Squadron Leader Daniels for an early morning "orientation" flight. The other WAAF were agog about the new Station Commander. "Gosh, he's gorgeous!" Natalie had exclaimed after seeing him for the first time.

"Yes, and married," Annie Bower reminded her.

"Nearly all officers over the rank of flight lieutenant are married," Violet commented. "You have to get them while they're young."

"That's when they're irresponsible and only interested in one thing," Lynne complained.

Kathleen shared their opinion of the WingCo's looks, but she'd met more than one good-looking man who was an absolute twit. It wasn't the Station Commander's looks that gave her a good feeling about him, it was the fact that when passing along the reception line on arrival he'd stopped to ask how many WAAF were on the station. When she'd told him, his response had been. "Jolly good. Glad to have you all." It had been such a spontaneous expression of support that it had made her stand taller. The fact that he'd been flying twice since his arrival less than two days ago also struck her as a good sign. This was no "wingless wonder" with his nose stuck in King's Regulations or obsessed with square-bashing as she'd experienced elsewhere. Priestman was a flier, and she liked that.

A little over an hour later, the WingCo and Danny returned and went together to Triple Two's dispersal, where the younger pilots had been dribbling in all morning. Smoke drifted up towards the dreary January overcast, showing that they had stoked up the coal stove for a cosy chat. Kathleen suspected they were mixing rum with their tea over there too, feeling a twinge of jealousy, not because of the rum but the comradeship that went with it all. Rufus, the Air Movement Assistant on duty with her, echoed her feelings by grumbling, "It's still a pilot's air force. The rest of us don't count quite as much."

"You know what they say: 'All airmen are equal, but some airmen are more equal than others.'" Kathleen quoted the popular paraphrase from Orwell's "Animal Farm" with a laugh. Rufus was right, of course, she just didn't mind. The men who flew in whatever capacity were special in some way, and it was to have an indirect role in flying that she had chosen air traffic control as her trade.

Willie arrived well before noon, and with no sign of Simpson anywhere, he told her to take the rest of the day off. "I'll think of an excuse for you if I have to," he promised.

Kathleen headed for the NAAFI to buy a chocolate bar for Hope. Everything was duty-free here, making such luxuries affordable. To her surprise, five of the other WAAF were waiting for her there already. They

90

had a basket full of presents for Hope. "We took a collection!" Lynne explained.

"You are angels!" Kathleen declared touched. "How thoughtful of you all!"

"We want Hope to be happy, so you'll want to stay!" Violet told her.

That was the nicest compliment anyone had ever paid Kathleen in her service career, and she gave the WAAF corporal a spontaneous hug. As the others identified who had given what, she reflected on what an extraordinarily genial group they were. Was it because they were so few? Or because they were isolated in an occupied country with threats just beyond the perimeter fence? Or maybe it was because they had such different jobs?

The gifts they'd brought for Hope were characteristic of each of them. Violet, the dowdy and domestic teleprinter operator, had knitted a little angel. Marie, the chic and saucy French translator, had contributed bright red satin ribbons. Annie the wireless operator, who was the joker in the little group, had contributed a yellow rubber duck which she claimed an ex-boyfriend had given her as a joke. Natalie the air movements assistant, who had grown up on a farm, had a little jar of honey sent from her mother. Lynne, the ambitious CO's secretary, gave two hair clips with paste diamonds in the shape of a flower.

But one WAAF was missing, Galyna Borisenko, the Russian translator. Kathleen wondered why. Up to now, she had not been stand-offish, and she had taken a keen interest in Hope all week long, asking lots of questions. At 25, Galyna was older than the others and decidedly more serious. Kathleen did not think she had yet heard her laugh, although she sometimes smiled solemnly. When the WAAF were off-duty together, she had spoken little but listened intently, as if she desperately wanted to be included but was too shy to speak up. It seemed odd that she hadn t wanted to join in welcoming Hope.

Kathleen focused on the WAAF collected around her, exclaiming, "I can't thank you enough! Hope will be so happy. Shall we have some tea and a bite to eat? The flight isn't due for another hour."

They bought tea and sandwiches and sat down together at a table near one of the tall windows. "Will you bring Hope around to meet us this evening?" Anne asked.

"Give poor Kathleen a little time alone with her daughter!" Violet answered frowning at Anne.

"Then, why not tomorrow at teatime? I could bake something," Natalie suggested.

Kathleen almost said yes but remembered seeing a notice that a bus would be going to the Commonwealth War Memorial tomorrow for a short prayer meeting at 3 pm. It was the perfect opportunity to visit Ken's grave without risking travel on the notoriously bad public transport. "Oh, I can't! I want to go to the Cemetery instead. Hope's father is buried there, and I want her to visit the grave with me. Or do they have these prayer services every Sunday?"

"No, it's the first time that I've ever heard about one. It's the WingCo's idea."

"Well, then let's do lunch?" Lynne suggested and they all agreed.

The conversation drifted to other topics and before she knew where the time had gone, Kathleen realized it was just fifteen minutes to the scheduled arrival of the BEA flight. She jumped up and reached for her overcoat. "I've got to go! Thank you all so much!"

"Don't forget the basket!" Lynne reminded her. Kathleen took it with a wide smile and a last wave and then hurried out. She had almost reached the admin building when Galyna intercepted her.

"Flight Sergeant Hart?"

"Galyna! Please call me Kathleen when we're off duty," she reminded her with a smile.

"Yes," Galyna answered earnestly but distractedly and held up her hands. "This is a little gift for your daughter," she declared solemnly. "I was looking for it all morning, which is why I did come over to the NAAFI earlier."

Although Kathleen's thoughts were flying ahead of her, she had no choice but to curb her impatience and look at what Galyna was offering. It appeared to be a brilliantly painted egg, except that it was wooden.

"It is a doll," Galyna declared and eagerly twisted the top and bottom in opposite directions to show that it unscrewed revealing another doll nestled inside. Galyna handed Kathleen the two pieces of the outer doll and proceeded to open the next and the next and the next. There were a total of five brightly painted dolls, one inside the other.

"These are wonderful!" Kathleen proclaimed, noticing that each was painted like a Russian peasant woman with a bright red scarf, vivid pink cheeks and a flowered apron. She knew Galyna had been born and raised in Ukraine until she left in 1937 never to return. She must have brought these dolls with her when she left, Kathleen surmised, noting out loud, "Galyna, these must be very precious to you!"

"I will find more," Galyna insisted without looking at her as she deftly screwed the dolls back together one after another.

"But Galyna," Kathleen protested, "You don't have to give them to Hope. She won't appreciate them. She's too little."

"I was six when my father gave them to me. I remember how I loved taking them apart and putting them back together again. Your daughter will love them too."

"Yes, but she might lose parts. She can be careless. I'd feel terrible if she lost anything. Please, I'd feel better if you kept them. You can show them to Hope when she comes to visit and let her play with them in your flat."

Galyna hesitated, looking down earnestly at the large doll in her hands. She looked so serious that Kathleen reached out and closed Galyna's hand around the doll. "Please. Keep them. I can see how much you treasure them."

Galyna did not deny that, but she looked distressed. "I will try to find others," she decided at last.

Kathleen smiled. "That would be wonderful. Now I must run. There's the BEA flight now."

The airliner was indeed visible coming over the perimeter fence as it sank toward the PSP runway. Kathleen arrived on the tarmac apron out of breath just as the engines wound down. Moments later the door swung open, and the stairs were rolled out to release a half dozen passengers, all male. Kathleen stared at the door. Where was Hope? Had she missed the flight? Had something come up at the last minute? Just when she was starting to panic, a smiling stewardess appeared holding Hope by the hand. The stewardess led the way down the stairs first, looking back to be sure Hope managed the large steps while clutching her teddy bear. Hope was concentrating so seriously on the steps that she didn't look up until she reached the bottom.

Kathleen flung open her arms and Hope ran to them with a loud squeal of delight. "Mummy! Mummy! They let me into the cockpit, and I saw the sea and the ships were so tiny!" She smothered her daughter in her arms and swung her back and forth in delight. How she had missed her!

Hope chattered non-stop. Kathleen didn't mind. She'd already arranged for Harry Wallace to bring Hope's suitcase over to the flat, and she took Hope in front of her on her bicycle. In the flat, Hope's eyes grew bigger and bigger with each fresh discovery. Her delight at seeing her bunny was nearly as great as for her mother, Kathleen thought. She showed Hope the presents from the other WAAF and let her eat one piece of the chocolate bar. Then she put the rest away in a cupboard Hope couldn't reach and suggested a walk to see the rest of the station. She knew Hope would tire before they had gone far, but they had time to see the enormous "duck pond" where Hope fed scraps of old bread to an excited flock of honking ducks.

By then, the early January day was fading, and the wind was turning cold. Kathleen put Hope on the seat of her bicycle and walked beside it back to the flat. Once inside, she set about warming up a can of soup and toasting bread for their supper. She had milk for Hope and put the kettle on to make tea for herself. Dinner together was a simple thing, but Kathleen loved it. By the time they finished, Hope was falling asleep in her chair. She'd had a busy day. "Go and get changed for bed, sweetheart, and I'll come and tuck you in."

"No! It's too early!"

"It's an hour later here, you know," Kathleen pointed to the wall clock. "I'll read you a bedtime story."

"Will you read Winnie the Pooh?"

"Yes, of course. The book is waiting on the bedside table."

Hope ran off without another word. Kathleen washed their dishes and the soup pan, put the bread away, and switched off the light in the kitchenette area. When she turned to go to Hope's room, she was startled to find Hope still in the sitting area staring at the photograph of the Lancaster crew. "Which one is Daddy?" Hope asked without introduction.

Instantly, Kathleen regretted hanging the photo. "None of them are, Sweetheart. I don't have a picture of your Daddy's crew. But that man there," she came and bent over Hope pointing, "is Kit Moran. He flew with your Daddy as Flight Engineer. Then after their skipper was killed, they went different ways. Daddy joined another crew, and Kit learned to fly and became the skipper of this crew."

Hope was looking at the picture with inexplicable intensity. Then she looked up at her mother. "Is he going to be my new Daddy?"

"What a silly question! Of course not! He's already married to a very nice lady called Georgina and they live in Yorkshire. Where did you come up with such a funny idea?"

"Grandma says it's time for you to marry again and for me to get a new Daddy," Hope told her.

"Well, Grandma was talking out of turn, Miss Hope Hart!" She retorted tartly, inwardly cursing her mother. It was bad enough that she harangued Kathleen about "finding a father" for her daughter; saying it to Hope was utterly unfair.

Kathleen took Hope by the hand and led her to her room to help her change into her nightie. She made sure she brushed her teeth before putting her to bed. Hope was so tired, she fell asleep long before Kathleen had finished reading, so Kathleen leaned over, kissed her forehead, and turned out the light. It was good to have her back, but as she curled up on the sofa to read a little before going to bed herself, she glanced over at the photo of Kit and his crew and wondered wistfully if Hope would ever have another Daddy.

Mad Dog Howley
Berlin — Zehlendorf (American Sector)
Saturday, 10 January 1948

The invitation from Colonel and Mrs Howley was for 7:30 pm and CO's driver picked the Priestmans up at their residence in the Station Commander's car, a confiscated Mercedes, at seven. It was already dark, so the drive revealed almost nothing of Berlin, certainly not to Emily sitting in the back seat. She was aware only of what seemed like an endless forest, followed by a long bridge over the Havel River. Shortly afterwards, Robin pointed out the Commonwealth War Cemetery, remarking it was the final resting place for nearly 3,000 RAF airmen who had been shot down over or near Berlin during the war.

"I mentioned, didn't I, that I've asked the padre to say a few words at a small, informal prayer meeting tomorrow afternoon?"

"Yes, along with church parade at 10 am, lunch with the padre and his wife at 12:30 and a welcome dinner at the Sergeant's mess at 7:30."

"Sorry, I have completely planned your Sunday, haven't I?"

"No worries. I was expecting it. We've done this before, remember? I didn't get the chance to ask earlier, 'though. Is there some special reason for the service at the Commonwealth War Cemetery?" Although Robin was devout in his way, he was not particularly pious.

"No. It's just something I wanted to do," he said curtly and looked out his window.

Emily felt brushed off and almost turned to look out the other window in mute protest but stopped herself. No, she wasn't going to let him do this. They had promised themselves a new start, and he'd promised to communicate more. She wasn't going to let him withdraw into his barbed shell. "Robin, you promised to *talk* to me, remember? What is this about?"

Robin was instantly contrite. "I'm sorry. It's just..." She could tell he was having difficulty overcoming something and so waited patiently. At last, he said, "It's just that several of the men I was in prison with were survivors from bombers shot down over Germany. They had lost most, if not all, of their fellow crewmates. It was a wrenching experience for them — something we fighter pilots never suffered in the same way. After seeing Berlin from the air yesterday, I decided I wanted to pay my respects."

Emily could sense that any memories of being a prisoner were painful and accepted that this was enough for now. "It's a good idea," she told him, and then leaned forward to speak to the driver, "Wallace, do you know where we could buy flowers?"

"Yes, Ma'am. I can pick up a wreath for you if you like at the shop in the Domaine Dahlem Underground Station near tonight's dinner venue. I can do it while you're at the dinner party and you can reimburse me."

Shortly afterwards they passed under a railway bridge and turned right. Emily saw a tall, radio tower half lost in low cloud. Then suddenly they stopped at a flashing light that marked a level crossing. Here they waited for a long time, with Robin irritably checking his watch until a train finally oozed past them.

"I'm sorry about the delay, sir," Wallace said looking at his CO in the rear-view mirror. "Nothing runs to schedule here and the Ivans are always halting trains along the way due to alleged railway repairs and the like."

Robin nodded but looked at his watch meaningfully again. He hated being late, and as this was his first meeting with the American commandant it was especially important to make a good impression.

Finally, the train had passed, and the flashing light stopped. Wallace drove carefully over the dangerously uneven railway bed and turned onto a broad avenue that led through what had once been a pleasant suburban area. Pointing to their right, Robin explained there was a large forest, Gruenewald, and a series of small lakes just beyond the villas lining the road. "Berlin must be huge!" Emily exclaimed.

"It is. The city limits incorporate three large lakes and many smaller ones. Next Saturday I'll have Danny give you an orientation flight as he did me."

It was almost 7:45 before they reached the imposing villa with a massive portico sporting four large white urns where the American commandant for Berlin lived. Already parked in front was a collection of luxury cars: Mercedes, BMWs, Audis, Horchs, a Rolls Royce, an Alfa Romeo and more. At the front door, they were met by a butler and a uniformed maid who took their overcoats.

The butler led them to a large reception room lit by two chandeliers and already crowded with what looked like forty or fifty people. A string quintette was playing classical music in the background. Uniformed maids with silver trays moved among the guests, offering drinks and hors d'oeuvres. Fresh flowers decorated the side tables. As her eye scanned the crowd, Emily was grateful for the clothing allowance the Ministry had granted them. They had used it for a shopping spree in London during which Robin had outfitted her for every occasion. On Robin's advice, she'd bought and was now wearing a burgundy, satin gown with a fitted waist and a wide skirt that fell to mid-calf. Compared to what the other women were wearing it was simple, but at least it was stylish, the material high-quality, and it had been tailored to her figure perfectly.

They had only stood a moment in the doorway before an elegant woman with her hair pulled severely away from her face emerged and offered her hand. Like Emily, her dress was more understated than flamboyant, and Emily guessed her age at nearly fifty. "Mrs Priestman? Wing Commander? I'm Edith Howley. I'm so glad you could join us on such short notice. Let me see if I can find Frank and introduce you." She looked over her shoulder, spotted her husband among a crowd of men and gestured for the Priestmans to follow her.

Clustered around the American Colonel were a couple of middle-aged civilians in dinner jackets with black bow ties, a British army major, and two American officers, one of whom wore the wings of the newly independent US Air Force. As they approached, Emily heard their host growling, "...they're liars, swindlers and cut-throats! Pretending otherwise won't change the facts but could get us in a lot of hot water!"

"Frank, stop complaining about our Russian friends long enough to meet Wing Commander Priestman, the new Station Commander at Gatow, and his wife," Edith interrupted the conversation.

"Ah!" The American Colonel turned to greet them. He had a rugged face with bushy eyebrows and ears that stood out on either side of his face. His hair was wavey, thick and light brown, and his smile was wide and infectious as he held out his hand to Emily. Rather than the hearty American handshake Emily expected, he bowed his head slightly in the European mode and murmured in perfectly accented French: "*Enchanté, Madame.*" Turning to Robin, Howley shook hands vigorously and reverted to sounding American. "Welcome to Berlin, Wing Commander. I hope we'll have a chance to talk a little later. Maybe after dinner. First, let me introduce these gentlemen."

The civilians were both Congressional staff members on a fact-finding trip from Washington. The overweight American Army captain introduced himself as a professor of art history. "Captain Norman Byrne is here to stop the Ivans from stealing every last piece of art left in Germany," Howley explained. "It's bad enough that they've plundered the German museums, but now the Ruskies are also trying to get their hands on everything that Goering, Goebbels and company robbed from the rest of Europe, too."

The captain bowed over Emily's hand, and Howley continued the introductions. "Do you already know Major Dickenson?" he asked, indicating the British officer. The Priestmans shook their heads simultaneously. "Dickenson is on General Robertson's staff with responsibility for cultural policy and works closely with Byrne."

The British officer looked very dashing in an immaculate uniform and wore a trim, dark moustache over a lean, handsome face with dark eyes. He too bowed over Emily's hand.

"Finally," Howley concluded the introductions, "this is Lt. Col. Charles Walker, he's the base commander at Tempelhof, so your immediate counterpart, Wing Commander."

The two airmen shook hands warmly. "I'd like to talk shop later," Robin suggested, and Walker responded by suggesting he come and visit Tempelhof airfield early the following week. As they settled into discussing details, Mrs Howley extracted Emily, taking her gently by the elbow and saying, "I'll introduce you to the ladies."

"Have you been here long?" Emily asked the elder woman.

"Almost from the first day. Frank arrived on July 1st, 1945. The children and I a couple of months later. It's been quite an adventure, to say the least, but I'm not as rattled as some of the women are. I served in France in WWI."

"Served?"

"I was a US Army nurse at a forward hospital treating shell-shock cases. We'd discovered that their condition deteriorated during the long sea journey, so the army requested that we deploy to France. We were based in Domrémy, famous for being where Joan of Arc was born."

Emily liked the sound of that. It meant Mrs Howley was neither a socialite nor a parasite. Out loud she asked, "Is that where you met your husband?"

Edith Howley smiled and shook her head. "No, Frank is younger than I by several years. We met in Paris, where we were both studying fine arts at the Sorbonne."

Emily's face betrayed her astonishment because Edith laughed. "I know, Frank has the reputation of a bull in a china shop among you Brits and the French. Meanwhile, the Russians' most complimentary description is 'cowboy.' Recently, he's been demoted — or Frank says promoted — to 'mad dog,' 'terrorist' and 'dictator.'"

Embarrassed, Emily tried to put things right. "I didn't mean to suggest — I mean, it's just he does seem surprisingly forthright, and —"

Edith waved her silent with a smile. "Frank has a big mouth and he's not afraid to open it. The problem is that too many people appear afraid to call a spade a spade, so Frank feels he has to — and to talk louder in order to be heard over all the people hushing him. I'm not sure he's using the right tactics, but I have no doubts that he knows what he's talking about. The Soviets aren't just trying to steal German art and industry from under our noses, they're trying to steal the whole country. The sooner people wake up to the fact that the Russians are not our friends and don't want to cooperate with us, the better. I hope I'm not shocking you?" Edith paused on the fringe of the crowd of lively women laughing and chatting together, evidently intent on finishing the conversation with Emily before plunging in among the others.

"No, not at all," Emily waffled. "It's only that I just arrived, and I haven't had enough time to find my bearings. I've been trying to read as much as I could ever since my husband received his assignment, but my German is very rusty and needs brushing up."

"Oh, do you speak German? That will be a big help I'm sure. Most of the wives here have no second language whatsoever and tend to interact only with one another. It makes them quite insular. You would be a wonderful asset to our Ladies' Club. It is open to the wives of all officers from the occupation powers, but the Russians never attend, of course, and very few French or British, either. I hope you will consider it. We meet once a month."

"Thank you, I'd be delighted," Emily lied. She hated 'women's clubs,' but didn't want to be rude to Mrs Howley.

"Please call me Edith."

Emily reciprocated with her name, and Mrs Howley led her among the other women to introduce her. There were too many new names and faces for Emily to remember anyone, although Mrs Byrne stood out by the flashy jewels she was wearing. Emily supposed she must be a millionaire's daughter. Mrs Howley was soon called away because her cook needed some instructions, leaving Emily alone among the others, feeling superfluous and lost.

Beside her, three women discussed the price of beer 'steins.' They seemed to know a great deal about these objects, which evidently had lids but were made of a variety of materials. "I never pay more than two packs of cigarettes for a pottery stein," one of the women declared firmly.

One of her conversation partners countered, "Surely that depends on the age? The oldest steins were of pottery, you know. If you get a really old one, it can be worth hundreds of dollars in the US."

"Well, two packs of cigarettes is the most I'm willing to pay," the first woman insisted. "There are so many on the market that I just don't think they're worth more than that."

Disgusted, Emily drifted away unnoticed to stand near another trio of women who, it turned out, were discussing how difficult it was to find servants with good English. "They all claim to speak English, of course, but when you try to give them instructions you might as well be talking to a brick wall. I've fired three maids since I got here."

Emily moved on, again. One of the uniformed maids stopped her to offer tiny squares of white bread spread with liver paté, devilled eggs or caviar. She shook her head.

"... have you ever been to one of the local shops? They're just terrible! They have practically nothing to sell at all! Old potatoes, carrots, celery roots, onions and cabbage are the closest they get to fresh produce at this time of year. In summer, they offer little beyond apples and pears."

"Thank God we have such a wonderful PX."

"Yes, what I love is that they have Betty Crocker cake mixes. My kids couldn't live without them, and they save so much time in the kitchen."

"The problem is with all the good food and so many dinners like this," her companion answered, "I've put on ten pounds since I got here!" She patted her ample hips.

Emily remembered reading that German rations were less than 2,000 calories a day. She continued drifting around the fringe of the crowd, wishing she could join the gentlemen. Surely they were talking about something more consequential than losing weight or making cakes? She glanced over and noticed that Robin, too, was observing more than participating. Sensing her gaze, her turned and raised his glass of scotch in salute. She smiled back and forced herself to stand beside the closest group of women.

"...I tell you, it was absolutely appalling! I've never been so insulted in my life! Do I *look* German?" The woman asked in outrage. "How could any GI mistake me for one of these *frauleins*? I wish I'd thought fast enough to demand his unit. He deserves to be court-martialled!"

"I'm telling you, we American women have to do something to protect ourselves! I heard some of the girls talking about wearing an armband with the American flag on it to advertise we're decent women."

"It's a thought. I mean it's bad enough that it's not safe to go into the Russian Sector, but if we aren't safe from our own GIs, it will feel like we're in prison."

A little bell rang, and voices fell silent as Mrs Howley announced dinner. Just like the school bell, Emily thought, relieved to rejoin the company of men.

She was seated between Captain Byrne and Major Dickenson, who entertained her with tales of their detective work tracking down stolen masterpieces. While fun, the conversation did not entirely distract her from the fact that she was served lobster tails from Maine, steak from Texas, and ice cream with pineapple drenched in rum mixed with brown sugar. She felt like a Christmas beggar at the lord's feast, her eyes popping out of her head at the sight, smell and taste of so much fine food. How would she ever be able to reciprocate?

As they drove back through the darkness to Gatow at the end of the evening, Emily confided her doubts to Robin. "I honestly can't entertain like that," she confessed.

"You don't have to. I'm not the British Commandant. We'll start small. I'd like you to have Danny and his flight lieutenants over first and then we'll have the whole squadron."

"You know that's not a problem. Just give me a week to sort our things out and learn my way around the house and then we can have Triple Two over. It's the Americans I don't think I can manage."

"Why not?"

"They're so, I don't know, spoilt. Except for Mrs Howley. I liked her. But the others seemed so shallow."

"Isn't it a bit early to judge? Give them chance." He paused and added, "Please."

"Mrs Howley wants me to join a Ladies Club that meets monthly. I've always avoided 'ladies' clubs.' I much prefer clubs and societies dominated by men. Ladies' clubs tend to talk about fashion, cooking and children —

three things about which I know nothing."

Robin laughed, then reached out and pulled her into the circle of his arm. He dropped a kiss on her cheek and exclaimed, "Thank God! If you start metamorphosing into a society gossip or chatty housewife I'll divorce you." He entwined his fingers with hers and squeezed her hand as he murmured in a low voice the driver hopefully wouldn't be able to distinguish. "This assignment is turning out to be much more complicated than it sounded in London. I'm still trying to find my bearings, too. So, let's take things slowly for now. Just play along and watch what the others are doing, then we'll reassess our objectives and priorities after a couple of weeks."

Emily nodded in agreement. She would do whatever it took to make this a success for him, she told herself. She just hoped there wouldn't be many more evenings like this.

The Battle for Berlin is Over...
Berlin — Charlottenburg (British Sector)
Sunday, 11 January 1948

To avoid trying Hope's patience, Kathleen skipped church parade and took her daughter to the stables instead. This proved a huge success — except for prompting the inevitable pleading to be allowed to take riding lessons. After consulting the riding instructor, she was reassured that Hope could start on an old pony and the lunge line.

Lunch with the other WAAF was an equal success — except that it went on too long for Hope to get a nap. With a tired and cranky child in tow, Kathleen went down to the main gate to catch transport to the Commonwealth War Cemetery. The bus was not crowded, and she found a seat at the back where Hope could lay her head on her lap and get a short nap.

The bus bounced out of the gate, and with the engine groaning and the gears grinding, started up the long straight road toward Spandau. Kathleen looked out at the gloomy mist that clung to the naked trees crowding the road and automatically registered that the visibility was inadequate for flying. She looked at her fellow passengers. All were men. Most sat alone. They too were lost in memories.

Kathleen turned her thoughts to Ken. She would never forget the day they met. She'd grown up in a post-war suburb made-up of semi-detached houses with tiny front lawns. She'd left school at sixteen and apprenticed as a shopgirl. Her first paying job was in the men's shoe department at Marks and Spencer's. One day a merchant navy officer wearing a double-breasted uniform with bright brass buttons and three gold stripes on his sleeve walked in. She had been bedazzled the moment he smiled at her. Because she'd been brought up very strictly, however, she would not give him her telephone number no matter how much he pleaded. Yet no sooner was he gone, than she regretted what she'd done. She'd been ecstatic when he turned up again the following morning asking to take her to lunch. She'd taken the risk and they had so much fun that they went to lunch together the rest of the week. When he'd asked to take her to the flicks on Saturday night, however, she made him come and meet her father first.

Hope squirmed in her lap, and Kathleen reached down to remove her hat so she would be more comfortable. As Hope settled back in her lap, Kathleen looked out of the window again. There was still nothing to see but fog in the wintry forest.

Her parents had never liked Ken because he was a sailor. Her father had warned her Ken would 'have a woman in every port,' Her mother thought he would simply disappear, leaving her penniless. They were utterly wrong. Ken had been devoted to her. He'd written to her daily when at sea and brought her gifts from every port he visited. Yet the greatest mark of his love had been giving up the sea he loved because she'd asked him to. Early in the war, his ship had been sunk under him and he'd barely survived in a lifeboat before being picked up by a westbound convoy. In the weeks while he was missing, she had nearly gone mad. So, when he finally turned up, she'd made him promise never to put to sea again. He'd volunteered for the RAF instead, as otherwise he'd have been conscripted into the army or navy. When he'd been shot down, Kathleen had blamed herself until gradually fatalism replaced her sense of guilt. Ken had always said they could not control the future and must simply snatch what happiness they could.

The bus came to a halt and the driver switched off the engine. Kathleen looked out of the window bewildered. They seemed to be in the middle of nowhere, but the other passengers were disembarking. She roused Hope, tied her hat back on, and took her by the hand. They followed the other passengers along a path between high, wet bushes until they turned a corner and in front of them was a simple, white stone structure with three arches flanked by low, square towers and stone bleachers facing one another. Beyond the arches, rows and files of identical white grave markers stretched into the distance. The WingCo, his wife, the padre and surprisingly two American colonels and a British Army major were already standing in the central arch. The arriving RAF personnel distributed themselves along the benches on either side. The WingCo and his wife sat down in the front row flanked by the two Americans. The padre stood in the central arch, and with a simple, "Let us pray," commenced the simple service.

The solemnity of her surroundings subdued Hope to both silence and stillness. She hardly moved beside her mother throughout the roughly fifteen-minute service. The padre then looked to the WingCo, who stood and went forward to say simply. "The men here gave their lives for our freedom. It is our duty to remember them — and the cause they died for. Their battle for Berlin is over and won. Ours continues. We must never forget that what we are doing here is securing by peaceful means what our colleagues gave their lives to defend."

That was very nicely said, Kathleen thought. She knew that many at the Station had been surprised that the new Station Commander would organize a service so soon. Kathleen had cynically wondered if he'd done it as a ploy to garner popularity. Yet after these remarks, Kathleen decided he simply took his mission here seriously.

Meanwhile, the WingCo had changed his tone to announce. "The bus will remain here for another half hour to give you time on your own." He rejoined his wife and shook hands with the Americans who were preparing to depart already.

"Where's Daddy?" Hope asked, breaking into Kathleen's thoughts.

"That's just what we're going to find out," she answered, indicating the Registry. Since several of the others were going through it, they had to wait a minute. When Kathleen's turn came, she found Ken's name and noted the plot number listed beside it. She located the plot on the map and asked

Hope to help her look. With Hope counting the rows, they walked down the wet, brown grass of the central aisle until they came to the right one. They turned in and began reading the names on the grave markers. When they found Pilot Officer Ken Hart they stopped, clinging to each other's hand. The marker was like all the others: white, the RAF wings carved at the head, then the rank, name, position (navigator), dates of birth and death. Unlike some of the others, there was no saying, poem or biblical reference at the foot because Kathleen hadn't been able to afford the extra cost.

Kathleen roused herself to point out the graves beside it. "That was your Daddy's skipper, Hope, Flight Sergeant Mark Grimsby, and that was the flight engineer…"

As she spoke, she reflected that Ken had been so much closer to his first crew. She was glad that Moran, at least, had survived the war.

"Do you think Daddy can see us now, Mummy? Does he know we're here?"

"I think so, sweetheart," Kathleen answered as she tried to conjure up Ken's ghost. Gazing at the grave marker she spoke to him in her mind. "Isn't Hope lovely, Ken? She's turning into such a bright and impish little girl. You would have had so much fun spoiling her."

Hope drifted off a little, looking at the other graves in the row, or was she looking for worms? Kathleen couldn't be sure, but she was contentedly amusing herself, so she remained where she was, talking to Ken. "As for me, I hope you're pleased that I've done well in the WAAF, that I've got a serious job, one involved in operations."

Staring at the grave she felt more certain than at any time since Ken's death that he didn't want her to stop living. He had always said that if he failed to return, he wanted her to remarry. He'd candidly said he would do the same. "As long as we can be together," he'd said, "that's all I want. But it's a lot of sentimental nonsense to think any human can love only one other person for their whole life.'"

Kathleen sighed. She agreed with him. It was time to move on. Much as she resented the pressure from her mother, who she suspected of wanting her to forget Ken, Hope deserved to have a father as well as a mother.

With a gust of cold wind, rain splattered down on her. What dreadful weather! "Hope, Sweetheart!" She called and held out her hand. "We need to get back to the bus."

As she waited for Hope, someone came up behind her and held an umbrella over her head. She turned around to thank him, expecting one of her colleagues and was surprised to find herself face-to-face with a British Army officer. He looked very smart in a tailored brown uniform and perfectly polished accoutrements that seemed to defy the rain. He had a clipped black moustache on an aquiline face under his peaked, brown cap that was beading with rain. Kathleen's trained eyes registered he was a major of the hussars.

"Thank you, sir!" Kathleen saluted.

"Not at all. My pleasure. Is someone you know here?"

"My husband," she indicated Ken's grave.

"My condolences, Mrs Hart."

"And you, sir?" Kathleen felt she had to ask. "Do you also know someone here?"

"Yes, my brother Homer. He was a bomb aimer on a Halifax shot down 15 February, '44." As he spoke he turned and pointed to the row just opposite. "I've been here before, but when Wing Commander Priestman said he was doing a reading today, I felt it would be good to come again. Of course, I didn't reckon with the rain."

Hope arrived, and Kathleen pulled her under the protection of the umbrella, her arms around her daughter to warm her too. "This is my daughter Hope."

"How do you do, Miss Hope Hart." The Major asked bending down to smile at the six-year-old. Hope gazed up at him with Ken's big blue eyes without answering and the major continued, "I'm Major Dickenson, by the way, Lionel Dickenson. May I escort you back to the bus?" The rain was getting heavier and more uncomfortable by the second.

"Thank you," Kathleen answered gratefully. With Hope between them and Major Dickenson getting wet as he held the umbrella over mother and child, they made their way back towards the entrance. Here they paused for a moment in the shelter of the arches to see if the rain would ease. Major Dickenson asked, "Have you been here long?"

"No. It will be a week tomorrow," Kathleen admitted, astonished. So much had already happened that she felt as if it had been at least a month.

"I'm afraid it looks like it's just getting worse," Dickenson concluded with an eye on the weather. "I think we'd better make a dash for the bus."

The driver had already started the engine and the whole bus trembled. Most of the other RAF had already boarded, and the CO's car was pulling away from the curb. Kathleen told Hope to hop aboard the bus and sit down, while she turned to Major Dickenson. "Thank you for sharing your umbrella, sir!"

"My pleasure, Mrs Hart."

Kathleen would have saluted, but he offered his hand instead, so she shook it hurriedly and then climbed aboard the bus.

As it pulled away, Kathleen plopped herself down beside Hope but gazed out of a window that was rapidly steaming up. She could just barely make out Major Dickenson. Something about him reminded her of Ken although they were not at all similar in looks, Dickenson being dark while Ken had been blond and blue-eyed. Then it struck her: the last time she said goodbye to Ken had also been in the pouring rain and fog on a January day just like this. Suddenly, Kathleen was crying.

"What is it, Mummy?" Hope asked.

Kathleen pulled her daughter into her arms and sobbed. "It's just that I miss your Daddy, Hope. I'm so lonely without him."

Hope hugged her back, pressing her head against her mother's breast. "Don't worry, Mummy. I'll keep you company until you find a new Daddy for us."

Chapter Three
First Encounters

Bullies
Berlin-Gatow
Saturday, 17 January 1948

The first week in Berlin had been frustrating for Emily. "Due to technical difficulties" the train with their personal effects had been delayed at the border to the Soviet Zone. Eventually, the passenger cars had been allowed transit but only after the car with their luggage had been decoupled from the train and side-tracked for two days. Their things hadn't arrived until late Thursday, meaning she'd spent all day Friday trying to sort things out. Because the house was completely furnished, they had only a few personal things, which Emily wanted to organize herself. In short, rather than being settled in the house by the weekend, there were half-empty boxes everywhere and more chaos than ever before.

Robin, fortunately, didn't seem to care. Weather permitting, he said they would do some flying Saturday morning and then go to the British Officers' Club for tea before joining Air Commodore Waite and his wife for dinner. When they awoke Saturday morning to a crystal-clear day perfect for flying, they were out of bed and off to the station in no time, despite temperatures below freezing even on the ground. They simply kitted up in heavy turtlenecks, fleece-lined Irvin flying jackets and boots, and two layers of gloves for their hands.

Danny was waiting for them out at the dispersal also in his flying jacket and boots. He smiled broadly at the sight of Emily and exclaimed, "I must say, sir, there's something a little exciting, about a woman in an Irvin jacket!"

"Good thing you'll be in separate cockpits," Robin growled, and Emily and Danny laughed.

"Did you have anything particular you wanted me to work on with Mrs

Priestman, sir?" Danny asked, still grinning.

"Work that out between yourselves. I'm not going to interfere." From the day she took up flying, Robin had left the instructing to her instructors because he felt strongly that they would be more objective. To Danny, he added, "For the next 90 minutes, she's Flying Officer Priestman, Danny. Try to forget she's my wife. Meanwhile, I'm going to go off on my own to get better acquainted with the Mark XII."

"Very good, sir," Danny agreed, saluting as Robin was already turning away, forcing the senior officer to turn back to return it. Emily saluted as well, enjoying the flash of amusement that lit Robin's eyes at the sight of her. Yet his mind was already in his Spitfire.

Danny turned his attention to Emily. "It's up to us then, Flying Officer. Where would you like to start?"

"You're the instructor, sir, but I thought maybe a familiarization tour of Berlin from the air would be a good start. It would allow me to become more comfortable with the Spitfire again before trying anything more difficult. I don't know if the WingCO mentioned it, but I've no training or experience in aerobatics or formation flying and only very little night flying, so those are the things I must master to get my RAF wings."

"What about instrument flying? The weather can close in quite suddenly." As he spoke, Danny looked around the sky, but there wasn't a cloud to be seen.

"Fortunately, I did many hours in the Link trainer to learn about instrument flying last year. It was something I could do even in bad weather, and the weather was terrible more often than not!" She laughed a little. At the time it had been infuriating and depressing to be cramped in a dark simulator rather than up in the air. In retrospect, Emily was grateful; there was no Link trainer at Gatow.

"Good, then let's do that tour. It's important to know where you are at all times because the Soviets are a bit silly about us not wandering into their airspace. We'll just 'do' Berlin today and the corridors another time. Keeping station with me will be the start of your formation flying. We'll fly low, so no need to go on oxygen. Just remember to put the mask to your face when using the R/T."

Emily nodded earnestly. The aircraft flown by the ATA had not been outfitted with radio telephones, so she was grateful for the reminder about the R/T.

"Have you ever flown Mark XIIs?"

"Yes, a dozen times or so. I ferried several across the channel to squadrons already deployed on the continent in the closing days of the war, but that was three years ago."

"Are you ready then?"

"As ready as I'm ever going to be," Emily answered.

"Good." Danny led her over to "G" for George that had already been warmed up by the ground crew; a parachute was waiting on the wing for her already, too. Danny introduced Emily to the erks as "Flying Officer Priestman," the erks grinned and saluted self-consciously to Emily. The entire station knew by now that the WingCo's wife was a qualified pilot, even if she did not yet have RAF wings. The number of ground crew loitering around in the cold on a Saturday morning was a tribute to what a curiosity that still was. Mentally, she prayed that she wouldn't make any stupid or obvious mistakes in front of the entire station!

The erks gave her a hand up, while Danny trotted over to his own Spitfire. Meanwhile, Robin had taken off and disappeared, which was — as he knew — the way she wanted it. She might be methodical and cautious, but she hated being treated like a child in need of parental oversight. With engines turning over, Danny led the way to the head of the grass runway with Emily following behind like a docile duckling. Because of the Spitfire's long nose, it was necessary to weave back and forth to see around it. So, despite the cold, she left the hood open and leaned out as far as she could to navigate her way across the field without mishap.

Danny checked in over the R/T. "Dragon Fly Blue One to Blue Two. Ready?"

"Dragon Fly Blue Two. Roger."

He addressed the tower: "This is Dragon Fly Blue Leader. Request permission for section take-off."

The tower answered in the affirmative, and Danny opened up the throttles on his Spitfire. Instantly, he seemed halfway down the runway, leaving Emily nervously aware she'd been taken off-guard. The ATA didn't do take-offs like that! Cautiously, she opened up her throttle and the engine snarled furiously as they hurtled along gaining speed until the tail came up and the lift of the wings started to carry the body. The rumble of the wheels faded away, and with an undying sense of wonder, she knew she was flying again. For a moment she revelled in that amazing feeling before returning to "business" by searching the sky for Danny.

"Catch up Blue Two!" Danny called into her ears. "Can't have you lagging behind like a lame duck. Cut across and tuck in close behind my starboard wing."

It was a second before Emily spotted the other Spitfire, but when she did, she retracted the undercarriage, opened up the throttle and banked around to chase after him. As she approached, she decorously eased off her speed and settled in a comfortable 100 yards to his right and behind him.

"Come in closer than that." Danny admonished. "I want to be able to see you smile when I tell jokes."

Emily drew a breath and pushed the Spitfire closer. She had never flown so close to another aircraft before, but she had to overcome her inner reluctance, or she would never earn her RAF wings. She wasn't flying for the safety-minded ATA anymore, she reminded herself. The RAF wanted pilots willing to take chances and hone their skills to the absolute limit.

"Good. Now look to port." Danny started the tour, this time flying counter-clockwise over the city, which meant they started by crossing the Havel. Danny kept them flying almost due east, over the southern boroughs of the city, pointing out the Sector border between the American and Soviet Sectors. Finally, he swung northeast and raced toward the city centre, the destruction becoming noticeably worse as they left the suburbs behind and flew over the older, denser working-class areas. Like Robin before her, Emily was inwardly appalled by the level of destruction, and like him concluded that the whirlwind had done its job. It was time to start rebuilding things.

Danny pointed out the Soviet HQ at Karlshorst with its red flags and the tanks and anti-aircraft batteries encircling it as if the war had only ended yesterday. They continued over the northeast suburbs and then turned toward the Frohnau beacon. This was located on the tip of a "peninsula" of territory jutting northwards into the Soviet Zone from the Western District of Frohnau. "What I'm going to do now," Danny explained over the R/T, "is lead you back to Gatow on one of the two standard approaches from Hamburg. If the wind is out of the west or south, the approach is over Grunewald with a turn into the wind over the Havel, but if the wind is out of the east or north, the approach is over the Soviet Zone almost the whole way. I'll show you that now."

"Very good, sir," Emily acknowledged. She was about to congratulate herself on starting to feel more comfortable keeping station beside him when for a heart-stopping second, her cockpit went abruptly dark. It was as if the world had suddenly come to an end. Emily instinctively let out a cry of shock and fear. An instant later an aircraft skimmed over the roof of her cockpit before it plunged downwards just off her starboard bow. Instinctively, she yanked the Spitfire to the left to avoid a collision with the strange aircraft. The sensitive fighter responded so readily that she came within inches of a collision with Danny's tail. With a gasp, she pulled back the other way, lifting her left wing in panic. Over her earphones, she could hear Danny cursing her. Then she heard him shout, "Here comes another one!" and decided maybe his cursing hadn't been directed at her after all.

Emily pressed her mask to her face and managed to ask, "What's going on?"

"Soviet fighters. They're just bullying us. Hold your station."

Emily grimly concentrated on flying in formation on Danny's flank as the next aircraft fell on them and shot past. This time as the cockpit darkened, she knew the cause and was not disoriented, but the belly of the other aircraft was so near she could see the rivets and oil stains. Her instinct was to flee not hold her course and speed.

"I hope they didn't do this to Wing Commander Priestman," Emily noted to Danny, as much to calm her nerves as anything.

"Why?" Danny asked back surprised.

"Because I don't know how he'd react," Emily admitted.

"Our orders are *not* to react," Danny answered, and Emily nodded. Somehow, she didn't think Robin would just sit there letting them figuratively shoot him out of the sky. She saw the sun blink and instinctively made herself smaller in the cockpit anticipating another Soviet fighter. This time as he whizzed by, she looked over the side to follow him down with her eyes. In the next instant, a Spitfire sliced over the Soviet's back in a curving dive from the beam, causing the Soviet aircraft to visibly lurch. Then one wing dipped, as the pilot searched the quadrant of the sky where the Spitfire should have been if it had dived down straight rather than arching in from the side.

Meanwhile, Robin had executed a flick 180-degree vertical roll that nimbly turned the Spitfire in the opposite direction to come racing back. It flew over the Soviet fighter close enough to make the Soviet pull his head down and push the stick forward into a dive.

"Ignore him," Danny advised and reported to the tower. "Cutty Sark. This is Dragon Fly Blue Leader. We're being harassed by a section of Soviet fighters and have now passed Frohnau on approach."

"Dragon Fly Blue Leader this is Cutty Sark. What is your altitude?"

"4,000 feet."

"Continue down to 2,000."

A loud "THAK, THAK, THAK!" sounded so loudly over the RT that Emily flinched. The Spitfire responded by lifting a wing and almost sliding down the sky. Adrenalin flooded her veins as she hastened to correct her unintentional manoeuvre and her heart was thundering in her chest as Robin's Spitfire flashed over her head to throttle back and settle down in front of Danny like a landing swan.

"Very funny," Danny commented.

"Dragon Fly Section, form a vic. Flying Officer, that means you formate on my port flank, with Squadron Leader Daniels on my starboard." Emily dutifully changed her position and Robin gave her a thumbs up. "Cutty Sark, this is Dragon Fly Section passing Staaken."

"Dragon Fly Section, turn left on 080 and descend to 1000 feet. Cleared for visual landing."

"Dragon Fly Section, we will land in formation on the grass runway."

Emily's breathing wasn't back to normal as they trundled, still in a vic, back towards the hangar. The entire ground staff of the station appeared to be on hand to receive them as if they'd seen or heard about the Soviet fighters. The pilots switched off their engines one after another, but Emily dutifully did all her cockpit checks before smiling up at the waiting fitter. He offered her a hand to help her out of the cockpit, which she accepted before decorously sliding off the wing to land on her feet. Here she paused ostensibly to remove her parachute but mostly to collect her shattered nerves. She was shaken both by the behaviour of the Soviet fighters and by the near collision. The worst of it, however, was knowing she dare not say a thing to either Robin or Danny. Both were combat veterans used to dogfighting.

Robin jumped down from his cockpit immediately after landing, leaving his parachute on the seat. With only a brief nod to the ground crew, he strode toward Danny's Spitfire, coming alongside as Danny shoved the hood back. Danny pushed himself up out of the cockpit and landed at his CO's feet to be accosted immediately. "Just how often do they do that?" Robin demanded with a glance toward his wife.

"Oh, maybe once a month, but it seems to be getting more frequent," Danny admitted.

"It's just plain bullying! They must know they can't shake us, but civilian passengers would have every right to be terrified." Again, Robin looked in Emily's direction. She had dismounted decorously like the lady she was, but he'd seen the way her Spitfire lurched when the first Soviet bounced her. She'd damn near been in an accident because of the irresponsible foolishness of some young Soviet pilot.

"They haven't done it to the BEA flight, yet," Danny noted, "but they tried it on the Anson the other day when Lt. General Herbert was inside. He was not amused. He was convinced they knew he was aboard and were intentionally trying to force him to return to Hanover."

"Were they?" Robin asked, dragging his helmet off and running his fingers through his dark hair.

"Not exactly, but they may have been testing to see whether the British Commandant would lose his nerve and scuttle back to Hanover just because they harassed his flight."

"Surely, we demanded an explanation. What did the Soviets say?"

"That it hadn't happened."

"What? But Herbert had experienced it first-hand! How could they just deny it?"

"As you'll see, they deny facts to our face all the time. In this case, they claimed the only aircraft in the air at the time had been my squadron, as if Herbert couldn't tell the difference between a Spitfire and a Yak -- not to mention we don't have red stars painted on our fuselage and wings." Danny paused and then cautiously noted, "Our standing orders are *not* to respond to any kind of provocation."

"I can imagine," Robin answered unrepentantly while casting a reassuring smile at Emily as she joined them. She looked shaken. Turning his attention back to Danny, he asked, "Who issued that order?"

"Your predecessor." Danny paused and then asked hopefully, "You wouldn't be rescinding it, would you?"

Robin thought about that, casting his eyes skywards and scanning the airspace that was now empty but for a half-dozen ducks. His first instinct was indeed to rescind the order. Sommerville, as a former bomber pilot, undoubtedly took pride in not even taking note of Soviet fighters. He would have flown through flak and hostile fighters on every wartime operational flight. Ignoring the Soviet Yaks would have been a sign of contempt. But Triple Two Squadron wasn't a bomber squadron. It had — or ought to have — a more aggressive ethos. Still, mock dogfighting was dangerous enough when everyone was playing by the same rules, and somehow Robin didn't think the Soviets would respect that. The risk of an accident was high, and an accident involving two fighter aircraft would probably raise issues of provocation that could easily escalate into an international incident. To Danny, he replied, "Can I be 95% certain that none of your pilots would cause an accident if they engaged the Soviets?"

"Meaning: are they good at judging a bounce and aerial dogfighting?"

"Correct."

"Not as good as you were just now."

That felt good, Robin admitted, and he allowed himself a ghost of a smile before noting more soberly, "Flattery will probably get you somewhere in this world, but seriously, just how much practice dogfighting have your pilots had?"

Danny shrugged a little nervously. "Almost none. As I told you, the flying we do is mostly reconnaissance in pairs. Sommerville was quite stingy with the aviation fuel."

Robin could believe that. Bomber boys tended to think mock dogfighting was nothing more than immature antics with no military purpose. In fact, it was the best way of preparing fighter pilots to do their job. The bulk of the pilots here had not flown in the war and even the flight commanders had only flown after the Luftwaffe's back was broken. Out loud he concluded, "In that case, we can't risk an accident just to make the point that this is a game two can play."

"Well, if you'll forgive my bluntness," Danny responded with surprising forcefulness, "*not* responding isn't getting us anywhere either! They just become more and more impudent. Bullies don't respect restraint. They respect force."

"Which is exactly what we don't have," Robin reminded him with a cynical smile.

"Well, you at least gave one Ivan a very bad moment just now. I wouldn't be surprised if Ivan's trousers needed laundering."

"The Ivans are tough and battle-hardened. I doubt I did more than surprise him — because he knows our standing orders as well as you do. Not responding to the Soviets is probably the wisest course of action for the present," Robin concluded despite not liking it. Some instinct rebelled against just being docile.

Something else bothered him too. Nobody — not HM's government, the French and certainly not the Americans — was happy with the current situation. Everyone knew the current arrangements were not sustainable and that something had to give. No one knew how or in what direction, but the risk of conflict — even if only a short clash, a skirmish more than a war — appeared high. And Gatow was a trip wire, which meant they might also be a pressure point.

"What are you thinking, Robin?" Emily asked, breaking in on his thoughts.

"The status quo appears dangerously fragile. The Soviets appear to be probing for weaknesses and testing our resolve — things like the harassment of our trains that prevented our personal effects from arriving on time, or this senseless beating up of aircraft flying inside our airspace. It all adds up to a situation that is unstable and likely to change very suddenly."

Danny and Emily nodded but waited for him to continue.

"On the one hand, as Lt. General Herbert stressed, that means we must walk softly and avoid provoking the Russian bear. On the other hand, the bear appears to be baiting us and batting us about like a cat with a mouse. If HM's government decides it's had 'enough,' and instead of withdrawing decides to stand up to the Soviets, we may find ourselves on the front line."

Danny looked a little taken aback, and Robin smiled at him. "And you thought you were posted to the back of beyond, didn't you?"

"It has been that way up to now."

"Yes, and we don't know yet what the government's policy for Berlin will ultimately be. They may still opt to withdraw rather than risk World

War Three. Nevertheless, I'd rather be prepared to fight than get caught flat-footed."

He paused as something else struck him. Up to now, he'd thought of the air show Waite wanted only as entertainment for the German public, but it could also serve a training function. It was always more effective to train towards a goal than to do exercises in an apparent vacuum. Out loud he said, "Air Commodore Waite seemed to think an air show would be a wizard public relations stunt. If we made a dogfight part of the show, it would give us an excuse to practice a bit."

"Roger!" Danny agreed enthusiastically, immediately catching his CO's drift. "You certainly have the experience to tell us what needs to be done. Let's put on a show that will make the Ivans sit up and take notice!"

Perfect Home
Kladow, Berlin
Tuesday, 20 January 1948

When Robin left for work, Emily remained at the breakfast table without a clue what she was to do with the rest of the day. She had completed unpacking the day before and all their things had been effortlessly swallowed by the large and elegant house. Their clothes were in the closets and dresser drawers. Their books had disappeared onto the floor-to-ceiling library shelves. Their photos had found spaces on desks and mantles and buffets. Yet when all was said in done, they had made no more impact than a handful of drops in a large lake. The character of the house had not changed.

Having seen Colonel Howley's mansion and also Air Commodore Waite's gracious residence, she knew that her housing assignment was "modest" by the standards of the Allied occupation. Generals Robertson and Clay lived in palaces with more than 150 rooms and employed a staff of twelve or more. Yet knowing that did not make her feel any more comfortable.

To be sure, Robin had been delighted. "Finally!" had been his commentary and Emily could readily see the resemblance — in ambience more than style — between this house and his grandfather's on the Isle of Wight. Robin had been apologetic to Emily about wartime housing. To him, this was nothing less than what they deserved.

But Emily had grown up in the slums of Portsmouth, and after marrying Robin, she'd lived mostly in RAF married housing. Nothing compared to this twenty-two-room house set in three acres of lawn stretching down to the shores of Berlin's great lake, the Wannsee. It had polished parquet floors and wood wainscotting painted in understated shades of greyish green or navy blue. It was elegantly furnished with a mixture of antique and early 20th-century furniture, accented by Persian carpets and works of art. A grand piano stood at the juncture between the grand salon and the winter garden, strategically placed to provide live background music to events in either location. Crystal and bronze chandeliers hung from ceilings with stucco mouldings. The mantlepieces were marble and the shelves and bookcases were custom-made to exactly occupy selected niches. Elaborate glazed-tile ovens stood ready to reinforce the central heating.

She considered the gleaming mahogany dining table at which she sat. It could comfortably seat twelve, and the place settings laid out for herself and Robin were made up with gold-trimmed, white porcelain flanked by heavy, silver cutlery. The matching neo-classical chairs standing at attention around the table had striped satin seats. Sliding glass doors opened onto a breakfast room at the far end, while the other three walls were hung with pairs of portraits going back to the 18th century. Looking through the breakfast room toward the lake, she could see swans waddling past the small boathouse that crouched at the far side of an expansive lawn.

But something wasn't right. Emily supposed she might have felt uncomfortable in so much grandeur anywhere. Yet as she sat sipping her slowly cooling tea, she felt her skin creep. Everything here had been carefully collected and lovingly displayed to create a harmonious composition. That was no accident. The Allies had imperiously tossed out the residents of the houses they requisitioned, which meant, quite simply, she was living *in someone else's house.* She couldn't help wondering who the real owners were. A professor, perhaps, or an orchestra conductor? Or had it been a factory owner, happy to use slave labourers or even an SS officer? No, everything was too tasteful and elegant to have been purchased by some Nazi thug, she told herself. Surely the owners had been men of culture and education. Or had they stolen the art and the tasteful furnishings from others? David Goldman claimed that many Jewish homes had been taken over by the Nazis wholesale.

Emily turned to look at the married couples who looked down on her from their golden frames. They didn't look particularly Jewish to her, but suddenly it seemed entirely plausible that the descendants of these elegant pairs of satin-bedecked ladies and gentlemen in gold-braided uniforms had been murdered in a death camp.

There was a soft clunk behind her, and she turned around to see one of the three maids, Frau Pabst, standing in the doorway leading from the kitchen. She wore a black dress trimmed with white collar, cuffs and bib-apron. Her grey-blond hair had been pulled back in a severe bun, and Emily estimated her age at anywhere between 40 and 60; it was hard to be more precise because hardship aged people prematurely. She wore two wedding rings, symbolic of widowhood, Emily had been told, but Emily hadn't a clue when Herr Pabst had died or how. Had he died fighting for Hitler, perhaps? Or in the inferno of death rained down by Anglo-American bombers? She would not have been comfortable with either answer, so she didn't ask.

A heavy silver tray in her hand, Frau Pabst asked in a voice that seemed to convey disapproval, "May I clear away the Herr Oberstleutnant's things, Madame?"

"Yes," Emily sat back to make way for her to set the tray down and load it with Robin's dirty dishes, wondering if she would ever be comfortable with the staff. At least, none of them lived in; they commuted from wherever they lived and worked five-and-a-half days per week.

Emily supposed she ought to be grateful, yet as she waited for Frau Pabst to disappear again, she couldn't help reflecting that she knew nothing about these people. The entire staff had been hired by one of Robin's predecessors and they were officially paid out of the BAFO representational budget. Robin said that hiring above need was an official policy to provide honest work to as many Germans as possible. Just like paying servants in the colonies. Fair enough, and yet....

The staff all spoke enough English to communicate about their respective jobs and presumably, they had undergone vetting to ensure they were not Nazi party members or war criminals. Yet that said nothing about who they had voted for in the last free election. Nor did it guarantee that they hadn't hailed Hitler with wild enthusiasm at his rallies. It certainly didn't mean they disapproved of his policies. They had almost certainly looked the other way while their neighbours were dragged out of their homes to be sent to slave labour camps and ultimately to the gas chambers.

"Would Madame like a fresh pot of tea?"

Did none of these women know how to smile? Had none of them a cheerful tone of voice? Or did they simply prefer not to use either with their new employer?

Emily tried to curb her rising resentment. Perhaps she was being unfair, she told herself. Frau Pabst was patiently awaiting her answer with an expression of stoic martyrdom, and Emily realised that the greater question was not whether she wanted a fresh pot of tea but what on earth was she going to do with the whole day, the rest of the week, and indeed with the next two years? She told Frau Pabst, yes, and settled down to think over her future more systematically.

The grace period was over and she was soon going to have to face the "diplomatic" entertaining that she dreaded. As Robin had suggested, she would start with Danny and his flight commanders and then the other officers from the Station. Which reminded her that David Goldman was arriving on Friday and would be staying with them for a week or two. She was looking forward to that and secretly hoped that she might be able to help him with his new company. They had worked together on helping a mutual friend turn his old barn into a bed-and-breakfast, and she felt there were things she could do to help with his ambulance business without being in the UK. Yet she knew better than to assume David would want her to get involved. Besides, even if he did, it wouldn't be full-time work.

She was going to have to find something useful and challenging to do here in Berlin because she would go mad if all she had to do was play hostess and go to "Ladies' Clubs" luncheons. After her encounter with the American wives at Colonel Howley's party, she knew that she did not want a life in the Allied community. She would be much happier if she could find work that entailed contributing to the reconstruction of Berlin in some way. At dinner with Air Commodore Waite this past weekend, he had stressed the need for a "charm offensive." While he'd directed most of his remarks to Robin, he had also turned to her to say, "Your face is much prettier than mine, Mrs Priestman. If you become the face of the RAF and Britain to even a small segment of the Berlin population, you will be doing exactly what His Majesty's Government wants."

"Find a charity you want to support — an orphanage, or a hospital, or a home for stray dogs." Mrs Waite had chimed in, adding that the fate of cats and dogs in the ruined city was particularly sad.

Emily recognized the wisdom of what they had said, but it required her overcoming her prejudices and it also entailed acquiring the ability to communicate with Germans more fluently than she now could. If she were more fluent in German, it would open doors. It would also enable her to assess her surroundings more intelligently. The things people said when they *didn't* think you could understand them were always the most revealing.

So German lessons sooner rather than later were the short-term answer to what to do with herself. A friend had given her the name, address and telephone number of a relative who might be able to offer conversational German. Where had she filed that information away? Her finger tapped impatiently and unconsciously on the table until she remembered: she'd put it into the pocket of her handbag where she kept her shopping lists, business cards and other odds and ends. She retrieved her handbag and inside the zippered pocket found the folded note. It read: Charlotte Countess Walmsdorf, Maybach Ufer 27, followed by a telephone number. It was time to contact Graefin Walmsdorf and see if she was willing to give German lessons.

Comrades in Arms?
Gatow/Staaken
Wednesday, 21 January 1948

The official request for a courtesy call by the new station commander at Gatow on his Soviet counterpart at Staaken had been submitted to the Soviet Military Government more than two weeks before Wing Commander Priestman's scheduled arrival. There had been no reply. Then suddenly on the morning of 21 January, Sergeant Andrews took a call from Staaken with the news that the Soviets expected Wing Commander Priestman at noon. She immediately went to inform him.

Priestman looked up from the work he had on his desk annoyed. As always, he had a long list of things to do today, not to mention a niggling guilty conscience about his response to the Soviet fighters this past Saturday. Surely they couldn't have found out he was flying the Spitfire that violated standing orders not to respond? Then again, who else but the Station Commander would risk ignoring the Station Commander's orders? He frowned at her. "Is this typical? That they say nothing and then expect us to jump like we are their lackeys?"

"I wouldn't want to say, sir," Andrews responded, uncomfortable with such a question.

"Send the Intelligence Officer into me, would you? Tell him to bring his tea with him. We need to talk."

"What should I tell the adjutant at Staaken, sir?" Andrews asked nervously.

"Pretend you couldn't find me and tell them you'll ring back as soon as you have my answer."

"Yes, sir." Andrews withdrew and shortly afterwards, Flight Lieutenant Boyd knocked softly on the door. Priestman invited him in as he stood and gestured towards the coffee table with his head. Despite being introduced and seeing him at briefings, this was their first one-on-one conversation and therefore Priestman's first opportunity to take the measure of his IO.

Flight Lieutenant Oliver Boyd was slender and bony with thick, dark-framed glasses that explained the absence of wings on his chest. He seemed young for an intelligence officer; Priestman judged him to be in his early twenties. He also seemed slightly nervous as he took the seat indicated by his CO. "I've just been informed that I'm expected at Staaken in—" Priestman glanced at the wall clock "— less than three hours. Andrews is stalling for me while I decide whether to go on this short notice. What do you recommend?"

"Well, sir, if I may speak plainly, I'm rather surprised you were invited at all. We always put in requests, but it's not usual for the Soviets to respond. Normally, they just say nothing. They seldom return our invitations to anything either. I've never heard of any of our chaps being invited into Soviet officers' homes or clubs. As far as I know, Group Captain Sommerville never went to Staaken, although he may have gone before I arrived. If you turn them down now, I doubt you'll have another chance to go. In short, sir, if you are serious about wanting to visit Staaken, you should take this opportunity."

"Very well." Priestman stood, went to his desk and rang through to Sergeant Andrews. "You may tell Staaken that I will be flying over in the Anson. Be sure we have clearance for that and ring through to the Chiefy to have it fuelled and ready for take-off by 11:30."

Returning to the coffee table, he picked up his tea and sipped it. Then he leaned back and said, "Now. Tell me everything you know about Staaken and my counterpart there."

"May I get my files, sir?"

"Of course," Priestman agreed. As the young man disappeared, the Wing Commander considered the fact that Boyd didn't have the affluent, public-school-boy accent that most intelligence officers had — something that suggested he'd worked his way up to this position the hard way. He didn't mind that, but he wondered if, given the delicacy of the situation with the Soviets, such a young man was experienced enough for the job.

Boyd returned with a thick file with a colour-coded cover indicating the level of classification. Opening this, he flipped through a couple of pages until he found what he was looking for. "Colonel Gregory Sergeyevich Kuznetsov was born in Moscow in 1914. His father was a coachman, who served in the artillery in the Great War and joined the Bolsheviks during the civil war. He lost a leg and was invalided out of service, dying some time in the thirties. Meanwhile, his son joined the Communist Party in 1932 and studied engineering in Moscow. He volunteered for the army in 1940. Was selected for the Air Force and earned his wings in 1941. He flew fighters, namely Mig-3s, Ilyushin-2s and finally Yak-3s. He served continuously on the front throughout the war receiving numerous decorations. Do you want me to list them?"

Priestman shook his head.

"He is credited with 29 kills against the Luftwaffe." Boyd stopped and looked up. "Is that more than you, sir?"

"Yes," Priestman admitted. "Is he married?"

"Yes. His wife Olga Federovna is a teacher. She is still in Moscow with their only child, a boy now aged three. The other person you should know about is Major Alexei Ivanovich Volkov. Technically, he is only the Personnel Chef, but he is known to be an agent of the NKVD, the Soviet State Police, and that means he controls Kuznetsov."

"I thought you just said he was a major and Kuznetsov was a colonel?"

"Yes, but as far as we can see, Kuznetsov has no ties to the NKVD, which means he is a pawn in their hands."

Priestman thought about that and decided it was something he would have to accept at face value for the moment and think more about later. "So, tell me more about the other man. What did you say his name was?"

"Volkov."

"Yes. What do we know about him?"

"Much less. He was probably born in 1909 or 1910. We know nothing about his background, and he may have been illegitimate. He has been a party member since 1926. He studied law but appears not to have completed his degree. Although he was in the army throughout the war, the positions he held were all unimportant yet notably in Moscow, which means he either had very high-placed protectors who could keep him out of the slaughter and misery of Soviet military service, or he had made himself indispensable to someone with influence over personnel assignments. In any case, he never served on the front." Priestman felt his skin starting to creep.

Boyd continued, "He did not come out to Berlin until March of last year, and officially held an innocuous position tasked with overseeing reparations. He travelled extensively around the Soviet Zone to factories whose industrial plant was subsequently sent to the Soviet Union. My superiors believe that he also identified workers for deportation. The move to Staaken is quite recent and may signal something — we just don't know what."

The more Priestman heard, the more out of his depth he felt. He already regretted agreeing to go to Staaken. It was bad enough dealing with hard facts like Soviet military might; trying to make sense of their internal politics was simply beyond his imagination. "You will be accompanying me to Staaken, Flight Lieutenant."

"Yes, sir. Um…"

"Yes?" Priestman prompted.

"Well, um, it might be advisable, sir, to take our Russian translator as well."

"I thought you spoke Russian?" Priestman countered surprised.

Shyly, his subordinate looked down and muttered. "I read and understand it quite well, sir, but I don't speak it fluently. What I mean is my accent isn't very good, and I prefer the Soviets not to know that I have any proficiency in the language whatsoever. When I'm with the Soviets, I always pretend not to understand."

Priestman thought about that and acknowledged the wisdom of it. "I suppose we better alert him to what is happening then."

"Yes, sir. There's, um.…"

"What?"

"There are some things you should know about Corporal Borisenko."

"Yes?"

"Well, she was born in Kyiv. Her father, Nicolai Andreyevich Borisenko was a high school teacher who was arrested for treason and disappeared in 1935 apparently in connection with the purge of Trotskyists although possibly due to opposition to collectivization. Or he may simply have fallen victim to jealousy or unfounded suspicions. His wife Anastasia Sergeyovna was an artist, engaged mostly in painting the large murals you often see on Soviet buildings."

"The hefty but happy harvesters and factory workers striding forward as they roll up their sleeves?"

"Yes, Socialist Realism. Anyway, after her husband's arrest, she was briefly arrested. Although she was later released, she was stripped of all her titles, and honours, and sent to work in a steel factory. Her works of art were painted over. Corporal Borisenko, was twelve or thirteen while this was going on. She underwent multiple interrogations but was eventually sent to a detention centre for the children of traitors."

Priestman was trying to remain impassive, but he found the story unsettling.

"She was there almost a year, and then her mother came to remove her. She had remarried a certain Maxim Dmitrivich Samenov. Galyna, however, could not get along with her stepfather and tried to run away to her grandparents. This led to new disciplinary measures and eventually to her being sent to her maternal grandmother, Ekaterina Alexeyevna Rogachova in Finland."

"Finland? I didn't think Soviet citizens could leave?"

"Not without the right papers that are very hard to come by. In short, Samenov was well connected enough to get rid of his troublesome stepdaughter for good, but one must add, in a humane way. She could simply have been sent to some 're-education' centre or collective farm in the middle of nowhere."

"Do you think she's some kind of mole?"

"No, we don't." Priestman noted that he said "we" implying that MI6 had made the assessment. Boyd continued, "Her mother's family were White Russians. Her grandfather Rogachov died fighting with the Whites. Her grandmother fled to England when the Soviets attacked Finland in 1939. Borisenko herself volunteered for the WAAF in 1940 and worked first as a stores clerk and then as a radio mechanic for Bomber Command until 1944. She did not apply to work as a translator until her CO recommended her for it. She has been with BAFO since 1946 and in Berlin for nearly a year."

Priestman considered his intelligence officer solemnly and then resting his elbows on his knees he asked, "Regardless of what her official status is, do *you* trust her, Boyd?"

"Yes, sir, I do." But he nervously pushed his glasses up his nose.

"What is it then? Why did you tell me all this?"

"I'm afraid *for* her, sir. I'm afraid the NKVD may find out about her father and target her in some way. According to Soviet law, she is technically still a Soviet citizen despite having a British passport. For most of her time with us, she has done nothing more than translate documents and newspaper articles internally, which is so low profile she is almost invisible. If we take her with us as an interpreter, on the other hand, she will be exposed."

"Then maybe we shouldn't take her with us."

Boyd looked down at his hands. "I'd rather not make that decision for her, sir."

Priestman thought about that and agreed. "Fair enough. Let's send for her." He stood, went to his desk and asked Andrews to send for Corporal Borisenko.

The corporal came promptly and saluted smartly. She was short, no more than five feet, and very solidly built. Not that she was plump, but she was square of face and body. The Station Commander sat down and indicated the chair before his desk. The Corporal sat down primly, her face serious. "Corporal, I've received an invitation to Staaken at very short notice and will be flying over at noon. Flight Lieutenant Boyd thought maybe it would help if you accompanied us."

The WAAF stiffened proudly in her chair and hardly breathed as she asked tensely but hopefully, "As an interpreter, sir?"

"Yes."

She nodded vigorously, "I'd be honoured, sir." She sounded very keen indeed, an impression reinforced by asking, "May I have your speech so I can read it through in advance? That will enable me to do a better job translating it, sir." She wanted to get things right.

"I don't have a prepared speech," Priestman admitted.

Borisenko looked confused, her head swinging toward Boyd as if for an explanation and then back to her CO as she stuttered, "But — But —"

"I had no warning of this invitation, and I'm only going over to introduce myself to my counterpart." From Priestman's point of view, this visit to Staaken had the same character as the one he'd made to Tempelhof the previous week, although he recognized that he wouldn't be received as warmly by the Soviets as he had been by the Americans.

"But, but, sir —" She again looked to Boyd for support.

Boyd responded to her mute plea by explaining, "I think Corporal Borisenko is worried that you may feel uncomfortable because the Soviets will certainly have prepared speeches."

"Well, they had time to prepare them! Besides, we only requested a courtesy call. Why would they prepare speeches much less expect one from me?"

"Because they can't risk being spontaneous."

"I'm not following you, Boyd."

"Sir, no Soviet officer would risk saying one word to us which has not been cleared by their political or party *apparatchiks*. They can only speak from scripts, but there's no reason why you have to respond in kind. You aren't going to be giving a policy speech."

"Most certainly not! I'm more interested in what I see and hear than in saying anything myself. I'm not ordering you to accompany us, Corporal." He returned his attention to Borisenko. "If you'd rather stay here, you may."

She caught her breath. "I very much want to come with you, sir. I have never visited a Red Air Force base before. It would interest me very much."

Priestman met her eyes, and they were unwavering. He glanced a Boyd, who nodded. He concluded, "Good. Then both of you report back here at 11:30."

Punctually at 11:30 the trio left the admin building and started walking across the expansive field toward the hangar apron on which the twin-engine Anson awaited them. Priestman and Boyd walked side-by-side with Corporal Borisenko trailing behind them. To get to know his intelligence officer better, Priestman conversationally asked Boyd how he'd acquired his knowledge of Russian.

Boyd looked down embarrassed, then tossed his CO a self-conscious smile as he admitted. "I'm afraid this is going to sound rather silly to you, sir."

"Why should it?" Priestman asked back baffled.

"Well, we were told you flew in the Battle of Britain, sir."

"Yes. I had a squadron then." He tried to keep the annoyance out of his voice. He did not want his whole being reduced to that single accomplishment.

Boyd meanwhile was explaining, "Well, I grew up in Canterbury, and in the summer of 1940, I was 16 years old. I got a kink in my neck from looking up at the sky so much of the time! I vowed then and there, I would join the RAF as soon as I was old enough. But being old enough to sign up, didn't give me the eyesight required for flight training." He shoved his glasses up his nose self-consciously. "I got mustered as a clerk and typist. That wasn't exactly what I had imagined while admiring you up in the sky."

Priestman laughed but then reminded him. "It wasn't all fun, you know. We lost roughly 70% of the squadron in four weeks. That was killed and wounded, so the bottom line wasn't as bad as it sounds, but it felt brutal at the time."

"Yes, sir, but when I found myself typing out requisition forms for ballpoint pens and toilet paper all day long, I became thoroughly browned off. Then I heard that they were going to train some clerks in Russian so we could communicate better with our new allies, and I volunteered. I did so well, that I was recommended for a commission and later transferred to intelligence, and here I am."

"How long have you been here?"

"In Berlin? Since the summer of 1947."

"And before?"

"I was at our Headquarters in Bad Oeyenhausen for two years."

They had reached the Anson, and Priestman told the others to go aboard while he consulted the crew chief. He was qualified on twins and had maintained his flying status while in his staff job by flying Ansons from Croydon. Still, he wanted to review the critical flying information before take-off. He then took the controls for the short hop to Staaken.

They landed two minutes ahead of the scheduled appointment, but to Priestman's dismay, what looked like hundreds of Soviet troops were lined up beside the runway on parade. The Soviet soldiers stood in perfect lines; the only movement was caused by the wind. This was not Priestman's notion of an "informal" visit.

As he rolled to a stop at the end of the runway, an American jeep with Soviet insignia rushed out to lead him around the taxiway to halt before the elegant terminal building. Red flags fluttered everywhere, and the troops remained rigidly at attention. Priestman looked over at Boyd chagrined. "This is not what I wanted or expected."

"Nor I, sir," Boyd answered embarrassed.

Priestman glanced over his shoulder at Corporal Borisenko and only then noticed she was bent over the airsickness bag. Feeling his gaze, she gave him a look of complete dismay. "This -- this was my first flight in an aeroplane, sir. I — I didn't know I would be sick."

"Don't worry about it. Leave the bag on the floor and go down the stairs first so you can introduce me and Ft. Lt. Boyd."

She gamely wiped her mouth clean with her handkerchief before descending from the Anson followed by Boyd, while Priestman collected himself. The spit-and-polish unnerved him. He had sincerely hoped to have an informal meeting with his counterpart during which he might have raised the issue of bouncing aircraft in the corridors. Any hopes of getting to know his Soviet counterpart, airman-to-airman, however, were shattered by this reception. Inspections like this were intended to impress and create distance rather than the opposite. Drawing a deep breath, he descended to the tarmac and saluted his reception committee.

The left breast of the senior officer meeting him was completely covered by dangling gold medals that danced in the wind, making Robin's modest ribbons seem unimpressive by comparison. The Russian uniform with the upright collar, stiff shoulder boards with rank insignia, riding breeches and boots was similar to the Luftwaffe uniform in style but brown like the Americans'. The man's face was squarish, with a blunt, short nose under pale blue eyes and red-blond hair cut very short.

Borisenko's low-pitched yet nervous voice spoke from Priestman's side, "Colonel Gregory Sergeyevich Kuznetsov welcomes you to Staaken, Wing Commander."

As the other ended his salute, Priestman held out his hand. "A pleasure to meet you, Colonel. I certainly didn't mean to cause so much trouble. I just wanted to introduce myself."

As Corporal Borisenko translated and the Colonel answered, Priestman's eyes took in the man standing two feet behind Kuznetsov. He was in a much simpler uniform without all the dangling medals, but he exuded hostility and self-assurance. His narrow face was abnormally pale, even for winter, and it was deeply lined, but his partially closed eyes were alert. He was not introduced, but Priestman glanced over at Boyd who nodded once. It was Volkov. He remained only two paces behind Kuznetsov throughout the ensuing ceremony.

Priestman first "inspected" the rows of soldiers. They looked very smart, with sparkling buttons and glowing leather. For the most part, they also looked older than the airmen he'd inspected over the years, which reminded him that many Russian troops stationed in Germany had fought throughout the war. The Russians had not demobilized to the same extent as the West. This, in turn, meant that many of these troops would have been here in the early months, participating in the plunder and rape. What an illusion military smartness was!

After the ground troops, came an inspection of the YAK fighters with their pilots standing at attention beside them in flying-kit. Priestman took the opportunity to get a close-up look at a Yak. The form reminded him most of a Mustang, but the Yak was noticeably smaller than the Spitfire — which explained why the Spitfire had more than twice the Yak's range. Yet nothing he could see on the exterior explained why it had a ceiling 10,000 lower than the Spitfire and a substantially greater turning radius. The fighter was simply second-rate compared to his own.

He turned his attention to the pilots instead, wondering which pilots had been involved in Saturday's little incident. None of them met his eyes, and as intended, they seemed interchangeable to an outsider.

The inspection over, Priestman was taken to the elegant top-floor dining room and led to a table on a raised platform bedecked with Soviet and British flags. The formal set-up was designed to quash the building of rapport. Women soldiers in tunics with brass buttons and leather boots under their straight skirts stiffly pulled out chairs for the guests, poured water and vodka, and served a meal. The stilted conversation did not extend beyond an exchange of wartime assignments and small talk about various aircraft. Priestman was relieved, however, that no reference was made to encounters in the corridors — recent or otherwise.

At the end of the meal, the Soviet Colonel got to his feet and read a prepared speech in a monotone voice while Volkov watched his every move, his every breath, and his every sip. Borisenko interpreted softly into Priestman's ear providing a fluent simultaneous translation, the gist of which was a lengthy account of the wartime sufferings the Soviet Union before emerging victorious. The Molotov-Ribbentrop Pact was not mentioned. The invasion of Finland was ignored. The invasion of Poland was forgotten. The Battle of Britain never happened. There had been no Allied strategic bombing offensive against Germany. Fifty-five thousand British airmen had not died hammering German cities to shatter German industrial production and break German morale. Nor had tens of thousands of Allied merchant seamen lost their lives bringing the Soviet Union tonnes of war material and humanitarian aid. Based on the Colonel's remarks, the Soviet Union alone had won the war against Germany. It was understandable, therefore, that he wound up his remarks by professing perplexity about the British and American insistence on stationing troops and aircraft inside the Soviet Zone of occupation. He concluded by saying while he was pleased to greet a fellow airman and pilot, he remained puzzled about his distinguished visitor's mission. Nevertheless, they should all drink to friendship among airmen! He raised his vodka glass.

Priestman stood, raised his glass and after clinking his tumbler with that of his Russian counterpart, he knocked the shot back just as deftly as his host. If nothing else, the RAF taught a man how to hold his liquor.

Colonel Kuznetsov sat down, but his eyes remained fixed on Priestman expectantly — along with that of all the other Russians in the echoing hall. A reciprocal speech was indeed expected. Priestman glanced at Borisenko and gave her a short nod to acknowledge she had been right. Then he drew a deep breath and addressed himself to his host.

"Thank you," Priestman opened, noting that a Soviet lieutenant leaned over to translate his words to Volkov. "Your remarks were extremely educational. They have given me much food for thought. As for why I'm here, there is a simple answer. I am a soldier and I obey orders. His Majesty's government sent me here to protect British interests in the capital of our mutual and defeated enemy — the enemy we fought for two long years while you were still drinking toasts to Herr Hitler. Let us drink again to friendship among airmen!" He lifted his glass.

Kuznetsov again got to his feet and raised his refilled vodka glass. They touched glasses, and for the first time, Priestman thought he caught a glimmer of emotion in the Soviet Colonel's eyes. He thought it might have been a look of amusement bordering on respect. Or not.

Penniless Countess
Berlin-Kreuzberg
Thursday, 22 January 1948

The sound of a car on the cobbled street brought Charlotte rushing into the salon. She knelt on the faded and stained cushion in the window seat and leaned against the plywood boards that replaced the broken panes. A single square of glass inset in the wood let in a little light and enabled her to look out.

On the street below a large, black Mercedes stopped, and a driver in an RAF uniform with grey gloves came around the car to open the back door. The passenger must be Mrs Priestman, her prospective language student. Charlotte was keen to teach German. It would be a more reliable source of income than chasing after "news" and writing articles that no one necessarily bought. Best of all, she could give lessons here in the safety of her apartment rather than having to go out into the streets where there were so many dangers.

Charlotte could not see the woman's face as she stepped out of the car, only that she wore a brown hat with a pheasant feather in it. How English! Her English grandmother had had a hat like that, she remembered.

Her English grandmother had married her Prussian grandfather in 1890 and lived in Germany for 46 years without ever losing her Englishness. To save money (of which the family was always short), Charlotte's parents had hired local girls to do the menial tasks of cleaning and feeding the children, while Grandma took over the more demanding tasks of nanny and governess. She'd taught the children English, etiquette, tennis, croquet, and more. Since Charlotte was the only girl in her generation, she'd received more of her grandmother's time and devotion than her brothers. The boys had gone off to cadet schools at seven, while Charlotte remained at home under her grandmother's wing. Because her grandmother did not think much of the village school, Charlotte had been subjected to a rigorous program of additional lessons that included reading "the classics" of German and English literature and philosophy. Charlotte hoped that education would be useful now. If only she had one or two of those books, she thought with a sinking heart as she looked around the nearly naked apartment.

The front door buzzer rang, and four flights below Theo Pfalz opened the door to let the visitor inside. Mrs Priestman would now be coming up the four flights of stairs, Charlotte thought with rising panic. The importance of this interview intimidated her. If she could convince the Englishwoman to come just once a week and pay in pounds, she might be able to afford a warm scarf or a new pair of shoes, she thought wistfully looking down at the scuffed and misshapen pair she was wearing. But first, she had to convince Mrs Priestman she was a competent teacher, and how could she do that without any experience or qualifications?

She tried to imagine what her grandmother would have advised, but all that came to mind were the terrible fights between her grandparents after the Nazis came to power. Her grandmother hated Hitler and wanted to go to England; Charlotte's grandfather and father, on the other hand, insisted that one didn't "abandon" one's country just because "the government didn't suit." Her father had said the Nazis would soon be gone because their insane policies would lead to an economic collapse. Her grandfather had added that the Nazi's adventurous foreign policy would lead to a showdown with France and Britain that could only end in humiliation for Hitler. Both insisted that Germany was greater than Hitler and his party and refused to "flee like cowards."

At the time, Charlotte had sided with her father and grandfather. She had been incensed when her grandmother chose to emigrate weeks after being widowed in 1936. Yet things looked different with the wisdom of hindsight. Her grandmother's assessment of the Nazis had proven correct. Furthermore, her self-imposed exile had become a lifeline for Charlotte. Not only did her grandmother send regular packages with things like tea, stock cubes, salt and sugar, her grandmother had also recommended her to Mrs Priestman.

The buzzer at the apartment door rang, indicating that Mrs Priestman had reached the top floor. Nervously, Charlotte made sure the tails of her brother's shirt were smoothed under her black skirt and her hand-knitted jumper was straight before opening the door as stiffly as a well-trained butler.

She immediately had a shock. Standing in front of her was a young, slender woman. Somehow she had assumed that the wife of a senior officer would be middle-aged and that she would be fat because the Allies had so much food.

The woman held out her hand. "Hello. Graefin Walmsdorf? I'm Emily Priestman."

"Please come in!" Charlotte backed up, holding the door so Mrs Priestman could enter. She saw her visitor look up at the naked bulb in the doorway and then look left into the salon.

"I'm sorry," Charlotte apologized at once. "The glass fell out in an air raid, and we have no money to replace it." Mrs Priestman stepped deeper into the hall to peer more intently at the salon. Charlotte knew what she was seeing: the parquet floors were relatively intact, while remnants of the ceiling mouldings suggested how elegant this room had once been. Yet the only furniture was a packing crate that served as a makeshift table, a couple of stools and a heavy Biedermeier buffet with a marble top and a mirror beyond the sliding doors that separated the salon from the dining area. "I'm afraid all the furnishings were taken by the refugees," Charlotte tried to explain.

Mrs Priestman turned to look at her uncomprehending.

"Toward the end of the war, the tenant in this flat was arrested by the Gestapo. When the people billeted on the first floor heard about his arrest, they rushed up here to take whatever they could carry. They were all bombed out, you see. That buffet, my bed and a couple of other objects were too heavy and bulky for them, but they took almost everything else."

"But what about your own things?" Mrs Priestman asked still confused.

Charlotte shrugged. "My home was in Mecklenburg but as the Red Army approached we heard what they were doing to German civilians. My father decided we had to flee." She could not meet Mrs Priestman's eyes as she explained, and she spoke as fast as she could. "It was winter and there was a lot of snow. We couldn't risk over-burdening the horses, so we took very little with us — just clothes and food. The rest," she shrugged. "The Soviets have it now."

"And this flat?" Mrs Priestman asked looking around again. "It doesn't belong to you?"

"Oh, no!" Charlotte shook her head vigorously. "Please come into the kitchen. It is warmer there. I can put the kettle on for tea."

"Yes, of course," Mrs Priestman smiled apologetically.

Charlotte led the way into the kitchen which felt warm after the salon.

She pulled out one of the straight-backed wooden chairs and indicated Mrs Priestman should take a seat, which she did, while Charlotte put the kettle on the stove, lit the gas, and then placed plates, saucers and cups on the table. None of it matched, of course, but she was careful to give Mrs Priestman an intact cup, not one of the ones glued back together again. They always leaked a little. She found two teaspoons which were not badly bent and two napkins. These at least were linen, clean and ironed.

"Are you renting this flat?" Mrs Priestman returned to the discussion.

"No, not really. My aunt Sophia married a wealthy man, Ferdinand Freiherr von Feldburg. When he was elected to the Reichstag in 1924, he bought this apartment house and moved into the first-floor flat — where all the bombed-out people live now. It goes all the way around the courtyard. My uncle died before the war, but his eldest son, my cousin Philip, inherited the house and he too rented out everything but the first-floor flat. Philip was a General Staff officer; when he was not on the front, he lived there. However, he was directly involved in the coup attempt against Hitler, and shot himself on the night of 20 July 1944—"

"In this house?" Mrs Priestman gasped.

"Yes, downstairs, in the family flat," Charlotte assured her, pointing toward the floor. "After that, the SD took over the flat, but as the end neared, they stole everything in it and disappeared. Refugees fleeing the Red Army like me were moved in instead. That was the situation when I —" she stumbled a little "— arrived here. Although I had only visited a couple of times in my life, the concierge recognized me and let me and the two servants who were with me live in the old coachmen's rooms over the stables in the second courtyard. Horst slept in the stalls with the horses at first, until this flat became free. That was when I moved in -- after the others had taken most of the furnishings."

"Why was the man who lived here arrested?" Mrs Priestman asked.

Charlotte shrugged. "I don't know. At the end of the war, people were arrested for almost anything or nothing. Just for telling a joke or saying something like 'too bad Stauffenberg failed' or for reporting the advances of the Red or American Army."

"Didn't you say your father and mother had left your home with you?"

"Yes. They were killed by a strafing Soviet fighter during the journey," Charlotte stated matter-of-factly.

Mrs Priestman caught her breath. "I'm so sorry! I shouldn't have asked. I'm sorry." She seemed so sincerely distressed, that Charlotte started to like her.

"Don't worry. It is better you know. My parents and two servants were killed. Three of us survived; Horst the coachman, Jasha our Polish cook and me — or is that I?" She asked, suddenly unsure of her English.

"What about other family members? Sisters and brothers…" Mrs Priestman focused on what had happened, not how she said it, which Charlotte liked.

"I was the only girl in my family. Both my brothers were killed in the war, but my cousin Christian, Philip's younger brother, arrived here just two weeks ago." Charlotte made no effort to disguise how relieved and delighted she felt. "He is trying to start up a wine business, selling wine from his family estate in Franken. He has been helping me with everything."

The kettle started to whimper, and Charlotte turned to take it off the heat and pour the steaming water over the tea leaves in her teapot. Even with her back turned, she sensed that Mrs Priestman was looking around the kitchen, no doubt noticing that some of the cupboards no longer closed properly, or that the countertop was gouged and stained as if she didn't clean it properly. Charlotte felt ashamed.

As she set the teapot down on the table, Mrs Priestman considered her from intelligent, observant eyes. Embarrassed, Charlotte ran her hand through her short-cropped hair, aware of what a ragamuffin she had become. She turned to withdraw a creamer already filled with milk from the refrigerator and set it on the table. "I am out of sugar, I'm afraid."

Mrs Priestman dismissed the missing sugar with a smile and "No worries." But her expression was serious. "I suppose we ought to get to business. First, German was my language a University, so I'm not a total beginner. I also have a sound grasp of the grammar, and I can still read it fairly well. However, I find it difficult to understand people, especially when they are speaking quickly, and my biggest problem is speaking. My primary objective with these lessons would be to become more fluent in spoken German."

Charlotte nodded vigorously, relieved. Talking was easier than teaching grammar.

Mrs Priestman continued. "I'd like to try to get my German up to speed as quickly as possible, which means I'd like to have frequent lessons at first if that is possible."

"Oh yes," Charlotte assured her.

"It won't interfere with your work as a journalist?"

"Oh, no. That is only part-time anyways," Charlotte explained.

"Oh, I'm relieved to hear that because, you see, I was hoping we might start with lessons three times a week, Monday, Wednesday and Friday." It was worded more as a question than a statement, so Charlotte nodded assent vigorously.

"Now, in terms of remuneration, does a shilling an hour sound reasonable to you?" Mrs Priestman asked next.

"Oh, yes. That would be fine," Charlotte agreed eagerly. Shillings were real money. Any amount of real money was better than any amount of occupation marks — or cigarettes. It might be old-fashioned snobbishness that she had no right to anymore, but she hated the thought of working for cigarettes. That was what whores did....

Mrs Priestman smiled. "Well, then I think that covers it! How soon could we get started?" Mrs Priestman asked. "Would next Monday be possible?"

"That would be very good. Only —" Charlotte cut herself off. She just couldn't be dishonest; it was against her upbringing. "I must confess to you, Mrs Priestman, that I'm not a trained language teacher. I trained as a secretary, you see, but even then I never worked in an office. When the war started, my father wanted me to come home. To the estate. We'd lost many of our workers and he wanted me to help. I could look after the horses so that the men could do the heavier work. And I helped in the kitchen, of course, and with the harvest."

Mrs Priestman was gazing at her with a strange expression. "Is something wrong, Mrs Priestman?"

"No, of course not, I just thought... I mean, I was told... Your title..." Her voice faded away. "I expected..."

Charlotte understood. In Berlin, too, she'd run into many people who assumed that just because she was a countess she had grown up in luxury and affluence. It seemed odd to Charlotte because all the landed noblemen she'd grown up around had been similarly poor to her parents.

She tried to explain to the Englishwoman. "That is my hereditary title, Mrs Priestman, and it's true that the family estate was quite large, over twelve hundred acres. Still, the soil was very bad, sandy, and only good for rye, oats and barley. Of course, the manor was grand, but it was austere too — and bitterly cold in winter. That's probably why I manage with so little coal now." She tried to make a joke of it, but it fell flat. So, she continued earnestly, "We had to live very frugally, Mrs Priestman. I never had a nightdress, I only wore hand-me-down nightshirts from my brothers. We did not have marmalade for breakfast except on Sundays, and hunting was for food as much as for sport. It was not a life of luxury — although," Charlotte paused to reflect, her eyes seeing things she had tried to forget "— it was a not brutal life either — not before the war. We all learned to play instruments so we could make music at home, and in the winter we took turns hosting dances." She smiled faintly. "But I never attended a proper concert or professional play or even visited a library until I went to secretarial school in Breslau. I certainly never attended a court ball or went to the opera." She paused and admitted. "I've never been West of Berlin either, Mrs Priestman. I have no idea about your world, except what I have read in books."

Mrs Priestman looked up at the naked lightbulb hanging over the battered kitchen table and then around the kitchen with its sagging cupboards and scratched floor until she was back where she'd started. She looked Charlotte straight in the eye and startled her with the words, "This looks almost exactly like the kitchen of the home where I grew up."

"But—" It was Charlotte's turn to be confused. "But your husband—"

"My husband comes from a good background and is a first-rate officer who has earned his stripes, but I grew up in the slums. I went to university on a scholarship and I'm much happier with a German teacher who *isn't* a grand, aristocratic lady, but someone I can talk to honestly. I've only been in Berlin for two weeks, and I have so many questions already. Do you think you can help me not only learn German but understand Germany and the Germans?"

Charlotte felt relief flood through her. Not because of the job and the income anymore, but because she felt this woman might become a friend. She had been battered down too much for hope not to be tempered by fear, however. She managed only a tentative smile and an honest answer,

"I'm not sure I can *explain* Germany or my countrymen to anyone, Mrs Priestman. I don't rightly understand them myself. Still, I think, we can discuss things together, perhaps, and seek answers?" Her hopeful look was answered by a wide smile from her visitor.

"That is exactly what I'd like best! My name is Emily, by the way, I hope I can call you Charlotte?" She held out her hand.

At last, Charlotte broke into a broad smile as she took Emily's hand and said with feeling, "I'm so glad we've met!"

Chapter Four
Wider Lens

Burying the Dead
Berlin, Kladow
Friday, 23 January 1948

When the flight attendant announced they were making their final descent into Berlin, David Goldman secured his seatbelt and leaned forward to look out of the small, oval window. All he could see was forest. Then he caught a glimpse of a wide, four-lane highway running straight as an arrow beside a railway track, and his heart missed a beat. The Avus! The Dakota banked to the right and craning his neck, David caught a glimpse of glimmering grey water as a river widened into a lake, but no matter how much he contorted himself, he could not see to the Schwanenwerder, where his uncle's lovely, lakeside home had once -- and maybe still -- stood.

Suddenly it all hit him, and David clutched the arms of the seat. The stewardess seeing his white knuckles smiled and assured him there was nothing to worry about. As an experienced pilot that would have amused him if he hadn't been so tense. His determination to stop Nazis from benefiting from family property had become a bit of an obsession. He was determined to clean the slate before focusing on his future, his air ambulance company. He'd just spent a week in Hamburg, where things had gone unexpectedly well, but Berlin was going to be more difficult. Here he was not dealing with the property of cheated survivors, but his memories of the murdered.

The aircraft sank steadily and with a loud clunk, the undercarriage dropped down and locked in place. They were buffeted by gusts of wind as they flew low over the Wannsee and seconds later, with a solid thump the wheels hit the earth. The loud rumble of rolling tyres reinforced the noise of the engines as they gradually slowed to a halt and turned to taxi toward the terminal. David looked out the window, bewildered by a sense of not having arrived after all. Gatow appeared to be surrounded by forest.

Taking his scuffed leather briefcase from the overhead compartment, David followed the other passengers out of the aircraft. At the foot of the stairs, he was surprised and delighted to be met by Wing Commander Robin Priestman. David hadn't expected that honour. He'd first met Robin in August 1940. At the time, David had been in the RAF only a few weeks after arriving from Canada to enlist. With nearly 1,000 flying hours as a civilian pilot, he'd been granted a short-service commission, and taught how to read rank, salute and march at an initial training centre in Brighton. But his first posting as an officer had been to an Operational Training Unit at Hawarden where he was supposed to learn how to fly Spitfires. When he entered the officers' mess for the first time, he was promptly told by one of his fellow trainees that "Jews did not belong in a first-class flying club." Stunned, he'd just stood there — until Priestman, then only a flight lieutenant and instructor, had walked into the mess. Priestman asked why he was drinking alone, and then proceeded to tear a stripe off the others. David couldn't remember exactly what he'd said, but he'd invoked the King and at one point declared "I thought I was *fighting* Nazi Germany not *living* in it!" They had been friends ever since.

"Welcome to Gatow, Banks!" Robin greeted. "You're going to have to go through customs over there and collect your luggage next door." He pointed toward a door in the building behind him where the other passengers were disappearing. "Emily is waiting for you in the lounge. She has a car and driver and will take you home. I'll come as soon as I can."

"That's perfect. Thank you, Robin. I appreciate being able to stay with you and Emily." David meant every word. Facing the gruesome fate of his favourite aunt and uncle without friends around him would have been bitter.

"I want to hear all about your new company. Who knows when I might find myself looking for work as a civilian pilot?"

"Very funny, WingCo!"

Because it was located in the British area of occupation, RAF Gatow was officially part of Britain, so David presented his passport to someone from HM Immigration Service and opened his bag for inspection by HM Customs. The formalities concluded, he went out into the lobby where he found Emily Priestman waiting as promised. As they touched cheeks in greeting, she exclaimed, "It's so good to see you, David! You look younger out of uniform!"

David looked down and fiddled awkwardly with the large, tortoiseshell buttons of the cashmere overcoat. He didn't like being out of uniform. It made him feel isolated and awkward. Too often, when he caught a glimpse of his reflection in a glass, he thought he saw his father's ghost looking back at him, smirking with contentment at his transformation into a businessman.

As they sank into the back of the large, black Mercedes that had been allocated to the Station Commander's wife, Emily asked, "How is Kiwi coping?"

David drew a deep breath, "Not as well as I wish. He doesn't want to accept that Betty's decision is final. He keeps trying to get her to meet up with him, hoping to make up."

Emily shook her head. "I never understood what he saw in her. She always seemed rather shallow and materialistic to me."

"I couldn't agree more, but he was besotted and can't seem to let her go."

"And you? Have you been seeing anyone?" Emily's tone was hopeful. Over the years she had discretely introduced him to several attractive and interesting women — other ATA pilots, WAAF and WRNS officers, and the like. David was not unappreciative. He did not want to spend the rest of his life alone. He would, very much, have liked to fall in love. But he had never found it easy to strike up friendships with ladies, and since losing the face he'd been born with he'd become even more reticent. It was hard to explain, but he could not kiss a woman without feeling as if a sheet of paper separated them.

David shook his head firmly in answer to Emily's question and was glad that she did not press him. Instead, she changed the subject. "And Sammy?"

Sammy was David's dog, adopted when he was still undergoing plastic surgery. Robin and Emily had looked after him whenever David was back in the hospital and called themselves his "aunt and uncle."

"Sammy is bossing Kiwi about," David said with a laugh, "and doesn't understand why he doesn't get to fly anymore."

"Hopefully, you'll have him back in the air soon," Emily suggested.

David nodded, happy to talk about his business rather than the reason he was in Berlin. "We're registered as a partnership, although if things go well I hope to transform it into a share company. Ideally, all our employees will be share-holders — non-voting shareholders, that is."

"Oh! Do you have employees already?" Emily asked sounding astonished.

David laughed. "None at all! All I managed to do was settle the legal issues and set up a bank account. Kiwi is working on finding us a suitable aircraft and identifying an airfield we can operate from at minimal cost. He's also started qualifying on twins and will hopefully have his license on them by the end of February. But until we know where we'll be based, we can't look for office space, a secretary, ground crews and the like. I have to find clients, too, and success will depend on what we charge, which in turn depends on our operating costs, which I can't work out until I know what aircraft we'll be using and where we'll be based."

"I wish I could help," Emily told him in a tone that made him look over sharply. She didn't meet his eyes, and he sensed latent tension.

"I thought you were going to be here in Berlin for the next two to three years?" He asked surprised.

"Yes, but I have no work here, and surely there are some things I could do to help with without being in the UK — like designing logos or writing marketing text?"

David hadn't thought that far, but he nodded tentatively. During the excruciatingly long recovery process from his injuries, Emily and he had worked together to convert a mutual friend's fifteenth-century barn into a charming bed-and-breakfast. Mr Bowles had been desperately poor and lonely after losing his only son in the war, and the project had given him something to do with his time and offered the prospect of a steady source of income in the future. While David handled all the financial aspects of the project, Emily had worked with the National Trust to be sure the old barn could be "modernized" in a way that nevertheless preserved its character so it could be listed. The project had been a success both psychologically and financially, and David had come to respect Emily's practical yet creative approach to problems. Among other things, she had thought up most of the advertising phrases they had used. Things like "Spend a night in the 15th Century."

Before David could answer, however, they pulled up beside a large, neo-classical villa and the driver stopped the car.

"Here we are," Emily announced, flinging the car door open. The driver removed David's luggage from the boot and followed them up the stairs to the entry hall, where a uniformed maid greeted them. While one maid led the driver up the curving marble stairs to put away the luggage, another took David's hat and coat, and a third announced that tea was laid in the "winter garden."

"Don't put the kettle on just yet," Emily answered. "I'll give our guest Mr Goldman a tour of the house first and then he will probably want time to freshen up before coming down. I'll ring when we're ready."

The maids disappeared and Emily conducted the tour ending at the upstairs bedroom she'd selected for David. It had a balcony looking out over the garden. Then she returned downstairs and rang for tea.

By the time David joined her, it was nearly five and the sun had already set. Darkness was gathering in the trees that clustered at the fringes of the lawn and a light drizzle had set in. He sat down on the sofa and Emily settled into one of the winged chairs while one of the maids brought the tea. "Did I tell you I've started German lessons?" Emily opened.

"Well done!" David praised, genuinely pleased that she was making this effort.

"Yes, Colin's great aunt suggested I get in touch with her granddaughter Charlotte."

"And things worked out?" He probed.

"We met for the first time on Wednesday, and I liked her very much. We're going to start with lessons three times a week. Her apartment was dreadfully cold and she had no books, so we agreed I'd send my driver for her and we'll have our lessons here. You'll have a chance to meet her yourself."

"Oh, that's nice," David agreed sincerely. He'd been curious about her from what their mutual friend Louise had said.

"She wasn't at all what I expected," Emily admitted as she finished pouring for both of them.

"What were you expecting?"

"Well, someone like you and your sister Sarah — you know, raised by nannies and governesses, someone who'd gone to a Swiss boarding school, spent her holidays on the Riviera and spoke five languages and the like." David laughed, but Emily continued seriously. "I suppose I expected someone older and more sophisticated, and a little arrogant."

"Arrogant? Why that? Louise isn't arrogant."

"I know, but Louise's English and Charlotte's father was a Junker."

"A Junker? What do you mean by that?"

"Isn't that the right term for the Prussians with large estates East of the Elbe?" Emily asked back surprised.

"It's a term that is often used — and more often misunderstood, particularly in America and Britain. Junkers are very rarely arrogant — proud, yes, but not arrogant. They are generally conservative in the sense of mistrusting change, which was why they were largely hostile to National Socialism. They are not particularly antisemitic — I faced more hostility to Jews in England. Hitler was an Austrian, remember? Goering and Himmler were both Bavarians. And it was the scions of some of the most famous so-called Junker families — Moltke, Yorck, Schulenberg and Tresckow — that gave their lives in the attempted coup against Hitler."

"But only to restore the Kaiser, surely? To regain their own power."

"I doubt that. Historically, the Junkers have shown an almost monastic devotion to duty and a degree of incorruptibility that made Prussian institutions work very well for a long time. They were bewildered, outmanoeuvred and ultimately repulsed by the Nazis because National Socialism accumulated power through lies and corruption. It is Germany's tragedy that the Junkers did not see the danger soon enough — and that General von Hammerstein was too much of a democrat to undertake a military coup d'etat in January 1933."

Smiling faintly, Emily shook her head and concluded, "It's a good thing you are here, David. Maybe you can help me understand this country better. I still feel lost and alienated. Maybe, we could—" Before she could say more, Robin poked his head into the winter garden to ask, "Shall I bring the champagne?"

"Oh! Did you get away so soon? That's wonderful!" Emily answered and a moment later one of the maids arrived with a silver tray laden with delicate champagne glasses and an ice bucket with a champagne bottle in it. As the maid withdrew, Robin poured for all three of them. Emily and David stood for the first toast.

"To old friends!" Robin suggested, and they clinked glasses before sipping, raising them again, and then sitting down. Robin turned to Emily to say, "The weather doesn't look good for flying tomorrow, I'm afraid. Intermittent sleet is forecast to continue throughout the night and into the morning." Then turning back to David, he asked, "What does your program look like while you're here?"

David had been avoiding thinking about it, but drawing a deep breath, he explained. "You may remember that in his will my father left me all family property in Germany. In Hamburg, that consisted of our family house on the Aussen Alster, the bank building, and various other investments from which my father had been parted at ludicrously low prices. The Allies recognize that contracts made under duress are invalid and I can reclaim the properties. However, my father had already transferred enough money to foreign bank accounts to assure that he could make a fresh start in Canada, and by the time he died, he'd rebuilt his fortune. My only concern was to ensure that no Nazi was directly benefitting from any of the family's former assets, and they weren't. The properties downtown had been obliterated in the firestorm and the family home had been taken over by a Danish shipping firm that happily paid me 5,000 pounds to settle all potential claims out of court."

"Well done," Robin remarked.

David drew a deep breath. "The situation here in Berlin is different. My father was one of just two children. His sister Anna married Dr Otto Kuczynski. Uncle Otto was an ophthalmologist, who had his practice and an optometrist office on the Kurfuerstendamm." He stopped speaking as the memories that he had been fighting back for so long were flooding back.

David swallowed and forced himself to continue, "Uncle Otto was very different from my father. He wasn't at all distant, stern or arrogant. He hadn't built himself a tower of financial success from which to look down on the rest of the world including his children. Uncle Otto was a wonderful, cheerful man who loved children, dogs and laughter. He made my Aunt very happy. In all my memories, she is smiling, laughing and bustling about to make others happy too. She was plump and loved large dinner parties, and going to concerts and plays. Uncle Otto didn't believe evil of anyone — which is why he didn't get out in time. He, my aunt Anna, and their two daughters were deported in mid-1942 and sometime later slaughtered like livestock at Auschwitz." The words burned the air.

After a moment of stunned silence, David looked down. "I'm sorry. I shouldn't have blurted it out like that. I didn't mean to ruin the mood."

Emily glanced at Robin and then said softly. "David, you don't need friends for small talk. We're for helping one another get through difficult times. Is there anything we can do?"

"Yes, it helps that I can stay here in your home rather than in a hotel. It helps to have a warm fire and people to talk to. Please just be patient with me, if I am tense or angry or even a little rude. I know this is going to be difficult. I am here to remember my aunt and uncle. To honour them. Figuratively to bury them. They were robbed and butchered, and their remains were incinerated. All that is left of them are the places where they once lived and worked. Then again, for all I know, every place associated with them has been swept away in the whirlwind."

Emily and Robin nodded, then Robin remarked softly, "About 40% of Berlin is in ruins."

David nodded, but his eyes were fixed on the teacup, his elbows on his knees. "My *hope* is that everything has been blown away or shattered beyond recognition. Then I can go to a synagogue, say prayers for the dead and arrange for a memorial, before getting on with my life." He paused and his friends remained silent, waiting for him to speak. "My *fear* is that something remains. If so I will have to sort through it, deciding what to do with it. My worst nightmare is that I must confront someone who is unjustly profiting from the cold-blooded murder of two kind-hearted people and their two innocent little girls."

A Lesson in History
Berlin-Kreuzberg
Saturday, 24 January 1948

"You think only capitalists commit mass murder?" Jakob Liebherr asked his son Karl incredulously.

As usual, Karl was home for Saturday dinner, but because Trude had been delayed at the hospital where she worked, the two men were cooking for themselves. This amounted to Jakob frying eggs and onions, while Karl sat at the kitchen table nursing a bottle of local beer in a brown bottle.

"Who killed the Kulaks?" Jakob asked his son.

"Don't try to change the subject!" His son protested frowning.

"I'm not changing the subject. You said only capitalism produces tyranny and mass murder. I'm simply pointing out you are wrong. Your "Great Socialist Motherland" has also carried out the slaughter of millions of people."

"Nothing comparable to the death camps, Vati! How can you, a victim of the Nazis, talk such nonsense?"

"Because it is true. Millions of kulaks were killed and many more millions died of starvation because of the forced collectivization of agriculture."

"That was nothing like what the Nazis did!" Karl insisted. "It was only because the Kulaks offered resistance that they had to be eliminated. That is the key difference that you either fail to understand or refuse to recognize," Karl insisted. "Fascists kill for their *own* benefit, for *individual* profit, not for the good of the working masses."

Jakob switched off the gas on the stove and with the handle of the skillet wrapped in a hot pad, carried it to the table. With a spatula, he dished half the eggs onto Karl's waiting plate and the other half on his own. Then he returned the skillet to the stove and put salt and pepper on the table before sitting down. His son had already started scooping the eggs and onions into his mouth with an evident appetite.

Taking advantage of his son's mouth being full, Jakob asked, "Aside from the fact that Hitler justified the slaughter of the Jews with the exact same argument, tell me who profited from the collectivization, Karl? Livestock was slaughtered on a massive scale and the meat rotted.

Agricultural productivity declined. Famine followed. Millions starved to death. Who profited? The masses? The peasants?"

"You're turning things on their head! The Kulaks killed the livestock and caused agricultural production to fall because they didn't cooperate! The famine was not the fault of collectivization but of the profit-seeking Kulaks!"

Jakob had not taken a bite to eat yet, but he leaned forward to speak more softly and directly to his son. "No one in Moscow starved, Karl. Or St. Petersburg. Or Kyiv. In Moscow, they gave banquets with caviar and white bread heaped in mounds."

"That's propaganda!" Karl protested angrily.

"I read it in *Pravda*, Karl, and so can you if you go to an archive. *Pravda* bragged and printed pictures of the receptions in Moscow, of Stalin at state dinners, of Molotov entertaining foreign dignitaries. At every opportunity, it claimed that the famine was Western propaganda, a fabrication, a lie. Agricultural production, *Pravda* said, had never been higher."

Karl frowned, recognizing too late that his father had laid a trap for him, but he doggedly fought back. "The Kulaks were capitalists, laying claim to land — which can only be held collectively for the common good of all people — and seeking to make profit from the sale of agricultural produce that belongs by rights to the entire people. They had to be eliminated."

"Why? It couldn't have been for the benefit of the people, Karl, because the rest of the population had *more* food when the Kulaks had farms than they have had at any time since the collectivization. In short, collectivization failed and failed miserably."

"That is not true!"

"It is true! It is a *fact* — an objective, verifiable fact and only wilful blindless prevents you from seeing and admitting it. Until you start facing facts, you will be living in a fantasy, following a mirage that will lead you to ever greater darkness and misery. Wake up!"

"Why do you assume that you have the facts, and I don't?"

"Because your so-called facts change if the Party says so. Real facts don't change. Let's start with something very simple. Something we can both personally observe. Did the majority of SPD members vote for a merger with the KPD or not?"

"We don't know because there was not a fair election!"

"There was a fair election, Karl. All across the Western Sectors of this city, there was a free and fair election."

"That's not true. The Western Imperialists pressured voters to vote against the merger."

"What is your evidence?"

"Everybody knows it was true! It was reported in the press—"

"The Soviet-controlled press."

"Of course! That is the only reliable press."

"But it is full of lies — like reports claiming agricultural production in the Soviet Union is higher than ever when *in fact*, Karl, people are starving by the million."

Karl refused to get dragged back on the topic of Soviet famine. Stubbornly, he insisted, "Vati, the elections were rigged! There was massive fraud! Ballot boxes were stuffed!"

"Where? When? By whom? Did you *personally* see any evidence of fraud?"

"Of course not, I was in the Soviet Sector."

"Where the polling places were closed so no election could take place at all. You call that democracy, Karl?"

"Democratic socialism has nothing to do with these silly shams of letting people vote. It doesn't need the trappings and façade of a multiparty system, competitive elections and independent parliaments —"

"Stop arguing! Both of you!" Trude Liebherr ordered as she swept into the kitchen. She was still in the greatcoat of her nurse's uniform and white nurse's hat. Her face was flushed with cold — or anger. "Listen to me! Both of you! Your arguments are pointless. We have a real crisis on our hands." She took a stand behind her chair that was still pushed up against the table, and she made no move to remove her overcoat or hat.

Turning to her husband, she addressed him. "Jakob, do you remember the little boy with leukaemia that I've been telling you about? Hans Riemann?"

"Yes, of course."

"His condition has deteriorated and is now critical. He was haemorrhaging much of the night, and he desperately needs a blood transfusion, but he has AB-negative blood. We called every single hospital and the Allies. No one has AB-negative blood in sufficient quantities. Finally, Dr Feuerbach called a colleague in Hamburg. They have AB-negative blood in their blood bank and have earmarked it for little Hans. However, we must get Hans to Hamburg as soon as possible. The next train to Hamburg leaves tomorrow morning. I need you to call the British liaison officer and explain the situation. Hans can only travel on a stretcher, so we'll need three seats, and also seats for the two stretcher bearers and myself."

"You're going with him?"

"Of course! His mother wouldn't know how to deal with any medical issues on the way, and I can explain his case history to the staff in Hamburg." Then without missing a beat she turned on her son. "Karl, I need you to help me, too. The Soviets board the trains as soon as they enter the Soviet Zone and all the German passengers are checked not only for ID but for other documentation as well. You must find out what we will need and help me get it. Today. Can you do that for me?" She looked him straight in the eye.

Karl seemed to swell before his father's eyes, evidently proud to be asked. "Yes. Mother. I can. I'll get to work on it immediately and be back as soon as I have everything together. You can count on me." Standing, he left his beer where it was, grabbed his cap and coat, and called "See you later!" to his parents as he departed.

As the sound of his footsteps faded in the stairwell, Trude smiled faintly at her husband. "You see, Jakob. He's still a good boy at heart."

"I know that — otherwise I wouldn't spend so much time and energy trying to help him see reason," Jakob replied.

153

Afternoon Tea in Tegel
Berlin-Tegel
Sunday, 25 January 1948

Lynne knocked on Kathleen's door with the news she had a visitor at the front gate.

"A visitor?" Kathleen asked back. "But I don't know anyone in Berlin who isn't stationed right here at Gatow."

"Well, he asked for you by name, and he's a British Army major."

Kathleen frowned for a second and then realized it must be the nice officer who had offered her an umbrella at the cemetery last Sunday. "Did he say what he wanted?"

"No, but if you don't want to go out with him, I will. He's quite a dish!"

"Could you possibly sit with Hope, while I go and see what it is he wants?"

Lynne readily agreed but called after her. "Do mention I'm available if you turn him down!"

At the main gate, Kathleen found a beautifully polished, bright green sports car like none she had ever seen before. It was all smooth, curved lines more reminiscent of a Spitfire than an automobile, she thought. The left-hand door flung open proving it was a continental vehicle, and Lionel Dickenson stepped out smiling. "Mrs Hart!" he greeted her.

Kathleen wanted to salute but wasn't in uniform so after a moment of indecision held out her hand. "Major Dickenson—"

"Please call me Lionel."

"Well, all right," Kathleen answered.

"Now, I hope you won't find this impertinent, but on the spur of the moment, I decided to pop by and see if you and your lovely little daughter might want to spend the afternoon with me. The French have an officer's club on the Tegler See with a large playroom for children staffed by four nannies. There are puzzles and colouring books and games, and sometimes one of the nannies reads children's stories. I'm sure Hope would love it."

"Yes, but I'm not an officer."

"No, but I am, and you'll be in civies." He grinned. "There's no reason anyone should think you aren't my wife and daughter. Do say 'yes.' The French also have a lovely tearoom and splendid food. While Hope is playing we could get a little better acquainted."

It was because he included Hope that Kathleen accepted. She would not have been inclined to leave Hope behind so soon after her arrival, but since Lionel planned something special for her too, Kathleen saw no reason not to take him up on the offer. Requesting fifteen minutes to change into something more appropriate and to get Hope ready, she departed.

Lynne was eagerly awaiting her. "And? Do I have a date?"

"No, we're going to a children's playroom for Hope."

"Alas. Always the bridesmaid...." Lynne remarked with feigned distress.

Forty-five minutes later, Kathleen, Lionel and Hope alighted before a large villa flying the French tri-colour and facing yet another large lake, this one northwest of the city centre. Although they'd driven past the 1936 Olympic stadium, which sat in a quiet suburb, and then through an industrial area that Lionel identified as "Siemensstadt," Kathleen had yet to see anything that qualified as a major urban area. "I've been in Berlin nearly three weeks and I still haven't seen anything of it but the outskirts," she complained.

"Don't worry. Downtown Berlin is mostly rubble and quite depressing." Lionel countered.

Lionel signed in at the French officers' club as Mr and Mrs Dickenson. Taking Hope by the hand, Lionel guided them to the children's playroom where he introduced Hope to one of the nannies. With exclamations of delight, she took Hope under her wing and led the six-year-old over to a table with colouring books on it. After Hope was happily settled, Kathleen allowed Lionel to take her by the elbow and escort her to a gracious lounge with low tables and splendid views of a lake dotted with low islands. The weather was still soggy, with mist clinging to the tops of the trees, but the room was comfortably warm and the waiters exquisitely polite. It all felt comfortably right, somehow; it was just the kind of place Ken would have taken her.

"Now, are you having tea or coffee? Or would you allow me to buy you a Hot Toddy or perhaps a brandy?"

"Thank you. I'll stick to tea," Kathleen told him with a gentle smile. She didn't like drinking alcohol when she was out with Hope.

Lionel spoke to the waiter in fluent French, evidently asking for some suggestions because there was a short exchange before, with a bow and a smile for Kathleen, the waiter withdrew. Lionel sat back in his chair. "Do you like it here, Mrs Hart?" He placed just enough emphasis on her name to remind her that she had yet not told him her first name.

"Very much," Kathleen agreed, adding with a smile, "and you may call me Kathleen."

"What a lovely name! Where are you from in the UK?"

"A place called Netley Abbey near Southampton. My father worked as a clerk for a building company there."

"I see, and you met your husband in the RAF?"

"No, I joined the WAAF after he was killed. I thought it would help me think about something other than what I had lost."

"Very wise. What sort of work do you do?"

"I'm an air traffic controller."

"How interesting!" Lionel exclaimed, sounding impressed rather than disapproving.

Pleased, Kathleen expanded a little. "Yes, it's responsible work, requiring skill and patience, especially radar controlling in bad weather."

Lionel laughed. "You'll get plenty of that here! And you like it?"

"Very much!" Kathleen stressed. "I don't work just for the money, you see. I genuinely like my work and hope to continue it indefinitely. I'm happy in the WAAF, but air traffic controlling is one of the few flying-related jobs that is expanding in civilian aviation as well." Then fearing she'd already talked too much about herself, she asked, "And you? What is your job here in Berlin?"

"I'm a Cultural Officer on General Robertson's staff."

"Oh." Kathleen was unable to imagine anything to go with such a title. As far as she knew, the RAF didn't have Cultural Officers. "What exactly does that mean?"

"Well, theoretically I advise General Robertson on cultural policy. Things like should we spend money to restore the opera house? How de-nazified should actors be before we allow them on the stage? Or is Wagner's music tainted with Nazism? Most of the time, however, I'm busy trying to recover stolen works of art."

"Stolen art?" Kathleen was surprised.

"You must have heard about how the Nazis plundered museums and palaces wherever they conquered."

"Of course, but can't we just give it back?"

"We could if we could find it, but you see the Nazis started hiding things when they realized they'd lost the war, so first we have to find where they hid it. Not just that, we have to find it faster than the Ivans do because they are less interested in restoring stolen art to the original owners and more interested in filling Soviet museums, palaces, and pockets."

"Oh, that's terrible!" Kathleen was sincerely shocked.

Lionel laughed. "You are so delightfully naïve, Kathleen."

"Am I? Is that a bad thing?" She wasn't sure.

"Not in my book."

"And have you been successful?" She asked anxious to deflect the conversation away from herself.

Lionel weighed his head from side to side before answering, "Up to a point. The Americans have an entire army unit dedicated to tracking down and rescuing artistic treasures called Monuments, Fine Arts and Archives, MFAA for short. It's headed by high-profile professors of art history and the like. They landed shortly after the fighting troops and were able to make some spectacular recoveries in the early months. You know the kind of thing: caves full of Rembrandts and van Goghs. However, it's gotten harder to find stolen objects with each passing month because the obvious masterpieces have been tracked down. Nowadays, we're looking less for the things stolen from the Louvre and more for things stolen from private collections."

Their tea arrived with an assortment of French miniature pastries such as Kathleen hadn't seen since before the war. She exclaimed in delight, and Lionel seemed pleased by the success of his surprise. After the waiter had retreated, she picked up the conversation. "How can you track down private thefts?"

"Good question. It is not an easy task by any means and is further complicated by questions of ownership that defy normal logic. For example, many things the Germans stole from the Russians had first been stolen by the Bolsheviks, who shot or drove into exile the rightful owners. But then, come to think of it, many French masterpieces," Lionel looked around the room with an amused smile, and then leaned closer to her, "were also effectively stolen from those who they sent to the guillotine, *n'est-ce pas?*"

Kathleen laughed with him amused by his daring turn of thoughts. She'd never met anyone quite like him. Encouraged, he continued. "And then there's the issue of Soviet theft. The Ivans brazenly cleaned out the Berlin museums and sent everything — lock, stock and barrel — back to Russia. Which, in my opinion, is hardly better than what the Nazis had done. In both cases, the theft was justified simply by being the victor. Much as I dislike the Germans, there is no justification for stealing their cultural heritage and their greatest works of art any more than for stealing Dutch or Danish masterpieces simply because they had the misfortune to be conquered. Or put another way, precisely *because* the Germans stole art when they were the victors, by repeating the crime, we effectively admit that what the Germans did was right after all, don't we?"

Kathleen had to think about that but decided that what he said was logical, so she nodded.

"So, we agree that the Soviets have no business stealing German art!" Lionel declared as if he had been anxiously awaiting her judgment. Then, leaning closer he asked with a frown of apparent puzzlement, "But what about Troy?"

"What do you mean 'Troy'?"

"The treasures of Troy — Helen's diadem, Hector's shield, Priam's gold. They were found by the famous German archaeologist Heinrich Schliemann at an archaeological site he identified as that of ancient Troy. They used to be on display in the Berlin Museum of Antiquities, but the Ivans took the lot, and those treasures are now presumably in a vault in the Soviet museum the Hermitage — or one of Stalin's residences."

"But that deprives the whole world of seeing them!' Kathleen protested.

"Indeed, but who do the treasures of Troy belong to? They were found, after all, in what is now Turkey. Does that not make them Turkish just as Stonehenge belongs to us?"

"But by that logic," she pointed out, "the Elgin marbles would belong to Greece."

"Quite right!" Lionel agreed with the delight of a teacher whose pupil has proved exceptionally bright. Before Kathleen could protest that she did not fully agree with this, he continued the conversation by saying, "Or what about my Porsche? It was abandoned by a drunken Soviet officer who drove down the Kant Strasse at nearly 100 mph and was stopped by British MPs. He was unable to show any proof of ownership, saying only it had been given to him by another Russian officer, who had since returned to Moscow. He claimed that his friend had 'found' the car on the street. Indeed. That is where cars are commonly parked, and since Russian officers believe that anything on a German street can be summarily declared 'reparations,' they take cars whenever they like."

"Just like that? Without any consequences?" She asked incredulously.

"Most of the time. Generally, they take them, use them until they run out of petrol or break down or there is an accident, and then they walk away and find another car to take."

"That's appalling," Kathleen insisted. "Can't the cars be returned to their owners?"

"Without licence plates (and the Russians always remove those) it is hard to prove the ownership of a mass-produced item. The same is true, by the way, of the prints from the engravings of famous artists like Duerer, or for pieces of jewellery. So, the Porsche is now mine and duly registered with the British military authorities in my name and has a British occupation licence plate, but is it really mine?"

"Well, no, but then if you don't know who it does belong to, I don't suppose there is any harm in using it, is there?" Kathleen didn't feel like she was on solid ground here, yet she didn't think Lionel deserved approbation for his behaviour. Nodding more to encourage herself than anything, she added more confidently, "I believe I heard somewhere that possession is nine-tenths of the law."

Lionel laughed delightedly. "Exactly!" He turned to signal to the waiter for more tea but caught his breath at the sight of the clock. "Good heavens! Look at the time! I think the playroom closes in five minutes. We best collect Hope and go down to the grille for dinner together."

Kathleen readily agreed. By the time they parted at Gatow's main gate three hours later, she was pleased that Lionel promised to call again.

HELENA P. SCHRADER

Corrected Vision
Berlin-Charlottenburg
Monday, 26 January 1948

Despite being told how terrible the destruction of Berlin had been, David stared at the ruins of the Kaiser Wilhelm Gedaechnis Kirche in stunned disbelief. The central spire was shorn off just above the neo-gothic windows and the nave was gutted entirely. Around it was a wasteland dominated by wrecked buildings, and things only got worse when he started to walk down the Kurfuerstendamm.

Once this had been the most fashionable commercial street in the city. David remembered the way he'd last seen it. Well-heeled people had strolled the wide sidewalks, shining cars had congested the streets, and streetcars with their jingling bells had travelled down the centre. The white, cream, pink and yellow facades of the buildings flanking the avenue had competed with one another for elegance. Their gables had been fancy with columns, pediments and spires, while the storefronts had brimmed with the finest products, all tastefully showcased in the shop windows. It had been summer, and flowerpots had flanked many of the entrances and laden the balconies. Tables draped in white linen and set with gleaming silver cutlery had beckoned passers-by to sit down for a Weiner schnitzel, apple strudel or Berliner Weisse.

Now half the buildings had been reduced to empty shells. The blackened facades gazed out like skeletons from beneath gutted roofs, whose jagged black remnants formed the skyline. Here and there an entire facade was missing, and one looked straight into individual rooms, where broken masonry, twisted iron, hanging cables and shattered furnishings lay exposed to the elements in eerie disorder.

Dazed, David walked along the broken sidewalk on the north side of the avenue. There had been a light snowfall during the night, but someone had scattered coal dust over the pavements to make them less slippery. As a result, instead of being white, everything was a dirty grey and coal dust blew with each gust of wind, getting into his eyes. He was miserable and with each step became more convinced that he was on a fool's errand. There was no way his uncle's property could have survived this carnage, he told himself. Soon he was chilled through, as much by the grey landscape

160

as by the damp, January wind. Yet he stubbornly continued walking, compelled by the need to close this chapter of his life.

Gradually, subtly, the damage lessened. Now and again, shops, even restaurants, crouched in the ground-floor remains of the buildings. Here and there buildings were intact up to two or even three stories. After walking for three-quarters of an hour, David stood before number 168, and stared up astonished at three stories of intact building with a fourth floor partially habitable as well. With a jolt, he noticed that on the ground floor to the right of the door — right where Uncle Otto had had his optician's office — a pair of glasses was childishly painted on the wooden plasterboard that replaced the glass. The words "Dr Dietmar Schlaer, Ophthalmologist" were painted under them.

What hutzpah! David thought furiously.

Angrily he pushed open the improvised door and looked around the cave-like room. With the windows boarded up, the only light came from the sparse lightbulbs. Still, he could see that there were a few old desks with chairs on both sides so people could be fitted with glasses. There were also stands with a handful of eye-glass frames displayed. An internal door led back to a second room — his uncle's examination room.

Even as he looked at it, it opened and a frail, young man wearing thick glasses under a shock of unkempt, reddish-brown hair emerged. "How can I help you, sir?" He asked cheerfully.

David's words stuck in his throat. This young man didn't look like one of the SA thugs that had smashed the shop windows on the so-called "Kristallnacht" of November 1938. Nor did he remind him of the Hitler Youth who had taunted and tormented him in his youth. He found himself asking in a wary but not overtly hostile tone, "Are you Dr Dietmar Schlaer?"

"Yes, are you looking for glasses, sir?" The young man sounded hopeful. Business couldn't be very good, David thought. Who could afford glasses in Berlin nowadays? David's perfect High German gave no hint that he now held a Canadian passport.

"No, I was looking for... How long have you had an office here?"

"Almost a year now. I got the lease in March last year."

"From whom?" David demanded indignantly, registering that this young man was merely a tenant. He had no issues with a tenant, it was the landlord who had stolen the property from his uncle and was now cashing in the rent.

"The City Administration. The Rental Office in Rathaus Charlottenburg. Are you new to Berlin?"

"Yes, I arrived Friday. What does the City have to do with renting private property?" David demanded.

"I presume the owners are dead or missing. Were you looking for someone? I used to live nearby. Maybe I can help you."

"You lived nearby? Where? When?

"In the Nestorstrasse. I was born there and lived there until I went to university. This was where I came to get my glasses when I was growing up. There was a wonderful ophthalmologist who had his offices here."

David caught his breath. "You remember Dr Otto Kuczynski?"

"Of course! I was extremely short-sighted from childhood. I had measles at ten months and was practically blind. It made me a timid and solemn child, but Dr Kuczynski made me feel special. He had a magical way with children. He had different noses — you know, the kind people put on for carnival, Pinocchio noses and noses with moustaches, things like that. He had me try them on with different glasses. It became a game, so much so that I looked forward to my visits to his office. It was because of him that I wanted to study ophthalmology."

"Did you decide that before or after they smashed the windows and wrecked everything inside? Or did you help yourself to the stock, the furnishings, the noses..." Even as he lashed out, David was ashamed of himself. He sounded far too bitter and emotional.

The young doctor did not become indignant or defensive; he simply gazed back at David sadly. At length, he said, "Whether you believe me or not, I was not here. I was at university. My parents were here, but they were very frightened of the SA. While the SA rampaged through the streets, they hid inside their apartment. They couldn't understand why the police didn't intervene. They were relieved to hear that no one was hurt."

Maybe it would have been easier on David if he'd thought Dr Schlaer was lying, but he didn't. Nor could David ignore what he'd said about Uncle Otto inspiring him to take up his profession. His uncle would have been pleased about that. Then again, an interest in ophthalmology didn't wipe the slate clean, he argued with himself. "The war," he burst out. "What did you do in the war?"

"I was in pre-medical studies when the war broke out. I was conscripted in the Wehrmacht. With my terrible eyesight, I was assigned to clerical duties, but as the situation deteriorated and they needed more medics, they allowed me to continue medical studies during the semester while serving on the front as a medic in between. It wasn't until after the war that I could finish my speciality studies. In Amsterdam. As soon as I had my qualifications, I came back here to set up my practice."

"Why here?" David demanded.

"Berlin is home. I had nowhere else to go."

"No, I meant, why did you set up a shop *here* — on the Kurfeurstendamm 168?"

"Because it seemed right. Because I had such good memories of this office. I thought it might bring me luck."

"Luck? Do you know what happened to Dr Kuczynski?" David shot back.

"Not specifically," Dr Schlaer waffled. "I hope he got out in time."

"No. He didn't. He and his entire family were gassed — because they loved Germany too much to leave when they could have." The anger and bitterness were raw in his voice.

Dr Schlaer did not look entirely shocked. He wasn't one of those who insisted he had "no idea" what was going on. He had the decency not to deny it. Instead, he simply said softly, "I'm sorry. I'm truly sorry. I don't know what I could have done, but I wish I had done it. Anything. I'm sorry." He paused and added, "I presume you are related to Dr Kuczynski, and I can understand if you are offended by me being here. But I would like you to know that I intended it as a tribute. I wanted to remember him and thought that being here, opening up a new optician's shop where his had been, was a way to keep his memory alive. It was meant to be an honour."

He sounded so sincere, that David believed him. He held out his hand to the young doctor. "I'm David Goldman. Dr Otto Kuczynski was my uncle."

"I'm glad to meet you, sir. I'm very pleased that you survived."

"Frau Dr Kuczynski was my father's sister. My father emigrated to Canada with his immediate family at end of 1933, so we all survived. However, I've been named sole heir to any family property still in Germany."

"I see, and you'd like me to vacate the premises." Dr Schlaer sounded sad but resigned to his eviction.

"No. While I plan to request restitution of this property from the Berlin city government, I have no immediate use for it personally. I live in the UK. No, I don't mind you remaining here — on one condition."

"Yes?" Dr Schlaer was tense, unsure if he should hope or fear the condition.

"That you name the shop for my uncle — as if he were your senior partner. You will be the sole proprietor, of course, but I want his name on the door and the window."

The young man nodded solemnly. "Yes, I could do that." Then he corrected himself. "I'd be happy to do that. It's the least I can do."

"Good. Here's my business card, and here is the telephone number of friends in Kladow." David turned the card over and wrote down the Priestmans' home telephone number.

"If for whatever reason, you need to get in touch with me — especially if you want to make changes here or move out or expand, please call that number and they will get a message to me."

"Of course, Herr Goldman."

They shook hands, and David went back out into the street.

The encounter left David emotionally drained. He couldn't hate Dr Schlaer, although he wasn't a particularly "good" German. He had stood by and let the German authorities humiliate, segregate, transport and ultimately kill his neighbours, and he'd served in the Wehrmacht. Yet he also remembered Uncle Otto with respect and affection. He felt guilty. Maybe that was enough? It was certainly more than many others were willing to do.

Unwilling to face the Underground which had been overcrowded, dirty and didn't feel safe, David flagged down a passing horse cart and offered two shillings sterling (hard currency) to be driven to Kladow and the Priestman's home. The driver turned his farm cart filled with sacks of potatoes around at once and happily set off. He was a garrulous man, no different from a London cabby, David admitted to himself. Like his British counterparts, the Berlin driver complained about the state of the roads, the rations, the lack of street lighting, and the weather. The German driver added the worthless currency, the Nazis, the Soviets and the Americans indiscriminately, or so it seemed. David made non-committal replies while letting the words run off him like shower water.

Tomorrow he'd find the city rental office and see what records they had for his uncle's other property as well, the house on Schwanenwerder in the American Sector. He would also find out where to submit his restitution claims. Whatever the status, he would try to visit his uncle's house to assess the damage to it. Situated on the east shore of the Havel amidst other elegant villas, it should not have been targeted in the bombing and was very likely intact — which meant it was probably requisitioned and occupied by some American officer. Since the Americans were cooperating actively with the Jewish Claims Committee, David felt confident that if the house was in American hands, he would eventually get it restored to him or receive fair compensation. With luck, he could fly back to the UK this Friday and focus on his business.

"You'll have to direct me from here, *mein Herr*," the driver broke into his thoughts. They had reached Kladow village.

David gave the necessary directions and alighted in the Priestmans' drive. He paid the driver and mounted the steps into the house. As he hung his hat inside the door, he heard women's voices coming from the den and remembered that Emily had said she was having her first German lesson today. He stopped to listen.

"... please speak slower. I can't understand what you're saying." Emily pleaded in her precise but stilted German.

"I'm sorry. I think I'm a terrible teacher," a woman answered. That would be Charlotte Walmsdorff, David registered, surprised that she sounded so unsure of herself. "It's just that I'm so upset," she added, and he supposed that explained her tone.

"Maybe you should tell me what happened in English, and then we can discuss it in German?" Emily suggested.

"Yes, yes."

David was curious to meet Charlotte because he'd spent many pleasant afternoons taking tea with her grandmother. Since he could offer his assistance with the translation, he had an excuse to interrupt. In the den, the tea things stood on a low coffee table while a fire burned in the open fireplace, making the room toasty warm. Emily had her back to him, and he had a good view of Charlotte. She was wearing a black woollen skirt that was far too wide for her and a man's sweater over a man's shirt. The effect was to make her look like a stick doll in a baggy sack. Her hair was cropped short, too. Yet despite the men's clothing and haircut, there was nothing masculine about Charlotte Walmsdorff. She put David in mind of a waif in need of rescue.

As David stepped into the room, Charlotte gasped and looked up in alarm. Her short, blond hair fell onto her forehead and their eyes met. He felt a shock go through him. The look in her eyes was gripping and he could not break free of it. "Forgive me, *gnadiges Fraulein*," he excused himself in German. "I did not mean to startle you. I'm the Priestman's houseguest, David Goldman." As he spoke he came deeper into the room.

Both women came to their feet, Emily with a smile of welcome relief, Charlotte gazing at him like a deer hypnotized by headlights.

"Did you want to join us, David?" Emily asked, and when he admitted he'd come to offer his translation services, she departed to tell Frau Pabst to bring another tea setting.

This left David alone with Charlotte, who still stood as if stunned. He smiled at her, wishing his face were more subtle and held out his hand. She took it limply, and he noted her hand was bony and cold. "You must be Charlotte Graefin Walmsdorf. Your English grandmother recommended you to Emily."

"Do you know my grandmother, too?" Charlotte asked in amazement.

"Yes. We're old friends — from when I lost my original face and was convalescing."

Charlotte's eyes widened, but she did not look away. Rather, she seemed only now to realise what was wrong with this face. "I am so sorry to hear you suffered. I would not have known...."

That was kind of her to say, David thought.

Emily returned and smoothly took over, inviting David to sit in the chair opposite the sofa where she and Charlotte were sitting. "Charlotte was trying to explain something that happened yesterday, but I'm afraid my German was not good enough to understand so she was just going to explain things in English."

Charlotte nodded. "Yes. Yesterday the Soviets stopped the British train to Hamburg."

"Yes, Robin mentioned that," Emily confirmed. "They side-tracked the train with our personal effects for several days last week as well."

Charlotte shook her head. "This was different. This is more — more —" she could not find the English words. Turning to David, she broke into a flood of German. "On that train was a young boy with a rare blood type. He needed a massive blood transfusion and there was not enough blood of his type in all of Berlin. The hospital had arranged for him to travel by train to Hamburg, where an ambulance was standing-by to take him to a hospital. The blood had already been set aside and was being held for him. It was all prepared. Frau Liebherr, my friend and neighbour, was travelling with the patient. Everything was very urgent and very risky, but it was his only chance. Now, because of the Soviets, it was all for nothing. The little boy died last night. Maybe he would have died anyway, but if they hadn't stopped the train, he might have had a chance. I've never seen Frau Liebherr so distraught. She looked after that boy for weeks. Then, just when everything finally seemed to have worked out, *the Ivans*—!" The bitterness in the last word was so eloquent that she did not need to finish the sentence.

"Please let me in on what is going on," Emily reminded David gently, and he hastened to explain the gist of the situation in English.

When he finished, Charlotte burst out in English, "We are so helpless! There is nothing we can do! The Ivans trample on us again and again, over and over. I know you will say it is our fault. That they have the right after what we did to them. I know...." The anger that had flared up suddenly dissolved and she seemed to melt into her sweater, her face down, her bangs shielding her eyes from view.

It was as if her spirit had been broken, David thought. Not now, not here, but in the past. By the Soviets — the Ivans, as she called them. Was it when they killed her parents before her eyes? Or something else? He noticed her hands were trembling, and he glanced at Emily helplessly.

Emily reached out a hand to Charlotte, but her thoughts had not followed his. She was still focused on the story of the sick little boy. "Charlotte, your grandmother told me you were a journalist. Can't you write about this?"

"Oh," Charlotte looked up, shaking her hair out of her eyes as a cynical, twisted expression spread across her face. "Everyone in Berlin knows a dozen stories like this. It would not interest the papers, I think."

"It would interest people in London," Emily countered.

"London?"

"You could submit it to the *Times*."

"Oh, I can't write so well English," Charlotte dismissed the thought with a weak smile of thanks to Emily.

"Then we can make it a language exercise. You write it down in German, and we translate it into English together."

Charlotte started to look intrigued. "Do you really think the *Times of London* might be interested?" She risked a tentative glance in David's direction.

"They will be if the wife of the RAF Station Commander submits it," David replied, turning directly to Emily to urge, "I think you need to send it, Emily. It will carry greater weight coming from a member of the occupation forces than from a German."

"Yes!" Charlotte agreed at once. "You don't have to put my name on it. I'm not — what is the word? I am not conceited."

"If you think that would make the difference between acceptance and rejection, I'm happy to send it. It seems to me that the important thing is that the story gets told."

Chapter Five
Ominous Omens

A Knock in the Night
Berlin-Charlottenburg
Night of 27/28 January 1948

The sound of men shouting in the street outside the house roused Charlotte from her sleep. For a moment, she lay in her bed staring at the ceiling and straining her ears, hoping she had imagined it. Then the shouts came again, this time accompanied by heavy banging at the front door.

Her heart started pounding with terror, and she sat bolt upright, overcome by panic. Ignoring the freezing temperature of the room, she threw back the heavy down counterpane. While searching with her feet for her shoes, her eyes found the wardrobe against the back wall where her clothes hung. She would hide inside behind the clothes she told herself.

The shouting and banging grew louder. Voices in both German and Russian demanded the door be opened. Charlotte could hear Theo Pfalz's voice answering in an unnaturally high pitch, asking what was going on.

"Police!" Came the answer. "Open up! Police!"

"What the devil...!" That was Christian's voice. She heard his footsteps in the long corridor. "Charlotte? Charlotte?"

"I'm here, Christian."

"There are Russian soldiers out front," Christian told her, confirming her worst fears. "Here!" He handed her a pistol. When she just gazed at it, he reminded her. "You know how to use it. I've seen you."

Yes, she'd learned to shoot with her brothers and cousins. Her grandfather had been acutely aware that his wife and mother had been left alone on the estate with unrest, revolution, deserters and criminals all around them during the Great War and the Revolution. After that, he had insisted that all the women in the house learn to shoot both rifles and pistols.

"Where did you get that?" Charlotte asked, taking the firearm from

Christian. It felt heavy and unwieldy in her hand. It was Russian.

"The Ivans would sell their own grandmothers for cigarettes." Christian answered dismissively, adding, "You'd better get your coat on before you freeze to death. If one of the Ivans tries to break in, shoot him — and shoot to kill. Understood?"

Charlotte nodded, but asked in alarm, "Where are you going?"

"To find out what's happening."

By now the noise had moved inside. Many pairs of boots were clomping up the stairs. Voices speaking Russian echoed in the stairwell.

"Christian! Don't!" Charlotte protested. "Stop! Stay with me!"

"I've got a second pistol," Christian answered as if that made everything all right. "Lock the door behind me!" He ordered. Then, pulling his cashmere coat on over his pyjamas, he left the apartment in his stocking feet.

Charlotte ran to lock, bolt and chain the door, but then stood indecisively in the hallway. Her initial explosion of panic had subsided. Christian was here; he was a deadly shot. The pistol he had given her was also a comfort. For a second, she even indulged in the thought of killing some of them and her hand closed more firmly around the pistol, starting to get the feel of it. She would kill as many of them as she could and save the last bullet for herself she decided. But meanwhile, she was shivering. She had to put her coat on. She put the pistol down long enough to pull her brother's heavy greatcoat on over her the brother's long underwear and the flannel shirt that she wore to bed. As she struggled to find the armholes, she was reminded of Monday's German lesson with Emily.

The encounter with Mr Goldman had been like an electric shock. It had left a lingering tingle of disturbed nerves. Not in a bad way. On the contrary, when their eyes had met, it had seemed to ignite a tiny flame of life inside her. Then, when she rose to leave, Mr Goldman had come with her to the door and helped her into her coat. It was such a simple gesture, so normal in the pre-war world, something Fritz had done a hundred times, and yet it had made her feel warm all over. It had made her feel like a lady again, *valuable* despite everything that had happened. "Let me help," Mr Goldman had said, and he'd taken the heavy coat and held it at just the right height for her. Maybe she would see him again at her lesson this afternoon?

Voices just outside her door brought her back to the present with a jolt. "Jakob! Be careful!" Frau Liebherr called.

"Soviet soldiers have no business in the American sector!" the Social Democratic Councilman answered firmly as he started down the stairs.

The sound of something heavy smashing wood came from the stairwell as a man continued to shout. "Open up! Police!"

With relief, Charlotte registered they had stopped on the floor below. This wasn't just Russian soldiers on a rampage. Probably it had to do with the black marketeers living one flight down.

"What's going on here?" Herr Liebherr demanded.

"Out of the way!"

"I'm an elected official of this city. You have no right to bring Soviet soldiers into the American sector."

"Take it up with the Chief of Police."

There was a loud crack and Christian shouted, "There's no need to break in! Can't you hear Herr Dr Hofmeier is coming?"

Hofmeier? Not the three shady characters in the apartment opposite? Dr Hofmeier asked in a frightened voice muffled by the closed door: "What is this about? What do you want?"

"You are to come with us at once!"

"Why? Where? For how long?" His voice was clearer now, as if he'd cracked open the door.

Rather than answer, the police simply declared. "You may pack a bag."

"A bag? What are you talking about? What is going on?"

"You will want underwear, toiletries and a change of clothes."

"But why? Where are you taking me?"

"You'll find out!"

"I protest—"

"Either you pack your things, or we take you the way you are."

After that, Charlotte heard a lot of clunks, crashes, bangs and scraping. Muffled Russian voices came through the floor, punctuated by laughs. The Soviets were probably plundering the apartment, taking whatever caught their fancy — as always. In the hallway, Herr Liebherr was still arguing with the police, demanding to see an arrest warrant. The policeman kept referring him to the Chief of Police.

In five minutes, it was over. Herr Dr Hofmeier was escorted out of the house carrying a suitcase with his personal belongings, while Christian and Herr Liebherr returned to the fourth floor. They stood on the landing separating their two apartments and talked. "I will go to the Chief of Police tomorrow," Herr Liebherr declared firmly.

"I think the Americans need to be informed as well," Christian added.

"Yes, I suppose so," Herr Liebherr agreed unenthusiastically, "Not that they'll do anything, but you can tell them about it. It's your property, after all. You have a right to be outraged about it being plundered."

"I don't care about the things. It's the arrest that bothers me. Can you tell me anything about Herr Dr Hofmeier that might make the case more comprehensible? The Americans are sure to ask. They'll want to know if he might be involved in criminal activities that justified his arrest. I haven't a clue. I've hardly seen him since I arrived."

Herr Liebherr drew a deep breath. "I doubt very much that Herr Dr Hofmeier is mixed up in anything illegal. He has a steady and well-paying job at AEG which means he has less reason than most to engage in shady activities. He was a solitary man, unmarried, with no children, but he was an engineer. Although he's been working for AEG for the last couple of years, during the war he was involved in the development of the V-2 rockets. I suspect that is what this is all about."

"Do the Ivans consider the rockets criminal?"

"No." Herr Liebherr replied wearily. "They simply want to build their own."

"So why arrest Hofmeier? Why not hire him?"

"They didn't arrest him. They kidnapped him. He will be sent to work in the Soviet Union. There have been thousands of similar incidents over the last couple of years. The West does nothing. They don't seem to care what is happening to the people of this city — unless it affects them directly. Since the Americans also want to build rockets, however, maybe they'll take an interest in this case. Be sure you stress he was a 'rocket scientist,' when you tell them about it. Maybe then they'll be annoyed the Russians got their hands on him before they did. But I doubt it."

On this gloomy note, they said good night.

Communist with a Swastika
Berlin-Mitte
Wednesday, 28 January 1948

The next morning Jakob Liebherr went to police headquarters on Alexanderplatz. The Berlin *Poliseipraesident* (Chief of Police) Paul Markgraf kept him waiting in the anteroom for almost an hour. When finally admitted to Markgraf's office, Liebherr was confronted by a lean man, only thirty-seven years old, whose dark hair was already peppered with grey. He wore it shorn short like Soviet soldiers, which emphasised his long lean nose and close-set eyes. He reminded Jakob of a wolf, but maybe that was because of his reputation rather than his looks.

Markgraf had once received a Knight's Cross from Hitler personally, but after being taken prisoner at Stalingrad, he switched his allegiance to Stalin. Not just nominally, but with so much zeal, cunning and loyalty that the German Communist leader Walter Ulbricht selected him to be one of just nine Germans sent into Berlin immediately after the fall of the city to the Red Army. Rumours suggested he was more trusted by the NKVD than Ulbricht — and maybe Sokolovsky. Although he had no police background whatsoever, he had been placed in charge of the Berlin police force by the SMAD.

It did not surprise Liebherr, therefore, that Markgraf received him without bothering to get to his feet. Instead, the Chief of Police remained sitting in a wooden armchair behind a large oak desk and gestured for the elected representative to sit down without a trace of hospitality. "I'm very busy," he declared without any facial expression. "Get to the point."

"Last night a man was dragged out of the apartment below me without a warrant. When I protested, your officers told me to take it up with you. Here I am."

"What was his name?"

"Dr Albert Hofmeier."

Markgraf shrugged. "Never heard of him." He said it as if that closed the case and he expected Liebherr to just leave.

"There was no arrest warrant," Liebherr repeated, refusing to be dismissed. "You cannot make arrests without warrants."

"I just did."

"Of what crime is Herr Dr Hofmeier accused?"

Without even sitting up straighter, Markgraf pushed a button on his desk, and at once the door opened and a young woman stood in the doorway. "*Jawohl, Herr Oberst?*"

"Bring me the files of Herr Dr Albert Hofmeier, who was taken into custody last night."

The young woman disappeared.

Liebherr didn't expect an answer about the charges. As he'd told Feldburg the night before, he believed this was a case of kidnapping rather than an arrest, so he continued to his next and more important question. "Why were your policemen accompanied by Soviet soldiers in the American Sector?"

Markgraf continued to show no expression whatsoever as he responded, "For their protection."

"Your police need protection?" Liebherr asked back, raising his eyebrows. "But everyone knows most of your police officers are former criminals."

"That's why they need protection," Markgraf countered equally straight-faced.

"Soviet soldiers have no business in the American Sector," Liebherr insisted.

"The Amis aren't complaining," Markgraf retorted, and for the first time the ghost of a smile flitted over his features before he added. "They haven't the guts to confront us anyway. Their days are numbered."

"What do you mean 'their days are numbered'?" Liebherr challenged with an uneasy tensing of his stomach. Much as he deplored the inaction and spinelessness of the Western Allies, the thought of them leaving was alarming.

"Surely a man as well informed as you, Herr *Stadtsabgeordnerter* Liebherr, is fully aware that the Americans and their British puppets will soon leave Berlin? They are committed to their policy of dividing Germany and setting up a capitalist puppet state in the West. Only the Soviet Zone will remain free and democratic. You can count yourself lucky that Berlin will naturally remain in the free and democratic part of Germany."

'Lucky' was not the word Liebherr would have used.

The secretary returned with a manila folder that she placed before

Markgraf. Without a word to Liebherr, he opened it and started skimming through it, leaving his visitor to contemplate his future. Liebherr reflected that the recent Communist coup in Prague appeared to be the blueprint for what was happening here. First, the police, firmly in the hands of the Communists, purged non-communist members from their ranks. Then they used the police to silence other opposition figures through arrests and kidnapping. If the non-Communist ministers in the government objected, the Communist agitators took to the streets, staging "popular" protests in favour of a Communist coup.

But Czechoslovakia had no Western Allied presence. For nearly three years, Liebherr had clung to the hope that the Western Allies would prevent a Communist takeover in Germany. He had no desire to end his days in Siberia or before a firing squad. He had no desire to see the merciless cruelty of a Soviet dictatorship strangle all that was left of Germany. He had put all his hopes in the Western Allies.

They had disappointed him again and again, yet faced with the thought of them withdrawing altogether, Liebherr suddenly discovered an intense fondness for them. They might be weak and naïve in the face of Soviet chicanery, but the West was not actively tyrannical. They had abandoned their original plans to keep Germany in perpetual poverty. They appeared committed to fostering German economic recovery. Furthermore, they had slowly and incrementally introduced a variety of ad-hoc measures which gradually delegated decision-making to elected German representatives. Slowly but systematically, they were paving the way for a return to German self-government. He had even seen reports indicating they had laid the groundwork for a German central bank and a sound currency. Most importantly, the US president had included the Western Zones of Germany in his request to Congress for funding Marshall Aid.

Yet in all this, the status of Berlin remained ambivalent. With each passing day, it appeared more and more likely that the West would defend their *Zones* from Soviet interference, but equally clear that they were prepared to jettison their Sectors of Berlin.

"You're quite right," Markgraf broke into his thoughts. "There is no arrest warrant in the file. But as I see here, it is not necessary. He has volunteered to work in the Soviet Union."

"Volunteered?" Liebherr asked, remembering Hofmeier's surprise and indignation on the previous night.

"Yes. There's a signed request here in the file." As he spoke, Markgraf held up a piece of paper with printed text and a signature attached. Liebherr had no chance to read the text or study the signature before Markgraf put it back in the file and closed the folder. "Was there anything else I can help you with, Herr Liebherr?" Markgraf asked in a voice that barely concealed his contempt.

"Not at the moment," Liebherr replied, mustering as much dignity as possible. He pulled himself to his feet. For a moment, the police chief remained sitting, and Liebherr could look down on him. Then the Communist got to his feet, and they stood eye-to-eye. Liebherr wished there were some threat or just some prediction of retribution that he could voice to take the smug expression off Markgraf's nearly impassive face. Yet, he could think of nothing with a shred of credibility. Anything he said — even "wait and see" — would sound like what it was: pathetic bluster.

Protected Squatter
Berlin, Zehlendorf
Thursday, 29 January 1948

David Goldman felt the same sense of helplessness. He was standing before the family home of his Aunt Anna and Uncle Otto, but officially it did not belong to him. The Soviets had given it to someone else, and everyone at the city land registry seemed to think that such allocations were untouchable.

The house sat ensconced in an overgrown garden and looked run-down in the way all property did after a decade of neglect. The wooden trellises that had once supported climbing roses were rotting away; the paint on the plaster façade was blistered where too much moisture had come through; a couple of attic windows were boarded over, apparently because window glass was not available. Yet for all its minor blemishes, the house was very much intact, liveable — and awakened memories.

David had loved coming here as a child. Unlike his father's formal house where children were to be seen and not heard, Uncle Otto loved the sound of children laughing and playing. At his father's home on the Aussen Alster in Hamburg, he was not allowed down to the water's edge; here he swam every day with his siblings and cousins. At home, dinner was a solemn, semi-formal affair in which the ticking clock had been the counterpoint to the discreet click of silverware on porcelain; here they had all talked at once. In a nutshell, David had been happier and more at *home* here, than ever in his father's house.

Now it was occupied by a dubious stranger. The records showed that the house had been sold twice after his uncle's name had been removed, and the current occupant, a certain Dr Jurgen Friedebach, had been entered in the registry in late May 1945 — after the Soviet occupation but *before* the arrival of the Western Allies. Whether the clerks at the land registry were willing to do anything about it or not, David was not prepared to simply give up. The house had been stolen from his uncle, which invalidated all those subsequent "sales," expropriations and allocations. In his eyes, the man inside was nothing but a squatter.

David boldly approached the front door and rang the bell. The sound was answered with surprising alacrity by a butler. Well, not a real butler, David concluded; the man would have looked more comfortable in an SS uniform and he was anything but friendly. "Who are you?" he barked, his eyes narrowed with suspicion and his jaw thrust forward out belligerently.

A friendly lady of the house or a kindly, old gentleman, would have elicited a more cautious approach, but the butler's tone and stance ignited David's full fury. He found himself retorting confrontationally, "I am the rightful owner of this house."

The butler responded with a scoffing sound and ordered David to go away.

David stood his ground and insisted, "I wish to speak to Herr Dr Friedebach."

The "butler" shrugged his big shoulders and his face became harder. "You can wish all you want. That doesn't mean Herr Dr Friedebach wants to speak with you."

"I am the sole heir to the last legal owner of this property. He can speak to me now or he can speak to me in court," David retorted, bluffing only a little. He *would* take it to court if he had to.

The door to the study swung open and a tall, sleek man with close-cropped black hair emerged. Wireless reading glasses perched part way down a fine aquiline nose that ended over a thin and neatly trimmed moustache more reminiscent of Errol Flynn than Hitler. He was immaculately dressed, right down to the gold cufflinks on his starched white shirt. "What's going on, Klein?" He spoke sharply, but David detected an Austrian accent .

"This man claims to be the legal owner of your house, Herr Dr Friedebach," the butler made it sound like a joke.

Friedebach was already looking his visitor up and down critically. David had the uncanny feeling that he even noticed that his face was reconstructed. "And what would your name be?"

"David Goldman."

"Goldman," Friedebach repeated the name with a small, contemptuous sneer. David remembered that tone of voice. The teachers had started using it in 1933 and the director of the glider club, too. A shiver crawled up his spine, and he felt his guts start to cramp again. It was irrational perhaps, but he knew Friedebach was a Nazi, a senior Nazi, one of the Nazis who'd been in some way involved in industry. To Friedebach he clarified. "I'm a nephew of Dr Otto Kuczynski, the legal owner of this property until 1942 — when his property was illegally confiscated by the corrupt and criminal Nazi regime. The Four Occupation Powers, in rare agreement, have judged such expropriations illegal, null and void. The Occupation Powers, most especially the Americans, in whose Sector this property lies, specifically recognise the right of the legal owners — or their estate if they are deceased — to claim restoration of any illegally expropriated property. That is what I am hereby doing."

Friedebach shrugged. "I don't know what you're talking about. This property was allocated to me by the SMAD in May 1945. If you have any complaints, take it up with them."

"The SMAD, as you well know, is no longer in control here in Zehlendorf. The US Military government is."

"Oh really?"

"You could hardly have failed to notice," David countered.

"Look, Mr Goldman, I'm a businessman and I mind my own business which is what I advise you to do as well — if you don't want unpleasant things to happen to you, that is. The Americans..." He shrugged eloquently. "Nice little schoolboys, aren't they? They agreed to respect all decisions made by the SMAD before they arrived here in Berlin, and they always play by the rules. In any case, they won't be here much longer. Meanwhile, Mr Goldman," his lips twisted as he spoke the name in that same contemptuous tone, "I manage three major pharmaceutical factories in Bitterfeld. Innocent children depend on the medicines I produce. No one in East or West is interested in seeing me inconvenienced, much less thrown out of my house. So, take your greedy little Jew-fingers somewhere else." He turned on his heel and disappeared back into his study, slamming the door in David's face. His butler took the hint and hustled David out the front door.

David stood on the front porch reproaching himself for bungling the entire confrontation. He didn't know what he *should* have done, but obviously not confront the man head-on like this. Of course, from the records, it had not been so obvious that he was dealing with a senior Nazi. Nor did he have a shred of evidence. He simply knew it in his bones. He'd heard rumours about SS generals who were given a new identity by the Soviet Secret Police. Presumably, it was because these high-ranking Nazis were useful to the Soviets in some way. Would an understanding of pharmaceutical production come under that category? And what exactly was covered by the term "pharmaceuticals"? Poisons? Drugs? Biological weapons? David didn't know, but he also recognised that he was up against something he could not handle on his own.

He needed help. Official help. And he needed time to find out more about who Friedebach really was and what crimes he had very probably committed. Only if he had solid evidence of war crimes could he expect any kind of help from the Western Allies. But time was exactly what he didn't have. He wanted to start a flying business, not spend his days sleuthing around for evidence of crimes that would inevitably nauseate him. Why couldn't this have been like the Danish shipping company and Dr Schlaer — a pleasant surprise requiring little further action?

But he couldn't let Friedebach get away with occupying Uncle Otto's house either. Maybe he should hire a professional detective to track down Friedebach's true identity. Then again, if Friedebach had Soviet protection, he would have an impeccable new identity too — that, or no detective would dare touch the job.

Shaken, David turned and walked back to the horse-cart taxi waiting for him. He climbed up beside the driver, who looked at him curiously but held his tongue. "Back to the S-Bahn station, sir?" The driver asked.

"Yes, back to the S-Bahn," David confirmed feeling weary and defeated.

A Meeting of the Allied Control Council
Berlin-Schoeneberg
Friday, 30 January 1948

Some men succeeded in staff jobs by being as invisible and attentive as a good butler. Others succeeded by sheer charm. Priestman, however, had done well because of the quality of his briefing notes and memoranda — and that meant hard work in advance. Because he felt out of his depth sitting in for Air Commodore Waite as the "Air Ministry Representative" at a session of the Allied Control Council, Priestman requested, received and read the transcripts of the meetings for the last six months before his scheduled attendance.

The day before the meeting, Air Commodore Waite's adjutant Fl/Lt. Abels brought Priestman the agenda of the following day's session and promised to meet him at the front entrance of the ACC at 9:30 am, half an hour before the sitting was due to start. Priestman took the station adjutant F/O Stanley and the Russian translator Corporal Borisenko with him to the meeting. True to his word, Abels met him out front and led the way inside and up the grand, central staircase. On the way, he spoke to the Wing Commander in a low voice, informing him that General Robertson had requested the French, who were chairing this session, to place the recent incident involving carriages decoupled from a British train en route to Hamburg on the agenda. It had not made it into the printed documents, but he had added it by hand.

After leaving their greatcoats in a cloakroom manned by two German women, Abels led them to the conference room with a high ceiling and a decorative marble mantle over a cold fireplace on the wall opposite tall windows. The walls had modest pilaster pillars, but the ceiling had no mouldings and no gilt, while the curtains framing the windows were a dull green colour; this was a room for working not representational display. Four tables formed a square in the middle of the room with three, straight-backed, functional chairs on the outside of each table. A small flag stuck in a stand designated where each delegation sat. The Americans were positioned with their backs to the cold fireplace, while directly opposite them the Soviets sat with their backs to the window. Priestman noted that this put the Soviets in silhouette, an old trick which made them seem more ominous and opaque. Facing one another while flanking the two "new" powers were the French and British.

Fl/Lt Abels indicated four upright chairs behind those at the British table and said two of these were for Priestman and Borisenko. "The economic advisor, Sir Horace Willis, will join you, and the last seat is reserved for the stenographer. Flying Officer Stanley and I will be waiting in the adjacent anteroom if you need us for anything."

Priestman thanked him and set about sorting himself out. Since he was not seated at a table, he would have to hold his briefcase on his lap to take any notes. He removed a pen from his case and slipped it into his inside breast pocket to have it handy. He spared a glance for his interpreter. She looked nervous and had gone to extra effort to look smart. Her uniform was newly pressed, and the buttons and shoes gleamed like those of a drill sergeant. Yet nothing could make the short, thick-set girl look elegant or sophisticated. He cast her an encouraging smile.

The room was gradually filling up. The French clustered together in a group gossiping and laughing. Sir Horace arrived, introduced himself, set his briefcase on a chair and disappeared to seek out the men's room. The stenographer, a severe-looking WRNS petty officer, took her place. General Robertson arrived, waived Priestman's salute aside and shook hands graciously. He settled into his seat at the table with an aide and an interpreter flanking him.

The Americans arrived in a gaggle, headed by the American military governor General Lucius D. Clay, who looked strikingly different from Howley. Receding dark hair and white sideburns framed a face dominated by a large nose and owlish eyes sunken deep in their sockets. Clay looked like he had not had enough sleep in a long time, and he lit up a cigarette almost before he'd taken his place at the table. The officers around him, however, looked as smart as their British counterparts. Priestman recognized and nodded to Lt. Colonel Walker from Tempelhof.

The Soviets appeared last yet in a larger group, and they instantly dominated the room. Dressed in breeches and boots, their footfalls pounded loudly on the wooden floors. Their upright collars and stiff shoulder boards flashed gold, while their myriad medals dangled and clanged on their chests whenever they moved. Priestman was reminded of the officers of certain Latin American countries who used to attend air shows when he was flying with the aerobatic team. At the time, he'd developed the theory that there was an inverse relationship between the ostentatiousness of medals for bravery and the courage required to obtain them. Since no one could question the Russians' courage, however, he supposed he had to discard his theory. Despite their abundance of medals and hard, leathery faces, however, the Russians still managed to look like children dressing up in their parents' clothes because of the ridiculously oversized design of their caps.

Beside him, Borisenko caught her breath, and he glanced over at her. In a low voice, she drew his attention to a young woman among the Soviet officers. The girl was shorter even than Borisenko and round-faced rather than elegant. She wore the same Red Army hat, tunic and boots as the other Russian delegates, but a straight skirt ended at the knee. "She's wearing the star of a 'Hero of the Soviet Union,' sir," Borisenko explained herself in a low, awestruck voice. "It's the very highest medal given by the Soviets. It's like a VC." Priestman looked again at the Russian woman with greater interest, but already the French were moving to take their places.

After the formalities of calling the session to order and greeting one another were over, The French Governor General Koenig turned to the agenda. "The first item of business is the establishment of more official kiosks for currency exchange. General Clay, did you want to expound on your proposal?" In the annotations to Priestman's agenda, it was noted that these were necessary to facilitate the 'eventual' introduction of a new currency. The existing number of official exchange offices was extremely limited, the notes explained. Such offices would be completely overwhelmed causing long lines and delays should the entire population be required to replace old currency with new.

"Yes," Clay leaned forward to speak, but he was cut off by Marshal Sokolovsky with a flood of Russian starting with a firm "Nyet!" Priestman frowned at that. Sokolovsky reputedly spoke excellent English and was fond of quoting Jane Austen.

Borisenko leaned closer to Priestman, and he bent in her direction as she provided the simultaneous translation directly into his ear making it nearly inaudible to others. "There is no need for these new kiosks whatsoever. People don't use the official exchange offices as it is," Borisenko rendered Sokolovsky's words in English.

Clay glanced at Robertson and might have responded had Sokolovsky not continued in a louder and more outraged voice. Boriskenko had to speak louder just to be heard. "This is all part of your machinations to subvert the German economy and make the Germans slaves of your capitalist industries! It is an insidious effort to pave the way for the introduction of your Marshall Plan! Well, we are not so stupid as not to see what you are doing! You are attempting to divide Europe in half, to carve it up into spheres of imperialist influence, robbing the Continental Europeans of their independence and making them dependent on hand-outs from you for all eternity!"

"Dear Marshal Sokolovsky, could you please explain to me how the European Recovery Act proposed by Secretary Marshall could possibly divide Europe when *any* European nation, including the Soviet Union, is welcome to apply for aid under its provisions?" Clay's voice was the very epitome of calm and reason. His Southern accent gave it an almost "folksy" charm.

"That is a sham! A trick!" Sokolovsky slammed his palm on the table so sharply that some of those in the room visibly flinched. "It is only open to countries willing to accept your central-banking system — a tool of capital to restore the chains of the working class! Your Plan is intended to take from the workers their hard-earned currency and replace it with monopoly paper controlled entirely from Washington!"

The accusation was so preposterous that Clay and Robertson exchanged another look before Clay answered in the same tone of patient understanding. "The real currency in Germany today is cigarettes, most of which originate in the United States. A currency reform would replace this barter economy, which benefits American GIs more than anyone else, with a sound currency backed by gold reserves and controlled by a German — and an American — central bank—"

"Nyet! Nyet! Nyet! Next item on the agenda!" Sokolovsky ordered frowning furiously at the French.

The French General looked questioningly towards Clay, who with a subtle gesture indicated he did not want to pursue the discussion. Turning to his notes Koenig read the next item on the schedule. "The increased circulation of heroin in Berlin. General Clay?"

"Thank you. Our military police have noted a dramatic increase in the amount of heroin in circulation in Berlin."

Sokolovsky demonstratively shrugged and murmured something to the man next to him without addressing the room at large.

"Did you catch that?" Priestman asked Borisenko.

"Something about what would one expect of American negro soldiers."

Clay either had not understood the remark or chose to ignore it and continued, "It is an astonishingly pure, white heroin and appears to come from a new source. Spot checks and search dogs on our trains and highway checkpoints, indicate it is not coming on the transit routes and it almost certainly originates in the Soviet Zone."

"Nonsense!" Sokolovsky dismissed the hypothesis with a wave of his hand. "Soviet soldiers are not drug addicts! They are disciplined and self-respecting. Drug addiction is an American problem."

Clay did not rise to the bait and continued doggedly, "We have evidence that the Germans produced heroin on an industrial scale in the closing days of the war and some of the German war criminals involved in the production of chemical, and possibly biological, weapons are still at large."

Priestman felt a chill run down his spine: just yesterday evening, David had told him about his encounter with the managing director of a pharmaceutical factory who he believed was a former SS officer. The man had been given David's uncle's house by the Soviets and obviously enjoyed their protection. His factories, furthermore, were located in the Soviet Zone.

"Curiously," Clay was continuing, "our clues all point to the Soviet Zone. Now, I'm not making any accusations," he stressed in his charming, Southern accent, "but my experts tell me that this heroin — and possibly other undesirable substances — appear to have been produced in one of the German pharmaceutical factories that have resumed production under

Soviet supervision in the Soviet Zone."

Priestman moved uneasily in his chair while Sokoklovsky snapped, "Impossible."

"In that case, I'm sure you'll have no objection to members of our counter-narcotics team inspecting all pharmaceutical factories operating in the Soviet Zone—"

"Nyet! Nyet! Nyet!"

"You are perfectly welcome to visit the pharmaceutical companies operating in the West. In fact, I seem to remember you have already done that—"

"That is our right! It is necessary to ensure we obtain our fair share of reparations from German industrial production throughout the country. You do not need to do the same in our Zone."

"No, not for reparations, but to track down the source of this heroin. The Soviet Union is a party to international protocols on controlling illegal drug trafficking—"

"No American police will be allowed into any factory in the Soviet Zone for any reason!"

"I see." As if in an aside to his aide, Clay remarked, "I'd say that confirms our suspicions, Baines." To the chairman, as he sat back and lit up another cigarette, he said, "You may proceed to the next point on the agenda."

"General Robertson, you wanted to discuss traffic accidents."

"Indeed. Thank you. There has been a noticeable increase in traffic accidents caused by drivers exceeding posted speed limits by as much as 40 mph."

"Is this seriously a subject for this august body?" Sokolovsky asked directly in English and looking left and right with an expression to suggest he thought he was in the wrong film.

"Yes," Robertson intoned solemnly, "because a disproportionate number of those accidents were caused by Soviet officers."

"My officers drink hard, love hard, and drive hard! That's just the way they are!" Sokolovsky answered with a wave of his hand and an indulgent smile for his entourage.

"One of your hard drinking, hard loving and hard driving officers killed a four-year-old child," Robertson told him in an ice-cold voice.

Sokolovsky made no pretence of shock or regret. He shrugged and replied. "Do you know how many Russian children died in the War, General Robertson? Millions. Millions of little Russian children died. What do I care about one German child?"

Robertson and Clay looked at one another speechless. After a moment, Robertson noted, "It could just as easily have been a British child, or a Russian one, for that matter." Then with resignation, he asked for the next item on the agenda.

"The removal of two passenger carriages from the British transit train this past Sunday."

Robertson turned to an aide, who handed him a file folder. Opening it, Roberston read prepared remarks that first outlined the bare facts of the incident, followed by a statement dictated in London. "His Majesty's government wishes emphatically to register a protest against members of the Soviet Armed Forces boarding one of His Majesty's trains and interfering with its transit through the Soviet Zone in violation of agreements on free access to and from Berlin for British forces."

This time Sokolovsky sat up straighter in his chair and punctuated his answer in Russian with stabs of his finger on the tabletop. "First, only German civilians were removed from the train, not any members of the British military. Second, there *are* no agreements about 'free access to and from Berlin for British forces' — or American or French forces, either. None of you," his eyes scanned the men sitting at the other three tables, "have any more right under international law to cross our Zone without our permission than you are entitled to cross into or over the Soviet Union itself. We *allow* you to transit our Zone, but we will control that transit as we see fit. Period." His eyes were hard, his expression stony, and the man next to him nodded agreement energetically. Something about the latter made Priestman's hair stand up. Bending closer to Borisenko he asked, "Do you know who the man sitting on Sokolovsky's left is?"

Borisenko shook her head sharply. "No, sir. I've never come to one of these meetings before, but he is wearing the uniform of a Colonel in the NKVD — the Soviet State Police."

By 13:30 they had worked through only two-thirds of the agenda and everyone at the Western tables was hungry, irritable and in need of a restroom break. However, instead of adjourning to the notoriously luxurious restaurant located a floor below, Robertson made a surprise and spontaneous suggestion for everyone to join him at his residence for an 'informal' luncheon. To Priestman's utter amazement, the suggestion was readily accepted by Sokolovsky.

Robertson swept out of the room, but Priestman caught Sir Horace just before he darted out. "Does he mean everyone? Including someone like me?"

"He does, yes. And your adjutant, interpreter and driver. There's a large servants' hall for those of lesser importance. Just follow along in the convoy."

"Does this happen often?"

"It hasn't happened for a long time, but in the first year, it was quite common, yes. I think the General is trying to get Sokolovsky to loosen up — or to get him away from his watchdog long enough for them to talk informally. Clay and Sokolovsky used to be good friends, you know. They went places together with their wives and frequented each other's houses. I suspect, General Robertson is planning to monopolize our friend from the NKVD while Clay tries to get Sokolovsky aside for a candid chat. If nothing else, maybe he can find out why the tone of these meetings has become more acrimonious of late."

That made sense. Priestman looked back to signal Borisenko over and noted the WRNS stenographer was also on her feet. He returned to the two women and asked the Wren if she also needed a lift.

"Oh, thank you!" She sounded surprised. "That's very kind, Wing Commander, but my office is just around the corner. I'd rather spend the break transcribing my notes. The more I get done today, the less I have to do tomorrow, ergo the more of a Saturday I might have."

Priestman had been a note-taker at enough meetings at the Ministry to know exactly how she felt. He smiled and told her, "Understood." He collected F/O Stanley from the anteroom and the trio from Gatow found their car and trailed behind the rest of the convoy of vehicles heading to the Dahlem residence of the British Military Governor. Arriving after most of the other guests, they parked almost two blocks away and then walked together to the imposing urban manor house with the British flag out front. As they passed the cars of the Soviet delegation, Priestman noticed that most had their engines running. He was startled until he realized that the drivers were sitting in all of them and many still had other occupants as well. They were running the engines to keep from freezing in the sub-zero temperatures.

At the door to the villa, General Robertson's adjutant, a butler and a housemaid received the guests. Hats, coats and side pistols were taken from those carrying them. Borisenko and Stanley were both directed toward a side door and told to take the stairs down to the staff dining hall, where a meal was being prepared for the junior officers and other ranks. Stepping into the larger salon where a buffet was hastily being prepared as maids circulated with drinks, Priestman overheard General Robertson speaking earnestly to Marshal Sokolovsky, "But Marshal, there's no need for your drivers and staff to sit out in the cold. There's food enough for all of them. Please," he urged, "the staff and drivers of the other delegations are all here."

Priestman did not hear the end of the conversation because Lt. Colonel Walker had caught sight of him and drew him a little aside. "What do you make of it all?" he asked.

"I'm beginning to understand Colonel Howley better," Priestman admitted, "and glad I'm not a diplomat, too."

"Same here."

A maid offered drinks and Priestman took a scotch and soda, before asking Walker as the maid receded, "But is that right? What Sokolovsky said about there being no official agreement for free access to Berlin — not even for our military?"

"Yes, it is, unfortunately."

"How did that happen? I mean, why didn't we insist the Soviets guarantee access?"

"It's a relic of the war. When Roosevelt, Churchill and Stalin met in Yalta to plan the occupation of Germany, they thought the border between the Soviet Zone and the British and American Zones would run through in Berlin."

"So, our respective Sectors of Berlin would have been an integral part of our respective Zones of occupation with no need to cross the Soviet Zone to move our troops in or out." Robin pictured the situation at once.

"Exactly. Then sometime during the fighting, the plans changed. The

Soviets surged forward faster than expected. Montgomery was held back. Eisenhower agreed to new Zones, and Berlin ended up in the middle of the Soviet Zone."

"And we still made no arrangements for access?"

"I wasn't there, but it seems that at the time everyone was focused on winning the war and they trusted in Stalin's good will."

That seemed terribly naïve in retrospect, but Priestman didn't doubt that it was true.

"The problem is," Walker concluded, "we're stuck with the mess they made. If the Soviets decide to be real bastards and close down the access routes, we could find ourselves up a creek without a paddle."

After the lunch break, the delegations of all four occupation powers returned to work through the rest of the agenda. The luncheon seemed to have improved the atmosphere. At least Solokovsky was less belligerent, although not less stubborn. In the end, no decisions were taken whatsoever, and all unfinished business was postponed to the next meeting set for Tuesday, February 10.

It was almost seven pm before Priestman was able to depart the ACC.

Stan sat in the front beside the driver and Borisenko took the seat beside Priestman in the back. He turned to her, "You did an excellent job today, Borisenko. Thank you."

Borisenko rewarded him with a grateful if modest smile. "Thank you, sir! Thank you for letting me come with you. It was very interesting."

"It certainly was!" Priestman agreed. He paused and then asked, "I'm curious. As a former Soviet citizen, why do you think Sokolovsky was so sharp and aggressive? Suggesting the European Recovery Act would 'enslave' European workers is ridiculous. It will be good for the American economy, too, of course, but first and foremost it will kick-start European industry and create jobs. If there was ever a policy enlightened by the spirit of mutual benefit, this is it."

"But it is a terrible threat to the Soviet Union, sir." Borisenko declared, her eyes wide.

"How?"

"Because it shows how rich America is! Not to mention that if the Soviet Union were to become part of an economic free trade zone with the other European countries, Western goods might flood into the Soviet Union. Inevitably there would be more contact between Russians and Europeans. The Russian people might start to understand that they have been lied to."

"About what?"

"About how terrible it is in the West."

Priestman thought about that a moment and reluctantly nodded. "Is that why Sokolovsky ordered his staff and drivers to wait in the cars although Robertson explicitly invited them into his house?"

"No," came the surprising answer, "That is because the marshal knew he would be having a friendly conversation with General Clay and wanted as few witnesses as possible."

"Witnesses?"

"People who might report back to the NKVD that he was too friendly with the Imperialists."

Priestman considered that. "Are you saying Marshal Sokolovsky is afraid?"

"Of course he is afraid!" Borisenko declared sounding genuinely astonished by her CO's naivety. "The higher one is in the Soviet Union, the more one has to lose and the more rivals one has."

"Rivals, I understand, but we're talking about his drivers, stenographers and lower-ranking officers?" Priestman protested.

"A Soviet marshal or general is especially afraid of his drivers, his batmen and the maids in his house," Borisenko told him solemnly. "Such people are most vulnerable to threats, and when you have almost nothing, the promise of only a little more — medicine for your sick parents or shoes for your growing children — makes you wax in the hands of those who want information against your boss."

Priestman stared at her. "Is it really that bad?"

"Bad?" She asked back. "No. It is not bad. It is hell."

A Risky Proposition
Berlin-Kladow
Saturday, 31 January 1948

David couldn't sleep. He was due to fly out on the next BEA flight, and suddenly he wasn't sure he should go. He had been hoping to discuss his feelings with Emily and Robin, but when his ex-CO arrived straight from a meeting of the ACC, the conversation had taken a different direction. They'd talked about Soviet intentions and Allied options, communism, democracy, tyranny and mob psychology, all of which interested him, but had not brought him closer to a decision about what to do next. No sooner had they had retired, than his personal concerns came back to haunt him.

After tossing in bed for an hour or so, he wrapped himself in his warm dressing gown, put on a pair of sheepskin slippers, and took the servants' stairs to the floor below so as not to wake his hosts. The stairs ended at the entrance of the dining room. Although darkened, he could still make out the pairs of portraits in their gold frames. His uncle's dining room had been similarly decorated, and he wondered what had happened to those portraits. Surely no SS officer would have wanted generations of Jews gazing down on him as he ate? Like the bodies of their murdered descendants, the paintings of his ancestors had probably been burned. Then again, David had heard the Allies were attempting to find and return stolen works of art. Maybe he should put in a claim? But that would require an inventory and exact description, which would take time and distract from his business. He was trapped in the same vicious circle.

A glance toward the front of the house confirmed that sleet was ticking against the tall windows facing the lawn and lake, so he sought out the den instead.

This windowless room tucked between the study and the library had an open fireplace. It was here they had spent the evening talking, and embers still glowed under the grate. David took some of the smaller twigs and branches stacked beside the fireplace and placed them on the embers. As they caught flame, he took a log from the stack on the other side and placed it on top of the kindling. Soon, flames leapt and curled around the heavier wood. They triggered associations: his burning Hurricane engine, the incinerators at Auschwitz, and the beautiful fireplace of his uncle's home as they gathered to toast the New Year with champagne.

Damn, damn, damn! His father had succeeded in forcing him out of the RAF by giving him a fortune he couldn't just leave lying around and by burdening him with the property — and so the memories and obligations — of the murdered. His facile plan to come, sell off anything remaining, say a few prayers and return to the UK had blown up in his face as surely as his Hurricane engine. He couldn't just walk away and forget about that dubious man occupying his uncle's house. David pounded his fist against the chimney, scraping his knuckles.

"Don't take things so hard," he heard his uncle advise him in his head. How often had he ended up unburdening his heart to Uncle Otto, telling him of his frustrations or admitting how he'd failed his father yet again? His memories of that house on the Schwanenwerder were heavily spiced with outbursts of pent-up juvenile rage against his father that his aunt and uncle gently and diplomatically soothed. That house had been his refuge.

"Don't waste time being angry about things you can't change," his uncle had often advised.

Did that include now? Should he just shrug and say there was nothing he could do to drive Friedebach out? Or should he put his business on hold to track down Friedebach's real name and bring him to justice? Yet even if he succeeded, it wouldn't bring his aunt, uncle or cousins back to life. So why bother?

Abruptly and without warning, the whole pile of wood toppled over and rolled onto the floor with a loud thud and rumble. He had disturbed the balance in some way by removing that one log. With an exasperated curse, David bent to collect the displaced logs and pile them up again. He then sank into a leather armchair to stare at the flames.

These last weeks, he'd been so focused on the past, that he'd almost lost sight of the future. The future lay with his air ambulance company, and Kiwi and he had myriad problems to solve before they could get started. He had to concentrate on that, he told himself. He owed it to Kiwi as much as himself. Kiwi was working on finding a suitable aircraft and identifying an aviation manufacturer that could make the modifications they would need, but they couldn't start looking for a base of operations without customers.

Too late, David realized he hadn't done a proper market survey before founding the company and hiring Kiwi. Good as the idea sounded in the bar of the Savoy, he'd gone off half-cocked. His father must be turning over in his grave from aggravation. Which, of course, was what he deserved, but it didn't make David feel any better about himself. Ultimately, the best revenge on his father would be to succeed with a flying business — not fail again.

The light in the den switched on and David spun about startled to find his host standing in the doorway in his pyjamas and morning gown. "Are you all right?" Robin asked.

"Yes, I just …" David shrugged and then decided on, "needed to think some things through."

"Can I help?"

"Not really. I'm confronting a lot of unpleasant facts." David offered a slightly crooked smile.

"Well, it's better to do that over a glass of scotch," Robin answered moving to the beautiful wooden secretary that disguised the drinks cabinet. He opened it, withdrew two crystal glasses, found the bottle of scotch and poured for both of them. Returning to hand one of the glasses to David, he urged, "Tell me."

"I told you about the man occupying my uncle's house."

"I thought of him today when Clay mentioned that some Nazi war criminals involved in the production of chemical and biological weapons are still at large. The Americans believe they might be mass producing the heroin that is flooding the city, but what most makes the Americans nervous is that these Nazis — like those who were part of the nuclear program — are being protected by the Soviets so that they can continue their research in the service of the Kremlin."

David almost choked on the scotch, and he stared at Robin. Of course! Why he hadn't thought of it. "But how do we prove that?"

"I haven't a clue. The only thing I can think of is to inform those bodies officially involved in tracking down Nazi criminals." Robin paused and then noted, "However, it might be good to have a little more evidence than inspired intuition as the basis for any accusation."

David sighed. "I know. Meanwhile, I need to concentrate on starting my air ambulance, and—"

"May I join you?" Emily asked timidly from the door. She too was in a dressing gown and slippers.

"Why not? The more the merrier," her husband answered. "Scotch? Sherry? Gin and tonic?"

"Just a glass of wine, if you wouldn't mind." While her husband devoted himself to the drinks, Emily sank into one of the armed chairs and directed her gaze at David. "I didn't mean to interrupt. You were saying that you need to get to work on your ambulance business."

"Yes. I've been so obsessed with clearing the decks here in Germany that I haven't done some of the most elementary things — like a proper market survey to test demand for our proposed service. I honestly don't know whether there *is* a need for an air ambulance service in the UK. Kiwi's experience was in Australia, which is a totally different market. There the low population density and vast distances involved justify using aircraft as ambulances, but the UK is densely populated and the next hospital is rarely far away. I feel as if my whole business idea just blew up in my face." As he admitted this out loud, he grasped what had been gnawing at him subconsciously for days.

"Yet there appears to be an acute need for such a service here in Berlin," Emily pointed out. "That little boy who needed to go to Hamburg for a blood transfusion wouldn't have died if there had been an air ambulance service here."

"No, but—" David stopped himself and looked back at her startled. Why hadn't he thought of that himself? Because it was such a radical proposal. "Would it even be possible?" He turned automatically to Robin.

"Would what be possible?" Robin had not followed his train of thought.

"Would it be possible for a civilian aviation company to fly patients out of Berlin for medical care elsewhere?"

"I don't know why not," Robin answered a little flippantly.

"Well, for a start, would it be possible for a civil aviation company to operate out of RAF Gatow?" David asked more pointedly.

"BEA is, and they have a hangar they hardly use," Robin reminded him, adding, "Three-quarters of Gatow's facilities are not in use. There is plenty of hangar, storage and office space available. The best thing would probably be to negotiate with BEA for a sublease of some sort. As a business, they'll be more agile than a government bureaucracy."

"Then again, maybe that incident with a child needing a rare blood type was exceptional. One case doesn't exactly demonstrate sustained demand sufficient to justify basing an air ambulance here," David argued with himself out loud.

"I could do some basic market research for you if you like," Emily offered. "It only entails going to the hospitals and asking how often they need to send patients out of Berlin for treatment, doesn't it?"

"Yes!" David agreed enthusiastically. Not only would this set him free to return to the UK, but it would also get Emily involved in his company. They were a good team, and she had a natural talent for marketing. "Excellent idea," he reinforced his original answer. "If you're willing to go around to the hospitals, we could do a proper survey identifying everything from the frequency to the kind of illnesses or conditions and the destinations, etc. etc."

"I'm not sure my German is that good," Emily admitted hesitantly but added hopefully, "but I could ask Charlotte to come with me—"

"Perfect!" David jumped at the idea. If Charlotte helped with the company, he would have a chance to get to know her better — and he wanted that.

But no sooner did he feel his heart start to soar with enthusiasm than some instinct yanked him back to the ground. Maybe it was the voice of his father, who always seemed to poison his moments of triumph, but he heard himself saying out loud, "But we mustn't get carried away. The Berliners are miserably poor, and an air ambulance is inherently expensive."

"If the Soviets continue to interfere with our ground transportation and interdict our access," Robin countered, "then flying patients out may be the *only* way of getting them across the Soviet Zone."

David looked over startled, as Emily remarked gently, "Of course, I could understand if you don't want to live here and devote your life to saving German lives."

"Odd as this may sound to you," David replied, "after two weeks here I can honestly say that Germany is still more 'home' to me than England, much less Canada. I grew up here. I know that not every German was a Nazi, and after I met Dr Schlaer and Charlotte, I found I don't hate the ordinary people who just tried to survive. Of course, I want to punish the war criminals and I want Friedebach out of my uncle's house, but for the rest..." He shrugged.

Sensing the incomprehension of his hosts, he added. "The active Nazis were always a minority. The anti-Nazis an even smaller minority. The vast majority of the population were simply selfish, little people looking for their personal advantage. Hitler's rise was enabled primarily by what we call *Mitlaeufer*, the people who rode on his coattails because it brought them advantages. They loved being the "Master Race," and they loved being victorious, but without Hitler, they would not have been murderers. They probably wouldn't even have been particularly antisemitic. Those people have been humiliated, and they're paying a high price for their hubris. That's enough."

"So, you wouldn't mind basing your company here?" Emily challenged hopefully.

"No, not at all. It would have several advantages," David admitted. "If you're right about the facilities at Gatow, Robin, and if there is sufficient demand for our services, then being based here would enable me to both build up a business and reckon with Friedebach. Maybe even put down roots...." He was irrationally thinking of Charlotte.

"You and Kiwi could live here," Emily spoke up eagerly. "At least while you're setting up and getting started. We have plenty of room and staff. It would be wonderful having friends in the house, working together to make the company a success...." David sensed that she sincerely wanted to be part of his company and for him to stay.

"Not to mention that Sammy would love chasing the ducks," Robin gave his consent to the invitation, and they all laughed at the thought of David's bird dog loose on the lawn.

"I can't say how much your support and invitation mean," David told his friends. He was on the brink of saying that they had solved his problems and it was time to go back to bed when again his father's ghost intervened. The cautious banker in his head spoke through his mouth. "On the other hand, it is extremely risky starting a business in an occupied city without clear legal status, no functioning currency and surrounded by the Red Army."

"As I recall," Robin replied, "it was extremely risky telling Hitler that we would not negotiate after he drove us off the Continent."

"Yes, but our only choice then was between 'fight' or 'surrender'. Now there are other, less risky options."

"Well, I'm not a businessman," Robin conceded, "but my maternal grandfather was wont to preach 'high risk, high gain.'"

"Wasn't he the one who ended up bankrupt?" David challenged.

Robin laughed, but countered, "Only because he fell in love with a French dancing girl. Stay away from loose women and you'll be fine."

Chapter Six
Deceptive Façades

Bargains
Berlin-Tiergarten
Sunday, 1 February 1948

Galyna Nicolaevna looked around nervously. She had never done anything like this before: agree to meet with a member of the Soviet forces of occupation. Until she had accompanied the WingCo to the meeting of the ACC two days ago, she had never even encountered members of the Soviet occupation. Yes, once she'd taken a bus tour of the sights: the gutted Reichstag, the battered Brandenburg Gate, the ruins of Hitler's chancery, the wreck of the Royal Palace and the "Rote Rathaus" or Town Hall, all of which lay in the Soviet Sector, and once she'd joined some of the other WAAFs and their RAF escorts on an outing to the East. They had all worn their uniforms and shown their ID to the Soviet soldiers at the Sector border. For an hour or more, they walked around Berlin Mitte. Yet the sound of Russian spoken and the Soviets in uniform and civilian clothes surrounding them on the streets had not made her happy or homesick as she'd hoped. Instead, it had filled her with near panic, so she had not returned.

During General Robertson's impromptu lunch, however, she discovered she was one of only two women in the staff dining room for the lower-ranking members of the respective entourages. Naturally, the women gravitated toward one another. Or rather, Mila Mikhailivna slipped around the room to introduce herself.

Although the Soviet woman was shorter and looked roughly five years younger than Galyna, she was a Hero of the Soviet Union, which intimidated Galyna. Mila laughed and said something in German to which Galyna replied in Russian that she didn't speak German. Mila's face lit up like a lantern as she asked, "Are you Russian?"

Galyna had hesitated with her answer. She had a British passport and she felt loyalty and gratitude to the country that had given her grandmother and herself refuge. She admired the British and even loved them, but she was not British. She could never be no matter how much she tried. So, she had nodded, adding by way of explanation, "My grandparents were émigrés." That was true but it also made her sound like the child of Tsarist refugees, conveniently ignoring her Soviet parents and childhood.

"You live in England? Fought for England?" Mila asked looking over Galyna's WAAF corporal's uniform.

"Yes, I am in the Royal Air Force. In the war, I was a radio technician." She explained proudly, pointing to the badge on her sleeve.

Mila looked up at her with what a look of wonderment. "A radio technician? That's amazing!" She exclaimed with apparent sincerity before adding in a tone of disappointment, "I'm hopeless with modern technology."

"But — but you are a Hero of the Soviet Union!" Galyna had protested, indicating the other's medals.

Mila had shrugged. "I killed a lot of Germans. I was a partisan."

"What is your position here?" Galyna asked cautiously.

Mila shrugged again. "Decoration. Marshal Sokolovsky likes to point to me when he talks about the sufferings and sacrifices of the Soviet Union and the courage of Soviet women."

Against her best intentions, Galyna liked Mila and before she knew what was happening they were chattering like old friends. Or, rather new friends, still learning about one another. Wasn't General Robertson kind to include them? Wasn't the food good? It seemed to be the same food that was being served upstairs; was that possible? They exchanged impressions of the Reichstag and Reichskanzlei etc. Cautiously, gradually, they risked more personal questions. Galyna asked where Mila had learned German, "From the enemy," she answered. "It was useful to be able to deceive them." Galyna had been intimidated by that answer and fell silent.

Mila persisted, unwilling to let the conversation die. She asked the question, "Are you married?" When Galyna said no, she volunteered that she wasn't either. "It was the war. There was no time for marriage and children." Mila looked momentarily wistful and added, "I fell in love many times, but..." She lifted her shoulders in a gesture of helplessness. "I would like to settle down now, but here…" she looked around the room at the others. All the men seemed intent on helping themselves to the generous platters of food and filling up with hot tea, coffee, or vodka.

Mila changed the subject, asking Galyna, "Does your family live in England?"

Galyna said 'yes'. That was not strictly true. Only her grandmother lived in England, while she did not know if her father was alive at all and her mother was still in the Soviet Union. But to Galyna, her mother was dead ever since she had remarried and tried to make Galyna forget her real father.

"And they are well?" Mila asked with big, concerned eyes.

"Yes, last I heard," Galyna answered without thinking.

"Has it been a long time since you heard from them?" Mila asked more anxiously still.

"Not really. My grandmother writes once a week."

"But isn't there a terrible famine in England?" Mila asked astonished. "And no one has any heat."

"Nonsense," Galyna answered irritated, remembering too late the articles from *Pravda* that made these claims. Understanding where Mila had her information, she'd made a point to speak firmly, "There have been some power shortages in London, but nothing lasting more than a few hours at a time. As for famine, that is pure propaganda. We still have rationing, which is tedious I admit, but no one in England is starving. Our last harvest was excellent. We're just all so spoiled," Galyna added, "that we want chocolate and coffee and oranges too!"

At this point in the conversation, an English officer put his head into the staff dining room and announced the break was over. It was time to get back in the cars and return to the ACC. Everyone stood and started looking for their overcoats, hats and gloves. In the commotion, Galyna risked asking Mila a favour. "I have a friend with a six-year-old daughter," she explained in a rush. "I would like to give her a set of Matryoshka dolls — as my father gave me when I was six. Is there somewhere in the Soviet Sector where I could buy a set?"

"Not for sale, no, but I can find you one. I will bring it to you next time."

"Oh, I won't be at the next meeting of the ACC. I'm only here with

Wing Commander Priestman, and he is a substitute for Air Commodore Waite."

"Then..." Mila started but cut herself off and stood frowning.

"Don't worry," Galyna assured her. "It was just a silly whim. It's not important."

"No, but—" Mila bit her lower lip and looked across the room toward the other Russians. They were laughing loudly and hastily pouring a last vodka down their throats. "If you want...." From the street came the sound of voices and car doors opening. Mila dropped her voice, "On Sunday. I could come to the Lehrter Bahnhof — in civilian clothing." She looked toward the other Russians, who were donning their caps and moving toward the door, joining the general exodus. "If you meet me there on the platform at noon, I'll bring the Matryoshka dolls..."

And so Galyna found herself standing in the cold on the platform at the Lehrter Bahnhof getting more and more nervous until amidst the grey crowd of shabby Germans she saw Mila striding towards her in baggy trousers, calf-high boots, and a backpack. Her hair was pinned up under a large wool hat and her hands were protected in men's mittens. She was all but lost in her clothing, but her smile was radiant.

"Galyna Nicolaevna!" She called and waved at the sight of the WAAF (also wearing civilian clothes) — as if they were long-lost relatives. It made Galyna's heartache. When was the last time anyone had been so glad to see her? She waved back, breaking unconsciously into a smile.

"I have three sets of Matryoshka dolls," Mila announced a little breathlessly as they shook hands in greeting. "You can choose which set you like best."

"Can we go someplace warm? Have some tea?" Galyna answered, expecting Mila to say no, that she must get back to the Soviet Sector.

To her surprise, the former partisan agreed, "Yes, yes! Do you know of a place?"

"A friend told me there is a café of sorts opposite the Reichstag if you can walk that far?" Galyna was certain that Mila would be afraid to stray far from the railway station.

"How far is it?" Mila asked with a look of concern.

"Half a mile or so."

Mila laughed. "Are you joking? In the war, I sometimes walked twenty miles in a day, though I preferred riding when we had horses." She hitched her backpack up on her back and looked expectantly at Galyna to lead the way. They left the noisy, dirty train station behind, crossed over the Spree on an improvised pedestrian bridge and continued down a broad street lined with ruins. As the Reichstag came into view, Mila stopped and gazed for what seemed like a long time at the scarred façade with the Soviet flag waving over it. Then she became pensive and marched silently beside Galyna with her thumbs hooked in the straps of her backpack until Galyna pointed toward a door in one of the ruins with a sign on it. "I think that's it," Galyna admitted uncomfortably. "It doesn't look very nice." That was an understatement. It looked horrible. A hole in the wall....

"As long as it's warm..." Mila answered, and taking the lead, she opened the door and stuck her head inside. Satisfied, she entered, going down two steps, with Galyna following hesitantly.

The windows were boarded up making it dark, and it was crowded with German men of all ages. Galyna's instinct was to flee; she did not feel safe among a crowd of rough men like these regardless of nationality. Mila, however, shouldered her way to a table and then turned back to face the men, all of whom were staring at them. Mila shrugged her pack back off her shoulders, put it on the seat of the chair beside her, yanked her mittens off and dropped them on the table. Then, still standing, she thrust her hand inside her double-breasted men's jacket. When she removed her hand it held a revolver which she pointed calmly at the gaping men. Her hand swept slowly from one side of the room to the other and back. "*Verstanden*?" (Have you understood?)

The men looked away, and Mila sat down. She put her pistol on the table with her hand still holding the handle. Galyna sank into the chair opposite unsure whether to be shocked or amused.

"Men," Mila said to her with a charming, almost childish smile, "generally understand guns better than words."

"Yes, I suppose," Galyna agreed, feeling both uncomfortable and safer.

An old man wearing an apron shuffled over and asked Mila a question in German. She checked if Galyna wanted tea or something else and Galyna confirmed tea. The man shuffled away.

Mila leaned back against the wall, sideways to the table, and propped one foot on the chair with her knapsack. She surveyed the room very carefully: like a policeman, Galyna thought. At last, satisfied, she turned and smiled at Galyna. "Do you know what I feel?" Mila asked. Galyna shook her head. "I feel free — free for the first time since the Red Army took over the control of the region where we partisans had fought for two years." She paused, considered Galyna and added softly. "You cannot understand that can you?"

"I don't know..." Galyna replied cautiously. She remembered feeling terrified after her father's arrest — afraid of a knock on the door, afraid of the ringing of the telephone, afraid of the people on the street. She remembered how she stopped talking to everyone and stopped looking people in the eye. She had not been brave. She had never stood up for her father, never defended him. She had condemned him publicly like they wanted her do. She had called him a traitor and said that he deserved to die. And even when the stranger who said she was her grandmother collected her at the train station in Helsinki, she had not trusted her for a long time. She had thought they would find her somehow, take her back, and send her to Siberia. Not until they got to England did she start to feel free, but only gradually.

"You don't have to tell me anything," Mila said into her thoughts. "Just let me talk. Please. I am so alone in Karlshorst. There is no one there I can talk to. Grisha... sometimes I think he understands. He's a good man. An honest and brave man. Yet, when I try to talk to him, he just says 'Don't talk like that, Milushka.' Or, 'You know better than to say such things.' He never tells me what he thinks. For a while, I thought we could be happy together. But how could I spend my whole life with a man who will not tell me what he truly thinks? Who will not let me say what is in my heart and mind?"

Galyna looked at Mila and they knew that they did understand each other, yet Galyna was still afraid to speak. She had learned her lessons too well and at too tender an age. Besides, she had not been a partisan who had learned to kill her enemies. She looked down at the revolver still held casually in Mila's hand.

"Two days before the meeting of the ACC where we met," Mila spoke so softly Galyna had to strain to hear her. "I received a message from my grandfather. It did not come by mail. He'd scribbled it on pages torn from a book and sent it with a conscript from our village who'd been assigned to the battalion guarding Karlshort. The boy found me and gave me the message, telling me in a whisper that what he wrote was true — before running away without telling me his name. Do you want to know what my grandfather wrote?"

Galyna nodded vigorously; she was hardly breathing.

Mila continued in her almost inaudible voice, "He wrote to tell me that my niece, my sister's three-month-old baby, had starved to death. She was not the only one in the village. They are all starving, he said. It is worse than during collectivization. He said there are no cattle left alive. He said they have no bread. They eat only potatoes and roots...." She fell silent, her hand stroking the pistol. "When Marshal Sokolovsky hosts dinners, he serves mountains of caviar, paté, game, turkey, lobsters and oysters...."

The waiter arrived with tall glasses of tea in metal holders. It was steaming hot. The two women held the glasses under their noses, breathing in the scent of the tea and letting the hot moisture stick to their faces. Mila started speaking again. "My sister weighs less than 70 lbs, my grandfather says. He says she is always cold because they have nothing but rags to wear. They don't live in Moscow, you see, or Kyiv or even Kharkiv. They are just peasants. Former Kulaks."

A shiver went down Galyna's spine despite the hot tea she clutched in her hands.

Mila looked over at her. "You understand?"

Galyna nodded. She almost gasped out that her father had been a teacher near Kharkiv, that he had spoken out against collectivization. For that, he had been arrested for treason and disappeared into a gulag. She wanted to tell Mila, but she couldn't overcome twelve years of silence. All she managed was to whisper, "You are Ukrainian, too."

Mila nodded.

"Did you have brothers?"

Mila looked at Galyna with a sad expression. "You put that question in the past tense."

Galyna looked down, "It is just that ... one hears, everywhere, about Soviet casualties...."

"You are right. I had three brothers. They are all dead. But I don't know who killed them. Maybe the Germans. Maybe not.... I think Nikita may have sympathized with the Germans. I don't know what happened to any of them.... Do you have brothers or sisters?"

Galyna shook her head. "Unless you count the children of my mother's second marriage, but I don't count them."

"Your father is dead?"

Galyna made a gesture. "Somewhere."

Mila nodded. She understood. For several moments they sipped their tea in silence and then Mila spoke again. "My sister and grandparents have no warm clothes. Do you think we could buy something here in the West? Good things, made in the West. Things that will last," she emphasized.

"Potsdamer Platz is the biggest barter market in the world. You can buy anything there if you have something to sell."

With a smile, Mila reached into her backpack and removed three Matryoshka dolls. "I have these, after you've taken the one you want, I can sell the other two and these." She dumped a handful of German iron crosses on the table. "I heard the Americans like to buy them," she explained.

Galyna nodded and reached out for the Matryoshka dolls. She inspected them carefully, treasuring the details on even the smallest doll. After comparing, she made her choice and asked, "How much do you want for it?"

"A pair of warm boots for my sister, or a fur hat for my grandfather, woollen underwear for my grandmother — things I can send home."

"We'll go to the black market. I have cigarettes from the NAAFI and with your Iron Crosses, I'm sure we'll find what you're looking for."

True Colours
Berlin-Kladow
Monday, 2 February 1948

"Frau Oberstleutnant!" the maid Frau Pabst pounced on Emily as she entered the breakfast room. "Frau Neuhausen has not arrived yet. We don't know where she is and what could have happened to her." She sounded more annoyed than upset.

Emily automatically looked at the clock that stood inside the door to the dining room. It was 8:05 am and the staff usually arrived at 7:30 am. Robin's car was due to pick him up in ten minutes, but the breakfast table was already set. Their boiled eggs, toast and tea awaited them. "It's early yet," Emily replied to the agitated maid.

Frau Pabst frowned and reminded her indignantly, "She's almost an hour late!"

"Have you tried to reach her house to see if she's ill?"

Frau Pabst shook her head. "She has no telephone."

Stupid question, Emily told herself; few Germans had telephones. "Do you know where she lives? Should I send my driver over?" Emily suggested.

Frau Pabst shook her head. "She lives in Babelsberg, in the Soviet Zone." She made it sound like a point of significance. Yet Kladow was nearly surrounded by the Soviet Zone, so Emily thought it was only logical that her staff lived there rather than farther away.

"I'm sure she has a good reason for being late and will show up eventually. Meanwhile, we'll manage without her. I'm perfectly capable of cooking my lunch and making dinner, if necessary," Emily assured the maid.

"Is something wrong?" Robin asked coming up beside her.

"Frau Neuhausen isn't here yet and she's never been late before."

They sat down for breakfast looking out at a lawn covered with a thin blanket of snow. Ducks waded cautiously out on the frozen surface of the lake, squawking and fluttering when the thin ice broke under their webbed feet. Robin poured himself some coffee and buttered his toast.

"Any chance this weather will hold so we can fly next weekend?" Emily asked scanning the cloudless blue sky.

"I'll check with the met office. You're meeting with Charlotte Walmsdorf this afternoon, aren't you?"

"Yes, we'll translate David's questionnaire and then hopefully start visiting hospitals."

"It would be best to —" The front doorbell rang causing him to frown and ask irritably, "Who could that be at this time in the morning?" They turned in their chairs to follow as Frau Pabst went to answer the door. A moment later, she returned with a grinning LAC Wallace in tow.

"I've brought yesterday's papers, sir," the CO's driver explained. "Ft/ Lt Boyd says your Letter to the Editor is on page 8, Mrs Priestman."

"What?" Excitedly, Emily took the paper and opened it as Robin got to his feet to look over her shoulder. Sure enough, the letter she and Charlotte had composed was prominently printed on the "Letters to the Editor" page. "Oh, I can't wait to show Charlotte!" Emily exclaimed.

"Well done!" Robin praised, putting on his cap. "I'll try to be back by 6:30." He bent to give her a quick kiss.

Robin and LAC Wallace departed as Emily re-read the letter. When she'd written it with Charlotte, she'd felt like she was doing something worthwhile, but now it seemed insignificant compared to the prospect of establishing an air ambulance business. If there was enough demand —

The sound of the ringing phone disrupted her thoughts and a moment later, Frau Pabst reported that Mrs Howley was on the line. Emily took the call in the winter garden. Mrs Howley was ostensibly calling to verify the time and dress code for Emily's dinner party on Thursday, but Emily suspected she was more intent on mentioning the upcoming meeting of the Ladies' Club and asking if Emily could help at the upcoming "fair" the Americans were hosting to celebrate Washington's Birthday.

"Oh dear," Emily exclaimed without thinking. "When is that?"

"Saturday 21 February."

Damn! Emily thought. Saturdays were the only day she could fly and if she had to spend all day at some sort of fair....

Edith Howley was still explaining over the phone, "... We drag out some old merry-go-rounds and a Ferris wheel and offer pony rides and popcorn and the like. We need volunteers to sell tickets to the rides and the raffle tickets etc. I'd really appreciate it if you could help."

Emily wanted to say no. She wanted to say she had more important things to do, but she bit her tongue. Pretending delight she didn't feel, she agreed to help. Edith Howley thanked her and rang off.

However, the call reminded her about her upcoming dinner party, her first international dinner. Although she was intentionally keeping it small: just the Howleys, Waites, and the French air attaché and his wife, it would be very awkward if Frau Neuhausen turned out to be seriously ill. She did not relish managing her first representational dinner without a cook.

When Charlotte arrived punctually at 2 pm, Emily proudly showed her their letter in the *Times*. She was disappointed that Charlotte seemed less pleased than expected until the Berliner explained, "It's good that the letter was published because the Soviets are up to new tricks."

"What do you mean?"

"Over the weekend they changed the document requirements for crossing in and out of the Zone. Do you remember? I told you about Horst, our former coachman, who collects milk from farmers in Brandenburg and brings it into Berlin?"

"Yes," Emily confirmed.

"Today he could not get across the border. The Ivans told him his papers were not valid, although they had been issued by the SMAD only a few months ago. He was told he needed new papers and had to go to an office near the town hall. It will no doubt take all day or more to get them and meanwhile, the children go without milk."

"Well, that explains what happened to Frau Neuhausen," Emily concluded, filling Charlotte in on the cook's absence.

"Yes," Charlotte agreed. "That will be the problem. She will have to get new papers. The Soviets do things like this all the time, you know? One day it is the drivers that need some new stamp. The next day the passengers are required to have a different ID or a letter from employers or something else. On the zonal border, Horst is constantly harassed and humiliated. Sometimes, the Soviets keep him waiting for hours without any explanation. Other times, they demand bribes. Once or twice, they have simply turned one of his churns upside-down and emptied it — supposedly to check for contraband, but in reality just to ruin it and reduce his already meagre income."

"What is the point of it all?" Emily asked appalled.

Charlotte drew a deep breath. "I think it is mostly just to humiliate us, to remind us that they are our masters. It is revenge for what we did to them as a nation. It doesn't matter that Horst never hurt anyone, or that little children need that milk."

"Yes, I suppose you're right," Emily conceded, troubled.

Charlotte broke into her thoughts. "There is nothing we can do."

"No," Emily agreed, "but I have some good news." She launched into an excited description of David's plans, ending by pulling out the questionnaire he had scribbled down on a legal notepad before departing. "He wants us to translate this," she explained, "and then go around to the hospitals in Berlin and ask them the questions on it."

The news brightened Charlotte's continence far more than the published letter. "Seriously?" she asked breathlessly. "Do you think it is possible he could — would — locate his aeroplane here?"

"If there is enough business," Emily stressed. "Do you think you can help me with the survey?."

"Yes, yes! We can get to work on the translation right away." Charlotte at once started removing a pen from her handbag as if to get to work.

"I was also rather hoping you could make the appointments for me," Emily confessed. "I hate trying speaking German over the telephone. Ideally, you would also come when I meet with the hospital managers. If we go together and each of us takes notes, we'll be much more likely to get everything right."

Charlotte eyes widened as Emily spoke and blood suffused her face; gradually a smile took shape. It was like watching her come to life before her eyes Emily thought as Charlotte nodded eagerly and declared, "I would like that very much."

"It will take a great deal of time. I fear your journalism would suffer."

"I don't care," Charlotte told her. "I would like to help."

"Mr Goldman is willing to pay ten shillings per completed questionnaire, and I thought we could split it 50/50, so five shillings a piece per hospital visit. Is that all right with you?"

"But there are more than forty hospitals in the Western Sectors of Berlin alone," Charlotte gasped out.

"Yes, and Mr Goldman needs the information as soon as possible. I'd like to get started right away and try to visit at least one hospital each workday. Do you think that's possible?"

"Yes — if we don't have to rely on public transport," Charlotte stressed earnestly.

"Of course not. I have the car and driver."

Charlotte nodded more vigorously, and although her tone was serious, she was still flushed and palpably excited when she added. "I would like to do this not just for the money, Emily, but because it would be very good for Berlin. I think—"

She was interrupted by the sound of a door crashing shut, followed by an explosion of German and excited voices. Startled, Emily and Charlotte looked towards the kitchen where they could now clearly hear sobbing. Emily jumped up and went to see what was going on. Frau Neuhausen sat at the kitchen table sobbing and shaking her head, while Frau Pabst and Fraulein Schilling tried to comfort her.

"Frau Neuhausen!" Emily exclaimed. "What is it? What has happened?"

"Die sowjetischen Schweine! Sie haben meinen Ehering gestohlen!" ("The Soviet pigs. They have stolen my wedding ring.") As Frau Neuhausen spoke, she held out her hand, the knuckle above the third finger was red and swelling. Frau Neuhausen drew her hand back to her breast and dissolved into a flood of tears.

Emily guided her cook to the breakfast table, sat her down and poured her some tea. There, with Charlotte's help, she extracted the story of what had happened. She explained that the Soviets had boarded her bus and demanded some papers that she didn't have. They then removed her from the bus and interrogated her for five hours. She sensed that they wanted a bribe of some sort, but all she had in her purse were worthless occupation marks. She had long since lost her watch to other Soviets and the only jewellery she owned was her wedding band.

Between snuffles into her handkerchief, Frau Neuhausen gasped out. "Rudi and I were married in 1915 he fell on 2 November 1917. Since the day I married, not once have I removed my Rudi's ring. Not once! And now! Gone! Stolen by Soviet pigs! And what does that make me?" She held her swollen finger in her other hand and sobbed miserably.

Emily understood only too well. She'd grown up surrounded by war widows. That wedding ring represented married status, respectability, and identity. Without it, Frau Neuhausen felt naked, humiliated, and vulnerable. Emily got up to put her arms around the older woman, and Frau Neuhausen broke down into tears again. She sobbed harder than ever as if releasing the misery of years.

Eventually, she pulled herself together, wiped the tears from her face, and gave Emily a forced smile. "Thank you, Madame," she whispered, adding a "Thank you, Frau Graefin," to Charlotte as well. "But..."

"Yes?" Emily prompted.

Frau Neuhausen drew a deep breath, shook her head, and then blew her nose in her handkerchief. "Please understand, Frau *Oberstleutnant,* I can't face them again! I'm very sorry, but I must give notice." She started sobbing again.

This time it was Charlotte who went to her. She sat beside Frau Neuhausen and put her arm over the older woman's shoulders. Charlotte held her close and let her sob. All the while, Frau Neuhausen gasped out, "*Ich kann nicht mehr. Ich kann nicht. Ich will nie wieder die Grenze ueberschreiten.*"

Emily waited helplessly, as the full import of Frau Neuhausen's words started to sink in. Frau Neuhausen was quitting, and she had her first diplomatic dinner in three days. Or should she offer to let Frau Neuhausen live in one of the vacant servants' rooms? There were four of them upstairs. Why on earth should Frau Neuhausen be forced to commute just because Emily selfishly liked having the house to herself?

Before she could make the offer, Frau Neuhausen got hold of herself. She squeezed Charlotte's hand, pushed her tear-soaked handkerchief into the pocket of her apron and got to her feet. "You know…" She started, broke off, and then resumed again, "You know, some of us have been trampled on our whole lives. First, we lost the Great War, then came the Inflation, and then the Depression, and then the bombers, and now the Ivans. No matter how hard we work or how honest we are, everything just gets taken away from us. Only Hitler ever gave us anything. *He* gave us our pride. That's why we loved him. He made us great. Now we are nothing again." Before Emily could recover from her shock, Frau Neuhausen had turned and disappeared into the kitchen.

For a moment they sat in stunned silence, and then Charlotte whispered. "Please don't think we all feel like that. Please."

Emily did not answer immediately. She took her time. She remembered David lecturing to her about how not all Germans were bad, and agreed, "No, I know that, but I hope you can understand that I don't want someone who *does* think like that living under the same roof."

"Did you not understand? She has given notice and does not want to come back to work," Charlotte replied softly.

"I understood that, but I was on the brink of offering her a room upstairs. I can't do that, now. Not after what she just said."

Charlotte nodded. "I understand. You are right. Just let her go."

Emily nodded and then remembered. "Except I have a major

diplomatic dinner on Thursday and now have no cook — just when I wanted to spend all my time going to hospitals. I don't want to spend the next three days preparing for this dinner, and I doubt very much I could even bring it off!" She started to wonder if it was too late to cancel, or if the maids could handle the cooking.

"Our old cook might be able to help," Charlotte ventured.

"Your old cook?"

"Jasha. She was a Polish forced labourer, who came to Walmsdorf during the war to cook for our Polish farm workers. She laughed so much and the scents from her cooking were so good that we asked her to cook for us too."

"But why is she here? Why didn't she return home at the end of the war?"

Charlotte shook her head sadly, "Because she has no home. The Soviets took it after they killed her husband and son. She was even more afraid of the Red Army than we were and pressed us to flee for months before we were ready. Naturally, she came with us when my father finally gave in. Now she works for an American family in Zehlendorf, but they are leaving at the end of next month and she will need a new job."

"The dinner is *this* Thursday," Emily countered fatalistically.

"She could probably get the evening off and work for you that one night. Then if you like each other, you could arrange to hire her full-time." Charlotte suggested hopefully.

That sounded much better than trying to manage everything herself, Emily conceded. "Could you arrange that?"

"If I may use your telephone," Charlotte answered with a slight smile.

"Yes, then we must finally get to work on translating this questionnaire and making our first appointments."

Investment Capital
Berlin
Wednesday, 4 February 1948

Clatter, banging, heavy breathing and cursing in the stairway drew Jakob Liebherr out of his apartment. Stepping out onto the landing, he leaned over the railing to look down the stairs. At the half-landing between the second and third floors, the three young men who lived in the apartment below him were huffing and puffing as they manhandled a large object up the stairs. Its weight was obvious from the way they strained and set the object down every few steps. Liebherr leaned farther over the railing, trying to figure out what on earth it was. It looked like a large refrigerator, not a small unit for domestic use but an industrial refrigerator.

His curiosity piqued, he descended the stairs and reached the landing just as the young men heaved the object up the last three steps. "My, my!" Liebherr affected a jovial tone. "What have you got there, Herr Meyer?"

All three young men looked over at Liebherr, and the eldest, who Liebherr had noted giving orders to the others, frowned at him. Then he straightened and pushed his long, dark hair off his brow with the back of his arm. Face to face like this, Liebherr sensed a strong, almost magnetic willpower bottled up in a body worn beyond its age. The young man's eyes were ringed with wrinkles. "It's just a refrigerator." He tried to make it sound innocuous.

"Indeed! I should say it is! And by far the largest refrigerator I've seen in years!" Liebherr exclaimed as he looked over the object with apparent interest. "In fact, I'd say that is the kind of refrigerator used in butcher shops," Liebherr simulated cheerful curiosity as he walked around it, pretending not to see the wary looks the young men were exchanging. "What kind of use do you have for something like this?" His tone remained light and nosy rather than interrogative.

"Oh, we have to take what we can find these days, don't we?" The tall blond youth at the far end of the refrigerator answered, tossing a charming grin at Liebherr.

"Yes, this was such a bargain, we couldn't resist it." The nervous acne-faced youth added with a titter.

"Hm. Maybe not such a good deal as you think," Liebherr noted like a kindly uncle, pointing to the electrical connections that had been torn out. The cord was frayed, exposing broken wiring and there was no plug. "You're going to have to get that repaired before you can use it," Liebherr concluded. "Which is just as well, since I doubt we have a socket anywhere in the entire house that could handle the power on something like this."

"It's not for here," the dark-haired ringleader hastened to explain. "We're just storing it until we can get it repaired and then it will go to my aunt in Neuruppin. She's got dairy cows and wants to start making cheese. She needs a large refrigerator."

"Ah," Liebherr nodded in feigned sympathy. Then smiling and nodding at the young men, he took his leave, "Well then, good day, Herr Mueller, Herr Schulz, Herr Braun."

Liebherr started up the stairs, while the three young men unlocked the door to their apartment and, grunting and cursing, attempted to shove the oversized refrigerator across the landing and into the apartment. As soon as one of them left the door to help lift the refrigerator, however, the door fell shut. Spotting his opportunity, Liebherr hastened back down the stairs to offer, "I'll hold the door for you while you get the refrigerator inside."

"We don't need—" The leader started to protest.

"It's no trouble at all!" Liebherr overruled him cheerfully, grabbing the door and slipping past the young man to hold it open from inside the corridor. He could hear angry whispering on the landing, but then with a command, the three men bent their backs to the refrigerator again. Meanwhile, Liebherr's gaze ranged as far into the apartment as possible, certain that he was not going to be allowed to remain long. The most obvious thing was that the interconnected rooms along the front of the building were all crammed with furnishings to the point of being more a warehouse than an apartment. Notably, the objects were not haphazardly dumped. Lamps were stacked in one corner, radios lined up along another wall, chairs were crammed beside a tower of tables, and paintings stood upright like folders in a filing cabinet.

When the refrigerator was far enough inside the door to keep it open, Liebherr let go of the door and wandered deeper into the apartment.

"Where are you going?" An angry voice called after him.

"Oh, just curious," Liebherr called over his shoulder as he drifted to the farthest room despite continued protests in rising volume. Before they could get truly angry, he returned to the door; he'd seen enough. One bedroom was filled with clothing, and in the other, the three narrow beds were almost lost among piles of neatly folded blankets, sheets, tablecloths, dishcloths, and boxed glasses. On the wall was a photo of Meyer/Muller and Schultz in long beards and dirty navy uniforms being draped with flower wreaths on a quay somewhere.

"What are you snooping around for?" The nervous, acne-faced man snapped at Liebherr as he re-joined the trio.

"I'm not snooping," Liebherr insisted calmly. Looking the dark-haired young man in the eye, he announced, "I'm a member of the City Council, and I'm working on a report about employment — or rather unemployment — in Kreuzberg. Could you describe the nature of your business and tell me your turnover, number of employees and wage rates?"

The young man, whom he had just addressed variously as Herr Meyer and Herr Mueller, answered in a staccato voice. "Our business is informal. It's just the three of us, and we can't afford to pay ourselves — much less anyone else. We just share out whatever we earn. Does that answer your questions?"

"Partially. What is the nature of your business?"

"We're a cleaning company," the blond youth answered straight-faced.

Liebherr raised his eyebrows eloquently in answer, and the ring leader replied, "When the police kidnap people, they bustle them out with what they can carry in one suitcase -- just as in the case of Herr Dr Hofmeier last week. The Ivans take whatever baubles attract them, but they rarely take clothes or furnishings. We just clean up a little."

"I see," Liebherr nodded, looking around again. Technically, of course, that was theft but with the Soviets stealing whole factories, their soldiers stealing anything that struck their fancy, and the Western allies turning a blind eye to both, who could blame Germans for joining the party? Stealing from the deported didn't hurt anyone, Liebherr supposed. That was the unspoken code of it all, that it was all right to cheat the Allies and each other as long as the destitute didn't get hurt any further.

"You seem to have a great deal of inventory. Doesn't that bind an excessive amount of liquidity?"

"Look, out there," Meyer/Mueller gestured with his head vaguely in the direction of a window. "People are selling silver, porcelain and Persian carpets for a ham or a barrel of pickled herring. If we sold this stuff on today's market, we'd be cheating ourselves. What you see here is our investment capital. We expect to make a return on it sometime in the future."

"After the Amis introduce a real currency, for example," the blond suggested.

Liebherr looked over at him and their eyes locked. No, these weren't ordinary street urchins, pickpockets, and petty criminals. At least Meyer/Mueller and Schulz weren't. "So how do you meet your daily expenses?"

"What business is that of yours?" the nervous Herr Braun lashed out, but Mueller/Meyer silenced him with a flick of his wrist and turning to Schulz ordered, "Go ahead. Show him."

Herr Schulz opened the kitchen door with a wary expression, and Liebherr looked inside. It took him a moment to figure out what the contraption stretching across the entire counter was, and then things fell into place. With the delight of understanding, he exclaimed: "A still! You're brewing schnapps!"

"Yes, would you like to try it?" Meyer/Mueller asked deadpan.

"God forbid! Anything that comes out of that still is likely to make a man blind sooner or later! What is the basis — Oh, I see. Potatoes. And your best customers are our dear friends the Ivans."

The three men nodded slowly, but by varying degrees, they were also starting to smile. Mueller/Meyer undertook the explanation. "Farmers know their bargaining power, and they won't exchange food for anything they don't want. Most of them have enough Meissen porcelain and Bohemian glass to feed the cows on it! They aren't willing to take any more. They want practical things. We got that refrigerator for a farmer with some illegal pigs."

"Yes, that makes sense. If he must slaughter unexpectedly, he needs to be able to keep the carcass cool — even in the summer. Understandable." Liebherr nodded thoughtfully. The network of illegal activities was amazingly comprehensive and complex. If he hadn't seen it with his own eyes, he would not have believed a barter economy could function as efficiently as it did. It was almost like a parallel universe to the official economy of rations and worthless paper currency. In many ways, it was a more optimistic world, Liebherr reflected, if only because it was inhabited by people who weren't starving, freezing, or prostituting themselves.

"Anything else?" Meyer/Mueller asked with controlled impatience.

"What about the clothing? That can't be particularly valuable. It will get moth-eaten or go out of fashion, while half the city wanders around in rags. Why not donate it to the poor?"

There was a moment of stunned silence as Schulz and Braun looked at Meyer/Mueller. His eyes met Liebherr's. After what seemed like an eternity, he answered, "You'd be surprised. Good clothes are one of the few things farmers still need. But I'll think about it."

"Thank you."

"Anything else?"

"Not really," Liebherr admitted, "but I am curious. You don't sound like Berliners. Where do you come from? What did you do before?"

"Before what? Before the capitulation, we were all good Germans."

"Meaning you were Nazis," Liebherr concluded.

"Is that how you define good Germans, Herr Liebherr?" Meyer/Mueller shot back, and it was not a joke.

Liebherr knew when he'd been bested, and he tipped his head in salute. "Your score, but would you mind clearing up one last, little thing?" The young man waited. "I called you Herr Meyer once and Herr Mueller the other time. You reacted to both. Just which is it? Meyer or Mueller?"

"Does it matter what our names are?"

"No, not really," Herr Liebherr admitted disarmingly, and with a smile, he shook hands with each of the young men in turn, "It was a pleasure meeting you all." He squeezed his way past the refrigerator and stepped out onto the landing.

Liebherr was half back to his apartment when Herr Mueller/Meyer called after him. "Where should I leave the clothes I decide to donate to the poor?"

With a smile, Liebherr turned back and met the young man's eyes. "Thank you, *Herr Kapitaenleutnant!*"

The other two men recoiled at the use of his rank, but Herr Meyer/Mueller only smiled cynically and asked, "Oh, did you see the photograph?"

Liebherr nodded. "You can drop the clothing off at my apartment anytime I'm home. I will see it gets to the Red Cross or the Salvation Army."

"Good," Mueller/Meyer answered, and when their eyes met Liebherr thought he saw a trace of respect in those weathered eyes. Pleased with what he had learned, and optimistic about receiving clothes for the poor, Liebherr continued up the stairs.

Creatures of the Night
Berlin
Friday, 6 February 1948

Kathleen and Lionel had repeated their afternoon outing to Tegel on the previous Sunday, but as the next weekend approached the Major called to ask if she could meet him Friday night instead "without Hope." Kathleen hesitated, but Lionel hinted that he had something special planned. She checked with Annie and Violet, and when they assured her it would be no imposition to have Hope for dinner and let her sleep in their apartment, she agreed.

Lionel advised her to wear a cocktail dress, but she didn't own one. She also only had a single pair of high-heeled shoes. Most awkward was the lack of an evening coat. She had no choice but to wear her WAAF greatcoat, but Lionel was understanding. "I don't expect anyone mentioned Berlin had much nightlife," he remarked with a grin as he helped her into his car.

It was the first time they'd been out at night, and as he drove through the poorly lit streets, Kathleen began to feel slightly unsafe. He drove a little too fast for comfort, but then again, there was little traffic. She told herself his daring driving added to the excitement of being alone with him.

"You aren't opposed to doing something a little off-limits, are you?" he asked with a crooked smile and a sideways glance, as they accelerated along the Heerstrasse.

Kathleen squirmed. She didn't relish putting a black up with the WingCo. That said, Wing Commander Priestman was neither a prude nor a hypocrite. He did not appear to have a double standard: one for men and one for women. He expected his personnel to do credit to their uniform when they were wearing it, and to be discrete when they were not. She would have preferred not to do anything he might take a dim view of, yet the look in Lionel's eyes also warned her that he was interested in a little adventure. She would spoil everything if she was her normal, tame self. Taking a hold of her courage, she declared gamely, "No, not if you aren't. You're in a more delicate position."

"Yes, Robertson can be quite the bore. Fortunately, he left for the Zone this morning and will be away all weekend." Lionel had never looked more dashing than now, with his cap set low and the light from the occasional streetlight gleaming on the polished leather strap cutting diagonally across his chest.

Conscious of her growing attraction for him, Kathleen commented, "Ah, while the cat's away...."

"Exactly." He grinned at her.

Lionel was racing down a wide avenue past the tall, metallic "Funkturm" — a modest Teutonic version of the Eifel Tower which served as Berlin's main radio transmission tower. They crossed under some railway tracks and suddenly seemed to become lost among the ruins as Lionel slowed the pace to twist and turn on narrow, darkened streets. Ahead of them, a train clacked past on raised tracks, the interior lit eerily by dim blue lights. They passed under the tracks via a short tunnel and emerged on the other side.

Despite her best intentions, Kathleen's apprehension was growing. What had she got herself into? She hardly knew Lionel. Yes, he was an officer of the crown and all that, but... She stopped herself. She was acting like some silly, sheltered girl. She was nearly thirty and widowed. It was time to be more adventurous. But there were no streetlights and the sidewalks seemed empty — until shadowy figures abruptly loomed up out of nowhere only to disappear again just as suddenly. Lionel was leaning forward looking for something, swearing steadily under his breath.

Finally, he exclaimed. "Here we are!" He pulled the car over, put on the handbrake and cut the ignition. Kathleen looked around bewildered. She could see nothing in the darkness except the cobblestone street and empty sidewalks lined by broken buildings.

Lionel laughed in apparent delight at her perplexity. He got out and came around to open her door, taking her elbow to walk back a dozen yards to a half-demolished façade. He pushed the doorbell and a buzzing sound went off inside. He let up, pushed again and again rapidly, and then added a long, last buzz.

Instantly the door cracked open, and a head poked out. "*Wie bitte?*"

"I'm here to see Charles," Lionel answered.

"*Allein?*"

"With my lady friend."

The door opened just enough to admit them one after another. Lionel indicated Kathleen should go first. Consciously overcoming her qualms, she slipped inside. Lionel followed and put his arm around her waist as he came abreast of her. It was a reassuring gesture and suggested he sensed how anxious she felt.

They found themselves in what had once been an elegant entryway, but the stairs leading to the second floor ended with a view of the night sky. The upper stories were no more. The man led them down a dark hall to a door that opened on stairs down to the cellar. "I'll go first," Lionel offered, stepping in front of her but taking hold of her hand in his firm, warm grip.

As they descended, her eyes adjusted to the darkness and the dampened sound of voices, laughter and music wafted toward them. At the foot of the stairs, a heavy, dark curtain confronted them, but Lionel pushed it aside to reveal a room that stretched under three or four houses. It was crammed with tables lit by hurricane lamps and surrounded by merrymakers. Waiters in tails rushed back and forth between the tables. Smoke clouded the upper reaches of the room, swirling and billowing. On a wooden platform in an alcove, a four-piece brass band played jazz. At the far end, another "stage" was occupied by women wearing lacy underwear, fishnet stockings and high-heeled shoes. They stamped and kicked in time to the music.

The head waiter intercepted them. "You have a reservation, sir?"

"Blimpson," Lionel said.

"Right this way, sir." Weaving around the clumps of laughing, smoking, flirting customers, he led them to a tiny circular table with two narrow, straight-backed chairs between the band and the stage. The white linen was already soiled with red wine and the ashtray was full to overflowing. The waiter deftly emptied the latter into a leather satchel tied to his coat and whisked away the former. Almost before Kathleen could grasp what had happened, a fresh tablecloth had been spread and the ashtray returned empty. "Your waiter will take your order immediately, sir," the magician said with a bow before he disappeared.

Lionel turned and offered to take Kathleen's coat, explaining in a murmur, "They collect all the cigarette stubs and roll new cigarettes with the tobacco. If you want to tip the waiter particularly well, just smoke more."

"Yes, of course," she felt stupid for having stared at the waiter as he emptied the ashtray.

Lionel removed his silver cigarette case from his breast pocket and flipped it open to offer her one. Feeling daring, she accepted. She had taken up smoking in the war, and despite several attempts to stop since, she still smoked now and again. She just hadn't done it in the presence of a man she fancied before.

Lionel lit her cigarette and then his own. "What do you think?"

Kathleen looked around more consciously. She directed her attention to the physical environment first. The walls were hung with curtains of some sort to cover the shattered plaster and the exposed bricks. The floor was uncovered concrete. Pipes and wiring wandered over the ceiling fully exposed. That was a commentary on the state of the economy, she supposed, but she couldn't blame the Berliners for trying to have fun regardless.

Turning her attention to the customers, the clientele consisted mostly of British, American and French soldiers accompanied by beautiful young women. Like every nightclub she'd ever visited, everyone seemed to be having a good time — on the surface. They were talking, laughing, smoking, drinking, flirting, and snogging. A closer look revealed that between the soldiers and their girls, other couples sat and there was something odd about them. At the nearest table, the woman was very heavily made up and her skin had large pores.... Kathleen felt a jolt of shock as she realized "she" was a man. She looked over at Lionel questioningly.

He burst out laughing, leaned closer and murmured. "Don't worry. They won't hurt you."

"No, no, of course not," Kathleen agreed embarrassed by her nervousness. She admonished herself that her discomfort with transvestites was silly and unsophisticated. She ought to be beyond that. Anxious to dispel an impression of provinciality, Kathleen remarked, "Aside from the unexpected venue — and some of the customers — it seems like any other nightclub I've seen. Why is it off-limits?"

"Well," Lionel leaned forward again, "let's just say that most of the things on sale here aren't entirely legal. Now, what would you like to drink?" The waiter had appeared with a bow.

Kathleen asked for a gin and tonic.

The music and dancing came to a halt to the sound of scattered applause. The dancers filed off the stage and the band took up a dance tune. From many tables, couples got up to crowd the little stage. A man pressed up against the table as if to let someone else pass, but when the other was gone, he opened his coat revealing a collection of items hanging from the inside. "Can I interest you in anything, sir? Madam?"

Kathleen glanced at Lionel. He simply stubbed out his cigarette and removed his case to get another. To the man looming over her, she shook her head vigorously without looking at what he was selling. She'd glimpsed only what looked like a pearl bracelet, a pair of gold earrings, and more bizarrely, a pair of scissors, a gold pen, and a typewriter ribbon."

"Is typewriter ribbon a scarcity here?" She asked Lionel.

He shrugged. "The only thing of which there is no scarcity in this city is, you'll pardon my bluntness, female flesh. Otherwise, this city is a giant flea market: one man's trash is another's treasure."

The next man who sidled up to their table didn't open his coat and didn't look at them. Instead, with his gaze directed at the far side of the room he muttered out of the side of his mouth. "Need a fix?"

"No, and tell your pals to stay away," Lionel told him brusquely. As he scuttled away, Lionel explained to Kathleen, "With the currency useless, everyone in Berlin is forced to use the black market, but drug dealers are the pawns of criminal gangs with big bosses from the underworld."

Kathleen looked over to try to catch a glimpse of the drug dealer, but he'd already disappeared into the background.

Kathleen and Lionel danced a little, but the dance floor was small and crowded. After being jostled and stomped on multiple times, they mutually agreed they weren't having much fun and returned to their table to order another round of drinks. Meanwhile, around them, the other couples were becoming drunker, their voices louder, the men bolder. Kathleen noticed the sergeant at the next table was openly fondling his girl's breasts. The girl took no notice of his hands as she blew her cigarette smoke toward the ceiling. She couldn't care less who was touching her or where, Kathleen thought with a shiver, and then looked down at her watch. It was nearing midnight.

Lionel balanced his chair on its back legs, and through the haze of the cigarette smoke considered her. "Why do I get the feeling you are not enjoying yourself?"

"Because I'm not," Kathleen retorted. "Did you seriously think I would?"

"Some women get a thrill out of places like this," Lionel defended himself.

"They must be bored; I get my excitement from my job. I don't need artificial stimulus like this." She wondered indignantly if he had seriously expected her to like it here.

The thought was hardly formed before he disarmed her with a charming smile and the announcement, "I'm glad you don't."

He turned, caught the waiter's eye and wrote with his finger on the palm of his other hand to indicate they wanted their bill. The waiter took a long time to come, but when at last he approached, Lionel took a last, long drag on his cigarette and stamped it out half unsmoked. "That" He indicated his unfinished cigarette, "represents 25% of the waiter's earnings for the night. They get two cigarettes for an eight-hour shift that lasts until six am."

"That's horrible!" Kathleen was shocked.

"Some people find the power it gives us intoxicating," Lionel answered, gesturing towards the other Allied guests with his head.

"And the girls?" Kathleen pressed him. "What do they get for an evening — that lasts to six?"

"I wouldn't know, but I've been told it's five cigarettes." Lionel didn't look at her as he answered. Instead, he turned away to retrieve her coat from the coat rack, ending the conversation.

As he helped her into her coat, Kathleen felt a new kind of unease. She couldn't convince herself that Lionel was pleased with her reaction. She sensed his disappointment. She had turned out to be unsophisticated and dull rather than adventurous and risqué. So, where did the evening leave them? Could they go back to tame afternoon teas in Tegel? And what about Hope, who had so obviously liked Lionel and kept hinting that he'd make an ideal "new Daddy"?

"Watering the Horses"
Berlin
Friday, 13 February 1948

Christian had not planned on staying in Berlin for so long. Part of him felt guilty for putting off his return since his wife asked when he would be back in every letter she wrote. Yet Berlin had a hold on him. For one thing, Charlotte needed him much more than his French wife, who was his best friend's widow rather than the woman he loved. Perhaps more compelling was the sense that he wasn't born to be a farmer. Being in Berlin reminded him of how provincial, boring and strait-laced Altdorf was. Berlin, ravaged as it was, still had a spark of life in it. It still had an indefinable cheeky quality that defied defeat — not on the surface, perhaps, but behind the grim façades and underneath the ruins.

Rather than helping his eminently competent mother on the family estate, Christian convinced himself that he could benefit the family fortunes better by cultivating a network of purchasers for their wine. To his surprise, he had discovered a remarkably resilient market for good wine ranging from restaurants and nightclubs catering to the cash-rich, arrogant and bored occupation troops to scarce but not insignificant numbers of wealthy private individuals.

It was one of the latter that Christian was trying to contact today, based on a tip he'd received two days earlier. He'd rebottled his wine, glued on the labels his mother had designed and printed, and resealed the bottles with old corks. With a sample bottle in his leather briefcase, the took the S-Bahn to Nicholassee.

At the S-Bahn station, he hired a horse-drawn taxi and gave the driver the address on Schwanenwerder. As they set off, he wound his woollen scarf closer and clutched his coat shut. Although the distance was not great, it was bitterly cold in the open air. On the other hand, the air here wasn't laden with brown-coal smoke as in Kreuzberg, and the bucolic clopping of the horse's hooves triggered memories of happier times. When he caught glimpses of the Grosser Wannsee, he was reminded of hot summer days when he and his older brother Philipp had gone swimming in the warm, brown lake waters. In retrospect, his childhood had been idyllic, and a soft melancholy enveloped him as he reflected that he'd probably never be able to offer anything similar to his children -- if he ever had any.

They crossed the narrow isthmus connecting the Schwanenwerder peninsula to the mainland and continued around almost to where the road turned back. The driver stopped before a once-luxurious house with an overgrown garden and some boarded-up windows on the top floor. Christian climbed down, took his leather case, and asked the driver to wait. As he made his way up the narrow brick walkway to the door, the driver put a blanket over his horse before settling down under a fleece to snooze while he waited.

Christian rang the front bell and a butler with short, dark hair over a squarish, hostile face greeted him. "What do you want?" He barked like a drill sergeant. Even five years after he'd been shot down, Christian knew instantly and instinctively that this man was SS.

"I'm Christian Freiherr von Feldburg, and I have an appointment with Herr Dr Friedebach."

The butler's countenance transformed instantly. Without a smile, he became subservient, clicking his heels together and bowing stiffly before stepping back to admit Christian. He closed and locked the door, and then with an "allow me, Herr Baron," he invited his visitor into the house. Christian's eyes scanned his surroundings attentively. It was easy to tell that this had once been an elegant house, and although it was less badly damaged than his own on the Maybach Ufer, something about it didn't seem right. It was a moment before he concluded it was the furnishings. They were either too large or too small for the space in which they had been carelessly shoved. Almost all were damaged — deep scratches disfigured wood surfaces that should have gleamed like satin; handles had been torn off leaving squares of broken, unfinished raw wood; here and there, legs were missing and replaced by stacks of bricks.

"Our Russian friends do not know how to treat good furnishings," a lilting Austrian voice broke in on his thoughts.

Christian turned to face a man with short black hair, a thin moustache and reading glasses. The host held out his hand. "Freiherr von Feldburg, I presume. You come recommended."

Christian shook hands, overcoming an irrational inner distaste by reminding himself that business was business. "You too, Herr Dr Friedebach. I was told you were a connoisseur of fine wines and frustrated by the offerings currently available in Berlin."

Friedebach snorted in what might have been either assent or dissent. "Come with me," he ordered and led deeper into the house. The condition of the furnishings improved noticeably — as if the damaged things were part of a façade.

They ended up in a large sunny room with a wide window offering a vista across a large, overgrown lawn half lost in old, crusty snow. This stretched gently down to the banks of the Wannsee. At the shore, tall weeds stuck up through a thin sheet of ice that clung to the shallows. Beyond the ruffled grey water of the wider lake, one could see boathouses strung along the far shore and hints of villas half lost in trees: Kladow. "Nice view," Christian remarked.

"It is, isn't it?" His host answered emotionlessly and indicated an armed chair before an exquisite, inlaid coffee table that reminded Christian of one they'd has in the Berlin apartment long ago.

"Take off your coat, if you like," his host suggested, drawing attention to the fact that the room was well-heated — a rarity for German homes in occupied Berlin. "Cigarette?" Friedebach offered, holding out a silver case with a coat of arms on it.

"Thank you," Christian leaned forward to help himself. He'd seen that coat-of-arms before, he thought, but couldn't place it.

Friedebach offered a light. Same coat of arms on the lighter.

Christian breathed in and the cigarette glowed.

"So, tell me about your wine."

"It is produced on our family estate in Altdorf, Franken."

"American Zone, then."

"Yes."

"How do you propose to get it across the Soviet Zone?"

"By train, of course. I can apply for a commercial license from the Americans."

Friedebach smiled cynically, "You may find that more difficult than you think, but it's not my problem. Let me try a sample."

"Of course. It's a light, table wine," Christian explained, as he reached down toward his leather case, "quite dry and crisp. A typical Franken." The wine was very good, but Christian thought it was better to understate his product to profit from the ensuing surprise.

Friedebach crossed to a sideboard to get some glasses, while Christian extracted the cork from the bottle. As he finished, he glanced over his shoulder to see where Friedebach was.

His breath caught in his throat.

Over the sideboard from which Friedebach was removing some crystal wine glasses hung a large, post-impressionist oil painting showing a Havel landscape with soft, blue water in the foreground. At the centre of the painting, two fine-boned, willowy, riding horses stretched out their necks to drink while their riders stood dismounted beside them. The riders were two young men in open-necked, white shirts, beige riding breeches and black boots. One of the riders, a handsome blond youth, looked straight at the observer with a faint yet self-confident smile on his lips; the other was dark, and his hair fell over his brow as he looked thoughtfully down at his horse.

Christian could neither move nor breathe.

Friedebach straightened and turned back towards him. He noticed the direction of Christian's gaze, and remarked, "Nice painting, isn't it?"

Christian knew he must control himself. He looked away and forced himself to focus on the lovely crystal glasses Friedebach set down on the table. Then letting out his breath slowly so Friedebach would not notice he had been holding it, he remarked as casually as he could, "Very nice indeed. Where did you get it?"

"Oh," Friedebach waved his hand vaguely. "You know how it was in '45. The Russians stole everything and anything. When I was given this house, it was completely plundered. I didn't even have a bed to sleep in or a toilet to sit on. I complained to the SMAD. They had allotted it to me, after all; I felt they had a duty to make it liveable. A few days later they brought over several truckloads of furnishings dumped on top of each other like rubbish. Everything must have been stolen from somewhere else. Much was too badly damaged to be used, but some things were quite astonishing — like that painting. Why?"

"Do you know what the painting is?" Christian asked cautiously.

"Not really. Should I?"

Christian shrugged. "I suppose not, but I'm surprised *you* like it. It's by a Jewish artist. Max Liebermann."

"Really?" Friedebach's eyebrows went up and he seemed to take a new interest in the painting. Then he asked sceptically, "You're sure? It's not what I would have expected of Jewish art." A frown hovered around his eyebrows, and he looked more critically at his visitor.

"I'm absolutely sure what it is," Christian answered with a touch too much steel in his voice.

Friedebach's expression went from sceptical to suspicious. "How do you know?"

"Oh," Christian gestured vaguely, "Once upon a time before the war and before I served the Fatherland, I moved in certain circles where art was appreciated. You may have forgotten, but Liebermann was once the President of the *Preussiche Akademie der Kuenste*; his paintings were popular among the upper classes."

"Before the Fuehrer came to power and threw him out of the Akademie," Friedebach concluded.

"Exactly. That painting was one of his last works. Painted when he was technically forbidden from working. It was a private commission and that's why it's not well known."

"So how do you know so much about it?" Friedebach pressed him.

"I knew the man who commissioned it. If you don't believe me, look at the back sometime. The title of the piece is "Watering the Horses," and it was painted by Liebermann in 1934." Conscious that if they discussed the painting much longer he might explode, Christian changed the subject. "Time to taste the wine."

Friedebach sat down and waited while Christian poured his wine into one of the small glasses and handed it over.

Friedebach sipped it and held it in his mouth to taste it thoroughly before swallowing. "Not as bad as I expected," he remarked condescendingly. Christian didn't bother responding. He knew the quality of his wine. He smiled cynically and waited. Friedebach took a second sip and then shook his head. "It is too dry for my taste, I'm afraid." He set the glass down again.

Christian shrugged. "Well, tastes differ." He took the cork, re-inserted it in the bottle and prepared to pack the bottle away in his briefcase again.

Friedebach leaned back in his chair and shook his head bemused. "I hope you were a better fighter pilot than salesman, Feldburg. Aren't you going to try to change my mind?"

"No. Why should I? I don't need your business. I can find other customers, who *do* recognize quality wine when they taste it." The bottle was back in his case. Christian stood and reached for his coat.

Friedebach watched, assessing him with sharp suspicious eyes, but Christian managed to maintain a façade of perfect indifference. He held out his hand. "No need to see me out. I can find my way. Have a good day, Herr Dr Friedebach."

By the time he reached the apartment on the Maybach Ufer, Christian was both furious and fractious. He pounded on Theo Pfalz's door. Startled, the concierge opened. "Is something the matter, Herr Baron?"

"What was the name of the SD man who took over the family apartment after my brother shot himself?"

"Standartenfuehrer Theirack, Herr Baron. Why?"

Christian made a distracted gesture. "I just discovered one of my father's paintings in a house on the Schwanenwerder. I'm trying to understand how it got there."

"It was probably stolen by the Ivans," Theo suggested.

"But you said this Theirack had all the valuable things from the family apartment packed and taken away *before* the Russians got here," Christian reminded him.

Theo shrugged. "Certainly, they were taken from Berlin, but who knows how far they got before the Reds caught up with them? Maybe no farther than Potsdam. Maybe, Brandenburg, Magdeburg or anywhere else before the Zonal border." Although what Theo said made perfect sense, irrationally Christian believed that "Friedebach" was himself the thief.

He nodded to Theo and turned away. In the entryway, he pulled a small, leather address book from the inside breast pocket of his blazer. He found the number he was looking for and picked up the phone in the foyer. Eventually, he was connected with his brother's widow, Alexandra, who now worked for the prosecution at the ongoing secondary war crimes trials.

"Alix? It's Christian."

"Christian! Where did you come from? What are you doing here?"

"I'm in Berlin, Alix. I'm calling because — because — Do you remember the large painting that used to hang in the dining room? *Watering the Horses* by Max Liebermann."

"Yes, of course. It was one of my favourite —"

"Alix, I just saw it in the home of a certain Juergen Friedebach. The man is allegedly one of the managers of a chemical or pharmaceutical plant in Leuna, but there's something fishy about him."

"He certainly has no right to that painting!"

"No, but I swear it is more than that."

"How did he say he got it?"

"From the Russians. He claims the Russians allocated the house to him before the Americans arrived. He's certainly still protected by someone for some reason. Can you see what you can find out about him?"

"Of course. What did you say his name was again?"

"Juergen Friedebach, Dr Juergen Friedebach, and he has an Austrian accent. He also had a cigarette case and lighter with a coat of arms that rang a bell. Of course, they could be stolen goods too, and yet something about him.... Forgive my language, but he stinks of brown shit, and it's making me sick."

"I'll call back as soon as I have anything. Is everything else all right? Your mother seemed distressed that you hadn't returned to Altdorf."

"If you talk to her, tell her I have very good reasons for remaining here, but I don't want to talk about them from a telephone in a foyer or write anything in a letter. She must trust me."

"Of course. I'll tell her. Take care of yourself, Christian."

"Nothing's going to happen to me. Goodbye for — no, wait! I just remembered! The coat-of-arms — they're the Aggstein arms."

"Aggstein? Should I recognise the name?"

"Not necessarily, but Theresa used to go on about a certain Max von Aggstein. He helped her husband get his factories in Warsaw, remember? Philipp met him and instantly hated him! He was a very senior in the *Deutsche Ausruestungswerke GmbH*, the Economic SS."

"I know, Christian," Alix reminded him gently but pointedly. She was the one drowning in the mountains of evidence against the SS's many business activities. "I'll see what I can find out about both Juergen

Friedebach and Max von Aggstein."

"You're an angel, Alix. Did I ever tell you—"

"At least one hundred times. Take care of yourself, Christian."

When Charlotte returned, Christian was pacing the apartment hallway in agitation. "What's the matter, Christian?" She asked alarmed. "Don't tell me you have to leave suddenly?" The question laid bare her constant fear of being left unprotected.

He gave her a short but hardy hug to reassure her, but he was too agitated to convey comfort. Instead, he announced, "No, I think I'm going to have to stay longer than ever. Let's talk where it's warm." He opened the door to the kitchen, and they sat down opposite one another. Charlotte looked at him expectantly, alarm over his behaviour written all over her face.

"Charlotte, today I went to the house of one of these odious parasites who have discovered how to manipulate the current situation to their advantage. I knew it wasn't going to be pleasant, but I'd been tipped off that the man might be willing to place a large wine order. I told myself that I don't need to *like* my customers, only the colour of their money. But I was still — I don't know how to say this."

"What?"

"Hanging in his salon was the Lieberman painting that my father commissioned of Philipp and me in 1934."

"The one that used to hang in the dining room of your apartment downstairs?" Charlotte remembered at once, her face lighting up at the memory of the lovely painting and the happier times that went with it.

"Charlotte! My brother —" Christian jumped to his feet and turned away.

Charlotte covered her mouth with her hand in distress and waited. When he spoke again, his voice was strained with the effort to hold back his tears. "It's the most beautiful picture of Philipp anyone ever made. All the other pictures we have are mere snapshots — hasty, often blurred, awkward or stiff, rarely expressive. And always in uniform. Even his wedding photos are in a damn uniform with the swastika on it! Liebermann's painting, on the other hand, captures his essence a hundred times better. Although it was done before the whole horror began, although he's still young and unravaged, it depicts his inner soul. I'm smiling at the artist like the naïve fool I was, but Philipp is looking down, his expression pensive, while he gently caresses the withers of his horse. Philipp not only saw what was coming, he cared about what it would do to all of us — right down to the innocent horses. It was the inhumanity of the regime — not the geopolitical consequences, not the economics, much less the lost war, as the idiot Americans think -- that appalled him! The *inhumanity* of the regime drove him to treason, and it was to save others that he killed himself rather than risk betraying their names to the Gestapo under torture."

Charlotte nodded mutely, sadly.

"Charlotte!" There was an urgency in Christian's voice that made her look up at him.

He met her eyes. "I don't think you, as a Protestant, fully understand what a sacrifice that was. Philipp was a devout Catholic. By taking his own life, he condemned his soul as well as his body." He paused. "I pray every day that God will forgive him because he did it for the right reasons, and *I — want — that — painting!*"

The intensity of his emotions frightened Charlotte. All she could do was nod again.

"If the painting had been destroyed that would have been different, but now that I have found it, I'm not going to let some thief — who doesn't even know who Philipp was — hang it in his stolen salon!"

Charlotte shook her head helplessly and whispered, "Of course not, Christian." Inwardly, she was grateful. It meant he wasn't going to leave her any time soon.

Chapter Seven
Friends True and False

Empty Promises
Leeds, England
Monday, 16 February 1948

The famous engineer Barnes Wallis had met Kit Moran while Kit was still flying with 617 Squadron and had offered to help him get a job after the war. Although Kit had opted for university instead, Wallis had told him to keep in touch. With the money his father had given them rapidly running out, Georgina unemployed and the baby due in April, Kit thought it was time to contact Wallis and get his advice about job opportunities.

"Flight Lieutenant Moran?" the engineer asked in an enthusiastic voice when Kit finally got through to him after several attempts. "It's been a long time! Good to hear from you."

"I'm glad you can remember me, sir."

"Of course, I remember you! I think of you — and the others from 617 — often."

"Mr Wallis, I'm calling because I've almost completed my degree. I have only one more semester and should be sitting for my final exams in June. I'll be ready to start work in July."

"Oh, well done! Time certainly does fly." There was an awkward pause and then Wallis said, "You wanted to remind me of my promise to help you get started in engineering."

It wasn't a question. Wallis clearly remembered his promise, but something in his voice warned Kit that he was unhappy with the situation. Kit tried to stay positive. "Yes, that's right. I thought maybe we could meet to discuss possible openings at Vickers or other options you might recommend?"

"I'd like to meet up with you, Moran, and hear how you are doing, but — this is very embarrassing — it's just that I wouldn't want you to come all the way down here with false expectations. You see," he sighed audibly, "the government contracts have all dried up. Civil aviation is expanding, of course, but orders for new aircraft are not coming at a rate to make up for the lost military contracts. There are too many serviceable old aircraft still about. Here at Vickers we may well be forced to lay off some of our staff, including engineering staff. As far as I know, the situation is the same at all British aviation companies."

A cold shiver ran down Kit's spine. He hadn't expected that. He had not dreamed that Vickers might be laying off workers. But he had a child to consider now and couldn't just take no for an answer. "But what about the new research facility, sir, the one in Weymouth that you're working at now?"

"Oh, you heard about my experiments with supersonic flight and variable-sweep aircraft?" Wallis sounded pleased. "It is very promising work. I'd like to get you involved with it at some point. I'm sure there will be a future in it. It's just — you see, it's still very much in the experimental stage. Which means, unfortunately, that at the moment we're looking more for mathematicians than engineers."

The chill was spreading from Kit's core to his extremities. His fingers and toes were going cold as Wallis continued in a distressed voice. "Of course, we will need engineers later — assuming all goes well, but for the foreseeable future, I don't know how I could justify hiring a recent engineering graduate. I'm hoping to win over Group Captain Cheshire to help with some of the theoretical aspects of command and control of pilotless aircraft," Wallis added this information as if Kit would find it good news in some way.

He didn't. It was bad enough that Wallis knew of no appropriate positions he might apply for. The mention of someone like Cheshire only added insult to injury. No, he didn't have a VC and three DSOs. No, he hadn't flown 100 operations. No, he hadn't commanded 617 Squadron or observed the drop of the atomic bomb on Nagasaki. He was just a disabled, veteran pilot with what was likely to be a Third-Class engineering degree.

On the other end of the line, Wallis was saying, "I'm very sorry about this, Moran. I wish I had better news. I wish I could help in some way. If you want, I can give you some names and addresses in America. You might also want to consider a master's degree. In another year, the situation may have changed again. In the meantime, learn as much as you can about rocket engineering. There are rumours that the Russians are recruiting all the German scientists that worked on the V-weapons and have plans to build more powerful rockets than ever before."

Kit stiffened as his resentment waxed. "As far as I know, sir, rockets have only one purpose: to deliver a cargo of high explosives. I've done more than enough of that already. It's not the future I envisaged for myself. I'm interested in civil, not military, aviation, and certainly not rockets."

"I understand," Wallis hastened to assure him, sounding contrite. "It is just — I'd like to be able to help you, Moran, but I don't know what else to suggest. Even if you're not interested in rocket engineering, I think your best prospects are in America. If you're willing to consider moving there, I would be happy—"

Kit cut him off. "No, thank you, sir. I'm not interested in going to America. Thank you, anyway."

"If I hear of anything, Moran, I'll certainly let you know," Wallis promised. "I sincerely wish I could help you."

The famous engineer sounded sincere, and Moran supposed he was. It just didn't help. Moran's hopes had been soundly shattered. He wasn't going to find an open door, he was going to have to go knocking. At least he'd found out now. This way he had four months to find another job.

With a Little Help from Our Friends
UK
Tuesday, 17 February 1948

Kiwi did not consider himself a wizard mechanic, but he knew enough to know that something was seriously wrong with his decrepit, twenty-year-old Vauxhall. It was making strange noises and steam was escaping from under the hood. He downshifted, slowed to a crawl and kept to the verge as much as possible, hoping to make the garage that he'd seen when driving the other way. It should be just over the crest of the next hill — or was it the one after?

Having trouble with his car was just his luck, Kiwi reflected. Banks had been generous so far, paying him a salary, covering company-related expenses and financing his flying lessons on twins, but he wasn't likely to foot the bill for a new car before the company started to operate. As for starting operations, that might be months away still.

Kiwi was discouraged but knew that much of his glum mood stemmed from the disastrous weekend he'd just put behind him. The weekends tended to leave him feeling lonely and full of regrets about losing Betty, but this past one had been particularly rocky. He'd asked Betty to meet with him for lunch, hoping he could show her he was on a new path. When she refused, he'd pleaded with her, and she'd become angry and insulting. He'd answered in kind, and it turned into a shouting match until she hung up on him. How had it come to this? They had been so in love in 1944…

The engine started coughing, and having crested the hill, Kiwi disengaged the gears and coasted. It was like gliding a Spit in after the engine stalled, he told himself. Luckily, he could see the petrol station at the foot of the hill. Unluckily, it was on the other side of the road, and there was oncoming traffic. If he had to put on the brakes, he'd never be able to roll into the station.

Concentrating and talking to the car at the same time, he judged the distance, his speed, and the speed of the approaching lorry. Just when he thought he was going to be able to turn in after it had passed, it slowed down. Kiwi had to slam on his brakes, and he came to a halt in the middle of the road, while the lorry continued obliviously on its way.

Traffic converged on Kiwi from both directions. Cursing colourfully, Kiwi tried to restart the engine, causing a bang followed by ominous hissing. The cars on either side of him started hooting their horns. Idiots! Surely, they could see he was dead in the water? One of the drivers started inching cautiously past his stern, but the other stuck his head out of the window to shout rude things at him.

Kiwi climbed out of his car and started pushing it off the road. He was relieved when a young man from the petrol station darted out to help him. The station attendant pointed to a garage behind the filling station, and they pushed the car in there. After putting on the brake, they looked under the hood together and Kiwi explained what he'd done and heard. As the young mechanic tinkered with this, that and the other, they chatted. The rapport between them was instantaneous, and in no time, Kiwi had his hands dirty as he helped.

They were so absorbed in their task, that neither of them took any notice of a car hooting behind them until a fat man came storming over shouting. "WOODWARD! What do you think I'm paying you for? Get out there and pump petrol!"

Too late, the helpful young man realised three cars were in line for petrol. Apologizing profusely to his boss, he rushed out to do his job, while Kiwi waited, feeling guilty for distracting him. After the customers had driven away, the proprietor started berating his young employee further. Thinking that unfair, Kiwi went over to interrupt the tirade by exclaiming, "Look! I'm a customer too, mate. Your employee has been very helpful! There's no need to tear a stripe off just because he was temporarily distracted."

"I'll kindly ask you to mind your own business! Woodward wasn't hired as a mechanic, and he's got no right sticking his nose under your hood!"

"He was doing a first-rate job, and if he wasn't hired to do it, then maybe he should be!"

"I'll hire who I please and with no advice from the likes of you!"

"Fine! In that case, I'd like a tow to the BP garage in Petersfield!" Kiwi retorted.

"That's fine by me," the proprietor snarled back, pointing toward the pay phone. "You can ring for a tow right over there!"

While the owner stalked back into the filling station office, the young employee remarked in a low voice, "BP will charge you an arm and a leg for a tow." Gesturing with his head toward the garage, he added, "If you give me another half hour, I think I can get her fixed up enough for you to get to Petersfield on your own power. The problem is the cylinder head gasket, and you'll need to get it taken off and reskinned at a proper garage."

"Thanks, mate, but I'd hate to get you in more trouble."

The attendant shrugged. "If it hadn't been you, it would have been something else. Mr Babbit doesn't think I'm worth the time of day let alone a shilling an hour! As he never tires of telling me, he only hired me as a favour to his sister, who happens to be my sister's mother-in-law." He shook his head in a gesture of apparent helplessness.

"In that case, if you're willing to risk his wrath, I would be grateful if you could get the car patched up enough, so I don't need a tow." Offering his hand he added, "Murray's the name, but I go by Kiwi."

"Woodward, but my friends call me Chips." They shook hands and started back in the direction of Kiwi's car.

"Problem is," Chips explained, "I've got no formal training on automobiles, and Babbit thinks a 'Merlin' is a mythical wizard rather than a wizard machine." He cast a disgusted look in the direction of the station office.

Kiwi laughed. "Fitter?"

"That's right. You with the mob, too?" Chips asked hopefully.

Kiwi nodded. "Best years of my life, but time goes on. You wouldn't by any chance be familiar with Cheetahs, would you?"

"Cheetahs? I tinkered around with the IX and XIX on the station Anson now and again. Why?"

"Well, a friend and I are setting up an air ambulance business and we're hoping to buy an Anson. Once we have an aircraft, we're going to need ground crew."

Chip's jaw dropped. "Are you serious, sir?"

Kiwi laughed, but before he could say more, a car drove into the station and Chips darted back to the pumps, leaving Kiwi to reflect on the fact that he still hadn't found the right aircraft and finding an aircraft was his first test as Banks' partner. He was terrified of making the wrong choice, yet time was running away from them too. Banks had made it clear he wanted an aircraft sooner rather than later, so they could move ahead with everything else.

After doing a lot of research, Kiwi selected the Anson as the ideal ambulance. He'd chosen the Anson in large part because it was still in production and so spare parts would not pose a problem, but it was in production precisely because there was continued demand for it. Kiwi thought he'd found the perfect aircraft, only for someone to make a better offer. Now he was returning to London empty-handed, and he feared Banks might lose faith in him. The fear of failing yet again was creeping into his soul and kept picturing his dreams going up in smoke.

Chips returned. "Sir, you were saying something about needing ground crew?"

Kiwi sighed. "I was jumping the gun a little, I'm afraid. Eventually, we'll need ground crew, but we haven't found the right aircraft yet."

"Have you considered a Wellington, sir?" Chips asked cheerfully as he bent over the auto engine and got back to work.

"It was one of our original ideas, but I think the Anson would be easier to modify."

"I don't know about that," Chips answered, reaching inside the engine and using his rag to unscrew something. "My mate Ron, who was a rigger on the Wimpy, claims they're very adaptable." Chips wiped his hands on his rag, stuffed it in his back pocket and went to the workbench to fetch a tool. He returned, leaned over the engine, and as he resumed work, he added, "Ron says the RAF is practically giving Wimpys away."

Kiwi snorted in disbelief. "Where did he hear that?"

"Ron's still matey with a Warrant Officer over at Shawbury, who says they're piling up there like bones beside a butcher's. It breaks Ron's heart."

Kiwi thought back to that first night at the Savoy. He'd suggested bombers could be converted into ambulances and hundreds of them had been decommissioned at the end of the war. "Do you think you could put me in touch with this friend of yours? After all, there's no harm in looking at a Wellington and finding out what it costs."

Chips grinned up at him. "I get off work at seven and usually meet up with Ron at the *Pig and Whistle* in Petersfield at about 8. You're welcome to join us if you like?"

Kiwi nodded agreement, not unhappy to delay telling Banks that he still hadn't found an aircraft. "Am I right that you'd be interested in working as ground crew?"

"Both of us, sir. We were a team for almost three years."

"What aircraft did you service?"

"Whitleys, Wellingtons, Sterlings, and Halifaxes."

"You know nothing is as good as it looks on the surface," Kiwi warned cautiously.

"What do you mean?"

"Well, my partner has got it into his head that we should base ourselves in Berlin."

"Berlin?" By the way, Chips said it, Kiwi might as well have said the moon. "Berlin, Germany?"

"That's right, operating out of RAF Gatow. I've been told we'll be able to use the station facilities, including the mess and quarters."

Kiwi could see Chips didn't like the idea of Germany very much, but after a moment or two while he continued tinkering with the car, he declared, "I can't say I ever wanted to go to Germany, but I suppose it couldn't be all that much worse than Scotland, could it?"

Kiwi laughed, but admitted, "Haven't the foggiest. Never been to Scotland, and last time I was in Germany we were pushing the Luftwaffe out of their messes and drinking their beer."

"Those were the days, eh?"

"Too right."

Chips nodded and gestured for him to get back into his car. "Try the ignition again. I think, if you don't drive over 30 mph, you should be able to reach Petersfield."

Kiwi settled in the driver's seat. Chips told him to prime the accelerator by flooring it once before trying the ignition. The engine coughed, almost caught and then died again. Chips held up his hand for Kiwi to stay where he was, fiddled with something under the hood and told him to try again. This time the engine caught. "Don't let it go out, sir!" Chips advised, shouting over the sound of the engine. "Drive straight to town, past the BP until you see another garage on your right. They're better and cheaper!"

Kiwi gave him a thumbs up and asked, "What do I owe you?"

"A job with your company, sir!" Chips grinned and winked.

"We'll discuss it at the *Pig and Whistle*!" Kiwi answered. As he got back on the road, Kiwi's blues had been blown away.

Bread and Circuses
Berlin-Dahlem (American Sector)
Saturday, 21 February 1948

How did the Americans do it, Robin asked himself. After almost six weeks of snow, sleet, rain and fog at temperatures hovering near the freezing point, the day the Americans had a "fair," the clouds disappeared, the sun beamed down, and temperatures soared at least 10 degrees. Clearly, the Lord looked down more favourably upon the Colonials than the Mother Country, he concluded.

The good weather had brought out the crowds, too. A queue three-to-four deep stretched the length of the long block. It was made up mostly of mothers with young children, although fathers or grandparents provided occasional variety. The women chatted as they shuffled forward, while the visibly excited children fidgeted, ran around or scuffled with one another. Given the conditions under which these children lived, Robin was impressed by how scrubbed and pressed they looked. Their clothes were faded, patched, darned and often too big or too small for them, but they weren't crumpled or dirty.

With only a twinge of shame, Robin walked past the patiently waiting Germans; they'd lost their war and victory had its privileges. The GIs selling entry tickets saluted smartly and let the senior RAF officer through without question. There were privileges to rank, too, he told himself. Red, white and blue balloons were being handed out to the children free of charge as they entered, and an American sergeant offered the RAF officer one with a grin. "Do you want a balloon, Colonel?" Robin smiled back but shook his head as he paused to get his bearings.

He had not been at a fair like this since he was ten or so, and he would much rather have been flying he thought, with a wistful glance at the pale blue sky overhead. However, this was the kind of publicity gimmick the Americans did so well and that Air Commodore Waite wanted to imitate, so it made sense to look it over. Furthermore, Mrs Howley had roped Emily into helping and she had been here all afternoon. Robin planned to take a quick look around and then rescue her at the end of her shift to take her out to dinner.

The main attractions of the fair were an ancient Ferris wheel, an even older Merry-go-Round and swings orbiting a rotating, central column. All could be seen looming above the rows of wooden booths selling food and trinkets. Immediately ahead of him stretched a line of stands selling fresh popcorn, hot dogs, chips, cotton candy, caramel apples and soft drinks. A little farther away were the booths with various games such as darts, ring tossing, and "high striker" as well as a pistol range. A sign pointed the way to pony rides. Finally, squashed between the darts and the pistol range, Robin spotted the booth selling raffle tickets at which Emily sat bundled up in scarves, mittens and a wool hat.

Robin went straight over to her, swept around the end of the table and dropped a kiss on her cheek. "Should I find you a hot coffee or chocolate someplace?" He asked, looking around.

"You're an angel, Robin! I'd love a hot chocolate," Emily admitted. "I think they sell them just up there a bit."

"Good. How's it going, by the way?"

"We've sold 87 tickets so far — which isn't very much."

"What's it for again?"

"An orphanage. Edith claims Berlin is overwhelmed by abandoned children. Some lost their parents in the bombing, others to the final assault by the Red Army, and yet others were refugees. Allegedly some of the children were put up for adoption after their parents were executed for treason, and others are the product of rape, abandoned by mothers who can't stand the sight of them or thrown out by husbands who won't raise their wife's bastards."

Robin reached out and put a hand on her shoulder. "You can't save the whole world, Emily. You have enough on your plate already," he reminded her. She had visited eight hospitals over the last two weeks and the experience had been intense, eye-opening and depressing. She candidly considered the situation 'catastrophic' — and she'd only just started the survey. "What do the tickets cost?" He asked her.

"Six pence."

"I'll buy four. Put my ticket stubs under the table to be sure I can't win." The transaction complete, Robin set off to find the hot drinks.

The tinkling music from the merry-go-round counter-pointed a waltz being blasted over microphones from the spinning swings. Bread and circuses, Robin thought. Did they really work? Did this kind of "friendship festival" have any impact on the way their former enemies looked at them? He found it hard to believe.

Or were the children being influenced unconsciously? Older minds were calcified. Look at Frau Neuhausen who still believed that Hitler had made Germany "great" again. Yet maybe those children giggling in delight as an American GI did magic tricks on an improvised stage would associate America with laughter, cotton candy and a brighter future.

He caught sight of WAAF Flight Sergeant Hart with her daughter returning from the pony rides. To his surprise, she was escorted by Major Dickenson. The adults each held one of the little girl's hands as she pulled up her feet and swung between them. Dickenson stopped and pointed to a stand selling cotton candy. Flight Sergeant Hart's daughter started clapping her hands and pleading with her mother. The responsible WAAF hesitated but then gave in. Major Dickenson went to the stand to buy the candy, and Robin continued.

A large crowd had collected around the pistol range and as he passed a round of applause swept the crowd. He paused to see what was happening. Standing before the target was a short, plump girl in trousers and boots who looked vaguely familiar although he couldn't place her. They had moved the target back another yard, yet she levelled the pistol and put another six shots into the bullseye with ease. As the applause sounded again, he remembered who she was: the Hero of the Soviet Union he'd seen at the ACC.

Quickly he looked around for other Soviet soldiers, but there were none in evidence. Of course, this girl was not in uniform either, so theoretically they might be mixing in the crowd although he'd been told that was strictly against SMAD orders. He looked more closely at the spectators. Most of the men in the crowd were either over sixty or American, French or British soldiers with their German girlfriends. Then, with a start, he caught sight of Corporal Borisenko in uniform close to the front of the crowd and clapping enthusiastically for the Soviet sharpshooter. Was that a coincidence? There was no prohibition against contact with the Soviets, of course, technically they were still Allies after all, and yet... Maybe he should mention it to the IO?

Robin continued, found the booth selling hot drinks and got in line. Progress was slow. When he finally reached the front, he ordered two hot chocolates and then retraced his steps, carrying the hot drinks in a cardboard tray. He caught sight of the Hero of the Soviet Union and Corporal Borisenko walking side-by-side, their heads together in earnest discussion. He changed course just enough to intercept them. Borisenko looked up surprised when he called her name but saluted without a trace of discomfort and promptly introduced her companion as "Mila Mikhailivna, who I met at the ACC luncheon."

"Are you enjoying the afternoon, Miss Mikhailivna?" Robin asked the Soviet heroine directly, and Corporal Borisenkov translated his question into Russian.

The young woman broke into a wide smile and gave a lengthy answer which Borisenko translated as: "Very much, sir. She's never seen anything like this before."

Interesting, Robin reflected. Maybe the bread and circuses had another audience as well? Out loud he asked, "Did she win a prize at the pistol range?"

Borisenko translated and Mila answered by removing a big teddy bear from her knapsack with a smile.

Robin congratulated her, wished them a pleasant afternoon, and continued to Emily's table.

"I thought you'd got lost!" Emily greeted him. He explained what he'd seen as he handed her one of the hot chocolates and took the other himself. She did not get a chance to drink much, however, before a crowd of four GIs and their girlfriends arrived to buy raffle tickets.

Robin was idly watching them when a deep, disgusted voice surprised him from behind. "Allied personnel are supposed to pay in hard currency and the Germans in occupation marks, but just behind the barracks they're trading their dollars on the black market and then converting it back again at the post exchange making a ten-fold profit without even getting their feet wet." Looking over his shoulder, Robin realized he'd been joined by Colonel Howley. The American Commandant continued, "They may arrive here honest and innocent, but after a month or two they're all currency sharks. We're not going to be able to stop it until we get a currency reform that holds."

Robin thought the American Commandant looked weary. "You sound like a man who's had a bad week, Colonel."

"You could say that. Some New York journalist discovered a Dutch masterpiece which belongs to the House of Orange at a New York art auction. All the evidence points straight at Berlin. The last place the painting was known to hang was in Jagdschloss Gruenewald, right here in the American Sector. Captain Byrne thinks Nazis still at large are being forced to sell off their ill-gotten treasures to pay off extortionists who would otherwise expose them, but the journalists are pointing their fingers at the MFAA itself."

"In other words, they think the gamekeeper has turned poacher?"

"Yep, although I find it hard to believe. Is that all you're drinking? Chocolate?"

"I couldn't find the scotch."

"Yeah, the ladies on the committee must be a bunch of prohibitionists," Howley agreed with a shake of his head, before offering, "I could find you a beer if you like?"

"No, I won't be staying much longer. Emily's been on duty all afternoon and her shift ends any minute." He checked his watch to be sure.

"Edith appreciated her volunteering to help. She likes our Allies to join in to show a common front. We also wanted to thank you and your wife for dinner the other night. It was great to have an evening like that with no other Americans present."

"We enjoyed it," Robin responded honestly. Emily's instinct to keep the numbers small had been spot on. The conversation had been much better than at the usual large receptions.

"Edith wants your wife to keep her informed about this air ambulance business, too — if it works out. She was a nurse, you know? If she can help in any way, just let us know."

"Gladly."

"Everything else all right?"

Robin felt he could best repay Howley's candour with some of his own. "I've been here six weeks and I still haven't sussed out what it is I'm supposed to be doing — other than squawk if the Russians kick too hard, and host events like this." He gestured to the carnival around them.

Howley laughed. "I've got bad news for you: I've been here almost three years and I can't figure it out, either. I thought I was sent here to stamp out Nazism, teach the Germans democracy and humanity, and with the help of our allies get the city working again. Instead, my allies — or one of them anyway — is doing all it can to stop everything from working, my troops are becoming corrupt and inhumane, and the Germans are teaching the Ruskies about democracy. It's a crazy place, I tell you." Then seeing Emily's replacement had arrived, Howley held out his hand. "Glad we ran into each other. We should get together again soon." With that, he disappeared again in the crowds.

Robin finished his now cold chocolate and found a rubbish bin to toss the paper cup away. By then, Emily had turned over her chair to her replacement, and she slipped her gloved hand through his elbow. As they started back toward the exit, the daylight was draining from the cloudless sky. "It looks like we'll be able to fly tomorrow," Robin observed.

Emily looked up surprised. "I thought there were no controllers on duty on Sunday."

"I've requested one." He told her, adding by way of justification, "Triple Two needs the flying as much as we do, and I've told the two sprogs to join us for some formation flying."

"Thank you, Robin. That's just what I need! It's been such a gruelling week."

"Let me guess: the dinner party and selling raffle tickets were the worst of it while visiting dilapidated, over-crowded and understaffed hospitals was fun."

"Am I that transparent?"

"To me. Look, Em, if you have to cut back on the 'diplomatic stuff,' do it! I'd rather have a wife who's helping an air ambulance get off the ground than the best hostess in Berlin."

She stretched upwards to give him a heartfelt kiss. "Thank you, Robin! Your understanding means the world to me!"

He squeezed her hand, glad that he could make her happy, but he felt a little apprehension as well. It wasn't as if he were in a secure position or could afford to offend anyone. He still needed her support, but not at the price of her being resentful or exhausted. Meanwhile, he had suggested that Danny and any other of the Spitfire pilots interested in dogfighting practice show up at dispersal tomorrow. He knew it would be good for them, but he couldn't entirely repress a certain trepidation either: the last time he'd been in a dogfight, he'd been shot down.

Old Dogs and New Tricks
RAF Gatow
Sunday, 22 February 1948

After the last two weeks, there was nothing Emily wanted more than a morning flying. Deep down, she would have been happiest on her own with only the Spitfire to answer to. She understood, however, that she was allowed to fly only on the condition that she learnt what the RAF wanted. Larking about at the expense of the British taxpayer was not her right. She accepted that she should do what she was told, but her 'revenge' was enjoying every minute of it.

When they arrived at the dispersal the two "sprogs" (most junior pilots) Pilot Officers "Benny" Benjamin and Neal Kennel, were already bundled up in their flying kit and eagerly — if a little nervously — awaiting their Station Commander. Robin explained what they were going to practice and assigned them their positions. Emily was "Red Four," and she knew that from now until they landed again, she would be addressed as nothing else. Robin told Benny and Kennel that they would swap positions after three-quarters of an hour, so each would get practice leading a section of two and being wingman to him respectively. After that, they went out to their respective Spitfires, which were fuelled, ready and waiting for them. They took off from the grass in formation.

What followed was an exhilarating ninety minutes of pure joy. It didn't bother Emily in the least that she was frequently admonished to close up, or that she was too wide on most turns, and sometimes slow to understand what was expected of her. She rather suspected that the sprogs welcomed her incompetence, as they might otherwise have been the butt of more criticism. Men, she reflected, were inveterately competitive; probably something to do with evolution and males having to compete for food and females. She was sorry when it was over, but tired from paying close attention. Although still lagging as they touched down, she took pride in her perfect three-point landing, something neither of the young RAF pilots managed. Benny bounced along rather badly.

They trundled back to their dispersal and found half the squadron standing about. As the sound of the Griffons cut off, Danny approached Robin, reaching him when he hit the ground. "I say, WingCo, weren't we supposed to do some of that dogfighting practice you promised?" After a fraction of a second, he added, "If you aren't too tired, that is."

Danny burst out laughing as Robin gave him a look of disgusted reproach before asking, "Who have you rounded up, Danny?"

Danny rolled off the names of the four other pilots waiting with him, which included one of the flight commanders, F/Lt "Lance" Knight.

Robin glanced over at Emily. "Do you mind?"

"Not at all. I'll get myself a cup of tea and a bun and warm up a bit in the dispersal."

"Good." He turned and asked the ground crews to refuel the four Spitfires that had just landed and invited the pilots to cluster around him. "Flight Lieutenant, I want you to lead a flight of six Spitfires composed of the rest of you without me and Danny. Start patrolling over the Western Sectors of Berlin, but don't cross into the air space of the East if you can avoid it. Danny and I will attempt to surprise and engage you. If any of us gets an opponent in his gun sights for the count of three, then signal that by transmitting 'thack, thack, thack' followed by the call sign of the victim. The latter must then return to Gatow and land. We'll keep it up until all but one of us has been 'shot down.' Understood?"

They dutifully chorused, "Yes, sir."

"And no cheating. It's not a kill unless you keep the target in your sights for three full seconds. Oh, and I don't mean with your sites on the trailing edge of the wing or the tail, either. I mean the cockpit. You must hold the cockpit in your sights for three seconds to claim a kill."

They nodded vigorously and ran to their respective aircraft like a pack of happy puppies, but Robin paused for a quick cup of tea. He drew it from the large urn on the iron stove. Since they were alone, Emily ventured to ask, "What if they shoot you down, Robin?" She was starting to wonder if this was such a wizard idea.

Robin smiled calmly, "I'm old bones, Em. They *should* be able to shoot me down. That's the point. The problem is that, except for Danny, none of them has been in combat. We'll soon see how they do." With that, he put his mug down and was gone.

Emily took Robin's mug, tossed out the dregs he'd left, and filled it with fresh tea for herself. She settled down in one of the armed chairs and propped her booted feet up on a crate filled with dog-eared periodicals. At first, she just contentedly soaked in the scene. She knew it could have been the dispersal of any RAF squadron practically anywhere in the world and being here subtly reinforced her bonds with Robin.

Like so many young pilots, he'd refused to get involved with any girl for years because he thought emotional entanglement might interfere with his flying and his career. She had broken down his defences by taking an interest in his passion and ultimately by learning to fly herself. Yet, despite all that, she knew that he only partially belonged to her. Flying, the squadron, and now the station would always come first. RAF wives who didn't accept that only made themselves miserable. Which was why it was so important for her to have a challenging and consuming job of her own. David's air ambulance company seemed a perfect fit because Berlin hospitals — at least the eight she'd visited — were in terrible condition. They lacked all kinds of modern equipment. Sometimes they didn't even have very basic machines and lab equipment. In the short term, flying patients out seemed the obvious solution.

But the decision wouldn't be hers, she reminded herself and tried to think of something else. She poured a second mug of tea and started picking through the magazines in the crate. With mild annoyance, she concluded that none of the journals was of any interest, and several were downright pornographic. She should have known.

The doorway darkened, and Benny stomped in. He answered her surprised look with a dejected, "He got me. Just like that!" He snapped his fingers. "And the CO got Hal." Another pilot was right behind him.

Emily was relieved that Robin hadn't been the first down. At least he'd put up a good fight. The pilots took their tea but went back outside to stare at the sky, so she joined them. In a surprisingly short space of time, another two aircraft landed. Kennel was one, but to everyone's surprise, Fl/Lt Knight was the other. "Did the WingCo get you, too?" Benny asked as the Fl/Lt arrived at the dispersal.

"No, the CO got me while I kept my eyes on the WingCo."

"So that leaves—" they broke off as another Spitfire put down on the runway and they strained to read the ID. "That's Mac."

"Who's still up there, then?"

"Just the WingCo and the CO," Benny told them pointing to the sixth aircraft setting down on the runway.

They could hear the engines straining not far in the distance, over the Havel, but no one could see the aircraft attached to them. The pilots and ground crews looked up, shaded their eyes, and squinted into the sun. The sound of the engines swept from left to right. The pitch changed, going up and down, louder, fainter. Now and then the engines seemed to stutter. A wisp of a contrail appeared and then faded away again. Once or twice, the sun glinted off something in the sky. Several times someone thought they saw a dot, but by the time the others followed the outstretched finger, whatever had been seen was gone again. Then finally two dots emerged side-by-side flying low. They grew into aircraft flying wingtip-to-wingtip. As they lined up on the runway, one throttled back and dropped lower to settle decorously on the grass, while the other pushed the throttles forward and roared over their heads at nought feet before lifting into a graceful "victory" roll.

It was P, and Emily felt a thrill of elation. She hadn't thought he would pull it off. This would buoy him up for days.

Around her, the others were muttering far less happily. They sounded put out and slightly ashamed. "How the devil..." the question wasn't finished. Another exclaimed, "I nearly blacked out and he was *still* on my tail!"

"I spun out completely and all I heard was that damn 'thack, thack, thack!'"

"It's crazy! He's got to be at least thirty," someone complained.

"Thirty-one going on thirty-two in June," Emily corrected. They'd forgotten she was there and looked over alarmed and then sheepish. She smiled at them.

Meanwhile, Robin made a circuit and landed. He trundled over to his waiting ground crew, cut the engine and shoved back the hood. The crew went up both wings and Emily could see him turning to talk to first one and then the other before climbing out onto the wing and jumping down. The ground crew were grinning as if *they'd* just shot down the entire flight. Danny was waiting at the wing root, and they came over to the dispersal together, pulling off their helmets despite the cold wind. Yes, Robin looked happy, Emily confirmed.

As he passed through the crowd of pilots, Robin remarked. "Come inside and I'll tell you what you were doing wrong."

Emily followed them inside but leaned against the windowsill at the back, while Robin went to the blackboard and started drawing diagrams. The discussion that followed was lively, with a great deal of hand-gesturing and no one paying much respect to rank, which was obviously the way Robin wanted it. After a few minutes of this, one of the pilots protested angrily, "But they *taught* us to turn, turn and turn again."

"In war, training is almost always out-of-date by the time you get it. Survival depends on adapting to reality. The Spit can out-turn almost any other aircraft in the world -- except another Spitfire. With us *all* flying Spits that advantage is neutralised. You have to adapt your tactics based on the capabilities of your enemy."

"Just how did you shake me off your tail?" Danny broke in to ask. "I had you in my sights for, I swear, two seconds — and then you were just gone!"

"Oh, that."

"Yes, that," Danny insisted, clearly annoyed.

"I corkscrewed."

"What?" The others exclaimed almost in unison.

"It's what our bombers did to escape German night fighters. I thought, if a Sterling could evade a Me110 with a corkscrew, it would be worth trying." Robin had that look on his face that suggested he was very pleased with himself.

"Worth *trying*?" Danny pressed him. "You mean you hadn't done one before?"

"No. I wasn't sure it would work, but I couldn't think of anything else." With a grin, he added, "That's how close you came to getting me."

Suddenly, Emily understood what this was all about: Robin had needed to prove to *himself* that he could still do this. Because he had, this little exercise had laid to rest the ghost of the FW190 that had shot him down five years ago. That not only made her happy, but she suspected it would also give Robin more inner confidence which would help him do his real job.

Chapter Eight
Close Calls

Off Course
Luton, London
Friday, 27 February 1948

Sunlight penetrated the room and Kiwi groaned. His head was throbbing, his mouth dry, and he needed to pee. But when he rolled over to get out of bed, he bumped into something. There was someone else in his bed. Oh, God! Where did she come from? The pub, of course; drinking with Chips and Ron. They'd chatted up those girls — well, not really girls anymore, Kiwi reflected as he eased out from under the covers without waking up his bedmate.

By the cold light of dawn with most of her make-up on the pillowcase, she looked older than he was. Her heavy breasts sagged shapelessly to either side, but her belly swelled up in two thick rolls. She lay on her back, her mouth hanging open, and she snored softly. She looked forty if she was a day, but who knew? Too many late nights, too many cigarettes, too much alcohol, too many lost friends and too many disappointments had left them all looking older than their age. Did anyone look "their" age anymore?

Kiwi stumbled over the cold floor to the bathroom, embarrassed to realise he was as naked as the woman in his bed. Their clothing was littered on the floor in a messy heap all mixed up together. He vaguely remembered the excitement of it, but the call of nature allowed no lingering.

He slipped into the bathroom and his reflection in the mirror made him groan. He looked an absolute wreck. God, he had to stop drinking like that. He couldn't handle it anymore — or the consequences. How the hell was he going to get rid of her? And what on earth was her name? Not to mention that his head was killing him!

After relieving himself, he turned on the tap and filled the basin with cold water. He leaned over, dipped his hands in the water and threw it at his face. He had the feeling he'd forgotten something — besides the name of the woman in his bed. What day of the week was it? What was he supposed to be doing?

Jesus Christ! He stood up so abruptly that he almost blacked out and had to clutch the washbasin to stop himself from losing his balance altogether. It was Friday! He was scheduled for his flight test today! At 9:30 am. What time was it?

Jesus! Jesus! He ran out of the bathroom and started frantically searching for his watch. Where had he put it? His hasty search made the stranger in his bed turn over with a little moan, but Kiwi didn't care. He had to find out what time it was. Finally, he spotted his watch lying atop the chest of drawers. 8:35!

No, no! He couldn't be late! His future depended on passing the qualifying exam on twin-engine aircraft. If he couldn't get his certificate for twins, he couldn't fly the Wellington, and he was no use to Banks, and he'd be tossed out of the company on his ear. Jesus! Jesus! The first objects he could put his hands on were his socks and he pulled one on after the other, then his undershorts and finally a pair of trousers.

The woman on the bed made a sound like she was awake.

"I've got to go, honey," Kiwi called over to her as he snatched up the house keys and stuffed them in his trouser pocket. "Just help yourself to tea or coffee and toast and let yourself out."

"What? Where—" She tried to sit up but flopped back on the pillow, apparently dizzy. Dishevelled hair framed a face on which smeared mascara gave her two black eyes.

"It was a great night," Kiwi flung at her as he made a dive for the door. "We'll have to do it again sometime, but I've got to go. I'm late."

He grabbed his flight jacket as he went out the door and continued buttoning up his shirt as he staggered toward his car parked on the curb out front. Only then did he realise he'd forgotten his car keys. Cursing, he ran back to the door, let himself in calling out as he entered, "It's just me! I forgot the car keys." He found them hanging by the door and ducked out again without another word. He fervently hoped she would be gone when he got back. What a mess if she decided to stay! But why should she? She must have a job somewhere.

He frowned, trying to remember. Yeah, she worked somewhere around here but had been a WAAF in the war. Seen one boyfriend after another buy it. Same old tough luck story they all told as an excuse for being so experienced in bed. It bothered him, though, that he couldn't remember her name. Judy? Rosie? Something with a "y" on the end he thought. Suzy?

He looked again at his watch. It was 8:45. Jesus! It would take him at least half an hour to get to the airport, then he had to park and check in, and...

Kiwi had never warmed to the Chief Flying Instructor at the flying school, who was also the certified examiner who awarded flying certificates. He was ex-Coastal Command and seemed to have a chip on his shoulder against "Fighter Boys." Maybe against "Bomber Boys" too, for all Kiwi knew. He certainly didn't like small talk. When Kiwi crashed into the flight school office five minutes late and dripping apologies, the look the man flung at him was full of contempt. "My next flight test is in 90 minutes. You'll have to prove to me that you can fly faster than if you'd been on time."

"Of course, of course," Kiwi promised, but things went wrong from the minute he sat down in the cockpit. His head still felt like it was splitting, and he had difficulty focusing. Maybe that was the reason he couldn't find the instruments as they went through the checklist? It was disconcerting and annoyed the examiner.

Finally, they completed the cockpit drill, contacted the tower and were cleared to taxi. At the runway, they waited while another aircraft landed, and then turned onto the broad tarmac before going through the final checks. Clearance was flashed at them, and with great concentration, Kiwi took them up into the pleasant morning sky. At least that was in his favour, he thought to himself as they lifted gracefully over the trees beyond the perimeter fence and gently gained altitude. So many of his training flights had been cancelled due to poor weather. Snow, sleet, high winds, and above all fog had closed the airfield half the time. He was lucky that today was such a fine day, although the aircraft seemed to be bouncing around more than necessary in such gentle winds.

"Don't you think it's past time to retract the undercarriage?" The examiner asked laconically.

It only got worse after that. By the time he was ordered to land, Kiwi was feeling disconnected from the whole world. His mind kept drifting back to when he'd learned to fly in New Zealand in an ancient but charmingly aerobatic biplane. He thought wistfully of his first flight in a Spitfire when he'd naively challenged one of the RAF's top aerobatics pilots to a flying duel. He'd done very well — only to forget the landing gear as he set down and he'd torn across the grass field on his belly doing substantial damage to the precious Spit.

"Are you landing or just doing a fly-past?" The examiner snapped at him.

Why couldn't he concentrate? Getting his twin-engine rating was vitally important. He was meeting up with Banks this afternoon because they had an appointment with the Ministry to transfer ownership of the Wellington they were buying. Banks expected him to have his qualifications in the bag because tomorrow they were supposed to take delivery of the Wellington at the RAF aircraft storage depot at Shawbury. They planned to fly it to its temporary home at Gravesend on Sunday, and on Monday they were to meet with Essex Aero, the company that was supposed to transform the bomber into an ambulance. Tuesday they had an appointment with Banks' tailor in the West End to get their uniforms. Finally, on Wednesday Banks was flying back to Berlin, while Kiwi was supposed to return to Gravesend to keep an eye on Essex Aero as they undertook the modifications.

"You're too fast and too high! Go around again!" The examiner ordered.

Kiwi responded instantly, pushing the throttles forward, pulling the column back, and putting the Anson into a tight lefthand bank.

"What the hell are you doing? This isn't a Spitfire! You don't need to curve around into the runway. Do a proper approach!"

Even as Kiwi diligently did what he was ordered, he knew it was hopeless. He wasn't going to get it right. It was as if someone or something was sitting between him and the controls. It was almost as if someone or something wanted him to fail. His head was throbbing, and his vision seemed to shift in and out. Why had he gone out drinking last night? Why had he taken some woman whose name he couldn't remember home with him? Why hadn't he prepared for this flight test like it was the most important thing in his life? Because it was.

After the third failed attempt at landing, the examiner took over the controls, made a fast but safe landing and taxied back to the hangar apron without saying another word. His face was a rigid mask. Kiwi sat with his hands in his lap waiting for the verdict, but it was obvious. He had failed. Wearily, as if he hadn't slept in a week, he climbed down from the Anson, returned the parachute, and continued out of the flying school. He still couldn't concentrate on anything.

David had no worries about the formal transfer of the Wellington to AAI and was already focused on the firm's next problems. Based on the questionnaires Emily had sent so far, he had already formed a picture of the kind of modifications they needed to make. One key problem, as he saw it, was providing heating in the fuselage where the stretchers would be slotted in like bunks. Providing oxygen there would be easy; the Wellington had been built for oxygen feeds throughout, but warmth had been considered a luxury for RAF aircrew. Not so for seriously ill patients. Another issue was facilitating intravenous feeding during flight, and ensuring medical staff had a safe place to sit and strap in during landing and take-off.

None of this would require huge structural changes, however, and David had been in touch with the company that had taken over Gravesend when it reverted to a civilian field. Before the war, Essex Aero had built racing aircraft and still hoped to get back into that business, which was why they had hangars equipped with everything necessary for custom building and modifying aircraft. Since the Wellington was in excellent condition and the modifications were moderate, David expected all modifications to be complete before April 1st, when he hoped to move AAI's operations — aircrew, ground crew and aircraft included — to Berlin.

David no longer had any doubts about the demand for an air ambulance. Emily and Charlotte had contacted more than thirty hospitals, and their research had readily established the need to send patients out of Berlin for medical treatment. Meanwhile, earlier this month, David had visited major hospitals in Hamburg, Hanover, Frankfurt, Munich and Wiesbaden to confirm they had capacity to receive patients from Berlin at short notice. The readiness of all hospitals to take emergency cases from

Berlin had been extraordinary.

David planned to return to Berlin next week to sign contracts with BEA for hangar and office space at Gatow and also see about getting Charlotte and Emily formally employed by the company. Fortunately, Robin had agreed that the ground crews could use RAF facilities, while Kiwi and he would stay with the Priestmans as suggested before he left. Eventually, he wanted to move into his uncle's house on Schwanenwerder. He could picture living there, hosting Robin and Emily, clients and city officials. He dreamed about hot summer afternoons with Charlotte wearing only a bathing suit as she shared a cocktail with him on the back terrace. He looked down at the long-haired, blond dog stretched out on the rug beside his desk, and assured him, "You'll like Schwanenwerder, Sammy. There are ducks and squirrels and feral cats and pigeons to chase, and lots of swimming too." Sammy lifted his head, blinked contentedly back at his human for a few moments, then flopped his head back down and closed his eyes.

Returning his focus to the present, David concluded that everything was on track with the aircraft, ground crew, and facilities. This left just two challenges. The smaller was that UK regulations required both pilots operating an air ambulance with patients on board to have at least thirty hours flying the aircraft type. That meant that Kiwi had only one month to get in thirty hours on the Wellington. Given the English weather in March, that might be challenging, but since Kiwi would be overseeing the modifications, David thought he'd find plenty of opportunity to fly.

The other issue, and the one that gave him headaches, was that he still had no clear answer about who was going to pay for their services. Many of the most desperate patients were precisely those who could *not* pay, and the German insurance industry had collapsed along with the rest of the economy, so most patients had no insurance either. This meant that someone else — either a major charity such as the Red Cross or the Knights of St. John or the Berlin city government — was going to have to pick up the tab. David personally favoured a contract with the Red Cross and had scheduled a meeting with the office head of the ICRC in Berlin this coming week. If nothing came of that, he would talk to the Knights of St. John. As a last resort, he would approach the Berlin government.

The clock struck three. It was time to leave for the ministry. David took his briefcase and checked that he had all the documentation required along with his passport, discharge papers, logbook, bank drafts and the like. He looked out the window. It had started to drizzle, so he took an overcoat and hat, thinking again how he longed to be back in uniform. Just a few more days, he reminded himself, and then he should have his own, unique AAI uniform.

David reached the Ministry early and settled down to wait. As the minutes ticked by, he became increasingly upset that Kiwi had not yet arrived. They both had to sign as they were both listed as owners in the articles of incorporation. Hopefully, there hadn't been some sort of accident....

"Mr Goldman and Mr Murray?"

David sprang to his feet and lifted his hand to indicate he was one of the individuals being called. "Yes, here. That is, I'm here, my partner—"

Just then Kiwi burst into the room, and David gestured for him to follow as the secretary turned and led the way into the inner chamber.

David sensed something was wrong immediately. Normally, the big New Zealander beamed like a lighthouse when they met. Now his smile was a rigid mask. Kiwi avoided his eyes altogether, and he kept swallowing nervously. He provided his passport and signed all the documents diligently, but he made no small talk and cracked no jokes. This behaviour was totally out-of-character.

With the aircraft registration signed over to AAI and in David's briefcase, they shook hands with the civil servant who had represented the Ministry and went back out into the anteroom. Only then did David ask in a low voice as they crossed the room, "What's wrong?"

Kiwi wouldn't look at him. "I — I have something to tell you. Let's go for a drink somewhere."

"I'd planned to celebrate at the Savoy—"

"There's nothing to celebrate," Kiwi cut him off, but wouldn't look at him and led the way back down the stairs and out into the street. His eyes scanned the street opposite, and he spotted a pub. "We can go there," Kiwi announced with a nod of his head.

David did not object. Kiwi had selected a city pub, the kind of place civil servants went for lunch or a quick pint after work. It was designed for the maximum number of nooks and crannies where customers could eat in small groups in maximum privacy. It was furnished with dark carpets, gleaming wood tables and leather chairs. They readily found a table and sat down.

Kiwi wanted to order something at the bar, but David held him back. "Sit down and tell me what's happened!"

"I failed."

"What?" David didn't know what he was talking about.

"I failed my flight test."

David stared at him. Not once had he considered that possibility. Kiwi was a brilliant pilot. He'd flown more kinds of aircraft than David had.

"I didn't get my license on twins," Kiwi clarified in the face of David's evident disbelief.

"How? How did you fail?"

Kiwi shrugged helplessly and stared at his folded hands. "I kept coming in too fast and too high to land."

"If you knew what the problem was, why didn't you correct it?" It was a rhetorical question. David could see that Kiwi was broken, just as he had been on that night in December when they had first conceived of this business idea. "Had you been drinking the night before?"

"Yes, goddamn it!" Kiwi lashed out furiously. "Yes, I went out and got sozzled — so blotto I don't remember the name of the girl I brought home with me or— It's all just a big black haze...." His anger fizzled out. He wasn't really angry, just ashamed and horrified by what he'd done.

David knew that. He also knew that he'd been relying on Kiwi, building his future on him. He hadn't just hired him, he'd given him equity. He'd made him a partner. He was furious. Too furious to speak.

"Please give me another chance, Banks. I swear, I won't touch a drop and I'll retake the test at my own expense—"

"When? How soon can you do that? Don't you realise you need more than the license? You need thirty hours flying the Wellington! We've been telling everyone — BEA, Essex Aero, Robin, Emily, Chips and Ron — that we're going to fly to Berlin on April 1. We're supposed to start operations almost immediately after that. We've been running up debts for three months, and if we don't start making some income soon, we're going to go bankrupt. Don't you realise that? How can you get plastered the night before your flight test?"

"I don't know," Kiwi answered honestly. "It just happened."

"Then how do you know it won't happen again?"

"I don't know," Kiwi admitted.

They stared at one another. David felt betrayed. He'd trusted Kiwi. He could have hired any one of the thousands of former Bomber Command pilots already qualified on twins and four-engine aircraft. He didn't have to take a down-on-his-luck ex-fighter pilot as his partner. Kiwi had brought nothing to their partnership so far — not money or business savvy or skills of any sort. Well, except for finding the Wellington and hiring the groundcrew, David reminded himself.

Kiwi stood. "I'll ask to retake the flight test tomorrow. I'll let you know the results."

"Do that," David snapped back and let Kiwi walk out of the pub. It was supposed to be a day for celebration and champagne. Instead, he was alone in the gloom no longer sure that everything was going to work out.

Early Landing
University of Leeds, UK
Monday, 1 March 1948

Kit's amputated foot was causing him trouble. He tried to make himself more comfortable in the wooden library chair, but nothing eased the aching and throbbing in the stump above the artificial limb. He must have walked too much yesterday, he told himself, but walking was one of the few pleasures they still had now that Georgina had lost her job. Besides, it had been an exceptionally warm and sunny day, filled with the promise of spring. With a glance across the partition separating him from the student in the next cubicle, he noted that today it was raining again.

Kit drew a deep breath and tried to concentrate on German grammar. He was required to pass a language proficiency exam to get his degree and had selected German because he thought he might find it easier than the other choices: French, Italian, or Russian. He'd grown up with Afrikaans spoken around him and had picked up some, but that didn't seem to help him much with German. The problem was he didn't particularly want to learn German. It was just a degree requirement, but he needed the degree, he reminded himself. Back to the genitive plural—

"Mr Moran?" The library assistant bent over his chair and whispered almost in his ear.

He looked over surprised. "Yes?"

"Could you please come with me?"

With a silent question, Kit indicated the books and notebooks spread out on the table. The assistant gestured for him to bring his things with him. Kit hurriedly closed the books with the notebooks inside to mark his place, put these into his leather knapsack and slung the latter over his shoulder before following behind the assistant. He couldn't imagine what this was about but understood that there could be no discussion in the library. Based on the number of frowns thrown in their direction, they'd already made too much of a disturbance.

As the heavy door clunked shut behind them, the assistant handed him a note folded in two. Puzzled, Kit opened it and read: "Your wife has been taken to St. James University Hospital. Labour started at two thirty." What? The baby wasn't due for another month! Was something wrong? This wasn't normal, was it? He had to get to the hospital as soon as possible. Calm down, he told himself. The doctor said labour usually took between four and eight hours, and it was only a quarter to five. No need to panic, he told himself, but he wanted to be there when the baby was born.

Thanking the assistant, he ran down the stairs to collect his overcoat in the cloakroom. He found his bicycle in the rack, tied his rucksack behind the seat and set off in the rain. The hospital wasn't far away, but the pouring rain made it an unpleasant bike ride. He parked the bicycle in the hospital lot, took his leather rucksack with him and went inside. At the main desk, they directed him to the maternity ward three flights up. Here he was greeted pleasantly and told to take a seat.

"Can't I go in to see my wife and at least let her know I'm here?"

"Of course not!" The sister sounded shocked, then paused and asked, "Is this your wife's first child?"

"Yes."

She softened up a little and assured him, "She's in the very best of hands, Mr Moran, and there's nothing you can do. Let the medical staff and your wife handle everything. I must warn you, however, that first births usually take longer. You might want to get a bite to eat and coffee or tea before you settle in for the vigil. It could be a long wait."

That sounded sensible, so Kit followed her advice and directions to a small tearoom. He considered calling his in-laws but decided against it. It made more sense to call them when it was all over. That way he could tell them if they had a grandson or a granddaughter.

Fortified he returned, asked if there was any news, and on receiving a negative answer settled himself in the waiting room to try to tackle German grammar again. It was the kind of study that could be interrupted at any second. Indeed, he would welcome any interruption, he admitted, as he tried to concentrate.

The sound of a wailing infant through a momentarily open door brought him eagerly to his feet, but a voice called out a different name and another man rushed across the waiting room to disappear behind the swinging doors. Kit looked at his watch. It was now nearly eight o'clock, so it should be any time now. He put his books away and looked at the other men waiting with him. They both looked older and more established, he thought. One looked like a clerk of some kind with a very neat suit, polished shoes, spectacles and straight dark hair meticulously parted and combed. The other man was poorer, older, and more relaxed. Probably the father of multiple children already, Kit surmised by the way he calmly read a sports magazine.

Kit tried to think about what needed to be done for Georgina and the baby at home. Georgina's parents had given them a crib complete with linens and also a trunk full of baby clothes with about two dozen nappies. But Georgina would need to rest a bit and shouldn't have to go shopping for a day or two. He set about making a grocery list.

The older man was called by a smiling nurse and disappeared through the doors. Kit stood to look at the dogeared magazines on the central coffee table. Listlessly, he scanned for something that might interest him. He took a journal on hunting and another on sports cars back to his seat and read through them. He leafed through the other magazines as well, frequently checking the large clock on the wall. The hands jerked their way around the face past ten o'clock and then eleven.

An ambulance wailed in the street. Shortly afterwards, a stretcher was wheeled in with a pregnant woman on top of it. With much bustle and a flurry of staccato orders, it disappeared through the doors. Later, there was a shift change and an older woman replaced the nurse who had greeted him. The clerk was called to see his new child. Another man came to join Kit in the waiting room. He looked nervous and kept wiping his face with his handkerchief.

It was past midnight and it had been almost ten hours since Georgina had been admitted to the hospital. Kit's nerves were starting to fray. Having nothing to do was like flying Second Dickie. He thought back to his Second Dickie flight, sitting uselessly beside Group Captain Fauquier as he flew through the barrage put up by the *Tirpitz*. The battleship's 15-inch guns had exploded at precisely the right altitude — but fortunately 200 feet ahead of them. Kit had found himself counting the seconds as they flew through the man-made turbulence. The bomb aimer laconically reported "No visual, Skip. You'll have to go around again." And they did. Seven times.

"Mr Moran?" The soft voice broke into his thoughts, and he flinched in surprise. The man beside him wore a white, surgical gown and cap. He was not smiling. Moran sprang to his feet, already sensing disaster.

"Your baby has been delivered and it is a healthy—"

"What's happened to my wife?" Kit demanded, responding to the gloom in the man's expression and demeanour.

"I'm afraid we haven't been able to stop the haemorrhaging, at least not yet. However, we wanted you to know that the baby has been safely delivered and is perfectly healthy. A lovely little girl."

Kit just stared at him.

"Please sit down and try to remain calm. We'll do our best to save your wife." The surgeon was gone.

Georgina was bleeding to death. Kit knew about that. He'd watched Reggie nearly bleed to death. But that had been in the war. How could this be happening to Georgina?

No. She couldn't die. She had given him the courage to keep flying after the disgrace of being posted for "Lack of Moral Fibre." She had been his reason for clinging to life when lying wounded in a Wehrmacht hospital so short on anaesthetics that the pain was almost unbearable. If not for her, he would not have been able to cope with losing his foot and part of his leg.

Without her, he would not have wanted to. If she was gone, he didn't want to go on. The baby was too abstract to even think about, much less hold on to. What would he do with a baby without Georgina? He didn't want it. He wanted Georgina.

After standing stunned for several moments, he recognised that he needed help. He couldn't cope with this alone. He turned and looked around the waiting room until he located a pay telephone at the back. Woodenly, he crossed to the telephone, found some coins in his trouser pocket, and inserted them. He dialled the vicarage in Foster Clough. It was nearly 1 am, so he let the phone ring until a gruff voice finally answered. Without preliminaries, Kit blurted it out. "The baby came early and Georgina's bleeding to death."

"Where are you?" His father-in-law asked back, sounding fully awake already.

"St James University Hospital."

"We'll be there as soon as we can," the Vicar promised and then Kit heard only the dial tone.

The man who had arrived after him was summoned by smiling nurses and he rushed away in a flurry of goodwill.

Kit sank into his thoughts. They were all dark. Georgina had been what motivated him to go on living. She was what made him happy. He didn't care what purpose God might have for him if he didn't have Georgina to share it with — and he'd tell the Reverend Reddings that to his face when he got here!

In the darkness and the stillness, the dead started to gather around him. Forrester, the Australian pilot, leaned back in the seat next to him. He had insisted on being Kit's rival from the day they met at an Operational Training Unit and had goaded him into competing. Now he stretched out his long legs and crossed them at the ankles. He locked his fingers behind his head. He wore his crooked grin as he mocked: "Did you think you'd have *all* the luck *all* the time, mate?" Howard, the aristocratic veteran pilot who had helped Kit integrate into the close-knit mess at 617 Squadron, came to sit on his other side looking sombre. With a look of concern in his eyes, he commiserated, "I'm so sorry, Kit." Sailor, the navigator on Don's crew, when Kit had still been a flight engineer, sat down opposite, playing with his cap as he so often did, "I know what you're going through, Kit. I would have felt the same if it had been Kathleen."

And then Don arrived. Don had loved Georgina first and no less intensely. His death had paved the way for her to fall in love with Kit, for Kit to marry her. Now Don and Georgina would be together again, while Kit was left behind. How had his father-in-law worded it in that sermon? Like the rubbish left by an outgoing tide. Don stood in front of him, and Kit gazed up at him. Don made no effort to disguise he wasn't entirely unhappy about this development — although he was gentlemanly enough to look sober as he replaced Forrester, who had disappeared again, in the chair beside him.

"It does take two to make a baby, Kit," Don remarked at length. Kit looked at him resentfully and Don smiled faintly, "I'm not saying you shouldn't have done it, but you have no justification for feeling like a victim."

Kit wanted to argue, to say that death in childbirth wasn't supposed to happen anymore, not in England anyway. But fair or not, it appeared to be happening.

At some point, the dead faded away and Kit became aware that his mother-in-law had her arm over his shoulders. He looked over at her, numb inside. "When did you get here?"

"About half an hour ago."

"What time is it?"

"It's almost five in the morning."

"Where's Edwin?"

"He's inside." She nodded toward the swinging door. "Professional privileges," Amanda explained with a faint smile.

"Is there any news?"

"No news is good news, Kit. If she'd died, they would have told us."

They didn't speak any more, just sat silently together side-by-side until Reverend Reddings emerged out of the doors. The dim hospital lights reflected off his glasses, making it hard to see his expression until he was beside Kit. He looked solemn, but not shattered. "Kit, they've stopped the bleeding, but Georgina hasn't come out of the anaesthetic as she should have done. We think you should try to reach her, wake her."

Kit jumped up. His remaining foot had fallen asleep, and he almost fell. His father-in-law caught him and would have given him an arm to lean on, but Kit shook him off in a fit of childish protest. He hated feeling like an invalid!

He limped forward a few steps until the feeling came back more fully. The doors parted in front of him, and Reddings guided him down a sterile corridor and into a narrow, white, over-lit hospital room.

Georgina lay peacefully on her back in a bed. Her belly was back to normal, and her hands were laid on it like a corpse. She looked thin and fragile and white as death. She did not seem to be breathing at all. Only the blood draining into her from a plastic bag suggested she was still alive.

Kit took one of her hands and crushed it in his own. "Georgina!" He gasped. Leaning closer to speak almost into her ear he pleaded, "Please don't leave me! We have a little girl now. She needs you."

The corpse stirred. Her eyes seemed to move, but she didn't wake.

Kit looked around the room. They were all just standing there like mourners at a funeral. "Where's the baby?" He asked. "Bring the baby for God's sake! It's a lifeline."

"That's not—" a nurse started to say, but the doctor waved her silent and in a low voice told her to fetch the baby.

Kit reached out to stroke the side of his wife's face with the back of his free hand. "Please, Georgina. Don't leave me."

There was still no real response.

The nurse returned with the little, squirming bundle, and Kit took his daughter into his arms. He was surprised by the surge of protectiveness that swept over him. Then he laid the baby on Georgina's stomach and lifted one of her hands, so it lay on the baby's head. All the while he kept talking softly to her. "She needs you, Georgina. I can't bring her up alone. And have you forgotten? You promised you would never leave me."

A small moan emerged from somewhere deep inside the woman on the bed. The eyes slowly opened, and Georgina smiled faintly, straight up at him. "How can you doubt me, Kit Darling?"

Kit bent and clutched her to him, baby and all. "I thought I'd lost you," he confessed.

"Ah, well, I know what that feels like," she reminded him with a teasing smile. "Don was here. Did you see him?"

"Yes. I think he was hoping you'd go with him."

"No, darling." She smiled up at him for another few seconds, but then looked down at the baby, her smile changing subtly, suffused with wonder. "Is this our baby?"

"Yes. A little girl."

"Oh, Kit! She's lovely, isn't she?"

He nodded, his throat too constricted to speak.

Georgina turned her head and noticed her parents. "Mummy! Daddy! What are you doing here? Did something go wrong?"

"Nothing serious," her mother assured her in a voice husky with tears.

"I'm sorry to cause so much trouble."

"Children do that sometimes, as you'll find out soon enough. It doesn't matter."

"You're lucky to have such a devoted husband," her father added, stepping closer. "The rest of us were giving up hope, but he brought you back to stay with us a little longer."

"Yes, there's so much to live for, isn't there?" Georgina told them, smiling down at her infant and then up at Kit.

As Kit met her eyes, he was gripped by an almost grim determination to make sure that that was true. He could not fail her now, not with their little girl to consider, too. He had to be sure that he found a job that would do more than just provide for them. He had to get work that would ensure that both his girls had everything they could ever hope for -- and more.

Air Supremacy
RAF Gatow
Tuesday, 2 March 1948

Kathleen glanced at the clock on the back wall, surprised by how late it was. She closed her book and got up to stretch. The BEA flight must be airborne from Hamburg by now, and Flight Lieutenant Simpson usually put in his appearance around this time. If he was sober that made no difference, but when he'd been drinking, he could be singularly unpleasant and disruptive. For the umpteenth time, she wondered if she should say something to the WingCo. Simpson's behaviour seriously undermined the efficiency and safety of the Station. Yet she felt awkward. She'd been here less than two months and she was a WAAF; she felt her more senior male colleagues ought to be the ones to approach the Station Commander with any complaints.

She settled down again, and her thoughts drifted, as they increasingly did, to Lionel. There had been no repeat of that bizarre evening at the nightclub. On the contrary, he'd been a model gentleman, and he'd completely captured Hope's heart. She called him "Uncle Lionel," and was always asking when they would see him next. Lionel called her "my little lady," (which she liked very much) and he over-indulged her with treats, yet Kathleen couldn't entirely fault him for it. When Hope was happy, so was she.

Because they did so much with Hope, however, they had not talked much, not even to talk through what had transpired that night. Kathleen strongly suspected that her response to the nightclub had made him lose interest in her as a woman. He certainly made no move to get more intimate. Yet if that was true, why was he so attentive and so kind to Hope? Reluctantly, she was beginning to wonder if he was the kind of man who only pretended an interest in women and children in order to disguise his homosexuality. Maybe that was the reason he had taken her to a bar frequented by transvestites? Or was it just —

A loud roaring shadow passed over the tower startling all the occupants.

"We've just been beaten up by someone!" Natalie exclaimed more amused than upset. Kathleen suspected that was because she'd been seeing rather a lot of Benny recently.

"That didn't sound like a Griffon engine to me!" Warrant Officer "Willie" Wilkins countered, and both he and Kathleen stood to get a better look across the runways to the grass field where the Spitfires were dispersed.

"Fourteen," Kathleen finished counting out loud while half a dozen pilots spilt out of the dispersal on the far side of the grass field, all searching the sky. Kathleen saw them point just before another aircraft roared overhead.

"Yanks!" Willie exclaimed.

"Yanks?" Kathleen asked back astonished.

"Not Yanks, *Yaks* — Soviet fighters. Look!" Willie pointed as the fighter banked to the right exposing the red stars on its wings.

"They have no business flying in our airspace — let alone at that height," Kathleen stated the obvious.

"Rufus, you better ask the FCO to come up here right away," Willie ordered his assistant.

While the corporal reached for the phone and asked the operator to connect him to Simpson's quarters, two more Soviet fighters skimmed over Gatow airfield.

The second telephone was ringing, and Natalie Vincent answered it. "Control Tower, Corporal Vincent....I'm sorry, sir, the FCO is not in the tower at the minute....I'll hand you over to Warrant Officer Wilkins." As she passed the receiver to the controller, she whispered, "The WingCo."

Willie took the telephone, stiffening automatically. "Yes, sir.... We're trying to find out, sir.... Yes, sir." He hung up and looked at Rufus Groom. "Did you get through to the FCO?"

"Yes and no."

"Meaning?"

"He answered but told me to go to hell."

"Wonderful."

"I'll call the Berlin Air Safety Centre and see what information they have," Kathleen volunteered.

"Good, I'll go switch on the radar and see what I can see," Willie disappeared inside the radar room, leaving the door open behind him.

When she had the Berlin Air Safety Centre on the line, Kathleen reported, "RAF Gatow here. Four Soviet fighters have just flown over the airfield at less than a thousand feet. Do you know what is going on?"

A French-accented voice drawled condescendingly on the other end, "Soviet aircraft are conducting manoeuvres in Berlin air space, but all aircraft will remain above ten thousand feet."

Kathleen spluttered. She was junior to everyone in the Berlin Air Safety Centre, and she suspected they weren't going to take her word for it, but the Yaks had barely scraped over the tower. Rather than argue, she opted to remind them instead, "The BEA flight is scheduled to arrive in—" she glanced at the clock "—less than thirty minutes."

"We have advised BEA of the manoeuvres, but there should be no interference with the incoming flight since the Soviets are flying far above corridor height."

Kathleen resisted the urge to say: "That's what you think!" She knew too well that the French did not approve of women in control towers and would not believe her. She resolved to ask Willie to call them and explain the situation, but she had barely hung up when another two fighters raced by overhead no higher than the first four. She turned and called through the open door to the open radar room. "Can you see anything, Willie?"

"Anything?" Wilkins asked back. "It looks like the whole Red Air Force is crowding into Berlin airspace. It's a flying circus!"

"What's going on?" The question came from Wing Commander Priestman as he entered the tower.

"Berlin Air Safety Centre is reporting Soviet manoeuvres, sir, but they are allegedly all flying over ten thousand feet."

"Ten thousand feet my — foot. They weren't an inch over 500. Where's Flight Lieutenant Simpson?"

"We've called him, sir," Groom answered. That didn't answer the question and the Wing Commander continued to look pointedly at the corporal until he looked down and mumbled, "He's still in his quarters, sir."

The Wing Commander made a single but very pointed and unprintable comment, and then looked around the tower noting that it was manned by only two corporals and one WAAF Flight Sergeant, all of whom he dismissed as insufficiently senior. "Who's in charge here?"

"Warrant Officer Wilkins is on the radar, sir," Kathleen answered, and the Station Commander immediately went into the radar room to look over Willie's shoulder, as yet another two fighters roared overhead. She could hear the WingCo and Willie muttering to one another in low tones. Then the Wing Commander called out to her. "How far away is the BEA flight?"

"According to the flight plan, sir," Kathleen spoke as Natalie passed her the strip of paper on which the filed flight plan was noted, "it is still 19 minutes out, roughly 40 miles from Berlin, flying at 6,000 feet."

"Someone get me a connection to Staaken and have Corporal Borisenko report up here immediately."

Groom grabbed one telephone and Natalie the other, Groom requested Staaken while Natalie asked for the translator.

Another two fighters had skimmed over the tower before Borisenko appeared in the doorway. She was handed the receiver Groom was holding as the CO ordered. "Inform Colonel Kuznetsov that our civilian airliner is on approach and scheduled to land in —" he paused to look at Kathleen.

"Sixteen minutes."

"— sixteen minutes. I want his fighters out of my airspace!"

Borisenko spoke into the phone in Russian. She nodded several times, acknowledged in the affirmative, then covering the receiver she reported to the Station Commander. "Colonel Kuznetsov says they are not his fighters, sir. They are from a visiting squadron which escorted a VIP from Moscow and are now taking part in manoeuvres."

"Well, tell him to get them out my airspace anyway!" Priestman snapped back.

"I don't think he can—"

"I didn't ask for your opinion, corporal. Tell Colonel Kuznetsov what I said."

Borisenko bit her lip in consternation but spoke firmly into the telephone. She nodded, thanked the Russian and hung up. "He said he would do what he could."

The radiotelephone in front of Willie's vacant seat came alive with a crackling sound followed by a voice calling, "Cutty Sark, Cutty Sark, this is Bealiner Seven-Seven. Do you read me?"

Kathleen glanced over her shoulder toward the radar room. Willie and the WingCo were again looking at the screen intently and pointing to this and that. Willie seemed to be explaining something to the Station Commander. She leaned across Groom to take hold of the radio receiver and answered, "Bealiner Seven-Seven this is Cutty Sark. We read you loud and clear."

"We are twenty miles from Frohnau and just passing through five thousand feet."

Kathleen glanced over her shoulder toward the radar room, but Willie and the CO were still preoccupied. "Continue descent to 3,500 feet at Frohnau."

"Continuing descent to 3,500 feet. What's the weather at Gatow?"

"Visibility three miles. Wind out of the NNE at 10 knots. Temperature 37 degrees Fahrenheit." Just as Kathleen provided the barometric pressure, she felt someone come up behind her and realised the Wing

Commander was standing behind her chair. She glanced up nervously, but he just nodded. As she released the radio microphone, he asked. "How far away is he now?"

"He's nineteen miles away and eleven minutes from landing."

"Can you handle him? I think Wilkins should remain on the radar to keep an eye on overall developments."

"Yes, sir."

"Well done." He returned to the radar room. Kathleen could hear Willie saying, "The Red Air Force seems to have withdrawn to the northeast but I've got this worrying plot down here. It could be an approach to Tempelhof from Frankfurt/Main — or a stray Russkie at God knows what height."

The CO called into the control tower. "Can you get hold of Berlin Air Safety Centre or Tempelhof and see if they're expecting an in-bound flight."

"Yes, sir!" Groom reached for the telephone at once.

"I'd also like to talk to Air Commodore Waite."

"Yes, sir." Natalie picked up her phone. Because her call went through first, she passed the receiver to the Station Commander.

"Sir, a squadron of Yak flew over Gatow tower at only a little over null feet. I was told by the Berlin Air Safety Centre they are taking part in manoeuvres allegedly at over ten thousand feet—" He paused as the Air Commodore spoke, nodding unconsciously. "No, the BEA airliner is on approach now." He glanced at Kathleen as he said this.

She nodded, just as the radio crackled again. "Cutty Sark, this is Bealiner Seven-Seven. Passing Frohnau."

"Turn right on 180 and continue your descent to 2,500 feet."

"Turning right on 180 descending to 2,500 feet."

When she finished speaking, the Station Commander passed the information to the Air Commodore. After a pause, while he listened, he nodded, said, "Very good, sir," and hung up. Speaking generally, he noted, "Air Commodore Waite says the entire purpose of these manoeuvres is to intimidate us."

"Sir?" Groom drew attention to himself.

"Yes?"

"Tempelhof is expecting an in-bound — apparently a military air transport carrying VIPs, Congressmen. It reported being 'buzzed,' as the Yanks say."

"That's intimidation all right." The Station Commander concluded, adding, "Although, I'm not sure terrifying US Congressmen is in Stalin's best interests." He fell silent and then turned again to Borisenko. "Call Kuznetsov again and inform him that there are two passenger planes inbound. Ask him in my name, airman-to-airman, to clear those Yaks out of the approach corridors."

"Yes, sir!"

While Borisenko carried out his orders, the WingCo took up a position standing directly behind Kathleen. She concluded he was here to stay until he'd seen the safe arrival of the BEA flight.

During the war, Kathleen had often handled returning bombers with technical difficulties or wounded on board. She found an echo of that tension as she anxiously awaited the arrival of the BEA flight.

"Cutty Sark, this is Bealiner Seven-Seven," the radio came to life again. "We've passed the Grunewald Beacon."

"Bealiner Seven-Seven, turn right onto 260 and descend to 1,000 feet. You are making a direct visual approach on runway 26."

"Turning right onto 260 for a direct visual approach on runway 26. Passing 1,200 feet."

"What the devil—?" the voice was that of Flight Lieutenant Simpson but one look from the WingCo silenced him.

The civilian airliner was in sight at last, flaps and undercarriage down as it lined up on the runway.

"Cutty Sark to Bealiner Seven-Seven, you are cleared to land on visual."

"Roger." The aircraft was noticeably settling down. The nose lifted slightly, and the wide undercarriage kissed the end of the PSP runway. As the pilot gently applied the brakes, it slowed until the tail wheel dropped and the aircraft came to a gentle halt at the end of the runway. After a short pause, it decorously swung around, and Kathleen let out her breath in relief.

Behind her, the WingCo remarked to the room at large. "Well done, everyone." Then in a clipped voice directed at the Flying Control Officer, he snapped, "Flight Lieutenant Simpson, accompany me to my office. We have something to discuss."

Meeting with a War Criminal
Berlin-Mitte
Wednesday, 3 March 1948

"He's a war criminal!" Emily objected when Charlotte announced the name of their next interlocutor.

"No, no," Charlotte protested vigorously and in obvious distress. "He was found 'not guilty.'"

"Charlotte, he was head of the Council that funded the experiments made at the concentration camps! Don't you know what they did? They experimented on living human beings! They injected people with diseases like typhus, typhoid, tuberculosis, and malaria. They tried out different experimental drugs on them. They severed limbs, gouged out eyes, smashed out teeth, punctured lungs and stabbed stomachs and intestines, so they could experiment with various means of wound treatment! A third of the victims died outright and others were left maimed for life. The medical experiments were one of the most inhumane and most perverse atrocities of the entire Nazi regime!" Emily had been too sickened by the press accounts from the Nuremberg Medical Trial to read them to the end.

"But Dr Sauerbruch's position on the Reich Research Council was nominal, honorary." Charlotte protested. "He is a man of science, not finance. I'm sure he just signed whatever they put in front of him."

"Oh, I see! He was just following orders," Emily scoffed sarcastically. She at once regretted it. Charlotte recoiled, her shoulders curled inward, and she lowered her face, so her short hair fell over her eyes like a curtain.

"I'm sorry. I shouldn't have said that," Emily admitted. "But is it really necessary to meet with him?"

"It is an honour!" Charlotte countered. Pulling herself together, she sat upright again and shook her hair out of her face to meet Emily's eyes. This was their first serious tiff and Charlotte continued, "Dr Sauerbruch is one of the most famous surgeons in all Germany! He did many wonderful things going back to before WWI. He found ways to make it safer to operate on hearts and lungs and made fake hands and feet — what do you call them?"

"Prostheses?"

"Yes, yes. That's the word. He did experiments with wooden limbs and found a way of making them so amputees could move them. It was very important after the last war when there were so many veterans without arms and legs. I think it was for that work that he was given the German National Prize for Art and Science before the war."

"All very impressive," Emily said without sounding impressed, "but it does not prove he was not a Nazi or that he opposed these experiments on living people."

"But he *wasn't* a Nazi," Charlotte insisted. "He never joined the Party, and he had many Jewish friends. He *publicly* opposed the euthanasia program. He saved the life of General Ludwig Beck, the leader of the coup attempt against Hitler in 1944, and his son was a friend of Graf Stauffenberg."

"Fine, but I still don't see why we have to meet him."

"Because he's the head of surgery at the Charité! That's the most prestigious teaching and research hospital in Germany. Many winners of the Nobel Prize have worked there. It would be a great honour for AAI to be associated with it in any way."

"Isn't the Charité located in the Soviet Sector?" Emily asked puzzled. Since she and Charlotte had started visiting hospitals, she had become increasingly familiar with the map and landscape of Berlin.

"Yes," Charlotte conceded and for the first time since broaching the topic she seemed unsure of herself. "It is located opposite the Lehrter Bahnhof, just inside the Soviet Sector." She paused only briefly and then looked straight at Emily to ask solemnly, "Doesn't David want us to help the people of the Soviet Sector too? They are in many ways worse off because the Red Army did more damage in the East."

"I haven't had a chance to ask him," Emily prevaricated. "I have the feeling that we have more business than we can handle as it is."

"But the Charité!" Charlotte insisted. "It is so prestigious, Emily. Surely, there is no harm in just talking to Dr Sauerbruch and leaving the questionnaire with him?"

Emily capitulated.

Two days later just after 10 am, Emily and Charlotte drew up in front of the heterogeneous collection of buildings clustered together behind a high chain-link fence that made up the Charité complex. Soldiers of the Red Army manned a sentry post controlling access, and Emily felt Charlotte stiffen beside her. Their RAF driver, however, announced their appointment with military self-confidence. The Soviet soldier made a telephone call, received confirmation, and told them to follow the signs to the main administrative building. The signs were in Russian, but their driver was familiar with Russian signage.

Although the temperatures were now consistently in the forties Fahrenheit, a cold wind blew out of the northeast. Grit and dirt swirled around their legs as they mounted a half-dozen steps to a large entrance. The façade of the building, like most others in Berlin, had not been painted in a long time, so it was a grimy, dark grey. Inside, they were met with the smell of strong, cheap disinfectant. An old woman wielding a mop was diligently wiping the tiled floor. Behind the reception desk sat a woman in a nurse's uniform. She asked them to sign their names in a register and gave directions to Dr Sauerbruch's office.

The corridors were poorly lit but unlike other hospitals they had visited, no patients lay on beds in the hallways. Indeed, the Charité seemed eerily empty and comparatively sleepy after the cramped, crowded and hectic hospitals they had seen over the previous month. Emily wondered if that was because it was so prestigious that one had to be referred here or because the Red Army controlled access. The few people they encountered sitting outside offices or in small waiting areas were all middle-aged, comparatively well-dressed, and male — hardly a cross-section of the population. Something about them made Emily's skin creep.

Finally, they reached Dr Sauerbruch's office and knocked on the door. A receptionist invited them in and told them to take a seat while she announced them. They were not kept waiting but invited in immediately. They found themselves in a small, cramped office over-stuffed with old wooden furniture. Framed documents — diplomas, awards, and the like — covered the walls between the tall cupboards. Almost lost among the things was a small, fragile, elderly man wearing a white doctor's coat over his suit. He jumped to his feet and started around his desk with his hand outstretched. He had little hair left, round glasses, and a grey moustache.

His gestures were welcoming, his smile kind, and his handshake dry and warm. He invited them to sit and asked his receptionist to bring tea. Finally, he sat down opposite them and smiled benevolently. No, Emily conceded, he did not fit her image of a war criminal.

"Welcome to the Charité," Dr Sauerbruch opened, "I am very pleased that you have come to see me. I have heard so much about this air ambulance scheme and was most anxious to learn more and meet the people involved. You can imagine my surprise to be told two *ladies* wished to talk to me about it!" He laughed delightedly. "It is the ladies who will put this world right, I think, no?"

Emily shook her head ambivalently, "Let's just say, we'd like to help. The owners of the ambulance are both men. Graefin Walmsdorf and I are simply doing the market research."

Dr Sauerbruch nodded approvingly. "I hope everything is going well. My colleagues are very excited about the idea. Although we have quite good facilities here at the Charité, of course, our capacity is limited. We cannot handle all the cases, and most Berlin hospitals are understaffed and lack proper surgical equipment. Many lack even basic machines -- much less specialized tools for complex surgery. Sending patients across the Soviet Zone by train takes time and can be fraught with danger. Flying them to better-equipped facilities outside Berlin would be marvellous."

"The company still faces several challenges," Emily warned, "First and foremost payment mechanisms."

"Yes, yes, of course," Dr Sauerbruch nodded earnestly and yet waived the issue aside. "Money is always a problem, although health care ought to be free."

"We have a questionnaire here," Charlotte took the form out of her purse and timidly passed it to the famous surgeon. He took it only to place it on his desk behind him without looking at it.

They could hear voices behind the door to the anteroom and then without a knock a second doctor swept in. He was young and vigorous, tall and upright, and his expression was exasperated. "Vati, did I hear—"

"Ah, Fritz. Let me introduce you. These ladies have come about the air ambulance."

"Ah," the younger doctor turned to Emily and Charlotte, who had both come to their feet. He bowed over their hands as he shook them, while the famous surgeon introduced his second son Friedrich. Then looking for a chair, the younger Sauerbruch seated himself, while his father explained, "These ladies were just telling me they have been tasked with assessing the demand for an air ambulance."

"None from this hospital," Friedrich Sauerbruch declared immediately and firmly — to the obvious astonishment of his father.

"Fritz, that's not true —"

"Father, listen to me. The air ambulance as I understand it —" he interrupted himself to turn to Emily and Charlotte and add, "Correct me if I am misinformed — would fly from Gatow to hospitals in the West."

Emily and Charlotte nodded, and the elder Sauerbruch asked, "So?"

The younger doctor drew an exasperated breath, and then attempted to sound patient as he explained, "The patients at this hospital are all either members of the Soviet occupation forces, who naturally prefer to be treated in the Soviet Union, or members of the Socialist Unity Party of Germany who likewise prefer to be treated in the Soviet Union. No one admitted to this hospital has any need or desire to be evacuated to a hospital in the capitalist Zones."

"Fritz, that is ridiculous—" the elder man started to say, but his son silenced him with a frown. The old man pressed his lips together and looked up resentfully at the younger man.

"Now, ladies, in the interests of saving everyone's time, allow me to escort you out," the younger Dr Sauerbruch concluded.

That was an order, not a request. Emily and Charlotte stood and turned to shake hands with the elder Dr Sauerbruch. The famous surgeon clasped their hands warmly between both of his in turn. He met their eyes one after the other as he assured them, "It is a wonderful project, an excellent service. It could save many lives. I wish you all the best. Good luck!" As they were ushered out of the office by the younger doctor, the famous man called out a second time "Good luck!" Emily thought she heard something plaintive in his wishes for them.

The younger Sauerbruch marched them down the dingy halls, past the pale-faced men in grey suits that gazed after them with expressionless faces. This time Emily noticed that many wore the same lapel pin as Friedrich Sauerbruch: two hands clasped. It was the symbol of the Soviet-controlled "German Unity Party."

The young Dr Sauerbruch maintained a pseudo smile and a forced friendliness as he escorted them. He made small talk with Emily without listening to her answers. When they reached the reception, they signed out while he waited for them. To Emily's surprise, he did not simply see them through the door, he came out to the car with them.

As Emily dropped into the back seat, he leaned down and spoke through the open door. "If you want my advice, Mrs Priestman, you will not try to start this business."

She was provoked enough to ask, "Why ever not?"

"Because, Mrs Priestman, it is only viable as long as the Western Allies have a military presence and control airfields in Berlin. Yet the imperialist powers have no business here whatsoever, and we Germans are fed up with them — most especially your air forces, which we came to know all too well when you rained terror on us day and night. We do not want your air ambulance or any other patronizing charities. Just leave and let us build back our own country the way we want it." Then he slammed the door shut before she could answer.

"I'm sorry," Charlotte whispered as they drove away.

"I'm not," Emily retorted. "That was a highly interesting and most educational meeting. Besides, you were right about the elder Dr Sauerbruch. I no longer believe he knowingly advocated cruel and painful experiments on living humans. We will, however, have to tell David what the younger Sauerbruch said."

Charlotte lifted her head in alarm and asked, "Must we? I mean, as you said yourself, the need for the ambulance from the West is great enough to justify the ambulance service. And Dr Sauerbruch senior confirmed that. His son was just trying to frighten us. He is a Soviet stooge! Did you see his party pin? He does not represent the real Berlin." Charlotte was emphatic both from conviction and fear that David might change his mind.

Emily nodded, "I suppose you're right, but we will still have to tell David."

Charlotte nodded unhappily, and they fell silent, lost in their separate thoughts.

After dropping Charlotte at her apartment house, Emily rode alone in the backseat if her car as her driver took her home. As the broken masonry of the battered city rolled by, her inner apprehension grew. She couldn't escape the feeling that Berlin was seething beneath the crust of its wounds. On the surface lay a dry, broken wasteland, inhabited by ordinary people struggling to survive, but underneath, like a festering wound, poisonous forces were at work — the black market, the prostitution of young mothers, kidnapping, institutionalised theft on the part of the Soviet state, sanctioned theft by the ordinary Soviet soldier and a clandestine campaign by Stalin to change the post-war balance of power by seizing control of Germany — if not the entire continent. The more she thought about it, the more absurd it seemed to try to start a business in this environment. Indeed, for the first time since their arrival, she wondered if it had been the right decision to come to Berlin at all. More than David's business was a risk. The Western Allies were under threat and RAF Gatow would be a prime target.

Chapter Nine
Deceptive Calm

False Expectations
Ministry of Civil Aviation, London
Tuesday, 16 March 1948

Kit felt the same nervousness as before oral exams. True, he was only facing one man sitting behind a solid oak desk rather than several on a platform, but the sense of his fate being decided from "on high" remained. He'd sent out dozens of job inquiry letters but so far he'd received only one invitation to an interview. It was for a position with the air crash investigation department of the Ministry of Civil Aviation. The work hardly sounded like what he'd dreamed about for the last three years, but it appeared to be the only kind he had a chance of getting.

The balding and bespectacled civil servant behind the heavy desk looked like the epitome of a bookkeeper. Since he was in a civilian suit, there was no way of knowing if once upon a time he had worn wings or not. Kit doubted it.

"So, Mr Moran," the civil servant opened the interview. "I see you have a commendable war record, but then so do all the candidates we see for jobs here." Really? Kit asked himself. They all had DFMs and DFCs? Most of his fellow students didn't.

The civil servant continued, "And I see you will obtain your BSc in Aeronautical Engineering this summer. Where was that from?" Although voiced nominally as a question, the civil servant did not look to Kit for an answer. Instead, he scanned the documents in front of him, confident that the information was already there. "Ah, yes, Leeds." He made it sound as if Leeds was an inferior institution. Kit supposed the man behind the desk had attended Oxford or Cambridge, or maybe he just wanted people to think he had.

The interviewer looked intently at Kit. "Do you have other qualifications that make you suitable for this job?"

No, Kit thought to himself, but he gamely answered, "I've survived three crashes."

"Oh? Interesting, but I'm not sure that is particularly relevant. Our work does not entail trying to *replicate* crashes, you understand, but rather explaining them. It is very meticulous, very tedious work in many ways. After a crash, we sift through the debris — literally thousands of pieces of shattered aircraft — trying to find the *one* piece that was defective or broke *before* the machine went down. One needs to discount all the damage done by impact or fire. It requires the utmost precision and attention to the tiniest details."

Why, Kit asked himself, did this man assume he was not capable of either? Out loud he remarked only, "I understand, sir."

"And you believe you can do that kind of work?"

"Of course. I was a flight engineer before I was a pilot and a fitter before that. I know engines very well."

"I see," the man did not sound convinced. Kit sensed this interview was not going well, but he didn't know why or what to do differently. Georgina had helped him draft his letter of application, giving it a stylistic polish that he did not possess, but she could not give him tips on how to answer these questions.

"Mr Moran, could you tell me why you applied for this position?"

Because I need a job, Kit thought to himself. "It sounded very interesting, sir. As I said, I've crashed three times myself."

"Surely you knew what caused your crashes? Presumably enemy action. Isn't that correct?"

"Yes," Kit admitted. Flak, night fighter, Me262. Why did he get the feeling that this man didn't want to talk to him, let alone listen to his answers?

"Mr Moran, what are you reading at the moment?"

"I'm reading for my exams, sir."

"Yes, of course. What I mean is what do you read for pleasure?"

Was this some sort of trick question? What answer did they want? Kit couldn't imagine.

"You do read for pleasure, don't you?" The man made it sound as if someone who did not was totally humid.

"I like reading very much, sir," Kit assured him honestly.

"So, what is it you like to read?"

Kit liked reading novels when he had time to submerge in a book, but he feared that didn't sound sophisticated enough. He considered saying something like biographies or economics but feared he'd be asked for an example. He opted for "literature."

"Literature? That's a bit vague, wouldn't you say? What sort of literature?"

"Classical literature. Joseph Conrad. Rudyard Kipling. G.B. Shaw. Remarque." Kit threw out the names of the first authors who came to mind, but he sensed he was digging himself into a hole.

"Not mysteries? Crime novels?"

"No, not particularly."

"A pity. We've found that many of our best employees have a police background or at least a keen interest in solving a mystery. They are the kind of people who like reading crime and mystery novels for fun."

Kit was beginning to think they had already identified the candidate they intended to hire. They were probably just going through the motions of an interview to fulfil some bureaucratic requirement. Doggedly, he pointed out. "There was no mention of wanting candidates who read crime novels in the advertisement. It said you were looking for an aeronautical engineer." He couldn't quite keep the tinge of resentment out of his voice; Georgina would have cringed had she heard him.

"We need an aeronautical engineer with an interest in investigations." The civil servant answered firmly. His smile was almost condescending.

"Yes, that's why I'm here," Kit lied. He was here because he didn't have any other alternatives at the moment.

"Mr Moran, I'm going to be perfectly honest with you. You have all the official qualifications for the job — assuming, of course, you get your degree — but my colleagues and I have the impression that you aren't quite the right fit for it. You know, 617 Squadron and all that. Rather a bunch of cowboys, weren't you?"

"Cowboys? No, sir. We were a Royal Air Force squadron specialized in precision bombing." Kit's temper was starting to simmer.

"Yes, but don't pretend you weren't very full of yourselves, taking unnecessary risks and doing all that low-level flying as much to impress your girlfriends as to defeat Germany." The man's smile was unquestionably condescending now.

"No, I didn't fly into flak at 600 feet to impress my girlfriend," Kit told him, his anger nearing the boiling point.

"Don't get me wrong, we here at the Ministry greatly admire what you Bomber Boys did, which is why I have been authorised to make you an alternative offer."

"I'm sorry. I don't think I take your meaning." Kit tried to keep himself from exploding.

"We don't think you're the right man for the job you applied for, but we are prepared to offer you a more junior position as assistant to the aeronautical engineer investigator. It would require disassembling engines and labelling the pieces of the wreck under investigation. It comes with a salary of five pounds a week."

That was half the compensation of the advertised position. It would barely replace the money his father had been sending them and certainly would not make up for the loss of Georgina's earnings. Furthermore, the cost of housing was much higher in London than in Leeds. They would never be able to make ends meet on five pounds a week plus his disability. Kit felt as if after six years of war and three years in university, he was right back where he started: earning apprentice wages.

But it would be a foot in the door at the Ministry, a rational voice in the back of his head reasoned with him. It would pay the bills while he looked for something better, and London had lots of schools. Georgina would have a better chance of finding work here than anywhere else — provided they could find someone to look after Donna. But how could they afford a nanny on slave wages?

Kit silenced the voice of reason in his brain, got to his feet and took his hat. "No, thank you!" he snapped at the astonished civil servant.

As he walked out the door, he heard another voice in his head. The CO at 617, Johnny Fauquier, was commenting: "Bloody minded, that's what you are, Moran. Bloody minded."

Commitments
Berlin Kreuzberg
Wednesday, 17 March 1948

Charlotte stood before the cracked and tarnished mirror of the wardrobe with a sense of despair. She looked like a scarecrow: a stick figure in ugly, mismatched and worn-out clothes. For a moment, her memory played tricks, superimposing an image of her at the Christmas ball of 1940. She'd worn an off-the-shoulder, blue velvet gown, and had pulled her long, blond hair away from her face to expose dangling earrings but let it hang down her back. As they danced the night away, the look in Fritz's eyes had told her she was beautiful — at least to him. His proposal followed only two days later.

And now? She simply could not go like this to the meeting with David Goldman. He had asked her to meet him at Café Kranzler at 3 p.m. for tea. She didn't fool herself that this was a personal invitation. He was not taking her to tea as Fritz might have done. He wanted to talk to her about his business. She hoped against hope that he was going to offer her a job, a permanent job, although she wasn't entirely sure what he would want her to do much less if she could do it. All she knew was that Mr Goldman had decided to go ahead, despite the younger Sauerbruch's warning and the various problems Emily had hinted at.

But she was getting ahead of herself. First, she had to make herself presentable for tea with a gentleman. There was nothing she could do about her hair except wash and comb it. She had found lipstick and rouge lying in a drawer somewhere and she would apply them to her pale face. But what should she wear? For so long, she had tried to disguise her sex behind shapeless clothing. Even when she visited hospitals with Emily, she tried to look "professional" and "serious." Now, for the first time since the end of the war, she wanted to look like a woman, if only for a few hours. That meant not wearing her brother's shirts but finding a proper blouse.

She lifted her eyes to the top of the wardrobe. There, lying side-by-side were two suitcases, her mother's suitcases. Horst had removed them from the shattered wagon and transferred them to their own. When they reached Berlin, he had placed them on top of the wardrobe, and she had not touched them since. She didn't even know exactly what was in them.

Her mother's clothes presumably. Clothes that hadn't been worn and washed, faded, torn, darned and patched and lost their buttons over the last three years.

Charlotte went to the kitchen and took one of the chairs. She placed it directly beside the wardrobe and with shaking hands pulled the first and then the second suitcase down. There were brown stains on the suitcases. Water stains? Horse blood? Her parents' blood? She stepped back, staring at them.

Images of the strafing returned: the roar of the aircraft engine so close overhead followed by the crunching explosions of the rounds of cannon going off. She'd put her hands over her ears and ducked down, but already it was over. The only sound was the high-pitched screaming of the injured horse thrashing in the traces. She opened her eyes to see her father hanging off the seat, and her mother flung forward, blood spreading across her back, her head gone.

Like slamming a book shut, Charlotte shut down her memories. All she allowed herself to think was that, no, the stains were not blood stains; the luggage had been behind the carnage.

Yet her hands trembled as her thumbs pushed the latches open and she flung back the lid. She was confronted by woollen stockings and long underwear. Her practical mother had packed these things on top for easy access. Charlotte pushed the underwear aside to find a stack of white and pastel blouses beside a stack of dark skirts. Nestled between the two piles was a long cardboard box. Frowning, she lifted the lid off the box and gasped. It contained her mother's pearls. A long necklace, a bracelet, a large brooch in an elaborate Jugendstil setting, a ring, pearl studs and dangling pearl earrings. Charlotte hastily closed the box. Pearls like these would buy a whole ham, five pounds of sugar, maybe even a crate of oranges or a bag of coffee on the black-market — ridiculous "riches" worth only a fraction of the jewellery's real worth — never mind the sentimental value. She did not want to be tempted.

She reached for the blouses instead and shook them out one after another. There were six altogether. They had collars, puffy sleeves, lace trim and deep cuffs in different combinations. Charlotte tried on each one. Although they were all too wide for her, they still made her feel pretty. She chose one with a broad, lace collar, and set it aside for ironing; after three years in a suitcase, it was badly creased. The skirts fitted poorly because her mother had been considerably wider than she, but she chose one that was belted and pulled the belt to the very last hole. That bunched up the waistline, but it gave her a bit more shape. Last but not least, she found two pairs of black silk stockings. It was a gift from beyond the grave, and she thanked her mother silently.

When she had finished dressing, she looked once more in the mirror and for the first time in years she saw a woman looking back at her rather than a formless, lost soul. Hopefully Mr Goldman would like what he saw.

The famous Café Kranzler on the Kurfuerstendamm had been utterly destroyed, but an enterprising Berliner had opened up a café on the ground floor of a neighbouring building and brazenly called his new establishment after the famous older one. The upper stories of this building on the corner of Uhland Strasse were still ruins, but the restaurant had a roof and glazed windows. The owner had also set up tables on the broad sidewalk out in front, and several hardy souls had seated themselves at them, wearing their overcoats in the still chilly March air.

David took a table inside, close to the window. He sent the attentive waiter away, telling him he was waiting for someone and sat back to watch the world pass by.

Kiwi had passed his flight test within a week of when they'd last met, and since then had been working hard to clock hours on their Wellington. Kiwi was a natural pilot, David acknowledged. The only problem was keeping him off the booze. Yet he hoped Kiwi had learned his lesson. To his credit, he'd found them some first-rate erks, and the modifications to the Wellington were moving forward as planned. So, all was on track on the operational side of things. Regarding the financial prospects, after sorting through the thirty-seven questionnaires Emily and Charlotte had collected from hospitals, David had no doubts about demand. Payment remained the only major unsolved issue, and he was optimistic. Although the International Red Cross had not committed to paying the costs, the local representative favoured the project and promised to advocate for it with his superiors. David was committed to moving forward to the next stage: establishing an office in Berlin.

He glanced around to see if Charlotte had arrived yet and became aware that many of the women strolling along the sidewalk in front of the café were looking for customers. As the waiters chased yet another woman away, he wondered whether this was the right place to meet with Charlotte after all. He didn't want her to think that he thought…. He searched his memory for an alternative, but it was too late. Charlotte was outside.

She looked enchantingly old-fashioned in a straight, dark skirt that reached almost to her ankles and a white blouse with a wide, lace collar. He had seen pictures of his mother dressed like that as a girl, he thought. Charlotte hung back, intimidated by the soliciting, and David jumped up and rushed outside. "Graefin Walmsdorf!"

Her face lit up with relief, and she came towards him.

She was roughly his height, yet she seemed to gaze at him admiringly. David thought it must be his new uniform. It was double-breasted like a navy uniform but black rather than blue, and the rank and wings were in red rather than silver or gold making it both subtle and striking. He was proud of how smart and distinctive it looked; it made him feel good. To Charlotte, he apologised, "Please, forgive me. I had no idea this neighbourhood was so — run down. Do you wish to go somewhere else? I believe there's a tearoom across from the British Embassy…"

"Oh, that's so far away. This is fine," she assured him.

He stood back to let her enter ahead of him, gesturing to the table he had selected. As they sat down the waiter appeared, and David asked Charlotte what she wanted to order, listing the offerings: "Coffee — although it's not real? Tea? Berliner Weisse? Wine?"

"Tea would be very nice."

"With cake of some sort, perhaps?" David prompted, indicating the vitrine where two cakes, already sliced into pieces, waited; one was chocolate and the other was a fruit tart of some kind.

"Oh, may I?" Charlotte replied in surprised delight as though she hadn't dreamed of such a treat.

David went to the vitrine, paid for a piece of each cake and returned with the chits that he gave the waiter. "You can try both and eat whichever you like best," he promised.

She thanked him, looking embarrassed. David wished he knew why. "You don't mind meeting me like this without Emily, do you?"

"Oh, no! I don't mind. Thank you for inviting me. You said you wanted to talk about something?" She looked at him earnestly, as if expecting bad news that she was anxious to get out of the way.

"Well, yes. We're getting very close to going operational, you know. I'm hoping we can move the aircraft to Berlin on April 1 and start taking patients one to two weeks after that."

"That is very exciting. It will help so many people."

"What I was wondering was whether you might be able to —"

The waiter chose this inconvenient moment to arrive with the tea and the two pieces of cake. He made a fuss of setting everything out and asking if there was anything else they needed. David told him 'No' firmly and he departed. Turning back to Charlotte, he asked, "Where was I? Yes, I was hoping you could join Air Ambulance International as an employee."

Charlotte's eyes grew large. "A — a permanent employee? Full-time?"

"Yes. We need several. Kiwi is my Chief Operating Officer; he's responsible for keeping the aircraft in top condition, managing the ground crew, handling the spare parts inventory, and ensuring all necessary maintenance is done in a timely fashion. In short, he's in charge of everything that has to do with the aircraft being operational. I've got my work cut out for me keeping track of the finances and ensuring that we have both the cash flow we need for operations and are profitable in the long run. For now, I'm also doing all the bookkeeping and the accounting, although I hope to hire someone to do both eventually. What I thought you could do was customer management. That is receiving requests, identifying requirements, setting priorities, working out a rational flight plan, handling the liaison with medical escorts and family members and, of course, dealing with customer complaints, if we have any." It was only as he laid it all out that he realised how much he was asking of her.

"That is a very responsible job," Charlotte echoed his thoughts, and her expression was serious rather than delighted. She stammered, "I — I ..."

"Yes?" He prompted, wondering — too late — if he'd overwhelmed her. She had trained as a secretary and her only work experience was as a freelance journalist.

"I'd be very happy to have a steady job." She seemed to think about her answer and added more forcefully, "I'd like this job *very* much — as long as Emily isn't angry. I think she hoped to stay involved in the business."

"Of course! She is responsible for marketing, personnel and facilities, that is liaison with BEA and the RAF and keeping personnel records, but her German isn't good enough for what I'm asking you to do."

"Oh, I'm glad to hear that!" Charlotte said with relief as her face broke into a smile. "It would be wonderful working together with Emily."

David smiled back at her and admitted, "She said the same thing about you."

Charlotte smiled more broadly but then seemed to catch herself, and in a voice that suggested she was almost afraid to ask, she inquired. "Do you have any idea what you might be able to pay?"

"I was thinking of starting at five pounds a week or 260 pounds a year. Does that sound reasonable?"

"Pounds? Not marks?" Charlotte's eyes were huge.

"Yes."

"That — that — would be wonderful!" Her face split into the biggest smile David had ever seen on her yet. "With so much money we could afford to heat the sitting room, and we could buy sugar and coffee and maybe some good detergent — oh, I'm sorry, I must be boring you with my silly list."

"No," David told her honestly. "But I am worried about one thing. Our office will be at RAF Gatow. We have just two desks and one telephone in a corner of the BEA office there. I understand that you live in Kreuzberg, so we need to discuss how you will get from Kreuzberg to Gatow."

Charlotte's smile had frozen, and the joy was draining out of her face.

David hastened to assure her, "I wouldn't want you to take public transport. I understand it is neither safe nor reliable."

Charlotte nodded agreement mutely, her expression sad although she did not dare speak.

"What would a taxi cost?" David asked.

"Oh, much too much!" She replied, shaking her head vigorously.

"I'll pay it," David declared in a tone that prohibited further discussion.

She looked at him with a mixture of awe and amazement, as if this offer was too good to be true. "You -- you would do that for me?"

"Yes. So, your salary would be 5 pounds a week plus a transport allowance to cover taxi fare to and from work daily. "

It seemed to take a moment before she dared believe him. Then she stammered out, "That is very generous. I would be very grateful." Yet she remained subdued rather than exuberant.

David was on the brink of asking what was wrong when he realized her eyes were watering. His offer had evidently overwhelmed her, and that embarrassed David. To overcome the awkwardness, he forged ahead in a professional tone. "Kiwi and I will fly the aircraft in with the ground crew on April 1, and I want the office fully functional by April 5 at the latest. The problem is there is a bit of bureaucracy to get you permission to work on an RAF facility."

Charlotte nodded seriously, understanding at once.

"I was therefore wondering if it would it be possible for you to come to Gatow tomorrow so we can start getting you an ID and station access? Emily and I could also show you the office space and explain the procedures. We'll also need to draft a contract that you can read through carefully and sign when ready."

"Yes, yes. Of course!" Charlotte assured him, brightening again as the reality of the job sank in. She'd swallowed down the tears and joy returned to her face. She was looking at David with so much gratitude, in fact, that he started to feel self-conscious. He hoped it wasn't just because she needed the money so badly. "Can you type by the way?" he remembered to ask.

"Yes, yes. I went to secretarial school," Charlotte assured him.

"Excellent!" David grinned with relief. Neither he nor Emily could type. "So, all we need is to find a typewriter."

"I have one," Charlotte told him. "I could not have worked as a journalist without it."

"Perfect. I will either buy it from you or lease it. We can include that in the contract. Now, why don't you try the cake?" David nodded in the direction of the untouched pieces of cake in front of her.

Charlotte looked down, surprised. After a moment she asked timidly, "May I have the chocolate cake?"

"Of course," David assured her and pushed the plate with the chocolate cake closer to her.

"Chocolate is my favourite," she admitted as, with great concentration, she cut off a little piece, pierced it with the prongs of the fork and put it into her mouth. When she closed her eyes in delight, David smiled. Her love of chocolate was a wonderful thing, he thought, because now he knew how to make her happy.

Mental Gulags
Berlin-Mitte
Thursday, 18 March 1948

Jakob Liebherr walked from the underground or U-bahn station "Stadtmitte" toward the tall, turreted, red-brick building that housed the Berlin City Council. Although referred to as the "Rote Rathaus" because of the red brick used in its construction, the name increasingly seemed like an ominous political omen. Here in the Soviet Sector, red flags flew from the roofs and huge banners of Stalin plastered the façades. Red Army troops stood guard outside all the government buildings, their Kalishnikovs over their shoulders.

Liebherr bought a copy of the Communist-controlled *Berliner Zeitung* to see what nonsense they were spouting today and perused it as he continued to the Rathaus. The lead article demanded an end to "Four Power" government in Germany. The heroic, long-suffering Soviet champions of the German people could not be expected to endure Western arrogance much longer. The former "terror bombers" were now terrorizing German workers not with bombs but with their devious tricks. Cartoons showed fat men with gold watches on chains and dollars falling out of their pockets pulling the strings of puppets that were skinny little men in rags who wore the faces of Germany's Social Democratic leaders.

A small 'spontaneous' demonstration condemning 'capitalist machinations' to divide Germany and calling for an end to 'Western interference' in the domestic affairs of Germany milled about at the foot of the front steps of the Rathaus. In the past, Liebherr had often stopped to talk to the demonstrators. Most freely admitted that they received extra rations for demonstrating. Others were former forced labourers, hoping to return to their home countries — something they could only do with Soviet permits.

Liebherr nodded and smiled at the pawns of the Soviet machine and mounted the steps to the front door of the Rathaus. Instead of being waved through by the Soviet soldiers (who knew him well), the Kalashnikovs came down. Scowling, the soldiers demanded his papers. Liebherr patiently handed over his ID and building pass. The Soviet soldier snatched them from his hand with a glance at his naked wrist. Seeing nothing to steal, the soldier made a great show of looking at Liebherr's papers upside-down and turning them this way and that before shoving them back with a decisive "*Nyet!*" He made a gesture indicating that Liebherr should go around to the side door.

With a sigh, Liebherr made his way to the side entrance where the farce was re-enacted. A gong from the clock tower struck the quarter hour reminding Liebherr that it was getting late. He started to get annoyed. Addressing the soldiers in Russian, he demanded to see an officer. A flicker of uncertainty passed over their faces, and they pulled aside to discuss what to do. Finally, one went to fetch an officer. After a fifteen-minute wait, a lieutenant appeared, glanced over Liebherr's papers cursorily and waved him inside.

Because of this treatment, Liebherr arrived late for the committee meeting he was supposed to attend. He slipped inside the chamber and found a seat just as the Chairman cleared his throat to announce, "The next item is medical infrastructure. Herr Dr Pelzner, do you have your report ready?"

Dr Pelzner nodded, removed a cardboard folder from his leather portfolio and proceeded to read a detailed account of Berlin's medical infrastructure. It listed the number of hospital beds, Intensive Care Units, ambulances, and operating theatres. The report noted that progress had been made in the last year to increase facilities and claimed there were now over 15,000 hospital beds, almost half pre-war levels. Furthermore, a new hospital was being built by the Soviets just outside Berlin in the Soviet Zone, which would add another 1,000 hospital beds to the capacity available.

Nevertheless, Dr Pelzner stressed, the demand for hospital care still far exceeded the capacity of the city to provide it. Despite 200 student nurses, who had commenced training in Berlin's hospitals there was an acute shortage of staff. "There is," he intoned, "not one doctor in the entire city qualified to conduct brain surgery — and no operating theatre equipped to handle such surgery. We have only two doctors capable of heart surgery, three who do lung surgery, and five who can conduct eye surgery. Blood banks remain woefully inadequate, with some types of blood in very short supply, or not available at all."

Dr Pelzner concluded by stressing that recruitment efforts to attract more qualified medical personnel to Berlin had produced extremely disappointing results. "The political situation here is viewed as unstable. Moreover, in anticipation of Marshall Aid pouring into the Western Zones, doctors and nurses are leaving Berlin to relocate to the West. Unless something is done to reverse this trend, the shortage of trained medical practitioners will soon reach catastrophic proportions, particularly among surgeons." He closed his folder.

"Any questions for Dr Pelzner?" The Chairman asked.

"Do you think paying a premium would induce more surgeons to move to Berlin?" One of the committee members asked.

"A thousand times nothing is still nothing," Dr Pelzner snapped. "As long as the currency is worthless, salaries are worthless. We've all heard the rumours of a possible currency reform, but to date, they are just that: rumours."

"If we cannot attract medical personnel here, we will be forced to send the sick out of the city for treatment," one of the councilmen noted. "We should ask the Allies to regularly provide dedicated hospital cars on their trains."

"At least an air ambulance service is due to start operations from Gatow next month," Jacob Liebherr noted incidentally. Charlotte Walmsdorf had been so excited and enthusiastic about her new job that she'd stopped by yesterday evening to tell the Liebherrs about it. When Christian came home, he joined them, bringing over some of his wine. It had turned into a little party -- something so rare that Liebherr was still cherishing the afterglow.

His colleagues stared at him astonished. "Is this service exclusively for the Allies?" Someone asked.

"No, it's being offered by a private British firm. They will charge, of course. I don't know the details, but I can find out more if you like."

The others nodded and tasked him to do that before continuing to the next item on the agenda. This turned out to be a report by an LPD member, who described in an angry yet frightened voice about being summoned to a police station in the middle of the night. He said the police threatened him with the confiscation of his ration cards and the cancellation of the operating license for his business unless he supported the side of "progress" with his vote and voice.

In a whining voice, he reminded them that he had a wife and a young family. His children had all grown out of their shoes. Were they supposed to go barefoot just to support the right of the Amis to be in Berlin?

Liebherr's good mood instantly vanished. All his senses snapped into a kind of overdrive as his instincts detected the whiff of panic in the air. So, this is what we've come to, he thought, angrily. Without asking to be acknowledged by the chairman he burst out. "If you think that is what this is about, you deserve whatever you get." All twenty committee members swung about to look at him. Liebherr continued sharply. "If you have no shoes for your children, it is because the Soviets have robbed us of our factories, our raw materials and even our labourers. How many is it now?" Liebherr turned to the colleague tasked with keeping track of Soviet kidnappings.

"We have verified 24,697 random workers, predominantly women, have been taken away," came the answer without hesitation. "Those are in addition to the 2,238 scientists and engineers specifically targeted because of their qualifications."

Liebherr nodded his thanks to his colleague but continued forcefully to the LPD member. "If you are short of rations, it is because the collectivization of agriculture produces famine year after year in Ukraine —the former breadbasket of Europe. If you lack clothes, it is because Soviet-printed banknotes are worthless and so we cannot import cotton or wool to produce clothing.

"But be my guest, Comrade, support the Soviets and increase your pitiable ration from 1,000 to 1,200 calories a day. Buy your wife and children cardboard shoes produced by slaves in Siberia and eat Soviet shit all day long, but don't expect the rest of us to pity you for it!"

"I didn't ask for your pity!" The man retorted angrily. "I'm simply telling you the facts. The Soviets control our access to food, clothes, electricity, transport, heat, and information. What is the point of resisting? What is the point of fighting? What good can come of it? We will all end up in a gulag!"

"You are already in a mental gulag," Liebherr scoffed, but inwardly his stomach was tying itself in knots. Just like when the Nazis came to power, he thought, most people were too frightened to fight for their freedom. The vast majority would cave into the pressure, and he would be alone with only a few other brave souls, too few to stop the red tide any more than the brown one.

Chapter Ten
The Ides of March

A Night at the Opera
Berlin-Mitte
Friday, 19 March 1948

Kathleen and Lionel had not spent an evening together without Hope since the disastrous episode at the nightclub, but the opening night of *Aida* at the Staatsoper with Gustav Furtwaengler conducting had been too great a temptation for Kathleen to refuse. Furtwaengler was one of those great musicians who everyone had heard about, but in Berlin, he was particularly famous. He was also the focus of a new controversy. Despite making several overtly anti-Nazi remarks, including direct insults about Hitler, he had been allowed to continue conducting throughout the Nazi era. Some said he'd clandestinely helped Jews, others that he had not done enough. Regardless of what they thought of his politics, however, the Berliners were united in adoring him as a conductor. The Western Allies' insistence on a "de-Nazification" trial had been dubbed "utter idiocy" by Lionel.

"He wasn't even a Nazi Party member," Lionel pointed out. "Certainly no one is accusing him of war crimes! The worst he did was conduct concerts in front of leading Nazis. The Berliners love Furtwaengler, and our shabby treatment of him makes us look like small-minded tyrants. Meanwhile, the Soviets garner all the credit for bringing *der Meister* back as conductor of the Staatsoper!"

Kathleen tended to agree with Lionel that Western small-mindedness had handed the Soviets a propaganda triumph on a silver platter. Yet mostly the prospect of attending the opera excited her simply because the famous musician would be conducting live and she would have a chance to see one of her favourite operas, *Aida*. She arranged for Hope to spend the evening with Anne and Violet and obtained permission to wear civilian clothes for the event.

At the last moment, Lionel called to say that General Robertson had decided to boycott the performance and had permitted Lionel to use his box. "You're going to have to dress up for this!" he warned. "You'll be seated front and centre, next to the royal box. A great many opera glasses will be trained on you!"

In a panic, Kathleen turned to Marie Casson, who wore the same size clothes. She came from a much more affluent family and had a larger wardrobe of evening attire. Marie graciously loaned Kathleen both a gown and a heavy evening cloak.

As always, Lionel was on time to the minute, and he smiled broadly at the sight of Kathleen. "Where have you been hiding that cloak?" he asked as he opened the car door for her.

"It isn't mine. I borrowed it."

"Ah. Good thinking. Let's swing by my quarters on our way. I have something I think you'll like."

"I thought we were in a hurry?"

"This won't take long. You'll like it."

Lionel raced up the Gatower Dam and "flew low" along the Heer Strasse. Near the Olympic stadium, he stopped at the villa he shared with two other officers of the Military Governor's staff and asked Kathleen to take a seat in the front sitting room. "Let me see what you're wearing under that cloak."

Kathleen dutifully untied the cord at her throat and drew the cloak away from her shoulders.

"Ah. Lovely! Absolutely stunning. But that little gold chain at your neck isn't quite the thing for such a generous neckline, do you think? I have something I can loan to you."

Kathleen instinctively felt the gold chain at her neck. It was the only jewellery she owned; she'd given no thought at all to whether it matched the neckline or not. Already Lionel was back with a black, velveteen box. He opened it and she gasped. Lionel laughed in delight at her surprise. "Turn around!" He ordered.

Kathleen did as she was told but a shiver ran down her spine as the icy cold jewels were laid around her neck. The necklace consisted of a very large amethyst surrounded by diamonds hanging from a choker of larger amethysts alternating with smaller diamonds. She had never seen — much less worn — anything like it. "Lionel! Where did you get this?"

"It's just on loan. Now give me your right arm. Here's the matching bracelet." He fastened an amethyst and diamond bracelet around her arm and then pushed two earrings into her hand. "There's a mirror in the hall. Go put those on — but screw them tight! We wouldn't want to lose one."

"Are you sure this is all right, Lionel?" Kathleen was feeling very out of her league.

He laughed. "Perfectly. We're going to the opera. Everyone is going to be showing off what they have!"

He was right, of course. Mercedes and BMWs, Voisins and Citroens, Roll-Royces, Buicks and Cadillacs. Most of the men climbing out of the polished cars were weighted down with gold braid and panels of medals in the Russian fashion, but Kathleen caught sight of some American Army and Air Force officers and other British Army officers, all less senior than the unending array of Soviet generals. As for the women, like her, they were in long gowns and cloaks and glittered with jewels. One could almost have forgotten one was in the ravaged corpse of a battered city; darkness hid the skyline of broken ruins.

The sound of the orchestra warming up wafted out of the open doors to the auditorium as they left their outer garments at the cloakroom. Shortly afterwards, a buzzer warned that the performance would start in ten minutes. Lionel bought a program from one of the ushers and escorted Kathleen into the magnificent inner chamber.

Kathleen suppressed a gasp of astonishment. Somehow the Soviets had restored the chamber to its earlier glory as if it had never been pounded into a shattered hulk by their artillery. How bizarre, she thought, people in Berlin were still receiving near-starvation rations. The ordinary people, the people the Soviets claimed to care about most, walked the streets in rags with cardboard soles on their shoes. Yet here, the rococo decorations gleamed with 14-carat gold gilding. Scores of silver candelabra lit the boxes and balcony. The light of the candles reflected off strings of crystals on dozens of chandeliers. Even the seats were newly upholstered with dark red velvet.

Lionel touched her elbow and directed her attention to the box on their left. "That is where Adolf Hitler always sat when he came here," Lionel commented, and Kathleen felt a shudder go down her spine. She had seen photos of Hitler in that box. He seemed near for the first time since she'd come to Berlin. She remembered reading somewhere that he'd loved opera, especially Wagner. She was glad they were seeing a Verdi opera instead.

The lights dimmed. The genial murmur of the audience died away, replaced with tense anticipation. In the orchestra pit, the last-minute squeaking and tweaking stopped. A door opened and the audience erupted into cheering and clapping. Furtwaengler entered briskly, bowed to the audience and then turned to bow to the orchestra. When he lifted his arms, the baton in his right hand, not a soul in the auditorium breathed. Then the magic began.

Kathleen could not remember enjoying an evening so much in years. The scenery was evocative with pyramids and sphinxes, the costumes were majestic, and the soloists were superb. Yet even as she was lost in the splendour of the opera, she was also aware of Lionel, handsome, attentive, witty, and amused, beside her. He seemed to be enjoying himself as much as she was, and he took delight in pointing out the various dignitaries around the room. Everyone who was anyone in the Soviet Military Administration was present, including Marshal Sokolovsky himself. The French Military Governor General Koenig and the French Berlin City Commandant General Jean Ganeval were both present, looking Napoleonic in their dress uniforms, but General Clay and Colonel Howley, like Generals Robertson and Herbert, had chosen not to attend. The senior British and American officers appeared to be making a statement of Anglo-American displeasure with the Soviet cultural policy of bypassing the de-Nazification procedures.

At the intermission, the foyer grew hot from the press of bodies. It was nearly impossible to get to the counters selling champagne and other refreshments. By the time their turn came, the fifteen-minute buzzer was already sounding. The sight of the artfully arranged caviar, oysters, deviled eggs, and chopped liver in pastry made Kathleen catch her breath in delight — until she saw the prices. They were astronomical even for members of the occupation forces. She looked around quickly and noted no one was eating anything and surmised the food was for display only.

The champagne on the other hand was cheap and abundant. From

Crimea, it was a dark pink and deliciously sweet, unlike French champagne that Kathleen had never learned to like. Lionel held up his glass. "To us!"

Kathleen liked that although she wasn't entirely sure what he meant or where they were going. Still, tonight represented a shift in their relationship, she thought. Clearly, his only interest was not Hope. She smiled and clicked her glass with his. "To us!"

The three-minute buzzer went off and they hurried back to their seats as the lights dimmed and the magic began again.

When the station gatehouse came into view, Lionel stopped the car. He turned off the engine and the lights and took Kathleen into his arms. They kissed as they had not done before. "I want you, Kathleen," Lionel admitted. "I've been a damned fool to pussy-foot around as if — I don't know." He pulled back just enough to look deep into her eyes.

She gazed up at him smiling gently, waiting for him to go on.

"This may sound like some sort of line, but you're the kind of woman I've been looking for all my life. Not cloying, not demanding, not dependent. I can't tell you how much it means to me that you have a life and a career of your own. It means we can be friends without, you know, all the paraphernalia of bourgeois relationships."

Now, what was that supposed to mean? She asked herself. Before she could ask him, however, he was speaking again.

"I'm afraid I'm going to have to go away for a while. You won't hear from me for at least two weeks, maybe longer, but when I come back...." His voice faded out.

After a moment of silence, she prompted, "Yes?"

"When I come back, I hope we can pick up where we left off."

What a disappointing conclusion, she thought, thoroughly confused.

He turned the key in the ignition but did not put the car in gear. "Maybe it would be best for you to give the jewels back here, rather than where someone might see us," he suggested.

"Yes, of course." Kathleen hastened to remove the earrings and bracelet before turning so he could unclasp the necklace. He stuffed the jewellery into his tunic pocket and then reached down and put the car in gear.

At the front gate, the guard saluted, and Lionel drove directly to the front of the Waafery. When he cut the engine, she thanked him for a wonderful evening, and he leaned over to kiss her again. "It was magical, wasn't it?" He whispered as he drew back, his large dark eyes searching her face. For what, she didn't know.

"Yes. Magical," she agreed, anticipating more.

Instead, he turned away and flung open his door to come around and help her out.

He kissed her again at the door after she'd unlocked it, then he got back into the car, gunned the engine once and oozed away from the curb.

Kathleen watched him drive away, feeling like Cinderella at the end of the ball.

Russian Roulette
Berlin-Mitte
Friday, 19 March 1948

Wearing her WAAF greatcoat and a thick shawl around her neck, Galyna caught the RAF bus to Spandau from the Main Gate. It was packed with other station personnel going out for the evening, and a nice corporal from the motor pool made space for her beside him. He asked her if she was alone, but when she assured him she was meeting up with a 'friend,' he left it at that. At Spandau station, she went to the ladies' room and removed her great coat and scarf, revealing civilian clothes underneath. She replaced her WAAF stockings and practical shoes with silk stockings and high heels, pulled a thick cardigan from her knapsack and stuffed the WAAF items into the backpack instead. Then she waited until the first eastbound train had left the station before re-emerging. By then there were no RAF personnel on the platform anymore. She boarded the next eastbound train and found a seat by the window from which she nervously watched the world clank by. When the train left the last station in the British Sector, the tension became almost unbearable, but she had crossed the point of no return.

The first stop in the Soviet Sector was Friedrichstrasse, but Mila had told her to continue to Hackescher Markt. Many Red Army soldiers boarded the train at Friedrichstrasse, however, and a couple tried to chat her up using terrible German. Galyna told them to leave her alone in a flood of angry Russian, and they backed off at once. Still, she was very glad to get off at the next station and even happier to see Mila waving vigorously.

They hugged in greeting as they now always did. Mila was flushed and excited to have Galyna in "her" part of the city. "Hurry!" she urged, "Before you catch a cold!"

Mila led Galyna through the entryway of a partially damaged and poorly restored building occupying a whole block, and out the back door into the courtyard. On the far side of the cobbled courtyard, a restaurant calling itself the "Comrade Stalin" crouched. The name was written in Cyrillic lettering, and it sported a large portrait of the Soviet leader over the door. Inside, a dark, wood-panelled room housed two dozen tables, all of which were full. A line of civilians speaking German waited for a table to come free. Mila guided Galyna passed the waiting Germans and up a stairway to a private dining room on the floor above.

This was packed with Russian officers and their female guests. Cigarette smoke hung low in the air, and an accordionist wandered between the tables playing popular Russian songs. Mila's arrival was greeted by shouts and waves from one of the tables, and one of the officers stood on his chair to whistle through his fingers.

"That's Grisha," Mila told Galyna blushing a little as they started to squeeze their way between the other tables towards him. He was certainly a good-looking man, Galyna thought. He had a square, open face, short blond hair and a heartfelt smile. He wore the shoulder tabs of a captain, and she knew from Mila that in civilian life he had been an engineer at a power plant. He had already squeezed two more chairs around his table by the time they reached it. Mila sat down directly beside him, and Galyna sat beside Mila.

"We thought you had forgotten us!" One of the others complained.

"Galyna's train was late," Mila said by way of explanation before she started the introductions. There was a Stephan, a Leonid, an Igor, a Dmitri and a Maxim in addition to Grisha. None had a rank higher than major, and all were introduced only with their first names and patronymics. Galyna was simply Galyna Nicolaevna.

"Where have you been hiding?" Maxim asked Galyna. "I haven't seen you around Karlshorst."

"That's because she works in Potsdam, stupid," Mila answered smoothly with a disgusted look as if this should have been obvious. Galyna marvelled at Mila's deft handling of the situation. She had promised that no one would know Galyna was from the West, but until this moment Galyna had not realized Mila's strategy. Her ruse was brilliant in its simplicity: because the NKVD had their headquarters in Potsdam, the vague reference to Potsdam suggested to the others that Galyna worked for the NKVD. She felt them internally distance themselves from her, even as Mila added, "We knew each other in primary school, but when her father got a new job in Kharkiv, she moved away. After that, we lost track of one another until I ran into her by chance a couple of weeks ago."

The officers nodded mute understanding, and someone poured her a drink. Although they competed in their efforts to appear friendly and welcoming, Galyna knew they would neither trust her nor risk asking questions about her work. She was safe from prying.

The awkwardness eased gradually as the others talked among themselves. Galyna simply smiled and nodded, saying little. The waiters came to take their orders. They collectively ordered borscht, cabbage piroshki, and chicken shashlik along with Crimean champagne. The vodka flowed, although Galyna and Mila both held back, substituting water whenever possible. Eventually, the lights dimmed, and the curtains were pulled back from a small, raised stage at one end of the room. The show which was the excuse for this party was presented by a visiting Soviet dance company and consisted of male and mixed choruses, balalaika players and folk dancers in traditional dress with bright embroidery. Mila kept leaning over to ask Galyna if she was enjoying herself.

"Yes, very much," Galyna assured her smiling. It was true; the Russian melodies and costumes made her happy at first. Only gradually did they trigger melancholy. The vodka was starting to affect the audience too. At other tables, some men were getting louder and rowdier. Some of the officers jumped onto the stage to compete with the dancers. This in turn brought others to their feet clapping and shouting encouragement. Some even stood on their chairs, their boots scratching the surface.

Galyna looked at her watch and in alarm realized it was almost eleven pm. She leaned closer to Mila. "I have to go soon, or I'll miss the last bus."

"OK," Mila agreed without hesitation.

"I'll just go to the ladies' room first," Galyna told her. Mila nodded understanding.

Galyna squeezed her way around the edge of the clapping and stamping crowd to the narrow hall leading toward the toilets. To her dismay, two women were in line already. They were officers' wives, gossiping about people Galyna didn't know. She tuned out their boring conversation and eavesdropped instead on the officers at the nearest table. They were not trying to keep their voices down, and one was very red-faced from too much alcohol already. Galyna glanced over at them, noting their rank insignia automatically. The toilet door opened, and a stunningly beautiful woman in a low-cut, tight-fitting dress emerged. Galyna heard one of the Russian women hiss "whore." The other answered, "Why doesn't anyone report her to the Party? Everyone knows that Ilya Dmitrivich has a wife and three children in Moscow. It's a disgrace for him to live openly with that snake!"

"The Party doesn't have any morals anymore! Look at Marshal Sokolovsky's! His new wife is younger than his daughter."

By the time Galyna got back to her table it was 11:08 and she was very nervous. Mila, however, had their coats and backpacks in hand. She waved goodbye to their tablemates, explaining, "I have to see Galyna home. It too dangerous for an unarmed woman to cross the American Zone alone."

"Do you want me to come with you?" Grisha offered, jumping to his feet.

"You think I can't handle this?" Mila asked back with a flash of anger, pulling her pistol partway out so the handle was visible between the buttons of her coat.

"I didn't mean to imply —" Grisha started, sensing he had blundered.

"I'll tell you when I need your help," Mila told him off. He looked duly chastened, and Mila at once relented. She gave him a smile and a peck on the cheek before asking, "Will I see you at the club tomorrow? Maybe we can go hunting?"

Grisha lit up and nodded vigorously. Without another word, Mila shouldered her way out of the dining room with Galyna in her wake.

They ran to the train station, and just barely caught a westbound train. As soon as the train crossed out of the Soviet Sector, Galyna removed her great coat from her backpack and put it on over her dress. Then she changed into her WAAF shoes and put on her cap as well. She felt much warmer after that but was still intensely grateful for Mila's company. They were practically the only women on the train, and it felt like every man -- regardless of age or nationality — leered at them. Sometimes men hesitated in front of them as if they were going to accost them, but then they'd catch sight of Mila's pistol butt and move along.

The two Ukrainians reached Spandau station just four minutes before midnight. Galyna was relieved to see other RAF personnel disembarking along the length of the train. She gave Mila a hasty hug, thanked her profusely for the escort, and left Mila on the platform to rush down the stairs to the RAF bus. Mila would take the next eastbound train back to the Soviet Zone. Meanwhile, Galyna boarded the bus bound for Gatow and plopped herself down in a window seat. As the bus pulled away, she sighed with relief. It was good to be back in the embrace of the British Empire.

A Matter of Intelligence
RAF Gatow, Berlin
Saturday, 20 March 1948

"Some potentially important intelligence has come to our attention, sir." The audibly uncomfortable voice of Flight Lieutenant Boyd rasped over the telephone line at the Priestman residence.

"Meaning you want me to come to the Station?" Priestman responded with just a touch of exasperation in his voice as he threw Emily a pained expression. Because a thick fog hugged the Havel, they had given up any hope of flying, but they had been looking forward to a quiet day alone together.

"I'm afraid so, sir."

"All right. I'm on my way." Priestman responded with resignation.

At Gatow, Preistman found Boyd awaiting him in the anteroom of his office, and he invited him inside straight away. In the hope this would not take long, he offered him a seat in front of his desk and sank onto his desk chair. "All right. What have you got?"

"Yesterday evening at a private party inside the Soviet Sector, Soviet officers said they expected to force the Western Allies out of Berlin by summer. If the policy of pinpricks didn't work, one said, then they would close down all access routes and starve us out."

"Slow down!" Priestman stopped his visibly excited intelligence officer. "First can you share with me the source of this information?"

"Corporal Borisenko, and—"

"What? What was she doing at a private party in the Soviet Sector?" The alarm in Priestman's voice could not be ignored.

"That's a very good question, sir, and I understand your concern but, I must say, that I think she pulled off a bit of an intelligence coup."

"Let's start with the facts," Priestman dampened his enthusiasm.

"It seems that on the day you sat in for Air Commodore Waite on the ACC, Borisenko met a Soviet partisan and Hero of the Soviet Union."

"Yes, she did," Priestman confirmed cautiously.

"Well, it turns out this Soviet heroine also comes from the same part of Ukraine as Borisenko. They agreed to meet up informally in civilian clothes and have done so on three or four occasions before last night."

"None of this is exactly ...." Priestman looked for the right word and decided on "orthodox, is it?"

"No, sir. But technically the Soviets are still our Allies. There is no policy, much less regulation, against contact and fraternization with the Soviets."

"No," Priestman conceded warily, "but the risks are obvious and as I remember it, you expressed particular concern about Borisenko's safety." He was moderately annoyed that his intelligence officer appeared to have changed his tune so dramatically.

"Yes, sir. I would most certainly have advised against this if Borisenko had asked me in advance. That said, it looks to me as if she's done a rare and first-rate job of piercing the Soviet shield and has obtained valuable intelligence. We'd be crazy not to take advantage of her unexpected access to Soviet sources."

"I'd like to speak with her myself."

"Yes, sir. I thought you might. She's waiting in my office." Boyd left the CO's office and returned with Borisenko. Each took a chair before the Station Commander's desk. Borisenko, as always, looked very serious but not particularly nervous, Priestman thought as he asked her to explain what had happened in her own words.

"You remember Mila Mikhailivna, who I met at the ACC?" Priestman nodded. "Well, she helped me find a set of Matrushka dolls for Flight Sergeant Hart's little girl, and I helped her find some fur-lined boots and gloves to send home to her family. I invited her to the American fair, as you know, and she reciprocated by suggesting I join her for a private performance of the Krasnoyarsk National Dance Company in a restaurant behind Hackescher Market. It was a program of Russian and Ukrainian folk music and dance. I was reluctant to go, but Mila promised that no one would know I was from the West and also assured me she would escort me safely back to the West, so I agreed."

"You were not in uniform, Fl/Lt Boyd says."

"No, sir." She looked down a little nervously as she had not received permission first. Then she looked up and met his eye. "I was afraid you would say no, so I changed into civilian clothing at Spandau station. Mila Mikhailivna met me at Hackescher Markt and introduced me to the others from her party as an old, school friend. She told the others I worked in Potsdam. We spoke only Russian. I do not think anyone had any idea I was not one of them."

"Yet Mikhailivna's companions proceeded to talk about driving the Western Allies out of Berlin? Don't you find that suspicious?"

"Oh, no, sir!" She shook her head vigorously. "I mean, that would have been suspicious if they had done that, but Mila Mikhailivna's friends avoided talking about *anything* political. They spoke only of the performance and their plans for the weekend and food and ..." she shrugged, "harmless things. I heard the conversation about plans to push us out of Berlin while waiting to use the ladies' room. Two officers who were already rather drunk were talking loudly at a table near the hallway."

"And what exactly did they say?"

"I can't remember the beginning. I know they were very insulting about the Americans first, calling them 'spoilt brats.' They referred to us as 'puppets' of the Americans. One said it was time to teach us a lesson and end our 'insufferable' interference in Berlin affairs. The other answered,

'They'll be gone by summer.' The first challenged him, asking how. The other man answered: 'Because if they don't go voluntarily, we'll close down all the access routes and starve them out.' The other made some remark about looking forward to watching that happen, and then the toilet became free and I heard no more."

Priestman thought about this. As far as he could tell the report was completely credible. The Red Army officers were meeting in the Soviet Sector at a private party and believed they were among their own. They were also already in their cups.

"Did you say anything about this to whats-her-name? Mila Mikhailivna?"

"No, sir. I thought it was better she didn't know I'd heard anything."

"Quite right!" Boyd assured Borisenko, nodding vigorously.

"Did you get a glimpse of the men who were speaking?"

"One was a colonel of artillery and the other was a *Zampolit* — what used to be called political commissars — of the same rank. Because I did not look at them while they were speaking, I don't know who said what, but I suspect the military officer was just complaining about us and the political officer was confident of success."

"That would be logical," Priestman agreed with a look toward Boyd, who also nodded. Addressing Borisenko again, he continued, "You understand this information will have to be reported. There may be questions. The fact that you were out of uniform without permission will not go unnoticed, and your WAAF superiors may decide on disciplinary action."

Borisenko nodded. "I understand, sir. I — it — just seemed worth it."

Priestman raised his eyebrows but said nothing. Every service member broke the rules now and again when it seemed "worth it." He'd certainly done it often enough, and given the potentially valuable information she had obtained, he had no interest in making an issue of a bagatelle. He simply wondered what about the escapade had made it worth taking risks for Borisenko. Was it just the music? Or the friendship with Mila Mikhailivna? Or was there more?

"Corporal, although I'm not in a position to assess this information just yet, as far as I can tell, you handled the situation correctly and I commend you for reporting it promptly." The corporal seemed to glow a little in the warmth of his praise. She gave him a shy smile.

"I am surprised, however," Priestman continued, "that you were willing to take such risks. I was led to believe that as a former Soviet citizen and daughter of a convicted traitor, you could be a target for the Soviet secret police. Indeed, you risk being kidnapped and, unless I'm mistaken, possibly deported to Siberia or worse."

Borisenko nodded earnestly, a faint frown shadowing her features. "That is true," she admitted, "I was very nervous, and I did not feel safe or happy until I was back on the RAF bus, but Mila has become a friend and...." Her voice faded away.

"Yes?" Priestman prompted.

"I don't know how to explain it exactly. I was curious. I wanted to see if they could detect me or if I could still pass for one of them. I wanted to see for myself what they were like."

"I'm not sure I understand what you're saying."

"For ten years I have been so afraid of them. They have become monsters in my mind. And then I met Mila and she's ... so normal. So like me. She isn't one of them. I wanted to see if there were others like her."

"You're playing a very dangerous game," Priestman warned.

"I know," she met his eyes as she answered.

"And you are prepared to keep playing? To report back to us all you hear while pretending to be what you are not? You understand that if you are arrested for spying in civilian clothes there is nothing we can do to help you?"

Borisenko nodded slowly. "Yes, sir. I understand."

Priestman looked at Boyd, who assured him, "I've explained everything to her, sir."

He turned back to Borisenko. "I want you to think about this very carefully. I don't want you to feel any pressure. When you've made your decision, let me know. You can remain a translator here, whether you undertake any further intelligence gathering or not. Understood?"

"Yes, sir. Thank you, sir."

"That will be all then." Borisenko saluted and retreated.

After going over the details once more with Boyd, Priestman dismissed the IO as well and asked the telephone exchange to put a call through to Air Commodore Waite. The latter was at a session of the Allied Control

Council, and so he left a message via his adjutant to call back as soon as it was convenient. He put on his cap and coat and was halfway down the hall when the telephone in his office started to ring. Damn! He reversed direction, pushed open the door and grabbed his phone from the far side of the desk at about the seventh ring. "Priestman!"

"Waite. You asked me to call you?"

"Yes. We've received some rather interesting intelligence and I —"

"It wasn't about the Soviets walking out of the Allied Control Council, was it?"

"No, it was— Wait! You don't mean they *did*?"

"That's exactly what I mean. The Soviets held the chairmanship this month and Sokolovsky didn't waste any time with niceties. He opened the session by accusing the Western Allies of treating the Germans with contempt. When Clay protested, Sokolovsky read off a prepared statement in which he railed against us in the most intemperate language. When Robertson objected, he was not allowed to finish. Sokolovsky announced that he 'saw no sense in continuing the meeting,' declared it adjourned, and the Soviet delegation stomped out in a closed group. After we'd recovered from our shock, General Clay concluded that the Allied Control Council is dead. Robertson thinks we're on the brink of WWIII. In light of these developments, is your intelligence still of any relevance, or is it OBE?"

Priestman thought about that a moment and replied. "I'd say it is more relevant than ever. Where can we meet and talk far away from walls?"

"There's is a lovely trail that wanders along the Havel just after the Glienicke Bridge. Can you meet me on the bridge in an hour and a half?"

"I'll be there, sir."

Chapter Eleven
Tightening the Screws

Harassment
RAF Gatow
Thursday, 1 April 1948

The guards saluted the Station Commander and waved his car through the main gate. Moments later, Priestman thanked his driver and climbed out in front of the admin building. In the ten days since the Soviets walked out of the ACC, nothing had happened. Nothing at all. Everything continued to function as if on autopilot, and Borisenko's intelligence report increasingly looked as if it were simply part of the propaganda war — nothing but a crude attempt to make the Western Allies nervous. Daily, the Soviets flooded the newspapers and radio programmes with absurd yet shrill insults and threats, but the tirades had become so ludicrous that Priestman doubted anyone took them seriously. To him, they seemed like nothing but irritating background noise — a kind of static — that no longer felt threatening.

With a glance at the clear blue sky overhead, he wondered if he ought to be focusing on bread and circuses instead. Maybe it was time to start planning and practising more seriously for the air show Waite wanted?

He entered the building and started up the stairs mentally organizing his day. There would be the usual reports, the airmen up on charges for one infraction or another, and then the press briefing, after which— Sergeant Andrews waved to him before he could even say good morning. "Lt. General Herbert rang and requested that I put you through to him as soon as you arrived."

"Go ahead and connect me. I'll take it in my office." Priestman signalled for Flying Officer Stanley to join him. He set his cap aside and went around the desk to take the phone still standing. "Priestman."

"Good morning, Wing Commander. I just wanted to let you know that late last night the Soviets announced the intention to 'check the papers' of all persons, civilian *and* military, transiting their Zone. They also said all freight would henceforth require SMA permits. We have rejected similar demands in the past and repeatedly informed the Soviet government that we do not recognize their right to control either passengers or goods on our trains. This morning, however, when we refused to allow their inspectors to board our train, they side-tracked it. It remains immobilised in Marienborn. We have a complete stand-off at the moment. General Robertson is currently in London for consultations, but he has been informed of the situation and will return as soon as possible. He might fly in any time today at very short notice."

Although his nerves had already gone on alert, Priestman kept his tone relaxed as he replied, "No problem, sir." Mentally, he calculated that the change of Soviet policy occurred on exactly the day the ACC should have met — if the Soviets hadn't walked out. Furthermore, these actions represented an escalation because they targeted not Germans using Allied trains, but the Allied forces themselves. Maybe Borisenko's intelligence had been correct after all.

In his ear, the British Commandant was saying, "There's no way of knowing if this will last only a couple of hours or all day." Herbert sounded as if he still didn't grasp the seriousness of the situation or wanted to downplay the provocative nature of Soviet actions. In fact, they had just taken a step closer to the invisible tripwire that would set off a confrontation. Knowing that Herbert was not interested in his opinion, however, Priestman confined himself to asking, "How have the other Allies responded?"

"The French have agreed to the Soviet demands," Herbert reported in an exasperated tone, "while the Americans are blustering about shooting their way through! Such talk is criminally irresponsible!" Apparently, while Herbert disapproved of French docility, he was more offended by American bellicosity.

Focusing on first things first, Priestman asked, "Did we have anything on the train that will need to be flown in?"

"We will send passengers with pressing business via the BEA flight or, if necessary, ask BAFO to lay on an RAF passenger flight. I don't know about goods yet, but if there is anything urgent, you'll be the first to know."

"Thank you."

They hung up, and Priestman stood for a moment thinking. If Borisenko's report was correct, and he thought it probable, then the Soviets were preparing to shut down all the access routes and "starve" the Western Allies out. As of this morning, however, they were only insisting on the right to check papers and manifests. His instincts said that the Soviets were just testing the waters, tightening the screws a little. Since the French had already caved in, the Western position was already undermined.

After only a moment's hesitation, he asked Andrews to put a call through to Colonel Howley. It was a little risky, as Herbert was Howley's counterpart, but he and Frank Howley had met informally several times now and got on better each time. Moments later, Andrews had the American Colonel on the other end of the line.

"Sorry to bother you, Colonel," Priestman opened. "I know how busy you must be."

"No more than you are, Wing Commander. What's up?"

"I was wondering if you could give me a read-out on how likely it is that your government will opt to use force to stop Soviet interference?"

"Between you and me: less than 50/50. The good news is that General Clay has had enough. He was as angry as I was. The bad news is that we have a bunch of old women in Washington who still think 'Uncle Joe' is our best friend. That or they think he's so dangerous that we have to tiptoe around him. I don't honestly think Washington's going to allow us to stand up to the Ruskies. When you get down to it, all they've asked for is information."

"In short," Priestman sought confirmation, "nobody's going to go to war over our right *not* to be subject to Soviet manifest checks."

"Yep. That sums it up nicely."

"Which means that we'll probably cave in sooner or later and allow the Soviets to check cargoes and passengers."

"That's where I'd put my money — even if it's not what I want."

"In which case, the Soviets will just raise the pressure in some other way until it becomes too much, and we quit and go home."

"Or we stop backing down. It's going to be one or the other."

"Thank you for your candour, Colonel. I won't take any more of your time."

"You can call me anytime you like, Robin. It feels good to talk to someone on the same wavelength I am. It bucks me up a bit." They laughed together and hung up.

Priestman remained standing for another moment, but he'd already made up his mind. The Soviet action signalled the intentional ratcheting up of tensions. While he could not make policy and would do whatever he was ordered when the time came, there was no excuse for not taking precautions. He needed to put Gatow on more of a war footing.

Turning to Stanley he announced, "I need to see all the department heads here in my office right away. Cancel all routine appointments for the next two to three hours."

"Yes, sir." Stanley nodded and withdrew.

The department heads clustered together around the Station Commander's coffee table exchanging snippets of information, while Sergeant Andrews brought in a tray loaded with tea things. Priestman joined them, sitting down at the head, and they looked over expectantly. "You will all have heard by now that the inbound train has been side-tracked due to a stand-off with the Soviets about our right to uncontrolled access to Berlin. General Robertson is expected to return from London sometime today, and there may be other extra flights coming in as well, but I'm not worried about that." He paused to be sure he had their attention. He did.

"Whether this particular action lasts only a few hours or a few days, it is part of a wider campaign to expel us from Berlin by making it too uncomfortable or too costly to remain. We must anticipate further Soviet interference in our operations and need to be prepared to cope with these sudden disruptions at all times." He paused to let that sink in before continuing, "Let's start with how Gatow will be affected if that train doesn't arrive any time soon." He turned his gaze to the Station Engineering Officer as he finished speaking.

Holt was prepared with his answer. "The most critical issue is aviation fuel. Two tankers were attached to today's train. Without them, we only have enough fuel for three days of routine operations. If we step up patrols or are asked to refuel incoming aircraft, it will be gone in a flash."

Priestman frowned slightly and glanced at Danny as he responded,

"As of now, operations are not routine. We need to increase our patrols to monitor Soviet troop and tank movements. Please make a note to increase your aviation fuel reserves as soon as possible."

"We don't have fuel tanks here, sir. We can only store fuel in tankers, which as you know pose severe fire hazards — particularly if parked near the runways."

"Point taken," Priestman conceded. "We'll have to come back to this at a future date. Go on."

"Petrol for ground transport and diesel for the generators is more plentiful. Both should last for a week at normal rates of consumption. Tyres and other spare parts are currently stocked in adequate quantities. It would take two weeks or more without resupply before shortages make themselves felt for isolated items. Most inventories are running between 75 and 80% and will last four weeks or more."

"Thank you. Go through your inventories and put together a list of critical items that might need to be flown in if the situation lasts. Be sure you know the weight of each item. As soon as transport is normalized, work at increasing inventory to the maximum."

"Yes, sir," Holt agreed, making a note to himself on a pad of paper.

Priestman turned to the Medical Officer next. "Anything you urgently need, Ashcroft?"

"Not really. I've kept inventories of medical supplies at high levels all along just because there is almost nothing available locally."

"Well done. Now, how are we for food?" Priestman directed his attention to Warrant Officer Pierce.

"We won't starve just yet, but we're going to need fresh produce — potatoes, cabbage, brussels sprouts, carrots etc. We can't buy that locally and it usually comes in daily by rail. We'll start to run out early next week. I could stretch the meat supplies a bit longer."

"How much booze have we got?" S/L Tucker asked. He was the commander of the 284th Field Squadron of the RAF Regiment, the unit responsible for protecting Gatow.

"That is a very good question!" Danny seconded, sitting up straighter.

"Well, we had an order in with the Commissary in Wunstorf that has not yet arrived. Whether it was on the train that was halted or is on lorries somewhere, I don't know."

"Meaning supplies are low?" Holt joined the conversation sounding alarmed.

"They aren't generous. If this situation lasts for more than a few days, we will have to consider rationing."

"That sounds dire!" Danny concluded.

Priestman ignored the commentary and asked, "Warrant Officer Wilkins? Anything from your perspective?"

"That depends on how long this lasts, sir. If air traffic increases substantially, we will need to institute shifts which would mean we'd need more air traffic controllers and assistants. Do you have any news yet on Ft/ Lt Simpson's replacement?"

"The new Flying Control Officer, S/L Garth, was due in today," Priestman remembered as he spoke. "Assuming he is not bumped off the BEA flight, you can show him the set-up and introduce him to the rest of the ATC staff, then we can have a three-way conversation later today. When you're ready to meet with me, call Sergeant Andrews and I'll fit you in."

"Yes, sir." Wilkins nodded vigorously, evidently relieved.

Priestman turned his attention back to the others with an implicit request for further questions or comments. No one spoke, and he let his eye scan them, trying to judge reactions. S/L Holt looked slightly confused; he tended to keep his head on his technical problems without paying much attention to politics. Boyd looked the most worried because he knew the Soviets best. The others kept their feelings hidden like good professionals. Priestman wrapped things up by saying, "Whatever happens, we need to prepare this station to receive as many cargo aircraft as possible."

The ground maintenance chief suddenly seemed to come to life. "Sir? Surely you don't think they'll try to fly in everything that has come by train up to now?"

"More or less," Priestman confirmed.

"But sir! The PSP runway wasn't built for cargo aircraft. The specifications were quite specific. I can go back and check on them, but they certainly weren't for dozens of freighters carrying up to 9 tons of cargo! I won't take responsibility for what happens if we have more than ten landings a day! The PSP is likely to simply disintegrate."

Priestman winced inwardly. This was his mistake. Because he'd never seen PSP before coming to Gatow, he'd over-estimated its capacity to withstand additional traffic. There was no point denying the problem, however, much less pretending he could order it away. "Understood. I will discuss the problem with BAFO and see if we can get authorization to lay down a proper concrete runway. Anything else?"

"Wing Commander?" The voice was that of Sergeant Andrews, who had gone to answer the phone while he spoke with the others. "Wunstorf has just rung through that General Robertson's Deputy, General Sir Neville Brownjohn, is airborne bound for Gatow. ETA: 10:25. Also, Soviet soldiers have occupied the Ritterfeld-Kladower Damm crossroads. They're stopping all traffic."

"What?" Priestman gasped in open alarm. That sounded like the prelude to an attempt to occupy the airfield. His blood ran cold.

To his astonishment, S/L Tucker spoke up in an annoyed voice. "Not again? You'd think they'd get tired of that silly game. I'll handle it right away."

"Can you?" Priestman asked astonished; the Squadron Leader sounded a bit over-optimistic to him.

"It's what we get paid for, sir," Tucker told him with a sigh of resignation, "and why we rotate out every six months, too. The Ivans used to do this at least once a month, but up to now, they've always backed down the moment we show up. Don't give it another thought."

Priestman hoped that Tucker was right. Don't lose your wool, he told himself; it wasn't time for panic bowlers yet.

First Flight
London, Northolt
Thursday, 1 April 1948

Kiwi felt both proud and smart in his new black uniform with three red stripes on the sleeve and an eagle carrying a red cross in its claws on his breast. What he liked best about the uniform was the use of a red cravat as an integral part of the uniform rather than a tie. It gave the otherwise conservative uniform a distinctly modern flair — and was more comfortable for flying too. Over the last month, he had not only stayed off the heavy booze, he had also gone to considerable effort to lose a half stone as well. As a result, his silhouette was much sleeker than it had been at the start of the year.

He picked up the latest weather report and scanned it as he left the met office. Clear weather all the way to Berlin. Although Kiwi was still thirteen hours short of the thirty he needed to carry patients, Banks had decided to go ahead and base their ambulance at Gatow. He reasoned that Berlin weather was better than British weather at this time of year and that flying the corridors for training would help familiarise them both with their future area of operations.

The market research showed that prospective patients were individuals with acute needs requiring special treatment. The hospitals to which they needed to be evacuated were not evenly distributed around the Western Zones. Eye surgery was best handled in Hamburg, for example, heart surgery in Munich, and cancer treatment in Hanover. In consequence, AAI's pilots needed to be familiar with all three air corridors and be prepared to fly to a variety of cities in the Western Zones.

Kiwi also looked forward to living with the Priestmans. They had been friends for eight years and he welcomed the chance to spend time with them. Of course, guests like fish stank if they stayed too long, but he was determined to worry about that tomorrow. In a pinch, they could bed down in RAF temporary quarters as their ground crew would be doing. For today, the start of a new phase of his life, he wasn't going to fret about it. He wanted to enjoy his new flying career.

"Mr Murray!" The voice sounded urgent, and he turned back to see who was calling. A BEA employee was running after him waving a telegram flimsy. "Mr Murray! This just came in for you!"

Puzzled, Kiwi took the telegram. It read: 'RAIL ACCESS TO BERLIN CLOSED STOP REQUEST INBOUND CARGO FOR MESS STOP DETAILS AT YOUR DISCRETION STOP PRIESTMAN"

Kiwi looked up at the BEA employee. "What's going on in Berlin?"

"I don't know exactly, sir, but we've been asked to make a stop at Wunstorf to take on military personnel that were thrown off the train. We'll also be picking up cargo in Wunstorf — cabbage, carrots and potatoes, last I heard." The employee grinned.

Kiwi shook his head. What the hell were they getting themselves into? He strolled over to their modified Wellington. It was painted white and sported red crosses under the cockpit window and on the tail, while "Air Ambulance International" in red lettering was written on the fuselage. David and the ground crew were going through the pre-flight checks. He stopped beside the nose and called up. "Banks! We've got a problem."

David poked his head out of the cockpit window. "What?"

"The Ivans have closed down rail traffic to Berlin and Robin's asking us to carry cargo inbound."

"OK. So, what's the problem? We're not under any time pressure. What does he want?"

"He didn't say — just 'for the mess.'" Kiwi reread the telegram. "I think we should take on a load of alcohol. There's always demand for that, it doesn't spoil, and it's high margin."

"Not to mention that you wouldn't want to arrive in Berlin and find the mess was short of the stuff!" David commented dryly.

"Never gave it a thought, Captain! I'm off the stuff, remember?" Kiwi put his hand on his heart melodramatically as he answered. Although the gesture was intended to elicit a laugh, it was only half in jest. Kiwi was determined not to have another incident. He knew Banks would not forgive him a second time.

David smiled weakly and shook his head ambiguously, then suggested, "Let's get cracking."

The four of them spent the next three hours purchasing and loading crates of whisky, vodka, rum, gin, and brandy. David refused to take beer aboard, certain that it could be produced locally. By then it was well past 1 pm, so they went for lunch together at a nearby pub. Soon after they arrived, the BBC news came over the radio reporting a "tense situation in Berlin, as the Soviets attempt to interfere with Western access to the former German capital."

"Are we sure we want to live there?" Ron asked generally.

"That's what you signed on for," David reminded him curtly.

"Well, the Soviets weren't closing down the railway when we signed up, were they?" Ron retorted pugnaciously. "Sounds like we could find ourselves in a bit of a pickle."

"If you want to jump ship, fine, but your contract calls for two weeks' notice," David answered coldly.

Ron backed down, but Kiwi saw him exchange a look with Chips. They were not happy about being based in Berlin — and that was before this trouble blew up. Kiwi could only hope the political tiff would blow over rapidly because if it didn't, they were going to face more trouble from their ground crew. Kiwi partially sympathised with them. He wasn't all that keen about living in Berlin either. It isolated them from family, friends and their familiar environment. But jobs flying or servicing aircraft were few and far between, so men like Kiwi, Chips and Ron swallowed the bitter pill. The question was: when did "bitter" become "poisonous"?

Back at the airfield, David climbed into the cockpit and sent Kiwi for an updated weather report. "Take Sammy with you so he can stretch his legs before the flight, will you?" David asked.

David's dog Sammy was making the move with them. He was almost ten years old, and David and the former stray were inseparable. Sammy had flown in the Wellington multiple times already. He'd rapidly discovered the bomb aimer's bubble and the tail turret, both of which offered splendid views through Perspex. Although Sammy seemed to prefer the bomb aimer's bubble, he sometimes wandered back to the tail turret for a change of perspective.

With Sammy on the lead, Kiwi returned to the met office and got the latest weather report. They were now reporting high clouds coming in from the West and more gusty winds, but nothing to worry about. He started back to the aircraft.

For a second time today, he was stopped by someone chasing after him. "Sir! Sir!" This time the voice calling to him was female, and Kiwi turned around to see a woman waving frantically while she tried to catch up with him. She was quite a sight! Tall and slender with short blond hair she was a corker all right, and not just that, she wore a raking hat and a fitted, double-breasted blazer that emphasised her slim waist. Yet these ladylike features were combined with baggy navy trousers and flat shoes. It was a curious mix of femininity and masculinity that intrigued him instantly.

As she came closer, he registered that she looked at least thirty, and although she wore make-up there was a hardness about her mouth. "Sir?

Is it correct that you are about to take off for Berlin?"

"Yes, the gen's correct," Kiwi answered warily.

"What a stroke of luck! I'm a reporter for the *Times* and I'm trying to get to Berlin to cover this breaking crisis. Unfortunately, BEA just bumped me off their flight — they say senior military officers from Wunstorf take precedence."

"Ah, I'm sorry, Ma'am, but we're not a passenger service. We're an air ambulance."

"I don't care about comfort, and I certainly don't need a meal. I just want to get to Berlin as quickly as possible. I'm perfectly happy to sit in the tail turret if that's the only space available."

Kiwi was torn. Part of him wanted to help a lady in distress, particularly one as unusual and attractive as this — and by her accent and the quality of the pearls at her throat, she *was* a lady. Yet another instinct suggested it wasn't wise to get involved with the press. "You'll have to come and talk to the captain," he told her. "I'm just the second pilot."

"Yes, of course!"

She flashed him a beautiful smile that made her seem vaguely familiar. He had the feeling he'd seen her somewhere before. "What did you say your name was?" Kiwi asked as they set off in the direction of the aircraft.

"I don't think I said," she admitted with a laugh. "I'm Virginia Cox. I write under V. Cox. Maybe you've seen my byline?"

"I can't say I remember seeing it," Kiwi admitted, "but I'm not terribly literate. Got my head in the clouds, my Mum used to say. I certainly haven't had much time for the papers in recent months. My partner and I have been busy getting our company launched. I'm Chuck Murray, Miss Cox." he offered her his hand. "Most people call me Kiwi."

As she shook his hand, she gave him another dazzling smile and added, "Just call me Vee — that's what most people do."

"Do you have any luggage, Vee?"

"Just this bag!" She patted a large leather bag that hung from her shoulder. It could have passed for a large handbag. Practical woman, Kiwi thought, remembering the way Betty always travelled with three or four bulky suitcases.

"Have you flown before?" Kiwi asked next.

"Good lord, yes! Bags of times! I was a war correspondent, and I wasn't joking about sitting in the tail turret. I've done it before." She laughed at that.

Kiwi assured her that, provided the captain approved, she could sit with them in the cockpit. He found her rather captivating, probably because she was refreshingly different from Betty.

They reached the aircraft and Kiwi bent to unclip Sammy's leash before telling him to "hop aboard!" The collie-mix clambered confidently up the steps into the aircraft and reappeared in the nose while Kiwi called up to the cockpit. "Banks!"

David looked out again. "Now what?"

"Miss V. Cox wants to hitch a ride to Berlin with us. She's a reporter for the *Times*."

"What? Wait!" David disappeared from the window and a moment later dropped down from the hatch. He came over to offer his hand politely, introducing himself. "David Goldman, Ma'am. I'm the founder and Managing Director of Air Ambulance International. Now how can I help you?"

"V. Cox, Captain," she introduced herself again and explained her need to get to Berlin to cover the unfolding crisis for the *Times*.

"I'm very sorry, Ma'am, but we are not licensed to carry passengers," David told her firmly.

"But, Captain, I'm not a passenger, I'm a hitch-hiker — though I'd be happy to compensate you for any inconvenience."

"You can't afford to compensate me for losing my license, Ma'am, and that is what I risk if the Ministry of Civil Aviation finds out that I have taken a passenger aboard an aircraft that is not licensed to carry them."

"But why should they find out? I'm certainly not going to tell them." She winked at him confidentially.

"There are people all over this airfield that may be watching, and there will be people watching when we disembark at Gatow. I'm truly sorry, Ma'am, but I cannot and will not risk it."

Kiwi noticed, not for the first time, that his friend Banks could be hard as nails when it came to protecting his business; it was a side of Banks he had not seen when they'd been together in the RAF.

V. Cox turned to look pleadingly at Kiwi, but he wasn't going to risk his future either. He'd put up one black already and didn't think he could afford a second. So, he shrugged and offered her a helpless smile. "I'm sorry, Miss Cox. He's the boss."

She looked from one to the other, and then turned on her heel and strode away without another word. There was fury and frustration in the set of her shoulders and the way her long legs ate up the distance. Kiwi regretted her departure, although he supposed it was for the best. Out loud he admitted, "I'm trying to remember where I've seen her before."

"Funny. I had that feeling too!" David exclaimed, but then he shrugged. "No matter. Time we got this crate to Berlin."

Nobody Likes Surprises
RAF Gatow
Thursday, 1 April 1948

"Sir! Air Commodore Waite for you."

Priestman returned to his office and picked up the phone. "Priestman."

"How are things going, Robin?"

"Fine. Any new developments?"

"Yes. I'm just off the phone with No 46 Group." That was Air Transport Command. "They plan to move two Dakota squadrons to Wunstorf. That would put 16 cargo aircraft there. They propose having the squadrons fly three sorties per aircraft per day on alternate days. Each squadron flies one day and does maintenance and rests the next, while Gatow receives 24 flights and 72 tons of cargo each day. Can you handle it?"

"Dakotas, you said. So, they'll be able to land on grass?"

"Yes. I've conveyed your concerns about the PSP runway just in case you needed a little support for your request regards a concrete runway to BAFO."

"Thank you. I very well *may* need it. Sanders did not sound particularly receptive."

"Leave it to 46 Group to make the case more compelling. They were on board immediately and thanked me for flagging the issue. Meanwhile, can you take the Dakotas?"

"No refuelling here, correct?"

"Correct. They'll depart with sufficient fuel for the return trip."

"In that case, we can certainly handle that number of flights for a few days, but it is going to put a terrible strain on our air traffic control staff. To avoid controllers becoming over-tired, we'll need to institute shifts and that will require more personnel. Just to complicate things, we've been without a Flying Control Officer since I had to post a man for drinking on duty. His replacement is supposed to be aboard today's BEA flight. Assuming he makes it, I'll sit down with him this afternoon to discuss the situation. My other concern is that I don't have ground personnel to off-load 72 tons of cargo nor the vehicles to move that much cargo to central warehousing."

"Don't worry about off-loading. As long as the situation lasts, Herbert proposes sending you the idle civilian workers from the rail depot. They have nothing to do at Westkreuz. He will assign the transport vehicles of the Berlin Brigade to shuttle the cargoes up to the warehouses."

"The workers have all been vetted, I presume?"

"Yes, and they have the appropriate IDs."

"How soon will this begin?"

"46 Group will send the squadrons across tomorrow. They'll probably initiate flights the day after at the latest. Unless the Soviets let our train through, of course."

"Good. We'll be ready for them."

"One other thing," Waite added.

"Yes?"

"The City Council contacted Lt. General Herbert with a request to fly out eleven seriously ill patients. They claimed there was an air ambulance service based in Gatow, which Herbert had never heard about. Neither had I. Is there?"

"Ah." Priestman squirmed. "BEA has sub-contracted space to a small company, which will operate a single air ambulance from here. They were due to fly in today, although my understanding was that they would not be operational for another couple of weeks. Via BEA, I requested they bring inbound cargo."

"Good thinking about the cargo, but I must say I would rather not have found out about this service by chance."

Robin winced. Despite Waite's pleasant tone, he was displeased --

with good reason. No senior officer liked being caught unawares, certainly not by civilians. Preistman apologised immediately. "I'm very sorry, sir. I was waiting until they materialised. I did not want to promise something that for one reason or another didn't work out."

"I understand. Nevertheless, if this air ambulance does go into service, it is something we will want — how should I word it? — to publicise. I don't want to sound like an American salesman or anything, but something like this reflects well on the United Kingdom. It's an example of British initiative and humanity both. You know, an example of British industry demonstrating ingenuity in mastering problems with modern technology for the sake of those in need — even our former enemies."

"Except that the founders are a Canadian and a New Zealander," Robin felt compelled to point out.

"In that case, it is an example of the resources and resourcefulness of the British Empire."

"I'm beginning to understand why you are so good at your job, sir."

Waite laughed. "Look. It's a good news story, and we're short of them at the moment. I want you to talk to my colleague in Press and Public Relations about this service as soon as things calm down a bit. Meanwhile, Lt. General Herbert has already assured the City Council that the patients will be put aboard the ambulance at the earliest opportunity. I believe he said, 'today' if possible."

Priestman looked at his watch. It was already 14:40. "We only have four and a half hours of daylight left, sir. I don't have an ETA for the ambulance, and assuming they have taken on cargo, they'll have to offload that before patients can go aboard. Furthermore, I believe the converted Wellington bomber's maximum capacity is six. To evacuate all eleven passengers, they would have to make two flights, which I doubt can be done."

"I thought of that. The issue is not 100% success but rather making a gesture. Just getting half the passengers out would show our goodwill and capability. Meanwhile, I presume the infirmary at Gatow can hold patients at the airfield overnight if necessary?"

"That would depend on what kind of care they need."

"Of course. Let's put the medical experts in touch with one another; I'll have my adjutant give the attending physicians the number of your MO."

"Very good, sir."

"Meanwhile, track down the ambulance's flight plan and get back to me with the details so I can pass them on to General Herbert and the City Council."

"Yes, sir."

Priestman hung up and sat looking at the phone for a second. He had a bad feeling about this. He left his office and took the flight of stairs up to the tower. At the sight of the Station Commander coming up behind them, Fl/Sgt Hart and Corporal Vincent started to get to their feet, but Priestman waved them back down. "Have you heard anything from Air Ambulance International? They were supposed to fly in today."

"Yes, sir," Corporal Vincent spoke up at once, indicating one of her slips with the flight plan. "It's already making its approach to Frohnau and is roughly fifteen minutes from landing."

"Excellent. Did they mention anything about what cargo they are carrying?"

"Indeed, sir! Vitally needed supplies for the mess." She risked a little grin.

"Meaning booze."

"Correct, sir."

"I'll see if I can find some volunteers to offload it," Priestman commented and left the tower. He paused outside his office to ask Stanley to find off-loaders for a cargo of alcohol and then continued down to the ground floor and out onto the airfield.

Sure enough, he could hear the incoming flight and shortly afterwards a white Wellington with red trim set down primly on the grass runway and swept past him as it applied the brakes. At the end of the runway, it swung towards him to taxi back, and he caught sight of Banks' dog in the bomb aimer's bubble. He shook his head in amusement and walked to the apron where the aircraft had been directed. He arrived as the engines wound down. Trolleys for off-loading cargo were already bouncing across the field and men were converging on the plane. Kiwi shoved open the cockpit window and waved to him cheerfully. "Good to see you, Robin!"

"Welcome to Berlin," Priestman replied. "I trust you had a good flight."

"Piece of cake," Kiwi assured him.

"Good. Can we chat?" It wasn't a question.

A moment later the hatch opened, and David dropped down onto the tarmac followed by Kiwi. They looked good in their matching uniforms, Priestman registered, as he again welcomed them to Berlin. There was little time for pleasantries, however, and he got straight to the point. "Unfortunately, news about your service has reached the City Council, which approached the British City Commandant with a request to evacuate eleven seriously ill patients. He wants you to take as many as possible out today."

"I'm sorry, Robin, but we can't possibly do that," David answered immediately.

"Why not? There's still plenty of daylight and we'll have the cargo offloaded in no time," Priestman glanced at the men already removing the crates of liquor with evident enthusiasm — and great care.

"Kiwi isn't qualified to carry patients. He needs another 13 hours on twins."

"I don't think anyone except you and Kiwi is counting," Priestman observed dryly.

"The Ministry of Civil Aviation is counting, and they can take away my license for a violation such as unqualified personnel in the cockpit — especially on my maiden flight. I can't risk my entire future for one flight."

Priestman could see Banks' point of view, but the British Commandant of Berlin had promised the Berlin City Council that patients would be flown out "at the earliest opportunity." A delay of a few hours due to weather or darkness would be understandable; a refusal to fly because of a technicality would not. Instead of a "good news" story, the ambulance could turn into a public relations disaster — just when world attention was focused on them. And the person to blame for the situation was Wing Commander Priestman who had not kept his superiors properly informed of the situation.

"I am sorry, Robin," David stressed, sensing that his friend was seriously upset. "I wish I could change the regulations. I wish Kiwi had more hours on twins. I wish —"

"Do the regulations require your pilots to be employees of the company?" Priestman interrupted as he was hit by a thought.

"I'm not sure — I —are you thinking of seconding an RAF pilot?"

"No, Emily. She has hundreds of hours on twins, including Wellingtons."

David lit up immediately. "Of course! Why didn't I think of that? And she already *is* an employee of the company. Is she—"

"I'll handle Emily. You prepare to turn the aircraft around as soon as possible. I'll authorise refuelling but be sure you refuel again wherever you land. We're very short here at the moment."

"Roger."

Emily had warned Fraulein Pabst that they were expecting two guests and a dog, all of whom would stay indefinitely and would occupy two of the guest bedrooms. Fraulein Pabst had spent most of the morning giving the selected rooms a thorough cleaning, making up the beds, setting out towels and the like.

Over lunch, Jasha the new cook gave Emily a long list of items to purchase from the commissary. She had done three dinners for Emily on an ad hoc basis since Frau Neuhausen's departure and Emily was delighted to have her full-time. She'd even agreed to let her live in, and she would be occupying one of the staff bedrooms. What Emily liked best about Jasha was that she was cheerful, with an infectious laugh, and the energy of two. She wanted not only more spices and herbs, but also an additional cutting board, and a variety of other things. A new regime was taking over.

When the phone rang mid-afternoon, Emily thought it must be Charlotte, who she knew was anxious to hear if David and Kiwi had arrived. "Priestman residence," she spoke into the receiver.

"This is your chance to save my career," Robin answered.

"I didn't know it was in trouble."

"It wasn't — until word of Banks' ambulance got out to the City Council who asked Lt. General Herbert to med-evac eleven patients on an aircraft without two pilots qualified for passengers."

"Meaning Kiwi doesn't have thirty hours yet?"

"Correct, but you do?"

"What?"

"Didn't you fly a lot of Wellingtons during the war?"

"Good heavens, yes. I don't remember how many exactly. I'd have to check my log book, but I certainly have more than thirty hours on them. Closer to a hundred, I should think."

"Air Ambulance International is offering you a position as First Officer, flying branch. Are you taking it?"

"It will take me ten minutes to change."

"Wizard! I'll send your car."

Kathleen noted the two-and-half stripes of the Squadron Leader, his signaller's air brevet, and the purple and white stripes of a DMF just under it. It was rare for a wireless op to earn a distinction like that. One day she'd like to know the story that went with it, but for now, she simply registered that there was no question this man was a veteran. He was stocky, shorter than she was, and weathered, with deep lines in his face to match that DFM. His hair was blond but greying and he wore a bushy moustache. His eyes were a vivid blue, very sharp and very quick to take in his surroundings.

"Garth," he introduced himself, adding in an Australian accent as he offered his hand after the salute, "You must be Flight Sergeant Hart," Kathleen admitted she was. His eyes shifted to her assistant. "And you're Corporal Vincent?"

"Yes, sir!" Natalie smiled as she shook his hand.

"And Corporal Groom." S/L Garth concluded shaking hands with Rufus before noting, "It has been quite a day, I understand." His eyes shifted to the airfield spread out before them. He scanned it expertly, and Kathleen could see him nod slightly at the sight of passengers filing up the stairs of the BEA Dakota from which he had disembarked only an hour earlier. He nodded at the sight of the dispersed Spitfires too and then stopped. "What the devil is that white Wellington?"

"It's an air ambulance, sir. It will be based here, leasing space from BEA."

"Air ambulance?" He looked back at the others frowning slightly.

"The hospitals here are in a deplorable state and desperately understaffed. They used to send patients in need of special treatment out by train, but..." Wilkins shrugged.

Squadron Leader Garth nodded. "Too right, not the best option, if the Ivans are mucking about with the railways."

As they watched, a decrepit-looking German ambulance rolled up beside the Wellington and a doctor and nurse disembarked. Medical staff spilt out of the station sick quarters wearing white coats and went to meet the people from the ambulance. After some handshaking all around and some discussion, the ambulance reversed and approached the building, leaving the Wellington in the hands of the ground crew that appeared to be preparing it for take-off again.

Meanwhile, the BEA airliner closed the cabin door, and the stairs were pulled away. Kathleen excused herself and sat down at the controller's table again, awaiting the BEA pilot's request to taxi. She could see the two men in the cockpit moving purposefully as they went through the final checks. She was vaguely aware that a car pulled up beside the air ambulance and disgorged a passenger in a dark uniform, but she took no particular notice. She was much more conscious that S/L Garth was directly behind her, watching her every move.

The BEA captain called in requesting permission to taxi and Kathleen approved. The airliner sedately moved away from the apron in front of the terminal building, gingerly crossed onto the runway and turned to face the wind. A pause followed as the captain and second pilot went through final pre-take-off checks.

Then the crisp voice of the captain announced, "Cutty Sark, this is Bealiner 78. Request permission for take-off."

Kathleen took the radio microphone and held it six inches from her mouth before replying in the affirmative. The Dakota started to shudder as the engines ramped up on the held brakes, and then the pilot released the brakes and the airliner accelerated until it was flying. As the Dakota gained altitude, Kathleen handed control of the aircraft over to the Berlin Air Safety Control.

Before they could relax, however, a tall man burst into the control room wearing an exotic black and red uniform. "'Scuse me, mates, but where does a man file a flight plan around here?"

The newcomer spoke with a broad down-under accent that brought a subdued smile to S/L Garth's face and the question. "Where did you come from, mate?"

"That air ambulance out there. The Berlin City government wants us to fly four patients out to Munich this afternoon, but I literally just landed an hour or so ago, and I haven't a clue where to file a flight plan."

"It's one floor down," Natalie told him with her ready smile. "I'll show you the way."

"Thanks, and sorry to burst in on you like this. The name's Murray. Chuck Murray, but I go by Kiwi. I'll probably be seeing you around because we're going to be operating out of here." Then he was gone.

On the tarmac in front of them, the petrol bowsers were being withdrawn and stretchers were being wheeled out to the white Wellington. Two pilots were again busy in the cockpit. Natalie returned with the flight plan entered on the appropriate slips.

S/L Garth, apparently satisfied that all was under control, suggested to Wilkins that he continue the tour and Wilkins willingly agreed, starting with the radar room at the back of the tower, and then down the stairs to the operations room. When they thought it was safe to speak, Natalie announced, "Squadron Leader Garth looks very nice."

"Yes, he looks competent to me," Rufus agreed.

"I'd like to know how he earned that DFM," Kathleen admitted, but then excused herself to go to the ladies' room, leaving Rufus to handle the ground movements of the Wellington.

When she returned, the Wellington was already on its way to the head of the grass runway and the light was starting to drain from the day. They would probably be landing in Munich after dark, she registered. The Wellington turned onto the runway and ran up its engines. They could see her vibrate and then relax. A click on the radio announced the transmission before it came, but it still gave Kathleen a shock. A well-modulated woman's voice that sounded vaguely familiar rang through the control tower. "This is AAI, Flight Double-Oh-Two for Munich. Request clearance for take-off."

Kathleen grabbed the radio and without even trying to suppress her excitement exclaimed. "I say! Is that a woman at the controls?"

"First Officer Priestman," came the answer.

Now Kathleen understood why the voice had sounded familiar; it was the CO's wife! It made her heart soar. So, there *were* men, who respected and enabled their wives to have serious aviation careers. Then she turned off her personal thoughts and focused on her job. "Well done, Ma'am! AAI, Double-Oh-Two, cleared for take-off, and Bon Voyage!"

Chapter Twelve
Civilians in the Crossfire

Business Not as Usual
Berlin-Kreuzberg
Friday, 2 April 1948

Christian fled from the chaos in the American freight forwarding office at Tempelhof. The American NCOs were overwhelmed by the frantic desperation of the Germans demanding information. The latter wanted to know when the rail connections would be restored, when they might see their consignments again, whether the Russians were going to be allowed to pilfer American trains, and a variety of similar questions. Fear made the Germans more aggressive and demanding. The lack of answers made the Americans short-tempered and rude. The result was a great deal of shouting back and forth. Christian saw no point in remaining in the midst of it; he was not going to get any useful information here.

He left Tempelhof, passing the gum-chewing guards at the entrance with ambivalent feelings. It was said that "to the victor go the spoils," but the Americans might be starting to wonder if the "spoils" of a broken city with half-starving inhabitants were worth having. Christian could remember arriving in Paris in 1940. It had been completely intact, the French hostile, of course, but too shocked to do much more than stare at the Wehrmacht. He'd found it easy to get on with the French simply by being pointedly polite and speaking French to them -- no matter how poorly. Paris had been such a prize! But Berlin? He looked around. Even the habitable buildings were filthy grey from years of coal dust and more often sported plasterboard than glass over the windows. Why would anyone fight to retain control of Berlin?

Well, he thought as he turned north to walk back to his apartment house, the Soviets would fight for it because battered and impoverished as it might seem, it was still better than most of what they had at home.

Besides, the Soviets were inherently greedy. They would grab and hold on to anything they could, even if their grasp strangled to death the very thing they wanted. Christian sincerely doubted the gum-chewing GIs would put up much of a fight.

The lack of information about what exactly was playing out between the Allies opened the floodgates to imagination and speculation. Christian knew that the Soviets had been playing cat and mouse with the Western Allies ever since they arrived. He knew that the chicanery usually lasted only a few days. Yet it seemed to have been getting worse of late, and the collapse of the Allied Control Council couldn't be dismissed as insignificant. It didn't matter that the Allies hadn't been able to agree on anything in the Control Council. The Control Council *symbolised* joint control. Soviet withdrawal signalled a rejection of the principle of shared responsibility for Germany.

The Soviets sought Communist control of Berlin, and after losing every kind of local election for three years, Stalin's patience had run out. If he couldn't create a Communist Berlin from the bottom up, he would impose it from the top down. To do that the Western Allies had to be booted out. The Soviet tactic for forcing the Western Allies out was to harass them and insult them until they got angry enough to withdraw in a huff.

Since that was not a very pleasant prospect, the logical thing to do would be to get out as fast and as soon as possible. Retreat to the family estate in Altdorf, which lay deep inside the American Zone. But Christian had spent three months building up a network of buyers for Feldburg wine. He had orders for over 700 bottles in his books already, and he had arranged for a shipment of 1,000 bottles to come in on the American train from Frankfurt. That consignment was now sitting on a railway siding somewhere along with everything else that had been on the train. With each day of delay, the risks of damage or theft increased.

More importantly, however, this incident highlighted the inherent vulnerability of his business model. There was no point in building up a client base in Berlin if he couldn't guarantee delivery, and he couldn't guarantee delivery if American trains could not transit the Soviet Zone unhindered. Christian remembered Herr von Aggstein aka Friedebach making some off-hand remark about transport being "more difficult" than he thought, and that suggested Friedebach had known what was coming

— which only made Christian more certain he was a criminal in need of exposure, arrest and preferably execution.

But that was beside the point — or at any rate secondary to immediate concerns. The issue at hand was that entire business, three months of work, had been built on false premises. It appeared to be time to concede defeat and go home to Altdorf. There were bound to be customers in the Western Zones. Then again, few of them would be willing to pay the premiums the luxury-starved Berliners seemed willing to pay.

Yet that wasn't the heart of the issue either, he acknowledged. His reluctance to leave Berlin was entirely emotional and irrational. The thought of returning to Altdorf depressed him. He was reluctant to face his wife because he did not love her and that was becoming an increasing emotional strain. He was also reluctant to return to the role of the dutiful son because much as he wanted to support his mother, he always felt inadequate, conscious that Philipp would have managed everything better. He wasn't a farmer by inclination, and he wasn't an exemplary pillar of the community either. He preferred the fast-paced, risky, and unpredictable life he had been living in Berlin.

And then there was Charlotte. Christian knew he could not leave her in Berlin alone, particularly not if the Western Allies were on the brink of departing and she was going to be left to the "tender mercies" of the Soviets. If he left, she must come with him. He knew she was terrified of crossing the Soviet Zone, but he believed he could have talked her into coming with him — if she hadn't had this new job.

The job with the air ambulance company had brought Charlotte back to life before his eyes. When she had been asked to conduct the market survey, she started to look after herself and take an interest in the world around her. She had started to smile now and again, even laugh a little. When she was offered a full-time, responsible job with a large salary, her joy erupted like a volcano, and it had been beautiful to behold. In no time, she had become completely devoted to her job. It had become her very reason for living. For the first time in three years, she was not looking back, but looking forward. Precisely because Christian understood all that, he hesitated to suggest she leave it. How could he say: give it all up and come to Altdorf, where you'll be the fifth wheel on the wagon instead of part of an exciting modern enterprise?

Then again, the ambulance company was British, and it had an aircraft. If the British pulled out of Berlin, surely the ambulance company would too? When they did, they might take Charlotte with them. Christian stopped to consider that. It sounded logical, but what if they didn't? What if she was stuck in Berlin alone after he'd already left?

He'd reached his apartment house and removed his key from his pocket to let himself in the front door. As he reached the landing before his apartment, Jakob Liebherr emerged from his flat.

"Ah, Guten Tag, Herr von Feldburg." The Social Democratic councilman consistently ignored Christian's title and always called him "Herr" rather than "Freiherr," but Christian didn't mind.

"Guten Tag, Herr Liebherr. I've just returned from Tempelhof. The Americans don't seem to have a clue about how long the situation might last."

"Why should they? The Soviets are the ones calling the shots. Only they know how long they plan to keep this up."

"And what is your assessment?" Christian asked, taking advantage of the opportunity to talk to the wily old politician.

"That the Soviets want the Western Allies out so they can eat us alive."

"Yes, I gathered that, but what about the Western Allies? Do you think they will cave in?"

Liebherr just shrugged. "Who knows." Then as if intent on finding something positive to say, he added, "Yet in the midst of all this, Charlotte's company managed to fly four passengers out of Berlin yesterday, and in two flights today they will deliver the remaining seven passengers to hospitals in the Western Zones. Quite a remarkable accomplishment, don't you think?"

"Yes," Christian remarked absently, and then he started and asked almost sharply. "They were flying patients out, but what were they bringing back in?"

"I wouldn't know. That would have been up to the British Military Government and the management of the company I presume. Now I must be on my way. Good day, Herr von Feldburg."

Jakob Liebherr continued down the stairs and Christian let himself into the apartment with his brain in overdrive. The ambulance was a modified bomber which very probably still had the winches for loading the bombs

337

on board. Christian hadn't a clue about the Wellington, but the Luftwaffe's medium bombers had routinely carried eight five-hundred-pound bombs. A barrel of wine weighed roughly 600 pounds and contained enough wine for 25 cases or 300 bottles of wine. Four barrels would constitute only slightly more than the average load of a medium bomber yet converted to 100 cases or 1,200 bottles of wine. He would only need to bring in that much wine every two months to stay in business — assuming he could find a bottling factory here in Berlin. He'd worry about that tomorrow. The first thing he had to do was convince Charlotte to introduce him to her employer.

Business as Usual
RAF Gatow
Saturday, 3 April 1948

David and Emily sat in a corner of the BEA office in the terminal at Gatow. After the frantic flying of the last two days, they were trying to bring order to the chaos left behind by their whirlwind first trips. The first eleven patients had been dumped on them directly by the City Council, but David did not want that to happen again. If nothing else, he had not been reimbursed for the flights, although many promises had been made. That was the main reason he'd asked Charlotte and Emily to come into the office on a Saturday to see if they could work out standard operating procedures for requests from the Berlin City Council — and the mechanisms for payment as well. Meanwhile, Kiwi and the ground crew were out in the BEA hangar checking over the Wellington to be sure she was 100% airworthy at a moment's notice.

David, Kiwi and Emily had come with Robin in his car, and it was only natural that Charlotte coming from Kreuzberg would not get in until later. She arrived, just after 9:30, and went straight to stand before David at his desk, "Herr Goldman?"

It upset David when she acted so deferential towards him. "I thought we had agreed on first names?" He admonished.

She nodded and smiled, still obviously nervous. "Yes, but...." Her voice fell away as if she was afraid to finish her thought.

"Yes?" He prompted.

"I have a favour to ask."

"Yes?"

"My cousin is with me and would like to speak to you."

"Your cousin?"

"Didn't I tell you my cousin is living with me?" She glanced at Emily.

David too looked over at Emily. He could not remember Charlotte mentioning anything about a cousin, but Emily nodded.

"He came in January and has been here ever since," Charlotte expanded.

David started to remember and frowned slightly. "Not the Luftwaffe officer?"

Charlotte nodded, "Yes, he was a pilot, but this has nothing to do with flying, David. It — it is a business proposition."

"Business?"

"Please. I would rather he spoke for himself."

"Where is he?"

"He's at the front gate. The guards would not let him through. My pass is not the right kind."

"I'll go get him," Emily volunteered at once, standing and reaching for her coat.

When she returned, she was laughing. David inwardly raised his eyebrows at the ease with which this German had broken through Emily's usual reserve, but there was no question the man was charming. He came straight towards David with an outstretched hand, and opened with, "Thank you for taking time to see me, Herr Goldman."

Extremely sensitive to patronizing, subservience and antisemitism, David was surprised to detect none of these as they shook hands. The German had a firm, warm handshake, and a straight-forward manner that David appreciated. "My name is Christian Freiherr von Feldburg," he announced, "I know you are very busy, and I promise not to take up more of your time than necessary."

David noted favourably the combination of respect and self-assurance. He gestured toward the vacant coffee table near the window. It was part of the BEA furnishings, but since the BEA flight wasn't due until the afternoon, none of the BEA employees had arrived yet.

"Should I try to see about getting us some tea and buns from the NAAFI?" Emily asked.

"There's no need for that, *gnaedige Frau*," Christian assured her with a smile. "I really won't linger. I know you have important work to do."

David sat down and Christian sat across from him with Charlotte and Emily at either end.

"What can I do for you?" David asked.

"To put it simply: save my business."

"Sorry?" David looked hastily between Christian and Charlotte. She was clutching her hands nervously.

"I have a wine business. My family estate in Altdorf in the American Zone produces dry, high-quality Franken wine. I've brought a sample with me if you want to try it?" Christian indicated his briefcase and included Emily in his invitation. She shook her head.

David answered, "Maybe later. First, I'd like to hear your business proposal."

Christian readily dropped the issue of a sample and explained, "There's a strong market for the wine here in Berlin. Much stronger than in the American Zone. There, many other estates produce good wine, but the Americans don't appreciate dry wine particularly."

David laughed and felt himself warming towards the German.

Christian continued, "The French would kill me if I tried to sell my wine in their Zone. That leaves the British Zone and Berlin. I focused on Berlin because Charlotte was here, and I had nearly a thousand bottles of wine on the American train that is now stopped on the Zonal border."

"And you want me to fly in those bottles with the ambulance." David surmised with obvious scepticism. He answered the implicit request without hesitation, "Out of the question. Bottles are too heavy, bulky and fragile."

"Agreed. I don't want you to fly the bottles in. We have barrels of unbottled wine in the cellar. I thought your bomber could easily handle four six-hundred-pound barrels of wine on one of its return flights."

"Theoretically, but we will be flying to different airports depending on the treatment needed by the patients we fly out. We have no schedule.

How could you get your barrels to the correct departure airport?"

"Charlotte thought," Christian glanced at her as he spoke, "that you were likely to have a flight to Munich at least once every two months. That's all I need. Whenever you happen to fly to Munich, you send me word, and I'll make sure the cargo is waiting for you."

"Once every two months, four barrels of wine?" David asked for confirmation. Feldburg nodded, but David pointed out, "Air freight is not cheap."

"I understand. You tell me what you want to charge, and I'll tell you if I can afford it."

They gazed at one another. David was tempted. Having return cargoes might be critical to the viability of the business. Wine was a high-margin business and using the winches to carry barrels meant there would be no damage to the facilities for patients. He glanced at Charlotte, who sat on the edge of her seat, clearly hoping he would approve. He turned next to Emily. She nodded and remarked, "It sounds like a good opportunity to me."

David still hesitated. He couldn't see any downside to the proposal, but before he could do business with this man he had to clear the decks of the ghosts between them. "You were in the Luftwaffe, I believe."

"That's right."

"Just what did you fly?"

"109s."

"Did you fly against England in 1940?"

"The whole bloody summer."

"You might have been the man who shot me down," David noted, and Charlotte audibly caught her breath.

"I doubt it," Christian answered evenly. "I wasn't particularly good. I didn't get my first confirmed kill until August 15th."

"I wasn't shot down — in flames — until Sept 15th."

"Couldn't have been me. By then I'd been repatriated for medical treatment. I'd been shot down in the Channel and suffered damage to my eye that grounded me for over six months."

"I suppose it was a Spitfire that shot you down," David remarked with a cynical smile.

"No, it was a Hurricane. Very good aircraft, the Hurricane, underrated by too many."

Feldburg had won; David couldn't resist his charm any longer and he smiled.

"You flew Hurricanes?" Christian correctly interpreted his reaction.

David nodded, "Until I was shot down and injured. After my face and hands had been reconstructed, I was posted as an instructor at our Central Flying School for the remainder of the war."

Their eyes met and Christian nodded. "They did a good job with your face."

"I was lucky to be handled by one of the best plastic surgeons of the century: Dr McIndoe."

"Ah, yes. I read about him when I was a POW in America. From New Zealand, I think?"

David nodded and brought the conversation back to business. "I'll do the calculations for the freight charges and Charlotte can pass them on to you. They won't be exorbitant, but I must warn you, that the RAF could commandeer our cargo space at short notice at any time. The needs of the RAF will take precedence over commercial partners."

"I understand. We can only take things one step at a time."

"Agreed," David concluded the meeting by standing up and offering his hand. As Christian took it, they both smiled. There was still a brotherhood among airmen. At least sometimes, David conceded.

Aggressive Airliner
RAF Gatow
Monday, 5 April 1948

The trains were rolling again. The Western Allies had buckled under and agreed to submit their passenger and cargo manifests to the Soviets. Because this procedure meant Soviet soldiers did not board the trains to inspect them, Lt. General Herbert was calling the compromise a "victory" for reason and diplomacy. Priestman thought it was a humiliating and unworkable concession. There was no reason why they should (or would) list everything in the manifests submitted to the Soviets and equally no reason why the Soviets would (or should) trust them. In short, they had done nothing but — as Colonel Howley worded it — "kicked the can down the road." The confrontation had not been avoided, merely postponed.

Which, Priestman reminded himself, was a good thing because his PSP runway was in shreds after just three days of intense use. Yet Sanders still pooh-poohed the need for a concrete runway, saying the situation was reaching a breaking point. He suggested that if things got worse, the UK would pull out of Berlin. Why should the British taxpayer build a concrete runway for the Soviets, he'd asked.

Fortunately, the CO of 46 Group, Air Commodore Mercer, not only disagreed but also weighed in on the issue. The poor landing conditions in Gatow meant more wear and tear on his aircraft, higher consumption of spare parts, and greater risks to crews. He had pointedly reminded Sanders that a decision to withdraw from Berlin would be made at the most senior levels. Until he heard otherwise, he insisted, he would assume that he *did* have to fly into Berlin. He wanted a concrete runway.

Sanders had reluctantly agreed that if Transport Command funded the construction out of their budget, he would authorize it. A typical bureaucratic waffle, in Priestman's book, but the important thing was he would get his runway. Mercer promised to have the paperwork to him by the end of the week.

His phone rang, and Priestman grabbed it. On the other end of the line, Corporal Groom from the control tower asked, "Sir? Could you come to the tower immediately, please? We have a problem."

Priestman left everything on his desk. Emily was due back in the ambulance later this afternoon from yet another medevac, and as he took the stairs two at a time he was already imagining some calamity that would prevent her from returning. As he entered the control tower, he was surprised by an alarmed voice crackling loudly over the intercom. It filled the entire room. "He's doing a loop right in front of me!"

"What's going on?" Priestman asked coming up beside Squadron Leader Garth, who was standing behind the seated controller and assistant.

"The incoming BEA flight claims a Soviet fighter is doing aerobatics in the air corridor in front of him."

Priestman cursed under his breath. Was this a coincidence or a calculated escalation? The Soviets had played silly games with the Spitfires at the end of January. At the start of March, they'd beat up the airfield — and also flown dangerously close to an inbound American passenger flight. This might just be part of that pattern. Before jumping to any conclusions, however, he asked, "Are we sure the BEA airliner is in the corridor? There's no chance he's off course, is there?"

"Now he's rolling off the top!" The BEA pilot reported loudly over the intercom.

"None whatsoever, sir," S/L Garth answered in his deep, reassuring voice. "I checked the radar myself before calling you up here. He's smack inside the corridor and steady on course. He's passed Frohnau and is approaching Spandau now."

"So, very close to the Soviet airfield at Staaken." Priestman grasped the situation.

Before anyone could reply, the BEA pilot exclaimed with a loud shout. "He's coming straight at me!" The sound of aircraft engines screaming reached a crescendo and then faded on the microphones. "He passed just feet overhead!" The BEA pilot reported, adding angrily, "I've got nine passengers on board. Can't you put an end to this madness?"

"Can we do anything, sir?" Garth asked softly.

"I'll do what I can. Maybe you or Wilkins should man the radar."

"I'll go, sir!" Wilkins jumped up and went to the radar room.

Meanwhile, Priestman ordered Groom to connect him to Triple Two Dispersal and then asked Garth to find out if the BEA airliner was being confronted by a single aircraft or a section.

"Cutty Sark to Bealiner Seven-Seven, is the fighter alone or operating in pairs?" Garth asked in his slow, inherently calming voice.

"I'm not sure — what? OK, my second pilot says he's alone. Now he's doing climbing rolls on our left."

Priestman addressed Corporal Vincent who was sitting on the far side of Flight Sergeant Hart looking shocked. "Get me a connection to Staaken, Corporal Vincent, and I need Borisenko as well."

Vincent nodded and picked up her phone, while Groom reported, "I've got Triple Two Dispersal, sir."

Priestman took the receiver from him. "Priestman. How fast can you get a section airborne?"

"We're on fifteen minutes readiness," Benny answered.

"You're going to have to be faster than that. I want you airborne in two minutes. The BEA flight is being harassed by a Soviet fighter. Scramble and report back to the tower once you're at the head of the runway ready for take-off."

"Yes, sir!"

Over the intercom, the BEA captain exclaimed, "He's stall turning. Coming back towards us." His voice switched to a yell. "He's sheering in—"

The explosion seemed to shake the entire tower. The clock read 1:57.

After a moment of stunned silence, Garth pressed the microphone button. "Come in, Bealiner Seven-Seven!" Nothing. "Bealiner Seven-Seven this is Cutty Sark. Do you read me?"

"Oh, my God!" Someone whispered, speaking for them all.

"Smoke, sir!" Flight Sergeant Hart pointed out of the window. Two columns of smoke could be seen rising north of the airfield. She stood, grabbed a pair of binoculars and directed them at the column of smoke.

"Put a call through to Lt. General Herbert at once." Priestman ordered Groom, adding to Vincent, "and put me through to Triple Two Dispersal."

Dispersal answered before he got through to Herbert and Priestman ordered the Section to stay on stand-by until he had joined them.

"Has something happened, sir?" a frightened voice asked at the other end of the line. "I thought I heard a tremendous explosion from not very far away."

"BEA's inbound aircraft appears to have collided with a Soviet fighter. We'll fly over to see what we can find." He hung up, thought a minute, and then ordered the station ambulance to attempt to reach the crash site overland.

"Lt. General Herbert's adjutant is on the line, sir." Groom handed him the receiver.

Priestman took the receiver. "This is RAF Gatow, Wing Commander Priestman. The BEA flight has crashed after reporting harassment from a lone Soviet fighter."

The Lieutenant on the other end of the line gasped. "Was it shot down?"

"We heard no gunfire prior to the explosion. Most likely it was a collision. I'm going to fly over the crash site now to see what I can find out from the air. Our ambulance will try to get there, but judging by the smoke, the crash site is nearer to Spandau and will be reached sooner from there."

"I'll get on that immediately, sir."

"I have Staaken on the line, sir," Groom reported.

Robin looked around but Corporal Borisenko had not yet arrived. "Tell them to wait. When Borisenko gets here have her request a meeting for me with my counterpart Colonel Kuznetsov at the earliest opportunity. You can relay the answer to me over the RT."

"Yes, sir."

Priestman left the tower and went down to his office to grab his flight jacket. As he crossed the outer office, Sergeant Andrews stopped him. "It's the police, sir," she explained, her hand over the receiver. "They are receiving numerous eye-witness reports of some sort of accident, sir. Some say mid-air collision, others just a crash."

"Ask them to protocol all eye-witness reports. We may need them. Stan?" He turned his attention to his adjutant, who was looking stunned. "Call BEA and ask for the manifest."

"Yes, sir."

Priestman descended the stairs and crossed the field briskly to his Spitfire "P" which had been rolled out for him. The bowser was alongside fuelling it and he asked the fitter if she was armed as well.

"Yes, sir," the Leading Aircraftman answered smartly, but the look he gave his Station Commander was one of alarm.

The two Spitfires of the duty section were at the head of the grass runway with their engines ticking over and their fuselages trembling. As Robin reached for the handhold to pull himself up onto the wing, Danny came running up. "Did I get the right gen? The BEA liner has crashed?"

"Yes — while being harassed by a Soviet fighter."

"Crikey! Does this mean war?" Danny looked stunned.

"Maybe, but not yet. Who's in the duty section?"

"Ah, Mac and Benny," the Squadron Leader answered.

"Would you mind replacing Benny and coming with me?"

"Done."

As Priestman climbed into the cockpit and went through the drill, Danny ran to one of the two waiting Spitfires and replaced the pilot. Priestman meanwhile taxied his Spit over to the others and took up position ahead of them. He switched on the RT. "Red Two, Red Three, ready?"

"Red Two, Roger." That was Danny.

"Red Three, Roger." Mac seconded him.

"Cutty Sark Control, Dragon Fly Red Section. Request clearance for take-off."

"Dragon Fly Red Section cleared for take-off," S/L Garth answered personally.

Priestman pushed the throttle forward and released the brakes. The Spit galloped over the grass and lifted into the air almost by herself. Then as they rose above the trees, he banked slightly to the right and flew straight for the two columns of smoke billowing up next to each other. Danny tucked in behind his right wing and Mac was on his left in a close vic.

Priestman did not bother laying on much altitude. Instead, they skimmed low over the forest north of Gatow. In the distance, the built-up area that marked Spandau jutted out, but the two columns of smoke rose from an open field no more than four miles ahead inside the Soviet Zone. The smoke of one column was increasing, belching up in puffs from the fuel tanks, while the other several hundred yards beyond was dying out. They reached the main wreck first. Flames were spreading out from the wreckage as the grass and crops of the surrounding field caught fire.

Priestman banked hard to circle the crash site, sweeping first to windward where he had a clear view. The wreckage was stretched over a considerable area, the fuselage broken into three pieces. The port wing was still attached, and it was the fuel tanks of this wing which were burning furiously and spewing great clouds of smoke into the sky. The entire port side of the Dakota was encased in flames. The starboard wing, however, had been severed from the fuselage and lay several hundred yards beyond the fuselage, closer to the outskirts of Spandau — and it was entangled with the remains of a Yak.

The tail of the Russian fighter stuck straight up into the air with the undercarriage folded into the belly. The nose of the fighter was buried into the earth and the cockpit collapsed into the main fuselage. The pilot had got what he deserved, Priestman thought furiously, as he flicked rolled and reversed his turn to fly back over the main wreck a second time, this time looking for possible survivors. "Anything moving down there?" He asked his wingmen.

"Not that I can see," Danny answered, "but passengers may have been torn out of the fuselage when the wing was ripped off. They might be scattered farther from the crash site."

They reversed again and widened the radius of their circle. As Danny had suspected, they found three lifeless bodies strewn across the field between the wing and the fuselage. One was a stewardess.

Priestman switched on the RT. "Cutty Sark. We've got the wreck in sight. The Soviet fighter is still entangled with the starboard wing. No question this was a collision. Any survivors would be a miracle."

"Roger. We reached Colonel Kuznetsov. He says you're welcome anytime. He — ah — Borisenko reports he sounded unusually receptive — not his usual ice-cold reserve. She thinks he may have seen the crash but not yet know a Soviet aircraft was involved."

Priestman digested that information. The Yak was flying alone, doing aerobatics. The pilot might not have been authorised to do aerobatics — or not inside the flight path of a civilian airliner. If that was the case, he might not have had his radio switched on and probably had not informed his superiors of what he was up to. To the tower, he answered. "That's good. Tell him I'll land in two minutes."

"Sir?" Garth sounded confused.

"You heard me. I'm turning to make my approach to Staaken now."

There was a pause before Garth asked, "Have you requested clearance from Area Control, sir?"

"I'll do that now," Priestman snapped back. He could sense that his actions unsettled S/L Garth — and would upset men like Herbert and Waite even more. He also understood *why* his actions were likely to agitate everyone. Direct contact with Soviet military leaders at a time like this was a huge gamble. The slightest misplaced word could be blown up into an 'incident.' Yet his instinct told him that he had to confront Kuznetsov before he'd had time to receive instructions from Moscow. He wanted to see what he had to say — airman to airman.

In all encounters to date, Kuznetsov remained reserved yet professional. He wore a 'fruit salad' of medals on his chest in the Soviet fashion, but they were not just bombast as in other cases. From their brief, translated conversations, Priestman knew that Kuznetsov had flown a variety of fighters during the war and claimed 29 victories against the Germans. Priestman considered him a genuine soldier rather than a party animal.

"Do you want us to come with you, sir?" Danny asked over the R/T.

"I want you to land with me, but not get out of your Spit. Be prepared to take off in a hurry if I am arrested. Mac, stay orbiting the airfield to watch what happens. If challenged in the air, scram."

"Yes, sir."

Only now did Priestman contact the Air Safety Centre, informing them that he was landing at Staaken "from the East." He did not ask for permission. He had already lowered the undercarriage and lined up with the outermost edge of the runway. If the Soviets wanted to stop him, they might push a truck or other vehicle on the runway, but the Spitfire could land almost as well on the grass beside it. All he had to do was sideslip.

Although he could see people running and hear sirens going off, nothing physically got in his way. He set the Spitfire down, and Danny clung to his inside flank. They rolled to the far end before turning around. Over the RT, he told Danny to stay there, where he had plenty of room to take off again if needed. Then slowly, he taxied back toward the terminal buildings.

The Spitfire did not get far. Soviet soldiers poured out onto the runway, waving at him to stop. Some of them had guns over their shoulders, but no one took aim. He applied the brakes and waited with the engine ticking over.

A jeep painted in the livery of a Red Air Force bounced across the field and screeched to a halt. Colonel Kuznetsov leapt out with agility. Only then did Priestman switch off the Spitfire engine, shove back the hood, and step out onto the wing root. When his feet touched the ground, Colonel Kuznetsov stood beside the Spitfire with his hand extended. The Colonel spoke in Russian, but an interpreter at his elbow said in English. "Allow me to offer my deepest condolences. This is a terrible accident."

Their eyes met. Priestman saw shock and sincere distress in the Russian's eyes. "There were nine passengers and four crew on that airliner. You *do* know that they have been killed by the shameless irresponsibility of one of *your* pilots? A Yak was doing aerobatics in the flight path of a civilian airliner on landing approach." His tone was sharp, and he did not take the outstretched hand as he waited for his words to be translated.

By Kuznetsov's reaction, Priestman surmised he'd already heard — or possibly had personally seen — what happened. Yet his distress seemed genuine as he said through the interpreter, "It was a tragic accident, Wing Commander. My pilot was very young and very keen. New to service in Germany."

"He had no business being in the air corridor. No business being in the landing path to Gatow." Priestman insisted.

Kuznetsov replied, "He has paid a high price for his foolishness."

"He got what he deserved — which is more than can be said for thirteen civilians, including at least two women, who were on a civilian airliner in peacetime." Priestman watched the interpreter closely, hoping he would faithfully convey his words.

The Russian commander nodded, and Priestman needed no translation of his, "Yes, yes." He followed with, "You are right. Please accept my condolences." Again, Kuznetsov offered his hand.

This time Priestman took it, but he did not become genial. Instead, he warned, "There will have to be a full investigation. Eye-witness reports were already coming in before I took off. I heard the communication between the pilot and the controller in my tower, and I have flown over the wreck. There is no question of what happened or who was to blame. I expect my government will demand a full apology and there may be other consequences as well."

"Let the political leadership deal with that as they may," the Russian officer replied with what Priestman thought was a sudden stiffness — almost distaste. He concluded with: "I have no say in the actions of my government."

That was true enough, Priestman thought to himself. Less than he had, and that was little enough, but at least he could vote against his government if he was angry with them. He drew another deep breath and answered while nodding. "We understand each other." He then saluted Kuznetsov smartly and turned to climb back into the Spitfire's cockpit.

Around him, orders were shouted, and the Soviet soldiers cleared the runway. Priestman restarted the engine and glanced to his left. Kuznetsov stood beside the runway still saluting him. He returned the salute and then pushed the throttles forward, confident that he had more than enough runway for take-off. Danny followed without awaiting orders.

They landed at Gatow minutes later, and Stan met Priestman as he dismounted from the cockpit. "Sir, General Robertson and General Clay have both ordered fighter escorts for all Allied aircraft travelling in the air corridors. No. 46 Group has suspended their flights for today until escorts can be organised at that end. The Air Ambulance is ready to return from Hamburg, but it was denied permission to take off due to the absence of an escort. Do you want them to hold there, or do you want to send an escort from Gatow to bring them in?"

"We'll send an escort," Priestman answered before calling over to the waiting ground crew to top up his Spitfire with fuel.

Danny joined them. "How many escorts do you want?"

"Two will do. It was Benny you kicked off the Spitfire earlier. Let him come with me."

"Yes, sir."

Danny disappeared but Stan asked anxiously. "You aren't planning to fly escort yourself, are you, sir?"

"Yes, I am," Priestman answered as he leaned back against the trailing edge of the Spitfire's wing and crossed his arms.

"But..." Stan looked shocked.

"Is BEA contacting the next of kin?"

"Yes, sir. Tragically, one of the passengers was the wife of a recently arrived American major, she was just joining him. There was also an American diplomat on board on a liaison assignment. The Americans have been informed and are handling both of those cases."

"Any French?" Priestman asked.

"No, the rest of the passengers and crew were all British."

"Air Commodore Waite was informed, I presume?"

"Yes, sir. I believe he and Lt. General Herbert are trying to reach the wreck by land rover."

"General Robertson knows, or he wouldn't have ordered the fighter escorts." Priestman continued.

"Correct. We were told he will confront Marshal Sokolovsky in person tomorrow."

"In that case, this incident is already being handled at the highest political levels in Germany, and I can see no reason why I must remain here," Priestman concluded. "I need to work off some anger, and I can do that best by flying. Also, I won't be at ease until my wife is back safely. By escorting her myself, I ensure that I don't get on everyone else's nerves. Understood?"

"Very good, sir," Stan gave him a wan smile and backed away.

The air ambulance arrived safely with its Spitfire escort later the same afternoon.

Avoiding WWIII
RAF Gatow
Thursday, 8 April 1948

Three days later, when Priestman arrived at work, his intelligence officer awaited him in the outer office.

He took one look at Boyd and braced himself inwardly for bad news. "Problems?"

"Not exactly. I just thought I ought to be the one to bring you these."

"What?"

"The latest Soviet-controlled press clippings about the crash."

"That bad?"

"They've changed their tune a bit. The first headline reads: 'British Aircraft rams Soviet Trainer!' The text continues: 'Bursting from low cloud without proper clearance, a British aircraft ploughed through an innocent Soviet training aircraft in the act of landing. The British aircraft was in complete violation of all air safety regulations—'"

"I don't want to hear any more. Is anyone going to believe that?"

"Not anyone who saw it happen — and probably not many others either. The free press has made quite a fuss already about an airliner being attacked — or at any rate endangered — by a fighter. I think most Berliners with an open mind will see this for the rubbish it is. The issue isn't really whether anyone believes it or not, but rather what it tells us about Moscow's attitude. Compared to the response that you had from Colonel Kuznetsov the day of the crash and what General Robertson reported regarding Sokolovsky's response the day after, this text represents an abrupt change of tone. It appears to have been dictated directly from Moscow, and as such tells us about the political atmosphere there."

"I'll subscribe to that. It's damn near a declaration of war. Any other thoughts?"

"Well, I wouldn't go quite that far, sir, but it is significant that the Soviet Leadership is unprepared to offer even commonplace and formal condolences for an accident. Usually, tragic accidents enable bitter enemies to bury their differences temporarily. The Soviets, on the other hand, seem intent on maintaining an image of perfection and strength. So much so, they cannot admit to a mistake by a young pilot. Such a response from Moscow does not bode well for the future of our relationship."

"That's one way of putting it," Priestman commented dryly.

Boyd continued earnestly. "They've closed the autobahns more than once. Since the start of this year, they've targeted the rail and barge links as well. We only just got the trains moving again by providing them with the passenger and cargo manifests."

"I know. And they're forcing the Germans who want to travel on our trains to obtain Soviet permission first. They have effectively established their right to decide who and what moves on the transit routes — without actually boarding the trains or carrying out inspections," Priestman summarized the situation as he saw it.

"My concern, sir, is that the air corridors may be next. Although the collision itself was an accident, they may have hoped the harassment would intimidate the BEA pilot into aborting the approach — or maybe they hoped to persuade BEA to suspend passenger service altogether. If that's the case, this might become a routine practice."

"I don't think our fighters will have any difficulty preventing something like this from happening again. I was perfectly prepared to shoot a Yak out of the sky if it so much as strayed into the corridor while I was escorting the ambulance back the other day."

"Ah. Yes." Boyd looked slightly uncomfortable. "I'm sure our fighters could provide effective defence — if we still had fighter escorts."

"You mean we don't?" Priestman asked flabbergasted.

"No, sir. General Robertson cancelled that order late last night after you went home. He felt that Sokolovsky's assurances about this being an accident ought to be trusted."

"We're supposed to 'trust' the Soviets after all the lies and insults and harassment we've been subjected to?" Priestman demanded furiously, feeling renewed sympathy for Colonel Howley. "What's wrong with the precaution of maintaining fighter escorts?"

Looking more uncomfortable than ever, Boyd reported, "Robertson said he didn't want to risk World War Three because — I think his exact words were — 'because of some trigger-happy fighter pilot.'"

Priestman stared at his Intelligence Officer. If he opened his mouth, he risked saying something that he might later regret. Only after he had his temper better under control did he snap, "I hope General Robertson flew over the wreck before he made that decision." Then he continued into his office and slammed the door.

Chapter Thirteen
In the Shadow of the Storm

Making the News
Berlin
Friday, 9 April 1948

"Air Ambulance International. How may I help you?" Charlotte answered in staccato, business-like German, which reflected how keen she was to do her job correctly.

To her astonishment, a female voice replied. "Yes, hello. This is Vee Cox of the *Times*. I'm trying to reach the Managing Director of Air Ambulance International for an interview."

Charlotte caught her breath. The *Times* was the best newspaper in the world! She felt as though she was speaking to a celebrity. If only David were here, but he wasn't. Into the receiver, she said apologetically, "I'm sorry. Mr Goldman is not in the office at present. Would you like to speak to his partner Mr Murray?"

"Oh, yes! Why not? Please."

AAI only had one phone, so Charlotte covered the receiver with her hand and whispered to Kiwi, who was doing calculations of some kind at the desk opposite her, "It's the *Times* calling!"

Kiwi looked surprised and then a little wary, but he held out his hand for the receiver. "This is Chuck Murray. How can I help you?"

"Chuck, darling! This is Vee! You must remember! We met at Northolt when I tried to hitch a lift with you at the start of the month. Your captain was quite emphatic about not taking a hitchhiker."

"I was very sorry about that, Ma'am."

"I know you were, darling! I could tell. Look, Chuck, I'm in Berlin for a couple of days. I've just come out of a meeting with Air Commodore Waite, and he was singing your praises. He says your air ambulance was an absolute sensation! He claims you lifted almost a score of seriously ill

355

patients out of Berlin right in the middle of this recent crisis and delivered them to hospitals in the West. Now, that's the kind of story my editors love to hear. Could we meet and talk about it in more detail?"

That sounded like free publicity to Kiwi, and he certainly didn't mind the idea of seeing Vee again, so he agreed. "Sure. Where?"

"I'm staying at the Adlon on Unter den Linden. It has a restaurant. Could we possibly meet there?"

"Why not? What time?"

"Well, when could you be here?"

Kiwi looked at his watch. It was 11 am. "I haven't a clue how long it will take to get to you, so let's just say whenever I get there. On the assumption it won't take all day, why don't we plan on lunch?" He was happy to get out of the office for a bit and liked the idea of lunch at a proper restaurant with an attractive woman.

"Perfect. Just ask for me at the main desk, and I'll come straight down."

Kiwi hadn't had much chance to see Berlin and taking a taxi to the Adlon was a sobering experience. Like Priestman, David, and Emily before him, he was shocked by just how little of the former German capital was still standing. The Adlon had survived the bombing, only to be badly damaged by Soviet artillery. The pock-marked, grey façade, naked of all embellishments, looked more like a prison than a hotel. The interior was somewhat more elegant, but the clientele consisted exclusively of Soviet military officers and Russians in grey suits. Kiwi had been warned about Russians in grey suits; allegedly, they were either Communist Party officials, Secret Police, or both.

He asked for V. Cox at the desk, and two minutes later she breezed into the lobby, a refreshing breath of fresh air. Today she wore a striking red suit with large white buttons and white "epaulettes" on the shoulders. As before, her shoes were flats, but today she wasn't in trousers. Instead, her skirt came to mid-calf and flared from the knee down. Besides being very stylish, it fitted as only tailored clothes do.

Vee greeted Kiwi like a long-lost cousin, touching her cheek to both of his and declaring, "It's lovely to see you again, Chuck! Shall we sit outside or in?"

Kiwi opted for the open air because of the large number of gloomy men in grey suits sourly glaring at them from around the room. At the handful of tables set up on the broad sidewalk out front, they were almost alone. A fresh breeze lifted the tablecloths and made the air chilly, but Vee was a good sport about it. "Just buy me a stiff cocktail and I'll warm up from the inside enough to stay for hours," she laughed.

Kiwi was happy to comply.

As soon as they had placed their orders, Vee remarked. "You must have been RAF in the war, no?"

"Spot on."

"Did you fly many Berlin missions?"

"No, flew fighters."

"Oh, lovely. I always did prefer fighters myself," Vee declared, and with a string of cheery questions she reeled Kiwi's life story out of him. They were halfway through lunch before she suggested they get down to 'business.' By then Kiwi had had three cocktails, and he was very happy to talk about AAI and its spectacular successes. Vee seemed so interested and she asked such good questions that he readily explained about the regulations they had to fulfil, the selection of the Wellington, his race to get a commercial license — the whole story. Vee seemed to share each triumph, smiling and commenting with words like "Good show!" and "Well done!" It was almost as intoxicating as the cocktails, of which he ordered another round.

Kiwi was sorry when after dessert and coffee he could drag out the 'interview' no longer. It was also getting increasingly chilly. He was just working up the courage to ask how much longer Vee planned to be in Berlin when they were distracted by shouting coming from further down the street. Turning, they saw a huge crowd surging towards them along Unter den Linden. The agitated and angry crowd was composed mostly of young men wearing the remnants of Nazi uniforms and chanting slogans in German. Kiwi's instinct was to get out of their path. "We'd better get back inside!" He urged Vee, pushing his chair back and taking her elbow.

The reporter would have none of it. "I've got to find out what this is about. Come on!" She started in the direction of the on-coming mob, leaving Kiwi calling anxiously to the waiter and paying the bill in haste so he could chase after her.

He was genuinely alarmed and worried about what might happen to Vee and at the same time exasperated by her audacity. Why couldn't she see that a mob of shouting Germans was dangerous? Why did she have to charge into the midst of it?

Vee plunged into the crowd of angry young men as it came abreast of the Adlon and Kiwi temporarily lost sight of her. Finally, he caught a glimpse of something red surrounded by wildly gesturing men. Elbowing his way through the crowd frantically, he came to the rescue, but by the time he reached her, the main crowd had moved on. Only five young men still stood around Vee all talking at once while the reporter struggled to take notes on a little pad of paper she held in one hand.

"...proctors in every hall!"

"And now they've closed down the paper!"

"For reporting the truth!"

"Vee! What's going on?" Kiwi reached her side.

"That's what I'm trying to find out. These young men are explaining it to me. Do you have any more paper?"

"No," Kiwi replied, glowering at the young men besieging Vee.

They nodded their heads to him, and one held out his hand. "I'm Hans Wilmer." Kiwi shook the offered hand automatically, if mistrustfully. The earnest young man continued in correct if accented English. "We are all students at Humbolt University. Did you know that more than 2,000 students have been arrested in the Soviet Zone? Six hundred of them have been sent to Sachsenhausen Concentration camp."

"I thought the concentration camps had been liberated." Kiwi protested.

"The *Nazi* concentration camps have been liberated — and taken over by the Soviets who are filling them again."

"That was 2,000 arrests?" Vee asked for confirmation, butting into the conversation.

The young man nodded irritably and wanted to say something else, but Vee got her question out first, "What did the students do?"

The young man looked extremely annoyed and directed his answer to the tall, burly and uniformed Kiwi rather than to the woman. "They were accused of anti-Soviet activities, 'reactionary' tendencies, and sabotaging the proletariat, but all they wanted was academic freedom, sir."

"That's all any of us want," another young man spoke up anxiously. He was very thin, almost skeletal, and his face had a hideous scar on it, presumably from a flame thrower or some such weapon. He had an intensity about him that made Kiwi nervous. "The Soviets make Marx, Lenin and Stalin the answer to every question — historical, political, or economic! They forbid analysis and discussion!"

"All the answers are dictated from Moscow!" A third student joined in. "Even the professors are allowed no freedom. They are required to teach only what Moscow wants — in the faculties of literature and art, no less than in politics and history!" This youth was still handsome and dreamy, Kiwi thought.

"What do you hope to achieve with your protest?" Vee entered the conversation again.

The third student turned to her and declared. "We want the Berlin City Council to give us a building where we can start a new university, a *free* university. We can't learn anything under the constant surveillance of Soviet agents!"

"Even in the canteen, they blast propaganda at us from the *Deutschlandsender*." A fourth student reported indignantly.

"We want a new university," the intense student repeated. "We are going to demand that Mayor Reuter give it to us! Come!" He turned away from Vee and led the others after the mob of students already streaming through the Brandenburger Gate into the British Sector. The young men ran to catch up, leaving Kiwi and Vee standing in the street.

"I've got to get this all written up before I forget!" Vee declared, tucking her notebook and pen into her leather handbag and striding in the direction of the hotel.

Kiwi chased after her. "Are you... I was wondering..." She was no longer paying any attention to him. She appeared to be completely obsessed with the story she wanted to write. "Vee!"

She paused and asked impatiently, "Yes?"

"Look, it's time for me to get back to the office, but I thought—"

She held out her hand to him with a wide smile that was ice-cold. A celebrity smile, Kiwi found himself thinking, the kind of smile people learned to give on command for admiring fans. "So, kind of you to take time for me, Chuck, and thanks for lunch, too!"

Sensing she was in a hurry to turn away, Kiwi struggled to keep her attention, "How much longer are you going to be in Berlin? I was thinking maybe we could—"

"Oh, I'm much too busy for anything social," she cut him off. "Thanks anyway, but I've got to get the university and air ambulance stories filed today. Nice seeing you." She held out her hand again. "Maybe another time."

Kiwi had rarely felt so roundly brushed off. Outwardly, he shrugged and returned to Gatow cursing 'working women' in his head. Inside he was deeply hurt— again.

Band of Brothers
Leeds, UK
Saturday, 10 April 1948

The tradition of meeting again on or about the anniversary of their last flight together had started two years ago. They'd all made that first reunion in 1946, but already in 1947, Stu had begged off. Now Adrian and Frank couldn't make it either and they were down to just four. Kit reserved a table for them and met Daddy MacDonald at the station.

Mrs MacDonald had put him on the train in Edinburgh, and Kit was on the platform ready to get the wheelchair off the train as soon as it pulled into the station. Kit's former flight engineer waved and smiled from the window when he caught sight of his skipper on the platform. Kit returned the gesture, hoping his face didn't betray his shock. He hadn't seen Daddy since his discharge from the RAF rehabilitation centre, and the difference was appalling. For two years after repatriation from the Wehrmacht hospital where they had both landed, the RAF had provided treatment and therapy, but eight months ago the RAF medical establishment had admitted defeat. Two months after his doctors decided that he would never walk again, Daddy was "demobbed." Kit was seeing him in civilian clothes for the first time in his life. They made the once stocky Scotsman look old and helpless, although he was just 39.

Daddy started giving Kit instructions on how to get the wheelchair off the train, but when the conductor and station master saw a man with an artificial leg trying to manhandle a wheelchair; they hastened to offer their assistance. The job done, they withdrew with nods of respect and smart salutes suggestive of wartime service. Daddy remarked rather cynically, "I could become fond of Leeds. They don't treat us invalids like that everywhere." Then he smiled up at Kit and remarked, "You're looking well, Skip. Being a father agrees with you, does it?"

"I haven't decided yet. Donna can be incredibly sweet and cuddly — and then the little monster screams half the night," Kit quipped back, handing Daddy his suitcase to hold on his lap before taking the handles of the wheelchair to spin it about and start for the exit.

Daddy laughed. "The little buggers can keep you awake at that age, can't they? But they get better as they grow up."

"Both your girls married now, Daddy?"

"No, only the older girl. Ailsa's training as a shop assistant, and she lives over the shop with a girlfriend."

"And how is Mrs MacDonald?"

"Just the same as ever," the tone was abruptly sharp, almost bitter, which surprised Kit. When they'd both been in therapy, Mrs MacDonald had visited every other weekend and she'd struck Kit as a quiet and competent woman who did not wear her heart on her sleeve yet cared deeply for her husband.

"Have you heard about Vade in Pace — or more commonly VIP?" Daddy asked looking up intently.

"Isn't that the crazy commune Group Captain Cheshire started?"

"Well, I certainly wouldn't call it crazy," Daddy rebutted with a frown. Fortunately, they had reached the exit and there were steps to navigate, so the conversation stopped for a bit. When they reached the sidewalk out in front of the station, Kit started to push the wheelchair towards his car, as Daddy returned to the topic. "VIP isn't communism or anything like that, Skip. It's an experiment in building world peace from the bottom up. The first community has done so well that Cheshire has bought a second property near Liss in Hampshire, and he needs colonists."

"Colonists? But Daddy..." Kit didn't know what to say to this absurd notion. Daddy had always been so reasonable and down-to-earth. How could he be taken in by all this 'building peace from the ground up' nonsense just because a celebrity pilot was the founder?

"Cheshire said specifically that anyone, regardless of their skills or health, was welcome. So, I wrote to him, told him all about myself and my injuries, and he replied with a beautiful, handwritten letter. He said he'd be delighted to have anyone from 617 Squadron at *his* home and that he'd find a place for me, but the Mrs won't hear of it. She's not willing to leave Edinburgh. She says Hampshire is too far from the girls and she wouldn't have a job, or friends or her own home anymore."

"She has a point," Kit noted, sympathizing entirely with Mrs MacDonald.

"You don't understand," Daddy told him bluntly. "Cheshire made me feel *wanted*. No, not just wanted, but *useful* for the first time since they tossed me out." The bitterness in his voice was unmistakable. Daddy had been a Halton apprentice. From the age of 15, the RAF had been his life; he had never *had* a civilian life, and he didn't want one. Yet the worst of it was that in his condition, he wasn't likely to have much of a civilian career either. Kit understood that, he just couldn't see how this commune of Cheshire's would help.

Daddy insisted, "He said he'd find me a *job*, Skip, something useful to do."

Suddenly, Kit understood. He, too, desperately wanted a job. Only it was worse for Daddy. Kit had only lost half a leg; Daddy had lost the ability to walk. If Daddy hadn't returned to the cockpit to find out what had happened to his skipper, he could have bailed out of the doomed Lancaster to safety. Instead, he'd still been in the cockpit when it crashed. If he hadn't tried to rescue Kit, he wouldn't be a cripple.

As if sensing where his thoughts had gone, Daddy spoke up gruffly. "Forget what I said, Skip. I shouldn't have mentioned it. I'm glad to be here. Let's focus on that."

Kit got Daddy out of his wheelchair and into his car. He then folded the wheelchair and put it in the boot before settling behind the wheel.

When they arrived at the restaurant, Terry was already waiting out front. Terry had been their wireless operator and had always been very near-sighted. He wore heavy glasses over a misshapen face, but he waved cheerfully at the sight of Kit and eagerly opened the door to help Daddy out. Kit retrieved the wheelchair and left Daddy in Terry's competent hands while he parked the car. When he returned, he found the two men already deep in conversation at the reserved table.

"Did you order a round?" Kit asked.

"Not yet. We were waiting for you."

Kit signalled the waiter over and they ordered. Daddy wanted a whisky, while Terry and Kit opted for a pint. That settled, Kit tried to make sense of the conversation he was joining in the middle. It sounded like Daddy was offering advice on work that did not require a school-leaving certificate, but Terry had been attending adult education for two years to make good what he had been denied as a lad. Even during the war, when they had been flying together, Terry had been a bookworm, reading nearly anything he could get his hands on. He had a good, sharp mind, and Kit had encouraged him to get school-leaving equivalency qualifications. Kit couldn't believe he had failed. "Terry, don't tell me you didn't pass your exams?"

Terry looked down ashamed and shook his head. "It was the maths that did me in, sir." His failure diminished him, and he slipped unthinkingly into the subordinate position. "I passed everything else."

"There must be something wrong with the exams!" Kit burst out. "You were wizard with the H2S and could plot fixes and back Adrian up on the navigation." Kit had never doubted that Terry would get his qualifications. Not only was he naturally inquisitive, but he was also diligent and hard-working.

"I'm sorry, Skipper."

"Terry, you don't have to apologise to *me*! I just can't believe it! You're smarter than half the people walking around with School Leaving Certificates."

"Not in maths."

"I don't believe that. It's probably just that no one ever taught them to you properly. Georgina always claimed that most people are put off maths by the way they're taught. She claims that once people have it in their heads that they 'aren't good with maths' they put up mental barriers. Don't you remember how she taught remedial maths to a dozen evacuees and almost all did brilliantly on their exams?"

Terry looked up at him through his dark-framed glasses and a flicker of a smile crossed his face. "Yes. And Nora Shields too. Remember her, Skip?" Kit nodded. "How is Mrs Moran, Skipper?" Terry asked softly.

"She's a little overwhelmed by motherhood at the moment, but I'm sure she'd want to help you. She misses teaching. There has to be some way we could...." Kit's voice faded away as he tried to think of some way to help both Georgina and Terry.

"Don't worry about it, Skip," Terry tried to smile. "Daddy was just saying that there are plenty of good jobs for men without a certificate. I'm a bit browned off with the Post Office, anyway. Maybe—"

A slight figure in a smart, navy-blue uniform with a single gold stripe on the sleeve emerged beside the table grinning widely. "Hello, everyone!"

"Crikey! Do I have to salute you *too*, Nigel!" Terry answered in awe tinged with envy.

"Well done, Lad!" Daddy thrust out his hand in congratulations, and Kit jumped to his feet to give his former tail-gunner his hand as well. "Congratulations!" He exclaimed as he pumped his hand.

"That stripe *does* mean you're an officer now, doesn't it?" Terry pressed him.

"Aye, it does. I passed my mate's exam and I'm registered on the seaman's list as a fourth mate. Just have to get my first berth. Frank wanted to be here," he continued seamlessly, referring to the mid-upper gunner, and focusing on Kit. "He called me 'special to say he was sorry to miss it, but he got a good berth. Purser on a P&O liner and shipped out six weeks ago. The last postcard I had was stamped in Malta, and he was outward bound for Hong Kong."

"We understand," Kit answered. "What are you drinking? It's on me. Or shall we all have a little champagne to celebrate Nigel's new status?"

"Champagne's my treat," Nigel announced, settling into the vacant seat. "I owe it to you, Skip, and Frank," he inserted honestly, "for encouraging me. It would have been easy to give up, but every time I thought about it, I remembered how much faith you had in me, and I said I couldn't disappoint you."

Embarrassed, Kit answered, "I'd have been blind not to see you could do better than your dad." He signalled the waiter over.

The jokes, the food and the alcohol flowed after that. It felt good to be together with these men. Kit supposed he would never forge such bonds again. Where in civilian life did you find men you were willing to die for?

Just after midnight, Kit excused himself. The others were staying at a small hotel near the restaurant. He wasn't as sober as he ought to have been, so he was relieved to get home without the police stopping him. He took off his shoes in the front hall and started up the stairs in his socks hoping not to disturb either Georgina or the baby. By the time he reached the landing, however, he could hear Donna whimpering softly. She seemed to do it a lot, usually as a prelude to screaming more vigorously. Sometimes a dummy would quiet her, however, so he pushed down the handle and shoved open the door to the nursery only to stumble over Georgina. Wearing only her nightgown, she sat on the floor beside the crib with her head on her knees.

"Georgina!" Kit exclaimed in surprise which turned instantly to concern. She looked exhausted and fragile. She hadn't been eating or sleeping properly since Donna was born. It was as if she were wasting away before his eyes.

Startled from her sleep, she gasped and looked up at him disoriented. Even in the darkness, he could see her face was streaked with tears.

"Georgina!" He went down on his heels beside her. "What's wrong?"

She turned away from him, wiping the tears from her face with the back of her hands while trying to get to her feet at the same time. "Nothing, nothing! I just came to feed Donna, and I must have fallen asleep—"

He caught her in his arms. "Georgina! What's the matter?"

She wouldn't look at him, she turned her face away. "It's nothing. I'm just tired. That's all," but she was crying.

He pulled her closer to him and held her as she sobbed. She tried to say, "I'm sorry," several times, but he shook his head and stroked her back.

"How was everyone?" She asked between hiccups.

"I'll tell you in the morning," he answered. "Where's the dummy? Oh, there. I see it." He reached over and gave it to his daughter, who sucked at once and with a sigh went contentedly still. Then he guided Georgina toward their bedroom and gently laid her down and covered her before changing into his pyjamas. The last thing he did was remove his artificial foot. As he lay back, Georgina snuggled up against him. "I'm sorry, Kit. I don't know what's wrong with me. I know I should be happy to have such a lovely daughter and the best husband in the world. I don't understand why I'm so unhappy."

"The doctor says it's not uncommon. He says you'll get over it."

"Of course. If only I could get a little more sleep."

"Try to sleep now," Kit urged.

Instead, she insisted on asking, "Did you have a good time?"

"Yes. I'll tell you about it in the morning."

"Did Nigel get his mate's papers and Terry his School-Leaving Equivalency?"

"Nigel did, but unfortunately, Terry failed his maths exam."

"Oh no!" She started to sit up and Kit held her down. It didn't stop her from saying, "Why didn't he tell me he was having trouble? I'm sure I could have helped him. I would have liked to help him."

"That's what I said. I told him to sign up to retake the exam in six months and that you'd help him prepare. The problem is when and where with him working in Manchester?"

"Surely we can work something out," Georgina insisted, and something in her voice caught Kit's attention. It sounded like energy and hope — things he hadn't heard from Georgina's mouth for months.

"Of course," Kit promised, "now try to sleep."

Charm Offensive
RAF Gatow
Tuesday, 13 April 1948

Priestman found Danny in the mess playing billiards with Lance. "Can I talk to you for a minute, Danny?"

"Of course, sir," Danny interrupted the game and followed the WingCo over to a table in the corner.

"Air Commodore Waite just rang me," Priestman opened. "Despite everything that's happened, he insists that we go ahead with the air show." He failed to keep the exasperation he was feeling out of his tone of voice. Despite the surface calm that had returned to daily operations,

Priestman could not expunge the image of the BEA stewardess flung like a broken doll on the field beside the burning wreck of a defenceless airliner. Without fighter escorts, he worried about Emily every time she took off in the ambulance. Yet he seemed to be the only one in the British occupation command who believed they were living on borrowed time. Or was he simply the only one who had the wind up so much that he couldn't pretend otherwise?

That self-doubt brought him up sharply. Had he lost his ability to stay calm in the face of a crisis? Was his very nervousness an indication of a crumbling capacity to cope with the pressure? He'd been posted to a sleepy backwater to show the flag. No one had consciously entrusted him with a pivotal position at a possible flashpoint for WWIII. Yet, he couldn't shake the feeling that that was where he'd landed.

Taking a deep breath, he explained to Danny, "Waite wants us to bring the date of the air show forward to the 8th of May to coincide with the third anniversary of VE Day. He says it will be part of a larger celebration including troop parades and a gala reception hosted at the Allied Control Council."

"I thought the Allied Control Council was dead." The Squadron Leader countered bluntly.

"You could be forgiven for thinking that, but as with so many things in politics, the carcass is still crawling. Meetings between the respective military governors have not been scheduled since March 20, but daily contact at the working level continues. Among others, the committee responsible for representational events is still functioning. That said, the Soviets are planning to unveil their massive war memorial out at Treptow—"

"Ah! The Monument to the Unknown Rapist?" Danny used the name the Berliners had already irreverently given the gigantic Soviet war memorial.

"Yes," Robin acknowledged, but continued seriously, "Waite expects the Soviets will move all their parades to Treptow, effectively boycotting anything we do, but we are going to go ahead with our celebrations all the same."

"Including an air show?" Danny wanted to be sure he understood.

"Yes, that's the idea. What's more, Waite seemed to think our proposed program was designed more for the benefit of our pilots than the audience. I countered that I was indeed using the air show as training and as a way of alleviating the boredom. While Waite acknowledged the validity of these concerns, he insisted he wanted our show to be a bit more — I think the word he used was 'fun' — for the audience."

Danny nodded and waited for his CO to continue.

"It seems that word has got out that the Americans responded more firmly than we did to the latest Soviet provocations. HM's government is accused of following a policy of 'appeasement' towards the Soviets. Colonel Howley, on the other hand, is perceived like a Wild West sheriff ready to shoot his way out of any situation, if he has to."

"Is there any truth to that?" Danny sounded outright hopeful.

"Confidentially, yes. General Clay suggested putting armed guards on the trains and shooting any Soviet soldier trying to board. Washington vetoed the plan, and Waite pointed out that shooting the guards would not have stopped the trains from being side-tracked — not to mention that we're out-gunned by astronomical numbers and no matter who *starts* the shooting, the Soviets are going to *end* it — because we'll all be dead."

"Only if they shoot back," Danny countered. "You know what I think of bullies and how to handle them."

Priestman conceded. "You and me both, but I've had my wings clipped. What surprises me is that the Berliners appear to prefer American belligerence to British caution. Given that they'll be caught in the middle if the shooting starts, I would have expected the opposite. Yet all that is beside the point at present. Waite wants the anniversary celebrations to cast Britain in a more positive light. He believes the air show might help."

"I'm not sure I can picture what he means by 'fun,'" Danny admitted. "Did he give you any indication of what he had in mind?"

"Well, he wants a flight of Daks from Wunstorf to land one after another and then for the first to open its doors to let off red, white and blue helium balloons. The next Dak, he suggested, might contain clowns, who would help offload the remaining Daks carrying rag dolls and toy aeroplanes that the clowns can hand out to the children attending."

"Roger." Danny nodded, and then grinned and admitted, "It does sound fun, sir. It might just be what people here need."

"Fair enough, and he said he'd organise the Daks and their cargoes.

He also wants to end the show, after our displays, with the air ambulance taking away an emergency patient."

"The orderlies will like that!" Danny pointed out. "I'm sure, they can be counted upon to have several airmen in bandages, splints, fake blood and suchlike."

"As for the core of the air show," Priestman continued, "Waite wants it reduced to just three events: formation flying, one low-level, short dogfight, and an abbreviated display of individual aerobatics."

"The chaps will be disappointed about that."

"I know. What I suggest, is that you retain squadron formation flying, so that they all get to fly at least once. Show two sections engaging for the dogfight; that will give eight pilots the chance to fly in that segment. As for who gets to do the individual aerobatics, I'll leave that to your discretion."

"If the show is scheduled for May 8, there's not much time to practice."

"It's not a competition. Most of the spectators won't know good from bad."

"The Frogs, Yanks and Ivans will. If we're going to put on a show, sir, we have to put up our best."

"Of course. Whoever you think."

"That would be you, WingCo."

Priestman stopped and looked over at the Squadron Leader. "That comes dangerously close to inappropriate flattery, Danny. You must have someone better than me. I'm very rusty."

"That's not the way it looked to me, sir."

"The dogfighting we did in March wasn't aerobatics, Danny," Priestman reminded him gently. "I out-witted you more than out-flew you. Besides, what about the others? Wouldn't they resent it? It's not fair for me to step in and nab the best for myself."

"How about making it a competition, sir? You decide on the program and then every pilot has to fly the sequence in front of the rest of the squadron. Everyone marks everyone else anonymously and the pilot with the highest overall score will fly in the show. That way every pilot has to learn and practice the manoeuvres, and the choice of candidate is objective and collective."

"Excellent suggestion, Danny. We'll do just that. I'll put together a program that is designed not for difficulty but for looking spectacular to the audience."

"I'm not following you, sir," Danny admitted candidly.

"Some of the most difficult manoeuvres don't look difficult to people who can't fly. Other things, like recovering from a spin, are things every pilot can do in his sleep but look dramatic to people who can't fly."

"Roger," Danny nodded understanding.

"I'll have the program to you by tomorrow. We'll do the judging a week before the event."

"But you *will* take part in the competition, won't you, sir?"

"Yes, I'll take part on 1 May." Priestman agreed. With surprise, he realised that he was keener to have one of the younger pilots win the honour than to fly himself and supposed that was called "maturing." The important thing was to encourage the young pilots to hone their flying skills in a systematic and concentrated way because it built confidence and encouraged risk-taking — two things they would need if they found themselves facing down the Soviets.

Chapter Fourteen
Distant Thunder

Clash of Partners
Air Ambulance International Offices, Gatow
Wednesday, 14 April 1948

As Kiwi cut across the grass towards the hangar, he had a spring in his step. Things were settling into a pleasant routine. After the first hectic days, they had flown twice a week and based on her conversations with the City Council, Charlotte thought this might be the normal pace of things for the foreseeable future. It was enough, combined with the office work, maintenance and test flights to feel engaged and not bored, but not so much as to be exhausting or nerve-racking. Meanwhile, he had accumulated his full thirty hours on Wellingtons by flying on the empty return flights. David had promised that he would command the next ambulance run with Emily as his second pilot. David was busy trying to find potential customers interested in flying cargo into Berlin at premium prices. This had become more important since they still hadn't seen anything but promises from the Berlin City Council concerning payment and a decision from Red Cross was still "pending" in Geneva.

The thought that he would soon be captain of an aircraft again might have been enough to make Kiwi whistle, but he was also sleeping better than he had in months. Being in a completely different environment helped put Betty behind him, and the Priestmans' hospitality was an added luxury. It was wonderful living in their gracious house, with its large lawn and peaceful views. With a full staff to look after them, he had no reason to feel guilty about making work for Emily, either. They arrived home after a day at work to find their rooms cleaned, their clothes washed and ironed, and a dinner waiting for them. If the Priestmans didn't have an invitation somewhere, they joined their house guests in the winter garden

371

overlooking the lake and talked of old times, current events, or future dreams. This past weekend, Robin and Kiwi had taken the boats out of the boathouse and determined that one rowboat and the sailboat both looked seaworthy. Being avid sailors, they were going to try to launch the sailboat this coming weekend — if another crash or a new Soviet provocation didn't get in the way.

Whistling unconsciously, Kiwi crossed out of the sun into the shadow of the hangar, where the sight of *his* Wellington lifted his spirits even further. Although the ground crew had named her "Moby Dick," Kiwi always thought of the Wellington as feminine. When they'd bought her, she'd been in her old battle dress, battered, scratched and drab. Now she was like, well, maybe not a fresh bride, but a pretty nurse. She seemed trim and competent and, above all, no longer malevolent in her white and red livery.

As Kiwi entered, Chips and Ron were sitting on a bench at the side of the hangar with mugs of tea in their hands. Crumbs on the empty plates beside them testified that breakfast was over. They, too, appeared to be in good spirits this morning. Ron, especially, had had a little difficulty settling in at first, but this past weekend one of the RAF corporals had shown them a slice of Berlin's nightlife, and their attitude had undergone a radical change. "There are girls everywhere!" Chips had confided in a tone of wonder. "I mean, you know, real lookers and, well, not too dear either."

Kiwi had laughed and winked at him with the fatherly admonishment to be careful. "Don't forget all those films we had to sit through on VD."

Based on their chipper and neat appearance this morning, the two mechanics had not been out on the town the night before. Yet their good mood was unmistakable as they called a cheerful "Morning, sir!" in unison. Chips added, "Have you seen the papers? The Engineering Officer brought these over to show us!"

"What have the Ivans done now?" Kiwi asked back.

"Nothing. You're in it!"

"What?"

"Come see!" Chips jumped up and came towards Kiwi with an open newspaper. "Right here on page five." He pushed the paper toward their pilot already open to the right place. With his finger, he pointed and then handed over the paper. Sure enough, there was a photo of Moby Dick under the heading. "British Air Ambulance Saves Children from Soviets." For the first time in his life, Kiwi consciously looked at the by-line. It read: V. Cox. So, she'd written up their interview after all.

"You come across like a real hero, sir!" Ron told him grinning with pride. That warmed Kiwi too; it was a good thing when ground crews identified with their pilots enough to bask in the latter's successes.

Kiwi sank onto the bench to read the article from start to finish. "We'll start the D.I., sir," Chips assured him, referring to the Daily Inspection required of every aircraft for it to be considered airworthy. Kiwi nodded absently already absorbed in the article. It was wizard. Vee certainly had a way with words. She made it sound like their arrival on the day the Soviets closed down rail transport hadn't been a coincidence, but a heroic act of mercy. Despite not being fully operational they had come to the rescue of five little children in need of medical care unavailable in war-ravaged Berlin. The remaining six passengers, all of whom had been old enough to be Nazis, were mentioned only in passing as Vee focused on the appealing tale of innocent children in need. The article even included small pictures of Kiwi and David, both still in RAF uniform and probably from a photo archive somewhere. All in all, it was a great article. David was sure to love the free publicity, Kiwi thought happily.

"Have everything under control, mates?" He called over to the two mechanics.

"Absolutely, sir!"

"Mind if I take your paper up to the office to show it to the others?"

"Of course not, sir. The *Times* isn't exactly our kind of reading, but I think it calls for a beer with lunch, don't you?"

"Definitely. I'll drop by again later."

Kiwi folded the newspaper together so the article about AAI was on top and returned to the terminal building. He took the stairs up to the first floor and strode down the hall to the joint BEA/AAI office at the end whistling unconsciously again. The BEA employees wouldn't arrive for another two or three hours, but Emily, David and Charlotte were all at their respective desks as he burst in. "We're in the *Times*!" He announced.

While the others expressed varying degrees of surprise, Kiwi crossed the room and put the paper down in front of David. As David read, Kiwi addressed Charlotte, "Remember that woman reporter who wanted to talk to me last week?"

"Oh, yes!" Charlotte's face flushed with excitement.

"Well, she wrote an article about AAI in the London *Times*."

"That's so exciting!" Charlotte exclaimed looking over to where Emily was trying to read over David's shoulder.

David, however, had started frowning and suddenly he exploded. "What the — Kiwi! How could you do this? How could you? You idiot!"

"What? What are you talking about?" Kiwi was blindsided. He thought it was a great article.

"You told the reporter you didn't have enough hours to fly!"

"Not with patients, but —"

"You fool! You stupid, goddamned fool! Don't you see this could get us closed down?"

"But I *didn't* fly. Emily—"

"That's not the way this article reads! It says, although you didn't have enough hours, you came anyway and then it starts talking about the flights out."

"Wait, wait!" Kiwi tried to calm him. "Let me see that!" He grabbed the newspaper and scanned down to the passage that had set David off. To his horror, he realised on re-reading that David was right. The article made no mention of Emily at all. "But I told her about Emily, Banks. I swear—"

"It doesn't matter what you said! The reporter has written the article, so it looks like you *did* fly and —" David struck out at the things on his desk, flinging them to the floor in a burst of fury that made both Emily and Charlotte jump back startled and shocked. Kiwi had the impression his partner would have buried him in foul language if the two women hadn't been within hearing. Yet their presence didn't spare him what David said next. "You had no business even *talking* to the press without my permission!"

That was going too far. Kiwi's temper flared. "You're *permission*? I don't need your permission to talk to anyone! We're partners, remember?"

"Some partner you are! You seem determined to ruin our business before we even get started! First, you can't keep off the booze—"

"I haven't had more than a half pint a day for the last two months!" Kiwi shouted back. He'd been rigorous about staying off the heavy booze for two and half months (well, except for those drinks with Vee at the

Adlon) and he felt he deserved credit for how well he'd done.

David didn't even acknowledge his protest. Instead, he forged ahead in a furious tone, "And you weren't qualified in time to fly our first operational flight, and then you go and brag about it to the press—"

"God damn it! I didn't brag about it! I gave an interview—"

"Oh, I'm sure, to that lady reporter that tried to hitch a ride with us from Northolt—"

"That's right, a reporter with the *London Times*. It was free publicity for God's sake! You should be grateful to me!"

"Free publicity like this will get our licence cancelled, you dimwit!"

"How can it, when we haven't done anything wrong?" Kiwi tried to reason with his partner. "Even if the Ministry opened an investigation, all they'll find is that Emily flew. It's all in the logbooks!"

David wasn't open to reason. "I've gone through thousands of pounds of my inheritance and all we have from the City Government is promises and silence from the Red Cros! We're running up bigger bills every single day, going deeper and deeper in debt, and all my so-called *partner* can think about is chasing a streamlined tart to get his name in the newspapers!"

"If that's the way you see me, then I'm through! I don't want anything more to do with you, Air Ambulance International, or that God-damned Wellington out there!" Kiwi stormed out of the office, slamming the door shut behind him. Taking the stairs at the double, he didn't stop until he was halfway to the hangar. Abruptly, in the middle of the airfield, he halted to let the sunlight and the breeze calm him down a little; his blood was boiling.

All his dreams had just crashed to earth at about 400 mph. It was a total wreck. His job flying, his steady income, his share in a company that made him someone important, his congenial life at the Priestman villa — and his eight-year-old friendship with David "Banks" Goldman. That was what hurt the most, Kiwi realised as he tried to calm his pounding heart. Banks had been his best friend ever since he'd left New Zealand and came to Europe. Banks and Sammy, Bank's beautiful dog. It was bad enough losing Betty, but she'd come into his life later than Banks.

Kiwi looked up at the sky. Dark clouds were gathering in the West, but they weren't likely to interfere with the BEA flight. He should go pack his things and get on that flight today. He couldn't spend the evening with

Banks after what had passed between them. He looked at his watch. It was only 10:40 am. Plenty of time to change out of his uniform.... That hurt too. He felt so good in the smart, black uniform. Going back to wearing his worn-out civvies would be another humiliation, another sign of defeat. But he couldn't wear the uniform if he wasn't part of the company. He'd need to check with BEA about a seat. If there was no seat available on the return flight, he'd ask Ron and Chips about sleeping in their quarters for the night. He couldn't face—

"Kiwi." The voice was so close it made him jump and look over. It was Emily. He gazed at her speechless. She'd heard it all and that meant Robin would know everything by nightfall. Two more friends lost.

"David wants you to come back. He's sorry he said those things. He didn't mean them. The fact that the City Council hasn't paid one penny for any of the flights has been — is — weighing on him far more than any of us realised. He shouldn't have blown up at you, but we all sometimes do and say things we shouldn't."

Kiwi stared at her. She looked so sincere, he wanted to believe her, but part of him didn't. He'd been hurt too deeply. "So why didn't he come himself?"

"Please, Kiwi. AAI means so much to all of us — and to a lot of very sick people in Berlin, too. David was wrong. He knows he was wrong. He's sorry he said what he said. Give him another hour or two and he'll say it himself."

"Meaning he wasn't ready to come out here and say it now," Kiwi concluded.

Emily answered by slipping her hand through his arm and walking him toward 222 Dispersal. "Come on, let's filch some tea off the boys of Triple Two. They might even have rum hidden in a locker somewhere."

"Rum at 10:30 in the morning? Don't tempt me," Kiwi answered but he didn't resist her. He could feel her benevolence and good intentions. If only he were convinced that Banks truly regretted what he'd said.

"That reporter," Emily was saying, "it wouldn't have been Virginia Cox-Gordon by any chance, would it?"

"She always called herself just 'Vee,' 'Vee Cox.' Why?"

Emily smiled wanly and nodded knowingly. "Don't you remember back in September 1940, before Robin and I married, a woman reporter from the *Times* came down to Tangmere and—"

"Of course!" Kiwi hit his forehead with his palm. "That's where I'd seen her before! She greeted Robin with champagne and a kiss, and it was all over the Portsmouth papers the next morning. Stuffy Dowding was furious, and AVM Park rang through to 606 dispersal to give Robin a ticking-off. They seemed to think it reflected poorly on the RAF for frontline squadron leaders to be dallying with socialites in the midst of the Battle of Britain. You mean that's who..." He thought about it. "Wasn't she some sort of an heiress?"

"That's right. Very rich. Very well connected. She'd been the debutante of the season in 1938, I believe. Robin and she had been seen together, shall we say, while he was doing air shows with the RAF aerobatic team."

"Yes, it's coming back to me now. Even the Auxiliary pilots were impressed. Robin's stock shot up in their eyes after Vee made a play for him like that."

"Let's just say she's good at getting a man in trouble." There was a flicker of a smile on Emily's face as she said that. Kiwi couldn't ignore it. He found himself smiling back.

Emily continued in a matter-of-fact tone, "Between you and me, she hates me for —as she sees it — taking Robin away from her. I suspect that's the main reason she made no mention of me in the article. She probably wanted to make me mad, not make life difficult for you. Just the reverse. She made you the hero of her article."

"Do you think Banks is jealous of that?"

"No."

"But you think he regrets what he said?" Kiwi pressed her.

"Yes. David Goldman is a very, very lonely man, Kiwi, and you are his closest friend after Ginger. Only Ginger's father and you have been close to him since Ginger died. You're closer than Robin and I because, well," she seemed to hesitate but then admitted it, "David fell in love with me when he was recovering from his injuries. Because he knows I love Robin and because he respects and likes Robin, he recognised it was hopeless. Yet it's an unspoken barrier between us just the same. Or it was. I don't think he's in love with me anymore, but he still feels embarrassed about his past feelings."

"So, if I'm his best friend, how could he say the things he just did?"

Kiwi's anger flared up again thinking about it.

"I think, we have all been misled by his apparent composure. We sometimes forget that his face is still part mask. It's become more flexible over the years. It has started to get lines and wrinkles, but it is still far less expressive than a real face. His face still disguises almost as much as it reveals.

"Beneath his apparent confidence and calm, I think he is both terrified of failing as a businessman and struggling to come to terms with the Holocaust. He is torn between a love for the good Germany — personified by Charlotte, her cousin and Dr Schlaer — and hatred for the bad, which we all know too much about. We all feel confused at times, at least Robin and I do, but for David it's a hundred times harder because part of him still *is* German, but it was his family that was slaughtered too."

Kiwi took a deep breath. "You're asking me to forgive what he just said?"

"Yes, I am."

"Let's take Moby Dick up for a test flight, while I think about it."

Emily smiled at that. "I'll go get my flight jacket and file a flight plan while you and the ground crew get her on the tarmac."

End of the Fairy Tale
Berlin
Thursday, 22 April 1948

Although the controllers had been absolved of culpability in the crash of BEA 77, the incident had added urgency to the station commander's request for additional air traffic controllers. S/L Garth had requested a full-time radar controller, and Sergeant Keel had been sent out. Garth had also put the CO on notice that if Soviet action against road or rail traffic again forced the British garrison to rely entirely upon air transport, they would need to institute a shift system and flat-out double or even triple ATC staff. Kathleen was relieved that Garth had taken such a forceful stand. She had been shaken by the crash precisely because this wasn't war.

Civilian airlines shouldn't be at risk in peacetime. Natalie, however, had taken it even harder and in a late-night session in Kathleen's apartment, she'd questioned whether she should continue in air traffic control at all. "I'm having nightmares," she said, "and I'm tense the moment I come into the tower. I'm afraid of what may happen every day."

Kathleen had assured her she would get over these feelings, but there was no way of knowing for sure. ATC took strong nerves, and many people just didn't have them. Kathleen felt she had what it took to be a good controller, but that didn't mean she wouldn't welcome shifts with the backup that inherently provided.

The telephone rang and Natalie answered it. "Control Tower…. Yes, sir." Covering the receiver, she turned to Kathleen. "It's the WingCo. He'd like you to go to his office when you have a break."

Kathleen nodded automatically, already tense. Why on earth would the WingCo want to see her in his office? "Are there any inbound flights on the boards?" She asked.

"Not for another ninety minutes," Natalie answered.

"Then tell him I'll be right down."

Kathleen liked and trusted Priestman, but no flight sergeant feels comfortable being summoned for a personal meeting with a wing commander. Kathleen was suitably nervous by the time she entered the CO's anteroom. Lynne nodded to her from her desk saying, "You can go right in, Kathleen. The WingCo's expecting you."

She knocked at the door nevertheless and entered only on his invitation. The WingCo was capless and already getting up from behind his desk, indicating the sofa under the window. Both gestures suggested this meeting was not strictly official, which only bewildered Kathleen more. Something was wrong.

"I'm afraid I have some bad news for you," Priestman opened, sitting down opposite her.

"Not my daughter!" Kathleen gasped out with sudden terror, but already Priestman was shaking his head and making calming gestures with his hand.

"No, no. Nothing like that. I was simply told that you had been seeing Major Lionel Dickenson socially."

"Yes," Kathleen admitted, her thoughts dashing around her head in confusion. Lionel had said he'd call her when he returned from wherever he'd gone. He'd warned her he would be gone for at least two weeks but probably longer. She'd been hoping for a call from him any day now. "Has something happened to him?" She asked with sudden alarm.

"Yes. He is suspected of being part of a smuggling ring led by Captain Byrne of the U.S. Monuments, Fine Arts and Archives unit. Along with Captain Byrne and others, he has been detained on suspicion of trafficking in stolen *objects d'art* and other goods of extremely high value — antiques, jewellery, rare manuscripts, things of that nature."

Kathleen caught her breath, and a shiver went down her spine as mentally she felt the chill of gold around her throat. That amethyst necklace! On loan.... She was shaking her head. "I had no idea," she stammered.

Then she had a second chilling thought. "Am I — am I under suspicion of being an accomplice? Do you want to search my quarters?" Then before he could even answer, she added forcefully. "You're welcome to. I have nothing to hide."

The full implications of Lionel's crime started to sink in. She thought back to that night at the opera, sitting there in the box beside Hitler's, wearing stolen jewellery for half of Berlin to see. For all she knew, it had been that very night, when he'd let her wear some of his stolen treasure to make her look more glamorous, that had led to Lionel's exposure and arrest.

Priestman was shaking his head. "A search won't be necessary. You are not under suspicion at this time. However, the inspector handling the case would like to ask you a few questions. He hopes you might be able to provide information that could lead to the recovery of some of the missing objects."

"Yes, of course," Kathleen assured him. "I'll cooperate in any way I can." She knew she had to, even as it hurt her. Lionel! Dashing, handsome, thrilling Lionel.... Oh, dear God, she thought, how could she ever explain this to Hope? Hope adored him. She was always asking about him. When was he coming back? When could they go to the playroom in Tegel again? Not to mention, Lionel had promised to take Hope to the upcoming horse show at the French Embassy.

At the same time, Kathleen acknowledged that she'd always sensed something wasn't quite right. She'd felt it most strongly that night at the nightclub, but because Lionel apologised and Hope had been so keen to meet with him she'd suppressed her misgivings.

And while she was being honest, it wasn't just Hope who had enjoyed the outings with Lionel. Except for that night at the nightclub, she'd enjoyed going out with Lionel, too. Somehow he'd made even mundane things feel a little thrilling. She'd missed him and had been looking forward to seeing him again. She'd even dared hope that maybe....

The last thing he'd said was that he wanted her. He said that knowing that she was proper and law-abiding. Maybe he had wanted to reform? Maybe if they'd been closer or if she'd had time to become a greater influence.... She stopped her thoughts to ask, "Is there any way I could see him?"

"I'm afraid not. He was detained in the UK."

"And he won't be coming back?"

"Not in the foreseeable future." The WingCo made it sound very definitive.

"Is there an address where I could write to him?" Kathleen asked next.

The WingCo looked down in evident discomfort. Then, taking a deep breath, he looked her in the eye. "Flight Sergeant Hart, Major Dickenson is a married man with two children."

Kathleen gasped and drew back. It was as if icy water had just been thrown over her. "You must think me an absolute fool," she managed to murmur at last, ashamed to meet Priestman's eyes.

"No," came the surprising answer, and Kathleen risked a sideways glance at him. There was not a trace of disdain or contempt on his face. Nor pity either. Just sorrow. "No, I don't think you're a fool. I think you are a decent, upright woman who had no reason to expect this kind of behaviour from an officer of the crown. I'm sorry that you had to learn that some of us are less honourable than we are expected to be. I deeply regret that a man holding the King's commission engaged in crimes of any kind — and deceived an honest woman to boot. In no way does this incident diminish my respect for you as a professional, and I hope that you will remain at Gatow. You have already demonstrated your capacity to withstand the pressures of your job, and I think you are officer material."

Kathleen felt tears in her eyes. That vote of confidence when she was feeling so ashamed and foolish was almost overwhelming. She thought she ought to say something, but all she managed to do was whisper, "Thank you, sir."

The Wing Commander got to his feet to indicate the interview was over. "Will you be all right, or do you want me to ask Sergeant Keel to report to the control tower immediately?"

Kathleen pulled herself to her feet and squared her shoulders. "I can do my job, sir."

He smiled at that. "I thought you could. Well done, Hart, and don't blame yourself for being blind to immorality. It is to your credit."

Facing Facts
Leeds, England
Friday, 30 April 1948

Georgina was giving Donna a bath when Kit called up the stairs, "I'm going out for a bit." The door clunked shut before Georgina could ask where he was going or when he would be back. Georgina was annoyed but told herself not to get upset. She was starting to come out of her depression. The spark that had set her on track had been Terry asking if she would help him. He came up from Manchester by train every other week and they spent an entire afternoon doing math exercises before the three of them had dinner together. It had become something to look forward to.

She had also learned that she needed to get out of the flat more. She needed sunshine and fresh air. So, she finished Donna's bath and dressed her in clean nappies and a pretty green dress that Aunt Emma had sent. She carried the happy baby downstairs on her hip to the front hall where the pram waited.

An envelope on the floor caught her eye, and she automatically bent her knees to reach it without bending over. As she went to put it back on the table under the mirror, she saw two other envelopes already lying there. One was a letter from Kathleen Hart that she happily slipped into her pocket to read in the park. The other, however, was already opened. Like the one she'd found on the floor, it was from an engineering firm. She knew what they were: more rejection letters.

For a moment she hesitated, tempted to read them, but it would be a breach of trust. Instead, she turned away and put Donna into the pram. It was a bright sunny day outside and she must take advantage of the weather. Besides, by reading in the park, Donna wouldn't disturb Kit's studying; his last exam was coming up. She tucked a sweater in the pram, in case it turned cold, and added her copy of *The Ides of March,* a book her father had lent to her.

The walk to the park was pleasant and she nodded to passers-by, stopping to let an elderly lady admire Donna. She tried to tell herself this was a pleasant life. Yet agreeable as it might seem, she couldn't help asking if this all life had to offer her — for tomorrow and tomorrow and tomorrow to the last syllable of recorded time. Was her future nothing but looking after Donna and Kit, cooking and cleaning, washing clothes and — as a reward — a walk to the park?

At least when she'd had a teaching job, Kit had made an effort to help out in the house. He wasn't very good at household chores, but his intentions had been good. He had recognised that if she was working, she couldn't carry the full burden of the household. Long ago, before the rejection letters started flooding in, he'd promised that after he got a proper job they'd have a maid and a nanny. Now he didn't talk about that anymore, and he didn't help much either.

At the park, Georgina made the effort to make small talk with the other young mothers, but she had to overcome her inner aversion to empty gossip, telling herself she was just being snobby. Soon the other women left and with Donna sleeping soundly, Georgina took out Kathleen's letter. She was stunned to learn that Kathleen's 'young man' had turned out to be not only married but detained for theft. Poor Kathleen! For the first time since the death of her husband Ken, she had tentatively risked striking up a friendship with a gentleman and it turned almost instantly sour. That was so unfair! Georgina resolved to respond in her first free minute, but for now, she fled into the Roman Empire. Reading fiction was one of her father's recommendations for fighting depression. "Stop thinking about your problems by getting immersed in someone else's. If you don't know anyone whose problems are worse than your own, find a book that creates fictional problems you can worry about."

When Donna started fussing, Georgina checked her watch and realised it was time to go home. At the flat, she let herself in as quietly as possible so as not to disturb Kit and took Donna in her arms to tip-toe upstairs to change her. She was surprised to find the door to the front bedroom open and the room empty. Kit had not returned. That was odd. His next exam was just days away.

With Donna changed, she started making dinner and as the time ticked by with still no sign of Kit, her thoughts turned inevitably to their situation. She'd lost her job when she became pregnant because the school had a policy against women teachers with children. Kit had been applying for engineer jobs for almost six months and had none. They could not live from Kit's small disability pension alone, and the lump sum Kit's father had given them had almost been used up. In the short term, they could move in with her parents, but they couldn't live indefinitely in a rural Yorkshire village. Kit needed a proper job, and until he had one, she couldn't start to look for work teaching.

She finished making shepherd's pie and put it in the oven but with still no sign of Kit, she did not turn the oven on. Instead, she nursed Donna and put her to bed. It was now 7:45, the sun was low in the sky, and Georgina was hungry.

She returned to the kitchen, turned the oven on and tried to write to Kathleen, but she couldn't concentrate. Kit had been gone all afternoon and Georgina vacillated between worry and anger. If he'd said where he was going and why, she would at least have been able to plan accordingly. It wasn't fair to just leave her not knowing where he was or when he would be back. She turned and looked toward the hall and the rejection letters again, then tried to focus her thoughts on Kathleen. What could she possibly say?

The door clicked open, and Kit walked in. "I was beginning to worry," Georgina called from the kitchen. When he didn't answer, she left everything standing and went to the hall.

Kit stood looking windblown and fragile in the front hall. For an instant, Georgina remembered the way he'd looked after the attack on the Kembs Barrage: the battle dress still smelling of cordite, the whistle glinting in the dark, his hair dirty and dishevelled like now. "What is it, Kit?" She asked softly as she moved closer. She wanted to touch him, but something held her back.

He did not look at her. He was looking down at his hands. "I don't think I'm going to get an engineering job."

"Kit, I know how you feel. Rejections are always discouraging, but it's too soon to assume that. You need to focus on your exam—"

"What I don't know now, I'm not going to learn in the next 36 hours!" Kit snapped.

"All right, but it's too soon to give up hope for a proper job."

"We can't afford this flat after next month!" He reminded her sharply.

"I know, but we can live with my parents for a month or two."

"If we knew it was only for a month or two, I'd agree, but there's no reason to think firms are going to be more willing to hire me in August or September than they have been the last six months. It's time to face facts, Georgina. I'm not going to get an engineering job. That's why I went to the airport. I think I could find work as an aircraft mechanic. Not that anybody offered me anything, but I was able to talk to a couple of people."

"Kit!" Georgina gasped. She knew he didn't want that. Taking work as a mechanic was worse than an apprenticeship. It was a dead-end job.

Kit was speaking, "A mechanic's job would pay better than five pounds a week, and if I can find something here or at another regional airport, the cost of living would be lower than in London."

"What about your leg? Wouldn't you have to be on your feet all day?" Georgina asked in concern.

"I'll manage," Kit answered tightly, not meeting her eye.

Georgina recognised that tone of voice and backed off. She slipped her arm around his waist and said, "You must be hungry. Come and have some dinner."

He let her lead him into the kitchen, and he sat while she set the table. Only after she had served and sat down herself did she speak again. "Kit, I don't think I told you that my Aunt Emma offered to let me sew for her. She has more customers than she can handle and has been turning work away. She says if I help her, she can take more orders and spend more time designing rather than sewing. She's willing to pay me two pounds ten a week, maybe more if things work out."

"You don't like sewing, Georgina," Kit reminded her sadly.

"And you don't want to be a mechanic."

He smiled faintly, then leaned forward and kissed her gently. "That's just my pride getting in the way. I didn't dislike being a fitter. You, on the other hand, are a teacher — a gifted teacher."

"Kit, you didn't mind being a fitter when you were 21 and hadn't learned to fly and hadn't commanded a Lancaster and hadn't spent three years at university beating things into your brain. You are now 28 and you will have an engineering degree and you will get an engineering job. Even if we have to go to America."

"You'd be willing to go to America?"

"I'd rather go to Canada or Australia, but if it has to be America, then, yes, I'd rather go to America than for you to take work as a mechanic. All I ask is that you give it at least a couple more months before we do anything radical, and meanwhile, I help Aunt Emma."

Kit drew a deep breath, reached to take her hand, and nodded. "All right. We can wait until the end of the summer to decide." Despite agreeing to her proposal, he didn't sound optimistic.

Second Rate?
RAF Gatow, Berlin
Saturday, 1 May 1948

Priestman was relieved that low cloud forced them to postpone the aerobatics competition to the afternoon because he had to sort out the issues delaying the construction of the concrete runway. It was nearly a month since the project had been approved, and yet nothing had been done on the ground. First, there had been bureaucratic hurdles to freeing up the funding. Now, the Ministry of Works claimed it did not have the capacity to address the runway at Gatow until, tentatively, October or November. Idiots! Priestman thought to himself. The Soviets might decide to shut down the access roads any minute — literally. His runway couldn't wait until October or November.

Priestman had, therefore, requested Sander's permission to speak with Air Marshal Mercer of 46 Group. Priestman had not spoken to him personally before; instead, Air Commodore Waite had acted as a go-between. Yet Priestman felt it would be better to put the case forward himself.

Just after noon, the connection with Harrow Weald went through and Priestman took the call. "Air Marshal Mercer?"

"Speaking."

"This is Wing Commander Priestman, Station Commander at RAF Gatow in Berlin. I know this is a bit unusual, but Air Marshal Sanders gave me the go-ahead to contact you directly."

"Um hm."

"As you know, sir, we currently only have a PSP runway here at Gatow, which was badly degraded during the short blockade of ground access routes to Berlin at the beginning of last month."

"I thought we approved funding for the construction of a concrete runway?" Mercer asked before Priestman had finished his planned introduction.

"You did, sir. Thank you. The problem is that the Ministry of Works says they can't start construction until September or October—"

"That sounds just like the Ministry of Works!" Mercer snorted.

"Sir, to be frank, the Soviets might shut down the access routes again at any moment. We don't have the luxury of waiting until September or October. Although I tried to explain the situation, I'm far too junior to carry much weight and I was hoping you might be able to persuade the Ministry—"

"Of Works? I'm sorry, Wing Commander, but they're a law onto themselves." His tone was sharp and Priestman sensed hostility. "It would be a waste of time trying to prod them into faster action. It's better to look into alternatives. Have you thought about contracting the work out to local firms?"

"German firms, sir?" Priestman was taken completely aback; he had not expected that suggestion.

"They built the autobahns," Mercer reminded him with a chuckle.

"Ah, yes," Priestman conceded, a weight falling from his shoulders as he registered that Mercer's earlier acerbity had been directed more that the Ministry of Works than at him. "Do you mean we could share the runway specs with them and allow them on the station to do the work?"

"You'd have to vet the firms and their employees carefully, of course, but there is no inherent reason why you couldn't contract the work to a foreign firm. We've done it around the world."

"All right. In that case, I'll get on that straight away." Already Priestman was envisaging the additional workload this would mean for his staff, but it was much better than just sitting on their hands and waiting for the Ministry of Works to get around to doing something.

"Meanwhile, Wing Commander, what I can do for you is send out a new PSP runway. We have some wartime surplus runways in storage. The Americans used to lay them down in three days. We don't have teams specialised in their construction, so it might take a bit longer, but not more than a week. If you're receiving 24 or more loaded freighters a day, the PSP will still break down fairly rapidly, but not as fast as the old one you had. I expect a new runway might stand up to the increased traffic for three to four weeks."

"That would be a great help, sir. Thank you."

"I'll ask one of my staff to handle this first thing on Monday," Mercer told him, "but don't see this as an alternative to the concrete runway. PSP has its value, but it's not a genuine substitute for concrete."

"Understood, sir. I will initiate the process of contracting out the construction of the concrete runway immediatcly."

"Was there anything else?"

"No, sir. Thank you again."

"Then good luck, Wing Commander. I don't envy you being in Berlin just now. Have a good day."

They hung up, and Priestman started making notes to himself on what they would need to do to turn the construction over to a German firm. For a start, he needed the detailed specifications and budget parameters. He mustn't forget to inform Sanders of what they were doing, either. They were going to have to request proposals and then vet not just the firms, but each construction worker which meant he needed someone to go over the security requirements for individuals granted access to facilities. Priestman put a call through to BAFO and left a message requesting Sanders call him back. He requested the specifications and parameters from 46 Group and then started drafting the Request for Proposal. His phone rang, and he grabbed it.

"Sir, the fog's lifted. We've got at least three miles of visibility. Couldn't we proceed with the aerobatics competition?" Danny asked at the other end of the line.

Priestman glanced out of the windows. The Squadron Leader was right. Triple Two's pilots had been practising diligently for today's internal competition and judging; it wouldn't be fair to postpone it to another day. He glanced at his watch. It was nearly two in the afternoon. If they didn't get started soon, they wouldn't finish. He told Danny he was on his way, hung up and changed into flying boots and a flight jacket.

On arrival in the dispersal, Priestman was pleased to find the squadron well organised. Aircraft assignments were posted on the blackboard and the order for take-off was to be determined by lottery. The squadron had also agreed that if there was a tie, there would be a run-off competition. Scorecards had been prepared in advance, and a box with a slit in the top for depositing the scorecards sat prominently on a table in the middle of the room.

The pilots were talking excitedly as their Station Commander entered, and Danny called them to attention. The WingCo signalled for them to stand at ease and asked if everyone was ready. There was a chorus of agreement. "Where's the Chiefy?" Priestman asked for the Ground Crew Chief.

"Here, sir!" Flight Sergeant Lowell stepped out from behind some of the pilots.

"Everything set from your end?"

"Yes, sir!"

"Well done. Then let's get cracking."

"You draw the aircraft that goes first, sir!" Benny stepped forward with a glass bowl containing folded pieces of paper. Priestman took one, opened it and read out: "D-Dog."

Groans of disappointment greeted the announcement except for the one pilot who, grinning sheepishly, pulled on his leather helmet and ran out of the door toward his waiting Spitfire. The others spilt out onto the grass before the dispersal to watch the demonstration.

Priestman let the young pilots cluster outside, chattering and making jokes at each other's expense. He hung back by the dispersal, confident he could see perfectly well from there. Danny came and joined him. "I hope you won't be disappointed with what they can do," the Squadron Leader cautioned.

"No, of course not. This isn't about aerobatics so much as confidence and risk-taking. Who do you think is the best of the lot?"

"Lance is good, and surprisingly Benny. He's a bit awkward otherwise and seems dreamy at times, but then, all of a sudden, he turns around and gets more out of his Spitfire than anyone else."

Priestman smiled at that and nodded without comment. Many of the best aerobatics pilots were loners like that.

The first pilot wasn't bad, Priestman noted, and he gave him four out of five on most manoeuvres and only one three for a very sloppy Immelman. The next pilot did only marginally worse, with two threes. Fl/Lt Swift was third and disappointed him, but then he'd noticed that Swift was not keen on aerobatics. Not everyone was. Danny gave a solid performance, mostly fives and a couple of fours. Mac was erratic, doing half the manoeuvres perfectly and then flubbing the others almost painfully. Priestman drew his own number next and flew the routine neatly without difficulty; this was not challenging stuff for an experienced aerobatic pilot. He returned to judging and was pleased by the performance of Lance and Benny, who both completed the program without error.

When all had flown, they removed the scorecards, stacked them by the aircraft ID, and added up the scores. Lance, Benny and Priestman had tied. Because it was nearly 6 pm, Priestman suggested they just draw straws to determine who would fly in the air show.

The suggestion was booed down soundly. "No, we agreed to a run-off," the others reminded him. "You three have to fly the routine again."

Priestman didn't fight them on it but announced, "We'll swap aircraft, so you don't know who you're judging. Danny, I'm trusting you to keep them inside and preoccupied with something while we go out to the aircraft." Then he led the other two contestants back outside, sent Benny to "P," Lance to Benny's "G-George" and took Lance's "K-King."

Benny again put in a superior performance, only to completely fumble the last stall-turn and sideslip badly. He recovered rapidly, but the error was disqualifying because it was so obvious. If that happened in the show, they would be laughingstocks. Lance made no mistakes, but Priestman missed rashness and daring in his performance. When all three had completed the run-off, they taxied back to their ground crews and dismounted. On the way to the dispersal, Priestman intercepted Benny. "What happened?"

"I waited too long before applying rudder," he answered morosely.

Priestman nodded understandingly. "An easy mistake to make. You have potential, Benny, you just need more practice."

"Do you mean that, sir?" He looked up hopefully, his whole face lighting up, and Priestman was glad he'd taken the time to talk to him.

"Absolutely. Don't be discouraged." He gave him a short clap on the shoulder, and they entered the dispersal.

"There's another tie, sir," Danny greeted them. "That sideslip on the stall turn put someone out."

"That was Benny, I'm afraid. Flight Lieutenant Knight will fly in the show."

"I don't agree with that," Lance answered.

"Why not, Flight Lieutenant?" Priestman challenged him with that edge on his voice that reminded them he might be flying with them, but he was still the Station Commander.

"Because you've been holding back. Sir."

"What makes you say that?"

"You only wrote two climbing rolls into the program, but we've all seen you do three."

They had him on that.

"You also didn't put in a double Immelman in the program, but we've seen you do that as well." Fl/Lt Swift pointed out.

"You can judge when to come out of a spin better than we can," Mac pointed out.

"And you can fly inverted lower without risk to the crowd," Kennel told him.

Priestman realised he'd been set up. "You never intended to let anyone else fly the aerobatics sequence, did you?" he asked Danny directly.

"No, sir. The Ivans and Yanks can be too damn arrogant. They think they own the sky. As I said when we first discussed this, if we're going to put on a show, we have to put up our best, and that's you."

The problem with that, Priestman acknowledged mentally, was that if the RAF wanted to keep up with the Soviets and the Yanks then it shouldn't have to rely on old bones like himself. That was the reason he had sincerely hoped one of the younger men would outperform him. He wanted to prove — at least to himself — that Britain (as represented by the RAF) wasn't declining into irrelevancy as they shed their empire and turned more and more world responsibilities over to the United States.

Maybe it was getting to him that the American response to the Soviets was consistently more vigorous. Yes, discretion could be the better part of valour and all that, but at what point did discretion melt into diffidence? When did caution become subservience? When did both end in humiliation and defeat? Had they won the war just to become a second-rate power, following in the wake of the Americans? And what happened when America's interests didn't align with Britain's?

The fidgeting of the men around him made him realise he had let his thoughts drift too far. He looked around the dispersal, letting his gaze linger on the faces of the young men awaiting his response. He liked what he saw. There was nothing wrong with these young pilots. Danny chafed under their orders not to respond as much as he did. They all did. And Benny and Lance had the potential to be good aerobatics pilots. All they needed was more competition, more motivation, and more practice. The problem was the short timeframe Waite had imposed on them.

"All right. This time I'll fly it, but next time, I want a real competition — with the Yanks, and I *won't* participate. Is that clear?"

They broke into a chorus of "yes, sirs" and "roger" and the like. Priestman announced he was buying the first round at the mess and harvested a second easy cheer. He told himself to enjoy it, and then glanced over at Danny, who was looking pleased with himself. "It still got them out of their rut, sir," Danny justified himself in answer to the unspoken question. "It was good for all of us."

Chapter Fifteen
Improving Visibility

VE Day Revisited
Berlin-Charlottenburg
Saturday, 8 May 1948

Despite — or was it because? — of the obvious and growing tensions between the four wartime allies, many outward displays of unity were meticulously maintained. That included not just the flags flying daily before the ACC and the Kommandatura, but also a joint evening reception to mark the anniversary of Germany's surrender in 1945. Not many Germans were invited to this gala affair at the Allied Control Council; members of the Berlin City Council were an exception.

Jakob Liebherr considered attendance at the reception an opportunity to observe the men controlling the fate of his city. If possible, he wanted to confront the representatives of the all-powerful occupation powers with their obligations to the people dependent on them. Since the evening clothes he owned were worn out, faded and dilapidated, Jakob knocked on the door of the apartment below and asked if they had anything suitable that he could wear. "You wouldn't want me to disgrace Germany, Herr Kapitaenleutnant."

"Don't call me that," the young man shot back.

"Why not?"

"Because it's not relevant anymore!" He answered irritably, but he invited Jakob inside and told him to take anything appropriate that fit him.

Trude preferred to ask Charlotte, and she had let Trude pick and choose from her mother's clothes. Trude had been outfitted in a full-length black skirt, lace-trimmed blouse and pearls.

Looking the best possible, they allowed themselves the luxury of a taxi and found themselves in the steady stream of guests showing their invitations to the soldiers at the main door of the imposing building that housed the Allied Control Council. Once inside, they joined the queue ascending the grand, curving stairs at a snail's pace towards the formal reception line at the entrance to the grand salon on the floor above. At the top of the stairs, they could, at last, see the four military governors standing in a row, and Jakob had plenty of time to study the men who held Berlin's fate in their hands as they inched forward.

Marshal Sokolovsky dominated the entire venue. He was big with a broad, square face divided by a straight nose. "He must have been a handsome young man," Trude murmured into Jakob's ear. "Can't you just see him modelling for some monumental work of Socialist Realism? A statue 20 feet high, perhaps, with a soldier holding a rifle over his head?"

Jakob concurred. Sokolovsky had just the kind of stern, soldierly face suited to a larger-than-life sculpture or painting on an official building in Moscow. Yet he was rendered a little ridiculous by the insane number of medals hanging from his chest. These were not just ribbons, as in the case of the Western officers, but large round medallions dangling from ribbons so that they clinked and jingled whenever he moved.

Beside Sokolovsky, the men representing the 'Old Powers', French General Pierre Koenig and British General Sir Brian Robertson, looked slight and weak. Their moustaches and comparatively longer hair made them look outdated as well. They appeared both intimidated and overshadowed by the Soviet marshal, offering a perfect microcosm of the current situation in Berlin.

Jakob turned his attention to the American General and received a slight shock. Although older, greyer, and uglier than the others, the American governor, General Lucius D. Clay, exuded an intangible dignity that subtly undermined Russian dominance. Scanning the line again, Jakob decided that all three Europeans were playing roles, the French haughty, the English gracious and the Russian commanding. Clay was the only one who couldn't be bothered pretending anything. Instead, he appeared to be alertly analysing everything around him. Jakob felt a tremor of hope. There was, he thought, more to this American General than one saw in the newspapers.

A strikingly good-looking RAF officer accompanied by a subtle beauty dressed in understated elegance stood directly in front of the Liebherrs.

When they moved forward to shake hands with Marshal Sokolovsky, the Russian chief of protocol smoothly stepped forward to murmur that the lady had been the pilot who flew the air ambulance in the British air show this afternoon.

"That must be Charlotte Walmsdorf's friend!" Trude whispered excitedly, understanding the Russian. "The one who got her involved in this air ambulance business. Her name is Emily something."

Of course, Jakob thought with a start, trying to get a better look at the woman who had been such a godsend to Charlotte. Solokovsky was pumping her hand and gushing at her in Russian at such a pace that the poor woman looked completely overwhelmed and confused. Jakob was on the brink of providing a translation when the official Russian translator stepped in to deftly convey his marshal's effusive praise. Liebherr watched as the Englishwoman smiled and assured the Soviet marshal that she was honoured by his compliments. She did it very well, Jakob thought, modestly and graciously. Almost too late, he remembered she was married to the RAF Station Commander and hastily turned his attention to her husband. The first thing that struck him was that he was much younger than Jakob had expected. Equally astonishing was the confidence he exuded — markedly more, Jakob thought, than Robertson. Jakob felt a tingle of inexplicable excitement run through him.

The British couple continued down the reception line to the French General, while Jakob and Trude came abreast of the Soviet Marshal. The Russian's eyes slid over the two Germans as his chief of protocol introduced them. The hand he offered Jakob was fleshy, his fingers short, and his grip unpleasantly harsh. He did not spare them a single word, only a nod. That said it all, Jakob thought; the Soviets had not the slightest interest in elected city officials. The Soviets undoubtedly wished that Liebherr and all his democratically elected colleagues did not exist at all.

The French General, while more genial, was almost equally disinterested. As a result of the dismissive reaction of both the Soviet and French governors, the Liebherrs had to wait while the British military governor spoke to Emily. "I must add my compliments to those of my Russian colleague," Robertson was saying. "It was indeed a delightful surprise to see a woman at the controls of the air ambulance in the show this afternoon."

"I was only Second Pilot, sir. The real honour goes to Captain—"

"I understand, but we're all used to seeing first-class male pilots. You on the other hand were a welcome surprise. Excellent show, Wing Commander, and I understand you flew the aerobatics yourself. Very impressive indeed." Robertson shook Emily's husband's hand, before turning to Liebherr.

The English General welcomed the Liebherrs formally and commented in surprise on Jakob's good English but didn't listen to his explanation of where he'd acquired it. Instead, his eyes were already focused on someone farther down the reception line. No, Jakob concluded, his first impression had not been wrong. Koenig and Roberston were not men of steel. They were malleable, adaptable, obedient and .... what? He sensed something more but couldn't put his finger on it. Maybe they were just tired? — tired of being here, tired of squabbling with the Russians, tired of waiting for progress and improvement.

Jakob turned his attention to General Clay, who looked as though he wasn't getting much sleep. Yet his voice was clear, soft and melodic. He spoke with an accent that was calming, rather than grating. It was not at all what one expected from an American, much less one with a "cowboy" reputation. Clay was saying, "Mrs Priestman, it would appear my colleagues have left me little to say." His eyes glimmered with amusement out of their darkly shaded sockets. "But it's a pleasure to meet you nevertheless, and attractive as you were in uniform, it is even more of a delight to see you out of it. Wing Commander, you are to be congratulated not only on your flying and the organization of a first-rate air show but also on your bride."

That didn't leave them a lot to say except "Thank you, sir," and they moved on.

The Liebherrs shuffled forward, and Jakob offered his hand to General Clay. "Jakob Liebherr, General," he introduced himself. "I sit on the Berlin City Council representing the borough of Kreuzberg."

The American General stunned Liebherr by replying, "That's a very important job, Mr Liebherr. May I ask what party you represent?"

"The SPD, sir." Since this might be his only chance to speak to the man who represented the United States of America in Germany, Jakob could not afford to be humble or reticent. He needed to get his message across, so he tacked on forcefully. "I was in the Reichstag before the war and voted against Hitler's Enabling law. I was rewarded with two years in a concentration camp, but I don't regret it." Jakob felt strongly that it was important not to bow and apologise just for being German.

"Then I am doubly honoured to meet you, sir." Clay replied courteously, adding, "Perhaps later we'll find time for you to tell me more about your career. I am interested in such things."

Liebherr understood that he was being asked to move on, but it had been done tactfully and respectfully. Clay, Jakob decided, was an ally. If he learned nothing else tonight, it had been worth coming for that single insight.

The Liebherrs entered the grand hall. Overhead, neo-Renaissance plaster mouldings framed a beautiful (if partly damaged) ceiling painting. Three huge chandeliers with electric candles provided the lighting. A massive fireplace with a magnificent, marble mantle dominated the inside wall, and opposite, a row of tall windows overlooked a park. At one end of the hall, white-jacketed waiters behind linen-covered tables stood ready to serve refreshments. At the other end of the hall, a chamber orchestra provided light background music as the guests arrived.

Jakob supposed he shouldn't begrudge the victors their celebration — but he did. There couldn't be anyone in this room who did not know that just outside people were living in ruins on inadequate rations while young mothers prostituted themselves to clothe themselves and youth scorned school to engage in pickpocketing and smuggling. Looking toward the buffet which included champagne chilled in silver ice buckets and mounds of caviar, he thought: If the people lack bread, let them eat caviar! Turning his head in the other direction, the scraping of the violins reminded him of Nero "fiddling" while Rome burned. Berlin was smouldering around them, and the Allies could think of nothing better to do than drink champagne and eat caviar?

Jakob sighed and Trude remarked, "It's bad enough that the Americans flaunt their wealth; they have an excess of everything. What offends me is the Russians putting so much food on display when half their population is starving."

Wearily, Jakob nodded. That was the most frightening nightmare of all: that they would be left in the hands of men who didn't care about the welfare of their people, let alone their former enemies.

As they continued in the direction of the refreshments, Liebherr looked for and spotted the Priestmans. He was curious about them and wanted to meet them personally, so he guided Trude towards them. Before he had a chance to introduce himself, however, Colonel Howley and his wife swept up to the table to congratulate the them.

"Great performance, Wing Commander!" The American announced in a loud voice, clapping the RAF officer on his shoulder.

"But I think *you* stole the show, Emily!" His wife declared, leaning forward to hug Mrs Priestman. "I was so delighted to see a woman in a cockpit!"

"I honestly didn't do that much," Emily protested.

Colonel Howley wasn't listening. He was asking her husband. "Any truth to the rumours I've heard that you're paving a runway at Gatow?"

Liebherr held his breath as he awaited the answer. Paving a runway was a significant investment and meant two things: the RAF planned on staying and expected more air traffic. In short, it also signalled a level of commitment to Berlin that Liebherr had not expected. The RAF Wing Commander answered, "I've got approval and a budget from the Ministry, but I'm going to have to contract the work locally. That is causing some delays and headaches."

"I can imagine. Look, I think we need to talk," Howley declared dropping his voice. For a man who usually spoke uninhibitedly, that spoke volumes, a point underlined by the American adding, "without walls or witnesses."

"Agreed," Priestman answered, and the look the officers exchanged made Jakob's blood run cold. These men appeared to know something he didn't know — and it wasn't good. "I have a 21-foot sailboat. Would you like to join us for a sail tomorrow?"

A sailboat was perfect for a talk without witnesses and Howley answered simply with, "What time?"

"Can you be at our residence at noon?"

"We'll be there!" Howley agreed and they took leave of one another, but another British officer caught the Priestman's attention before Liebherr could step forward. "Congratulations, Robin! Everything went like clockwork! I was impressed with your aerobatics. As for you, Mrs Priestman, I must say I was a trifle put out that you had not shared your secret with me. How many times have we met? Not once did you breathe a word about being a pilot. You are a tremendous asset that I would like to exploit much more extensively. You *did* know you enlisted in the RAF when you married this handsome fellow, didn't you?"

"Actually, no," Emily admitted. "At the time, I thought I'd married a whirlwind that would be gone long before I had a chance to get to know him properly."

"Ah, a wartime romance," the older officer concluded.

"Worse, sir," the Wing Commander answered for his wife, "Middle of the Battle of Britain and I'd just been given a Tangmere Squadron."

"You deserve a DSO for taking that on, my dear," the older man smiled benevolently before adding, "Unfortunately, I'm not authorised to give them out."

"She is in the Voluntary Reserve, now." Wing Commander Priestman made a point of telling the other man.

"So much the better! Then we can use you for press and public relations events without the least inhibition. As I've said before, your face is much prettier than mine." Fortunately, someone came to speak to the older officer at last giving Liebherr a chance to step up and introduce himself. "Excuse me, my name is Jakob Liebherr—"

"Oh!" Emily recognised the name. "You're Charlotte's neighbour, the city councilman!"

"Yes, that's right," Liebherr smiled, pleased to think Charlotte had talked about him. He bowed his head as he shook hands first with Emily and then her husband. Jakob liked the feel of both handshakes, particularly that of the Wing Commander. There was energy in this man, bridled and impatient energy. He would have liked to talk more with Priestman, but Marshal Sokolovsky chose this moment to bear down on them like a battleship. The band had started playing a waltz and the Marshal, with a bow, indicated that Emily should join him on the dance floor. She was not given a choice.

Liebherr could sense the Wing Commander's apprehension as the Soviet Marshal took his wife into his arms. It didn't help that Sokolovsky was soon holding her so close that she was bending over backwards to try to keep a little distance. Sokolovsky only bent farther forward to compensate. Inevitably, they lost their footing more than once, and Emily appeared to be trying to extricate herself from dancing, while the Soviet Marshal insisted on continuing. Looking from Emily to her husband, Jakob could not decide who looked most alarmed.

Then Liebherr heard a low, lilting voice behind him declare, "Wing Commander, I fear your lady is in distress." General Clay was standing between them with a bourbon in his hand.

"I agree, sir, I'm simply not sure how to rescue her without causing an international incident."

"With your permission, Wing Commander, I'll step in." Clay handed Priestman the bourbon and crossed the dance floor to cut in on the Soviet Marshal with a bow.

Very interesting, Liebherr thought to himself as he turned to his wife and suggested they join the dance. General Clay, it seemed, was a man of many parts, and the RAF was worth watching too. There was more mettle here than he had dared hope.

A Chill Wind off the Havel
Berlin-Kladow
Sunday, 9 May 1948

"Do you have a sweater or something to wear over your blouse?" Emily asked Edith Howley. "It's always colder on the water," she explained. In the interest of meeting privately with the Howleys sooner rather than later, Robin was taking a risk with the weather. Although it was a warm, sunny day, there was a strong, gusty wind out of the northeast. Emily feared it might be too much., but Robin insisted they'd be fine. Sailing in a small open boat ideally served the purpose of enabling the American Commandant to speak to the RAF Station Commander far from the public, their subordinates — and the telephone.

While Emily went back to the house to get Edith something warmer to wear, Frank Howley and Robin pushed the boat into the water, lowered the centreboard, inserted the ruder and prepared but did not hoist the sails. It amused Emily that Robin took command without any deference to the American's senior rank — and that Frank willingly took his orders. The women stepped aboard from the rickety dock to avoid getting their feet wet, and Emily took the tiller, while Frank and Robin pushed the boat into deeper water before scrambling in over the stern. Robin went forward to hoist the mainsail, while Emily held the bow into the wind. On Robin's order, Emily fell off the wind and at once a gust hit them. They heeled hard to port, eliciting a tiny shriek from Edith. Her husband ordered her onto the high side of the boat and wedged himself against the edge of the cockpit to take the spray crashing over the bow on his broad back. Meanwhile, Robin hoisted the jib, and at his signal, Emily eased out on the main sheet and swung the stern more into the wind. The boat righted itself and all seemed calmer, quieter and warmer as they ran down-wind toward the Pfaueninsel.

"That's much better," Edith exclaimed as she relaxed and turned her face to the sun, soaking in the heat and the tanning rays.

Robin took over the tiller and Frank bent to remove his wet shoes. As he straightened he turned to Emily sitting opposite him on the low side of the boat, "Speaking as an old advertising executive, Emily, that was one heck of a publicity stunt flying the ambulance at the air show yesterday!"

"I suppose I should be flattered by all the praise," Emily replied cautiously, "but between you and me, it strikes me as a trifle condescending the way people reacted. What is so special about a woman flying an aircraft? Every other pilot in the entire show did more than I did."

"That's not the point," Howley told her with a smile. "Because women pilots are rare, you drew more attention to the ambulance than a male pilot would have done, and that's smart marketing."

"Besides, as I told her," Robin addressed himself to Frank, "it never hurts to get a little unearned praise. Normally, things are the other way around."

Frank laughed and declared, "Too true! As every military man knows."

"There speaks a man with a great deal of experience in that regard!" Edith quipped and then turned to Emily, "Still, you're being far too modest. Why didn't you say something to me? If I'd known that you were flying for this firm, I wouldn't have kept pestering you to come to our various social events."

"Well, I didn't want to seem standoffish," Emily explained. "It's true, however, that since the company went operational, it demands more and more of my time."

"Emily isn't just a pilot, she's Director for Marketing, Personnel and Facilities," Robin explained proudly.

While the Howleys looked suitably impressed, Emily corrected, "For a company with two partners, four employees and a single aircraft."

"At the moment. It might grow," Robin sounded optimistic. "Banks is a born businessman and Kiwi's just the partner he needs to knock some common sense into him when he gets too wrapped up in his numbers."

"Yes, they're a good team," Emily agreed, thinking how glad she was that David had managed enough of an apology to convince Kiwi to stay on. Still, latent tension remained between them, and it worried her. To the Howleys she stressed, "There's more than enough demand for our services. Unfortunately, there are serious challenges as well, but I wouldn't want to bore you with the details."

"You're not boring us!" Edith insisted. "Tell us more."

"Our biggest problem is that the patients can't pay for evacuation, German health insurance companies haven't reorganized, the Red Cross keeps giving us the run-around, and the Berlin city government doesn't have any hard currency. We're covering operating costs by flying cargoes into Berlin and doing the air ambulance work effectively as a charity. We're not breaking even that way, let alone making a profit, and that can't go on indefinitely."

"No, of course not." The Americans understood about profits.

"The other problem is the patients need to be accompanied by a nurse. We assumed that the hospitals would simply send along an escorting nurse when they sent us patients, but it turns out that many German nurses are afraid to fly." Emily's disbelief was reflected in her tone of voice. "We've repeatedly had delays and complications because a substitute nurse had to be found at the last minute. Then half the time, they're still so frightened or airsick that they can't do their job."

"Wouldn't it make more sense for the company to hire a nurse?" Edith asked.

"Yes, I think so, but as long as we're still making losses the Managing Director won't hear of it."

Edith nodded. "If you change your mind, I know just the nurse for you."

"Who?" Frank asked.

"Anna Savage," Edith answered her husband, and he exclaimed, "Ah" and nodded approvingly, while Edith turned to Emily to explain, "Anna's coloured and comes from the worst slums imaginable, but she fought her way to a high school diploma and then trained as a nurse. She was one of just a few hundred black women accepted into the Army nursing corps. Like most of them, she was assigned to a hospital in a POW camp. It was a rough assignment because she was sent to a camp where there is segregation in the surrounding area. Anna, however, took it as an opportunity to teach herself some German — enough so she realized the Nazis were bullying some of the prisoners. When they beat up one young man so badly that he landed in the hospital, she learned from him about a planned escape attempt and tipped off the camp authorities."

"If she'd been white, she would have been given a commendation and a promotion," Frank interjected forcefully. "The fact that she got nothing is shameful. It still makes me mad when I think of it." He shook his head in disgust and sat frowning for a moment. Then turning to Robin, he declared, "There's a tendency among the Americans, Brits and French to think that we could never have done what the Germans did — that we're fundamentally morally superior to them. Yet you only have to experience one incident with the Ku Klux Klan to know that — given the opportunity — there are many Americans who would have no trouble running concentration camps to kill their fellow Americans — just as long as the inmates have a different skin colour from their own," Frank answered soberly.

"As I remember it, we British invented concentration camps in the Boer War," Robin took up the theme, "And British history is littered with examples of arrogance, aggression, and brutality. Yet I still find it hard to believe British inhumanity was ever as bad as what happened here."

"Maybe it wasn't as bad because the technology didn't allow for atrocities on the same scale? I think I heard someone call it 'the industrialization' of mass murder." Frank suggested.

No one had a chance to answer because with a shout Emily drew Robin's attention to a motorboat bearing down on a collision course.

"Prepare to come about!" Robin ordered sharply, and Emily jumped to release the lee jib sheet. Unsurprisingly, the motorboat was manned by Soviet officers.

After a short zig-zag, they resumed their earlier, comfortable down-wind tack and Edith picked up the conversation. "Just to finish what I was saying about Anna Savage, she's now back in southern Georgia dealing with the consequences of poverty and prejudice and she's miserable. I think she'd jump at the opportunity to come to Europe and maybe even use some of her German again."

"I'd certainly like to work with someone like that," Emily confirmed. "If the Managing Director ever agrees to hire someone."

There was a short lull in the conversation, and then Frank asked the question that had occasioned the entire outing. "So, tell me about your runway, Robin."

Robin kept his eye on the wind, waves and their heading, the tiller clamped under his arm and one foot braced on the opposite seat as he answered, "Back in April when the Soviets closed the land access routes, fully loaded Dakotas were landing just thirty minutes apart with the result that our PSP runway started to disintegrate. It wasn't in the best of condition to start with, but the point is it couldn't have taken much more traffic. So, I asked and received funds to lay down a proper 2,000-foot concrete runway."

"Correct me if I'm wrong, Robin," Frank started with a smile on his lips but deadly serious eyes, "but that sounds to me like you *expect* the Ruskies to close the land routes again."

"Don't you?"

"I'm surprised they haven't already done it! It's like waiting for the second shoe to fall!" Frank answered in exasperation. "I don't know what they're waiting for and it's driving me crazy! Then again, the more alarmist captains on my staff think that the Ruskies may not bother with the access routes next time and will just send in the tanks." Although not worded as a question, Emily sensed that the American was probing.

"Nothing's impossible, I agree, but we have no indications that such a development is likely. My Spitfire patrols have reported no concentration of Soviet ground forces on the borders to Berlin. We'll see something building up before they strike."

"The women are getting nervous, though," Edith volunteered. "You missed the luncheon in April, Emily, but some of the wives were almost hysterical. They insisted that they and their children ought to be sent home 'before it was too late.'"

"Yeah, a bunch of officers put in requests to send their families home," Frank admitted, flashing a grin at his wife. Turning to the Priestmans he reported, "General Clay said he'd be happy to send any *officer* home who was 'uncomfortable with the situation' — but only after telling them it was 'unbecoming' of an American officer to 'show signs of nervousness.'"

The Priestmans laughed and Edith concluded, "So *that's* why they were all so subdued at this last meeting!"

"*'He who hath no stomach for this fight, let him depart. His passport shall be made and crowns for convoy put into his purse. We would not die in that man's company, who fears his fellowship to die with us.'*" Robin quoted.

It took only a couple of seconds for Edith to identify the source but then exclaimed delightedly, "Shakespeare's *Henry V*!"

"Yes," Robin confirmed, flashing her a grin of approval before adding, "The quote from the same play that used to upset us during the Battle of France, however, was: '*Once more onto the breach, dear friends, once more — or fill the wall up with our English dead.*'"

They laughed, but there was an edge to the laughter too. Robin ended it by soberly telling Frank, "To date, the Soviets have consistently taken incremental steps. Suddenly sending in the tanks would be a break with that pattern. They don't want to take control of our Sectors against heroic resistance. Armed resistance, no matter how futile, would expose them as the aggressors they are, result in casualties on both sides and probably spark a greater response. My guess is they want to humiliate us -- as well as force us out of Berlin. They want to make us strike the flag and retreat with our tails between our legs so they can ridicule, taunt and laugh at us as we go."

Howley nodded thoughtfully. "I hadn't thought of that, but you're probably right."

Robin continued, "I also think they're looking for a pretext to strike. They're waiting for us to make some move which they can cast as aggressive. That way, they can depict their actions as defensive." For a moment, nobody spoke, and the sound of water racing past the hull of the boat and wind in the rigging seemed louder. Waves had built up on the Havel and raced after them. Curling and hissing, the agitated water overtook the sailboat causing it to corkscrew increasingly uncomfortably.

Frank drew a deep breath and declared. "If you're right, then the currency reform is the most likely trigger. They know we can't allow them to keep printing money without controls, but if we introduce a new currency that they can't print, they lose a very lucrative means of enriching themselves at our expense."

Robin nodded. "A sound currency is certainly key to getting the economy working again. Any idea when the new currency is going to be introduced?"

Frank looked uncomfortable, like a man who knew more than he was at liberty to say. "Let's just say we're talking weeks not months."

Robin nodded but he looked worried. Emily remembered him saying it would be six weeks or more before the concrete runway could be finished, and even the new PSP runway wouldn't arrive until this coming week, meaning it was ten days away from being ready.

Frank picked up the conversation. "Whatever the cause, whenever the Ruskies close down the access routes again, Clay isn't going to take it sitting down. He's had enough."

"Meaning he'd risk war?" Robin asked, for a moment taking his eyes off their course to meet Frank's eyes.

"He doesn't think it will come to that. He thinks if we show any backbone, they'll back down. So do I." Frank underlined firmly.

Robin nodded. "*D'accord*. But to be on the safe side, I did some calculations on whether — with a concrete runway — we could fly in enough food, fuel and ammo to keep the garrison operational. We can. That means we wouldn't have to fight — just fly."

"Why don't my flyboys think like you?"

Robin laughed. "What I don't know is where the Germans stand in all this. If the Soviets try to push us out of Berlin and we resist, whose side will the Berliners take? Will they be out in the streets yelling 'Yankee Go Home! And 'Down with British Imperialism'?"

"Maybe, but in my opinion, it doesn't matter. We still have to stand up to Stalin or he's just going to keep on gobbling up countries."

Robin squinted up at the sails, looked into the wind then downwind toward their destination, which was rapidly approaching. Finally, he looked over at Frank and shook his head. "I disagree. I think it does matter where the Germans stand. If we are surrounded not only by the Soviets but also by a hostile population, then it makes no sense to take a stand in Berlin. We'd be better off spending our scarce resources to defend Greece or Denmark or the Channel Islands — wherever the Soviet expansion runs up against grass-roots resistance."

Howley took a moment to digest that answer and flashed Robin a grin. "Good point, but I think you'll find we've got more support here than you think."

VIP
Liss, Hampshire
Sunday, 13 June 1948

A letter from Maisy MacDonald reached Kit in early June. Aided and abetted by their eldest daughter and son-in-law, Daddy MacDonald had left her to join the VIP community at Le Court in Liss, Hampshire. Daddy did not answer Maisy's letters. In her despair, she turned to Daddy's former skipper, a man he admired, Kit Moran. Could he drive her down to Liss so she could try to persuade Daddy face-to-face to return home with her?

Kit showed the letter to Georgina, who urged him to go at once. His father-in-law offered to cover all the expenses of the trip. Thus, Kit found himself driving up the gravel drive of Le Court Manor with considerable internal trepidation.

After Maisy's appeal for help, Kit made an effort to learn more about "Vade in Pace" or VIP as the project was called. From what Kit could decipher, although the founder was not politically a Communist or an admirer of the Soviet Union, his two VIP communities operated on the fundamentally communist principle of "from each according to his ability and to each according to his needs." The self-contained colonies were intended to give everyone, particularly ex-servicemen, a "fair deal." No one was turned away, and everyone had a job to do — which, Kit remembered, was what had appealed to Daddy.

Kit had briefly heard a faint siren suggesting that if he and Georgina joined VIP, he could stop his futile job search and would never have to face another rejection letter. Yet Kit couldn't quite overcome his scepticism about it all. The concept called for not one such community, but for communities replicated across England, the Commonwealth and eventually the world. As Daddy had worded it, the vision was to "build peace from the ground up." It all sounded too ambitious and idealistic to Kit. It also smelled a little bit like a famous man trying to retain the limelight and gain new laurels. Kit wouldn't have approved of that in any case, but he particularly had doubts about the celebrity behind VIP, Group Captain Leonard Cheshire.

Cheshire had flown 100 operational sorties. He had commanded three squadrons, including 617. He had the DFC, three DSOs and the VC, the latter awarded not for an individual act of bravery but for sustained courage throughout the war. He'd experimented with low-level target marking, on one occasion telling the bombers to aim at his aircraft when they couldn't see the target flares. Unsurprisingly for a man with such an abundance of personal courage, Cheshire had no tolerance for anyone who "funked." He was on record saying that any pilot who showed signs of hesitation or reluctance was immediately posted; he had no time for anyone suffering from a "lack of moral fibre" (LMF).

Given that Kit had been labelled LMF temporarily in late 1943, the prospect of facing the RAF's most highly decorated officer grew more daunting the closer the moment drew. Nor did Kit think a man with a personality as forceful as Cheshire's would take kindly to Kit and Maisy questioning him or anything he'd done. Maisy and his best hope was that Cheshire would be absent from Le Court -- off advising the government or giving an important speech at the UN or whatever. Ever since serving as the British observer aboard an American bomber during the nuclear attack on Nagasaki, Cheshire had been elevated to celebrity "expert" on all aspects of war and peace. He wrote a weekly news column, was active on various committees and flitted from one speaking engagement to the next. If Cheshire was away from Le Court, Kit thought Maisy and he stood a chance of convincing Daddy to return home. If not, they were probably on a fool's errand.

They turned off the A-3 and started up the long drive through the grounds of Le Court. Tall trees cast shadows, and the dense underbrush seemed like a natural fortification designed to keep the uninitiated out.

The poor condition of the road reinforced the sensation of being warned off; visitors, Kit sensed, were not wanted. Kit slowed to a crawl to navigate the ruts and puddles, while beside him Maisy MacDonald nervously clutched her handbag. She soundlessly moved her lips, either praying or practising what she wanted to say to her husband.

Then suddenly the trees stopped, and a dry lawn of close-cropped grass opened up to reveal a neo-Tudorian mansion. It was just two stories high and crowned with eight tall, brick chimneys. Two bay windows flanked a glassed-in entry hall, and four dormers sat on the steep roof to either side.

Kit stopped the car before the entrance. There was no sign of any other human. Kit climbed out of the car and looked around. Nothing. Maisy MacDonald slipped out of her side of the car and stood looking at the house in obvious despair.

"Come," Kit gestured for her to join him as he approached the door and knocked. There was no response. "Wait here, I'll see if I can find someone around the back."

Kit left Maisy on the doorstep and skirted around the side of the building looking for any sign of life. At the back of the house, there were several large greenhouses and in front of these an open vegetable garden. Rows of sticks supporting tomato plants and heads of lettuce stood in neat lines. A gardener wearing an old, straw hat was busy pulling weeds.

"Good afternoon!" Kit called as he made his way between the lanes of lettuce.

The gardener looked up and then stood, dusting off his trousers. He looked vaguely familiar as he came to his full height and too late but with a sense of near panic, Kit realised he was face to face with the legendary Cheshire himself. He looked much thinner and older in his baggy gardening clothes than in dress blues with the medals below his wings. There was something almost cadaver-like in his thinness; all his bones seemed to be sticking through his skin.

Yet Cheshire was smiling at him mildly. "I'm sorry," he opened the conversation, trying to wipe his hands clean on his trousers before offering one. "I didn't hear you arrive. Can I help you in any way?"

"I hope so. I'm Kit Moran—"

"As in: Flight Lieutenant Kit Moran? Formerly of 617 Squadron?" Cheshire's face brightened, and when Kit admitted his identity, it cracked into a winning smile. "Gordon has told me so much about you already!"

That knocked Kit off his stride entirely and he found himself stammering awkwardly, "Well, yes, Daddy — Flight Sergeant MacDonald, that is, and I flew together—"

"So, I've heard! Let's go inside and get out of the sun," Cheshire suggested with a smile and a gesture. "Gordon is in the kitchen doing the washing up."

"His wife's out front," Kit hastened to explain his presence and the situation. "I brought her here so she could talk to him."

"Ah. I understand." Cheshire nodded, but the smile didn't fade. "We'd best let her in as well, then, hadn't we? Would you bring her around to the back door, while I go wash my hands and warn Gordon?"

Kit dutifully returned and took Maisy MacDonald by the elbow. "I ran into the Group Captain," he explained, "He asked me to bring you around to the back entrance."

She nodded and let Kit guide her. She was, Kit noted, trembling a little.

The back door led into a spacious, Victorian kitchen where Daddy sat in his wheelchair before the large, low sink drying his hands on a dishcloth. He looked warily at his wife as she entered, but Cheshire intervened before a word was exchanged. "Moran, what do you say we go for a walk and leave the MacDonalds to themselves for a bit?"

There was no need for Kit to answer, Cheshire had a firm hand on his elbow and was directing him through a door into the interior of the house. As the Group Captain led down a long hallway, Kit found himself asking. "Where is everyone else?"

"Who else?" Cheshire stopped to ask.

"The other colonists?"

"Oh." Cheshire looked down. Sadness settled on his features and weighed on his shoulders. "They've left. All of them." He paused and then admitted. "It was a failure. First Gumley Hall and now Le Court as well."

Despite his earlier scepticism, the revelation made Kit sad. Now that he'd met Cheshire personally, Kit understood that the project hadn't been about a famous man trying to stay important and relevant. He sensed that Cheshire genuinely wanted to help others and sincerely wanted world peace. He just didn't know how to go about it.

"Why?" Kit asked. "Why did it fail?"

"I don't know," Cheshire answered with a slight shrug as he gestured through an open door toward a desk heaped with correspondence. "People have suggested a variety of reasons: That I put too much trust in others. That I don't understand finances. That I'm a dreamer. That I can't focus. That I'm over-ambitious. That I'm a bad judge of character. That I'm mad. I suppose it's all true."

Kit shook his head in incomprehension. How could the forceful, famous, dynamic and indomitable Cheshire have failed so completely?

"Shall we go for a walk?" Cheshire suggested leading Kit through a side door back into the sunny day. From the cracked doorstep he pointed toward fields planted with crops. "I don't own the estate anymore, but I don't think anyone would mind us just walking around the edges."

"I'm afraid I can't walk very well on uneven ground, at least not long distances." Kit indicated his foot, lifting his trouser enough to expose the wooden limb.

Cheshire blushed. "How inconsiderate of me! I'm so sorry. Do you want to sit down?" He looked around helplessly and then noticed Kit's car parked in front. He smiled at the sight of it. "Why don't we take a drive instead?"

Kit agreed and they climbed in. "Just tell me where to go," Kit told Cheshire.

"Go down the drive and turn right. Gordon thinks the world of you, you know."

"I don't know why. He wouldn't be in that wheelchair if it hadn't been for me."

"Don't belittle his greatest deed. It uplifts him and is fundamental to his self-esteem."

"I don't understand," Kit admitted, taking his eyes off the drive long enough to look questioningly over at Cheshire.

"MacDonald claims he saved your life. Isn't that true?"

More confused than ever, Kit tried to remember everything that had happened on their last flight together while keeping his eye on the road ahead. To Cheshire, he explained, "When I came to, I was still in the cockpit and MacDonald lay inert beside me. I thought he was dead. The fuel tanks had exploded behind us, and the flames seemed to be getting nearer. The ammo from the guns was going off. When I tried to move, I realised that my left foot was trapped under the instrument panel and that my hip and ribs were broken too. I was bleeding badly from a gash over my left eye. I thought I was trapped and would soon be consumed by the flames. All I could think about was how horrible it would be for my fiancé. She'd already lost one young man, and now, because of me, she was going to suffer that horrible grief all over again. Then suddenly, Wehrmacht soldiers were in the cockpit. They dragged MacDonald out first and then roughly tried to pull me free. The pain was excruciating, and I lost consciousness."

Cheshire didn't answer immediately, but then he said softly. "What Gordon told me was that after pushing your wireless operator out of the forward hatch, he returned to the cockpit to find you had unbuckled your harness, apparently in preparation for bailing out. When he urged you to hurry, you said the autopilot couldn't cope and shouted at him to get out before it was too late. He again urged you to leave the controls and bail out. You answered that the aircraft was vibrating too badly, and you could barely hold it; if you let go of the controls, it would dive straight into the ground. Gordon insisted on strapping you back into your seat before seeing to himself. He says if he hadn't done that, you would have been killed in the crash."

Kit forced himself to recall the final minutes *before* the crash. He remembered trying to leave his seat only to realise that the autopilot was worthless. He remembered Daddy returning to the cockpit and he knew he'd shouted furiously at him to get out. He remembered some kind of scuffle in which he tried to shove MacDonald away while screaming at him that he was running out of time. He remembered struggling with the controls so fiercely that he was sweating and out of breath. Then abruptly they were in the trees, the Perspex shattered, and everything started spinning so fast that he blacked out. In retrospect, the scuffle might have been triggered by MacDonald taking the time to strap him in, when he wanted him to just get out. If that was true, then he did owe him his life — which only made things worse.

Cheshire was speaking again. "He's proud of saving your life, Moran. He says it was the most important thing he did in his whole life. The problem for him isn't the past but the future. What are *your* plans for the future?" Cheshire asked looking at Kit intently.

Kit could only shrug as he kept his eyes on the winding road. "I finished my degree, but I can't get an engineering job anywhere. I've been looking for months, and I must have had a hundred rejection letters. I'll probably end up taking a job as an aircraft mechanic somewhere." He tried not to sound bitter, but he had the distinct feeling that Cheshire saw right through him. Cheshire said nothing except to give more directions.

They were in open countryside again and Cheshire said to turn onto a dirt road. Suddenly a hangar loomed up in front of them and a windsock blew out in the stiff breeze. Kit put on the brakes and looked at Cheshire bewildered. Why were they at an airfield?

Cheshire smiled mildly and suggested, "Why don't you park over there?"

Kit did as he was told without question.

Cheshire climbed out of the car and started toward the hangar. Men came out to greet him eagerly. He gestured for Kit to join him, and Kit heard him ask, "Is she serviceable?"

"Of course, sir!"

Cheshire indicated Kit. "Moran's another pilot from 617. You don't think anyone would notice if we took her up do you?"

They laughed. "No, sir, but I don't know how much petrol is left in her tanks."

"Would you mind taking a look-see?"

They were all moving towards a hangar containing a de Havilland Mosquito. Cheshire explained. "I owned it until — I don't know. I sold the other one, but I tried to hold on to this one. It needed maintenance, however, and had trouble paying for the repairs and then I was so sick my parents sent me to Canada for six months. When I returned, everyone at Le Court was fighting with one another, the crops were rotting in the fields, and people started leaving. I was twenty-thousand pounds in debt. That's when I sold off the estate to pay my debts. I'm not entirely sure if the bank foreclosed on the Mossie in the meantime or not. I must sound terribly irresponsible," he noted with a sad smile.

Kit thought about that. No, not so much irresponsible as lost. Before he could say anything, however, Cheshire suggested with an infectious smile. "Shall we go for a flip?"

Kit took one look at the Mossie, back at Cheshire who was smiling infectiously and couldn't resist the temptation. Flying had meant so much to him and he'd thought he might never do it again. He grinned at Cheshire. "Why not?"

Around them, the men, whoever they were, gave them the thumbs up and set to work pushing the Mossie out and preparing her for take-off. Kit offered to give them a hand, but they brushed him off. "We can handle it!"

"Have you ever flown a Mossie?" Cheshire asked as they climbed up the flimsy ladder into the nose.

"No."

"Wimpys?"

"About 270 hours."

"When was the last time you flew?"

"When I crashed in Germany, crushed my foot and put Daddy in a wheelchair."

"In a Lanc?"

"Yes."

They were in the cockpit and Cheshire dropped into the righthand seat and smiled up at Kit. "You fly it."

"I only have one foot."

"No, you have two, one flesh and one wood. You drive a car perfectly well. Bader flew with two artificial legs, remember?"

"My license isn't up to date."

"Then don't prang it, and no one will find out."

"Aren't you worried?"

"No. I trust you," Cheshire replied with his utterly irresistible, crooked smile. Then getting down to business he declared. "Let's not keep everyone waiting. I'll show you where everything is."

The next thing Kit knew, he was flying again over the English countryside in the late summer sunshine. The fields below were green and gold, the villages tidy, the churches solid, the streams glistened and the Channel in the distance was a brilliant blue. To Kit's amazement, he had no difficulty with the controls. After three years with the artificial foot, he had learned to feel through it. Furthermore, the Mossie was light compared to the Lancaster, and he found it easy to fly. All in all, Kit thought flying was easier than driving, it came to him more instinctively.

For nearly an hour, Kit and Cheshire knew no trouble, no doubts, and no cares. They had severed all ties with the earth and with their past and future. Only the setting sun and draining gas tank drove them back to the airfield.

Kit set the Mossie down on the grass field. It was not a great landing, and they bounced a bit, but not dangerously. They taxied toward the hangar. Although the Mossie had only two Merlins instead of four, they were nearer and seemed just as loud. They certainly kept the entire light frame of the "wooden wonder" vibrating. It wasn't until he'd shut down the engines and the aircraft became still that he felt reality return. He turned to Cheshire and said simply. "Thank you."

They climbed out of the cockpit, thanked the ground crew, and Kit tried to tip them, but they wouldn't accept it. He climbed back into the driver's seat of his car and started to drive back to Le Court.

"What are your plans?" Kit asked Cheshire as dusk closed around them.

Cheshire shrugged. "I was thinking of going to the Soviet Union to get arrested."

"What?"

Cheshire shrugged again. "People in the Soviet Union don't seem to know how close the world is to a new war. I thought something dramatic might alert them to the danger. But then I realized that I'm not nearly important enough for my arrest to attract attention much less make any difference."

"I have a friend stationed in Berlin," Kit reflected. "She says the Soviets are trying to push us out."

"Berlin," Cheshire repeated. "I was there after the war, you know. It is…" He seemed to hesitate, searching for the right word. "It is full of contradictions. So much power and powerlessness, so many reminders of cruelty and depravity and yet hope and self-reliance as well. Perhaps I should go back, but first, a friend has asked if he can park his caravan here at Le Court while he recovers from cancer. Of course, I said he could, because he's not going to recover. He's dying. I'll just see him through to the end, so he isn't alone when it happens. After that, I don't know. I'll just wait and see if anyone else needs me for something."

What a remarkable yet depressing plan, Kit thought. How lucky he was to have Georgina and Donna who needed him. They gave him something to live for, work for, and fight for every day.

Speaking into his thoughts, Cheshire remarked. "I think it would be better for Gordon, if he returned with his wife, don't you? I didn't want to say that to him for fear he would feel rejected, but I think he is better off with his family. Especially now that I've met Mrs MacDonald. She does care for him a great deal, doesn't she?"

"Yes, very much. The problem is she has a job and she's always been quite independent. On the one hand, I suspect she's unintentionally made him feel quite superfluous. On the other, she's inclined to coddle him like an invalid, and he doesn't like that, either."

"No, I can see that. You'll stay the night, won't you? Both of you. I'll find sheets and blankets somewhere and we'll cook something together."

Kit nodded and agreed. He and Mrs MacDonald had been prepared to spend the night in a guest house somewhere, but neither had money to spare. Besides, the thought of the four of them making dinner together in this rundown old manor appealed to him.

They left the car out front, and Cheshire led them inside. "We're back!" he called out as they entered, pausing to listen for an answer.

"We're in the sitting room," Daddy's gruff voice replied.

Cheshire led the way. When Kit and he entered, they found the MacDonalds sitting side-by-side on a sofa holding hands. "I'm going home with Maisy," Daddy announced as they entered.

"What excellent news!" Cheshire agreed with a wide smile and a wink for Kit.

Kit found himself thinking what a strange world this was. The house was falling down around Cheshire's ears. He had neither income nor fortune nor work. Just, apparently, an insatiable and disproportionate need to be useful to someone else, to be serving a good cause, and preventing another war. It sounded so grandiose in the newspaper articles, but it amounted to letting Daddy do the washing up, letting him fly again — and ensuring that a man didn't die alone.

Kit resolved to try to follow that example and found the thought liberating. His failures didn't matter quite so much anymore. What mattered was that he and Georgina were together. Somehow they would give Donna a wonderful childhood so she would grow up happy. Most important, rather than seeking success, he told himself, he should concentrate on being useful.

Chapter Sixteen
A City Divided

Money Matters
Berlin-Kreuzberg
Tuesday, 22 June 1948

"Jakob! Jakob!" Louise Schroeder, the Deputy Mayor of Berlin called breathlessly as she put her head around the door of Jakob Liebherr's office in the Kreuzberger Rathaus. "Are you here?"

The sixty-one-year-old Louise wore rimless glasses and a navy-blue suit with a white blouse and lace collar. Jakob Liebherr jumped to his feet to come around his desk, pulling out his wooden visitor chair for her. "My dear! What brings you here? What has happened?"

Because the Soviets still refused to recognise Ernst Reuter, Schroeder was the acting mayor. In Liebherr's opinion, she was doing an outstanding job — as one would expect of the first woman ever elected to the German parliament. Liebherr had known her since she first came to Berlin during the Weimar Republic, and she had been a staunch friend even in the worst years of his life. Although frequently arrested and interrogated by the Nazis, Louise had somehow avoided being sent to a concentration camp. This enabled her to support Trude while Jakob was incarcerated. Jakob knew that Louise had provided his wife not only with moral support and a shoulder to cry on but often with much-needed food and cash as well.

"Jakob, have you read Sokolovsky's statement?" She asked, her eyes enlarged by her thick glasses.

"Which one?"

"The one issued late last night. The one that says the Soviets are unilaterally introducing a new currency in the Soviet Zone and that it will henceforth be a crime for anyone to possess Western currency anywhere in the Soviet Zone *and throughout Berlin.*"

"They don't have any say over what currency is used in the Western Sectors of Berlin," Liebherr countered.

"You're missing my point! Whether they have the right to say it or not, Solokovsky just *explicitly* claimed that Berlin — all of Berlin — was 'part of the Soviet Zone.' They've seized Berlin right out from under us!"

"No, they haven't, Louise," Jakob tried to calm the deputy mayor, noting he'd never needed to do this before. Louise Schroeder was not the kind of woman who easily panicked. "They can't steal it. The Western Allies are still here."

"Do we know that a deal wasn't struck behind our backs? The Four Powers are meeting at the Control Council this very minute. Officially only the financial experts are meeting but who knows what instructions they have from their respective governments. I fear — what is that American expression? — that we've been 'sold down the river.'"

"I don't believe it," Liebherr insisted, remembering his impression of General Clay. "Clay has long been spoiling for a fight and Ernst told me just yesterday that he senses a stiffening on the part of the British as well."

"I hope you're right, Jakob, but Major Otschkin has summoned me to report to him at the Town Hall immediately. Will you come with me?"

"Of course! Why didn't you say so straight away?" Jakob reached for his hat, told his secretary where he was going, and took Louise by the elbow as they made their way down the central stairs to the street below. Louise, as acting Mayor, had a car and driver — a Volkswagen Beetle. They climbed together into the narrow back seat.

After months of talking about it and weeks of wild speculation, the day before the Western Allies had at last introduced a new currency in the Western Zones, the so-called Deutsche Mark. People living in the Western Zone could now exchange their old marks for these "D-Marks" — as people were already calling them — at set rates. Since this morning, reports were flooding in that the stores in Bizonia (the combined British and American Zones) are suddenly full of goods — and not just butter, eggs and vegetables, but silk stockings, leather shoes, radio sets, and more. So far, however, Berlin had been excluded from the currency reform. That seemed an ominous development and inwardly Jakob shared Louise's alarm.

They pulled up before the Rote Rathaus and together went up the steps. They showed their ID to the Soviet soldiers guarding the door and made their way to the sumptuous office of the Soviet liaison officer to the City Council, Major Otschkin.

Exceptionally, they were not kept waiting long. Nor did Otschkin comment on Liebherr accompanying Schroeder. Instead, he appeared to be in a hurry. He handed over several prepared documents. One was Sokolovsky's official decree on the introduction of a new Soviet currency throughout the Soviet Zone 'including Berlin.' The second was a set of technical guidelines for the introduction of the new marks. Finally, there was a handwritten note from the Chief of Staff of the SMAD laconically stating that he "expected no trouble" from the Berlin City Council.

Schroeder asked for time to read the documents, and the Soviet Major frowned but agreed. He sat back in his chair drumming his thumbs on the arms of his chair while the two Germans read through the documents carefully.

Schroeder was correct. Sokolovsky's statement explicitly laid claim to all of Berlin, but Liebherr was equally disturbed by the detailed instructions for the introduction of the Soviet currency. These allowed members of the SED, the FDJ (the Socialist Youth Organization), managers of collective farms and expropriated factories now run by the Soviet administration to exchange their old marks on more favourable terms than other categories of citizens. At one extreme, the privileged few deemed 'progressive' could exchange their old marks at a rate of one-to-one. At the other extreme, 'capitalists,' (anyone who owned a business) 'warmongers,' 'enemies of the people,' 'reactionaries,' — effectively anyone the SMAD didn't like — would receive no new currency at all. That amounted to the expropriation of all money held by 'reactionary' elements. The decree was as much a political assault on opponents of Soviet control as a currency reform.

Pretending surprise, Louise asked as if confused, "But these orders appear to apply to *all* of Berlin."

"Of course," Otschkin answered brusquely.

"But they have been issued solely by the SMAD," she pointed out, frowning and turning the documents over as if looking for the usual seals. "Our mandate requires us to follow only properly constituted decrees issued by all four powers," the acting mayor reminded the Soviet officer.

"That is not going to happen in this case," Otschikin told them in an indifferent tone underlined by a shrug.

"But what if we receive contrary orders from the Western Allies?" Liebherr spoke up for the first time.

"You won't," Otschkin dismissed the question irritably and directed his next remarks to Schroeder in a firm, commanding tone, "We insist that you present this decree to the City Assembly. You must do so later than tomorrow afternoon and you must obtain full legislative support for the measure. Need I outline the consequences of failure to comply with SMAD orders?"

"No, that won't be necessary," Louise answered and got to her feet. With a nod of her head to Otschkin, she walked out of the office with Liebherr in her wake.

They did not speak until they were back inside her car. Louise then announced grimly, "We must get these documents to Mayor Reuter at once."

Precisely because the Soviets refused to recognize Reuter, his fellow elected representatives were meticulous about giving him the respect due to a governing mayor. Reuter, not Schroeder, summoned the City Council to the Schoeneberg Town Hall later that same evening. The Soviet decree and technical instructions were shared with all Council Members. Reuter then surprised the others by reading a joint statement drafted by the Western Allies, which he said, would be issued later the same evening or early the next morning.

The key element was a clause which read: "The unilateral SMAD decree violates the Four-Power Agreements and is null and void." The text went on to promise that a new Western currency would be issued in the Western Sectors the following day. Rather than imposing penalties for possession of the Soviet-issued notes, however, the Western Allies explicitly allowed both currencies to circulate throughout the city simultaneously. Most importantly, the rate of exchange was the same for everyone and was set at one-to-one for essential commodities such as food, rent and utilities, rising to a steep ten-to-one for "luxury" goods.

As soon as Reuter opened the floor to discussion on how to respond to the situation, one of the SED members jumped to his feet and declared, "There is nothing to discuss. The SMAD has spoken."

Reuter told him he was out of order, and again opened the floor to discussion.

Another SED councilman spoke up. "Our Soviet friends have put forward a brilliant and generous plan. The Soviet exchange rate of one-to-one (except for criminals and reactionary elements) is far more generous than this scandalous and exploitive exchange rate of ten-to-one with insignificant exceptions—"

"You think food, clothing and housing are insignificant?" Liebherr called out, but the speaker ignored him, and Reuter frowned at the interruption and called Liebherr to order as well.

"The Western Allies are transparently trying to divide Germany." Another SED councilman insisted.

He was echoed by a colleague who declared passionately, "They want to tear the country apart so they can keep Germany impoverished and weak forever. Anyone who touches one of these D-Marks is a traitor to Germany!"

Liebherr was on the brink of pointing out that the Soviet terms expropriated wealth, but Reuter gestured for him to remain silent and insisted firmly that the Council was constrained to comply only with decrees issued by all four powers. If they accepted the SMAD decree, they violated their mandate.

"In that case, there is nothing to discuss," the SED spokesman declared, and the faction got up and walked out of the meeting. Reuter looked relieved, but it was only when one of his aides reported that the SED faction had left the building that he announced, "I propose convening the entire City Assembly tomorrow. At that Assembly, the City Council should recommend the rejection of the SMAD decree as illegal. We should not attempt to discuss the respective merits of the currencies. Our argument must remain simple. The unilateral nature of the Soviet degree makes it invalid. All opposed?"

Liebherr wanted to protest. He felt the conditions were important and shouldn't be ignored. They succinctly revealed the nature of the Soviet regime. But around him he sensed a reluctance to oppose Reuter. They had learned to trust his pollical instincts.

Reuter was asking, "All in favour?"

Liebherr lifted his hand with the others.

"Done." Reuter declared. "Tomorrow before the full assembly we will recommend rejection of the Soviet decree as illegal."

Filial Affection
Berlin-Kreuzberg
Wednesday, 23 June 1948

Karl Liebherr burst in on his parents just as his father was putting on his jacket. "Don't go to this Assembly, Vati!" Karl ordered.

"What do you mean?" His father asked astonished. "I'm a member of the City Council. I voted last night on the decision that is to be debated today. Of course, I must attend."

"It's a waste of time!" Karl countered. "By going, you only make a public spectacle of yourself! You will be photographed by the press, and everyone will know where you stand."

"I'm not ashamed of where I stand, Karl."

"This is like voting against Hitler's Enabling Law all over again, isn't it?" The way Karl asked the rhetorical question made it sound like something shameful.

Jakob, however, was proud of having voted against Hitler's Enabling Law. "Yes," he answered steadily. "There are many parallels, which is exactly why I intend to go." He started for the door, but his son blocked his way.

"Don't you remember where your vote against Hitler's Enabling Law got you?"

"Do you think I can forget two years in a Concentration Camp?"

"Apparently you can! And the worst of it is that you never give a thought to anyone but yourself and your image! You don't care about the consequences of your grandstanding for Mutti and me, do you?"

"Oh, so *that's* what this is all about," Jakob scoffed. "You think my public opposition to the SMAD might hurt your career in the SED. Well, I'm sorry, Karl. You're a big boy now. You'll have to deal with that yourself."

"I can! I'm not worried about myself! It's Mutti, I worry about. You honestly don't give a damn about what happens to her, do you? No, of course, not! Just like in '33! All you think about is your public image!"

"Karl! How dare you talk to your father like that!" Trude reared up.

"Dare? It's *past* time that *someone* stood up to him! I watched you suffer while he was in the KZ!" Karl told his mother furiously. "I watched you cry in despair. I watched you beg neighbours and relatives for help. I watched you humble yourself before the Nazis and try to play 'nice little Hausfrau' in the hope—"

Trude slapped her son hard. "Stop it! I'm not proud of what I did, but you have no right to judge me!"

"I'm not judging you!" Karl shouted. "I'm trying to stop it from happening all over again. Don't you see? Are you both idiots? The SMAD has issued a decree and they will enforce it. The SED will enforce it. The police will enforce it. The Red Army will enforce it. Why do you have to go through this puppet theatre of defiance?"

"You think a meeting of the City Assembly is 'puppet theatre'?" His father asked back. He did not raise his voice, yet he asked the question with acute intensity. He spoke slowly and deliberately, the apparent calm of his voice underlining the depth of his shock and outrage.

"What else is it?" Karl shot back unintimidated. "Such quaint institutions have no place in a Farmers and Workers State. The Vanguard of the Proletariat knows what is best and should be obeyed without this bourgeois charade of democracy."

"In that case, we can at least go on record as standing up for the Four-Power Agreements that the Soviets themselves signed."

"Why?" Karl insisted. "What difference will that make? Four-Power government is dead. The Western Powers have ripped it up in favour of protecting the interests of their monied classes."

Jakob refused to discuss his son's Soviet disinformation. "Our stand will show the world that we know what is at stake and that we care about liberty."

"Vati! I'm warning you not to go!" Karl was still shouting. He sounded enraged, but something in his tone had subtly changed. Both his parents recognised it. Jakob's eyes locked with his son's, and he saw terror in them. His son was afraid for him.

Trude touched his elbow. "Jakob...."

He looked at her and saw his son's fear reflected in her eyes. "How many men have already disappeared? Even Herr Dr Hofmeier, who was utterly unpolitical, has never been heard from again. I don't want to lose you — not now."

"Trude," he said her name gently. "You, of all people, must know that if I stay, you will have lost me more certainly than if I go. If I stay home, I abandon my principles. You would not want what is left of me after I have done that." Turning back to his son, he said gently, "Thank you for warning me, Karl. Now, let me go."

Defeated, Karl backed away from the door and let his father out.

End of an Illusion
Berlin-Mitte
Wednesday, 23 June 1948

The streets leading up to the Rote Rathaus were clogged with lorries disgorging men. Their overalls and heavy boots identified them as factory workers and some of the trucks had signs in the windscreens with the names of various "Peoples' Factories" (*Volkseigener Betriebe*). Many workers waved red flags, some with the hammer-and-sickle on them. Others carried banners with slogans such as "Unity!" or "Down with the Capitalist Oppressors!" Still others held up pictures of Stalin.

From loudspeakers mounted on a lorry, a recorded speech by Walter Ulbricht, the leader of the Socialist Unity Party, boomed out. Ulbricht harangued and shouted in tones reminiscent of Adolf Hitler. Only, in place of "the Fatherland" he extolled the virtues of the "Great Soviet Motherland." Rather than bragging about the Wehrmacht's victories, he blessed the "Heroic Red Army" for "liberating" Germany. Instead of shrieking about the evils of Communism, he condemned the "Capitalist powers," and instead of vowing to destroy the "stranglehold of international Judaism," he promised to thwart the efforts of the "West" to divide Germany. All that was missing, Liebherr reflected, was the call for "Total War."

In the side streets, the "spontaneous" demonstration was still being organised, but in front of the Rathaus, the mob had already been unleashed. As Liebherr came around the corner he saw men surge up the steps, shoving the handful of policemen aside to burst through the main entrance into the foyer. For the first time since the surrender of Berlin to the Red Army, Liebherr noted, there was not a single Soviet soldier in sight.

With rioters flooding the main stairs, entrance, and foyer, Liebherr diverted his steps toward a side entrance. A sudden eruption of shouting stopped him. Although many men had already forced entry into the Town Hall, hundreds of others were still converging from the back streets. They had spotted something that attracted their rage. Swarming around and gesturing threateningly, they broke out into a chant that sent a shudder down Liebherr's spine. "Judensau! Judensau!" (Jewish sow.)

Liebherr had last heard it chanted by the SA during the pogrom of November 1938. Then Hitler's thugs attacked Jews in their shops and homes, smashing, stealing, punching, kicking and trampling. Now, the chant was directed at one of his fellow SPD councillors, Jeannette Wolfe. Wolfe had spent six years in a concentration camp. She was a grandmother as old as Louise Schroeder. Liebherr pushed, shoved and kicked his way forward, reaching her just as the crowd started to use their fists. Fortunately, he was not alone. Several of his colleagues from the City Council also came to Jeannette Wolfe's rescue.

The men formed a protective shield around their colleague, linking arms. Together they tried to shuffle their way toward the building. Liebherr felt fists punch into his shoulders. Someone kicked him hard in the shin. Someone else aimed at his ankle, making him stagger. They were spitting too and continued to chant "Judensau! Judensau!" Jeannette had her arms crossed over her bent head.

"Under the stairs. The emergency exit!" Someone shouted into his ear.

Liebherr nodded and glanced over to direct their steps in the right direction. A fist hit him on the chin. It flung his head to the side, sending a sharp pain down his neck, but it failed to knock him down or out. Before a second blow fell, a younger colleague came to his assistance, striking back.

Still, Liebherr was not sure they would have made it if the crowd had not been distracted. Suddenly, half their attackers went chasing after something else, and Jeannette Wolfe's defenders pushed and shoved their way free of the others to reach the doorway. One of the porters cracked it open and reached out to pull Jeannette inside. Her colleagues followed one at a time, before the porter slammed the door shut in the face of their pursuers. He threw the bolt, and the sound of fists pounding on the door almost drowned out the noise coming from overhead where the mob was vandalizing the main lobby.

The porter, an old man who had worked at the Rote Rathaus for decades, signalled for the councilmen to follow him. He started up a fire escape that led past the lobby to the floor beyond. They found, however, that the mob had already invaded the Council Chamber. Louise Schroeder was shouting for the rioters to clear the chamber, but Karl Mewis, a SED assemblyman, jumped onto a bench shouting, "Stay! Stay! You are the People! Speak for the People!"

From overhead in the visitors' gallery voices chanted: "Down with the Secessionists! Kill the pigs! Kill the pigs! Kill the pigs!"

Something in that chant triggered visceral fear in Liebherr — fear he had not felt as he faced his son or he helped Jeannette Wolfe reach safety. He felt a chill run down his spine, and he saw again the look in his son's eyes when he warned him not to attend today's session. His eyes scanned the room again. Not a single policeman. Not a single Soviet soldier. Nor a Western officer either. Since the town hall was in the Soviet Sector, the Western Allies could not sent troops, but they might have sent some observers, Liebherr thought. Yet they had not. The City Council had been abandoned -- thrown to a mob incited by the SED. They would be silenced either by brute force or by the simpler method of reporting only "unanimous" support for their "Soviet brothers" in the press.

Just then Mewis spotted Jeannette Wolfe among the occupants of the room and took up the chant of "Judensau!" His mouth was as wide and dark as the worst caricature of Goebbels. "Traitors aren't allowed in here! Out! Out!"

Before anyone could stop her, Wolfe rushed forwards and shoved him backwards off the bench. He crashed down, hitting his head so hard that he was temporarily dazed. Louise Schroeder took advantage of his fall to grab the gavel and pound it on the podium. "Clear this chamber of visitors," she shouted, "or we'll reconvene in the American Sector!"

The rioters started to hoot and whistle their contempt, but Schroeder had caught sight of the Chairman of the Communist Trade Unions, apparently one of the organisers of this 'demonstration,' who was standing just in front of the podium. "I'm serious, Herr Chawalak!" Schroeder intoned, "You have to the count of ten to clear your goons out of this chamber, or we'll withdraw to the American sector where we have police protection!"

Chawalak climbed onto the podium. "Comrades! Comrades!" It took several seconds before the crowd quietened enough for him to speak. "Comrades! You've made your point loud and clear! Go outside and await the decision of this Chamber! You will be informed as soon as the vote is taken!"

Claps and cheering greeted his statement making a mockery of claims that the riot had been "spontaneous." Liebherr had never seen a genuine mob that changed character so rapidly from violent to docile. Someone took up the *Internationale* and singing loudly the rioters streamed out of the Chamber waving their banners and flags in time to the music like well-drilled schoolboys. Yet the fact that they just as willingly attacked an old women and smashed furniture on command was chilling.

As the doors closed behind the last of the rioters, Schroeder called the Assembly into session. They had lost two hours to the staged disruption, but as though nothing had happened, Schroeder presented the Council's case for rejecting the SMAD ultimatum.

"Traitors! Traitors!" The SED faction protested. "Stooges of the Western Capitalists!"

Schroeder ignored the shouting but recognised a SED assemblyman who asked for the floor. "Madam Mayor," he opened in a polite voice, "you *do* realise that the City's accounts are held in the Soviet Sector of Berlin, don't you? Surely you recognise that these will be frozen, if we are so foolish as to ignore the SMAD directive?"

An LPD Assemblyman requested recognition. "What currency are those deposits in?" he asked back rhetorically, answering his own question. "Worthless occupation marks! Madam Chairman, I move that we open our accounts in a bank in the American Sector — in D-Marks!"

His suggestion was met with a flurry of seconds and cheers.

Another SED assemblyman asked for the floor. "Comrades!" He called out. "Comrades! Don't be blinded by prejudice! You think the Soviets have been high-handed. You are angry about the reparations and some minor incidents of indiscipline on the part of the long-suffering Red soldiers, but don't let these bagatelles blind you to what is happening here." He paused dramatically to be sure everyone was listening. When all were silent, he continued, "The Western powers are trying to tear Germany in two! They are going to set up a puppet state in their Zones. Why? So that Germany can never again be whole and strong!" A chorus of "hear, hear!" erupted from the ranks of the SED benches.

"Maybe we can't stop that," he continued when the shouts faded, "but we can stop them from tearing *Berlin* apart. Do you want a wall to be built through the heart of our beloved city? Think about that, comrades. Think what that would mean. Don't allow them to do that, comrades!" He pleaded passionately. "For all our differences, you must see that we are one people, one nation, one city."

It was a powerful appeal, Liebherr conceded mentally and glanced at his fellow SPD assemblymen to see whether anyone was preparing to respond. None appeared to want the floor, so he stood himself. His fit of nerves had passed. The courage of the women — Wolfe and Schroeder — had made him brave again. "Madam Deputy Mayor, Fellow Councilmen, Fellow Members of the Berlin City Assembly," he opened. "Comrade Thiele has made an important point. He has reminded us that we are one nation, one people, one city. I daresay, there is not one person in this room who wishes to see Germany divided — torn in two — as Comrade Thiele worded it." He paused to let the nodding of heads and calls of agreement die out.

Then he continued, "So, we agree on the goal. Now let us look a little closer at the means. Comrade Thiele would like to preserve the unity of the city by breaking the framework under which this assembly operates. He would have us stop recognizing the authority of the Western Powers and, instead, adhere solely to the directives of the Soviets." He looked over at the SED leader, who nodded vigorously.

Liebherr continued. "That would indeed preserve the unity of Berlin. But at what price?" He paused, but not long enough for anyone to interrupt him. "Is it in the best interests of our constituents to accept a Soviet ultimatum that will leave them no richer than before? Is it in the interests of our constituents to cut them off from Marshall Aid and Western military protection?" He paused again as across the room men and women shook their heads and even the SED faction looked at one another in irritation or alarm.

Theile jumped up to speak, but Liebherr cut him off by continuing. "We have a choice. It is not a grand choice because our power is very limited. We cannot make Germany whole again, or rich again, or strong again, or respected again. What we can do, however, is not succumb to intimidation, mob violence, and the shouts of hatred and racism that met us as we tried to assemble peacefully today!" His voice had risen to a forceful crescendo. "That crowd out there! Shouting 'Judensau!' and 'Traitors!' should not be allowed victory! If it is, we have proven to the whole world that that crowd is us — all of us. If we give in to the mob, then racist, fascist mobs are still the face and essence of Germany — a Germany that deserves to be utterly destroyed!"

The City Assembly voted 106 to 24 to uphold the decision of the City Council and ignore the Soviet ultimatum.

Chapter Seventeen
Technical Difficulties

Milk Run
Berlin-Kreuzberg
Thursday, 24 June 1948

June 24th dawned clear and sunny, promising an exceptionally warm day. Christian paused just in front of his apartment house and looked up at the pale blue sky. The pleasant weather made him reluctant to travel by underground train and he checked his watch, trying to decide whether he could make his appointment on time if he walked part of the way. His thoughts were interrupted by a wagon drawn by two well-groomed horses driven by the coachman Horst with his great handlebar moustache.

Christian had made a point of taking Horst out for a weekly beer ever since his arrival. It was mostly to thank him for looking after Charlotte, but also out of gratitude for saving the horses. Too many had been killed, starved to death or slaughtered by people desperate for food, particularly in the final months of the war. To Christian, Horst's well-kept team represented a tiny victory — or maybe the promise of a better future.

The sight of the wagon at this time of the morning, however, grated a nerve. "Horst!" Christian called out. "Shouldn't you be collecting milk from the Zone?"

"Can't get across the border, Herr Baron," Horst answered, shaking his head and looking worried. "Nothing I could do or say would budge the Ivans. I even offered them bribes. *Nyet!*" He made an emphatic gesture. "Maybe it's nothing more of their usual shenanigans, but I didn't like the way a Red Army lieutenant smugly told me to find a different 'line of work.'" Horst shook his head, his expression darkening. "I fear the Ivans have something up their sleeve, and, God help us, it won't be good for us."

430

Russian News
Berlin-Kladow

At the Priestman villa in Kladow, Jasha turned on the radio as she started washing up. All the "gentlefolk"— Mr and Mrs Priestman, Mr Goldman and Mr Murray — had left for work and the house belonged to the servants. Jasha tuned into a program that featured Russian music because, much as she hated the Russians, she preferred their music to the horrible jazz the American-controlled Radio in the American Sector (RIAS) played so much of the time.

As the sink filled with water, the music was interrupted by a news bulletin. "Due to technical difficulties, the Transport Authority of the Soviet Military Administration in Germany has been forced to suspend all road and rail traffic for both passengers and goods between the Western Zones and the Western Sectors of Berlin until further notice."

Jasha turned and stared at the radio. *All* road and rail links? Closed simultaneously? Indefinitely? She turned the radio dial to the official Red Army station. This, however, only repeated the earlier message, adding: "Coal shipments to Berlin from the Soviet Zone have been halted. A shortage of coal at the Czernowitz Power Station has made it imperative that electricity supplies from the Soviet Zone to the Western Sectors of Berlin be terminated."

Jasha stared at the radio, stunned. A moment later the fear set in.

American News
RAF-Gatow

Charlotte had finished translating a new brochure and was typing it up. She flinched and jammed her fingers between the keys painfully when someone burst into the BEA office calling, "The Ivans have shut down all the access routes — even the canals!"

Exclamations of disbelief and surprise erupted from across the room. "Turn the wireless on!"

The man closest to the radio switched it on, tuning in to RIAS. "... Since late last night, the Western Sectors of Berlin are receiving no electricity from the Soviet Zone or Sector. Power will be cut across the city as the power plants in the Western Sectors cannot cope with demand. The electricity shortage will also affect public transport, water supply and sewage disposal—"

"They can't be serious!" One of the BEA employees exclaimed stunned.

Charlotte went cold. She'd heard David and Kiwi speculate about the access routes being closed again, but no one had expected them to shut down the flow of electricity. This changed everything. The Soviets were strangling them. The Western Allies would be forced to withdraw. They didn't have a choice. They couldn't fight because there weren't enough of them. Besides, why should they? Who would go to war over something as unimportant as half a ruined city full of half-starved former enemies?

Charlotte started trembling in spasms. Without the Western Allies, there would be no one to protect them, no one to turn to, and nowhere to escape or hide. The Soviet soldiers would go everywhere and do whatever they liked. She pushed herself to her feet and walked in a daze to the ladies' lavatory. She locked herself in one of the stalls and started crying uncontrollably. She couldn't face it. She couldn't. She wouldn't. She would kill herself before she let it happen again.

Fake News
RAF-Gatow

"Sir!" Flight Lieutenant Boyd stood in the doorway of the Station Commander's office and announced, "We have reports coming in of rioting in central Berlin. An angry mob is allegedly breaking shop windows and stealing food."

Priestman sat straighter at his desk and shot back. "Who's reporting that? Do we have confirmation?" He'd been expecting a Soviet move for nearly three months, and just as Frank Howley had suggested, the introduction of the D-Mark had triggered it, but he had not expected riots

-- or not right away.

"All the radio stations are repeating the same information, sir, but I can't track down the source. They're saying things like 'we're hearing reports' and 'it is being alleged.' No one seems to have first-hand information, and, no, I don't have any confirmation from any authority."

"I'll see what I can find out," Priestman agreed, but before he could take further action, the phone on his desk rang and he answered it.

"Sir? This is the Tower. Triple Two's duty patrol is reporting armour clogging the inbound autobahn."

Damn, he thought. He hadn't expected either the electricity to be cut off or the tanks to move. In short, he'd made two miscalculations. Just to be sure the report was reliable, he asked, "Who's reporting?"

"Flight Lieutenant Knight, sir."

"Thank you." Priestman disconnected with his finger without replacing the receiver on the base, and dialled his WAAF secretary in the outer office, asking her to connect him to General Herbert. As he waited, he looked at Boyd again. "Do we have confirmation that all access routes by land and water are interdicted?"

"Yes, sir. No question about that. We have the official SMAD notification of the measures — 'due to technical difficulties'." Priestman nodded and glanced out the window toward the long shallow ditch filled with rainwater where his paved runway was supposed to be. The new PSP runway had been laid down three weeks ago, but the concrete runway was still two weeks away from completion. No, wait! If they couldn't ship in concrete and steamrollers, he might not be able to get it finished at all.

"Sir!" Stan burst into the office.

Priestman just looked at him waiting.

"The radio is reporting that Allied troops have fired on rioters in Charlottenburg, killing dozens!"

"*That* is not credible," Priestman answered. "What station was reporting that?"

"I don't know, sir. I heard it down in the mess. A bunch of German workers were standing around and staring at the radio in horror."

"Boyd, would you please go down and find out what station they're listening to? If it is Radio Berlin — or any other Soviet-controlled station — make them turn it off or listen to RIAS."

Boyd nodded and departed as from the telephone receiver Sergeant Andrews informed Priestman that she had a connection to the British City Commandant. Priestman opened: "Wing Commander Priestman here, sir. I wanted you to know that my duty section has reported Soviet armour blocking the autobahns. Also, we're hearing rumours of riots and casualties. Can you provide me with any insight into the situation?"

"The city is completely calm. Tense, but calm. No riots, so no reason to shoot and certainly no casualties. I'll pass on your information about the tanks. Meanwhile, I suggest you join me in my office with your IO for a full briefing."

"Yes, sir. Should I come straight away?"

"Let me see..." Herbert's muffled voice consulted someone before he ordered, "Can you be here in an hour? I'll hold a general briefing then."

Behind the News
Berlin-Charlottenburg

An hour later, Priestman and Boyd were ushered into General Herbert's office, where Air Commodore Waite and other officers already waited. The others made room for the two RAF officers on the settee as extra cups and saucers were brought. The last person to arrive was a liaison officer from the Foreign Office in an elegant pinstriped suit.

Once everyone was settled, Herbert commenced. "As you already know, the Soviets have cut off electric power to the Western Sectors of the city and closed the autobahns, railways, and canals connecting our Sectors to the surrounding Soviet Zone. Traffic cannot move either in or out of Berlin.

"While we believe that these measures are ultimately directed at us, the civilian population of Berlin is directly and immediately affected. After all, we can and have supplied the British garrison by air." He nodded acknowledgement to the RAF as he spoke. "However, the current measures deny the *entire* civilian population in the three Western Sectors of all supplies necessary for survival. It is easy to focus on food, but the issue is not one of food alone. Medicines and medical equipment, clothing, soap, detergent and disinfectant, lavatory paper, newspapers, not to mention the raw materials necessary to keep factories operating -- everything -- is impacted."

"However, as noted earlier, the most dangerous aspect of this current situation is that the Soviets have stopped supplying electricity from their Sector and the surrounding Zone."

That was indeed the point, Priestman thought to himself. He had never expected nor planned for a situation without adequate energy.

Herbert was continuing, "You will remember that the Soviets dismantled the only modern power plant in Berlin before we were allowed into the city. Although plans to build a new generating facility have been approved, construction has not begun. The existing power stations in our Sectors are obsolete and cannot meet demand. Furthermore, it is impossible to produce electricity even at these inadequate levels without coal, and coal deliveries have also been suspended. The Berlin Electrical Works informed us this morning that with electricity cut to the absolute minimum, existing coal reserves will be depleted in ten days. Without electricity, the city's underground and trams cannot operate, the water pumping stations cannot function, and the sewage plants will shut down." The audience stirred uneasily.

Hebert continued. "Deliveries of liquid fuels have likewise been suspended. Without liquid fuels, the city's buses cannot move. Last but not least, none of the factories can operate without coal, electricity or diesel power, so people will soon be out of work."

One of the officers asked. "Do we have any idea how long this could last?"

"No, but we must assume that the Soviets know exactly what our coal, fuel, and food reserves are. They know that within two weeks, everything will effectively stop running. I think we can presume that they are prepared to keep this up for two weeks or more."

"Do we know what London is thinking?"

"Would you care to answer that, Mr Cartwright?" Colonel Herbert directed the question to the gentleman from the Foreign Office.

"At this point, London is still digesting the news, sir. I expect there will be consultations with the Americans and French before a final position is announced. Meanwhile, it is safe to say that, while we will not retreat with our tails between our legs, neither can we resolve the impasse with force. In short, only a diplomatic solution is possible. The Soviets are betting on the fact that — because we won't let more than two million people starve — we will withdraw gracefully. But if we *do* attempt to stay, they have created a situation which is designed to turn the Germans against us.

"The very fact that Soviet and SED radio stations are spreading rumours of riots, reveals Soviet expectations. The Soviets believe that the measures they have taken will cause the German population to protest against our presence. They've failed to convince the Germans to vote for Communism, and they most emphatically failed to stop them from taking our money. They're last hope for turning the Berliners against us by creating a situation in which the Germans suffer for our rights. The plan is not without its merits," he concluded as if he almost admired the Soviets.

Shortly afterwards the meeting broke up, and as Priestman rose to leave, Air Commodore Waite stopped him. "Stay a moment, if you would please, Wing Commander."

Priestman dutifully waited as the others departed although baffled by Waite's request. Herbert looked from Waite to Priestman and back again.

"I wanted to return to the topic we discussed yesterday, General," Waite addressed Herbert. "If you don't mind, I'd like to show you some calculations I've completed in the meantime."

General Herbert looked displeased but acceded. Waite pushed three sheets of paper over the table towards him. With a closed pen, he tapped on one sheet. "Now, here you see a breakdown of the supplies we've been bringing in every day by road, rail and barge — general categories, tonnages etc. Here you see some calculations of minimum daily requirements for basic goods: primarily food, fuel and other absolute necessities. And here are some estimates of what could be delivered by air." As he said the latter he glanced at Priestman. To Herbert, he added, "I'm not saying this would be easy or that an airlift could fully replace surface transport, but every 100 tons of food or fuel we fly in postpones the date at which our reserves run out. An airlift would buy us time to negotiate."

Herbert's face was eloquently sceptical, but he did Waite the courtesy of looking over his documents before announcing with a sigh, "I don't think it can be done, Air Commodore, but I'm not going to stand in your way if you wish to present these figures to General Robertson."

"Thank you, sir!" Waite responded with evident relief, collecting his papers again, and withdrawing with Priestman in his wake.

In the outer office, Priestman asked softly, "What was that all about?"

"When you asked me to support your request for a concrete runway, you left me with some estimates of the impact the runway would have on Gatow's capacity to receive cargo. Those numbers proved that the concrete runway would eliminate our vulnerability to Soviet interdiction of the access routes."

"My calculations did not include flying in coal to run the powerplants, and furthermore were for maintaining our *garrison,*" Priestman protested, "*Two thousand* men and their dependents — not more than two million people!"

"Quite right. I understand. But I took your numbers, added the capacity of Tempelhof and then did some calculations on just how often a heavy transport would have to land to meet the needs of the civilian population. When I learned the electricity had been shut down as well, I crunched the numbers again, adding in coal transport. I'd like you to look my numbers over and see if have made any glaring errors." He handed Priestman his sheets of paper.

Standing where he was, Priestman scanned Waite's numbers. He shook his head as he finished, "Rex, my calculations were based on having a concrete runway, and I don't have one yet. All I have at the moment is a perfectly level, 2000-foot-long hole in the grass filled with rainwater. The concrete and the construction equipment were due to arrive by rail next week, but that is no longer going to happen."

Waite considered him and then said calmly. "I take your point, Robin, but we have to be creative and — given our other options — I think we have to give an airlift a try. As I said to General Herbert, it might just buy our diplomats the time they need to find a compromise. I'm confident we can find a way to complete your runway with equipment and concrete from Berlin. If we take your runway as a given, are the other calculations correct?"

Priestman nodded cautiously.

"Then you'll support me on this?"

Priestman nodded again, this time more firmly. Waite was right; there had to be concrete and construction equipment somewhere in Berlin. Most importantly, even if they could not supply the entire city, they could stretch the available supplies and buy time.

"General Robertson is, unfortunately, at our HQ in Bad Oeyenhausen today. Could you organize an aircraft for me?"

"Of course. You can have the Anson."

"I'd like you to come with me. As moral support — and because you know the situation at Gatow best."

"Of course. Do you want to join me in my car back to Gatow?"

"Yes, let's get this to Robertson as soon as possible."

The Mayor's Decision
Berlin-Schoeneberg

The Social Democratic faction of the Berlin City Council congregated spontaneously at Rathaus Schoeneberg, drawn by the need for solidarity and mutual support during this breaking crisis. Mostly, they clustered in Louise Schroeder's office, but some spilt out into the hallway. Jakob Liebherr went into the hall to stretch his legs, where he found Jeannette Wolfe standing by a window. She had cracked it open to allow the smoke from her cigarette to escape and smiled sheepishly at Jakob. "I know, 100 Reichsmarks going up in smoke."

An ugly bruise on her temple and the cane she was leaning on testified to the previous day's riot. Liebherr noted, too, that the hand holding the cigarette was trembling. He understood. She was more shaken today than she had been in the midst of the attack. Yesterday, her outrage had overwhelmed her fear; today the full measure of the antisemitism and violence had sunk into her consciousness.

Liebherr deflected the conversation away from what was weighing on their minds. "What's the black-market rate for D-Marks today? Are people speculating on the rapid withdrawal of the Western Allies and anxious to get rid of their D-Marks?"

"You want to know the exchange rate of D-Marks to wallpaper marks or dollars?" Wolfe asked back with a raised eyebrow.

"Wallpaper marks? Is that what the Berliners call the new Soviet currency?" Liebherr asked, amused.

"Yes, or the sticker mark — for the little stickers the Soviets glued on the old Reichsmarks. The glue isn't very good, and the stickers fall off and can easily be counterfeited, I'm told."

"And the exchange rate?" Jakob pressed her.

"One to five, last I heard."

Liebherr would have liked to know if the D-Mark was trending up or down, but a young man flung himself out of one of the offices farther down the hall and shouted: "Colonel Howley's on the air! He's making a statement on RIAS!"

In a swarm, they surged toward the office where the young man turned up the volume on the radio to the maximum. The voice of the American commandant crackled over the airwaves. "...are hogwash. My wife isn't packing her silver! The Americans are *not* leaving Berlin. Period. I don't know how we're going to resolve this situation, but this much I do know: The American people are not going to stand by and allow German people to starve."

The American Colonel paused while an interpreter delivered his words in clipped German. Then he continued: "And now I will give the Russians something to chew on besides black bread. If you try to come into our Sector, we are ready for you — and believe me, many a comrade will go across the golden Volga."

"He's bluffing," Wolfe murmured into Jakob's ear, while the translator delivered Howley's words in German.

Liebherr glanced at the white-haired, Jewish survivor of the Thousand Year Reich. "Of course, he's bluffing, but his heart is in the right place. That's the kind of defiant spirit we need right now. It was a strong statement of commitment."

"I agree," Reuter spoke up. He was standing directly behind Liebherr and Wolfe. "That was the strongest statement yet."

"Certainly better than General Robertson's 'Steps are being taken to address this emergency' without a clue as to *what* steps," Wolfe complained.

"The French Foreign Ministry has also issued a statement saying the French plan to remain in Berlin." Schroeder pointed out.

"*For now*. None of them has said anything about how they intend to feed us or keep the electricity on, or the factories working…."

"Let's not complain," Reuter interceded. "All three Western Allies have issued statements of commitment to Berlin. That is the essential prerequisite to finding a solution to this crisis. We need to give them time to consider their options — and coordinate a response. It's time for *us* to do *our* part."

The others stared at him blankly.

"We should stage a rally. The SPD leadership must loudly and publicly protest against these cynical Soviet moves. We need to be sure that every Berliner knows exactly what is at stake. Berliners must be made to understand that this is nothing short of an attempt to force *us* — not the Allies but we Berliners — to accept Communist rule. It is an attempt to starve *us* into submission," the elected mayor reminded them forcefully.

"The reason the Soviets want the Western Allies to withdraw is so they can fully control Berlin. Willy?" Reuter looked around for one of his assistants. "See if you can find us an appropriate venue — the Olympic Stadium or the Hertha Sports Stadium. Somewhere big enough for 50,000 people to gather. Once we have a venue, ask RIAS to start broadcasting the message: All freedom-loving Berliners are to gather at five-thirty this afternoon to demonstrate their refusal to submit."

"Do you seriously think 50,000 people will gather on a day like this?" Louise asked with a glance out of the window. The beautiful sunny day had given way to low cloud cover from which a steady drizzle fell dolefully.

"We shall see. If people care more about their bellies than their future, it's better to find out now rather than later. I, for one, don't think that is the case. For the last three years, the Soviets and the SED have been bribing people with better rations, clothing coupons, and a host of other privileges while threatening and intimidating anyone who resisted the bribes. What have they reaped? One in five votes! Eighty per cent of Berlin's population isn't buying their lies. We owe it to that 80% to say we have heard them. We need to state clearly and plainly that we're not going to lie down and let the Soviets walk all over us."

The men and women around him murmured their support, glad to have something to do in a situation where, in fact, they were completely helpless.

An Alternative Option
British Military Government HQ,
Bad-Oeyenhausen near Hanover, British Zone

General Robertson burst into the outer office of his HQ at Bad Oeyenhausen, a pre-occupied and angry expression on his usually mild and dignified features. He was slightly flushed and did not welcome the presence of two unexpected RAF officers in his anteroom.

He acknowledged their presence with a curt, "Air Commodore, Wing Commander." Waite and Priestman had come to their feet respectfully, but the General's expression discouraged any pleasantries. "I presume you've come to see me, so you might as well come on in," Robertson conceded and preceded them into his office, angrily dumping his battered briefcase onto a leather chair beside his desk. Priestman, entering last, closed the door behind them.

Robertson glared at the two RAF officers and then admitted candidly. "You've caught me at rather a bad moment, I'm afraid. I'm just back from a meeting with General Clay and the American General is threatening to punch his way down the autobahn by force. He was talking about two hundred lorries escorted by an engineer battalion to eliminate any 'technical difficulties' — and riflemen to shoot any Russians who might try to stop them. It would be an outright provocation, and it would trigger war. I told him flatly that HM's government would not support such a measure."

Although Robertson's words were forceful, his expression was uneasy. In the circumstances, he could not have had a chance to consult with London before making that statement to Clay. In a situation fraught with such severe political implications, no general liked to act without his government's backing.

Waite and Priestman exchanged a look, and then Waite moved closer to Robertson's desk. "Maybe there is an alternative, sir. We've been working on some calculations," as he advanced, he pulled his three sheets of paper out of his breast pocket and unfolded them. "I admit these figures are very rough, and there is much that would have to be adjusted and modified as things play out, but they show that an all-out effort by RAF Transport Command could move up to 2,000 tons of goods into Berlin each day by air."

"Two thousand tons? A day?" Robertson sounded incredulous and glanced at Priestman for confirmation.

"Yes, sir. And that's just the RAF. We believe the USAF has considerably greater capacity. They have a large fleet of four-engine Skymasters which can carry 10 tons and a few C-74 Globemasters with twice that capacity. Together we should be able to deliver 4,500 tons of goods a day — the absolute minimum, as you see on the second sheet, needed to supply the civilian population at minimum levels."

Robertson glanced at Priestman. "Can Gatow handle the traffic?"

"Assuming we can complete the new concrete runway, triple the number of Air Traffic Controllers, build additional hard-standings, and install night lighting as well as deploy either army transport staff or local civilians for off-loading, there's no inherent reason why we couldn't handle the volume of air traffic Air Commodore Waite is talking about."

Robertson was frowning. "Those were a lot of assumptions, Wing Commander!" He snapped tetchily. "Aren't you assuming rather too much — including that everything will go like clockwork? By the ribbons you're wearing, you ought to know that things never go according to plan in the real world. What happens when one of your aircraft crashes, or just gets stuck in the mud and blocks the runway? And if we don't have electricity, how do you keep the lights on and the radar and R/T working?"

"You're absolutely correct, General," Waite replied smoothly diverting Robertson's wrath, "Nothing will go exactly according to plan. But what are our alternatives? You have already rejected Clay's idea of an armed convoy."

"Most definitely!"

"Are you suggesting we should withdraw from Berlin?" Waite pitched the question perfectly, Priestman thought, without a hint of sarcasm or rebuke.

Robinson scowled and snapped back, "That's not my decision to make." For a moment, he faced them grimly, his teeth clenched under his moustache, his fingers drumming on his desk. They waited tensely

442

as he mentally reviewed his options. Finally, he drew a deep breath and announced. "I suppose it doesn't matter if it can work in the long run or not. An airlift is a damn sight better than shooting our way across the Soviet Zone and starting a war! But the Americans must be on board with this, so we'll have to pitch the idea to General Clay."

He picked up the phone and asked for a connection to his American counterpart. While waiting for the call to go through, he covered the receiver and addressed Waite. "Whether the Americans embrace this action or not, I'll pass your proposal to Air Marshal Sanders immediately. The sooner we start working on it, the better and the more leverage we'll have with Clay and Koenig." Waite nodded and would have spoken but Robertson held up his hand for silence as something was said into the phone at the other end. "What? Already? Damn! Thank you!" He hung up and announced. "Clay has already left Heidelberg for Berlin."

Robertson looked at his watch. "Let's drop by Air Marshal Sanders' office and then we can fly together to Berlin and approach Clay there."

America Speaks
Berlin-Tempelhof

The SPD rally had been called for 17:30, the same time that General Clay's aircraft was scheduled to land at Tempelhof; Vee Cox had opted to meet Clay's plane. Clay, however, was delayed and while waiting for him she listened to RIAS. Reporting from the Hertha Sports Stadium, an enthusiastic radio journalist reported that the stadium was overflowing. He claimed 80,000 people or more had responded to Mayor Reuter's summons. They were giving the speakers an enthusiastic response. Vee began to regret her decision to come to Tempelhof. Eighty-thousand people shouting defiance at the Soviets was a great story. She looked at her watch, wondering if she had time to get to the stadium and catch the end of the rally. She could interview people coming out, get a sampling of public opinion, the "man-in-the-street" perspective perhaps?

Her thoughts were interrupted by her colleague Margaret Higgins of the New York Herald Tribune. "That's General Clay's plane now," the American journalist gestured toward a USAF Dakota taxiing toward the terminal.

Tempelhof terminal was a massive Nazi structure with five floors both above and below ground. It was also more than a kilometre long and curved gently, embracing the northwest corner of the airfield. Along the length of the terminal, tall windows provided vistas of the field, hangars and aircraft movements. A concrete canopy stretched over the apron so passengers could disembark without getting wet in the rain. The Nazis had understood a thing or two about airport construction, Vee admitted grudgingly.

The two women journalists watched as the Dakota decorously taxied up to the apron and then swung about to stand sideways to the terminal. The pitch of the engines dropped sharply and the airscrews started to wind down.

"What questions do you want to ask Clay?" Vee asked her colleague. Because their male colleagues didn't treat Higgins or Cox as equals — much less "one of the boys" — the only two women in the press pool had forged an informal alliance.

"Everybody's been focusing on '*will*' the Allies stay. What I want to know is *how*? What about you?"

"Well, I'd like more clarity on how long existing supplies can last and if they couldn't be stretched by bringing things in by air?" Vee admitted.

"Air? Seriously? You think that might be possible?'

"I don't know, but why not?"

Higgins shrugged. "OK, let's ask! Whichever one of us gets Clay's attention puts that question to him. Deal?"

"Absolutely."

A gaggle of journalists awaited the American Military Governor as he came into the waiting area. Cameras flashed loudly, and questions were flung at him from all sides. Vee had never seen him look so tired or so grim, yet he lifted his chin and declared firmly and loudly. "The Russians are trying to make us uncomfortable — but they can't drive us out of Berlin by anything short of war."

That sounded like an echo of Colonel Howley's earlier statement, but the journalists weren't satisfied. "General, just how do you intend to feed over two million people, if you can't bring supplies in from the Western Zones?"

"Our right to transit the Soviet Zone was established and recognised before the War ended," Clay reminded them. "We will exercise our rights."

That sounded nice, Vee thought, but it didn't answer the question.

"Does that mean you are prepared to use force to get convoys and trains through? To risk war?"

"I think we all need to keep things in perspective," Clay told the reporters in a patient voice. "We know the Soviets would like to see us, along with our British and French friends, out of Berlin. But the Soviets don't want war any more than we do. These new measures were meant to make us panic and go home. Well, we aren't panicking, and we aren't going home. So, the Soviets will come to their senses and face reality. We aren't leaving. Period." Clay clearly wanted this to be his last word. He made a salute-like gesture directed at the room at large, then lowered his head so the visor of his military cap covered his eyes as he walked vigorously toward the exit.

Vee wormed her way through the throng of journalists to put herself in Clay's path, but Margaret Higgins opted to raise her voice and call across the heads of her fellow journalists: "General! General! Just one more question!"

Because it was a lady asking, Clay paused and looked over expectantly.

"Would it be possible to supply Berlin's population with its needs by air alone?" Higgins asked.

"Absolutely not!" Clay answered definitively and continued on his way.

A Change of Heart
Berlin-Dahlem

It was nearly midnight before Clay's car pulled up outside his home on the quiet residential street Im Dol in Berlin-Dahlem. The sight of a British car with the fender flags of the British Military Governor elicited a weary sigh from the American General. His wife met him as he entered and told him that General Robertson and two RAF officers were waiting to see him in the living room. He nodded and handed her his cap.

As he entered the living room, the British officers got to their feet and Clay acknowledged them by asking, "What are you drinking, gentlemen? Because whatever it is, I'll join you."

"Lucius, believe me, I wouldn't be here at this time of night if I didn't think this was important," Sir Brian replied.

"I understand, Brian. Kentucky Bourbon?" He asked holding up a bottle.

"Yes, thank you," all three British officers agreed in unison.

Clay poured for them and for himself and then sank on the sofa and stretched out his legs. He looked utterly exhausted, and his eyes were sunk deep in their darkened sockets.

"Been talking to Washington?" Robertson asked in an understanding tone.

"It would be one thing if the State Department was afraid. Caution is what one expects of diplomats, but the Secretary of the Army is no damned better! They started asking me if we couldn't roll back the currency reform!" He paused, glanced at Waite and Priestman and noted. "What I say in this room doesn't leave this room, understood?"

"Yes, sir," Waite and Priestman agreed in unison.

"We can't," Robertson answered the substance of Clay's remark.

"No, we can't, we shouldn't, and we won't," Clay agreed. "What I don't understand is that Washington could even broach the topic! We talked through the needs and risks of the currency reform ten thousand times *before* we implemented it. It's as if they don't listen to a goddam thing I say! We knew the Ruskies were going to be hopping mad. We knew they'd try something. But we also know they aren't ready for war and every intelligence source we have says they don't *want* one either — at least not yet."

"Quite right, but they are very thin-skinned, arrogant and quick to bluster. Anger and boasts can all too easily spiral out of control. There is always the risk that the Ivans will start to believe their propaganda and allow things to escalate. We don't need to respond like frightened rabbits, but we mustn't do anything provocative either." Robertson reiterated his position.

Clay sat nursing his bourbon, his expression sour yet resigned. Washington had punched most of the fight out of him.

Robertson reached over and lightly touched his knee. "Lucius, I want you to listen to what Air Commodore Waite has to say." Robertson gestured for Waite to take over.

Waite launched into his short presentation, with Priestman chiming in at appropriate moments without prompting. Clay looked from one to the other, his bourbon in his hand. He was slouching more than sitting on his sofa, and he was far too tired to muster any enthusiasm, but when they finished speaking he didn't look quite as discouraged.

He looked Waite straight in the eye. "Do you honestly think this can be done? Supplying more than two million people with all the things they need — food, fuel, medicines, toiletries, clothing and the rest?"

"Sir, I'm not suggesting they can be supplied with *all* the things they need. But I do believe we can airlift in survival levels of essentials during the summer months when the days are long and the weather generally good. I admit an airlift won't be sustainable through the winter. But it could buy us a few weeks, possibly a month or two, time in which we have a chance to work something out with the Soviets."

Clay turned to Robertson. "What does your government say to the whole thing?"

"You want the exact words of my instructions?" Roberson asked.

Clay just waited with raised eyebrows in anticipation.

"'Do the best you can.' I kid you not."

Clay laughed. "They want you to improvise."

"We did it at Dunkirk," Robertson retorted with a touch of pride in his tone. It wasn't until that moment that Priestman knew that Robertson had truly bought into the idea and would back them 100%. Meanwhile, Clay lifted his glass in salute and drank deeply.

Robertson continued seriously. 'We're going ahead, Lucius. HQ RAF Transport Command has promised that squadrons of freighters will start deploying to Wunstorf tomorrow morning. We'll keep building up the fleet as Gatow's capacity to receive the cargo increases. That means getting more air traffic controllers, installing more lighting, and completing the concrete runway currently under construction. It might take a week or more to get things fully running, but meanwhile, we'll be bringing in enough cargo to push back the date when Berlin runs out of anything essential."

Clay shook his head ambiguously. Then he drained his tumbler to the bottom and declared. "We'll do it — but only if the Berliners are prepared to face the hardships that will go with it. I don't want us flying our guts out only to face riots because the Berliners think they aren't getting enough of something."

Chapter Eighteen
Taking a Stand

A Meeting with the Military Governor
Berlin-Kreuzberg/Dahlem
Friday, 25 June 1948

Reuter called Liebherr to announce, "Jakob, General Clay has requested my presence in his office at 10 am."

Liebherr started in astonishment. Clay, as Military Governor, was responsible for all American-occupied territories and did not normally deal with the Berlin City Council directly. Up to now, they had always met with the American Commandant Colonel Howley. On the other end of the line, Reuter was saying, "I'd like you to come with me. Can you meet me at Rathaus Schoeneberg in the next half hour?"

"I'll do by best."

Under normal circumstances, the U-bahn or subway was the fastest means of getting anywhere, but the blockade-induced power cuts had completely disrupted schedules. Liebherr asked Horst whether he could reach Rathaus Schoeneberg by milk cart in half an hour. The old coachman said he'd try.

Dressed in his best suit, Liebherr climbed up beside the coachman as they trotted along the Landwehr canal and turned south on Mehringdamm. He noted the absence of traffic except for an unusual number of American jeeps. The GIs were kitted out in combat gear and had rifles over their shoulders. So far, despite reports of Soviet troop and tank movements in the surrounding Zone, the Soviets had not sent additional troops into Berlin.

But if the streets were empty, the sidewalks were full. Some people hurried along to their destination, but many more stood about talking. The gesturing and uneasy body language suggested the discussions were animated and intense. Liebherr heard no laughter, saw no smiles and children were scarce.

Liebherr tried to pay Horst when they arrived at the Rathaus, but the coachman waved the offer aside. "Just get the Ivans to open the border again," he demanded.

"Do you want the Western Allies to pull out?" Liebherr asked, always interested in the opinions of the 'average' Berliner.

"Are you out of your mind?" Horst asked back flabbergasted. "I didn't bury the good baron, his wife and two friends just to surrender to the damn Ivans! I'd rather die fighting than submit to those bastards!"

"Well, let's hope it won't come to that," Liebherr answered.

Reuter and his aide Willy Brandt were already waiting for Liebherr out front. He smiled inwardly to find Reuter wearing his iconic brown beret and tweeds rather than a formal business suit. Liebherr supposed he wanted to signal to the American General that he was not awed by his invitation.

Louise Schroeder came down to see them off with the reminder, "Be sure the General understands that while we've had no riots yet, we *will* have them if supplies don't start to flow. People don't have any reserves — not in their pantries or on their bodies." She was right, of course; most Berliners were already underweight.

The three men climbed into Reuter's rundown Opel, with Brandt behind the steering wheel and Reuter and Liebherr in the back. Riding headlong toward a date with destiny altered perceptions, Liebherr noted. Petty concerns and mundane thoughts evaporated. Looking out of the window, he seemed to be wearing new eyeglasses; his vision had become clearer. In the densely populated boroughs of Schoeneberg and Wilmersdorf, he noticed that the heaps of rubble were smaller than he remembered them. He registered that life was returning with greater energy than he recalled. Shops and restaurants had sprouted up like blades of grass in a desert. After they passed under the autobahn and S-bahn bridges to turn onto the broad Hohenzollerndamm, however, the American military presence became ominously dominant. By the time they reached the imposing complex built to house Luftwaffe Military District III HQ, Liebherr felt the same queasy feeling he had known on the eve of the last war. Not again, he found himself thinking. Weren't two world wars more than enough for any man's lifetime?

The grey buildings in the monumental style of the Third Reich had survived the war almost intact. A barbed wire fence 12 feet tall and patrols of armed American soldiers protected it. A Sherman tank and a jeep with a manned machine gun flanked the gate. The alert and punctilious guards at the gatehouse carefully checked the IDs handed over by the Germans, and an American MP directed the city council members to a parking place in the shadow of two large anti-aircraft guns. Although the flagpole flying the American flag rose high above the guns, Liebherr was uncomfortable. He and his colleagues were the only men in civilian clothes in the complex.

The MP led them inside, along corridors and up a set of stairs to Clay's office on the second floor. Soldiers with weapons had given way to officers carrying briefcases, manila folders, and telegrams. The sound of clacking typewriters escaped from every door they passed. Liebherr felt as if he were in the centre of a beehive, with the khaki-clothed American military men buzzing around him.

At last, they were ushered into a large waiting room with several sofas, coffee tables and two secretaries at desks flanking the room like sentries. All the other men waiting in the outer office were American officers. One of the officers politely moved so they could sit together around one of the coffee tables. Liebherr glanced at the magazines offered: *Life, Time, Saturday Evening Post, Newsweek*. Newspapers displayed large headlines: "Berlin under Siege!" and "Russians Strangle Berlin!"

Liebherr picked up one of the papers. The front page story claimed that the Berliners "were not physically or emotionally equipped to withstand a siege." The American newspaper predicted the Berliners would "crack." Silently, he passed the newspaper to Reuter. Reuter snorted in disgust.

A smart, young officer with trouser creases so sharp they looked as though they might draw blood, came out of the General's office, "Mayor Reuter?"

Reuter got to his feet. "That's me."

"General Clay will see you now, sir." The young officer indicated the open door and the Germans filed through.

General Clay came around his desk to meet them but indicated that Reuter should take a seat in a well-padded leather chair before his desk while two additional, less comfortable, chairs were found for Liebherr and

Brandt.

"Mayor Reuter, thank you for joining me this morning at such short notice. I thought it was important that we speak face-to-face about the current situation."

"I'm delighted to have the opportunity, General," Reuter replied with a smile.

"Yes, well, you've probably read in the newspapers that I have promised the US will remain in Berlin and not be pushed out by any measures short of war. Now, I have to say, that what was printed in the newspaper was taken a little out of context. At no time did I wish to imply that we would stay here regardless of what the Berliners want or that we would insist on our rights at the price of intolerable hardships for the civilian population."

"I did not misunderstand your intentions for a moment, General," Reuter assured him.

"Now, although I believe we might be able to force our way through to Berlin with an armed convoy, there are risks associated with such a tactic. So, before we try that, we're looking at something else. Namely, while I may be the craziest man in the world, I'm going to try to supply this city by air."

Liebherr was stunned and looked over at Reuter and Brandt to judge their reaction. They looked as dumbstruck as he was. Clay continued, "Obviously, there is no way we'll be able to supply the city at the same levels as before, but we think we can fly in enough essentials to make immediate surrender unnecessary. What I'm trying to say, is that an airlift could buy us time for negotiating with the Russians, but if we do that the Berliners are in for a rough time. They're going to have only sporadic electricity and minimal public transport, and they're going to have to live on things like powdered milk and powdered eggs. Unless the Berliners are willing to put up with all that, there's no point in trying to call the Soviet bluff at all."

Reuter opened his mouth to speak, but Clay didn't notice and continued firmly. "I honestly don't think the Soviets intend to let more than two million Berliners starve, but if we're going to make them back down, we're going to have to show them we're determined to stay. I'm prepared to do that, but only if it is what the Berliners *want*. What I'm trying to say is we're only going to go through with this, if the Berliners can and will take it." At last, Clay paused with his eyes fixed on Reuter.

Reuter nodded. "General, I can assure you, and I do assure you, that the Berliners will take it. After yesterday's rally, there can be no question of where the Berliners stand. They will make sacrifices. They will resist Soviet pressure. They will fight for their freedom in any way they can and for as long as they can."

"Thank you, Mayor. That was a firm commitment, and I appreciate it." General Clay nodded, but he wasn't finished. "In that case, we need to discuss how and who sets the priorities. I do not think it appropriate or practical that my headquarters, or any other body associated with the occupation authorities, dictates things like meat versus bread, coal versus food, medicine versus milk and so on. It seems to me, Mayor, that it would be more appropriate for the elected government of Berlin to determine demand by category and to set priorities. In coordination with our allies, the American military government will do all in its power to undertake the transportation of those items that *you* identify as essential, and we will do so in accordance with the priorities that *you* set — to the best of our abilities. Do you agree with that?"

Liebherr noted that this was a cunning move to shift some of the blame for shortfalls onto the civilian government, but it was only fair. If the Allies, their former enemies, determined needs and set priorities, people were more likely to suspect a lack of goodwill or devious ulterior motives.

Reuter, meanwhile, had already smiled and responded. "Absolutely, General. The City Council will undertake to do exactly that, and we will do it promptly," Reuter promised. Meeting and holding General Clay's gaze, Reuter concluded, "You see to the airlift, General, and I'll handle the Berliners."

Clay considered that and smiled faintly as he nodded. "Very good, Mayor Reuter. That's a deal." General Clay rose to his feet and offered Reuter his hand.

Reuter and his companions stood, shook hands with the American General and departed. They did not speak while they were escorted back through the rabbit warren of corridors to their car. Only as they drove off in the old Opel did Reuter turn to his companions to declare: "Clay's determination is wonderful!" He paused, shook his head and added, "I just don't believe it can be done."

"Neither do I," Liebherr agreed. "But we're lucky they're willing to try."

Good-Byes
RAF Gatow
Saturday, 26 June 1948

A heavy shower darkened the sky and Galyna reached over to turn on her desk lamp. It was almost two pm and most of her fellow translators had gone off duty an hour ago since it was Saturday afternoon. Only a couple of the German translators lingered in the other room talking in low, worried tones. Galyna sighed as she looked over the long article in *Pravda* that she wanted to finish before leaving. It was so tedious that she couldn't concentrate. Always the same rubbish, she thought with disgust. The same hackneyed phrases, the same bombast, the same hate. She was sick of it. Why weren't the people in the Soviet Union sick of it, too?

Did they seriously believe that the West wanted to destroy the Soviet Union? Surely it was obvious that if they wanted that, they would have supported Hitler. They could have sent Hitler the guns, jeeps, trucks, tanks and aircraft that had been sent to the Soviet Union instead. Or the West could have remained neutral and let the Soviet people starve. Or if the West was still intent on destroying the Soviet Union, all they need do was drop an atomic bomb on Moscow.

On top of fabricating a Western threat that did not exist, the voice of the Communist Party of the Soviet Union insisted on whining and whimpering about being a victim. Poor us! Poor Russia! Poor Socialist Motherland! Always the victim of brutal aggression and evil plots. Yet it shouldn't take a genius to notice that victims don't get bigger and stronger. The Soviet Union was expanding rapidly — across the Baltic States and into Poland, setting up puppet regimes in Hungary and Czechoslovakia and Germany — or as much of Germany as they controlled.

Did anyone in Moscow seriously think that the Soviet Union was *forced* to cut Berlin off from all supplies in "self-defence"?

No. The answer was much simpler. For *Pravda* and therefore for the Communist Party and the Soviet state, there *was* no blockade. Just "technical difficulties."

Disgusted, Galyna pushed her pad of paper away and rolled her shoulders to ease the tension. Maybe she should leave the translation until Monday? Who cared about such drivel?

No, she stopped herself. She had told Flight Lieutenant Boyd that she wanted to be more than a translator; she was on informal probation for the intelligence branch. She had to prove she could do more than produce a perfect translation. She had to show she could filter out the window dressing and boilerplate language to recognise the subtle hints hidden underneath. She had to prove she could detect a change of policy or tactics signalled by some unusual turn of phrase. It was like looking for clues in a treasure hunt. While possible to find, one had to be patient and meticulous.

A telephone started jingling, and Galyna reached across the desk opposite hers to pick up the receiver. "Translation."

Only silence greeted her.

"Hello? This is the translation section. Is someone there?"

"Galyna Nicholaevna?" A female voice whispered her name.

"Yes. This is Corporal Borisenko."

"Galyna! Thank God! I was afraid I'd miss you!" Only now did Galyna recognise the breathless voice of Mila Mikhailivna.

"Mila?" She asked just to be sure.

"I'm calling from a public phone box," came the whispered answer. "I don't dare speak any louder."

"Is something wrong?" Galyna asked alarmed.

"I just — I wanted to say how much our friendship meant to me. I'm so glad we met. I will always remember you."

"Mila! Where are you going? Are they sending you back to the Soviet Union?"

"No, no, but you will be leaving soon. I was afraid we might not have a chance to talk before you go."

"What makes you think I'm leaving?" Galyna asked bewildered.

"You'll all be going," Mila answered. "They're saying in a week or two at most."

"We're not going, Mila," Galyna told her firmly.

"No! Galyna, don't be stupid or stubborn. Go! Please!"

"Both the British and American governments have announced they will not withdraw from Berlin."

"Galyna! Don't you see how foolish that is? If you stay, you'll be crushed. I don't want to think what could happen to you! Please, Galyna, even if the others stay, find a way to go. Say you are sick or your grandmother is sick or something! Anything to make them send you to safety, back to England. Please!"

Before Galyna could answer, Mila gasped. "I have to go!" and hung up. The dial tone droned in Galyna's ear. Slowly, still in a daze, she replaced the receiver. Was Mila being used to spread fear among the British, or was she genuinely concerned for Galyna's safety?

Galyna closed her notebook and put her pencil and erasers away. She left the office closing the door behind her and made her way to Flight Lieutenant Boyd's office. Unsurprisingly, he was still working, and he invited her into his office. She explained what had just transpired, and he told her to sit down.

"What's your gut feeling, Borisenko? Do you think Mila's a Soviet agent?"

"No, I don't," Galyna answered without hesitation. "I know that may make me seem naïve, but I don't." Galyna hoped her conviction would not spoil her chances of being considered for intelligence work.

Boyd drew a breath to answer but was cut off when the door opened and the WingCo walked in. Boyd and Borisenko sprang to their feet.

"Am I interrupting something?" the WingCo asked.

"Only something you should know about anyway," Boyd answered, summarizing the situation, and ending with, "We were just discussing if the information was planted or not."

"Um," the WingCo nodded but then remarked, "If it was, what could they hope to achieve? Threats like this aren't going to budge HM's government. Might they undermine morale?" He looked at Galyna. "Are you frightened, Corporal? Do you want a transfer out?"

"No, sir!" Galyna assured him, hot with indignation. For the first time in her life, she felt she was in an important job with the chance of fighting back against the regime that had killed her father. She was not going to run away!

"Corporal, I'm asking you because I will take a dim view of requests for transfer at this time. However, because you would be treated as a traitor if you fell into Soviet hands, and the Soviet state does not treat traitors kindly, you are an exception. If you wish to leave Berlin, I will authorize a posting elsewhere."

Galyna shook her head. "I do not want to leave, sir. I'm tired of running away. I'm tired of them getting their way in everything. I want to fight back, and I think I can do that best by staying here." She glanced a little nervously at Ft/Lt Boyd as she concluded, but he nodded encouragingly.

"Well said, Borisenko," the WingCo replied. Then he nodded once and withdrew saying, "Come see me when you're finished here, Boyd."

Boyd turned to Galyna. "Is there anything to add?"

She shook her head.

"In that case, have a seat and draft a memcon — that's a memorandum-of-conversation — noting everything that was said in your telephone call with Mila Mikhailivna as exactly as you can remember it. I'll go see what the WingCo wanted, but if you finish before I come back, please wait for me." He paused and then added, "I do hope you know what you're getting yourself into."

"Yes, sir!" Galyna assured him, but as she began to write her report, she felt a chill run down her spine. Was it ever possible to know what we are getting ourselves into?

Choices
RAF Gatow
Saturday, 26 June 1948

It was after 10 pm before Kathleen let herself into her flat. It had been one of the most exhausting days of her career, and she couldn't decide if she needed sleep or the proverbial "soaking glass of wet" first. The sight of her daughter standing in her nightie at the doorway to her bedroom banished all other thoughts.

"Hope! Sweetheart! What's the matter?" She rushed to her child and swept her into her arms. Hope's face was wet with tears. "Hope! What is it?"

"Don't send me away, Mummy! Please don't send me away! I don't want to go back to Grandma. I want to stay here with you."

How on earth had Hope learned or guessed that she might send her home? "Oh, sweetheart!" She hugged her and swung back and forth.

Hope started crying again. "I like it here, Mummy! I have lots of friends and Mrs Carter and Mrs Pierce are both so nice! And then there's Rosie!" Rosie was the pony she was learning to ride, which reminded Kathleen that Hope had her riding lesson tomorrow and she wasn't going to be able to take her to it. The station air traffic control unit was in an 'emergency modus.' They would be working sixteen-hour days until reinforcements arrived. At least the WingCo had promised a tripling of air traffic control personnel to enable three, eight-hour shifts a day, each manned by two controllers and two assistants. Once all were in place, things would be manageable, but it wasn't clear when the extra personnel would arrive. Meanwhile, Gatow was landing aircraft every fifteen minutes from six am to ten pm.

Kathleen sank exhausted onto the sofa in her sitting room and lifted Hope up beside her, pulling her close. She didn't want to frighten her child, but she had to make her understand why it was better for her to go back to the UK. "Sweetheart, the Russians have done a very bad thing. They won't let any food, fuel, or medicine into Berlin by train or lorry, so everything must be carried in aeroplanes."

"I know!" Hope told her frowning and using an irritated voice to protest being talked down to. "That's why there have been so many Daks flying in today. But they fly out empty," Hope informed her. "If it gets bad, we can fly out in them. None of the other children are leaving!" Hope's tone was reproachful.

"No, I know, sweetheart, but other children have Mummies to look after them, and I have to work very long hours. I won't be able to take you to your riding lesson tomorrow, for example."

Hope didn't like that. She frowned and kicked at the sofa in inarticulate frustration. Before Kathleen could say any more, however, loud, rapid knocking at the door made her flinch and call out in exasperation. "Who's there?"

"It's me! Natalie!"

Just what she didn't need, Kathleen thought. Natalie had been a bundle of nerves all day leading to mistakes. Fortunately, today they had been caught in time; another day they might not be so lucky. Natalie was becoming a serious liability, and Kathleen was in no mood to hear her apologies. "Can't this wait until tomorrow?" she called through the door.

"Please, Kathleen! I have to talk to you!"

With a sigh, Kathleen kissed Hope and asked her to go back to bed. "As soon as I'm done with Miss Natalie, I'll come and we can continue our talk. Then, if you like, you can sleep in my bed tonight."

Hope jumped down without answering and disappeared into her room. She didn't exactly slam the door behind her, but she closed it loudly enough to express displeasure. Kathleen mentally promised to make it up to Hope with some late-night hot chocolate and went to open the door to Natalie.

Her fellow WAAF burst in still in uniform and declared almost aggressively, "I can't take it anymore! I can't! You know how frazzled I've been ever since the BEA crash, but now, with all this traffic — There's going to be another crash. I know it. We can't handle aircraft every ten minutes as the CO wants!"

"That's only after the concrete runway is complete and we go on three shifts with double staffing," Kathleen reminded her.

"I don't care! Didn't you hear what Squadron Leader Garth said? For all our work and stress, we only landed 188 tonnes of supplies in Gatow today. The goal is 2,250! Twelve times as many aircraft, twenty-four times as many air movements! Kathleen, they're crazy! It can't be done."

"Yes it can, Natalie. You're not taking into account that the Yorks can carry three times as much cargo as the Daks."

"So, instead of twenty-four times as many movements it's only eight times as many. That's still crazy, Kathleen. We can't handle it." She paused and then corrected herself. "Well maybe you and Willi and Garth can handle it, but I can't!"

"Calm down, Natalie. Sit down and let me get you a drink," Kathleen indicated Natalie should take a seat on the sofa and went to her kitchenette to take down two tumblers. "Gin and tonic, all right?"

"Yes, fine," Natalie answered, and Kathleen poured for both of them. Returning to the sitting room, she found Natalie curled in the corner of the sofa with her shoulders hunched up and tears streaming down her face.

Kathleen sat beside her, pushed the glass of alcohol into her hand and

459

then put her free hand on Natalie's shoulder.

"I can't take it anymore!" Natalie repeated. Her tone was no longer belligerent just miserable. "It's not just that I want a posting away from Gatow, I want to change trades altogether. I want to get out of air traffic control and into something else — maybe maps or cypher work."

Kathleen drew a deep breath. Natalie had been hinting at this for three months, and Kathleen had advised her not to make a hasty decision. After three months, it wasn't 'hasty' any more. More importantly, in the current situation, they couldn't afford to have anyone in the tower who was as frayed and nervous as Natalie was. She was a danger to them all. If only she'd made this decision before the blockade had started and before the CO had announced he would not be accepting transfer requests.

Yet Kathleen guiltily acknowledged she was partially to blame for Natalie's delayed decision. She shouldn't have tried to talk her into staying. She should have let her go the first time she proposed getting out of ATC.

"Couldn't *you* request that I be posted?" Natalie asked softly. "If you and Squadron Leader Garth want me out of Gatow, the CO won't have any choice but to let me go."

"That would be a terrible black on your service record, Natalie," Kathleen reminded her.

"I can't go back to the tower, Kathleen! Either you help me or I'm going to just — break down."

Kathleen drew a deep breath and nodded. "I'll talk to Squadron Leader Garth first thing in the morning."

Natalie thanked her and Kathleen saw her out. Going to her daughter's room, she found Hope had already fallen asleep again, so she turned out her light and went to bed herself. Despite her exhaustion, she couldn't sleep.

Before making a more general announcement that transfers out of Berlin would not be entertained for the foreseeable future, the CO had called Kathleen into his office to say that she was one of his few exceptions. She *could* request a posting if she wanted. But the thought of being part of the largest airlift in history excited her. Squadron Leader Garth claimed that the need to funnel a large volume of traffic through limited air space would require innovation and creative thinking. "We're going to have the chance to experiment with and test new systems and methods for air traffic control," he'd announced with obvious keenness. Kathleen wanted to be part of that, but to do so she either had to send Hope home to her parents or put her at risk.

Her first instinct was to send Hope home, and no sensible woman should be swayed by a seven-year-old's tears and pleas. And yet, Hope had struck a nerve when she said none of the other children was going. The CO had been quite clear on that point. Dependents were not being evacuated. The school would remain open. Why should Hope be treated differently just because she didn't have a father? Hadn't she been uprooted often enough? She had made friends here and she was happy here — happier than at any time Kathleen could remember. Of course, there was a risk of something going wrong, but Kathleen had the utmost trust in the WingCo. He would get the children out, even if he and other officers were fighting alongside the RAF regiment at the perimeter.

The door opened and Hope slipped inside her room whining, "You said I could sleep in your bed tonight."

"Of course, sweetheart," Kathleen answered, moving over and opening the covers for her. Hope climbed in and snuggled close. They had started doing this more often ever since Lionel had left. Hope had been angry to learn that "Uncle Lionel" had another family in England. "I guess we were just substitutes!" she'd declared indignantly. Kathleen had teased her about "such a big word," but Hope had shrugged irritably and never mentioned Lionel again. Lionel's betrayal had brought them closer together, she reflected, and coming here had been the right decision in the first place. Staying together was just as important now, she concluded. They would both be happier that way. On this thought, she drifted off to sleep with her daughter cuddled happily in her arms.

Chapter Nineteen
Allies No More

The Devil in the Details
Berlin-Kreuzberg
Sunday, 27 June 1948

It was all very well for Mayor Reuter to promise General Clay that the City Council would determine the requirements of the civilian population but that was far easier said than done. How did the old expression go? The Devil was in the details.

It was not even clear what methodology they should apply. Did they start from the top down, looking at the average tonnage of goods by category that had been consumed in the past and reduce these by the same factor across the board until the total tonnage matched what the Allies believed they could airlift into the city? Or should they try to construct needs from the individual level to the aggregate?

The top-down approach did appear rational to Jakob. If nothing else, up to now many items such as fresh vegetables, milk and coal had been brought from the surrounding Soviet Zone rather than from the West. These items now had to be factored into the calculations, and coal was heavy. To make way for coal shipments, other items would have to be decreased or taken off the list altogether.

Jakob concluded it was better to work from the bottom up, calculating the absolute necessities for each human and then multiplying that by the number of inhabitants. The risk to that method was that it might produce astronomical numbers that the Allies could never put on aircraft. Still, he had to start somewhere.

Fuel requirements were the easiest to calculate. Everyone knew how much coal was needed to produce how much electricity and how much electricity was consumed to run a train from A to B, or to heat an oven or to light x-number of the streetlamps for y-number of hours. Berlin's electricity company had been tasked with breaking down their requirements into specific categories, with priority for sanitation, transportation and industry, while household needs came last in the ranking.

Calculating food requirements was trickier. Yes, the population lived on predetermined rations in which a set number of calories were derived from categories of food such as proteins, fats, sugar, carbohydrates etc. Yet problems remained. For example, was it more efficient to fly in processed meat, or to keep herds of animals alive by flying in feed for livestock? Ditto with butter and milk. Or what about bread? Flying in loaves of bread sounded silly since they were light and bulky *ergo* the capacity of the aircraft would not be utilised. On the other hand, baking bread in Berlin required not only importing the flour but also the coal to fire the bake ovens. Maybe not such a great idea after all....

Moving beyond food and fuel, how was one to calculate, say, clothing requirements? For example, not everyone needed a new pair of shoes each year, but *some* people had been wearing the same shoes for three, four or even five years. If their shoes wore out, replacing them was an absolute necessity. Likewise, blankets and overcoats might not sound like consumables, but the warmer people could dress, the less coal would be needed to heat their homes and workplaces. But making space for the clothing and blankets on transport aircraft meant there was less space for flying in coal.

Medicine and medical equipment likewise sounded uncontroversial — unless it would make more sense to fly the sick and injured out. Charlotte Walmsdorf's air ambulance couldn't take on the entire burden, obviously, but if the Allies were flying scores of planes into the city every day, then surely they could take sick people back out again? Or maybe not, Jakob reflected as he tried to imagine windowless freighters without seats packed with sick people. He couldn't remember ever seeing the inside of a cargo plane, but he knew what a freight-train hauling coal looked like. The coal dust got into everything. It was inconceivable that seriously ill patients — people with wounds that could get infected or people with congested lungs that would become clogged with coal dust — could be transported in an aircraft that had brought in coal. And going aboard after a load of dead fish or freshly butchered meat wasn't going to be much better. Jakob decided to defer thinking about that for a few more days.

Looking again at the list of categories in front of him, his eye fell on "paper". Now that was another ticklish issue. On the surface, paper sounded quite superfluous, but it wasn't. People needed to know what was going on, and that meant they needed newspapers. The Soviets were sure to print papers with their "facts" and these facts were guaranteed to deceive people about what the Western Allies and the City Council were doing. Claims about riots that weren't happening was just the latest and most obvious example of such disinformation. Jakob believed that people needed to hear the City Council's version of what was happening — not just the Soviet or, for that matter, the American version of events. The best means of getting the Berlin government's message to the citizens of Berlin was through newspapers.

Then there were hygiene items — soap, detergent, toilet paper, sanitary towels, toothpaste and the like. Was toothpaste to be considered a luxury? Or shampoo? Surely, they were more important than alcohol, but men without their beer would be more likely to get angry and aggressive. It was nice to preach sobriety, but politics was the art of the practical. This was a battle for the hearts (and votes) of Berliners, and alcohol would play a role whether one wanted it to or not. The Soviets could be counted on to exploit ready access to liquor to sway popular opinion in their favour. Jakob suspected alcohol needed to be given an almost medicinal priority as an elixir that could keep people content despite other hardships. Yet what could he leave off the list to enable the transport of something as heavy as alcoholic beverages?

The deeper Jakob delved into these problems, the more confused he became. What had started as a straightforward task had become a nightmare of uncertainty and reflection on the value of practically everything. He was so lost in his thoughts that he started when Trude knocked on his study door and announced that Karl had arrived.

"Karl? What does he want?" Jakob asked frowning and already defensive.

"It's Sunday, Jakob and time for dinner. Seeing as I have no idea if we'll have anything much to eat a week or two from now, I made chicken fricassee."

"Ah, my favourite! Can we afford it?"

"Jakob, the chicken is already four days old, if we don't eat it, it will rot. The same is true of the cream. Let's enjoy a good meal since it may be our last for a long time to come."

Jakob willingly left the chaos of his incomplete calculations behind, washed his hands quickly in the little water closet, and then joined his wife and son in the kitchen, where they always ate. The smell of the chicken in cream, onion and mushroom sauce was mouth-watering, and Trude had set the table with their best things: matching china, linen napkins, water and wine glasses. "Do we have any wine?" Jakob asked surprised by the latter.

"Freiherr von Feldburg gave you one of his bottles of wine as a thank-you for some introduction you gave him a few weeks ago. I decided now was a good time to try it."

"I'm so relieved to see you are both so calm," Karl exclaimed, looking from one parent to the other. "I feared you would be angry and full of recriminations and that we would just fight again."

Trude shook her head and declared. "You're my only child, Karl."

Jakob took his time answering. He was moderately surprised to realise that he wasn't feeling any animosity toward his son. After a moment's thought, he realized it was because, for the first time in almost a year, he was feeling optimistic. So much so, he reflected with an impish smile, he looked forward to baiting his son a little bit. Out loud he remarked, "I'm most eager to hear how you justify this latest demonstration of brute force by your friends the Soviets."

"Force?" Karl asked in a tone of mock (or was it genuine?) astonishment. "But that's the *beauty* of this tactic, Vati. It is completely non-violent. Not a shot has been fired. Not a bomb dropped." As he spoke, Karl seated himself and shook out his napkin. Trude set a bowl with rice in front of him, put the tureen with the fricassee beside it, and placed serving spoons next to both before taking her place between her two men.

While his son heaped the food on his plate, Jakob remarked in a slow, friendly tone, "You're quite right, Karl. But don't you think it's a bit extreme to besiege an entire city because you've issued a worthless currency that no one is willing to take seriously?"

"The Soviets had no choice. The Western warmongers were not willing to act reasonably and withdraw without pressure. Something had to be

465

done," Karl told his father smugly.

"Hm," Jakob answered ambiguously as he helped himself to the delicious-smelling fricassee in the centre of the table. "What I'm trying to understand, Karl," he noted without looking up from serving his dinner "is why you seem so gleeful about the prospect of all of us starving to death. I admit it doesn't seem very real as we gorge ourselves on a splendid meal of delectable chicken, but by cutting us off from all our sources of food, the Soviets have demonstrated a willingness to let us starve for the sake of kicking the Allies out."

"Nonsense!" Karl scoffed. "The Soviets don't want us to starve. They are only waiting for people to come to their senses. Already the shops are practically empty and soon people's household reserves — like what we're eating here — will be used up as well. When hunger becomes real rather than theoretical, people will stop being deceived by your fine but misleading words like 'democracy' and 'freedom' and 'self-determination.' They will finally recognise these phrases are an empty charade and will accept the hand of friendship offered by our Soviet brothers."

"The hand of friendship that is taking away our food?" Jakob asked scratching his head in a time-honoured gesture of puzzlement.

"Vati, you know that's not true! You know it's the Western capitalists who are forcing you to go without food just because they selfishly want to stay in Berlin! Why? Why should they have soldiers here in the middle of the Soviet Zone?"

"Because it was part of the wartime agreements."

Karl rolled his eyes, "Spare me! That is history. It's time to look to the future. We want a bright, Socialist future. No one wants to be a slave of Capital."

"I do!" Jakob answered instantly.

"No, you don't!" His son responded. "You're just trying to provoke me. But I'm not going to let you. This whole laughable affair will be over in days. The Amis are spoilt little brats and won't be able to stand any hardship and if they go the Brits will toddle along behind them. I'll wager that one week from today we can have an even better dinner with more fresh meat and new potatoes purchased from the exemplary collectives that are already springing up all across the Soviet Zone! Soon, we'll have all our food produced on well-organised collective farms and sold in government-controlled retail points so that we will never again be subject to the price gouging of reactionary farmers or profit-maximizing of shopkeepers."

"You think that one week from today this will all be over?" Jakob asked his son for confirmation.

"One or two. Certainly not more than three weeks. By then, all the coal stored in the Western Sectors will be gone and we'll have no electricity and so no public transport, no pumps for the water or the sewage system. Civil society will break down. There will be protests everywhere! The Western Allies will be booed and attacked by outraged citizens whenever they venture out of their compounds. The Amis and Brits will lose their taste for occupying such a hot and dangerous corner of the world and will scuttle back where they came from."

Jakob nodded thoughtfully, but then warned his son, "Maybe, but then again maybe not. The Western Allies are committed to keeping us supplied by air."

"That's the most ridiculous thing I've ever heard in my whole life! It shows just how stupid and irresponsible the Amis are. Supply a city of two million people by air! The Luftwaffe couldn't even supply a couple hundred thousand men at Stalingrad. Keeping a whole city alive by air is impossible. Only a capitalist with no idea how much a litre of milk or a bag of coal weighs would be stupid enough to suggest it. What are they going to do? Drop barrels of beer from their bombers and herd pigs into their airliners? They have lost touch not just with the suffering masses but with reality itself."

"Maybe," Jakob conceded. He wasn't entirely convinced an airlift would work either, but whether it worked as planned or not it had already achieved something magnificent: it had demonstrated the determination of the West to defend Berlin and the Berliners. Six months ago, Jakob had been afraid of defeat; now he knew that the fight was not over. Most astonishing of all, contrary to his fears, he and his fellow Berliners were not alone in their struggle against new oppression. They had immensely powerful friends in the form of two of their former enemies.

The Show is Over
Berlin-Kreuzberg
Monday, 28 June 1948

The City Council was too preoccupied with establishing guidelines and priorities for airlift cargoes to give a thought to the air ambulance. Charlotte was told by her contact in the town hall that there would be no more medical evacuations until "further notice." All they could do was wait until the situation stabilized.

At home, Charlotte tried to focus on making an inventory of the necessary consumables that she and Christian had on hand. Except for wine, they were not well supplied. They had exactly half a loaf of bread, three eggs, two sticks of butter, half a litre of milk and 200 grams of salami. In addition, they had a sack of onions and a some old potatoes. They had neither fruits nor vegetables because Horst normally brought fresh things from the farmers outside the city, but it was four days since he had been able to cross the zonal border. In terms of basic non-edible necessities, they had only a couple of bars of soap, half a box of detergent, and two extra light bulbs.

The inventory complete, Charlotte sank onto one of the chairs at the kitchen table and let her thoughts consume her. How long would Western Allies stay? How long would David stay? At the latest, he would pull out when the British left, but might he leave earlier? She was a little surprised he had not decided to leave at once. His entire business model was predicated on Western presence. Once Berlin was integrated into the Soviet Zone, there would be no need for an air ambulance.

A loud crashing noise at the front door startled her so violently that she leapt to her feet with a short scream that fortunately escaped her throat only as a faint whimper. The noise was just Christian kicking the door open because he had his arms full. He had been out shopping.

"Did you find anything?" she asked anxiously.

"Well, not much," he admitted. "The stores are pretty barren." He dumped the two shopping bags on the table and started unpacking them. "I got these four bags of spaghetti."

"Spaghetti?" Charlotte had only eaten spaghetti once long ago in an Italian restaurant. It didn't qualify as "real food" to her.

Christian, on the other hand, had eaten it often during his stay in an American POW camp. "It's high in calories and can be stored almost indefinitely," he pointed out. "Also, I managed to snatch these packages of dried mushrooms and some dried tomato soup," he narrated as he tossed the packages on the table.

"No butter or cheese?"

"No, nothing left. Nor bread nor meat of any kind, though I found these cans of sardines and a jar of pickled herring."

Charlotte gazed at these latest items with distaste. She hated fish.

"I snapped up this salt and pepper, this tin of flour and bottle of olive oil, too," he told her, putting the items on the table. "And I found an overlooked stash of dishwashing liquid and detergent, so I took two of each." He straightened and surveyed their stores. It was pathetically little. Charlotte just stared at it.

"We'll still be getting rations," Christian reminded her, "and I've got almost three hundred bottles of wine we can trade for food."

"You can only trade if someone else has food to give you in exchange," Charlotte reminded him as he pulled out the chair opposite her. "If everyone is cut off, everyone will be starving." She knew what that was like; she'd been in Berlin in 1945.

"No blockade is perfect. Food will get through. Too many farmers in Brandenburg stand to gain too much from selling food at inflated prices. I guarantee you there will be a huge amount of illicit trading going on." Christian sounded self-assured (as always), but Charlotte was not impressed. He didn't know what he was talking about because he had been safely in an American POW camp during the worst phase of the post-war chaos and crisis.

"Our other option, of course, is to get out," Christian reminded her.

They had discussed this several times in the past, and because Charlotte felt everything had already been said on the subject, she reacted tetchily. "Only via the Soviet Zone! I've told you again and again that I won't set foot in the Soviet Zone!"

Christian did not allow her raised voice to rattle him. He answered in a tone intended to calm her. "Charlotte, you work for a company with an aircraft. If they want to fly you out *over* the Soviet Zone to the West, they can."

"You don't know Mr Goldman." she countered in frustration. "He is very particular about regulations. He is, well, very *German* in that regard. He will not do anything that might endanger his license. He will not let me fly out unless it is allowed by the Occupation authorities."

"Well," Christian continued reasonably, "why wouldn't the Western Allies authorise some evacuation? Everyone who leaves is one less mouth to feed."

"Because *everyone* would want to leave if only they could!" Charlotte retorted sharply. "If they let one person go, they'd have let everyone go, and they can't fly two million people out any more than they can fly enough food and coal for two million people in!"

Just as suddenly as her anger had flared, it died away again. Reality was the tiny collection of things on the table and the knowledge that they could not sustain life. Staring at the pathetic pile, all her hope for the future started to drain out of her — her visions of AAI's success, her budding friendship with Emily, her dreams of a career, and her longings for a normal life with both work and pleasure.

For a short time, she had allowed herself to believe Berlin was coming back to life. She'd imagined a city with restaurants and cafes on the broad avenues again, shops full of goods for sale, and places to have fun like operas, theatres, concerts and tea dances. For almost two months David's activities and successes had persuaded her that Berlin would return to what it had been.

She had also secretly imagined being together with David more, not just working together but enjoying life together too. That was because sometimes, just once or twice, she had caught David looking at her, and he had smiled embarrassed and looked down. She had sensed — or had she just imagined? — warmth and gentleness, and, yes, affection in his eyes.

That image went abruptly dark — as if someone had switched off the projector in a movie theatre. The beautiful world she had pictured was nothing but a foolish illusion. When the Allies left, they would take David and Emily and the world they had created with them. With the Western Allies gone, there would be no one and nothing to restrain the Ivans anymore. They would go back to the way they had been before. Arrogant, contemptuous, triumphant and utterly uncontrolled. In the U-bahn, on the streets, at the door....

Christian would be here, of course, she reminded herself. He would try to protect her. Yet he was not as strong as he thought he was. They would kill him.

She said nothing. There was no point in telling Christian how horrible their end would be. Let him hope a little longer and imagine escape. Charlotte knew better because she was mortally wounded. Her energy and hope were haemorrhaging out of the invisible wound in her womb.

She was startled out of her thoughts by Christian. He laid his hand on hers. She looked up at him confused.

"Charlotte, Mr Goldman is in love with you. He is not going to leave you here to your fate, even if he has to knock you out and evacuate you as a critical 'casualty.' An action which, by the way, I would heartily assist."

"You think David is in love with me?" Charlotte asked astonished.

"Charlotte, it's written all over his face every time he looks at you. So, pull yourself together and don't give into despair. You and I are going to survive this crisis just as we survived the war, and we're going to have a better future."

She gazed at him. "You sincerely believe that don't you?"

"I do, and so should you."

Charlotte thought about it. No, she didn't believe it. Not like he did. But she felt a gentle reawakening of hope. If David could love her... That would be something to live for, even fight for. But David didn't know the truth about her. He didn't know what had happened... Don't think about that now, she admonished herself. Christian was right. They had to survive first. For the moment, she would concentrate on surviving and worry about everything else later.

Flight Cancelled
Berlin-Kladow
Monday, 28 June 1948

Jasha responded to the news of a complete blockade by deciding they must turn the lawn of the Station Commander's residence into a vegetable farm. "We can hire young men to tend it and sell vegetables in Berlin," she told Emily optimistically. "We'll make good money."

Emily said 'no'. Aside from a reluctance to tear up her serene environment and have strange men traipsing over her property every day, she didn't need to consult with Robin to know that it would be against King's Regulations to transform an RAF property into a commercial enterprise.

Reluctantly, Jasha scaled back her ambitions to a large "kitchen garden" intended to produce fresh things that they could consume themselves, including, Jasha announced next, fresh eggs.

"Where are you going to get hens in times like these?" Emily countered. "Everyone who has a hen will be keeping it for themselves."

"Then we will pen-up some of those ducks and geese," Jasha replied unperturbed, with a vague gesture in the direction of the Havel where, as usual, a half dozen wild fowl stood about cleaning their feathers or dozing in the sun. "Duck eggs," Jasha insisted, "taste excellent and are larger anyway."

"You'll have to catch them first," Emily pointed out, "and if you do, you'll have to protect them from Sammy and put them in a pen far away from the boathouse." Robin would have a fit if he had to wade through smelly and squawking ducks when he wanted to go for a sail.

Herr Krueger, the gardener, entered the conversation for the first time, pointing to a spot at the foot of the garden near a stand of trees. Krueger spoke a dialect of German that Emily found hard to understand, but after some discussion, Jasha announced they would build the duck coop by the Havel but on the opposite side of the lawn from the boathouse. With a frown of disapproval at Sammy who had chosen this minute to bound down toward the lake, Emily warned they would need to do more than just put up a coop, they would have to fence Sammy out. The collie-mix with tail wagging excitedly made a leap towards one of the ducks and the whole flock took the air with a wild flapping of their wings.

A moment later, with an ear-splitting roar, a Spitfire shot over the roof of the house only a few feet overhead. It wheeled on wingtip just as it reached the water and went into a climbing turn. Emily strained to follow it with her eyes, trying to see if it was "P". Could Robin possibly have found time to fly in the middle of all this? But already two more Spitfires roared over the roof at no more than fifty feet, with two more chasing after them. It was the whole squadron, she realised as three more pairs followed the leader. That meant Danny rather than Robin was probably in the lead and she wondered vaguely what he was up to. For now, it was time to let Jasha and Herr Krueger get on with creating a kitchen garden and building a duck coop.

Nodding to them, she called Sammy back to her as she started towards the house. Sammy bounded up the slope of the lawn, careful to shake himself only after he was close enough to splatter her with water. Then he happily looked up expecting a hand-out of some sort. "You are so spoilt," Emily told him indulgently.

In the kitchen, Emily put the kettle on for some tea. She'd hardly seen Robin since the Russians had laid siege to Berlin, and today Group Captain Biggar, who had been appointed by BAFO to coordinate and command all RAF airlift activities, was flying in with his Army counterpart, Brigadier Lucas. The latter had been appointed by the British Army on the Rhine to coordinate all the land movements associated with the airlift. Robin had a separate meeting with an officer from the Royal Corps of Engineers with expertise in airfield construction; he had been sent to Berlin with orders to expedite the completion of the concrete runway. Kiwi, meanwhile, had gone to the airfield on the pretext of keeping an eye on "Moby Dick" and checking how Ron and Chips were bearing up. Secretly, Emily suspected he simply liked the excitement down at the airfield and was itching to be part of it.

David, on the other hand, had been called to a meeting with Mayor Reuter. The call from Reuter's assistant Willy Brandt had come late yesterday evening, and Brandt had stressed that with public transport in disarray, it would be impossible to set a time for the meeting. He'd asked David simply to come. "Whenever you get here, I'll make sure you see the Mayor."

Emily had rather hoped David would invite her to join him for this seminal meeting with Reuter, but he didn't. Objectively, she admitted she had nothing to add. David understood the capacity and constraints of AAI better than she did and also spoke better German. She simply would have liked to meet the already legendary mayor of Berlin and hear first-hand what he had to say with respect to their operations. She hoped the meeting signalled support for the ambulance service from the highest level of civil government, and David was hoping for a breakthrough on the issue of payment.

The telephone started ringing just as the kettle started to whistle, so Emily switched off the stove and went out into the hallway to take the phone. "Hello!" When neither Robin nor David answered her, she added, "This is Emily Priestman."

"Emily?" It was an unfamiliar female voice.

"Yes?"

"This is Cheryl Walker, Lt. Col. Walker's wife."

"Oh, hello!" Emily was surprised. She had met Mrs Walker at most a half-dozen times and they'd never gone beyond small talk.

"I was so sorry you couldn't make it to the Ladies' Club Luncheon yesterday," Mrs Walker told her. Emily had completely forgotten about it. Edith had made it clear she wasn't expected in the circumstances. Before she could even explain her absence, Mrs Walker continued, "It was an important meeting because, you see, we wives feel we have to put forward a united front. The Soviets are going to take over Berlin any day now, and we and our children need to get out of here before that happens. Frankly, I think the men should pull out too! President Truman was a fool to let us get into this ridiculous trap! He certainly can't be trusted to get us out! Unfortunately, until the next election, he's still the President of the United States so the men will have to obey his orders. We women and children, however, are *not* under military discipline and we shouldn't be subjected to a siege. I'm sure you agree."

Although Edith had warned her that such sentiments were simmering among the Americans, Emily was still taken somewhat aback. She tried to respond as diplomatically as possible, "I can certainly sympathise with your position, Mrs Walker—"

"Please call me Cheryl," the American insisted.

"Of course, Cheryl. As I was saying, I understand your concerns, however, my position is quite different. I have no children and it looks as if my job will require me to remain here for the foreseeable future."

"But what about the other British women? Aren't they being evacuated?" From her tone, Emily surmised that the American had hoped that a British evacuation of dependents would set a precedent which might force Clay's hand.

"I'm very sorry, Cheryl, but no," Emily informed her.

"Not even those with small children?"

"No."

"I must say, I'm *astonished*. I thought you Brits were more cautious and less, you know, gung-ho about confronting the Soviets."

"I wouldn't want to comment on that, Cheryl."

"Don't you realize we're completely surrounded by Soviet troops? I've heard men saying we won't last fifteen minutes if they send in the tanks. What is the point of staying? Why get us all killed?"

Cheryl seemed to be working herself into greater agitation and Emily felt she ought to try to calm her. "For what it's worth, Cheryl, our assessment isn't quite as negative as that. We don't believe the Soviets want war."

"What have you been doing? Talking to Edith?" Cheryl asked sharply.

"Not recently," Emily waffled.

"Well, I don't share your opinion. Time will tell which of us was right. Goodbye." She hung up in a huff, and Emily sighed. She wasn't sure she'd handled that very well.

Returning to the kitchen, she glanced at the clock. It was 4:30 already. Robin's meeting had been set for 11 am, but of course, whatever instructions the senior officers brought would have a myriad of implications for Gatow. Robin would need to break down the overall orders into specific action items and brief his subordinates. He would probably work until late into the night again.

The kettle started to whistle, and she poured the steaming water over the loose tea in the pot. She put the teapot, milk and sugar onto a silver tray and took it out to the back terrace. Mrs Walker's call left Emily vaguely unsettled. Was she being naïve? She was troubled by the Russian ability to disengage from reality and live in a world of their own making. The Russians insisted that oppression was freedom, that dictatorship was democracy, and that everything they did was justified by the march of history toward communism. She did not want to be here if the Russians walked through the front door because she knew there would be no defence: neither pleading nor pride. Not even avowals of political sympathy would stop a Russian intent on proving his mastery over another human being.

She had let her imagination go too far and she recoiled in alarm at the sound of someone in the house behind her. Then Sammy jumped up barking with wild delight and bounded toward the house. It could only be David or Kiwi. A moment later, David emerged.

"David! How did it go?" Emily asked eagerly getting to her feet. Then realizing she had brought only one cup and saucer out to the terrace, she gestured for him to hold his answer. "Wait! I'll get another cup and you can join me for tea."

"I'll get it," David answered and disappeared inside again. By the time he reappeared, Emily had registered that he didn't look triumphant. Indeed, he looked so sober that she asked anxiously, "Did something go wrong?"

David sighed and removed his cap, tossing it on a vacant chair as he sat down. He avoided looking at her as he poured milk into his cup and helped himself to tea.

"Surely Mayor Reuter didn't summon you only to say we should suspend operations?" Emily pressed him.

David shook his head. "No, Reuter is committed to evacuating as many sick people from Berlin as possible." He looked at Emily and met her eyes. "He believes that this siege makes it imperative that we remove not only emergency cases but people with severe chronic medical conditions as well. He pointed out that under current conditions, there is no way to ensure the hospitals will have sufficient diesel for their generators, which means that life-support systems might fail at any time."

Emily thought she was beginning to understand David's mood. No matter how good the news might be for AAI, as a human being, the situation was grim and depressing. Berlin was facing an extremely dark and dangerous period — even if the Russians weren't about to walk in as she had been foolishly picturing to herself moments before.

David continued. "In principle, he'd like us to shuttle people out of Berlin as fast as we can, but there are two obstacles."

"Aviation fuel," Emily answered instantly. There was no storage capacity for aviation fuel in Berlin and no means of flying it in either. All aircraft had to refuel in the West and the RAF needed all available fuel for its own operations for the foreseeable future.

"That's one," David agreed, nodding as he absently fondled Sammy behind the ears. "The other is still the confounded issue of payment. As has been the case for the last three months, the City Council accepts their obligation to pay us *in principle*, but they have no means to do so *in fact*. They are in debt up to their eyeballs. They have no access to hard currency. All they have are promissory notes, and those won't buy aviation fuel or pay salaries." Emily nodded tensely, waiting for him to finish.

"What's new is that Reuter thinks neither London nor Washington would want headlines about dying children or newspaper images of hospital patients rotting away without proper treatment. He believes the Western Allies can be persuaded to pick up the tab for our services."

"That would be splendid!" Emily enthused.

"Yes, it would be," David agreed without sounding at all convinced. "It would mean that we'd be paid in sterling or dollars directly into our London bank account. Furthermore, if the Allies buy into the notion that the evacuation of seriously ill Berliners is part of the overall effort to keep Berlin viable, we'll be able to get access to aviation fuel."

"Then what's the problem?" Emily pressed him, reading his mood rather than his words.

"How on earth are we supposed to convince HM's government — much less the United States — to pick up the tab? I don't have access to the corridors of power in London or Washington!"

"But surely Mayor Reuter would make the request? It was his idea. Why can't he go to Generals Clay and Robertson?"

Before David could reply, Kiwi burst out onto the terrace and declared. "We can all pack up and go home. AAI is finished! Done! *Kaputt!*"

They had not heard a car pull up, and even Sammy was taken by surprise and scrambled to his feet to greet Kiwi with leaps of joy. The humans just stared at Kiwi astonished and uncomprehending.

Kiwi was dressed in greasy overalls and his hands were dirty as if he'd been working on Moby Dick, but it was his face that shocked Emily. He wore a grimace intended to hide the fury and hurt behind it. No one cared more about the success of AAI than Kiwi. If something went wrong, she still had Robin and David still had a fortune, but Kiwi had nothing.

David recovered from his shock first, "What do you mean we're finished? What's happened? Has there been an accident? Is something wrong with Moby Dick?"

"No. The aircraft's fine, but the ground crew refuses to stay in Berlin another day. I've been arguing with them for the last six hours straight and nothing — absolutely nothing! — will change their minds. They say they are getting on the BEA flight tomorrow and they don't care if you pay them for the last two weeks or not."

David sprang to his feet and started cursing and pacing. While Sammy chased after him in distress, Emily held her breath, afraid that he would blame Kiwi.

David stopped in front of his partner and asked angrily, "Were they trying to get danger pay?"

"I don't think so. I didn't ask that explicitly because I didn't want to suggest we might do it. But I asked if there was *anything* we could do to make them stay and they said: 'Get the Ivans to go home!'"

"Right!" David snorted sarcastically. "As if they didn't know this could happen! They knew from the start where we would be based."

"And they never liked it," Kiwi reminded him.

"Neither did you! Are you taking their side?" David flared up.

"Of course, I'm not!" Kiwi snapped back. "But maybe we should think about operating from somewhere else — at least until the blockade is lifted."

"It's *because* of this siege that we're more useful here than anywhere else in the world!" David countered furiously.

"All right, but why couldn't we keep Moby Dick somewhere in the West and fly into Berlin to pick up patients as needed? That way Ron and Chips could live in the West—"

That sounded like a good idea to Emily, but David exploded. "That would nearly double operating costs — and what about emergencies? Patients could die while we fly in from Hamburg or Hanover! I'm not moving out of Berlin! Ron and Chips can go to hell! I'll find ground crew willing to work in Berlin, even if I have to hire German aircraft mechanics."

"Germans don't know a thing about Merlins!" Kiwi flung back at him furiously. His nerves were so raw, he was nearly shouting. "If you think—"

"Pack it up! Both of you," Robin interceded sharply. He was still in his best blues, his cap on his head, and his authority was sufficient for both of his former subordinates to obey instantly, although they glared at him resentfully. He dissipated the latter by adding, "I need at least a double scotch and it sounds like you could use one too. What are you drinking, Emily?"

"Gin and tonic, if you don't mind, Robin."

Robin disappeared into the winter garden where the alcohol was kept, and Emily collected the tea things on the tray to carry them back to the kitchen. From the foot of the garden came the sound of voices as Jasha, having noticed Robin, hurried back to make dinner.

Jasha took the tray from Emily and shooed her out of the kitchen. "I make dinner," she assured her employer as she washed her hands rigorously in the sink and then grabbed her apron. Emily left her to it and went back out onto the terrace.

The three men were standing, each with a crystal tumbler in their hands. Although Kiwi looked the most shattered, Emily could see how strained David looked, too. His reconstructed face stretched tighter than ever across the fine bones of his face, and his eyes were hard. Robin stood with one hand in his trouser pocket and a casual observer might have thought he was completely at ease; Emily knew better. He was tense and tired and easily looked ten years more than 32.

As she joined them Robin was saying, "...I'm not going to be able to allow employees of a private company to live in RAF quarters any longer anyway. The Army is establishing what they call the Rear Airfield Supply Organisation, or RASO, to collect, store, organise and load cargoes at the airfields in the West and a Forward Airfield Supply Organisation, FASO, here at Gatow, to off-load and distribute cargoes in Berlin. The bulk of the loading and off-loading will be done by Germans, but they will be supervised by Army personnel, who will live on the Station. Meanwhile, we'll also be getting support with our runway from the Army Corps of Engineers. Lt. Col. Russel was a pleasant surprise. Not at all pushy or, you know, full of bumpf. We walked out to have a look at the runway, and he thinks he can get it completed in a couple of weeks, but he'll be bringing in some sappers to help supervise the work. On top of that, I need to expand staffing almost across the board, starting with air traffic control, communications, inventory and accounting, personnel and payroll, catering — everything. Everything superfluous must go. Triple Two Squadron has already pulled out."

Emily caught her breath. "So that's why the squadron beat up the house this afternoon!"

Robin nodded, "Yes. Danny asked me to give you his regards and best wishes. He was very sorry not to have a chance to say goodbye in person."

"And that means all the Spits are gone," Emily registered with a sense of loss. It meant the end of formation flying, mock dogfights, air shows and aerobatics. It was the end of having fun flying together with Robin. It signalled the seriousness of the situation at a personal level and made her sad.

"They left me R, but as I was trying to explain, I'm going to need all the available quarters on the station for official personnel both permanent and temporary."

Kiwi nodded understanding, but David protested acidly, "So, we're just supposed to fold? Now, when we're needed most? Mayor Reuter just told me he wants to see all seriously ill patients out of Berlin, so they won't be at risk — or become an embarrassment — if things go very wrong."

Emily thought David's tone was inappropriate. Robin had been extremely generous up to now. Fortunately, Robin didn't snap as he sometimes did. Instead, he considered David critically and drew a deep breath before announcing, "No, I don't think you have to fold. In the short term, Kiwi's suggestion about temporarily relocating your base of operations to somewhere in Bizonia and flying into Berlin as needed sounds reasonable. Your thought about German mechanics who could live on the economy might also be worth exploring — if this goes on for more than a few weeks. You want to bear in mind, however, that both Clay and Robertson exceeded their authority when they committed to this airlift. Although the PM and President Truman have backed them, neither government has obtained legislative approval for what we are doing — and we're going to need that given the enormous costs involved. So, this could all be stopped at very short notice."

"Meaning we just cave to the Ivans?" Kiwi asked flabbergasted.

"If we pull out, all the decent Berliners starting with Mayor Reuter get thrown in concentration camps — or maybe just shot outright!" David echoed his partner's outrage.

Instead of answering either of them, Robin turned to his wife. "Emily, what the devil is going on in the garden? Why is our gardener tearing everything up?"

"He's not. He and Jasha have simply decided we should produce as many fresh things as we can — you know, tomatoes, beans, parsley, cucumbers, lettuce, eggs and the like. I can't imagine why, but they seem to think rationing is going to be very meagre during an airlift."

Robin stared at her. "You mean they're planting a Victory Garden?"

"Yes, that's one way of looking at it."

Robin burst out laughing leaving the others to look at each other baffled.

"Don't you see?" Robin looked from one to the other and then pointed at the gardener still diligently at work as the sun slipped down the sky turning the Havel a golden colour. "That is a vote of confidence in the airlift. There's no point planting if you don't think you'll harvest. We're talking about quitting and he's digging a garden." Then, shaking his head, he took a sip of scotch and declared, "What a world! Three years ago, we'd just finished off Hitler and here we are going on rations and tearing up our lawns for vegetables again." He lifted his glass for another swallow and noticed it was empty. He turned around looking for the bottle. Kiwi reached it first, and Robin held out his glass for Kiwi to fill it, indicating halfway with a finger.

Emily exploited the pause in the conversation to announce, "I had a call from Mrs Walker, one of the Americans I met at the luncheons. Just as Edith warned, the American wives are in a dither and want to be evacuated." Robin raised his eyebrows eloquently. "Do you think I should call all the wives of Gatow personnel to a meeting? Try to find out what they're thinking?"

"If you don't think it will lead to a mutiny...." Robin sounded a little sceptical.

"I seriously doubt it, Robin. There isn't a wife on this station that didn't go through the war. Many were in the services or worked in munitions factories. Not only have we lived on rations and tended Victory Gardens, but we've also been bombed and faced the V1s and V2s. We're not as easily intimidated or frightened as our American counterparts. But even if I'm wrong, it's better to confront any fears and discontent head-on, rather than try to sweep things under the carpet. That way, you'll know what you're up against and won't be taken by surprise. If the wives feel they can talk to me, we'll hear about discontent in time to counter it."

"Well said. Thank you. Do it." Despite the terseness of his words, the gaze he gave her was so full of appreciation and admiration that it made Emily warm inside. Was it just a little over six months ago that she didn't have a clue what to do with herself? That she'd felt superfluous and intimidated by her role here? That her greatest worries had been failing as a diplomatic hostess and ruining Robin's career? She felt like a different person.

David's tense voice broke in on her thoughts. "I want to return to what you were saying, Robin, about this airlift being terminated before it even gets off the ground. Do you think that's a serious possibility?"

"From our side no. The government will put its case to Parliament on Wednesday and Robertson is confident of full backing. Clay, however, admitted that Truman's decision is opposed by both his Department of State and the Pentagon. The State Department would rather abandon Berlin and put pressure on the Soviets elsewhere, while the Pentagon simply doesn't think the airlift will work. Meanwhile, both air forces have been told to "do the best you can." We are frantically trying to do exactly that, but, frankly, it might not be good enough. We could very well fail no matter how much political will there is."

That was a sobering thought, but Emily realised that unlike Mrs Walker she still wanted to be here. She wanted to be a witness to this unprecedented attempt to keep a city alive from the air, and even more, she wanted to help keep the ambulance flying. Most importantly, whatever came, she wanted to be with Robin, helping him in any way she could. They were a team, and she wanted it to stay that way.

Partners
Kladow
Monday, 28 June 1948

David couldn't sleep. He tossed and turned so much that Sammy got off the bed in disgust and went to sleep in an armchair. Keeping him awake was the realization of his commitment to the Berliners. It was ridiculous. At least half of them must be Nazis and some of them, like the man occupying his uncle's house, were antisemitic war criminals who had contributed to the slaughter of his family. He ought to be glad to turn his back on Berlin. Yet he couldn't. He'd given his word to Mayor Reuter, and he felt genuine sympathy with the children caught up in this nightmare. He'd come to like men like Dr Dietmar Schlaer, Jakob Liebherr and Christian von Feldburg. And he'd fallen hopelessly in love with Charlotte.

He might as well admit it, at least to himself. He loved her and he couldn't bear the thought of leaving her here. Of course, if he left, he could ask her to come with him. She might even *want* to leave Berlin, but he was profoundly afraid of asking too much of her too soon. She was so fragile, so wounded, so vulnerable. He could see, too, that she was insecure and desperately afraid of something. He wanted to find out what it was. He wanted to ease her fears. He wanted to win her trust. He wanted to win her *love*. But he wasn't the kind of man who could do that all at once. He needed time. He needed to approach things in his own way. This crisis had come at all the wrong time!

Acknowledging that he was not going to get any sleep, David threw the covers back and got out of bed. The moon was rising over the Havel, casting a sheen of silver across the water and casting light onto the lawn through the trees on the shore. Grabbing his dressing gown, David left his bedroom and tip-toed down the back stairs, through the dining room and across the salon to exit by the French doors onto the terrace. The air was humid, and moisture made the flagstones cool, almost cold. It was refreshing, and he pulled his dressing gown more tightly around himself as he sat down in one of the iron garden chairs, indifferent to the condensation on the seat.

Was he deluding himself? Could a Countess Walmsdorf ever fall in love with a Jew? He considered the question carefully and concluded that neither Charlotte nor Christian had ever shown a trace of antisemitism.

483

The problem with Charlotte wasn't class or racial prejudice; it was far more elusive. Feldburg had hinted that she had not been able to "put the past behind her." He'd mentioned a fiancé who was still MIA. David understood how difficult that was; it would have been much easier if her old love was dead and buried.

And then there was his face. He put his fingers to his forehead and cheeks. It was eight years since his face had melted away and six and a half since Dr McIndoe had finished fashioning a replacement. His new face fitted on his bone structure well enough without discolouring nor prominent scars, yet his hair had grown back coarser and darker, and he could not have grown a beard if he wanted to. He knew his face looked human enough, yet it lacked something too, and that made it difficult to connect with women. He had not had an intimate relationship since his accident. Would he be able to overcome his inhibitions with Charlotte?

Something clicked behind him, and he turned in his chair. Someone had entered the winter garden and was lighting up a cigarette. It was Kiwi.

David got to his feet and walked back into the house calling "Kiwi?"

Kiwi recoiled visibly and then answered in his New Zealand drawl. "That's right."

"You couldn't sleep either?"

"How the hell am I supposed to sleep when everything I've worked for these last six months is on the rocks!" Kiwi told him off.

Mentally, David accepted that he'd earned that bitter retort, and he wanted to make amends. "Kiwi, I'm sorry I was so angry earlier. I'm not angry at *you*. I know AAI means as much to you as it does to me —"

"Too right!" Kiwi did not sound mollified, and David felt terrible.

"Kiwi, you're right. We should pull back, forget Berlin and all the connections we've built up here. If you want we can try to start over in the UK—"

"That's not what I want! This is a huge opportunity. We'd be crazy to give up now!" Kiwi's cigarette burned intensely as he inhaled, and then it fell away from his face as he continued. "And I'm not so dumb that I don't see it's more expensive and less effective to fly in from the West, but this situation has to be temporary. Either, as Robin says, we fail and there is no business here anymore, or we force the Ivans to the negotiating table and then things will stabilise again. We're only talking about a stop-gap measure for the next few weeks, about finding a way to keep the groundcrew from deserting us."

"Yes," David agreed. "You're right." David felt a jolt of inspiration, and he repeated himself, not in resignation but with energy. "You're *absolutely* right, Kiwi, and that's what we're going to do. I mean, that's what *you're* going to do. Tomorrow, I want you to fly Moby Dick out of here and take Ron and Chips out with you." Everything seemed to be falling into place. Nodding to himself, he added, "In fact, fly them back to the UK to cool off for a couple of days. Tell them to go home. Let them think about being without a job for a day or two. Meanwhile, you can make enquiries about replacement crews. There have to be other fish in the sea."

"Yeah, I was thinking that too," Kiwi admitted nodding and inhaling again. Then he paused. "Did you want a smoke?" His tone was reconciliatory.

Relief flooded David's veins, and he agreed at once. "Yes. Thanks." Kiwi stepped closer, his pack of cigarettes extended. David took a cigarette and put it to his lips. Kiwi lit it for him. That felt better.

"I was thinking," Kiwi started and paused to see if David would cut him off.

"Go on. Your thinking has been clearer than mine recently," David admitted.

"I don't know about that, mate, but on second thought it occurred to me that maybe German ground crews wouldn't be such a bad idea, either. All we'd need is a former ground crew chief who can show them the idiosyncrasies of Merlins and keep an eye on them."

"Yes," David agreed, nodding.

"There just has to be a way to make this work," Kiwi stressed. "The need for our services is extraordinary, and we're on the brink of getting reliable payment."

"Agreed," David replied as he felt a huge weight lift from his shoulders. No, they didn't have all the answers yet, but they could and would find the solutions if they worked together as a team. Kiwi had certainly been doing his part. Moby Dick was a good, reliable aircraft, and Ron and Chips had been good, cheap and up to now reliable. Kiwi's flying was first-rate too, and he'd laid off the bottle almost entirely. David took a deep breath and admitted, "I'm sorry I'm such an ass sometimes, Kiwi. I inherited it from my father. Maybe the reason I didn't want to go into business was that I feared it would warp me like this. So, well, when I get on my high horse, just knock me off, would you?"

Kiwi didn't answer right away. He seemed to think David's words over and then he nodded. "All right, mate, but try to cut me some slack sometimes too. I know I'm not perfect, but I do want AAI to succeed."

"I know," David assured him.

They nodded to one another, and slowly they both started grinning. The friendship had won. Kiwi suggested, "Let's go get some sleep, mate. Tomorrow we need to get AAI back off the ground."

A Wing and a Prayer
Foster Clough, Yorkshire
Wednesday, 30 June 1948

Kit and Georgina could cram all their worldly goods into Kit's car, although Donna's crib had to be dismantled. As they pulled away from the rented flat for the last time, Kit felt only relief. One less-than-satisfying episode in his life was over; it was time to move on, even if the future remained shrouded in an impenetrable fog. Still, he'd managed to scrape by to a second-class degree and had agreed to spend two months with his in-laws, while he continued to look for work in the UK. At the end of that time, if he still had no job offer, he planned to contact Barnes Wallis about his American connections. As they left Leeds behind, both he and Georgina felt so good they started singing songs together, an old pleasure.

It was a sunny day with only intermittent showers, and they arrived at the vicarage in Foster Clough in the early afternoon. Georgina's mother Amanda met them with such a welcoming smile all remaining doubts about the move were blown away. Amanda took her granddaughter into her arms with the kind of glow that only a grandmother has, and Georgina and Kit unloaded the car together. As they finished unpacking, Georgina turned to Kit and asked hopefully. "Do you think we have time for a ride before dark?"

Georgina had been an avid horsewoman all her life and her parents still kept two horses. During Kit's recovery from his injuries, Georgina had helped him master riding with his artificial leg. They had many good memories of riding together in the surrounding countryside.

After checking with Amanda that she wouldn't mind looking after Donna, they changed clothes and tacked up the two horses, Hannibal and Hester. The horses were eager, and Georgina led the way confidently; Kit just followed along content to see her so happy again. When they reached one of their favourite picnicking spots, they drew up to enjoy the view, dropping the reins on the withers to let the horses graze. "Kit Darling?" Georgina opened, and Kit thought 'Oh dear. Now what?' She always called him 'darling' when she wanted to say something she thought he wouldn't like. "I've been thinking."

"Always advisable," Kit quipped.

"Yes," Georgina acknowledged with a quick smile before continuing more seriously, "I've been thinking about Africa."

"Have you been writing to my mother again?" Kit asked suspiciously. Georgina had corresponded with his mother before they were engaged, let alone married. They were both dedicated teachers, and the relationship between them was exceptionally good. Not for an instant had Georgina treated his mother as less of an authority merely because she was half-black. Kit's parents lived in Nigeria, where his father was in the Colonial Service.

"Yes," Georgina answered his question. "She was telling me that there are many children in Africa who don't go to school at all. The need for teachers is huge, and no one cares if a teacher is married or has children or not. Your mother thought that schools in Africa might prefer to hire a married woman with children than a single girl who, she said, might be less committed. She thinks there is a need for engineers in Africa too."

"Of course Africa needs engineers," Kit replied calmly, his gaze on the Yorkshire vista spread out before him but seeing the Great Rift Valley instead. "That's why I wanted to be an engineer in the first place — to build bridges over the wild gorges and railway lines to the remotest cities. I pictured myself designing daring aqueducts and developing complex irrigation systems that transformed the savannah into an agricultural gold mine — all those childish things little boys imagine engineers can do."

"But they *can* do them, can't they?" Georgina asked innocently.

Kit shook his head. "That's civil engineering, and your idiot husband just completed a degree in aeronautical engineering."

"But they must need aeroplanes in Africa too?" Georgina persisted.

"Yes, old ones, but they don't build them there. Besides, you know I said I would never go back."

"You said you would never go back to *South* Africa, which I understand, but you miss East Africa."

"How do you know that?" He asked surprised.

"Because sometimes you talk in your sleep and if you aren't flying a Lancaster, then usually you're on safari with your father."

Kit nodded slowly, thinking for a few minutes about Africa, his childhood, and his love/hate relationship with the continent. Finally, he admitted. "You're right. I do miss East Africa sometimes. I miss the dry heat, the acacia trees, the music, the colours of the women's dresses..."

"Then couldn't we..." Her voice drifted away.

He looked over at her. "Go on," he prompted.

"Yesterday, in the newspaper, I saw an advertisement for Ethiopian Airlines. They are recruiting pilots and flight engineers both."

"Ethiopian Airlines?" Kit was instantly intrigued. When Kit was a child, his father had served as District Officer in Moyale in Kenya, near the Ethiopian border, and his father had always expressed admiration for the Ethiopians. After all, Ethiopia had never been a colony, and the Ethiopians were both fiercely proud and reputedly incorruptible. Maybe it was an option, he told himself. "It's worth thinking about," he told Georgina, "But we better get back to the house before Donna wears out her welcome."

They arrived at the vicarage just as the sun sank behind the hills leaving the stable yard in shadow. Georgina went straight inside to take her daughter off her mother's hands, while Kit saw to the horses. When Kit entered by the kitchen door, he found that his father-in-law Reverend Edwin Reddings had returned home in their absence.

Edwin greeted his son-in-law enthusiastically. "I've been keeping champagne cooled for the last week and counting the days 'till you got here! Come, help me pour."

"No, Edwin," his wife stopped him. "We'll have the champagne *after* Donna's been put to bed. Go drink your usual and listen to the news.

We'll call you when dinner's ready."

"We have our orders," Edwin sniffed, and he and Kit retreated to the library where Edwin made them each a whisky sour before settling down for a chat. "You're looking more relaxed," Edwin observed.

"My exams are behind me. I managed a second-class degree. I'm more resigned to my fate."

"What fate?"

"I don't know yet, but I've told myself to accept whatever it is."

"Where did this new wisdom come from?"

Kit just shrugged, ashamed to admit he'd learned it from Leonard Cheshire VC.

Edwin didn't press him. "Shall we listen to the news?" At Kit's nod, Edwin got up to switch on the radio.

"*This is the BBC Home Service. At the top of the news, the House of Commons today debated the government's policies concerning Germany and especially Berlin. Speaking on behalf of His Majesty's government, Foreign Minister Bevin declared:* (a recording of the Foreign Minister speaking was blended in) "*We cannot abandon those stout-hearted Berlin democrats who are refusing to bow to Soviet pressure. We are fully conscious of the task that is before us and all the hindrances that may be put in our way, but His Majesty's Government have decided to place at the disposal of the combined effort every possible resource we have.*"

The BBC Commentator continued,

"*Speaking for the Opposition, Mr Eden noted:* (again the original voice recording was blended in) "*Whatever effort the Royal Air Force and the joint air forces make, they will be making that effort not in war but in the cause of peace; they will be working to supply a civilian population exposed to cruel suffering; and this time they will be dropping on Berlin not bombs, but food.*"

"I wish I were doing that," Kit declared abruptly.

He no longer heard the radio, only the droning of the Merlins as Berlin crawled unbearably slowly beneath their wings. Blacked out, it was lit only by the sharp flashes of flak that blinded more than illuminated. Then quite unexpectedly, the rising moon slid out from between the clouds to shine down on lakes that suddenly glistened. Two lakes were separated yet connected by several narrow rivers or canals.

"That's the Spree," the bomb aimer reported calmly. "We should be getting a marker flare soon."

Anxiously they peered out of the Plexiglas enclosing them. The water below was so calm that it reflected the moonlight like polished silver. Then flak exploded, ruining their night vision and knocking the Lancaster around.

"Green marker flare! Three o'clock." The bomb aimer reported.

"Navigator to pilot: Steer 085."

Loaded down with 6,000 lbs of explosives, the heavy bomber banked gracefully to starboard. A complex of large industrial buildings with smokestacks eased slowly into sight.

"Target Indicators dead ahead, Skip," the bomb aimer reported sounding satisfied.

"Bomb doors open," Don answered.

The flak edged closer again. The Lanc bounced and shuddered. The smell of cordite penetrated the interior and shrapnel clattered like metallic rain on the metal fuselage. Bursting explosives lit up the cockpit enough to see every detail in black and white but drained the colour away. Below them clusters of bright flashes erupted as bombs released from other bombers exploded on the city below. The incendiaries rapidly took hold and flames started to spread out across the darkness. The drops of flame slowly merged into a lake of fire.

"Left, Skipper. Left. Left. Right. Steady. ... Bombs gone."

The Lancaster bounced upwards, relieved of her load, but they held their course for the photo flash. Below them, the smoke spreading over the flames dulled the glare from the incendiaries, transforming the image. It was as if a layer of molten lava was oozing over the city. Quite abruptly, the smoke shredded apart for an instant revealing, in the midst of the inferno, a graceful Gothic church with a tall spire. It had made Kit gasp.

Gradually, Kit noticed that he was surrounded by silence as he stood in the library at his father-in-law's house. Edwin had turned off the radio. Kit remembered what he was doing here, the BBC announcer and the recording of the Parliamentary debate in which Mr Eden had said that the RAF would be bringing food rather than bombs to Berlin. He knew he'd said he wanted to do that, and he felt silly. "I'm sorry. That must have sounded childish," he apologised with an embarrassed smile.

"That's not the word I would have chosen," Edwin replied dryly, "and it's not the reason I turned off the radio." Kit waited for what he would say next. "I felt a shiver run down my spine when you said that. I think you will be doing it — even if I can't imagine how it will come about."

War
RAF Gatow
Thursday, 1 July 1948

Priestman summoned all station personnel to the auditorium. The design of the hall suggested it had been used by the Nazis not only for lectures but also for rallies and speeches. It was easy to imagine red banners with white circles enclosing swastikas hanging from the lofty ceiling and between the tall, narrow windows. No doubt the conspicuously vacant pedestal behind the stage had once held a bust of Adolf Hitler, Goering or a Luftwaffe eagle.

The auditorium had been built for 500 - 600 people and it was filled nearly to capacity. Men of the RAF Regiment stood guard at the doors and IDs were checked as personnel entered. Priestman could not remember ever addressing such a large audience before.

At 9:00 pm sharp, the RAF Regiment closed the doors, and the Station Commander mounted the steps to the stage. His subordinates got respectfully to their feet and the rustling and murmurs died away. From the podium, Priestman looked out at a room full of men and women standing still and attentive, though not rigid as at a parade.

"Thank you. You may be seated." He pulled his notes from inside his tunic and put them in front of him on the podium. He had worked on them most of the afternoon and knew them almost by heart. He did not want to read from them but having his text before him made him less nervous.

He looked out at the expectant faces and began. "Ladies and gentlemen, I have called you together because I think it imperative that you understand the situation we are in and what will be expected of you in the days to come. I'm sure you've been following the news and many of you may already know what I am about to tell you. Still, I think it best that you hear it from me and not second-hand.

"Last Thursday, the Soviets interdicted access to Berlin by road, rail and canal. They also stopped all natural gas and electricity deliveries to the city. This means that in addition to the Allied garrisons, the civilian population living in the Western Sectors of Berlin has been deprived of virtually all necessities needed to live a normal life from fresh milk to scotch." As intended, they laughed.

"The ostensible purpose of this blockade is to force us and our American and French allies to withdraw our garrisons from Berlin. This would mean that the civilians living in the Western Sectors of Berlin would come under Soviet domination and the entire city would be absorbed into the Soviet Zone."

Priestman paused and looked out across the room. "I am sure that many of you don't see anything wrong with that. Why should His Majesty's armed forces be stationed in the middle of the Soviet Zone? Why shouldn't Berlin, which lies deep inside the Soviet Zone, be an integral part of it?" He scanned the faces in front of him and was surprised that only a minority of them seemed to express agreement with his words.

"For those of you who think like that, let me remind you that much the same was said just under ten years ago at Munich. Then people asked: Why shouldn't the ethnically German population of the Sudetenland be part of Germany? What could be more reasonable than to allow the Sudeten Germans to be absorbed into the Greater German Reich?"

"The situation now is similar. The absorption of the Western Sectors of Berlin into the Soviet Zone is not a logical adjustment of a geopolitical anomaly, but rather a crass violation of international agreements and understandings. It represents not a 'reasonable' solution to an earlier mistake. It is most certainly not a case of self-determination." He saw heads start to nod solemnly across the room.

"On the contrary, the blockade is a cold-blooded and transparent attempt to expand Soviet power at the expense of the West in the face of fierce opposition from the affected population. I cannot overstate the similarities between this crisis and that which Hitler manufactured in September 1938." Priestman could sense that the mention of Munich had struck a nerve. Many more in the audience were now nodding solemnly.

"Let me also remind you that the Western Powers surrendered territory already occupied by our troops in exchange for our presence here in Berlin. The Soviets are *not* offering to reverse that exchange. They want it all.

"Our reason for being in Berlin was to ensure that we had a say in the reconstruction of Germany. This being the German capital, it was believed that any future German state would be ruled from here. Allied oversight of new German institutions was deemed vital to ensure the complete denazification and democratization of the former Nazi state.

"Yet for months, even years, the Soviet Union has been eating away at the very basis of Four-Power rule in Germany. The Soviets have systematically broken the instruments necessary for implementing joint policies. They long prevented the introduction of a sound currency essential to a viable economy and equally critical to ending the wholesale corruption and criminal activities endemic in a collapsed state.

"His Majesty's government has had enough. The Foreign Secretary declared unequivocally before the House of Commons yesterday that we would not withdraw from Berlin. His words were greeted with cheers from both sides of the chamber. Mr Bevin noted soberly that our decision to remain in Berlin may have grave consequences. It could, conceivably, lead to war between Great Britain and the Soviet Union." Priestman paused to let that sink in. His audience was very sober and very still.

Priestman resumed, "The Conservative Spokesman Harold Macmillan, responded bluntly by asserting that grave as the risk of war is, the alternative — to shirk from the issue, as he put it — involves not merely the *risk*, but the *certainty* of war." Priestman knew that many would have already read this exchange in the morning newspapers.

"Although I am merely a relatively junior RAF officer," the Wing Commander noted in a more relaxed tone, "I beg to differ with the honourable Mr Macmillan." This brought a titter of surprised amusement from some and uncomfortable wriggling from others. Priestman waited until everyone was again still before resuming.

"From the vantage point of Westminster, war may appear a distant — if distinct — possibility. In contrast, from here at Gatow, ladies and gentlemen, I submit that *we* are *already* at war with the Soviet Union.

"No, this is not a shooting war — at least not yet — but it is a war nevertheless. It is a war of nerves that will be won, hopefully, not with bloodshed, but with intelligence, innovation, improvisation and ingenuity. It will be won by determination, diligence, and discipline — mixed, I hope, with a sense of humour.

"I'm not an expert on the Russian character, but from what I've seen thus far, there is nothing the Russians hate quite so much as us not taking them as seriously as they take themselves. They most certainly don't like to see us smiling, joking and laughing at them." To his relief, many in the audience laughed, and Priestman risked a smile himself before becoming serious again.

"The job we have set ourselves is unprecedented. No one has ever supplied a city of two million entirely by air. We are all going to be experimenting with the limits of our abilities — and imagination. We will make mistakes. We will sometimes fall short. But we will not simply surrender. At least I won't."

Someone at the back of the room shouted. "We will never surrender, sir!" This was met with cheers from most of the other occupants in the room. Some men even jumped up to cheer while most confined themselves to enthusiastic clapping.

Priestman waited until things had calmed down before he concluded simply with, "Thank you, Ladies and Gentlemen. That's all for tonight."

As he descended from the podium, Priestman was acutely aware that he had come to Berlin reluctantly and with thoughts only of saving his career. Now his concerns were for everyone in this room — and, indeed, the fate of the entire city.

Principal and Historical Characters

Principal Characters
(in rough order of appearance)

- Wg/Cdr Robert "Robin" Priestman, DSO, DFC and Bar, RAF Station Commander Gatow
- Emily Pryce Priestman, his wife
- Charlotte Graefin (Countess) Walmsdorf, freelance journalist
- Christian Freiherr (Baron) von Feldburg, her cousin, former Luftwaffe pilot, wine merchant
- Christopher "Kit" Moran, DFC, British engineering student, former Lancaster skipper
- Reverend Edwin Reddings, his father-in-law
- Georgina Reddings Moran, his wife
- Jakob Liebherr, Social Democratic Berlin City Councilman
- Trude Liebherr, his wife
- Karl Liebherr, his son, active member of the Soviet-controlled SED (German Unity Party)
- David "Banks" Goldman, German-Canadian Jew
- Charles "Kiwi" Murray, DFC, life insurance salesman, former RAF pilot
- Kathleen Hart, RAF, air traffic controller
- Hope, her daughter

Secondary Characters

RAF Gatow

- Adjutant F/O "Stan" Stanley
- Intelligence Officer Fl/Lt Oliver Boyd
- Medical Officer S/L Bertram Ashcroft
- CO of Field Squadron, RAF Regiment, S/L Tucker

Air Traffic Control and Operations

- Flying Control Officer Fl/Lt Simpson, later S/L Garth
- Senior Air Traffic Controller W/O "Willie" Wilkins
- Assistant Air Traffic Controller WAAF Fl/Sgt Kathleen Hart
- Air Movement Assistant Cpl "Rufus" Groom
- Air Movement Assistant WAAF Cpl. Natalie Vincent
- Operations Control Officer W/O Bob Tyler
- Wireless Operator WAAF Cpl Annie Bower
- Teleprinter Operator WAAF Cpl Violet Moore

222 (Spitfire) Squadron

- Squadron Leader "Danny" Daniels
- Fl/Lt Swift
- Fl/Lt "Lance" Knight
- P/Os "Benny," "Mac"

WAAF

- Sgt Lynne Andrews, Clerk General Duties, CO's secretary
- Cpl Galyna Nicolaevna Borisenko, Russian translator
- Cpl Marie Cresson, French translator
- Cpl Natalie Vincent, air movements assistant
- Cpl Annie Bower, wireless operator
- Cpl Violet Moore, teleprinter operator

House on the Maybachufer 27

- Top (4th) Floor Right: Charlotte Graefin Walmsdorf and Christian von Feldburg
- Top (4th) Floor Left: Jakob and Trude Liebherr, City Councilman and his wife
- 3rd Floor Right: Dr Hofmeier, engineer from AEG
- 3rd Floor Left: Mr Meyer, Braun and Schmidt, black marketeers
- 1st and 2nd Floors: refugees
- Ground Floor Left: Mr Pfalz, the concierge
- Ground Floor Right: Horst, coachman and milkman

Staff at Priestman Residence in Kladow

- Mr Krueger, the gardener
- Mrs Neuhausen, the cook, later replaced by
- Jasha Wisniewski
- Mrs Pabst, Misses Schilling and Gruen, the chamber maids

Miscellaneous

- Lieutenant Colonel Charles Walker, USAF Base Commander Tempelhof
- Cheryl his wife
- Colonel Gregory Sergeyevich Kuznetsov, Red Air Force Base Commander Staaken
- Major Alexei Ivanovich Volkov, NKVD Officer at Staaken
- Mila Mikhailivna Levchenkova, former partisan and sharpshooter, now with Soviet Mission to the ACC

Relevant Historical Personages

- US President **Harry S. Truman**, Democratic Party
- British Prime Minister **Clement Attlee**, Labour Party
- Soviet Head of State **Josef Stalin**, CPSU
- US Secretary of State **George C. Marshall**
- British Foreign Secretary **Ernst Bevin**
- Soviet Foreign Minister **Vyacheslav Molotov**
- American Military Governor **General Lucius D. Clay**
- British Military Governor General **Sir Brian Hubert Robertson**
- French Military Governor General **Joseph-Pierre Koenig**
- Soviet Military Governor Marshal **Vassili Sokolovsky**
- American City Commandant Colonel **Frank Howley**
- British City Commandant Lt. General **Otway Herbert**
- French City Commandant General **Jean Ganeval**
- Soviet City Commandant General **Alexander Kotikov**
- Lord Mayor of Berlin **Ernst Reuter** (SPD)
- Air Commodore **Reginald "Rex" Waite**, RAF Liaison Officer to the ACC

RAF Rank Table

RAF	USAAF
Marshal of the Airforce	Five Star General
Air Chief Marshal	General (4 Star)
Air Marshal	Lt. General (3 Star)
Air Vice Marshal	Major General (2 Star)
Air Commodore	Brigadier General (1 Star)
Group Captain	Colonel
Wing Commander	Lt. Colonel
Squadron Leader	Major
Flight Lieutenant	Captain
Flying Officer	First Lieutenant
Pilot Officer	Second Lieutenant

Because the USAAF had ten non-commissioned ranks to the RAF's seven, it is not possible to provide exact equivalents, however, the lowest rank in the RAF was Aircraftman. This is the term that was corrupted in RAF jargon to "erk" based on the cockney pronunciation.

The RAF non-commissioned ranks from highest to lowest were:
- Warrant Officer
- Flight Sergeant
- Sergeant
- Corporal
- Leading Aircraftman (LAC)
- Aircraftman 1st and 2nd Class

Key Acronyms

ACC	Allied Control Council
AVM	Air Vice Marshal
BAFO	British Air Forces of Occupation
BAOR	British Army on the Rhine
CPSU	Communist Party of the Soviet Union
CDU	Christlich Demokratische Union Deutschlands — Christian Democratic Union of Germany
Fl/Lt	Flight Lieutenant
Fl/Sgt	Flight Sergeant
F/O	Flying Officer
GC	Group Captain
KPD	Kommunistische Partei Deutschlands — The German Communist Party
NKVD	Soviet Secret Police
P/O	Pilot Officer
RAF	Royal Air Force
RAFVR	Royal Air Force Volunteer Reserve
R/T	Radio Telephone, the radio sets used in aircraft at this time
SED	Sozialistische Einheitspartei Deutschlands — The Socialist Unity Party (Soviet Controlled Party)
Sgt	Sergeant
S/L	Squadron Leader
SPD	Sozialdemokratische Partei Deutschlands — The German Social Democratic Party
SMAD	Soviet Military Administration in Germany
USAF	United States Air Force
USAFE	United States Air Forces Europe
Wg/Cdr	Wing Commander

Historical Note

Although the principal characters in this novel are fictional, the main events are historical fact. The extraordinary Soviet siege of Berlin 1948-1949 and the Allied response are well documented. There are many excellent accounts of the Berlin Blockade and Airlift, some of which are listed under "Recommended Reading." In this short note, I simply wish to highlight some of the facts that may seem incredible and also note conscious deviations from the historical record.

- Wing Commander Robert Priestman is a fictional character. The historical Station Commander at Gatow during the Airlift was Group Captain Brian Yarde, who arrived in July 1947 and departed in November 1949. I have extended the term of his predecessor Group Captain Duncan Somerville to December 1947, to accommodate the plot of the novel. The decision to make the RAF station commander the main character of this book was dictated by the fact that Gatow became the world's busiest airport in this period and Gatow led with innovations in air traffic control and air safety.

- The date of the construction of Gatow's concrete runway is inconsistently recorded in the available literature. Some sources claim a concrete runway was already laid down in Gatow by March 1947; other sources say the concrete runway was not completed until 16 July 1948. The earlier date of 1947 is not credible because prior to the start of the mini-airlift in April 1948, Gatow had almost no traffic and laying down a concrete runway would not have been a priority to a British government heavily in debt and cutting back on defence spending. After the mini-blockade of April 1948, in contrast, construction of a concrete runway became imperative. Furthermore, the exceptional challenges associated with the construction of the runway are described in great detail in a number of first-hand accounts, all of which support the thesis that completion of the concrete runway did not take place until after the start of the Airlift in 1948. Throughout this series, therefore, this later date is accepted, and the challenges of its construction are described in detail in the next book in this series *Cold War*.

- Because I was unable to find diagrams or precise descriptions of the manning and configuration of the Control Tower at Gatow before and during the Airlift, the set-up described in this novel is based on available photos of the tower and descriptions of ATC operations at Gatow during the Airlift supplemented by consultations with an RAF veteran with decades of experience in British civilian air traffic control.

- The summary of the situation in Berlin at the time the Western Allies arrived provided in the chapter "Berlin, Berlin" is based on the historical record. The estimate of the number of rapes is likewise based on historical materials.

- The Allied Occupation forces did live in luxury and abundance in a city where daily rations were roughly half what Americans considered "minimum." As noted, senior officers had large staffs of twelve or more and even junior married officers employed multiple servants. All lived in lavishly furnished confiscated houses.

- The harassment of women by American GIs was so widespread that some American women started wearing armbands with the stars-and-stripes on them to distinguish themselves from the local population.

- German civilians travelling in passenger carriages attached to a British train travelling from Berlin to the British Zone were prevented from continuing their journey on 24 January. I moved the date by one day to Sun 25 January to accommodate the storyline.

- Although Dr. Hofmeier is a fictional character, kidnappings of this kind occurred throughout the Soviet occupation and escalated in the months before the Blockade. Frequent targets were policemen not willing to do Soviet bidding, students that challenged the ideological straight-jacket imposed at universities, scientists and engineers, as in this fictional case. Two thousand three hundred German scientists and their families are known to have been deported for work in the Soviet Union. In addition, roughly 25,000 ordinary workers, mostly women, were also deported on short notice to work in Soviet factories often for years on end.

- The sitting of the Allied Control Council depicted in Chapter 5 is fictional. That said, the Soviets officially rejected Marshall Plan Aid and forced the East European countries under their control to reject it. The Soviets repeatedly and vehemently condemned the entire program as an anti-Soviet plot. Drug dealing was a major problem in post-war Berlin. Traffic accidents involving Soviet officers driving too fast and under the influence of alcohol were a perennial problem. Last but not least, Robertson's "spontaneous" invitation to luncheon at his home — including the initial exclusion of lower-ranking Soviet officers and drivers at Sokolovsky's insistence — did happen, albeit more than a year earlier.

- The situation in Berlin's hospitals was precarious, but the specific statistics used to describe the situation are fabricated.

- The increasing harassment of Germans transiting the Soviet Zones or crossing Sector borders is well documented. As noted, changes in the documents required while petty in themselves cumulatively amounted to a growing psychological and economic burden on the German civilian population.

- The black-market prices and exchange rates mentioned are based on historical accounts. Likewise, the wages for prostitutes and waiters are based on the historical record.

- The sordid nightlife and cigarette economy depicted in the chapter "Creatures of the Night" is based on historical accounts.

- A number of high-ranking SS officers did receive new identities and enjoyed Soviet protection in the post-war period for a variety of reasons, not all of which are transparent.

- The illicit participation of Allied officers in black market and criminal activities is, sadly, also well-recorded. Captain Norman Byrne was a real person. A sensational article in *Newsweek* magazine exposed the large quantities of stolen art being trafficked by American officers. This led to an investigation and the arrest of Byrne, who was a senior officer at the US Army organization "Monuments, Fine Arts and Archives" (MFAA) made famous by the Hollywood film "Monuments Men." As shown in the film, the organization was charged with finding, safeguarding and/or returning works of art plundered by the Nazis or Soviets. Byrne, unfortunately, used his official position to enrich himself by selling off some of the looted masterpieces and keeping others for his personal collection. Because I wanted include this plot thread, I invented Lionel Dickenson as a character that would involve Kathleen indirectly and unsuspectingly in this underworld.

- There are several recorded instances of off-duty Soviet officers bragging about the Soviet intention to throw the Allies out of Berlin during the Spring of 1948. The incident described here, while fictional, is based on the report from an American medical officer who overheard Soviets talking among themselves at a Christening and referring to the Americans as "pigs."

- The "mini-blockade" of 1-4 April is a historical event as is the British response of moving two Dakota Squadrons of No. 46 Group forward to Wunstorf and flying in 72 tons of supplies per day as depicted.

- The collision between a Soviet fighter (Yak) and the BEA airliner on 5 April was a historical event. The fighter was seen doing aerobatics in the landing-approach corridor to Gatow by many, primarily German, eye-witnesses. The bulk of the wreck fell into the Soviet Zone and the British were initially denied access to it, while the Yak still entangled with pieces of the Dakota landed in the British Sector. Although the

Soviets were initially apologetic, within two days they had changed their tune and were publicly blaming the "aggressive" airliner while pretending the Yak had been a "training aircraft" on a routine landing.

- After the fatal accident involving the BEA airliner, both the British and American Military Governors temporarily ordered fighter escorts for their aircraft in the Berlin corridors. They rescinded the order after being convinced by Marshal Sokolovsky that the crash had been an accident rather than an attempt to close the corridors.

- It is recorded that during the mini-blockade in April some American officers asked to have their families evacuated from Berlin. Clay responded by saying such behaviour suggested "nervousness" which was "unbecoming" an officer. He added that anyone uncomfortable with the situation could submit his request for a transfer out. The RAF position was identical.

- Although Kit's encounter with Cheshire is fictional, the depiction of Cheshire's situation at this time is based on his biography. In June 1948, his VIP project had collapsed, he'd sold off the estate of Le Court to pay off twenty thousand pounds in personal debt. He'd sold one Mosquito, although the status of the other is unclear. He was living alone in Le Court after the other colonists had left, and sometimes wandering the roads like a mendicant friar. It was in this period that he talked about going to the Soviet Union in order to get arrested and draw attention to the risk of war. He had not yet converted to Catholicism, but soon Arthur Dykes, a terminally ill cancer patient, would join him at Le Court.

- Louise Schroeder was summoned to receive orders from the Soviets on 23 June, and was accompanied by her deputy Ferdinand Friedensburg. I substituted the fictional Liebherr, but the content of the discussion is based on the historical record.

- The introduction of competing currencies, Soviet claims to control all of Berlin, and the occupation of City Hall by Communist-controlled thugs are all historical facts, including the antisemitic attacks on Jeannette Wolfe and her pushing an SED councilman backwards of a bench. The concluding vote was as recorded, but the speeches in the text are fictional.

- The Blockade began 24 June with the measures described. Similar to Putin calling the war in Ukraine a "special military operation," the Soviets never admitted that they had instituted a blockade. Instead, the bulletins cited in the novel are based on the actual Soviet announcements which referred only to "technical difficulties" and coal shortages. For months, the Soviets also insisted that the "technical difficulties" would miraculously disappear if the West made political concessions.

- The Soviets broadcast reports of riots and Western troops shooting and killing demonstrators which were entirely fictional.

- Air Commodore Waite suggested supplying the city by air to General Herbert on 23 June, only to be turned down brusquely. He worked all night on putting together precise figures which he showed to Herbert the next day — after the start of the Blockade.

- Herbert gave Waite permission to present his plans to General Robertson. The place and timing of this are uncertain, but Robertson was impressed enough to "share the information" with Clay — in what way and when is not stated. Given the fact that Clay categorically denied the possibility of supplying the city by air in a press conference at 5:30 pm on 24 June but suggested the option to Ernst Reuter on the morning of 25 June, I've hypothesised a late-night meeting between Clay and Robertson/Waite on 24 June.

- Clay's meeting with Reuter on 25 June is legendary, but accounts vary. Clay himself did not include the encounter in his memoirs. Willy Brandt, who is most commonly quoted, only recorded key statements rather than a full transcript. The dialogue used here is constructed from multiple accounts and attempts to encompass all important elements while retaining a coherent dialogue.

- As in the novel, the British Parliamentary debate on the airlift, took place on 30 June. The quotes from Bevin and Eden are extracted from the Parliamentary protocol but have been edited to make them more concise than the original.

Recommended Reading

- Auer, Peter. *Ihr Voelker der Welt: Ernst Reuter und die Blockade von Berlin*. Jaron, 1998.

- Cherny, Andrei. *The Candy Bombers: The Untold Story of the Berlin Airlift and America's Finest Hour*. G.P.Putnam's Sons, 2008.

- Clay, Lucius D., *Decision in Germany*. William Heinemann Ltd, 1950.

- Collier, Richard. *Bridge Across the Sky: The Berlin Blockade and Airlift 1948-1949*. MacGraw Hill, 1978.

- Gere, Edwin. *The Unheralded: Men and Women of the Berlin Blockade and Airlift*. Trafford, 2003.

- Halvorsen, Gail. *The Berlin Candy Bomber*. Horizon Publishers. 1997.

- Haydock, Michael D. *City under Siege: The Berlin Blockade and Airlift, 1948-1949*. Brassey's, 1999.

- Jackson, Robert. *The Berlin Airlift*. Patrick Stephens, 1988.

- Keiderling, Gerhard. *Rosinenbomber ueber Berlin: Waehrungsreform. Blockade, Luftbruecke, Teiling*. Dietz Verlag, 1998.

- Koenig, Peter. *Schaut auf diese Stadt! Berlin und die Luftbruecke*. Be.Brag Verlag, 1998.

- Miller, Roger G. *To Save a City: The Berlin Airlift 1948 — 1949*. Univ. Press of the Pacific, 2002

- Milton, Giles. *Checkmate in Berlin*. Henry Holt & Co, 2021.

- Parrish, Thomas. *Berlin in the Balance 1948-1949: The Blockade, The Airlift, The First Major Battle of the Cold War*. Perseus Books, 1998.

- Percy, Arthur. *Berlin Airlift*. Airlife, 1997.
- Prell, Uwe and Lothar Wilker. *Berlin-Blockade und Luftbruecke 1948-1949: Analyse und Dokumentation*. Berlin Verlag, 1987.
- Rodrigo, Robert. *Berlin Airlift*. Cassel & Co., 1960.
- Scherff, Klaus. *Luftbruecke Berlin: Die dramatische Geschichte der Versorgung aus der Luft June 1948 — Oktober 1949*. Motorbuch Verlag, 1998.
- Schrader, Helena P. *The Blockade Breakers: The Berlin Airlift*. The History Press, 2008.
- Tunner, William H. *Over the Hump*. Office of Air Force History: USAF Warrior Studies, 1964.
- Tusa, Ann & John. *The Berlin Airlift*. Sarpedon, 1998.

About
Helena P. Schrader

Helena P. Schrader is an established aviation author and expert on the Second World War. She earned a PhD in History (cum Laude) from the University of Hamburg with a ground-breaking dissertation on a leading member of the German Resistance to Hitler. Her non-fiction publications include *Sisters in Arms: The Women who Flew in WWII*, *The Blockade Breakers: The Berlin Airlift*, *Codename Valkyrie: General Friederich Olbricht and the Plot against Hitler*, and *The Holy Land in the Era of the Crusades: Kingdoms at the Crossroads of Civilizations*.

In addition, Helena is the author of nineteen historical novels and winner of numerous literary awards. Her novel on the Battle of Britain, *Where Eagles Never Flew*, won the Hemingway Award for 20th Century Wartime Fiction and a Maincrest Media Award for Historical Fiction. RAF Battle of Britain ace Wing Commander Bob Doe called it "the best book" he had ever seen about the battle. *Traitors for the Sake of Humanity* was a finalist for the Foreword INDIES awards. *Grounded Eagles* and *Moral*

Fibre have both garnered excellent reviews from acclaimed review sites such as Kirkus, Blue Ink, Foreword Clarion, and Feathered Quill. In addition, *Moral Fibre* won the Hemingway Award 2022, was awarded a Maincrest Media Award for Military Fiction and was a finalist for a Book Excellence Award.

Over Aviation Books
by Helena P. Schrader

For readers interested in the backstory to Robin and Emily:

Where Eagles Never Flew:
A Battle of Britain Novel

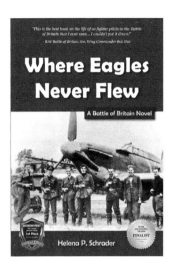

Winner of a the Hemingway Award for Twentieth Century Military Fiction, a Maincrest Media Award for Military Fiction and Finalist for the Book Excellence Award.

This superb novel about the Battle of Britain, based on actual events and eye-witness accounts, shows this pivotal battle from both sides of the channel through the eyes of pilots, ground crews, staff — and the women they loved.

Summer 1940: The Battle of France is over; the Battle of Britain is about to begin. If the swastika is not to fly over Buckingham Palace, the RAF must prevent the Luftwaffe from gaining air superiority over Great Britain. Standing on the front line is No. 606 (Hurricane) Squadron. As the casualties mount, new pilots find a cold reception from the clique of experienced pilots, who resent them taking the place of their dead friends. Meanwhile, despite credible service in France, former RAF aerobatics pilot Robin Priestman finds himself stuck in Training Command — and falling for a girl from the Salvation Army. On the other side of the Channel, the Luftwaffe is recruiting women as communications specialists — and naïve Klaudia is about to grow up.

For readers interested in the backstory to Kit and Georgina:

Moral Fibre:
A Bomber Pilot's Story

Winner of a Hemingway Award for 20th Century Wartime Fiction 2022 and a Maincrest Media Award for Military Fiction. It was also a finalist for the Book Excellence Awards for Historical Fiction.

Riding the icy, moonlit sky—
They took the war to Hitler.
Their chances of survival were less than fifty percent.
Their average age was 21.
This is the story of just one Lancaster skipper, his crew,
and the woman he loved.
It is intended as a tribute to them all.

Flying Officer Kit Moran has earned his pilot's wings, but the greatest challenges still lie ahead: crewing up and returning to operations. Things aren't made easier by the fact that while still a flight engineer, he was posted LMF (Lacking in Moral Fibre) for refusing to fly after a raid on Berlin that killed his best friend and skipper. Nor does it help that he is in love with his dead friend's fiancé, who is not yet ready to become romantically involved again.

Finally, for those interested in the back story of David and more on Kit:

Grounded Eagles:
Three Tales of the RAF in WWII

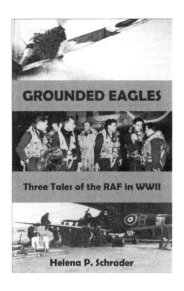

Disfiguring injuries, class prejudice and PTSD are the focus of three heart wrenching tales set in WWII by award-winning novelist Helena P. Schrader.

A Stranger in the Mirror: David Goldman is shot down in flames in September 1940. Not only is his face burned beyond recognition, he is told he will never fly again. While the plastic surgeon recreates his face one painful operation at a time, the 22-year-old pilot must discover who he really is.

Lack of Moral Fibre: In late November 1943, Flight Engineer Kit Moran refuses to participate in a raid on Berlin, his 37th 'op.' He is posted off his squadron for "Lacking Moral Fibre" and sent to a mysterious NYDN center. Here, psychiatrist Dr Grace must determine if he needs psychiatric treatment — or disciplinary action for cowardice.

A Rose in November: Rhys Jenkins, a widower with two teenage children, has finally obtained his dream: "Chiefy" of a Spitfire squadron. But an unexpected attraction for an upperclass woman threatens to upend his life.